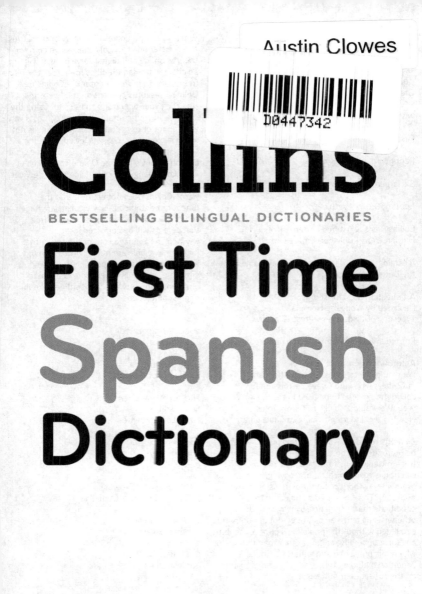

# Collins

BESTSELLING BILINGUAL DICTIONARIES

# First Time
# Spanish
# Dictionary

Collins

**HarperCollins Publishers**
Westerhill Road
Bishopbriggs
Glasgow
G64 2QT
Great Britain

www.collinslanguage.com

First Edition 2008

Reprint 10 9 8 7 6 5 4 3 2 1

ISBN 978-0-00-726111-6

A catalogue record for this book is available from
the British Library

Art direction by Mark Thomson
Designed by Wolfgang Homola
Typeset by Davidson Pre-Press, Glasgow

Printed in Italy by Rotolito Lombarda S.p.A.

**Acknowledgements**
We would like to thank those authors and
publishers who kindly gave permission for
copyright material to be used in the Collins Word
Web. We would also like to thank Times
Newspapers Ltd for providing valuable data.

PUBLISHING DIRECTOR
Catherine Love

MANAGING EDITOR
Gaëlle Amiot-Cadey

PROJECT MANAGEMENT
Susie Beattie
Sinda López Fuentes

EDITORS
Cordelia Lilly
Julie Muleba
José María Ruiz Vaca
Malihé Forghani-Nowbari
José Antonio Gálvez Castiella

TECHNICAL SUPPORT
Thomas Callan

ILLUSTRATIONS
Cordelia Lilly

ILLUSTRATED SUPPLEMENT
Marcella Grassi
© Boroli Editore 2008

SERIES EDITOR
Rob Scriven

William Collins' dream of knowledge for all began with the publication of his first book in 1819. A self-educated mill worker, he not only enriched millions of lives, but also founded a flourishing publishing house. Today, staying true to this spirit, Collins books are packed with inspiration, innovation, and practical expertise. They place you at the centre of a world of possibility and give you exactly what you need to explore it.

Language is the key to this exploration, and at the heart of Collins Dictionaries is language as it is really used. New words, phrases, and meanings spring up every day, and all of them are captured and analysed by the Collins Word Web. Constantly updated, and with over 2.5 billion entries, this living language resource is unique to our dictionaries.

Words are tools for life. And a Collins Dictionary makes them work for you.

**Collins. Do more.**

# Contents

The **Collins First Time Spanish Dictionary** is a new bilingual dictionary aimed at primary school children who are starting to learn Spanish.

Access to a dictionary which is pitched at an appropriate level is a vital part of the language-learning process. The content of this dictionary has been carefully selected to reflect current trends in primary education and help children with acquiring basic language-learning skills.

The key aims of the **Collins First Time Spanish Dictionary** are:

- to develop both language skills in Spanish and language learning skills in general
- to cover the four key areas of language attainment: listening, speaking, reading and writing
- to reinforce key aspects of the language by the use of notes and feature boxes throughout the entries
- to extend cultural awareness by providing information about Spain, especially where traditions differ from those in Britain

The **Collins First Time Spanish Dictionary** supports language learning in a number of specific ways:

- it develops children's knowledge of how language works by encouraging them to understand, analyse and use simple aspects of grammar
- it develops children's individual learning skills by using a wide range of notes that explain things in a simple but interesting way
- it enables children to make comparisons between Spanish and English by encouraging them to explore the similarities and differences between the two languages and cultures
- it introduces young learners to all the basic elements of a bilingual dictionary and provides detailed instructions on how to get the most out of using the dictionary

The **Collins First Time Spanish Dictionary** is presented in an easy-to-use format which is intended to appeal to children of primary school age. It provides lots of simple, relevant examples and tips on how to remember words, and how to avoid some of the pitfalls of translation. It also features key phrases, illustrations and information about life in Spain, making it an invaluable and exciting new resource.

**Step one:**
**Pick the right side**
Remember there are two halves to the dictionary. If you want to know what a Spanish word means, look in the first half of the dictionary.

If you want to translate an English word into Spanish, look in the second half, which is English-Spanish. It comes after the supplement in the middle of the dictionary.

1 Which of these words would you look up on the Spanish-English side of the dictionary?
**ver brother horse teléfono**

2 Look at page 51 of the dictionary. Is this the Spanish side or the English side? How can you tell?

3 Look at page 150 of the dictionary. What is shown at the top of the page, down the side?

4 Is **invite** the first or the last word on page 437?

Remember that you do not read across the whole page in a dictionary – you have to read down the columns.

5 Which word comes immediately after **aburrido** on page 3?

**Step two:**
**Find the right word**
A B C D E F G H I J K L M N O P Q R S T U V W X Y Z
Words are in alphabetical order in the dictionary – like names in the phone book, and in a school register. The alphabet is shown down the edge of each page of the dictionary. You can sort words into alphabetical order by looking at the first letter of each word.

6 Can you put these names in alphabetical order?
**María, Isabel, Juan, Jorge, David, Arturo, Carmen**
When two words start with the same letter, look at their second letters.

7 In alphabetical order which comes first – **Juan** or **Jorge**?

8 This is the order of the days of the week on a calendar:
**Monday, Tuesday, Wednesday, Thursday, Friday, Saturday, Sunday**
Which day comes first in a dictionary? Which comes last?

9 **Thursday** comes before **Tuesday** in a dictionary. Why?

10 Put the seven days of the week into alphabetical order.
If the first letters are the same, and the second letters are the same, look at the third letters.

11 **June, July, August**: which comes last in the dictionary?

**Step three:**
**Pick the right translation**
The translations are easy to spot in this dictionary because they are blue on the English-Spanish side and red on the Spanish-English side.

Spanish words can be masculine or feminine, and singular or plural. In the dictionary you will come across the abbreviations *masc* and *fem*, which tell you the gender of a Spanish word. PL tells you the word is plural. The dictionary also shows you the Spanish word for 'the' (this can be **el**, **la**, **los** or **las**). In the Language plus supplement, NOUN is abbreviated to N and ADJECTIVE is abbreviated to ADJ.

When you look up 'doll' you can see that the word for 'doll' in Spanish is **muñeca**. You can tell that the Spanish word for 'doll' is feminine because it is given with **la** and the dictionary says that it is '*fem*' (feminine).

So 'the doll' is **la muñeca** and 'a doll' would be **una muñeca**.

Sometimes there is more than one translation, and each one has a number. If there is more than one translation, don't just pick the first one! Check to see which is the right one.

**12** Which is the Spanish word for **a ball** that you kick – **la pelota** or **el balón**? Look for the clue.

**ball** NOUN
1 la **pelota** *fem* (for tennis, golf, cricket)
**Hit the ball!**
¡Dale a la pelota!
2 el **balón** *masc* (PL los **balones**) (for football, rugby)
**Pass the ball!**
¡Pasa el balón!

## Step four:
## Parts of Speech

Sometimes, to pick the right translation, you need to know the part of speech of a word, for example whether a word is a noun, an adjective, an adverb or a verb.

## NOUNS

**Nouns** are naming words for things or people. You often use the words 'a' or 'the' with a noun – eg a **girl**, a **boy**, the **school**, the **windows**.

Nouns can be singular, eg an **accident**, the **playground**, my **dad**, **football** – or plural, eg **sweets**, the **children**, my **friends**.

**13** How many nouns are there in this sentence? What are they?
*The car has got a flat tyre and a big dent in the door.*

## ADJECTIVES

An **adjective** is a describing word which tells you what things are like: **flat** shoes are shoes that don't have high heels. A **flat** tyre is a tyre with no air in it.

**14** How many adjectives are there in this sentence? What are they?
*She's got brown hair and blue eyes.*

Some words have a **noun** meaning and an **adjective** meaning. In the dictionary there is a box to tell you about this. The different meanings usually have different translations in Spanish.

## patient

> **patient** *can be a noun or an adjective.*

**A** NOUN
el/la **paciente** *masc/fem*
**B** ADJECTIVE
**paciente** *masc & fem*
**The teacher is very patient.**
El maestro es muy paciente.
**Be patient, Joshua.**
Ten paciencia, Joshua.

## ADVERBS

An **adverb** is a word which describes a verb or an adjective:
She writes **neatly**. The film was **very** good.

**15** How many adverbs are in this sentence? What are they?
*The children sat quietly and played happily.*

## VERBS

**Verbs** are sometimes called 'doing words'. They often go with words like 'I' and 'you', and with names, eg I **play** football, what **do** you **want**?, Hugo **likes** mashed potato.

Verbs tell you about the present, eg I'm **listening** – the past, eg I **scored** a goal – and the future, eg I'm **going to get** an ice cream.

**16** How many verbs are there in this sentence? What are they?
*School starts at 9.00 and finishes at 3.30.*

Some words have a **noun** meaning and a **verb** meaning. In the dictionary there is a box to tell you about this. The different meanings have different translations in Spanish.

## rain

rain *can be a noun or a verb.*

**A** NOUN
la **lluvia** *fem*
**in the rain**
bajo la lluvia

**B** VERB
**to rain**
**llover**
**It's going to rain.**
Va a llover.
**It rains a lot here.**
Llueve mucho aquí.

**It's raining.**
Está lloviendo.

**17** What is the Spanish word for 'rain'?

**18** Why is 'It's going to rain.' in part **B**?

**19** How do you say 'It's raining.' in Spanish?

**20** Is 'llover' a noun or a verb?

### Learn useful phrases
In the dictionary you'll see phrases that are especially important in orange boxes. Try to learn these when you come across them, and you'll soon know lots of useful things to say in Spanish.

**What time is it?**
Qué hora es?
**It's lunch time.**
Es la hora de comer.
**How many times?**
¿Cuántas veces?
**Have a good time, Amanda!**
¡Que lo pases bien, Amanda!

### Find out about life in Spain
There are also boxes which tell you about Spanish customs, and about differences between life in Spain and Britain.

*Did you know?*

**churros** *are a kind of fritter that people often eat on the streets in a paper bag or order in a café typically with a cup of thick, hot chocolate:* **chocolate con churros**.

### Even more words
At school you will learn to talk about subjects such as the time and the weather, your family, your pets, and your clothes. The most important words for talking about these subjects are shown in the dictionary itself, and even more words are given in **Language Plus**, the middle part of the dictionary. Have a look!

## Answer key

1 ver and teléfono
2 It is the Spanish side. It has Spanish words on it and Spanish–English written at the side near the top.
3 Spanish-English
4 The last word
5 aburrirse
6 Arturo, Carmen, David, Isabel, Jorge, Juan, María
7 Jorge – because 'o' comes before 'u'
8 Friday; Wednesday
9 Because the second letter of Thursday is 'h', which comes before 'u', the second letter of Tuesday.
10 Friday, Monday, Saturday, Sunday, Thursday, Tuesday, Wednesday
11 June
12 el balón – The clue is (for football, rugby).
13 four – car, tyre, dent, door
14 two – brown and blue
15 two – quietly and happily
16 two – starts and finishes
17 la lluvia
18 It is an example of the verb and so is in the verb section of the entry.
19 Está lloviendo.
20 a verb

# Spanish - English

**a** PREPOSITION

> **Language tip**
>
> When **a** is followed by a masculine noun, **a** and the article **el** turn into **al**.

1 **to** *(with places)*
**Fueron a Madrid.**
They went to Madrid.
2 *(with movement)*
**Me caí al río.**
I fell into the river.
**Se subieron al tejado.**
They climbed onto the roof.
**Marta llegó tarde a la estación.**
Marta arrived at the station late.
3 *(with distances)*
**Está a quince kilómetros de aquí.**
It's fifteen kilometres from here.
4 **at** *(with time, ages, speed)*
**a las diez**
at ten o'clock
**a medianoche**
at midnight
**a los veinticuatro años**
at the age of twenty-four
**Íbamos a más de noventa kilómetros por hora.**
We were going at over ninety kilometres an hour.
5 *(with dates)*
**Estamos a nueve de julio.**
It's the ninth of July.
6 *(with prices)*
**Los huevos están a un euro con cincuenta la docena.**
Eggs are one euro fifty a dozen.
7 *(before an infinitive or a direct object)*
**Voy a verla.**

I'm going to see her.
**Vine a decírtelo.**
I came to tell you.
**Me obligaban a comer.**
They forced me to eat.

**Nos cruzamos al salir.**
We bumped into each other as we were going out.
**Se lo di a Ana.**
I gave it to Ana.
**Le enseñé a Pablo el libro que me dejaste.**
I showed Pablo the book you lent me.
**Se lo compré a él.**
I bought it from him.
**Vi a Juan.**
I saw Juan.
**Llamé al médico.**
I called the doctor.

**abajo** ADVERB
1 **below**
**Los platos y las tazas están abajo.**
The plates and cups are below.
**La montaña no parece tan alta desde abajo.**
The mountain doesn't seem so high from below.
**Mete las cervezas abajo del todo.**
Put the beers right at the bottom.
**El estante de abajo.**
The bottom shelf.

**2 downstairs**
**Abajo están la cocina y el salón.**
The kitchen and lounge are downstairs.
**Hay una fiesta en el piso de abajo.**
There's a party in the flat downstairs.

la **abeja** NOUN
**bee**

el **abeto** NOUN
**fir tree**

**abierto**

> **abierto** *can be an adjective or a verb.*

**A** (FEM **abierta**) ADJECTIVE
**1 open**
**¿Están abiertas las tiendas?**
Are the shops open?
**2 on**
**No dejes el gas abierto.**
Don't leave the gas on.
**B** VERB ▷*see* **abrir**
**He abierto la puerta.**
I've opened the door.

**abrazar** VERB
**to hug**
**Al verme me abrazó.**
He hugged me when he saw me.
**¡Abrázame fuerte!**
Give me a big hug!
■ **abrazarse**
**to hug**
**Se abrazaron y se besaron.**
They hugged and kissed.

el **abrazo** NOUN
**hug**
**¡Dame un abrazo!**
Give me a hug!

> **un abrazo**
> love

> **Did you know…?**
> *Did you know that Spanish speakers sometimes end e-mails, postcards and letters to friends with* **un abrazo***?*

**abrigar** VERB
**Esta chaqueta abriga mucho.**
This jacket's really warm.
■ **abrigarse**
**to wrap up well**

el **abrigo** NOUN
**coat**
**un abrigo de pieles**
a fur coat
**ropa de abrigo**
warm clothing

**abril** MASC NOUN
**April**

> **Language tip**
> *Months are not spelled with a capital letter in Spanish.*

**Nació el veinte de abril.**
He was born on the twentieth of April.

> **en abril**
> in April

**abrir** VERB
**1 to open**
**Las tiendas abren a las diez.**
The shops open at ten o'clock.
**Abre la ventana.**
Open the window.
**¡Abre, soy yo!**
Open the door, it's me!
**2 to turn on**
**Abre el gas.**
Turn the gas on.

■ **abrirse**
**to open**
**De repente se abrió la puerta.**
Suddenly the door opened.

**abrocharse** VERB
**to do up**
**Abróchate la camisa.**
Do your shirt up.
**Abróchense los cinturones.**
Please fasten your seatbelts.

la **abuela** NOUN
**grandmother**
**mi abuela**
my grandmother
**¿Dónde está la abuela?**
Where's Gran?

el **abuelo** NOUN
**grandfather**
**mi abuelo**
my grandfather
**¿Dónde está el abuelo?**
Where's Granddad?
**mis abuelos**
my grandparents

**aburrido** (FEM **aburrida**)
ADJECTIVE
1 **bored**
**Estaba aburrida y me marché.**
I was bored so I left.
2 **boring**
**No seas aburrida y vente al cine.**
Don't be boring and come to the cinema.
**una película muy aburrida**
a very boring film

**aburrirse** VERB
**to get bored**
**Me aburro viendo la tele.**
I get bored watching television.

**acabar** VERB
**to finish**
**Ayer acabé de pintar la valla.**

Yesterday I finished painting the fence.
**Acabo de ver a tu padre.**
I've just seen your father.
■ **acabarse**
**to run out**
**La impresora te avisa cuando se acaba el papel.**
The printer tells you when the paper runs out.

**acaso** ADVERB
**por si acaso**
just in case

el **accidente** NOUN
**accident**
**los accidentes de carretera**
road accidents
**Han tenido un accidente.**
They've had a car accident.

la **acción** (PL las **acciones**) NOUN
**action**
**una película llena de acción**
an action-packed film

el **aceite** NOUN
**oil**
**el aceite de oliva**
olive oil

la **aceituna** NOUN
**olive**
**aceitunas rellenas**
stuffed olives

el **acento** NOUN
**accent**
**'Té' lleva acento cuando significa 'tea'.**
'Té' has an accent when it means 'tea'.
**Tiene un acento cerrado del sur.**
He has a strong southern accent.

**aceptar** VERB
**to accept**
**Acepté su invitación.**
I accepted his invitation.
**Acepté ayudarles.**
I agreed to help them.

la **acera** NOUN
**pavement**

**acerca** ADVERB
**acerca de**
about
**un documental acerca de la fauna africana**
a documentary about African wildlife

**acercar** VERB
1 **to pass**
**¿Me acercas la sal?**
Could you pass me the salt?
2 **to bring over**
**Acerca la silla.**
Bring your chair over here.
**¿Acerco más la cama a la ventana?**
Shall I put the bed nearer the window?
**Nos acercaron al aeropuerto.**
They gave us a lift to the airport.
■ **acercarse**
1 **to come closer**
**Acércate, que te vea.**
Come closer so that I can see you.
2 **to go over**
**Me acerqué a la ventana.**
I went over to the window.
**Acércate a la tienda y trae una botella de agua.**
Go over to the shop and get a bottle of water.

**acertar** VERB
1 **to get ... right**
**He acertado todas las respuestas.**
I got all the answers right.
**No acerté.**
I got it wrong.
2 **to guess**
**Si aciertas cuántos caramelos hay, te los regalo todos.**
If you guess how many sweets there are, I'll give you all of them.

el **acierto**

> acierto *can be a noun or a verb.*

**A** NOUN
**right answer**
**Tuve más aciertos que fallos en el examen.**
I got more right answers than wrong ones in the exam.
**B** VERB ▷*see* **acertar**
**No acierto a entenderlo.**
I can't understand it at all.

**aclarar** VERB
**to clear up**
**Necesito que me aclares unas dudas.**
I need you to clear up some doubts for me.
**Con tantos números no me aclaro.**
There are so many numbers that I can't make head nor tail of it.

**acompañar** VERB
**acompañar a alguien**
to come with somebody/to go with somebody

> *Language tip*
> **acompañar a alguien** *has two meanings. Look at the examples.*

**Si quieres te acompaño.**
I'll come with you if you like.
**Me pidió que la acompañara a la estación.**
She asked me to go to the station with her.

**aconsejar** VERB
**to advise**
**Te aconsejo que lo hagas.**
I'd advise you to do it.

**acordarse** VERB
**to remember**

**Ahora mismo no me acuerdo.**
Right now I can't remember.
**acordarse de**
to remember
**¿Te acuerdas de mí?**
Do you remember me?
**Acuérdate de cerrar la puerta con llave.**
Remember to lock the door.

**acostado** (FEM **acostada**)
ADJECTIVE
**estar acostado**
to be in bed

**acostarse** VERB
1 **to lie down**
2 **to go to bed**

**acostumbrarse** VERB
**acostumbrarse a**
to get used to
**No me acostumbro a la vida en la ciudad.**
I can't get used to city life.
**Ya me he acostumbrado a trabajar de noche.**
I've got used to working at night now.

el **acto** NOUN
**ceremony**

**en el acto**
instantly

el **actor** NOUN
**actor**

la **actriz** (PL las **actrices**) NOUN
**actress**

la **actuación** (PL las **actuaciones**) NOUN
**performance**
**Fue una actuación muy buena.**
It was a very good performance.

**actual** (FEM **actual**) ADJECTIVE
**present**
**la situación actual del país**
the country's present situation
**uno de los mejores pintores**

**del arte actual**
one of the greatest painters of today

**Language tip**
Be careful! **actual** does not mean **actual**.

**actualmente** ADVERB
1 **nowadays**
**Actualmente apenas se utilizan las máquinas de escribir.**
Typewriters are hardly used nowadays.
2 **currently**
**Es geólogo, pero actualmente está en el paro.**
He's a geologist but he's currently out of work.

**Language tip**
Be careful! **actualmente** does not mean **actually**.

**actuar** VERB
1 **to act**
**Es difícil actuar con naturalidad delante de las cámaras.**
It's hard to act naturally in front of the cameras.
**No comprendo tu forma de actuar.**
I can't understand your behaviour.
**No actuó en esa película.**
He wasn't in that film.
2 **to perform**
**Hoy actúan en el Café del Jazz.**
Today they'll be performing at the Café del Jazz.

el **acuario** NOUN
1 **aquarium**
2 **fish tank**

el **acuerdo**

**acuerdo** can be a noun or part of the verb **acordar**.

**A** NOUN
### agreement

**llegar a un acuerdo**
to reach an agreement
**¡De acuerdo!**
All right!

**B** VERB ▷*see* **acordar**
**Ahora no me acuerdo.**
I can't remember it now.

## acusar VERB
### to accuse
**Su novia lo acusaba de mentiroso.**
His girlfriend accused him of being a liar.

## adelantado (FEM adelantada)
ADJECTIVE
**1 advanced**
**Suecia es un país muy adelantado.**
Sweden is a very advanced country.
**los niños más adelantados de la clase**
the children who are doing best in the class
**2 fast**
**Este reloj va adelantado.**
This watch is fast.

## adelantar VERB
**1 to bring ... forward**
**Tuvimos que adelantar la boda.**
We had to bring the wedding forward.
**2 to overtake**
**Adelanta a ese camión cuando puedas.**
Overtake that lorry when you can.
**3 to put ... forward**
**El domingo hay que adelantar los relojes una hora.**
On Sunday we'll have to put the clocks forward an hour.

## adelantarse VERB
### to go on ahead
**Me adelanté para coger asiento.**
I went on ahead to get a seat.

## adelante

**adelante** *can be an adverb or an exclamation.*

**A** ADVERB
**Se inclinó hacia adelante.**
He leant forward.
**más adelante**
further on/later

*Language tip*

**más adelante** *has two meanings. Look at the examples.*

**El pueblo está más adelante.**
The village is further on.
**Más adelante hablaremos de los resultados.**
We'll discuss the results later.
**B** EXCLAMATION
**1 come on!**
**2 come in!**

## adelgazar VERB
### to lose weight
**¡Cómo has adelgazado!**
You've really lost weight!
**He adelgazado cinco kilos.**
I've lost five kilos.

## además ADVERB
**1 as well**
**Es profesor y además carpintero.**
He's a teacher and a carpenter as well.
**2 what's more**
**El baño es demasiado pequeño y, además, no tiene ventana.**
The bathroom's too small and, what's more, it hasn't got a window.
**3 besides**
**Además, no tienes nada que perder.**

Besides, you've got nothing to lose.

**adentro** ADVERB
**inside**
> **Empezó a llover y se metieron adentro.**
> It began to rain so they went inside.

**adhesivo**
(FEM **adhesiva**)
ADJECTIVE
**sticky**
> **cinta adhesiva**
> sticky tape

**adiós** EXCLAMATION
**goodbye!**

> **decir adiós a alguien**
> to say goodbye to somebody

**adivinar** VERB
**to guess**
> **Adivina quién viene.**
> Guess who's coming.
> **adivinar el pensamiento a alguien**
> to read somebody's mind

el **adjetivo** NOUN
**adjective**

**admirar** VERB
**to admire**
> **Todos la admiran.**
> Everyone admires her.
> **Me admira lo poco que gastas en ropa.**
> I'm amazed at how little you spend on clothes.

**admitir** VERB
**1 to admit**
> **Admite que estabas equivocado.**
> Admit you were wrong.
**2 to accept**
> **La máquina no admite monedas de dos euros.**
> The machine doesn't accept two-euro coins.

**Espero que me admitan a la universidad.**
I hope I'll get a place at university.

el/la **adolescente** NOUN
**teenager**

**adónde** ADVERB
**where**
> **¿Adónde ibas?**
> Where were you going?

**adornar** VERB
**to decorate**

el **adulto**
la **adulta** NOUN
**adult**

el **adverbio** NOUN
**adverb**

**advertir** VERB
**to warn**
> **Ya te advertí que sería difícil.**
> I warned you it would be difficult.
> **Te advierto que no va a ser nada fácil.**
> I must warn you that it won't be at all easy.

**aéreo** (FEM **aérea**) ADJECTIVE
**air**
> **un ataque aéreo**
> an air raid

el **aeropuerto** NOUN
**airport**

**afectar** VERB
**to affect**
> **Esto a ti no te afecta.**
> This doesn't affect you.

**afeitar** VERB
**to shave**
> ■ **afeitarse**
> **to shave**
> **Voy a afeitarme.**
> I'm going to shave.
> **Se afeitó la barba.**
> He shaved off his beard.

la **afición** (PL las **aficiones**)
NOUN
**hobby**
Su afición es la filatelia.
His hobby is stamp collecting.
Tengo mucha afición por el ciclismo.
I'm very keen on cycling.

**aficionado**
**aficionada**

aficionado *can be a noun or an adjective.*

A MASC/FEM NOUN
1 **enthusiast**
un libro para los aficionados al ciclismo
a book for cycling enthusiasts
2 **amateur**
un partido para aficionados
a game for amateurs
B ADJECTIVE
1 **keen**
Es muy aficionado a la pintura.
He's very keen on painting.
2 **amateur**
un equipo de fútbol aficionado
an amateur football team

**aficionarse** VERB
aficionarse a algo
to take up something/to become interested in something

**Language tip**
aficionarse a algo *has two meanings. Look at the examples.*

Raúl se aficionó al tenis.
Raúl took up tennis.
Me he aficionado al teatro.
I've become interested in theatre.

**afirmar** VERB
afirmar que ...
to say that ...
Afirmaba que no la conocía.
He said that he didn't know her.

**aflojar** VERB
**to loosen**
■ aflojarse
**to come loose**
Se ha aflojado un tornillo.
A screw has come loose.

**afónico** (FEM **afónica**) ADJECTIVE
Estoy afónico.
I've lost my voice.

**afortunado** (FEM **afortunada**)
ADJECTIVE
**lucky**
Es un tipo afortunado.
He's a lucky guy.

**afuera** ADVERB
**outside**
Vámonos afuera.
Let's go outside.

las **afueras** NOUN
**outskirts**
en las afueras de Barcelona
on the outskirts of Barcelona

**agacharse** VERB
**to crouch down**

**agarrar** VERB
1 **to grab**
Agarró a su hermano por el hombro.
He grabbed his brother by the shoulder.
2 **to hold**
Agarra bien la sartén.
Hold the frying pan firmly.
■ agarrarse
**to hold on**
Agárrate a la barandilla.
Hold on to the rail.

la **agenda** NOUN
1 **diary**
2 **address book**

**Language tip**
*Be careful!* agenda *does not mean* agenda.

**agitar** VERB
**to shake**

**Agítese antes de usar.**
Shake before use.

**agosto** MASC NOUN
**August**

> **Language tip**
> Months are not spelled with a capital letter in Spanish.

**en agosto**
in August
**el ocho de agosto**
the eighth of August
**Nació el ocho de agosto.**
He was born on the eighth of August.

**agotado** (FEM **agotada**)
ADJECTIVE
1 **exhausted**
**Estoy agotado.**
I'm exhausted.

2 **sold out**
**Ese modelo en concreto está agotado.**
That particular model is sold out.

**agotar** VERB
1 **to use up**
**Agotamos todas nuestras reservas.**
We used up all our supplies.
2 **to tire out**
**Me agota tanto ejercicio.**
All this exercise is tiring me out.
■ **agotarse**
**to run out**
**Se está agotando la leña.**
The firewood's running out.
**Se agotaron todas las entradas.**
The tickets all sold out.

**agradable** (FEM **agradable**)
ADJECTIVE
**nice**

**agradecer** VERB
**agradecer algo a alguien**
to thank somebody for something
**Te agradezco tu interés.**
Thank you for your interest.

la **agresión** (PL las **agresiones**)
NOUN
**attack**

el **agricultor**
la **agricultora** NOUN
**farmer**

la **agricultura** NOUN
**farming**

el **agua** FEM NOUN
**water**
**agua corriente**
running water
**agua potable**
drinking water

**aguantar** VERB
1 **to stand**
**No aguanto la ópera.**
I can't stand opera.
**Su vecina no la aguanta.**
Her neighbour can't stand her.
**Últimamente estás que no hay quien te aguante.**
You've been unbearable lately.
2 **to take**
**La estantería no va a aguantar el peso.**
The shelf won't take the weight.
3 **to hold**
**Aguántame el martillo un momento.**
Can you hold the hammer for me for a moment?
**Aguanta la respiración.**
Hold your breath.
**No pude aguantar la risa.**
I couldn't help laughing.

**Si no puede venir, que se aguante.**
If he can't come, he'll just have to lump it.

**agudo** (FEM **aguda**) ADJECTIVE
1 **sharp**
2 **high-pitched**
3 **witty**

la **aguja** NOUN
1 **needle**
2 **hand**

el **agujero** NOUN
**hole**
**hacer un agujero**
to make a hole

**ahí** ADVERB
**there**
**¡Ahí están!**
There they are!
**Lo tienes ahí mismo.**
You've got it right there.

*Language tip*

*por ahí has several meanings. It can be translated as* **over there**, **somewhere** *and* **thereabouts**. *Look at the examples.*

**Tú busca por ahí.**
You look over there.
**¿Has visto las tijeras? – Andarán por ahí.**
Have you seen the scissors? – They must be somewhere around.
**doscientos o por ahí**
two hundred or thereabouts

**ahogarse** VERB
**to drown**
**Se ahogó en el río.**
He drowned in the river.

**ahora**
ADVERB
**now**

**¿Dónde vamos ahora?**
Where are we going now?

**Ahora mismo está de viaje.**
He's away on a trip right now.
**Ahora te lo digo.**
I'll tell you in a moment.
**Por ahora no cambies nada.**
Don't change anything for the moment.
**Ahora mismo voy.**
I'm just coming.

**ahora mismo**
right now
**de ahora en adelante**
from now on
**por ahora**
for now

**ahorrar** VERB
**to save**

el **aire** NOUN
1 **air**
**Necesitamos aire para respirar.**
We need air to breathe.
**aire acondicionado**
air conditioning
2 **wind**
**El aire se le llevó la gorra.**
The wind blew his cap off.
**al aire libre**
outdoors/outdoor

*Language tip*

*al aire libre has two meanings. Look at the examples.*

**Comimos al aire libre.**
We had lunch outdoors.
**una fiesta al aire libre**
an outdoor party

el **ajo** NOUN
**garlic**

**al** PREPOSITION (= *a + el*) ▷ *see* **a**
**Fui al cine.**
I went to the cinema.

el **ala** FEM NOUN
**wing**

**alargar** VERB
1 **to make ... longer**

Hay que alargar un poco las mangas.
We'll need to make the sleeves a bit longer.

**2 to extend**
Decidieron alargar las vacaciones.
They decided to extend their holidays.

■ alargarse
**to get longer**
Ya van alargándose los días.
The days are getting longer.

la **alarma** NOUN
**alarm**
Saltó la alarma.
The alarm went off.
dar la voz de alarma
to raise the alarm
alarma de incendios
fire alarm

el **alboroto** NOUN
**racket**
¡Vaya alboroto!
What a racket!

**alcanzar** VERB
**1 to catch up with**
La alcancé cuando salía por la puerta.
I caught up with her just as she was going out of the door.

**2 to reach**
alcanzar la cima de la montaña
to reach the top of the mountain

**3 to pass**
¿Me alcanzas las tijeras?
Could you pass me the scissors?

**alegrar** VERB
**to cheer up**
Intenté alegrarlos con unos chistes.
I tried to cheer them up with a few jokes.
Me alegra que hayas venido.
I'm glad you've come.

■ alegrarse
**to be glad**
¿Te gusta? Me alegro.
You like it? I'm glad.
Me alegro de su éxito.
I'm glad about his success.
alegrarse por alguien
to be happy for somebody
Me alegro por ti.
I'm happy for you.

**alegre** (FEM **alegre**) ADJECTIVE
**cheerful**

la **alegría** NOUN
Sentí una gran alegría.
I was really happy.

¡Qué alegría!
How lovely!

**alejarse** VERB
**to move away**
Aléjate un poco del fuego.
Move a bit further away from the fire.

la **alergia** NOUN
**allergy**
¿Tienes alguna alergia?
Have you got any allergies?
alergia al polen
hay fever

las **aletas** PL NOUN
**flippers**

la **alfombra** NOUN
**1 rug**
**2 carpet**

**algo**

**algo** *can be a pronoun or an adverb.*

**A** PRONOUN

**1 something**
Algo se está quemando.
Something is burning.
¿Quieres algo de comer?
Would you like something to eat?
¿Te pasa algo?
Is something the matter?
Aún queda algo de zumo.
There's still some juice left.

**2 anything**
¿Algo más?
Anything else?

**B** ADVERB
**rather**
La falda te está algo corta.
The skirt's rather short on you.

el **algodón** (PL los **algodones**) NOUN
**cotton**
Me puse algodones en los oídos.
I put cotton wool in my ears.
el algodón de azúcar
candyfloss

**alguien** PRONOUN
**1 somebody**
Alguien llama a la puerta.
There's somebody knocking at the door.
¿Necesitas que te ayude alguien?
Do you need somebody to help you?

**2 anybody**
¿Conoces a alguien aquí?
Do you know anybody here?

**algún** ADJECTIVE (FEM **alguna**, MASC PL **algunos**)
**1 some**
Algún día iré.
I'll go there some day.

**2 any**
¿Compraste algún cuadro?
Did you buy any pictures?
¿Quieres alguna cosa más?
Was there anything else?

algún que otro …
the odd …

**alguno** PRONOUN (FEM **alguna**)
**1 somebody**
Siempre hay alguno que se queja.
There's always somebody who complains.
Algunos piensan que no ocurrió así.
Some people think that's not what happened.

**2 some**
Solo conozco a algunos de los vecinos.
I only know some of the neighbours.
Tiene que estar en alguna de estas cajas.
It must be in one of these boxes.

**3 any**
Necesito una aspirina. ¿Te queda alguna?
I need an aspirin. Have you got any left?
Si alguno quiere irse que se vaya.
If any of them want to leave, fine.
¿Lo sabe alguno de vosotros?
Do any of you know?

el **alimento** NOUN
**food**
alimentos congelados
frozen food

**allá** ADVERB
**over there**
Tu libro está allá.
Your book is over there.
Échate un poco más allá.
Move over that way a bit.

**allí** ADVERB
  **there**
> **Allí está.**
> There it is.
> **Allí viene tu hermana.**
> Here comes your sister.

el **alma** FEM NOUN
  **soul**
> **Lo siento en el alma.**
> I'm really sorry.

la **almohada** NOUN
  **pillow**

**almorzar** VERB
  **to have lunch**
> **No he almorzado todavía.**
> I haven't had lunch yet.
> **¿Qué has almorzado?**
> What did you have for lunch?

el **almuerzo** NOUN
  **lunch**

**alrededor** ADVERB
  **alrededor de**
  around/about

> **Language tip**
>
> **alrededor de** *has two meanings.*
> *Look at the examples.*

> **El satélite gira alrededor de la Tierra.**
> The satellite goes around the Earth.
> **Deben de ser alrededor de las dos.**
> It must be about two o'clock.

los **alrededores** PL NOUN
> **Ocurrió en los alrededores de Madrid.**
> It happened near Madrid.
> **Hay muchas tiendas en los alrededores del museo.**
> There are a lot of shops in the area around the museum.

**alto** (FEM **alta**)

> **algo** *can be an adjective, a pronoun or an exclamation.*

**A** ADJECTIVE
1 **tall**
> **Es un chico muy alto.**
> He's a very tall boy.
> **un edificio muy alto**
> a very tall building

2 **high**
> **El Everest es la montaña más alta del mundo.**
> Everest is the highest mountain in the world.
> **Sacó notas altas en todos los exámenes.**
> He got high marks in all his exams.

3 **loud**
> **La música está demasiado alta.**
> The music's too loud.

**B** ADVERB
  **high**
> **subir muy alto**
> to go up very high
> **Pepe habla muy alto.**
> Pepe has got a very loud voice.
> **¡Más alto, por favor!**
> Speak up, please!
> **Pon el volumen más alto.**
> Turn the volume up.

**C** EXCLAMATION
  **stop!**

la **altura** NOUN
  **height**
> **Volamos a una altura de quince mil pies.**
> We're flying at a height of fifteen thousand feet.
> **La pared tiene dos metros de altura.**
> The wall's two metres high.

el **alumno**
la **alumna** NOUN
  **pupil**

**amable** (FEM **amable**) ADJECTIVE
  **kind**

**amanecer**

> **amanecer** *can be a verb or a noun.*

**Spanish English**

a b c d e f g h i j k l m n ñ o p q r s t u v w x y z

**A** VERB
**to get light**
**Amanece a las siete.**
It gets light at seven.

**B** MASC NOUN
**dawn**

**al amanecer**
at dawn

**amar** VERB
**to love**

**amargo** (FEM **amarga**) ADJECTIVE
**bitter**

**amarillo** (FEM **amarilla**)
ADJECTIVE, MASC NOUN
**yellow**

el **ambiente** NOUN
**atmosphere**
**Se respira un ambiente tenso.**
There's a tense atmosphere.
**el medio ambiente**
the environment

**amenace** VERB ▷ see **amenazar**
**No voy a hacerlo aunque me amenace.**
I'm not going to do it even if he threatens me.

la **amenaza** NOUN
**threat**

**amenazar** VERB
**to threaten**
**Le amenazó con decírselo al profesor.**
He threatened to tell the teacher.

el **amigo**
la **amiga** NOUN
**friend**

**hacerse amigos**
to become friends

el **amor** NOUN
**love**

**ancho** (FEM **ancha**) ADJECTIVE
1 **wide**
**una calle ancha**
a wide street
2 **loose**
**Le gusta llevar ropa ancha.**
He likes to wear loose clothing.
**Me está ancho el vestido.**
The dress is too big for me.

**anda** EXCLAMATION
1 **well I never!**
**¡Anda, un billete de cincuenta euros!**
Well I never, a fifty-euro note!
2 **come on**
**¡Anda, ponte el abrigo y vámonos!**
Come on, put your coat on and let's go!

**¡Anda ya!**
You're not serious!

**andar** VERB
1 **to walk**
**Anduvimos varios kilómetros.**
We walked several kilometres.
**Iremos andando a la estación.**
We'll walk to the station.
2 **to be**
**Últimamente ando muy liado.**
I've been very busy lately.
**No sé por dónde anda.**
I don't know where he is.
**¿Qué tal andas?**
How are you?
**andar mal de dinero**
to be short of money

**anduve** VERB ▷see **andar**
**Anduve dos horas.**
I walked for two hours

el **ángel** NOUN
**angel**

el **ángulo** NOUN
**angle**
**en ángulo recto**
at right angles

el **anillo** NOUN
**ring**
**un anillo de boda**
a wedding ring

**animado** (FEM **animada**)
ADJECTIVE
1 **cheerful**
**Últimamente parece que está más animada.**
She has seemed more cheerful lately.
2 **lively**
**Fue una fiesta muy animada.**
It was a very lively party.
**dibujos animados**
cartoons

el **animal** NOUN
**animal**
**los animales domésticos**
pets

**animar** VERB
1 **to cheer up**
**Lo ha pasado muy mal y necesita que la animen.**
She has had a rough time and needs cheering up.
2 **to cheer on**
**Estuvimos animando al equipo.**

We were cheering the team on.
**animar a alguien a que haga algo**
to encourage somebody to do something
**Nos animaron a que fuésemos a la fiesta.**
They encouraged us to go to the party.
■ **animarse**
**to cheer up**
**¡Vamos, anímate hombre!**
Come on, cheer up mate!
**animarse a hacer algo**
to make up one's mind to do something

**ánimo** EXCLAMATION
**cheer up!**
**¡Ánimo, chaval, que no es el fin del mundo!**
Cheer up mate, it's not the end of the world!

**anoche** ADVERB
**last night**
**antes de anoche**
the night before last

**anochecer** VERB
**to get dark**
**En invierno anochece muy temprano.**
It gets dark very early in winter.

**anteayer** ADVERB
**the day before yesterday**

la **antena** NOUN
**aerial**
**una antena parabólica**
a satellite dish

**anterior** (FEM **anterior**)
ADJECTIVE
**before**
**La semana anterior llovió mucho.**
It rained a lot the week before.
**Su examen fue anterior al nuestro.**
Their exam was before ours.

**antes** ADVERB
1 **before**
   **Esta película ya la he visto antes.**
   I've seen this film before.
   **antes de la cena**
   before dinner
   **antes de que te vayas**
   before you go
   **Él estaba aquí antes que yo.**
   He was here before me.
   **Antes no había tantos juguetes.**
   People didn't use to have so many toys.
2 **first**
   **Nosotros llegamos antes.**
   We arrived first.

**lo antes posible**
as soon as possible

**antiguo** (FEM **antigua**) ADJECTIVE
**old**
   **Este reloj es muy antiguo.**
   This clock is very old.

**antipático** (FEM **antipática**)
ADJECTIVE
**unfriendly**

**anual** (FEM **anual**) ADJECTIVE
**annual**

**anunciar** VERB
**to announce**
   **anunciar una decisión**
   to announce a decision

el **anuncio** NOUN
1 **advertisement**
   **Pusieron un anuncio en el periódico.**
   They put an advertisement in the paper.
2 **announcement**
   **Tengo que hacer un anuncio importante.**
   I have an important announcement to make.

**añadir** VERB
**to add**

el **año** NOUN
**year**
   **Estuve allí el año pasado.**
   I was there last year.
   **¿Cuántos años tiene?**
   How old is he?
   **Tiene quince años.**
   He's fifteen.

**¡Feliz Año Nuevo!**
Happy New Year!
**el año que viene**
next year
**el año pasado**
last year
**los años ochenta**
the eighties

**apagar** VERB
**to switch off**
   **Apaga la tele.**
   Switch the TV off.

**aparecer** VERB
1 **to appear**
   **De repente apareció la policía.**
   The police suddenly appeared.
2 **to turn up**
   **¿Han aparecido ya las tijeras?**
   Have the scissors turned up yet?

el **apartamento** NOUN
**flat**

**apartar** VERB
**to move out of the way**
   **Aparta todas las sillas.**
   Move all the chairs out of the way.
   **¡Aparta!**
   Stand back!
■ **apartarse**
   **to stand back**
   **Apártense de la puerta.**
   Stand back from the door.

el **apellido** NOUN
surname

**apenas** ADVERB, CONJUNCTION
1 **hardly**
No tenemos apenas nada de comer.
We've got hardly anything to eat.
Apenas podía levantarse.
He could hardly stand up.
2 **hardly ever**
Apenas voy al cine.
I hardly ever go to the cinema.
3 **barely**
Hace apenas diez minutos que hablé con ella.
I spoke to her barely ten minutes ago.
Terminé en apenas dos horas.
It only took me two hours to finish.

el **aperitivo** NOUN
aperitif

**apestar** VERB
to stink
Te apestan los pies.
Your feet stink.
apestar a
to stink of

**apetecer** VERB
¿Te apetece una tortilla?
Do you fancy an omelette?
No, gracias, ahora no me apetece.
No, thanks, I don't feel like it just now.

el **apetito** NOUN
appetite
Eso te va a quitar el apetito.
You won't have any appetite left.
No tengo apetito.
I'm not hungry.

**aplastar** VERB
to squash
Me senté encima del regalo y lo aplasté.
I sat on the present and squashed it.

**aplaudir** VERB
to clap
Todos aplaudían.
Everyone clapped.

el **aplauso** NOUN
applause
Los aplausos duraron varios minutos.
The applause lasted for several minutes.

**aplazar** VERB
to postpone

**apostar** VERB
to bet
apostar por algo
to bet on something
¿Qué te apuestas a que ... ?
How much do you bet that...?

**apoyar** VERB
1 **to lean**
Apoya el espejo contra la pared.
Lean the mirror against the wall.
2 **to rest**
Apoya la espalda en este cojín.
Rest your back against this cushion.
3 **to support**
Todos mis compañeros me apoyan.
All my colleagues support me.
■ **apoyarse**
to lean
No te apoyes en la mesa.
Don't lean on the table.

**aprender** VERB
to learn
Ya me he aprendido los verbos irregulares.

I've already learnt the irregular verbs.

**aprender a hacer algo**
to learn to do something
**Estoy aprendiendo a tocar la guitarra.**
I'm learning to play the guitar.

**aprender algo de memoria**
to learn something off by heart

**apretado** (FEM **apretada**)
ADJECTIVE
1 **tight**
**Estos pantalones me están muy apretados.**
These trousers are very tight on me.
2 **cramped**
**Íbamos muy apretados en el autobús.**
We were very cramped on the bus.

**apretar** VERB
1 **to tighten**
**Aprieta bien los tornillos.**
Tighten up the screws.
2 **to press**
**Aprieta este botón.**
Press this button.
**Me aprietan los zapatos.**
My shoes are too tight.

**aprobar** VERB
**to pass**
**aprobar un examen**
to pass an exam
**aprobar por los pelos**
to scrape through

**aprovechar** VERB
1 **to make good use of**
**No aprovecha el tiempo.**
He doesn't make good use of his time.
2 **to use**
**Aprovecharé los ratos libres para estudiar.**
I'll use my spare time to study.
**aprovecharse de**
to take advantage of

**Me aproveché de la situación.**
I took advantage of the situation.
**Todos se aprovechan del pobre chico.**
Everyone takes advantage of the poor boy.

**¡Que aproveche!**
Enjoy your meal!

**apruebo** VERB ▷ see **aprobar**
**Si no apruebo, mis padres se enfadarán.**
If I fail, my parents will be angry.

**apuesto** VERB ▷ see **apostar**
**Te apuesto a que no le va a gustar.**
I bet you she won't like it.

**apuntar** VERB
1 **to write down**
**Apúntalo o se te olvidará.**
Write it down or you'll forget.
**Apunta mis datos.**
Can you take a note of my details?
2 **to point**
**Me apuntó con el dedo.**
He pointed at me.
▪ **apuntarse**
**to put one's name down**
**Nos hemos apuntado para el viaje a Marruecos.**
We've put our names down for the trip to Morocco.
**apuntarse a un curso**
to enrol on a course

**¡Yo me apunto!**
Count me in!

los **apuntes** NOUN
**notes**

**tomar apuntes**
to take notes

**aquel** (FEM **aquella**) ADJECTIVE

Spanish English
a b c d e f g h i j k l m n ñ o p q r s t u v w x y z

**that**
> **Me gusta más aquella mesa.**
> I prefer that table.

**aquél** (FEM **aquélla**) PRONOUN
**that one**
> **Aquél no es el mío.**
> That one isn't mine.
> **Dame aquélla de allí.**
> Give me that one over there.

**aquello** PRONOUN
> **aquello que hay allí**
> that thing over there

**aquí** ADVERB
1 **here**
> **Aquí está el informe que me pediste.**
> Here's the report you asked me for.
2 **now**
> **de aquí en adelante**
> from now on
> **por aquí**
> around here/this way

> *Language tip*
>
> **por aquí** *has two meanings. Look at the examples.*

> **Lo tenía por aquí en alguna parte.**
> I had it around here somewhere.
> **Pasa por aquí, por favor.**
> Please come this way.

la **araña** NOUN
**spider**
> **¡Hay una araña en la bañera!**
> There's a spider in the bath!

**arañar** VERB
**to scratch**
> **El gato me arañó.**
> The cat scratched me

el **árbitro**
la **árbitra** NOUN
**referee**

el **árbol** NOUN
**tree**
> **un árbol frutal**
> a fruit tree
> **el árbol de Navidad**
> the Christmas tree

el **arco** NOUN
1 **bow**
2 **arch**
> **el arco iris**
> the rainbow

**arder** VERB
**to burn**
> **Ese tronco no va a arder.**
> That log won't burn.
> **¡La sopa está ardiendo!**
> The soup's boiling hot!

la **ardilla** NOUN
**squirrel**

el **área** FEM NOUN
**area**

la **arena** NOUN
**sand**
> **arenas movedizas**
> quicksand

**armar** VERB
1 **to assemble**
> **El juguete viene desmontado y luego tú lo armas.**
> The toy comes in pieces and you assemble it.
2 **to make**
> **Los vecinos de arriba arman mucho jaleo.**
> Our upstairs neighbours make a lot of noise.
> **armarse un lío**
> to get in a muddle
> **Me voy a armar un lío con tantos números.**
> I'm going to get into a muddle with all these numbers.

el **armario** NOUN
1 **cupboard**
**un armario de cocina**
a kitchen cupboard
2 **wardrobe**

**arrancar** VERB
1 **to pull up**
**Estaba arrancando malas hierbas.**
I was pulling up weeds.
2 **to pull out**
**Le arranqué una espina del dedo.**
I pulled a thorn out of his finger.

**arrastrar** VERB
**to drag**
**Arrastraba una maleta enorme.**
He was dragging an enormous suitcase.
■ **arrastrarse**
**to crawl**
**Llegaron hasta la valla arrastrándose.**
They crawled up to the fence.

**arreglar** VERB
**to fix**
**¿Sabrás arreglarme el grifo?**
Could you fix the tap for me?

**arreglarse** VERB
1 **to get ready**
**Se arregló para salir.**
She got ready to go out.
2 **to work out**
**Ya verás como todo se arregla.**
It'll all work out, you'll see.

el **arreglo** NOUN
**repair**
**El tostador sólo necesita un pequeño arreglo.**
The toaster only needs a minor repair.
**Esta tele no tiene arreglo.**
This TV is unrepairable.
**Este problema no tiene arreglo.**
There's no solution to this problem.

**arriba** ADVERB
1 **above**
**Los platos y las tazas están arriba.**
The plates and mugs are above.
**Visto desde arriba parece más pequeño.**
Seen from above it looks smaller.
**Pon esos libros arriba del todo.**
Put those books on top.
2 **upstairs**
**Arriba están los dormitorios.**
The bedrooms are upstairs.
**los vecinos de arriba**
our upstairs neighbours

**más arriba**
further up

**arriesgado** (FEM **arriesgada**)
ADJECTIVE
**risky**

la **arroba** NOUN
**at**
**Mi e-mail es loveday arroba collins punto E-S (loveday@collins.es).**
My email address is loveday at collins dot E-S (loveday@collins.es).

**arrojar** VERB
**to throw**
**Arrojaban piedras y palos.**
They were throwing sticks and stones.

el **arroyo** NOUN
**stream**

el **arroz** NOUN
**rice**
**arroz blanco**
white rice
**arroz con leche**
rice pudding

la **arruga** NOUN
1 **wrinkle**
2 **crease**

el **arte** (PL las **artes**) NOUN
**art**
>el arte abstracto
>abstract art

el **artículo** NOUN
**article**
>el artículo determinado
>the definite article
>el artículo indeterminado
>the indefinite article

**artificial** (FEM **artificial**)
ADJECTIVE
**artificial**

el/la **artista**
NOUN
1 **artist**
2 **un artista**
an actor
**una artista**
an actress

**asar** VERB
**to roast**
>asar algo a la parrilla
>to grill something

Me aso de calor.
I'm boiling.

el **ascensor** NOUN
**lift**

el **asco** NOUN
>El ajo me da asco.
>I think garlic's revolting.
>La casa está hecha un asco.
>The house is filthy.

¡Qué asco!
How revolting!

el **aseo** NOUN
>el aseo personal
>personal hygiene
>los aseos
>the toilets

**así** ADVERB
1 **like this**
>Se hace así.
>You do it like this.

2 **like that**
>Es así: como lo hace Jorge.
>It's like that: the way Jorge is
>doing it.
>¿Ves aquel abrigo? Quiero
>algo así.
>Do you see that coat? I'd like
>something like that.
>un tomate así de grande
>a tomato this big

el **asiento** NOUN
**seat**
>el asiento delantero
>the front seat
>el asiento trasero
>the back seat

la **asignatura** NOUN
**subject**
>Tiene dos asignaturas
>pendientes.
>He's got two subjects to retake.

**asomar** VERB
>No asomes la cabeza por la
>ventanilla.
>Don't lean out of the window.
>Asómate a la ventana.
>Look out of the window.

**asombrar** VERB
**to amaze**
>Me asombra que no lo sepas.
>I'm amazed you don't know.
■ **asombrarse**
**to be amazed**
>Se asombró de lo tarde que
>era.
>He was amazed at how late it
>was.

**el aspecto** NOUN
**appearance**
> **A ver si cuidas más tu aspecto.**
> You need to take a bit more care
> with your appearance.

**la aspiradora** NOUN
**vacuum cleaner**

**asqueroso** (FEM **asquerosa**)
ADJECTIVE
1 **disgusting**
2 **filthy**
> **Esta cocina está asquerosa.**
> This kitchen is filthy.

**el asunto** NOUN
**matter**
> **Es un asunto muy delicado.**
> It's a very delicate matter.
> **No me gusta que se metan
> en mis asuntos.**
> I don't like anyone meddling in
> my affairs.
> **¡Eso no es asunto tuyo!**
> That's none of your business!

**asustar** VERB
1 **to frighten**
> **No me asustan los
> fantasmas.**
> I'm not frightened of ghosts.
2 **to startle**
> **¡Huy! Me has asustado.**
> Goodness! You startled me.
■ **asustarse**
**to get frightened**
> **Se asusta por nada.**
> He gets frightened over nothing.

**atacar** VERB
**to attack**

**el atajo** NOUN
**short cut**
> **Cogeremos un atajo.**
> We'll take a short cut.

**el ataque** NOUN
**attack**
> **un ataque contra alguien**
> an attack on somebody
> **Le dio un ataque de risa.**
> He burst out laughing.

**atar** VERB
**to tie**
> **Ata al perro a la farola.**
> Tie the dog to the lamppost.
> **Átate los cordones.**
> Tie your shoelaces up.

**atardecer**

> **atardecer** *can be a verb or a noun.*

**A** VERB
**to get dark**
> **Está atardeciendo.**
> It's getting dark.
**B** MASC NOUN
**dusk**

> **al atardecer**
> at dusk

**el atasco** NOUN
**traffic jam**

**atención**

> **atención** *can be a noun or an
> exclamation.*

**A** FEM NOUN
> **Hay que poner más atención.**
> You should pay more attention.
> **Escucha con atención.**
> Listen carefully.
> **El director del colegio le
> llamó la atención.**
> The headmaster gave him a
> talking-to.
> **Estás llamando la atención
> con esa ropa.**
> You're attracting attention to
> yourself in those clothes.

**B** EXCLAMATION

**¡Atención, por favor!**
May I have your attention please?
**'¡Atención!'**
'Danger!'

el **atentado** NOUN
**attack**

**un atentado terrorista**
a terrorist attack

**atento** (FEM **atenta**) ADJECTIVE
**thoughtful**

**Es un chico muy atento.**
He's a very thoughtful boy.
**Estaban atentos a las explicaciones del profesor.**
They were paying attention to the teacher's explanations.

el **aterrizaje** NOUN
**landing**

**un aterrizaje forzoso**
an emergency landing

**aterrizar** VERB
**to land**

**atiendo** VERB ▷ see **atender**
**Ahora mismo la atiendo.**
I will be with you right away.

la **atracción** (PL las **atracciones**) NOUN
**attraction**

**una atracción turística**
a tourist attraction
**sentir atracción por algo**
to be attracted to something
**Sentía atracción por él.**
I was attracted to him.

**atractivo** (FEM **atractiva**)
ADJECTIVE
**attractive**

**un hombre muy atractivo**
a very attractive man

**atrapar** VERB
**to catch**

**Mi gato atrapa pájaros.**
My cat catches birds.

**atrás** ADVERB

1 **Los niños viajan siempre atrás.**
The children always travel in the back.
**la parte de atrás**
the back
**el asiento de atrás**
the back seat

2 **Mirar hacia atrás.**
To look back.
**Está más atrás.**
It's further back.
**ir para atrás**
to go backwards

3 **El coche de atrás va a adelantarnos.**
The car behind is going to overtake us.
**Yo me quedé atrás porque iba muy cansado.**
I stayed behind because I was very tired.

**atrasado** (FEM **atrasada**)
ADJECTIVE

1 **backward**
**Es un país muy atrasado.**
It's a very backward country.

2 **behind**
**Va bastante atrasado en la escuela.**
He's rather behind at school.
**Tengo mucho trabajo atrasado.**
I'm very behind with my work.

3 **El reloj está atrasado.**
The clock's slow.

**atravesar** VERB
**to cross**
**Atravesamos el río.**
We crossed the river.

**atreverse** VERB
**to dare**
**No me atreví a decírselo.**
I didn't dare tell him.
**No me atrevo.**
I daren't.

**atropellar** VERB
**to run over**
> Un coche atropelló al perro.
> The dog was run over by a car.

el **aula** FEM NOUN
**classroom**

el **aumento** NOUN
**increase**
> Ha habido un aumento de los precios.
> There's been an increase in prices.

**aun** ADVERB
**even**
> Aun sentado me duele la pierna.
> Even when I'm sitting down, my leg hurts.

> aun así
> even so

**aún** ADVERB
1 **still**
> Aún me queda un poco para terminar.
> I've still got a little bit left to finish.
> ¿Aún te duele?
> Is it still hurting?
2 **yet**
> Aún no ha llegado mi madre.
> My mum hasn't arrived yet.
> Y aún no me has devuelto el libro.
> You still haven't given me the book back.
3 **even**
> La película es aún más aburrida de lo que creía.
> The film's even more boring than I thought it would be.

**aunque** CONJUNCTION
1 **although**
> Me gusta el francés, aunque prefiero el alemán.
> I like French, although I prefer German.
> Estoy pensando en ir, aunque no sé cuándo.
> I'm thinking of going, though I don't know when.
> Seguí andando, aunque me dolía mucho la pierna.
> I went on walking, even though my leg was hurting a lot.
> No te lo daré, aunque protestes.
> You can complain all you like but you're not getting it.
2 **even if**
> Pienso irme, aunque tenga que salir por la ventana.
> I shall leave, even if I have to climb out of the window.

**ausente** (FEM **ausente**)
ADJECTIVE
**absent**

**auténtico** (FEM **auténtica**)
ADJECTIVE
1 **real**
> Es un auténtico campeón.
> He's a real champion.
2 **genuine**
> El cuadro era auténtico.
> The painting was genuine.

el **autobús** (PL los **autobuses**)
NOUN
**bus**

> en autobús
> by bus

**automático** (FEM **automática**)
ADJECTIVE
**automatic**

la **autopista** NOUN
**motorway**
> autopista de peaje
> toll motorway

el **autor**
la **autora** NOUN
**author**

la **autoridad** NOUN
**authority**

**autorizar** VERB
**to authorize**
>No le han autorizado la
>entrada al país.
>His entry into the country hasn't
>been authorized.

**auxilio** EXCLAMATION
**help!**

**avanzar** VERB
**to make progress**
>Isabel avanzó mucho el
>pasado trimestre.
>Isabel made a lot of progress last
>term.

el **ave** FEM NOUN
**bird**
>un ave
>de rapiña
>a bird of prey

la **aventura** NOUN
**adventure**
>Te contaré nuestras
>aventuras en la playa.
>I'll tell you about our adventures
>at the beach.

**avergonzar** VERB
**to embarrass**
>Me avergonzaste delante de
>todos.
>You embarrassed me in front of
>everyone.
>Me avergüenzan estas
>situaciones.
>I find this sort of situation
>embarrassing.
>**avergonzarse de algo**
>to be ashamed of something
>**No hay de qué avergonzarse.**
>There's nothing to be ashamed
>of.

la **avería** NOUN
>El coche tiene una avería.
>The car has broken down.

**averiarse** VERB
**to break down**

el **avión** (PL los aviones) NOUN
**plane**
>**ir en avión**
>to fly

**avisar** VERB
**1 to warn**
>Ya nos avisaron de que haría
>mucho frío.
>They warned us that it would be
>very cold.

**2 to let ... know**
>Avísanos si hay alguna
>novedad.
>Let us know if there's any news.

el **aviso** NOUN
**notice**
>Había un aviso en la puerta.
>There was a notice on the door.

la **avispa** NOUN
**wasp**

**ay** EXCLAMATION
**1 ow!**
>¡Ay! ¡Me has pisado!
>Ow! You've trodden on my toe!

**2 oh no!**
>¡Ay! ¡Creo que nos han
>engañado!
>Oh no! I think they've cheated
>us!

**ayer** ADVERB
**yesterday**
>**ayer por la mañana**
>yesterday morning
>**ayer por la tarde**
>yesterday afternoon/yesterday
>evening

**Language tip**

**ayer por la tarde** *has two
meanings. It can be translated as*
**yesterday afternoon** *and*
**yesterday evening**.

>**ayer por la noche**
>last night

**antes de ayer**
the day before yesterday

la **ayuda** NOUN
**help**
> **Gracias por tu ayuda.**
> Thanks for your help.

el/la **ayudante** NOUN
**assistant**

**ayudar** VERB
**to help**
> **¿Me ayudas con los ejercicios?**
> Could you help me with these exercises?
> **Me está ayudando a hacer los deberes.**
> He's helping me do my homework.

el **ayuntamiento** NOUN
1 **town hall**
2 **city hall**

la **azafata** NOUN
**air-hostess**

el **azúcar** NOUN
**sugar**

**azul** ADJECTIVE, MASC NOUN
**blue**
> **una puerta azul**
> a blue door
> **azul celeste**
> sky blue
> **azul marino**
> navy blue
> **Yo iba de azul.**
> I was wearing blue.

# B b

el **bache** NOUN
1 pothole
2 bump

el **Bachillerato** NOUN

> **Did you know…?**
> The **Bachillerato** is a two-year secondary school course leading to university.

la **bacteria** NOUN
bacterium

la **bahía** NOUN
bay

**bailar** VERB
to dance
sacar a bailar a alguien
to ask somebody to dance

el **bailarín**
la **bailarina** NOUN (MASC PL
los **bailarines**)
dancer

el **baile** NOUN
dance
Me han invitado a un baile.
I have been invited to a dance.

**bajar** VERB
1 to go down
Bajó la escalera muy despacio.
He went down the stairs very slowly.
2 to come down
Baja y ayúdame.
Come down and help me.
3 to take down
¿Has bajado la basura?
Have you taken the rubbish down?
4 to bring down
¿Me bajas el abrigo?
Could you bring my coat down?

5 to fall
Han bajado los precios.
Prices have fallen.
6 to turn down
Baja la radio.
Turn the radio down.
7 to download
■ bajarse de
to get off/to get out of/to get down from

> **Language tip**
> **bajarse de** has three meanings. Look at the examples.

Se bajó del autobús antes que yo.
He got off the bus before me.
¡Bájate del coche!
Get out of the car!
¡Bájate del árbol!
Get down from the tree!

**bajo** (FEM **baja**)

> **bajo** can be an adjective, a preposition or an adverb.

A ADJECTIVE
1 low
una silla muy baja
a very low chair
la temporada baja
the low season
Hablaban en voz baja.
They were speaking quietly.

**2 short**
Mi hermano es muy bajo.
My brother is very short.

**3 ground**
Viven en la planta baja.
They live on the ground floor.

**B** PREPOSITION
**under**
Juan llevaba un libro bajo el brazo.
Juan was carrying a book under his arm.

**C** ADVERB

**1 low**
El avión volaba muy bajo.
The plane was flying very low.

**2 quietly**
¡Habla bajo!
Speak quietly!

la **bala** NOUN
**bullet**

el **balcón** (PL los **balcones**) NOUN
**balcony**

la **baldosa** NOUN
**tile**

la **ballena** NOUN
**whale**

el **ballet** (PL los **ballets**) NOUN
**ballet**

el **balón** (PL los **balones**) NOUN
**ball**
balón de fútbol
football

el **baloncesto** NOUN
**basketball**
jugar al baloncesto
to play basketball

el **balonvolea** NOUN
**volleyball**
jugar al balonvolea
to play volleyball

el **banco** NOUN
**1 bench**
**2 bank**

la **banda** NOUN
**1 band**
Toca la trompeta en una banda.
He plays the trumpet with a band.

**2 gang**
La policía ha cogido a toda la banda.
The police have caught the whole gang.
la banda ancha
broadband
la banda sonora
the soundtrack

la **bandeja** NOUN
**tray**

la **bandera** NOUN
**flag**

la **banqueta** NOUN
**stool**

el **banquillo** NOUN
**bench**
El entrenador está en el banquillo.
The trainer is sitting on the bench.

el **bañador** NOUN
**1 swimming trunks**
**2 swimming costume**

**bañarse** VERB
**1 to have a bath**

Me gusta más bañarme que ducharme.
I prefer having a bath to having a shower.

**2 to go for a swim**
Estuve en la playa pero no me bañé.
I went to the beach but I didn't go for a swim.

la **bañera** NOUN
bath

el **baño** NOUN
**1 bathroom**
La casa tiene dos baños.
The house has two bathrooms.
darse un baño
to have a bath/to go for a swim

> **Language tip**
>
> **darse un baño** has two meanings. It can be translated by **to have a bath** or **to go for a swim**.

**2 toilet**
¿Puedo usar el baño, por favor?
Can I use the toilet, please?

el **bar** NOUN
bar

la **baraja** NOUN
pack of cards

**barato** (FEM **barata**)

> **barato** can be an adjective or an adverb.

**A** ADJECTIVE
**cheap**
Esta marca es más barata que aquélla.
This brand is cheaper than that one.

**B** ADVERB
**cheaply**
Aquí se come muy barato.
You can eat really cheaply here.

la **barba** NOUN
beard

dejarse barba
to grow a beard

la **barbaridad** NOUN
**1 atrocity**
Hicieron barbaridades en la guerra.
They committed atrocities during the war.
**2 Pablo come una barbaridad.**
Pablo eats an awful lot.

la **barbilla** NOUN
chin

la **barca** NOUN
boat

el **barco** NOUN
**1 ship**
**2 boat**
un barco de vela
a sailing boat

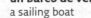

la **barra** NOUN
bar
una barra metálica
a metal bar
Me tomé un café en la barra.
I had a coffee at the bar.
una barra de pan
a French stick
una barra de labios
a lipstick

**barrer** VERB
to sweep

la **barrera** NOUN
barrier

la **barriga** NOUN
belly
Estás echando barriga.
You're getting a bit of a belly.
Me duele la barriga.
I've got a stomachache.

**Spanish English**

a b c d e f g h i j k l m n ñ o p q r s t u v w x y z

el **barrio** NOUN
**area**
> **Ese chico no es del barrio.**
> That boy's not from this area.

el **barro** NOUN
**mud**
> **Me llené los zapatos de barro.**
> My shoes got covered in mud.

el **barullo** NOUN
**racket**
> **armar barullo**
> to make a racket

la **báscula** NOUN
**scales**

la **base** NOUN
**base**
> **la base de la columna**
> the base of the column

**básico** (FEM **básica**) ADJECTIVE
**basic**

**bastante** (FEM **bastante**)

> **bastante** *can be an adjective or an adverb.*

**A** ADJECTIVE
1 **enough**
> **No tengo bastante dinero.**
> I haven't got enough money.
> **¿Hay bastante?**
> Is there enough?

2 **quite a lot of**
> **Vino bastante gente.**
> Quite a lot of people came.
> **Se tarda bastante tiempo en llegar.**
> It takes quite a while to get there.

**B** ADVERB
**quite**
> **Son bastante ricos.**
> They are quite rich.

**bastar** VERB
**to be enough**
> **Con esto basta.**
> That's enough.

> **¡Basta ya de tonterías!**
> That's enough of your nonsense!

> **¡Basta!**
> That's enough!

la **basura** NOUN
1 **rubbish**
> **Eso es basura.**
> That's rubbish.
> **tirar algo a la basura**
> to put something in the bin
2 **litter**

el **basurero** NOUN
**dustman**

la **bata** NOUN
**overall**

la **batalla** NOUN
**battle**

**batería**

> **batería** *can be a feminine or masculine noun.*

**A** FEM NOUN
1 **battery**
> **Se ha agotado la batería.**
> The battery is flat.
2 **drums**
> **¿Tocas la batería?**
> Do you play the drums?
**B** MASC/FEM NOUN
**drummer**

el **batido** NOUN
1 **milkshake**
> **un batido de fresa**
> a strawberry milkshake
2 **smoothie**

**batir** VERB
1 **to break**
2 **to beat**

el **baúl** NOUN
1 **chest**
2 **trunk**

el **bautizo** NOUN
**christening**

**beber** VERB

**to drink**
> **Hay que beber mucha agua en verano.**
> You need to drink a lot of water in the summer.

la **bebida** NOUN
**drink**
> **bebidas alcohólicas**
> alcoholic drinks

la **beca** NOUN
1 **grant**
2 **scholarship**

el **beicon** NOUN
**bacon**

la **belleza** NOUN
**beauty**

**bello** (FEM **bella**) ADJECTIVE
**beautiful**

**bendecir** VERB
**to bless**

la **bendición** (PL las **bendiciones**) NOUN
**blessing**

las **bermudas** NOUN
**Bermuda shorts**
> **Le compré unas bermudas.**
> I bought him a pair of Bermuda shorts.

**besar** VERB
**to kiss**
> **Ana y Pepe se besaron.**
> Ana and Pepe kissed each other.

el **beso** NOUN
**kiss**
> **Dame un beso.**
> Give me a kiss.

> **besos**
> love

**Did you know...?**

*Did you know that Spanish speakers sometimes end e-mails, postcards and letters to friends with un beso (a kiss) or besos (kisses)?*

la **bestia** NOUN
**beast**

la **Biblia** NOUN
**Bible**

la **biblioteca** NOUN
**library**

el **bicho** NOUN
**insect**
> **Me ha picado un bicho.**
> I've been bitten by an insect.
> **David es un bicho raro.**
> David's weird.

la **bici** NOUN
**bike**

la **bicicleta** NOUN
**bicycle**
> **una bicicleta de montaña**
> a mountain bike

**bien**

**bien** *can be an adverb or a noun.*

**A** ADVERB
1 **well**
> **Habla bien el español.**
> He speaks Spanish well.
2 **good**
> **Huele bien.**
> It smells good.
> **Lo pasamos muy bien.**
> We had a very good time.
> **Ese libro está muy bien.**
> That's a very good book.
> **Has contestado bien.**
> You gave the right answer.

**Hiciste bien en decírselo.**
You were right to tell him.
**¡Está bien! Lo haré.**
OK! I'll do it.
**3 very**
**un café bien caliente**
a very hot coffee

**¡Qué bien!**
Excellent!

**B** MASC NOUN
**good**
**Lo digo por tu bien.**
I'm telling you for your own good.
**los bienes**
possessions
**todos los bienes de la familia**
all the family's possessions

la **bienvenida** NOUN
**dar la bienvenida a alguien**
to welcome somebody
**una fiesta de bienvenida**
a welcome party

**bienvenido** (FEM bienvenida)

**bienvenido** *can be an adjective or an exclamation.*

**A** ADJECTIVE
**welcome**
**Siempre serás bienvenido aquí.**
You will always be welcome here.
**B** EXCLAMATION
**welcome!**

el **bigote** NOUN
**moustache**

el **bikini** NOUN
**bikini**

**bilingüe** (FEM bilingüe)
ADJECTIVE
**bilingual**

el **billar** NOUN
**billiards**
**el billar americano**
pool

el **billete** NOUN
**1 ticket**
**un billete de metro**
an underground ticket
**un billete de ida y vuelta**
a return ticket
**2 note**
**un billete de veinte euros**
a twenty-euro note

el **billón** (PL los **billones**) NOUN
**un billón**
a million million

*Language tip*
Be careful! **billón** *does not mean* **billion**.

**biodegradable**
(FEM **biodegradable**) ADJECTIVE
**biodegradable**

la **biografía** NOUN
**biography**

la **biología** NOUN
**biology**

**biológico** (FEM biológica)
ADJECTIVE
**1 organic**
**2 biological**

el **biquini** NOUN
**bikini**

la **bisabuela** NOUN
**great-grandmother**

el **bisabuelo** NOUN
**great-grandfather**
**mis bisabuelos**
my great-grandparents

el **bistec** (PL los **bistecs**) NOUN
**steak**

**bizco** (FEM bizca) ADJECTIVE
**cross-eyed**

el **bizcocho** NOUN
**sponge cake**

**blanco**

**blanco** *can be an adjective or a noun.*

**A** (FEM **blanca**) ADJECTIVE
**white**
un vestido
blanco
a white dress

**B** MASC NOUN
**white**
**Me gusta el blanco.**
I like white.
**Me quedé en blanco.**
My mind went blank.

**blando** (FEM **blanda**) ADJECTIVE
**soft**
Este colchón es muy blando.
This mattress is very soft.

el **bloc** (PL los **blocs**) NOUN
**writing pad**
un bloc de dibujo
a drawing pad

el **blog** NOUN
**blog**

el **bloque** NOUN
**block**
un bloque de pisos
a block of flats

**bloquear** VERB
**to block**
La nieve bloqueó las
carreteras.
The snow blocked the roads.

la **blusa** NOUN
**blouse**

la **bobada** NOUN
Este programa es una
bobada.
This programme is stupid.

**decir bobadas**
to talk nonsense

**bobo** (FEM **boba**) ADJECTIVE
**silly**

la **boca** NOUN
**mouth**
No debes hablar con la boca
llena.

You shouldn't talk with your
mouth full.
**No abrió la boca en toda
la tarde.**
He didn't open his mouth
all afternoon.
**Me quedé con la boca
abierta.**
I was speechless.

**boca abajo**
face down
**boca arriba**
face up

el **bocadillo** NOUN
**sandwich**
un bocadillo de queso
a cheese sandwich

*Did you know...?*

In Spain, a **bocadillo** is usually
made with a baguette.

el **bocado** NOUN
**bite**
Dame un bocado de tu
bocadillo.
Let me have a bite of your
sandwich.
**No he probado bocado desde
ayer.**
I haven't had a bite to eat since
yesterday.

el **bocata** NOUN
**sandwich**
Ya me he comido el bocata.
I've already had my sandwich.
un bocata de queso
a cheese sandwich

*Did you know...?*

In Spain, a **bocata** is usually made
with a baguette.

la **boda** NOUN
wedding

la **bofetada** NOUN
slap
**Le dio una bofetada.**
She slapped him.

la **bola** NOUN
1 ball
**una bola de nieve**
a snowball
2 scoop

el **boli** NOUN
pen

el **bolígrafo** NOUN
pen

el **bollo** NOUN
bun
**Me he comido un bollo para desayunar.**
I had a bun for breakfast.

los **bolos** NOUN
tenpin bowling

la **bolsa** NOUN
bag
**una bolsa de plástico**
a plastic bag

el **bolsillo** NOUN
pocket
**Sacó las llaves del bolsillo.**
He took the keys out of his pocket.
**un libro de bolsillo**
a paperback

el **bolso** NOUN
bag

la **bomba** NOUN
bomb

el **bombero** NOUN
fireman

la **bombilla** NOUN
lightbulb

el **bombón** (PL los **bombones**) NOUN
chocolate

la **bombona** NOUN
gas cylinder

**bonito** (FEM **bonita**) ADJECTIVE
pretty
**una casa muy bonita**
a very pretty house

el **borde** NOUN
edge
**al borde de la mesa**
at the edge of the table

**borracho** (FEM **borracha**) ADJECTIVE
drunk
**Estás borracho.**
You're drunk.

el **borrador** NOUN
1 duster
**Usó un trapo como borrador.**
He used a rag as a duster.
2 rough draft
**Escribe primero un borrador.**
First write a rough draft.

**borrar** VERB
1 to rub out
**Borra toda la palabra.**
Rub out the whole word.
2 to clean
**Borra la pizarra.**
Clean the blackboard.
**borrarse de**
to take one's name off/to leave

### Language tip
borrarse de *has two meanings. Look at the examples.*

**Voy a borrarme de la lista.**
I'm going to take my name off the list.
**Se borró del club.**
He left the club.

el **bosque** NOUN
1 wood
2 forest

**Spanish English**

**bostezar** VERB
to yawn

la **bota**
NOUN
boot

**botar** VERB
to bounce
Esta pelota no bota.
This ball doesn't bounce.

el **bote** NOUN
1 boat
un bote salvavidas
a lifeboat
2 jar

pegar un bote
to jump

la **botella** NOUN
bottle

el **botón** (PL los **botones**) NOUN
button
He perdido un botón de la
camisa.
I've lost a button off my shirt.
pulsar un botón
to press a button

**boxear** VERB
to box

el **boxeo** NOUN
boxing

las **bragas** NOUN
knickers
unas bragas
a pair of knickers

la **bragueta** NOUN
fly

**bravo** EXCLAMATION
well done!

la **braza** NOUN
breaststroke
nadar a braza
to do the breaststroke

el **brazo** NOUN
arm
Me duele el brazo.
My arm hurts.
Estaba sentada con los
brazos cruzados.
She was sitting with her arms
folded.

**breve** (FEM **breve**) ADJECTIVE
short
un relato breve
a short story

**brillante**

brillante can be an adjective or
a noun.

A (FEM **brillante**) ADJECTIVE
shiny
Tenía el pelo brillante.
Her hair was shiny.
B MASC NOUN
diamond

**brillar** VERB
1 to shine
Hoy brilla el sol.
The sun is shining
today.
2 to sparkle

el **brillo** NOUN
1 shine
2 sparkle

**británico**
**británica**

británico can be an adjective or a
noun.

A ADJECTIVE
British
B MASC/FEM NOUN
British person
los británicos
the British

la **brocha** NOUN
paintbrush

a b c d e f g h i j k l m n ñ o p q r s t u v w x y z

el **broche** NOUN
1 clasp
2 brooch

la **broma** NOUN
joke
> **Le gastamos una broma al profesor.**
> We played a joke on the teacher.
> **decir algo en broma**
> to say something as a joke
> **una broma pesada**
> a practical joke

**bromear** VERB
to joke

el/la **bromista** NOUN
joker

la **bronca** NOUN
1 row
> **Tuvieron una bronca muy gorda.**
> They had a huge row.
2 fuss

**echar una bronca a alguien**
to tell somebody off

el **bronce** NOUN
bronze

el **bronceado** NOUN
suntan

el **bronceador** NOUN
suntan lotion

la **bruja** NOUN
witch

el **brujo** NOUN
wizard

la **brújula** NOUN
compass

**bruto** (FEM **bruta**) ADJECTIVE
rough
> **¡No seas bruto!**
> Don't be so rough!

**bucear** VERB
to dive

**buen** ADJECTIVE ▷ see **bueno**

*Language tip*
When **bueno** goes in front of a masculine singular noun it is shortened to **buen**.

> **Es un buen hombre.**
> He's a good man.

**bueno** (FEM **buena**) ADJECTIVE
good
> **Es un buen libro.**
> It's a good book.
> **Hace buen tiempo.**
> The weather's good.
> **Es buena persona.**
> He's a good person.
> **un buen trozo**
> a good slice
> **ser bueno para**
> to be good for
> **Está muy bueno este bizcocho.**
> This sponge cake is lovely.
> **¡Buenos días!**
> Good morning!
> **¡Buenas tardes!**
> Good afternoon!/Good evening!
> **¡Buenas noches!**
> Good evening!/Good night!

*Language tip*
Did you know that the Spanish use **¡buenas tardes!** in the afternoon and early evening and **¡buenas noches!** when it starts to get dark as well as when they say good night?

> **¡Bueno!**
> OK!

la **bufanda** NOUN
scarf

el **búho** NOUN
owl

el **bulto** NOUN
lump
> **Tengo un bulto en la frente.**
> I have a lump on my forehead.

la **burbuja** NOUN
**bubble**
> **un refresco sin burbujas**
> a still drink
> **un refresco con burbujas**
> a fizzy drink

la **burla** NOUN
> **Siempre hacen burla de mí.**
> They are always making fun of me.

**burlarse** VERB
> **Siempre se burlan de mí.**
> They are always making fun of me.

la **burrada** NOUN
> **Siempre andan haciendo burradas.**
> They're always messing around.

**burro**

> **burro** *can be a noun or an adjective.*

**A** MASC NOUN
1 **donkey**
2 **idiot**
> **Eres un burro.**
> You're an idiot.

**B** (FEM **burra**) ADJECTIVE
1 **thick**
2 **rough**

el **buscador** NOUN
**search engine**

**buscar** VERB
1 **to look for**
> **Estoy buscando las gafas.**
> I'm looking for my glasses.
2 **to pick up**
> **Mi madre siempre me viene a buscar al colegio en coche.**
> My mother always picks me up from school in the car.
3 **to look up**
> **Busca la palabra en el diccionario.**
> Look the word up in the dictionary.
> **Él se lo ha buscado.**
> He was asking for it.

la **búsqueda** NOUN
**search**

la **butaca** NOUN
**armchair**

el **buzo** NOUN
**diver**

el **buzón** (PL los **buzones**) NOUN
1 **letterbox**

> **Did you know...?**
> *Spanish **letterboxes** tend to be American-Style boxes in which the postman leaves any mail rather than the hole in the door that is common in the UK.*

2 **postbox**
> **echar una carta al buzón**
> to post a letter
> **buzón de voz**
> voice mail

# C c

el **caballo** NOUN
**horse**
> **¿Te gusta montar a caballo?**
> Do you like horseriding?

el **cabello** NOUN
**hair**

**caber** VERB
**to fit**
> **No cabe en mi armario.**
> It won't fit in my cupboard.
> **No cabe nadie más.**
> There's no room for anyone else.

la **cabeza** NOUN
**head**
> **Se rascó la cabeza.**
> He scratched his head.

la **cabina** NOUN
**phone box**

el **cable** NOUN
**cable**

la **cabra** NOUN
**goat**

**cabrá** VERB ▷ see caber
> **No sé si cabrá.**
> I don't know whether it will fit.

el **cachorro**
la **cachorra** NOUN
**1 puppy**

**2 cub**

**cada** (FEM **cada**) ADJECTIVE
**1 each**
> **Cada libro es de un color distinto.**
> Each book is a different colour.
> **cada uno**
> each one
**2 every**
> **cada año**
> every year
> **cada vez que la veo**
> every time I see her
> **Viene cada vez más gente.**
> More and more people are coming.
> **Viene cada vez menos.**
> He comes less and less often.
> **Cada vez hace más frío.**
> It's getting colder and colder.

la **cadena** NOUN
**1 chain**
> **una cadena de oro**
> a gold chain
**2 channel**
> **Por la cadena tres ponen una película.**
> There's a film on channel three.

> **tirar de la cadena**
> to flush the toilet

**caer** VERB
**to fall**
> **¡Cuidado que vas a caer!**
> Careful or you'll fall!
> **Su hermano me cae muy bien.**
> I really like his brother.
> **Eva me cae muy mal.**
> I can't stand Eva.
- **caerse**
**to fall**
> **Tropecé y me caí.**
> I tripped and fell.
> **Se me cayeron las monedas.**
> I dropped the coins.

el **café** (PL los **cafés**) NOUN
**1 coffee**

un café con leche
a white coffee

**2 café**

**caigo** VERB ▷ *see* **caer**
¡Ahora caigo!
Now I remember!

la **caja** NOUN
**1 box**
una caja de zapatos
a shoe box
**2 checkout**

el **cajón** (PL los **cajones**) NOUN
**drawer**

el **calcetín** (PL los **calcetines**)
NOUN
**sock**

la **calculadora** NOUN
**calculator**

la **calefacción** NOUN
**heating**
calefacción central
central heating

el **calendario** NOUN
**calendar**

el **calentamiento** NOUN
el calentamiento global
global warming
ejercicios de calentamiento
warm-up exercises

**calentar** VERB
**1 to heat up**
¿Quieres que te caliente la
leche?
Do you want me to heat up the
milk for you?

**2 to warm up**

**calentarse** VERB
**1 to heat up**
Espera a que se caliente el
agua.
Wait for the water to heat up.
**2 to warm up**
Deja que se caliente el
motor.
Let the engine warm up.

**caliente** (FEM **caliente**)
ADJECTIVE
**hot**
Esta sopa está muy caliente.
This soup is very hot.

la **calificación** (PL las
**calificaciones**) NOUN
**mark**
Obtuvo buenas
calificaciones.
He got good marks.
boletín de calificaciones
school report

**callado** (FEM **callada**) ADJECTIVE
**quiet**
una persona muy callada
a very quiet person

**callar** VERB
**to be quiet**
Calla, que no me dejas
concentrarme.
Be quiet, I can't concentrate.
■ callarse
to keep quiet/to stop talking

---
***Language tip***

**callarse** *has two meanings. Look at
the examples.*

---

Prefirió callarse.
He preferred to keep quiet.
Al entrar el profesor, todos se
callaron.
When the teacher came in,
everyone stopped talking.

la **calle** NOUN
**street**

**Viven en la calle Peñalver, 13.**
They live at number 13, Peñalver Street.
**Hoy no he salido a la calle.**
I haven't been out today.

**calmar** VERB
**to calm down**
**Intenté calmarla un poco.**
I tried to calm her down a little.
**¡Cálmate!**
Calm down!

el **calor** NOUN
**heat**
**No se puede trabajar con este calor.**

It's impossible to work in this heat.

**Hace calor.**
It's hot.
**Tengo calor.**
I'm hot.

los **calzoncillos** NOUN
**underpants**
**unos calzoncillos**
a pair of underpants

la **cama** NOUN
**bed**
**Está en la cama.**
He's in bed.

**hacer la cama**
to make the bed
**irse a la cama**
to go to bed

la **cámara** NOUN
**camera**
**una cámara digital**
a digital camera

la **camarera** NOUN
**waitress**

el **camarero** NOUN
**waiter**

**cambiar** VERB
1 **to change**
**No has cambiado nada.**
You haven't changed a bit.
**He cambiado de idea.**
I've changed my mind.
**Voy a cambiarme.**
I'm going to get changed.
2 **to swap**
**Me gusta el tuyo, te lo cambio.**
I like yours, let's swap.

**cambiar de idea**
to change one's mind

el **cambio** NOUN
**change**
**un cambio brusco de temperatura**
a sudden change in temperature
**¿Tiene cambio de veinte euros?**
Have you got change of twenty euros?

**caminar** VERB
**to walk**

el **camino** NOUN
1 **path**
2 **way**
**¿Sabes el camino a su casa?**
Do you know the way to his house?
**La farmacia me pilla de camino.**
The chemist's is on my way.

el **camión** (PL los **camiones**)
NOUN
**lorry**

la **camisa** NOUN
**shirt**

la **camiseta** NOUN
1 **T-shirt**
2 **vest**
3 **shirt**

el **campamento** NCUN
**camp**

un campamento de verano
a summer camp

la **campana** NOUN
**bell**

el **campeón**
la **campeona** NOUN
**champion**

el **camping** (PL los **campings**)
NOUN
1 **camping**
Fuimos de camping este
verano.
We went camping this summer.
2 **campsite**
Estamos en un camping.
We're at a campsite.

el **campo** NOUN
1 **country**
Prefiero vivir en el campo.
I prefer living in the country.
2 **pitch**
un campo de fútbol
a football pitch

el **canal** NOUN
1 **channel**
Por el canal dos ponen una
película.
They're showing a film on
channel two.
2 **channel**
el Canal de la Mancha
the English Channel

la **canción** (PL las **canciones**)
NOUN
**song**

el **cangrejo** NOUN
**crab**

**cansado** (FEM **cansada**)
ADJECTIVE
**tired**
Estoy muy cansado.
I'm very tired.

Estoy cansado de hacer lo
mismo todos los días.
I'm tired of doing the same thing
every day.

**cansarse** VERB
**to get tired**
Está muy débil y enseguida
se cansa.
He is very weak and gets tired
quickly.
Me cansé de esperarlo y me
marché.
I got tired of waiting for him and
I left.

el/la **cantante** NOUN
**singer**

**cantar** VERB
**to sing**

la **cantidad** NOUN
1 **quantity**
La calidad es más importante
que la cantidad.
Quality is more important than
quantity.
¡Qué cantidad de gente!
What a lot of people!
2 **amount**
una cierta cantidad de dinero
a certain amount of money

la **capa** NOUN
**layer**
la capa de ozono
the ozone layer

el **capitán**
la **capitana** NOUN
**captain**

el **capítulo** NOUN
**chapter**

la **capucha** NOUN
**hood**

la **cara** NOUN
1 **face**
Tiene la cara alargada.
He has a long face.
Tienes mala cara.
You don't look well.
No pongas esa cara.
Don't look like that.
2 **cheek**
¡Qué cara!
What a cheek!
3 **side**
un folio escrito por las dos caras
a sheet written on both sides

¿Cara o cruz?
Heads or tails?

el **caramelo**
NOUN
**sweet**

la **carga** NOUN
**refill**

**cargar** VERB
1 **to load**
Cargaron el coche de maletas.
They loaded the car with suitcases.
2 **to charge**

la **caries** (PL las **caries**) NOUN
1 **tooth decay**
2 **cavity**

**cariñoso** (FEM **cariñosa**)
ADJECTIVE
**affectionate**
Es muy cariñosa con los niños.
She is very affectionate towards the children.

la **carne** NOUN
**meat**
No como carne.
I don't eat meat.
carne de cerdo
pork
carne picada
mince
carne de ternera
veal
carne de vaca
beef

el **carnet** (PL los **carnets**) NOUN
**card**
el carnet de identidad
identity card
un carnet de conducir
a driving licence

**caro** (FEM **cara**) ADJECTIVE, ADVERB
**expensive**
Aquí todo lo venden tan caro.
Everything is so expensive here.

la **carpeta** NOUN
**folder**

la **carrera** NOUN
**race**
una carrera de caballos
a horse race

la **carretera** NOUN
**road**

el **carrito** NOUN
**trolley**

el **carro** NOUN
1 **cart**
2 **trolley**

la **carta** NOUN
  1 **letter**
    **Le he escrito una carta a Juan.**
    I've written Juan a letter.
  2 **card**
    **jugar a las cartas**
    to play cards

el **cartel** NOUN
  1 **poster**
  2 **sign**

la **cartera** NOUN
  1 **satchel**
  2 **wallet**

el **cartero** NOUN
  **postman**

el **cartón** (PL los **cartones**) NOUN
  **cardboard**
    **una caja de cartón**
    a cardboard box

el **cartucho** NOUN
  **cartridge**

la **cartulina** NOUN
  **card**

la **casa** NOUN
  1 **house**
  2 **home**
    **Estábamos en casa.**
    We were at home.
    **Nos vamos a casa.**
    We're going home.
    **Estábamos en casa de Juan.**
    We were at Juan's.

**casado** (FEM **casada**) ADJECTIVE
  **married**
    **una mujer casada**
    a married woman
    **Está casado con una francesa.**
    He's married to a French woman.

**casarse** VERB

**to get married**
    **Quieren casarse.**
    They want to get married.

la **cascada** NOUN
  **waterfall**

la **cáscara** NOUN
  1 **shell**
  2 **skin**

**casi** ADVERB
  **almost**
    **Casi me ahogo.**
    I almost drowned.
    **Son casi las cinco.**
    It's nearly five o'clock.
    **Casi no comí.**
    I hardly ate.

la **casilla** NOUN
  **box**

el **caso** NOUN
  **case**
    **En casos así es mejor callarse.**
    In such cases it's better to keep quiet.
    **El caso es que no me queda dinero.**
    The thing is, I haven't got any money left.
    **No le hagas caso.**
    Don't take any notice of him.

la **caspa** NOUN
  **dandruff**

la **castaña** NOUN
  **chestnut**

**castaño** (FEM **castaña**)
  ADJECTIVE
  **brown**
    **Mi hermana tiene el pelo castaño.**
    My sister has brown hair.

**castigar** VERB
  **to punish**
    **Mi padre me castigó por contestarle.**

Spanish English

a b **c** d e f g h i j k l m n ñ o p q r s t u v w x y z

My father punished me for answering him back.

el **castigo** NOUN
**punishment**
> Tuve que escribirlo diez veces, como castigo.
> I had to write it out ten times, as punishment.

el **castillo** NOUN
**castle**
> un castillo de arena
> a sandcastle

la **casualidad** NOUN
**coincidence**
> ¡Qué casualidad!
> What a coincidence!
> Nos encontramos por casualidad.
> We met by chance.

el **catarro** NOUN
**cold**
> Vas a pillar un catarro.
> You're going to catch a cold.

la **catástrofe** NOUN
**catastrophe**

**catorce** (FEM **catorce**) ADJECTIVE, PRONOUN
**fourteen**

> **el catorce de enero**
> the fourteenth of January
> **Nació el catorce de enero.**
> He was born on the fourteenth of January.

la **causa** NOUN
**cause**
> No se sabe la causa del accidente.
> The cause of the accident is unknown.

> **a causa de**
> because of

**causar** VERB
**to cause**

**La lluvia causó muchos daños.**
The rain caused a lot of damage.

**cayendo** VERB ▷see **caer**
**Está cayendo nieve.**
It's snowing.

la **cazadora** NOUN
**jacket**

la **cebolla** NOUN
**onion**

la **ceja** NOUN
**eyebrow**

**celebrar** VERB
**to celebrate**

el **celo** NOUN
**Sellotape®**

los **celos** NOUN
**jealousy**
> Lo hizo por celos.
> He did it out of jealousy.
> Tiene celos de su mejor amiga.
> She's jealous of her best friend.

**celoso** (FEM **celosa**) ADJECTIVE
**jealous**
> Está celoso de su hermano.
> He's jealous of his brother.

el **cemento** NOUN
**cement**

la **cena** NOUN
**dinner**
> La cena es a las ocho.
> Dinner is at eight o'clock.

**cenar** VERB
**to have dinner**
> No he cenado.
> I haven't had dinner.
> ¿Qué quieres cenar?
> What do you want for dinner?

> **Did you know...?**
> *In Spain, people generally eat later than in the UK. Lunch is usually around two and people tend to have dinner around nine or ten.*

el **cenicero** NOUN
  ashtray

la **ceniza** NOUN
  ash

**centígrado** (FEM **centígrada**)
  ADJECTIVE
  centigrade
    **veinte grados centígrados**
    twenty degrees centigrade

el **centímetro** NOUN
  centimetre

el **céntimo** NOUN
  cent

**central** (FEM **central**) ADJECTIVE
  central

el **centro** NOUN
  centre
    **un centro comercial**
    a shopping centre
    **Fui al centro a hacer unas compras.**
    I went into town to do some shopping.

**cepillar** VERB
  to brush
    **Se está cepillando los dientes.**
    He's brushing his teeth.

el **cepillo** NOUN
  brush
    **un cepillo de dientes**
    a toothbrush

la **cera** NOUN
  wax

**cerca** ADVERB
  near
    **El colegio está muy cerca.**
    The school is very near.
    **cerca de la iglesia**
    near the church
    **cerca de dos horas**
    nearly two hours

    **Quería verlo de cerca.**
    I wanted to see it close up

el **cerdo** NOUN
  1 pig
  2 pork
    **No comemos cerdo.**
    We don't eat pork

el **cereal** NOUN
  cereal

    **Los niños desayunan cereales.**
    The children have cereal for breakfast.

el **cerebro** NOUN
  brain

la **cerilla** NOUN
  match
    **una caja de cerillas**
    a box of matches

el **cero** NOUN
  zero
    **Estamos a cinco grados bajo cero.**
    It's five degrees below zero.
    **cero coma tres**
    zero point three
    **Van dos a cero.**
    The score is two-nil.
    **Tuve que empezar desde cero.**
    I had to start from scratch.

**cerrado** (FEM **cerrada**) ADJECTIVE
  closed
    **Las tiendas están cerradas.**
    The shops are closed.

la **cerradura** NOUN
  lock

**cerrar** VERB
  1 to close
    **No cierran al mediodía.**
    They don't close at lunchtime.

**Cerró el libro.**
He closed the book.
**Cerré la puerta con llave.**
I locked the door.
**Se me cierran los ojos.**
I can't keep my eyes open.
**No puedo cerrar la maleta.**
I can't shut this suitcase.
**2 to turn off**
**Cierra el grifo.**
Turn off the tap.

la **cerveza** NOUN
**beer**

el **césped** NOUN
**grass**
'no pisar el césped'
'keep off the grass'

el **chaleco** NOUN
**waistcoat**
un chaleco salvavidas
a life-jacket

el **chalet** (PL los **chalets**) NOUN
**1 house**
**2 cottage**

el **champú** (PL los **champús**)
NOUN
**shampoo**

el **chándal** (PL los **chándals**)
NOUN
**tracksuit**

la **chaqueta** NOUN
**1 cardigan**
**2 jacket**

**charlar** VERB
**to chat**

el **chat** NOUN
**chatroom**

la **chatarra** NOUN
**scrap metal**

la **chica** NOUN
**1 girl**
**2 girlfriend**
Fui al cine con mi chica.
I went to the cinema with my
girlfriend.

el **chichón** (PL los **chichones**)
NOUN
**bump**
Me ha salido un
chichón en la frente.
I've got a bump
on my forehead.

el **chicle** NOUN
**chewing gum**

el **chico** NOUN
**1 boy**
Fueron todos los chicos de
la clase.
All the boys in the class went.
**2 boyfriend**
Iré con mi chico.
I'll go with my boyfriend.

**chillar** VERB
**to scream**

la **chimenea** NOUN
**1 chimney**
**2 fireplace**

la **chincheta** NOUN
**drawing pin**

el **chiste** NOUN
**joke**
El maestro nos contó un
chiste.
The teacher told us a joke.

**chocar** VERB
chocar contra
to hit/to bump into/to crash
into

*Language tip*

**chocar contra** *has various
meanings. Look at the examples.*

**El coche chocó contra un árbol.**
The car hit a tree.
**Choqué contra una farola.**
I bumped into a lamppost.
**Chocó contra un muro.**
He crashed into a wall.

el **chocolate** NOUN
chocolate

el **chorizo** NOUN
chorizo

> **Did you know...?**
> **Chorizo** *is a kind of spicy sausage.*

el **chubasquero** NOUN
cagoule

**chulo** (FEM **chula**) ADJECTIVE
1 **cocky**
2 **cool**
**¡Qué mochila más chula!**
What a cool rucksack!

**chupar** VERB
**to suck**
**Se chupaba el dedo.**
He was sucking his thumb.

los **churros** PL NOUN
**long sweet fritters**

> **Did you know...?**
> **churros** *are a kind of fritter that*
> *people often eat on the streets in a*
> *paper bag or order in a café typically*
> *with a cup of thick, hot chocolate:*
> **chocolate con churros**.

el **cíber** NOUN
**Internet café**

el **cibercafé** NOUN
**Internet café**

el/la **ciclista** NOUN
**cyclist**

**ciego**
**ciega**

> **ciego** *can be an adjective or a*
> *noun.*

**A** ADJECTIVE
**blind**
**Mi abuelo es ciego..**
My grandfather is blind.

> **quedarse ciego**
> **to go blind**

**B** MASC/FEM NOUN
**un ciego**
a blind man
**una ciega**
a blind woman
**los ciegos**
the blind

el **cielo** NOUN
**sky**
**No había ni una nube en el**
**cielo.**
There wasn't a single cloud in
the sky.

**cien** (FEM **cien**) ADJECTIVE,
PRONOUN
**a hundred**
**Había unos cien invitados en**
**la boda.**
There were about a hundred
guests at the wedding.

> **cien mil**
> a hundred thousand
> **cien por cien**
> a hundred percent

la **ciencia** NOUN
**science**
**Me gustan mucho las**
**ciencias.**
I really enjoy science.

**ciento** (FEM **ciento**) ADJECTIVE, PRONOUN
**a hundred**
> **ciento cuarenta y dos libras**
> a hundred and forty two pounds
> **Recibimos cientos de cartas.**
> We received hundreds of letters.
> **el diez por ciento de la población**
> ten percent of the population

**cierro** VERB ▷ see **cerrar**
> **Cuando cierro al puerta hace un ruido extraño.**
> When I close the door it makes a funny noise.

**cierto** (FEM **cierta**) ADJECTIVE
**true**
> **No, eso no es cierto.**
> No, that's not true.

**por cierto**
by the way

el **ciervo** NOUN
**deer**

la **cifra** NOUN
**figure**
> **un número de cuatro cifras**
> a four-figure number

el **cigarrillo** NOUN
**cigarette**

**cinco** (FEM **cinco**) ADJECTIVE, PRONOUN
**five**
> **Tiene cinco años.**
> He's five.

**el cinco de enero**
the fifth of January
**Nació el cinco de enero.**
He was born on the fifth of January.
**Son las cinco.**
It's five o'clock.

**cincuenta** (FEM **cincuenta**) ADJECTIVE, PRONOUN
**fifty**
> **Tiene cincuenta años.**
> He's fifty.

el **cine** NOUN
**cinema**
> **Mañana voy al cine.**
> I'm going to the cinema tomorrow.

la **cintura** NOUN
**waist**
> **¿Cuánto mides de cintura?**
> What's your waist size?

el **cinturón**
(PL los **cinturones**)
NOUN
**belt**
> **el cinturón de seguridad**
> the safety belt

el **circo** NOUN
**circus**

el **círculo** NOUN
**circle**
> **Dibuja un círculo.**
> Draw a circle.

el **cisne** NOUN
**swan**

la **cita** NOUN
**1 date**
> **No llegues tarde a la cita.**
> Don't be late for your date.
**2 appointment**
> **Tengo cita con el médico.**
> I've got a doctor's appointment.

la **ciudad** NOUN
**1 city**
**2 town**

la **clara** NOUN
**white**

**claro** (FEM **clara**)

**claro** can be an adjective or an adverb.

**A** ADJECTIVE
**1 clear**
> **Lo quiero mañana. ¿Está claro?**
> I want it tomorrow. Is that clear?

**Está claro que esconden algo.**
It's obvious that they are hiding
something.

**2 light**
**una camisa azul claro**
a light blue shirt

**B** ADVERB
**clearly**
**Lo oí muy claro.**
I heard it very clearly.
**¡Claro!**
Of course!
**¿Te oyó? –**
**¡Claro que me oyó!**
Did he hear you? –
Of course he heard me!

la **clase** NOUN
**1 class**
**A las diez tengo clase de**
**física.**
I have a physics class at ten.
**Mi hermana da clases de**
**inglés.**
My sister teaches English.
**Hoy no hay clase.**
There's no school today.
**clases particulares**
private lessons
**2 classroom**
**3 kind**
**Había juguetes de todas**
**clases.**
There were all kinds of toys.

**clásico** (FEM **clásica**) ADJECTIVE
**classical**
**Me gusta la música clásica.**
I like classical music.

**clasificar** VERB
**to classify**
■ **clasificarse**
**to qualify**
**Esperan clasificarse para la**
**final.**
They hope to qualify for the
final.
**Se clasificaron en tercer**
**lugar.**
They came third.

la **clave** NOUN
**code**
**un mensaje en clave**
a coded message

el **clic** NOUN
**click**
**hacer clic en algo**
to click on something

el **clima** NOUN
**climate**
**Es un país de clima tropical.**
It's a country with a tropical
climate.

la **clínica** NOUN
**hospital**

el **clip** (PL los **clips**) NOUN
**paper clip**

**cobarde** (FEM **cobarde**)
ADJECTIVE
**cowardly**
**¡No seas cobarde!**
Don't be such a coward!

el **coche** NOUN
**car**
**Fuimos a Sevilla en coche.**
We went to Seville by car.
**un coche de carreras**
a racing car
**los coches de choque**
the bumper cars
**un coche de bomberos**
a fire engine

la **cocina** NOUN
**1 kitchen**
**Comemos en la cocina.**
We eat in the kitchen.
**2 cooker**
**una cocina de gas**
a gas cooker
**la cocina vasca**
Basque cuisine
**un libro de cocina**
a cookery book

**cocinar** VERB
**to cook**

**Spanish English**

**No sabe cocinar.**
He can't cook.
**Cocinas muy bien.**
You're a very good cook.

el **codo** NOUN
elbow

**coger** VERB
1 **to take**
**Coge el que más te guste.**
Take the one you like best.
2 **to catch**
**¡Coge la pelota!**
Catch the ball!
**La cogieron robando.**
They caught her stealing.
**He cogido un resfriado.**
I've caught a cold.
**Voy a coger el autobús.**
I'm going to get the bus.

el **cohete** NOUN
rocket

el **cojín** (PL los **cojines**) NOUN
cushion

## cojo

*cojo can be an adjective or a verb.*

**A** (FEM **coja**) ADJECTIVE
**Es algo cojo.**
He has a bit of a limp.
**B** VERB ▷*see* **coger**
**¡Si te cojo!**
If I catch you!

la **cola** NOUN
1 **tail**
2 **queue**
**Había mucha cola para el baño.**
There was a long queue for the toilets.
3 **glue**

**hacer cola**
to queue

**colarse** VERB
**to push in**
**No te cueles.**
Don't push in.
**Nos colamos en el cine.**
We sneaked into the cinema without paying.

el/la **colega** NOUN
1 **mate**
2 **colleague**

el **colegio** NOUN
school
**¿Todavía vas al colegio?**
Are you still at school?
**un colegio público**
a state school

**colgar** VERB
1 **to hang**
**Colguemos el cuadro en esta pared.**
Let's hang the picture on this wall.
**¡No dejes la chaqueta en la silla, cuélgala!**
Don't leave your jacket on the chair, hang it up!
2 **to hang up**
**¡No cuelgues!**
Don't hang up!
**Me colgó el teléfono.**
He hung up on me.

el **collar** NOUN
1 **necklace**
2 **collar**

el **colmo** NOUN
**¡Esto ya es el colmo!**
This really is the last straw!

**colocar** VERB
**to put**
**Colocamos la mesa en medio del comedor.**
We put the table in the middle of the dining room.

**¡Colocaos en fila!**
Get into a line!

la **colonia** NOUN
**perfume**
**¿Qué colonia llevas?**
What perfume are you wearing?

**una colonia de verano**
a summer camp

el **color** NOUN
**colour**
**¿De qué color son?**
What colour are they?
**un vestido de color azul**
a blue dress

la **columna** NOUN
**column**

el **columpio** NOUN
**swing**

la **coma** NOUN
**comma**
**Separa las palabras con una coma.**
Separate the words with a comma.
**cero coma ocho**
zero point eight

*Did you know...?*
In Spanish you use a comma instead of a point in decimal numbers.

la **comba** NOUN
**skipping rope**

**saltar a la comba**
to skip

el **comedor** NOUN
**1 dining room**
**2 refectory**

**comenzar** VERB
**to begin**

**Comenzó a llover.**
It began to rain.

**comer** VERB
**1 to eat**
**¿Quieres comer algo?**
Do you want something to eat?
**Le estaba dando de comer a su hijo.**
She was feeding her son.
**2 to have lunch**
**Comimos en el hotel.**
We had lunch in the hotel.
**Hemos comido paella.**
We had paella for lunch.
**¿Qué hay para comer?**
What's for lunch?

*Did you know...?*
In Spain, people generally eat later than in the UK. Lunch is usually around two and people tend to have dinner around nine or ten.

**cometa**

*cometa can be a masculine or a feminine noun.*

**A** MASC NOUN
**comet**
**B** FEM NOUN
**kite**

el **cómic** NOUN
**comic**

la **comida** NOUN
**1 food**
**La comida es muy buena en el hotel.**
The food in the hotel is very good.
**2 lunch**
**La comida es a la una y media.**
Lunch is at half past one.

*Did you know...?*
In Spain, people generally eat later than in the UK. Lunch is usually around two and people tend to have dinner around nine or ten.

a
b
c
d
e
f
g
h
i
j
k
l
m
n
ñ
o
p
q
r
s
t
u
v
w
x
y
z

**51**

**Spanish English**

a
b
c
d
e
f
g
h
i
j
k
l
m
n
ñ
o
p
q
r
s
t
u
v
w
x
y
z

**3 meal**
**Es la comida más importante del día.**
It's the most important meal of the day.

**comienzo** VERB ▷*see* **comenzar**
**Yo comienzo y después tú me sigues.**
I go first and then you follow me.

**como** ADVERB, CONJUNCTION
**1 like**
**Tienen un perro como el nuestro.**
They've got a dog like ours.
**blanco como la nieve**
as white as snow
**Es tan alto como tú.**
He is as tall as you.

**2 as**
**Como ella no llegaba, me fui.**
As she didn't arrive, I left.
**Lo usé como cuchara.**
I used it as a spoon.

**3 if**
**Como lo vuelvas a hacer se lo digo a tu madre.**
If you do it again, I'll tell your mother.

**4 about**
**Vinieron como unas diez personas.**
About ten people came.
**como si**
as if
**Siguió leyendo, como si no hubiera oído nada.**
He kept on reading, as if he had heard nothing.

**cómo** ADVERB
**how**
**¿Cómo se dice en inglés?**
How do you say it in English?
**¿Cómo están tus padres?**
How are your parents?
**¿Cómo es de grande?**
How big is it?
**¿Cómo es el clima?**
What's the weather like?
**Perdón, ¿cómo has dicho?**
Sorry, what did you say?
**¡Cómo! ¿Mañana?**
What? Tomorrow?

**cómodo** (FEM **cómoda**)
ADJECTIVE
**comfortable**
**un sillón cómodo**
a comfortable chair

el **compañero**
la **compañera** NOUN
**1 classmate**
**2 workmate**
**3 partner**

la **compañía** NOUN
**company**
**Ana vino a hacerme compañía.**
Ana came to keep me company.

**comparar** VERB
**to compare**
**Siempre me comparan con mi hermana.**
I'm always being compared to my sister.

**compartir** VERB
**to share**

el **compás** (PL los **compases**)
NOUN
**compass**

la **competición** (PL las **competiciones**) NOUN
**competition**

el **complejo** NOUN
**complex**
**Tiene complejo porque está gordo.**
He's got a complex about being fat.

**un complejo deportivo**
a sports complex

**completo** (FEM **completa**)
ADJECTIVE
**full**
  **Los hoteles estaban completos.**
  The hotels were full.
  **Me olvidé por completo.**
  I completely forgot.

**complicado** (FEM **complicada**)
ADJECTIVE
**complicated**

la **compra** NOUN
**shopping**

  **ir de compras**
  to go shopping

**comprar** VERB
**to buy**
  **Quiero comprarme unos zapatos.**
  I want to buy a pair of shoes.

**comprender** VERB
**to understand**
  **¡No lo comprendo!**
  I don't understand it!

**común** (FEM **común**) ADJECTIVE
**common**
  **un apellido muy común**
  a very common surname
  **No tenemos nada en común.**
  We have nothing in common.
  **Hicimos el trabajo en común.**
  We did the work between us.

la **comunidad** NOUN
**community**

**con** PREPOSITION
**with**
  **Vivo con mis padres.**
  I live with my parents.
  **¿Con quién vas a ir?**
  Who are you going with?
  **Lo he escrito con bolígrafo.**
  I wrote it in pen.
  **Voy a hablar con Luis.**
  I'll talk to Luis.
  **con tal de que no llegues tarde**
  as long as you don't arrive late

la **concha** NOUN
**shell**

el **concurso** NOUN
**competition**

la **condición** (PL las condiciones) NOUN
**condition**
  **a condición de que apruebes**
  on condition that you pass
  **El piso está en muy malas condiciones.**
  The flat is in a very bad state.
  **No está en condiciones de viajar.**
  He's not fit to travel

**conducir** VERB
**to drive**
  **Mi madre no sabe conducir.**
  My mum can't drive.

el **conductor**
la **conductora** NOUN
**driver**

**conduzco** VERB ▷ see **conducir**
  **Siempre tomo mucho cuidado cuando conduzco.**
  I'm always very careful when I'm driving.

el **conejo** NOUN
**rabbit**

la **conferencia** NOUN
**lecture**

**confesar** VERB
**to admit**
  **Confesó que había sido él.**
  He admitted that it had been him.

la **confianza** NOUN
**trust**
  **Tengo confianza en ti.**
  I trust you.

a b **c** d e f g h i j k l m n ñ o p q r s t u v w x y z

a
b
c
d
e
f
g
h
i
j
k
l
m
n
ñ
o
p
q
r
s
t
u
v
w
x
y
z

No tiene confianza en sí mismo.
He has no self-confidence.

**confiar** VERB
**to trust**
No confío en ella.
I don't trust her.

**confieso** VERB ▷see **confesar**
Confieso que estaba equivocado.
I admit I was wrong.

**conformarse** VERB
conformarse con
to make do with
Tendrás que conformarte con uno más barato.
You'll have to make do with a cheaper one.

**confundir** VERB
1 **to mistake**
La gente me confunde con mi hermana.
People mistake me for my sister.
2 **to confuse**
Su explicación me confundió todavía más.
His explanation confused me even more.
Confundí las fechas.
I got the dates mixed up.

**congelado** (FEM **congelada**)
ADJECTIVE
**frozen**

el **congelador** NOUN
**freezer**

**congelar** VERB
**to freeze**
Me estoy congelando.
I'm freezing.

el **conjunto** NOUN
**group**
un conjunto de música pop
a pop group

**conmigo** PRONOUN
**with me**

¿Por qué no vienes conmigo?
Why don't you come with me?
Rosa quiere hablar conmigo.
Rosa wants to talk to me.
No estoy satisfecho conmigo mismo.
I'm not proud of myself.

**conocer** VERB
1 **to know**
Conozco a todos sus hermanos.
I know all his brothers.
Nos conocemos desde el colegio.
We know each other from school.
2 **to meet**
La conocí en una fiesta.
I met her at a party.

**conocido** (FEM **conocida**)
ADJECTIVE
**well-known**
un actor muy conocido
a well-known actor

el **conocimiento** NOUN
**consciousness**
perder el conocimiento
to lose consciousness

**conozco** VERB ▷see **conocer**
No la conozco.
I don't know her.

**conseguir** VERB
**to get**
Él me consiguió la entrada.
He got me the ticket.

el **consejo** NOUN
**advice**
¿Quieres que te dé un consejo?
Would you like me to give you some advice?

**consigo**

**consigo** can be a pronoun or part of the verb **conseguir**.

**A** PRONOUN

**1 with him**
Se llevó a Marta consigo.
He took Marta with him.

**2 with her**

**3 with you**

**B** VERB ▷ see **conseguir**
No consigo olvidarme de lo que pasó.
I can't forget what happened.

## constipado

*constipado* can be and adjective or a noun.

**A** (FEM **constipada**)
ADJECTIVE
**estar constipado**
to have a cold

**B** MASC NOUN
**cold**
coger un constipado
to catch a cold

*Language tip*
Be careful! **constipado** *does not mean* **constipated**.

## construir VERB
**to build**

la **consulta** NOUN
**surgery**
horas de consulta
surgery hours

## consultar VERB
**to consult**
Deberías consultar a un médico.
You should consult a doctor.
Tengo que consultarlo con mi familia.
I need to discuss it with my family.

## contagioso (FEM contagiosa)
ADJECTIVE
**infectious**

la **contaminación** NOUN

**pollution**
la contaminación del aire
air pollution

## contar VERB

**1 to count**
Sabe contar hasta diez.
He can count to ten.

**2 to tell**
Les conté un cuento a los niños.
I told the children a story.
Cuéntame lo que pasó.
Tell me what happened.
Cuento contigo.
I'm counting on you.

el **contenido** NOUN
**contents**
el contenido de la maleta
the contents of the suitcase

## contento (FEM contenta)
ADJECTIVE
**happy**
Estaba contento porque era su cumpleaños.
He was happy because it was his birthday.
Estoy contento con la bici nueva.
I'm pleased with my new bike.

## contestar VERB
**to answer**
Contesté a todas las preguntas.
I answered all the questions.
Me escribieron y tengo que contestarles.
They wrote to me and I have to reply to them.

## contigo PRONOUN
**with you**
Quiero ir contigo.
I want to go with you.
Necesito hablar contigo.
I need to talk to you.

el **continente** NOUN
**continent**

**contra** PREPOSITION
**against**
 Eran dos contra uno.
 They were two against one.
 El domingo jugamos contra
 el Málaga.
 We play against Málaga on Sunday.

**contrario** (FEM **contraria**)
ADJECTIVE
1 **opposing**
2 **opposite**
 Los dos coches iban en
 dirección contraria.
 The two cars were travelling in
 opposite directions.
 Ella opina lo contrario.
 She thinks the opposite.
 Al contrario, me gusta mucho.
 On the contrary, I like it a lot.
 De lo contrario, tendré que
 castigarte.
 Otherwise, I will have to punish
 you.

la **contraseña** NOUN
 **password**

el **control** NOUN
 **control**
 Nunca pierde el control.
 He never loses control.

la **conversación** (PL las
conversaciones) NOUN
 **conversation**
 Necesito clases de
 conversación.
 I need conversation classes.

**convertir** VERB
**to turn**
 Convirtieron la casa en
 colegio.
 They turned the house into a
 school.
■ convertirse en
 **to become/to turn into**

*Language tip*

convertirse en *has two meanings.
Look at the examples.*

 Se convirtió en un hombre
 rico.
 He became a rich man.
 Se convirtió en una pesadilla.
 It turned into a nightmare.

la **copa** NOUN
 **glass**

la **copia** NOUN
 **copy**
 hacer una copia
 to make a copy

**copiar** VERB
**to copy**
 copiar y pegar
 to copy and paste

el **corazón** (PL los **corazones**)
NOUN
 **heart**

el **cordón** (PL los **cordones**)
NOUN
 **shoelace**

la **corona** NOUN
 **crown**

la **correa** NOUN
1 **lead**
2 **strap**

**correcto**
(FEM **correcta**)
ADJECTIVE
 **correct**
 Las respuestas
 eran correctas.
 The answers were correct.

el **corredor**
la **corredora** NOUN
 **runner**

**corregir** VERB
1 **to correct**
Corrígeme si me equivoco.
Correct me if I'm wrong.
2 **to mark**
El profesor corrigió los exámenes.
The teacher marked the exams.

el **correo** NOUN
**post**
Me lo mandó por correo.
He sent it to me by post.
**Correos**
the post office
**correo electrónico**
email

**correr** VERB
1 **to run**
Tuve que correr para coger el autobús.
I had to run to catch the bus.
2 **to hurry**
Corre que llegamos tarde.
Hurry or we'll be late.
3 **to go fast**
No corras tanto, que hay hielo en la carretera.
Don't go so fast, the road's icy.
4 **to move**
Córrete un poco hacia la izquierda.
Move a bit to the left.

la **corriente** NOUN
1 **current**
2 **draught**

**corrijo** VERB ▷ see corregir
Ahora mismo lo corrijo.
I'll correct it right away.

**cortado** (FEM cortada) ADJECTIVE
1 **sour**
2 **chapped**
3 **closed**

**cortar** VERB
**to cut**
Corta la manzana por la mitad.

Cut the apple in half.
**Me corté el dedo.**
I cut my finger.
**Te vas a cortar.**
You're going to cut yourself.
**Estas tijeras no cortan.**
These scissors are blunt.
**Fui a cortarme el pelo.**
I went to get my hair cut.

el **corte** NOUN
**cut**
Tenía un corte en la frente.
He had a cut on his forehead.
**un corte de pelo**
a haircut

**Me da corte pedírselo.**
I'm embarrassed to ask him.

la **corteza** NOUN
**crust**

la **cortina** NOUN
**curtain**

**corto** (FEM corta) ADJECTIVE
**short**
Susana tiene el pelo corto.
Susana has short hair.

la **cosa** NOUN
**thing**
¿Qué es esa cosa redonda?
What's that round thing?
Cogí mis cosas y me fui.
I picked up my things and left.
¿Me puedes decir una cosa?
Can you tell me something?
¡Qué cosa más rara!
How strange!

**cualquier cosa**
anything

**Spanish English**

a b **c** d e f g h i j k l m n ñ o p q r s t u v w x y z

**coser** VERB
to sew

las **cosquillas** NOUN
**hacer cosquillas a alguien**
to tickle somebody
**Tiene muchas cosquillas.**
He's very ticklish.

la **costa** NOUN
coast
**Pasamos el verano en la costa.**
We spent the summer on the coast.

**costar** VERB
to cost
**Cuesta mucho dinero.**
It costs a lot of money.
**Me costó diez euros.**
It cost me ten euros.
**Las matemáticas le cuestan mucho.**
He finds maths very difficult.

**¿Cuánto cuesta?**
How much is it?

la **costilla** NOUN
rib

la **costumbre** NOUN
1 **habit**
**Tiene la mala costumbre de mentir.**
He has the bad habit of lying.
2 **custom**
**una costumbre británica**
a British custom
**Se le olvidó, como de costumbre.**
He forgot, as usual.

**cotillear** VERB
to gossip

**crecer** VERB
to grow
**Me crece mucho el pelo.**
My hair grows very fast.
**¡Cómo has crecido!**
Haven't you grown!

**creer** VERB

1 **to believe**
**Nadie me cree.**
Nobody believes me.
**¿Crees en los fantasmas?**
Do you believe in ghosts?
2 **to think**
**No creo que pueda ir.**
I don't think I'll be able to go.

**Creo que sí.**
I think so.
**Creo que no.**
I don't think so.

la **crema** NOUN
cream
**Me pongo crema en las manos.**
I put cream on my hands.
**la crema solar**
suncream

la **cremallera** NOUN
zip
**Súbete la cremallera.**
Do your zip up.

el **cristal** NOUN
1 **glass**
**una botella de cristal**
a glass bottle
**En el suelo había cristales rotos.**
There was some broken glass on the floor.
2 **window pane**
**Los niños rompieron el cristal.**
The children broke the window pane.
**limpiar los cristales**
to clean the windows

el **cromo** NOUN
picture card

la **croqueta** NOUN
croquette
**croquetas de pollo**
chicken croquettes

el **cruce** NOUN
crossroads

En el cruce hay un semáforo.
There are traffic lights at the crossroads.
**un cruce de peatones**
a pedestrian crossing

**crudo** (FEM **cruda**) ADJECTIVE
**raw**
**las zanahorias crudas**
raw carrots

**crujiente** (FEM **crujiente**)
ADJECTIVE
**crunchy**

la **cruz** (PL las **cruces**) NOUN
**cross**

**cruzar** VERB
1 **to cross**
2 **to fold**
**Nos cruzamos en la calle.**
We passed each other in the street.

el **cuaderno** NOUN
**notebook**
**un cuaderno de ejercicios**
an exercise book

la **cuadra** NOUN
**stable**

**cuadrado** (FEM **cuadrada**)
ADJECTIVE, MASC NOUN
**square**
**dos metros cuadrados**
two square metres

el **cuadro** NOUN
**painting**

**cual** PRONOUN (PL **cuales**)
1 **who**
**el primo del cual te estuve hablando**
the cousin who I was telling you about
2 **which**
**la ventana desde la cual nos observaban**
the window from which they were watching us

**cuál** PRONOUN (PL **cuáles**)
1 **what**
**No sé cuál es la solución.**
I don't know what the solution is.
2 **which one**
**¿Cuál te gusta más?**
Which one do you like best?
**¿Cuáles quieres?**
Which ones do you want?

**cualquier** ADJECTIVE ▷ *see* cualquiera

**cualquiera** (FEM **cualquiera**)

cualquiera *can be an adjective or a pronoun.*

**A** ADJECTIVE
**any**
**Puedes usar un bolígrafo cualquiera.**
You can use any pen.
**No es un empleo cualquiera.**
It's not just any job.

**cualquier cosa**
anything
**en cualquier sitio**
anywhere

**B** PRONOUN
1 **anyone**
**Cualquiera puede hacer eso.**
Anyone can do that.
**cualquiera que le conozca**
anyone who knows him
2 **any one**
**Me da igual, cualquiera.**
It doesn't matter, any one.
**en cualquiera de las habitaciones**
in any one of the rooms
**cualquiera que elijas**
whichever one you choose
3 **either**
**¿Cuál de los dos prefieres? – Cualquiera.**
Which of the two do you prefer? – Either.

**cuando** CONJUNCTION
**when**
    **Lo haré cuando tenga tiempo.**
    I'll do it when I have time.
    **Puedes venir cuando quieras.**
    You can come whenever you like.

**cuándo** ADVERB
**when**
    **¿Cuándo te va mejor?**
    When suits you?
    **No sabe cuándo ocurrió.**
    He doesn't know when it happened.

**cuanto** (FEM **cuanta**) ADJECTIVE, PRONOUN
    **Termínalo cuanto antes.**
    Finish it as soon as possible.
    **Cuanto más lo pienso menos lo entiendo.**
    The more I think about it, the less I understand it.
    **Cuantas menos personas haya mejor.**
    The fewer people the better.
    **En cuanto oí su voz me eché a llorar.**
    As soon as I heard his voice I began to cry.
    **Había sólo unos cuantos invitados.**
    There were only a few guests.

**en cuanto a**
as for

**cuánto** (FEM **cuánta**) ADJECTIVE, PRONOUN
1 **how much**
    **¿Cuánto dinero tienes?**
    How much money do you have?
    **Me dijo cuánto costaba.**
    He told me how much it was.
2 **how many**
    **¿Cuántas sillas?**
    How many chairs?
    **No sé cuántos necesito.**
    I don't know how many I need.

    **¿A cuántos estamos?**
    What's the date?
    **¡Cuánta gente!**
    What a lot of people!
    **¿Cuánto hay de aquí a Bilbao?**
    How far is it from here to Bilbao?
    **¿Cuánto tiempo llevas estudiando inglés?**
    How long have you been studying English?

**cuarenta** (FEM **cuarenta**)
ADJECTIVE, PRONOUN
**forty**
    **Tiene cuarenta años.**
    He's forty.

**cuarto**

**cuarto** can be an adjective, pronoun or noun.

**A** (FEM **cuarta**) ADJECTIVE, PRONOUN
**fourth**
    **Vivo en el cuarto piso.**
    I live on the fourth floor.
**B** MASC NOUN
1 **room**
    **Los niños jugaban en su cuarto.**
    The children were playing in their room.
    **el cuarto de estar**
    the living room
    **el cuarto de baño**
    the bathroom
2 **quarter**
    **un cuarto de hora**
    a quarter of an hour

**Son las once y cuarto.**
It's a quarter past eleven.
**A las diez menos cuarto.**
At a quarter to ten.

**cuatro** (FEM **cuatro**) ADJECTIVE, PRONOUN
**four**

**Son las cuatro.**
It's four o'clock.
**el cuatro de julio**

Spanish English
a b c d e f g h i j k l m n ñ o p q r s t u v w x y z

• • • • • • • • • • • • • • • • • • • • • • •

the fourth of July
**Nació el cuatro de julio.**
He was born on the fourth of July.

## cuatrocientos
(FEM **cuatrocientas**) ADJECTIVE, PRONOUN
**four hundred**

## cubierto

**cubierto** *can be an adjective or part of the verb* **cubrir**.

**A** (FEM **cubierta**) ADJECTIVE
**covered**
**Estaba todo cubierto de nieve.**
Everything was covered in snow.
**B** VERB ▷*see* **cubrir**
**Ha cubierto el piano con una lona.**
He's covered the piano with a tarpaulin.

los **cubiertos** NOUN
**cutlery**

el **cubito de hielo** NCUN
**ice-cube**

el **cubo** NOUN
**bucket**
**el cubo y la pala**
the bucket and spade
**el cubo de la basura**
the dustbin

## cubrir VERB
**to cover**
**Tenemos que cubrir los cuadernos.**
We have to cover our exercise books.
**El agua casi me cubría.**
I was almost out of my depth.

la **cuchara** NOUN
**spoon**

la **cucharada** NOUN
**spoonful**
**una cucharada de jarabe**
a spoonful of syrup

la **cucharilla** NOUN
**teaspoon**

**cuchichear** VERB
**to whisper**

el **cuchillo** NOUN
**knife**

el **cucurucho** NOUN
**cone**

**cuelgo** VERB ▷*see* **colgar**
**¿Dónde cuelgo el abrigo?**
Where can I hang the coat?

el **cuello** NOUN
**neck**

la **cuenta** NOUN
**1 bill**
**El camarero nos trajo la cuenta.**
The waiter brought us the bill.
**2 account**
**una cuenta de correo**
an email account
**darse cuenta**
to realize/to notice

*Language tip*

**darse cuenta** *has two meanings. Look at the examples.*

**Perdona, no me di cuenta de que eras vegetariano.**
Sorry, I didn't realize you were a vegetarian.
**¿Te has dado cuenta de que han cortado el árbol?**
Did you notice they've cut down that tree?

## cuento

**cuento** *can be an adjective or part of the verb* **contar**.

**A** MASC NOUN
**story**

a
**b**
**c**
d
e
f
g
h
i
j
k
l
m
n
ñ
o
p
q
r
s
t
u
v
w
x
y
z

**La abuela nos contaba cuentos.**
Grandma used to tell us stories.
**un cuento de hadas**
a fairy-tale

**B** VERB ▷*see* **contar**
**Si quieres te cuento lo que pasó.**
If you want, I'll tell you what happened.

la **cuerda** NOUN
**1 rope**
**Le ataron las manos con una cuerda.**
They tied his hands together with a rope.
**2 string**
**Necesito una cuerda para atar este paquete.**
I need some string to tie up this parcel.

el **cuero** NOUN
**leather**
**una chaqueta de cuero**
a leather jacket

el **cuerpo** NOUN
**body**
**el cuerpo humano**
the human body
**el cuerpo de bomberos**
the fire-brigade

## cuesta

**cuesta** *can be an adjective or part of the verb* **costar**.

**A** FEM NOUN
**slope**
**una cuesta muy empinada**
a very steep slope

**ir cuesta abajo**
to go downhill
**ir cuesta arriba**
to go uphill

**B** VERB ▷*see* **costar**
**¿Cuánto cuesta esa bicicleta?**
How much does that bicycle cost?

la **cueva** NOUN
**cave**

el **cuidado** NOUN
**care**
**Conducía con cuidado.**
He was driving carefully.

**¡Cuidado!**
Careful!

**cuidar** VERB
**to look after**
**Ella cuida de los niños.**
She looks after the children.
■ **cuidarse**
**to look after oneself**
**Tienes que cuidarte.**
You need to look after yourself.

**¡Cuídate!**
Take care!

la **culpa** NOUN
**fault**
**La culpa es mía.**
It's my fault.
**Siempre me echan la culpa a mí.**
They're always blaming me.

## culpable

**culpable** *can be an adjective or a noun*.

**A** (FEM **culpable**) ADJECTIVE
**guilty**
**Yo no soy culpable.**
I'm not guilty.
**B** MASC/FEM NOUN
**culprit**
**Ella es la culpable de todo.**
She is to blame for everything.

la **cultura** NOUN
culture

la **cumbre** NOUN
summit

el **cumpleaños** (PL los cumpleaños) NOUN
birthday

> **¡Feliz cumpleaños!**
> Happy birthday!

**cumplir** VERB
1 **to carry out**
2 **to keep**
  **Mañana cumplo dieciséis años.**
  I'll be sixteen tomorrow.

la **cuna** NOUN
cradle

la **cuñada** NOUN
sister-in-law

el **cuñado** NOUN
brother-in-law

**cupo** VERB ▷see caber
  **No cupo por la puerta.**
  It wouldn't go through the door.

el **cura** NOUN
priest

**curar** VERB
1 **to cure**
  **un remedio para curar una pulmonía**
  a treatment to cure pneumonia

  **Espero que te cures pronto.**
  I hope that you get better soon.
2 **to heal**
  **Ya se le ha curado la herida.**
  His wound has already healed.

**cursi** (FEM **cursi**) ADJECTIVE
1 **affected**
2 **twee**

el **cursillo** NOUN
course
  **un cursillo de informática**
  a computer course
  **hacer un cursillo de natación**
  to have swimming lessons

el **curso** NOUN
1 **year**
  **un chico de mi curso**
  a boy in my year
  **Hago segundo curso.**
  I'm in Year two.
2 **course**
  **Hice un curso de alemán.**
  I did a German course.

la **curva** NOUN
bend
  **Hay algunas curvas muy cerradas.**
  There are some very sharp bends.

Spanish English

a
b
c
d
e
f
g
h
i
j
k
l
m
ñ
n
o
p
q
r
s
t
u
v
w
x
y
z

# D d

la **dama** NOUN
**lady**
**damas y caballeros**
ladies and gentlemen
**las damas**
draughts
**jugar a las damas**
to play draughts

el **daño** NOUN
**damage**
**El daño producido no es muy grave.**
The damage isn't very serious.
**¡Me estás haciendo daño!**
You're hurting me!

**hacerse daño**
to hurt oneself

**dar** VERB
**to give**
**Se lo di a Teresa.**
I gave it to Teresa.
**Se me dan bien las ciencias.**
I'm good at science.

**de** PREPOSITION

*Language tip*
**de + el = del.**

**1 of**
**un paquete de caramelos**
a packet of sweets
**un vaso de agua**
a glass of water

**las clases de inglés**
English lessons
**un anillo de oro**
a gold ring

**la casa de Isabel**
Isabel's house
**2 from**
**Soy de Madrid.**
I'm from Madrid.
**una carta de mi tía**
a letter from my aunt
**Son del año pasado.**
They're from last year.
**3 than**
**Es más difícil de lo que creía.**
It's more difficult than I thought.

**dé** VERB ▷ *see* **dar**
**Quiero que me dé el móvil.**
I want him to give me the mobile phone.

**debajo** ADVERB
**underneath**
**Levanta la maceta, la llave está debajo.**
Lift up the flowerpot, the key's underneath.
**debajo de**
under
**debajo de la mesa**
under the table

## deber

**deber** *can be a noun or a verb.*

**A** MASC NOUN
**duty**
**Sólo cumplí con mi deber.**
I simply did my duty.
**los deberes**
homework
**B** VERB
**1 must**
**Debo intentarlo.**
I must try it.
**No debes preocuparte.**
You mustn't worry.
**No deberías haberla dejado sola.**

You shouldn't have left her alone.
**deber de**
must
**Debe de ser canadiense.**
He must be Canadian.
2 **to owe**
**¿Cuánto le debo?**
How much do I owe you?

**hacer los deberes**
to do one's homework

**débil** (FEM **débil**) ADJECTIVE
**weak**

**decidir** VERB
**to decide**
**Tú decides.**
You decide.
**Me decidí a aprender inglés.**
I've decided to learn English.
**¡Decídete!**
Make up your mind!

**décimo** (FEM **décima**) ADJECTIVE,
PRONOUN
**tenth**
**Vivo en el décimo.**
I live on the tenth floor.

**decir** VERB
1 **to say**
**¿Qué dijo?**
What did he say?
**¿Cómo se dice 'casa' en inglés?**
How do you say 'casa' in English?
**No sé lo que quiere decir.**
I don't know what it means.
2 **to tell**
**Nunca me dice la verdad.**
He never tells me the truth.
**Me dijo que esperara fuera.**
He told me to wait outside.

**es decir**
that's to say
**¡No me digas!**
Really?

el **dedo** NOUN
1 **finger**
2 **toe**
**el dedo gordo**
the thumb/the big toe

*Language tip*
**el dedo gordo** *has two meanings. It can be translated as* **the thumb** *or* **the big toe**.

**dejar** VERB
1 **to leave**
**He dejado las llaves en la mesa.**
I've left the keys on the table.
**No me dejes sola.**
Don't leave me on my own.
2 **to let**
**Mis padres no me dejan salir de noche.**
My parents won't let me go out at night.
**dejar caer**
to drop
**Dejó caer la bandeja.**
She dropped the tray
3 **to lend**
**Le dejé mi libro de matemáticas.**
I lent him my maths book.
**dejar de**
to stop
**He dejado de morderme las uñas.**
I've stopped biting my nails.

**del** PREPOSITION ▷see **de**
**Vengo del colegio.**
I'm coming from school.

**delante** ADVERB
**in front**
**Siéntate delante.**
You sit in front.
**la parte de delante**
the front

**de delante**
front
**la rueda de delante**
the front wheel
**Se inclinó hacia delante.**
He leaned forward.
**delante de**
in front of/opposite

*Language tip*

**delante de** *has two meanings.*
*Look at the examples.*

**No digas nada delante de Anna.**
Don't say anything in front of Anna.
**Mi casa está delante de la escuela.**
My house is opposite the school.

## delgado (FEM delgada)
ADJECTIVE
**thin**
**Estás muy delgado.**
You're too thin.

## demás

**demás** *can be an adjective or a pronoun.*

**A** (FEM **demás**) ADJECTIVE
**other**
**los demás niños**
the other children
**B** PRONOUN
**los demás**
the others
**lo demás**
the rest
**Yo limpio las ventanas y lo demás lo limpias tú.**
I'll clean the windows and you clean the rest.

## demasiado

**demasiado** *can be an adjective or an adverb.*

**A** (FEM **demasiada**) ADJECTIVE
**too much**

**demasiado tiempo**
too much time
**demasiados libros**
too many books
**B** ADVERB
**too much**
**Hablas demasiado.**
You talk too much.
**Es demasiado pesado para levantarlo.**
It's too heavy to lift.
**Caminas demasiado deprisa.**
You walk too quickly.

el **dentífrico** NOUN
**toothpaste**

el/la **dentista** NOUN
**dentist**

**Mi madre es dentista.**
My mum is a dentist.

## dentro ADVERB
**inside**
**¿Qué hay dentro?**
What's inside?
**dentro de**
in
**Métdelo dentro del sobre.**
Put it in the envelope.
**dentro de tres meses**
in three months
**por dentro**
inside
**Mira bien por dentro.**
Have a good look inside.
**Está aquí dentro.**
It's in here.

**dentro de poco**
soon

**depender** VERB
**depender de**
to depend on
**El precio depende de la calidad.**
The price depends on the quality.

**Depende.**
It depends.

el **deporte** NOUN
**sport**
**No hago mucho deporte.**
I don't do much sport.

**deportista**

deportista *can be an adjective or a noun.*

**A** (FEM **deportista**) ADJECTIVE
**sporty**
**Alicia es poco deportista.**
Alicia is not very sporty.
**B** MASC NOUN
**sportsman**
**C** FEM NOUN
**sportswoman**

**deprisa** ADVERB
**quickly**
**Acabaron muy deprisa.**
They finished very quickly.
**Lo hacen todo deprisa y corriendo.**
They do everything in a rush.

**¡Deprisa!**
Hurry up!

la **derecha** NOUN
**1 right hand**
**Escribo con la derecha.**
I write with my right hand.
**2 right**
**doblar a la derecha**
to turn right
**a la derecha**
on the right
**Coge la segunda calle a la derecha.**
Take the second turning on the right.

**derecho**

derecho *can be an adjective, an adverb or a noun.*

**A** (FEM **derecha**) ADJECTIVE
**1 right**
**Escribo con la mano derecha.**
I write with my right hand.
**2 straight**
**¡Ponte derecho!**
Stand up straight!
**B** ADVERB
**straight**
**Siga derecho.**
Carry straight on.
**C** MASC NOUN
**right**
**los derechos humanos**
human rights

**¡No hay derecho!**
It's not fair!

**desagradable**
(FEM **desagradable**) ADJECTIVE
**unpleasant**
**un olor muy desagradable**
a very unpleasant smell
**Fuiste muy desagradable con tu prima.**
You were really nasty to your cousin.

**desaparecer** VERB
**to disappear**
**La mancha ha desaparecido.**
The stain has disappeared.

el **desastre** NOUN
**disaster**
**La función fue un desastre.**
The show was a disaster.

**Soy un desastre para la gimnasia.**
I'm hopeless at gymnastics.

**desayunar** VERB

**1 to have breakfast**
**Nunca desayuno.**
I never have breakfast.

**2 to have ... for breakfast**
**Desayuné café con leche y un bollo.**
I had coffee and a roll for breakfast.

el **desayuno** NOUN
**breakfast**

**descalzarse** VERB
**to take one's shoes off**
**Descálzate.**
Take your shoes off.

**descalzo** (FEM **descalza**)
ADJECTIVE
**barefoot**
**Paseaban descalzos por la playa.**
They walked barefoot along the beach.
**No entres en la cocina descalzo.**
Don't come into the kitchen in bare feet.

**descansar** VERB
**to rest**
**Tienes que descansar.**
You must rest.

el **descanso** NOUN
**1 rest**
**He caminado mucho, necesito un descanso.**
I've done a lot of walking, I need a rest.

**2 break**
**Cada dos horas me tomo un descanso.**
I have a break every two hours.

**descarado** (FEM **descarada**)
ADJECTIVE
**cheeky**
**¡No seas descarado!**
Don't be cheeky!

**descargar** VERB
**to download**
  ■ **descargarse**
  **to go flat**

**desconectar** VERB
**to unplug**

el **descubrimiento** NOUN
**discovery**

**desde** PREPOSITION
**1 from**
**Desde Burgos hasta mi casa hay treinta kilómetros.**
It's thirty kilometres from Burgos to my house.
**2 since**
**La conozco desde niño.**
I've known her since I was a child.
**¿Desde cuándo vives aquí?**
How long have you been living here?

**desde entonces**
since then
**desde luego**
of course

**desear** VERB

**to wish**
> Te deseo mucha suerte.
> I wish you lots of luck.

**desenchufar** VERB
**to unplug**

el **deseo** NOUN
**wish**

el **desfile** NOUN
**parade**

la **desgracia** NOUN
**tragedy**
> Su muerte fue una auténtica desgracia.
> His death was an absolute tragedy.
> por desgracia
> unfortunately
> Por desgracia he vuelto a suspender.
> Unfortunately I've failed again.

**deshacer** VERB
**to untie**

el **desierto** NOUN
**desert**

**desnatado** (FEM desnatada)
ADJECTIVE
**skimmed**

**desnudarse** VERB
**to get undressed**

**desnudo** (FEM desnuda)
ADJECTIVE
**naked**

**desobedecer** VERB
**to disobey**

**desobediente**
(FEM desobediente) ADJECTIVE
**disobedient**

el **desodorante** NOUN
**deodorant**

**desordenado**
(FEM desordenada) ADJECTIVE
**untidy**
> Tengo la habitación muy desordenada.
> My room's really untidy.

**despacio** ADVERB
**slowly**
> Conduce despacio
> Drive slowly.

> ¡Despacio!
> Take it easy!

**despedir** VERB
**to say goodbye to**
> Se despidieron en la estación.
> They said goodbye at the station.

el **despertador**
NOUN
**alarm clock**

**despertar** VERB
**to wake up**
> No me despiertes hasta las once.
> Don't wake me up until eleven o'clock.

**despierto** (FEM despierta)
ADJECTIVE
**awake**
> A las siete ya estaba despierto.
> He was already awake by seven o'clock.

**después** ADVERB
1 **later**
> Ellos llegaron después.
> They arrived later.

**un año después**
a year later
**2 next**
**¿Qué viene después?**
What comes next?
**después de**
after
**Tu nombre está después del mío.**
Your name comes after mine.
**Después de comer fuimos de paseo.**
After lunch we went for a walk.

el **destornillador** NOUN
screwdriver

**destrozar** VERB
to wreck
**Tu perro ha destrozado la silla.**
Your dog has wrecked the chair.

**destruir** VERB
to destroy
**Los huracanes destruyen edificios enteros.**
Hurricanes can destroy whole buildings.

la **desventaja** NOUN
disadvantage

el **detalle** NOUN
detail
**No recuerdo todos los detalles.**
I don't remember all the details.

**detener** VERB
**1 to stop**
**¡Detenlos!**
Stop them!
**2 to arrest**
**Han detenido a los ladrones.**
They've arrested the thieves.

■ **detenerse**
**to stop**
**Nos detuvimos en el semáforo.**
We stopped at the lights.

el **detergente** NOUN
detergent

**detrás** ADVERB
behind
**El resto de los niños vienen detrás.**
The rest of the children are coming on behind.
**detrás de**
behind
**Se escondió detrás de un árbol.**
He hid behind a tree.

**devolver** VERB
**1 to give back**
**¿Me puedes devolver el libro que te presté?**
Could you give me back the book I lent you?
**2 to take back**
**Devolví la falda porque me iba pequeña.**
I took the skirt back as it was too small for me.
**3 to throw up**

**di** VERB
**1** ▷ *see* **decir**
**Di, ¿qué te parece?**
Tell me, what do you think?
**2** ▷ *see* **dar**
**Se lo di a ella.**
I gave it to her.

el **día** NOUN
day
**Pasaré dos días en la playa.**
I'll spend a couple of days at the beach.
**Es de día.**
It's daylight.
**¿Qué día es hoy?**
What day is it today?/What's the date today?

**Language tip**

**¿qué día es hoy?** has two meanings. It can be translated as **what day is it today?** and **what's the date today?**

> **un día de fiesta**
> a public holiday
> **el día de los enamorados**
> Saint Valentine's Day
> **el día de los Santos Inocentes**
> the Feast of the Holy Innocents

**Did you know…?**

In Spanish-speaking countries the day people play April-Fool-type practical jokes on each other is 28 December, **el día de los Santos Inocentes**.

**al día siguiente**
the following day
**¡Buenos días!**
Good morning!
**todos los días**
every day

el **diablo** NOUN
devil

**diagonal** ADJECTIVE, FEM NOUN
diagonal
> **en diagonal**
> diagonally

el **diamante** NOUN
diamond

el **diámetro** NOUN
diameter

**diario**

**diario** can be an adjective or a noun.

**A** (FEM **diaria**) ADJECTIVE
**daily**
> **la rutina diaria**
> the daily routine
> **la ropa de diario**
> everyday clothes
> **a diario**
> every day
> **Va al gimnasio a diario.**
> He goes to the gym every day.

**B** MASC NOUN
**diary**

la **diarrea** NOUN
**diarrhoea**

**dibujar** VERB
**to draw**
> **No sé dibujar.**
> I can't draw.

el **dibujo** NOUN
**drawing**
> **Me hizo un dibujo.**
> She did me a drawing.
> **los dibujos animados**
> cartoons

el **diccionario** NOUN
**dictionary**

**dicho** VERB ▷ see **decir**
> **Ya te he dicho que no lo quiero.**
> I've already told you that I don't want it.

**diciembre** MASC NOUN
**December**

**Language tip**

Months are not written with a capital letter in Spanish.

**en diciembre**
in December
**Nació el seis de diciembre.**
He was born on the sixth of December.

**diciendo** VERB ▷ see **decir**
> **Como iba diciendo …**
> As I was saying …

**diecinueve**
(FEM **diecinueve**) ADJECTIVE, PRONOUN
**nineteen**
> **Tengo diecinueve años.**
> I'm nineteen.

**el diecinueve de julio**
the nineteenth of July
**Nació el diecinueve de julio.**
He was born on the nineteenth of July.

**dieciocho** (FEM **dieciocho**)
ADJECTIVE, PRONOUN
**eighteen**
> **Tengo dieciocho años.**
> I'm eighteen.

**el dieciocho de abril**
the eighteenth of April
**Nació el dieciocho de abril.**
He was born on the eighteenth of April.

**dieciséis** (FEM **dieciséis**)
ADJECTIVE, PRONOUN
**sixteen**
> **Tengo dieciséis años.**
> I'm sixteen.

**el dieciséis de febrero**
the sixteenth of February
**Nació el dieciséis de febrero.**
He was born on the sixteenth of February.

**diecisiete** (FEM **diecisiete**)
ADJECTIVE, PRONOUN
**seventeen**
> **Tengo diecisiete años.**
> I'm seventeen.

**el diecisiete de enero**
the seventeenth of January
**Nació el diecisiete de enero.**
He was born on the seventeenth of January.

el **diente** NOUN
**tooth**
> **Me lavo los dientes tres veces al día.**

I clean my teeth three times a day.
**un diente de leche**
a milk tooth
**un diente de ajo**
a clove of garlic

la **dieta** NOUN
**diet**
> **una dieta vegetariana**
> a vegetarian diet

**estar a dieta**
to be on a diet

**diez** (FEM **diez**) ADJECTIVE, PRONOUN
**ten**
> **Tengo diez años.**
> I'm ten.

**Son las diez.**
It's ten o'clock.
**el diez de agosto**
the tenth of August
**Nació el diez de agosto.**
He was born on the tenth of August.

la **diferencia** NOUN
**difference**
> **¿Qué diferencia hay entre los dos?**
> What's the difference between the two?

**diferenciar** VERB
> **¿En qué se diferencian?**
> What's the difference between them?
> **Sólo se diferencian en el tamaño.**
> The only difference between them is their size.

**diferente** (FEM **diferente**)
ADJECTIVE
**different**

**difícil** (FEM **difícil**) ADJECTIVE
**difficult**
> **Es un problema difícil de entender.**

It's a difficult problem to understand.

la **digestión** NOUN
digestion

**hacer la digestión**
to digest

**digital** (FEM **digital**) ADJECTIVE
digital
**una cámara digital**
a digital camera
**una huella digital**
a fingerprint

**digo** VERB ▷see **decir**
**Porque lo digo yo.**
Because I say so.

**dije** VERB ▷see **decir**
**¡Yo no dije eso!**
I didn't say that!

el **dinero** NOUN
money
**No tengo más dinero.**
I haven't got any more money.
**dinero suelto**
loose change

**dio** VERB ▷see **dar**
**Me dio un libro.**
He gave me a book.

**Dios** MASC NOUN
God

el **dios** (PL los **dioses**) NOUN
god

**dirá** VERB ▷see **decir**
**¿Qué dirá mi madre cuando se entere?**
¿What will my mother say when she finds out?

la **dirección** (PL las **direcciones**) NOUN

1 direction
**Íbamos en dirección equivocada.**
We were going in the wrong direction.
**una calle de dirección única**
a one-way street

2 address
**Apúntame tu dirección aquí.**
Can you write your address down here for me?
**dirección de correo electrónico**
e-mail address

**directo** (FEM **directa**) ADJECTIVE
direct
**Hay un tren directo a Valencia.**
There's a direct train to Valencia.
**una pregunta directa**
a direct question

el **director**
la **directora** NOUN
1 headteacher
2 manager
3 director

el **disco** NOUN
record
**un disco compacto**
a compact disc
**el disco duro**
the hard disk

la **discusión** (PL las discusiones) NOUN
argument
**Tuve una discusión con mi madre.**
I had an argument with my mother.

**discutir** VERB
to argue
**Siempre discuten por dinero.**
They're always arguing about money.
**Discutió con su madre.**
He had an argument with his mother.

el **disfraz** (PL los **disfraces**)
NOUN
**costume**
  **un disfraz de vaquero**
  a cowboy costume
  **una fiesta de disfraces**
  a fancy-dress party

**disfrazarse** VERB
  **disfrazarse de**
  to dress up as
  **Mi amiga se disfrazó de hada.**
  My friend dressed up as a fairy.

**disfrutar** VERB
**to enjoy oneself**
  **Disfruté mucho en la fiesta.**
  I really enjoyed myself at the
  party.
  **Disfruto leyendo.**
  I enjoy reading.

**disgustado** (FEM **disgustada**)
ADJECTIVE
**upset**

> **Language tip**
> Be careful! **disgustado** does not
> mean **disgusted**.

**disimular** VERB
**to hide**
  **Intentó disimular su enfado.**
  He tried to hide his annoyance.
  **No disimules, sé que has sido
  tú.**
  Don't bother pretending, I know
  it was you.

el **disparate** NOUN
**silly thing**
  **He hecho muchos disparates
  en mi vida.**

I've done a lot of silly things in
my life.
**No digas disparates.**
Don't talk rubbish.

el **disparo** NOUN
**shot**

la **distancia** NOUN
**distance**
  **la distancia entre dos coches**
  the distance between two cars
  **¿Qué distancia hay entre
  Madrid y Barcelona?**
  How far is Madrid from
  Barcelona?
  **¿A qué distancia está la
  estación?**
  How far's the station?
  **a veinte kilómetros de
  distancia**
  twenty kilometres away

**distinguir** VERB
**to distinguish**
  **Resulta difícil distinguir el
  macho de la hembra.**
  It's difficult to distinguish the
  male from the female.
  **No distingue entre el rojo
  y el verde.**
  He can't tell the difference
  between red and green.
  **Se parecen tanto que no los
  distingo.**
  They're so alike that I can't tell
  them apart.

**distinto** (FEM **distinta**)
ADJECTIVE
**different**
  **Carlos es distinto a los
  demás.**
  Carlos is different to everyone
  else.

**distintos**
several
**distintas clases de coches**
several types of car

la **distracción** (PL las distracciones) NOUN
**pastime**
Cocinar es mi distracción favorita.
My favourite pastime is cooking.

**distraer** VERB
1 **to keep ... entertained**
Les pondré un vídeo para distraerlos.
I'll put a video on to keep them entertained.
**Me distrae mucho escuchar música.**
I really enjoy listening to music.
2 **to distract**
No me distraigas, que tengo trabajo.
Don't distract me. I've got work to do.

**distraído** (FEM distraída)
ADJECTIVE
**absent-minded**
Mi padre es muy distraído.
My father is very absent-minded.
Perdona, estaba distraído.
Sorry, I wasn't paying attention.

la **diversión** (PL las diversiones)
NOUN
**entertainment**

**Language tip**
Be careful! **diversión** does not mean **diversion**.

**divertido** (FEM divertida)
ADJECTIVE
**funny**
Fue muy divertido.
It was great fun.

**divertir** VERB
**to entertain**

**Nos divirtió con sus cuentos.**
He entertained us with his stories.

■ **divertirse**
**to have a good time**

**dividir** VERB
**to divide**
El libro está dividido en dos partes.
The book is divided into two parts.
**Divide cuatro entre dos.**
Divide four by two.
■ **dividirse**
**to divide/to share**

**Language tip**
**dividirse** has two meanings. Look at the examples.

**Nos dividimos el trabajo entre los tres.**
We divided the work between the three of us.
**Se dividieron el dinero de la lotería.**
They shared the lottery money.

**divierto** VERB ▷see **divertir**
**Me divierto mucho con ellos.**
I have a good time when I'm with them.

la **división** (PL las divisiones)
NOUN
**division**
en primera división
in the first division
**Ya sabe hacer divisiones.**
He already knows how to do division.

Spanish English

a
b
c
d
e
f
g
h
i
j
k
l
m
n
ñ
o
p
q
r
s
t
u
v
w
x
y
z

75

**Spanish English**

a b **c** d e f g h i j k l m n ñ o p q r s t u v w x y z

el **DNI** ABBREVIATION
(= **Documento Nacional de Identidad**)
**ID card**

e **doble** NOUN
**twice as much**
**Comes el doble que yo.**
You eat twice as much as I do.
**Trabaja el doble que tú.**
He works twice as hard as you do.

**doce** (FEM **doce**) ADJECTIVE, PRONOUN
**twelve**
**Tengo doce años.**
I'm twelve.

**Son las doce.**
It's twelve o'clock.
**el doce de diciembre**
the twelfth of December
**Nació el doce de diciembre.**
He was born on the twelfth of December.

la **docena** NOUN
**dozen**

el **doctor**
la **doctora** NOUN
**doctor**
**Cuando crezca me gustaría ser doctor.**
I want to be a doctor when I grow up.

el **documental** NOUN
**documentary**

el **documento** NOUN
**document**
**un documento oficial**
an official document
**el documento nacional de identidad**
the identity card

**doler** VERB
**to hurt**
**Me duele el brazo.**
My arm hurts.

**Me duele la cabeza.**
I've got a headache.
**Me duele la garganta.**
I've got a sore throat.

el **dolor** NOUN
**pain**
**Gritó de dolor.**
He cried out in pain.

**Tengo dolor de cabeza.**
I've got a headache.
**Tengo dolor de garganta.**
I've got a sore throat.
**Tengo dolor de estómago.**
I've got a stomachache.

**doméstico** (FEM **doméstica**)
ADJECTIVE
**domestic**
**para uso doméstico**
for domestic use
**las tareas domésticas**
the housework
**un animal doméstico**
a pet

el **domingo** NOUN
**Sunday**

**Language tip**
*The days of the week are not spelled with a capital letter in Spanish.*

**La vi el domingo.**
I saw her on Sunday.

**todos los domingos**
every Sunday
**el domingo pasado**
last Sunday
**el domingo que viene**
next Sunday

**don** MASC NOUN
**don Juan Gómez**
Mr Juan Gómez

**donde** ADVERB
**where**
**La nota está donde la dejaste.**
The note's where you left it.

**dónde** ADVERB
**where**
**¿Dónde vas?**
Where are you going?
**Le pregunté dónde estaba la catedral.**
I asked him where the cathedral was.
**¿Sabes dónde está?**
Do you know where he is?
**¿De dónde eres?**
Where are you from?
**¿Por dónde se va al cine?**
How do you get to the cinema?

**doña** FEM NOUN
**doña Marta García**
Mrs Marta García

**dorado** (FEM **dorada**) ADJECTIVE
**golden**

**dormir** VERB
**to sleep**
**Antonio durmió diez horas.**
Antonio slept for ten hours.
**dormir la siesta**
to have a nap
**estar medio dormido**
to be half asleep
■ **dormirse**
**to fall asleep**
**Me dormí en el tren.**
I fell asleep on the train.
**Se me ha dormido el brazo.**
My arm has gone to sleep.

el **dormitorio** NOUN
**bedroom**

**dos** (FEM **dos**) ADJECTIVE, PRONOUN
**1 two**
**Tenemos dos gatos.**
We have two cats.

**2 both**
**Al final vinieron los dos.**
In the end they both came.
**Los hemos invitado a los dos.**
We've invited both of them.

> **Tiene dos años.**
> He's two.
> **Son las dos.**
> It's two o'clock.
> **el dos de enero**
> the second of January
> **Nació el dos de enero.**
> He was born on the second of January.

**doscientos** (FEM **doscientas**)
ADJECTIVE, PRONOUN
**two hundred**
**doscientos cincuenta**
two hundred and fifty

**doy** VERB ▷see **dar**
**Si quieres, te doy uno.**
If you want, I'll give you one.

el **drogadicto**
la **drogadicta** NOUN
**drug addict**

la **ducha** NOUN
**shower**

> **darse una ducha**
> to have a shower

**ducharse** VERB
**to have a shower**

la **duda** NOUN
**doubt**

**Tengo mis dudas.**
I have my doubts.
**Tengo una duda.**
I have a query.
**¿Alguna duda?**
Any questions?

## dudar VERB
**to doubt**
**Lo dudo.**
I doubt it.
**Dudo que sea cierto.**
I doubt if it's true.
**Dudó si comprarlo o no.**
He wasn't sure whether to buy it or not.

## el dueño
la **dueña** NOUN
**owner**

## duermo VERB ▷ see dormir
**Duermo ocho horas todos los días.**
I sleep eight hours every day.

## dulce

dulce *can be an adjective or a noun.*

**A** (FEM **dulce**) ADJECTIVE
**sweet**
**B** MASC NOUN
**sweet**

## durante ADVERB
**during**
**Tuvo que trabajar durante las vacaciones.**
He had to work during the holidays.
**durante toda la noche**
all night long
**Habló durante una hora.**
He spoke for an hour.

## durar VERB
**to last**
**La película dura dos horas.**
The film lasts two hours.

## durmiendo VERB ▷ see dormir
**Me estoy durmiendo.**
I'm falling asleep.

## duro

duro *can be an adjective or an adverb.*

**A** (FEM **dura**) ADJECTIVE
**1 hard**
**Los diamantes son muy duros.**
Diamonds are very hard.
**2 tough**
**Esta carne está dura.**
This meat's tough.
**B** ADVERB
**hard**
**trabajar duro**
to work hard

# E e

**e** CONJUNCTION

*Language tip*

**e** *is used instead of* **y** *in front of words beginning with 'i' and 'hi', but not 'hie'.*

**and**
> Pablo e Inés.
> Pablo and Inés.

**echar** VERB
1 **to throw**
> Échame las llaves.
> Throw me the keys.
2 **to throw out**
> Me echó de su casa.
> He threw me out of the house.
3 **to expel**
> Lo han echado del colegio.
> He's been expelled from school.
> Echo de menos a mi familia.
> I miss my family.

**ecológico** (FEM **ecológica**)
ADJECTIVE
**ecological**
> un desastre ecológico
> an ecological disaster
> un producto ecológico
> an environmentally friendly product

**ecologista**
**ecologista**

**ecologista** *can be an adjective or a noun.*

**A** ADJECTIVE
**environmental**
> un grupo ecologista
> an environmental group
**B** MASC/FEM NOUN
**environmentalist**

la **edad** NOUN
**age**

> Tenemos la misma edad.
> We're the same age.

**¿Qué edad tiene?**
How old is he?

el **edificio** NOUN
**building**

la **educación** NOUN
1 **education**
> educación física
> PE
2 **upbringing**
> Rosa recibió una educación muy estricta.
> Rosa had a very strict upbringing.
> Señalar es de mala educación.
> It's rude to point.
> Es una falta de educación hablar con la boca llena.
> It's bad manners to speak with your mouth full.

**educado** (FEM **educada**)
ADJECTIVE
**polite**
> Es un chico bien educado.
> He's a polite boy.

**egoísta** (FEM **egoísta**)
ADJECTIVE
**selfish**

el **ejemplo** NOUN
**example**
> ¿Puedes ponerme un ejemplo?
> Can you give me an example?

**por ejemplo**
for example

el **ejercicio** NOUN
**exercise**

La maestra nos puso varios ejercicios.
The teacher gave us several exercises to do.

**hacer ejercicio**
to do exercise

**el** (FEM SING **la**, MASC PL **los**, FEM PL **las**) ARTICLE
**the**
Perdí el autobús.
I missed the bus.
Yo fui el que lo encontró.
I was the one who found it.
Ayer me lavé la cabeza.
I washed my hair yesterday.
Me puse el abrigo.
I put my coat on.
Tiene unos zapatos bonitos, pero prefiero los míos.
Her shoes are nice but I prefer mine.
No me gusta el pescado.
I don't like fish.

**él** PRONOUN
1 **he**
Me lo dijo él.
He told me.
2 **him**
Se lo di a él.
I gave it to him.
Su mujer es más alta que él.
His wife is taller than him.
**él mismo**
himself
No lo sabe ni él mismo.
He doesn't even know himself.
**de él**
his
El coche es de él.
The car's his.

la **electricidad** NOUN
**electricity**

**eléctrico** (FEM **eléctrica**) ADJECTIVE
**electric**
una guitarra eléctrica
an electric guitar

el **elefante** NOUN
**elephant**

**elegir** VERB
**to choose**
No sabía qué color elegir.
I didn't know what colour to choose.

**elijo** VERB ▷ see **elegir**
Yo elijo el blanco.
I choose the white one.

**ella** PRONOUN
1 **she**
Ella no estaba en casa.
She was not at home.
2 **her**
El regalo es para ella.
The present's for her.
Él estaba más nervioso que ella.
He was more nervous than her.
**ella misma**
herself
Me lo dijo ella misma.
She told me herself.
**de ella**
hers
Este abrigo es de ella.
This coat's hers.

**e-mail** NOUN
1 **email**
2 **email address**

**embarazada** ADJECTIVE
**pregnant**
Estaba embarazada de cuatro meses.
She was four months pregnant.

**Language tip**

*Be careful!* **embarazada** *does not mean* **embarrassed**.

**embarazoso**
(FEM **embarazosa**) ADJECTIVE
**embarrassing**

la **emergencia** NOUN
**emergency**
**la salida de emergencia**
the emergency exit

**emocionante**
(FEM **emocionante**) ADJECTIVE
**exciting**
**El partido fue muy emocionante.**
The match was very exciting.

el **empaste** NOUN
**filling**

**empatar** VERB
**to draw**
**Empatamos a uno.**
We drew one-all.

el **empate** NOUN
**draw**
**un empate a cero**
a goalless draw

**empezar** VERB
**to start**
**Las vacaciones empiezan el día uno.**
The holidays start on the first.
**Ha empezado a nevar.**
It's started snowing.
**volver a empezar**
to start again

el **empleo** NOUN
**job**
**Ha encontrado empleo en un restaurante.**
He has found a job in a restaurant.
**estar sin empleo**
to be unemployed

**empollar** VERB
**to swot**
**Me pasé la noche empollando.**
I spent the whole night swotting.

el **empollón**
la **empollona** (MASC PL los empollones) NOUN
**swot**

la **empresa** NOUN
**firm**
**Mi padre trabaja en una empresa de informática.**
My dad works for a computer firm.

**empujar** VERB
**to push**
**Empuja la puerta.**
Push the door.

**en** PREPOSITION
1 **in**
**en el armario**
in the wardrobe
**Viven en Granada.**
They live in Granada.
**Nació en invierno.**
He was born in winter.
**Lo hice en dos días.**
I did it in two days.
**Está en el hospital.**
She's in hospital.
2 **into**
**Entré en la cocina.**
I went into the kitchen.
3 **on**
**Las llaves están en la mesa.**
The keys are on the table.
**La librería está en la calle Pelayo.**

a
b
c
d
e
f
g
h
i
j
k
l
m
n
ñ
o
p
q
r
s
t
u
v
w
x
y
z

81

The bookshop is on Pelayo street.
**La oficina está en el quinto piso.**
The office is on the fifth floor.
**4 at**
**Yo estaba en casa.**
I was at home.
**Te veo en el cine.**
See you at the cinema.
**5 by**
**Vinimos en avión.**
We came by plane.

**enamorado** (FEM **enamorada**)
ADJECTIVE
**estar enamorado de alguien**
to be in love with somebody

**enamorarse** VERB
**to fall in love**
**Se ha enamorado de Yolanda.**
He's fallen in love with Yolanda.

**encantado** (FEM **encantada**)
ADJECTIVE
**Está encantada con su abrigo nuevo.**
She loves her new coat.

**¡Encantado de conocerle!**
Pleased to meet you!

**encantar** VERB
**to love**
**Me encantan los animales.**
I love animals.

**Les encanta esquiar.**
They love skiing.

**encargar** VERB
**to order**
**Encargamos dos pizzas.**
We ordered two pizzas.

**encender** VERB
**1 to light**
**2 to switch on**

**encendido** (FEM **encendida**)
ADJECTIVE
**on**
**La tele estaba encendida.**
The telly was on.

el **enchufado**
la **enchufada** NOUN
**Amelia es la enchufada del profesor.**
Amelia's the teacher's pet.

**enchufar** VERB
**to plug in**
**Enchufa la tele.**
Plug the TV in.

el **enchufe** NOUN
**1 plug**
**2 socket**

**enciendo** VERB ▷ see **encender**
**¿Cómo enciendo la calefacción?**
How do I switch the heating on?

**encima** ADVERB
**on**
**Pon la taza aquí encima.**
Put the cup on here.
**encima de**
on/on top of

*Language tip*

**encima de** *has two meanings. Look at the examples.*

**Ponlo encima de la mesa.**
Put it on the table.
**Mi maleta está encima del armario.**
My case is on top of the wardrobe.

**encontrar** VERB
**to find**
> No encuentro las llaves.
> I can't find the keys.

**encontrarse** VERB
1 **to feel**
> Ahora se encuentra mejor.
> Now she's feeling better.
2 **to meet**
> Nos encontramos en el cine.
> We met at the cinema.
> **Me encontré con Manolo en la calle.**
> I bumped into Manolo in the street.

el **enemigo** (FEM la **enemiga**)
ADJECTIVE, NOUN
**enemy**

la **energía** NOUN
**energy**

**enero** MASC NOUN
**January**

> *Language tip*
> *Months are not written with a capital letter in Spanish.*

> **en enero**
> in January
> **Nació el seis de enero.**
> He was born on the sixth of January.

**enfadado** (FEM **enfadada**)
ADJECTIVE
**angry**
> Mi padre estaba muy enfadado conmigo.
> My father was very angry with me.

**enfadarse** VERB
**to be angry**
> Papá se va a enfadar mucho contigo.
> Dad will be very angry with you.

la **enfermedad** NOUN
**illness**

> Adelgazó mucho durante su enfermedad.
> He lost a lot of weight during his illness.

el **enfermero**
la **enfermera** NOUN
**nurse**
> Mi madre es enfermera.
> My mother's a nurse.

**enfermo**
**enferma**

> **enfermo** *can be an adjective or a noun.*

A ADJECTIVE
**ill**
> He estado enferma toda la semana.
> I've been ill all week.
B MASC/FEM NOUN
**patient**
> un enfermo del Dr. Rojas
> one of Dr Rojas' patients
> **Los enfermos deben tomar precauciones especiales.**
> Sick people need to take special precautions.

**enfrente** ADVERB
**opposite**
> Luisa estaba
> sentada enfrente.
> Luisa was sitting
> opposite.

> **La panadería está enfrente.**
> The baker's is across the street.
> **de enfrente**
> opposite
> **la casa de enfrente**
> the house opposite

**enfriarse** VERB
1 **to get cold**

**La sopa se ha enfriado.**
The soup has got cold.

**2 to cool down**
**Deja que la sopa se enfríe un poco.**
Let the soup cool down a bit.

**3 to catch cold**
**Ponte el abrigo que te vas a enfriar.**
Put your coat on or you'll catch cold.

**engordar** VERB
**1 to put on weight**
**No quiero engordar.**
I don't want to put on weight.
**He engordado dos kilos.**
I've put on two kilos.

**2 to be fattening**
**Los caramelos engordan mucho.**
Sweets are very fattening.

la **enhorabuena** NOUN
**¡Enhorabuena!**
Congratulations!

**enorme** (FEM **enorme**) ADJECTIVE
**enormous**
**Tienen una casa enorme.**
They have an enormous house.

la **ensalada** NOUN
**salad**

**enseguida** ADVERB
**straight away**
**La ambulancia llegó enseguida.**
The ambulance arrived straight away.

la **enseñanza** NOUN
**1 teaching**
**2 education**

**la enseñanza primaria**
primary education

**enseñar** VERB
**1 to teach**
**Ricardo enseña inglés en un colegio.**
Ricardo teaches English in a school.
**Mi padre me enseñó a nadar.**
My father taught me to swim.

**2 to show**
**Ana me enseñó todos sus videojuegos.**
Ana showed me all her video games.

**ensuciar** VERB
**to get ... dirty**
**Vas a ensuciar el sofá.**
You'll get the sofa dirty.

**No quiero ensuciarme.**
I don't want to get dirty.
**Me he ensuciado las manos.**
I've got my hands dirty.

**entender** VERB
**to understand**
**No entiendo el francés.**
I don't understand French.
**¿Lo entiendes?**
Do you understand?

**enterarse** VERB
**1 to find out**
**Me enteré por Manolo.**
I found out from Manolo.
**Se enteraron del accidente por la tele.**
They heard about the accident on the TV.

**2 to notice**

Me sacaron una muela y ni me enteré.
They took out a tooth and I didn't notice a thing.

**entero** (FEM **entera**) ADJECTIVE
**whole**
> Se comió el paquete entero de galletas.
> He ate the whole packet of biscuits.
> Se pasó la noche entera estudiando.
> He spent the whole night studying.

**entiendo** VERB ▷ see **entender**
> No lo entiendo.
> I can't understand it.

el **entierro** NOUN
**funeral**

**entonces** ADVERB
**then**
> Me recogió y entonces fuimos al cine.
> He picked me up and then we went to the cinema.

la **entrada** NOUN
1 **entrance**
> Nos vemos en la entrada.
> I'll see you at the entrance.
2 **ticket**
> Tengo entradas para el teatro.
> I've got tickets for the theatre.
> 'prohibida la entrada'
> 'no entry'

**entrar** VERB
1 **to go in**
> Abrí la puerta y entré.
> I opened the door and went in.
2 **to come in**
> ¿Se puede? – Sí, entra.
> May I? – Yes, come in.
> Le entraron ganas de reír.
> She wanted to laugh.
> De repente le entró sueño.
> He suddenly felt sleepy.

Me ha entrado hambre al verte comer.
Watching you eat has made me hungry.

**entre** PREPOSITION
1 **between**
> Lo terminamos entre los dos.
> Between the two of us we finished it.
> Vendrá entre las diez y las once.
> He'll be coming between ten and eleven.
2 **among**
> Las mujeres hablaban entre sí.
> The women were talking among themselves.
> Le compraremos un regalo entre todos.
> We'll buy her a present between all of us.

**entregar** VERB
**to hand in**
> Marta entregó el examen.
> Marta handed her exam paper in.

el **entrenamiento** NOUN
**training**

**entrenarse** VERB
**to train**

**entretenerse** VERB
**to amuse oneself**
> Se entretienen viendo los dibujos animados.
> They amuse themselves watching cartoons.
> No os entretengáis jugando.
> Don't hang about playing.

la **entrevista** NOUN
**interview**

**entrevistar** VERB
**to interview**

**entusiasmado**
(FEM **entusiasmada**) ADJECTIVE

**excited**
> Estaba entusiasmado con su fiesta de cumpleaños.
> He was excited about his birthday party.

**entusiasmarse** VERB
**to get excited**
> Se entusiasmó con la idea de hacer una fiesta.
> He got very excited about the idea of having a party.

**enviar** VERB
**to send**
> Envíame las fotos.
> Send me the photos.

la **envidia** NOUN
**envy**
> ¡Qué envidia!
> I'm so jealous!
> Le tiene envidia a Ana.
> He's jealous of Ana.

**envidiar** VERB
**to envy**
> ¡No te envidio!
> I don't envy you!

**envolver** VERB
**to wrap up**
> ¿Quiere que se lo envuelva?
> Would you like me to wrap it up for you?

**envuelto** VERB ▷ see **envolver**
> Estaba envuelto con papel de embalar.
> It was wrapped in brown paper.

el **equipaje** NOUN
**luggage**
> equipaje de mano
> hand luggage

el **equipo** NOUN
**team**
> un equipo de baloncesto
> a basketball team

**equivocado** (FEM **equivocada**)
ADJECTIVE
**wrong**
> Estás equivocada.
> You're wrong.
> Elena me dio el número equivocado.
> Elena gave me the wrong number.

**equivocarse** VERB
1 **to make a mistake**
> Perdona. Me equivoqué.
> Sorry. I made a mistake.
2 **to be wrong**
> Si crees que voy a dejarte ir, te equivocas.
> If you think I'm going to let you go, you're wrong.
> Perdone, me he equivocado de número.
> Sorry, wrong number.

**era** VERB ▷ see **ser**
> Era yo.
> It was me.

**eres** VERB ▷ see **ser**
> Eres muy amable.
> You're very kind.

el **erizo** NOUN
**hedgehog**

el **error** NOUN
**mistake**
> Fue un error contárselo a Lola.
> Telling Lola about it was a mistake.

Cometí muchos errores en
el examen.
I made a lot of mistakes in the
exam.

**es** VERB ▷*see* **ser**
Es un árbol.
It's a tree.

**esa** ADJECTIVE ▷*see* **ese**
Dame esa raqueta.
Give me that racket.

**ésa** PRONOUN ▷*see* **ése**
Ésa es mía.
That one is mine.

la **escalera** NOUN
**stairs**
   **bajar las escaleras**
   to go down the stairs
   **una escalera mecánica**
   an escalator

el **escándalo** NOUN
**scandal**
   **La pelea produjo un gran
   escándalo.**
   The fight caused a huge scandal.

**escaparse** VERB
**to escape**
   **El ladrón se escapó de la cárcel.**
   The thief escaped from prison.

la **escayola** NOUN
**plaster**
   **Mañana me
   quitan la
   escayola.**
   I'm getting my
   plaster taken
   off tomorrow.

la **escoba** NOUN
**broom**

**escocés**
**escocesa** (MASC PL **escoceses**)

**escocés** *can be an adjective or a
noun.*

**A** ADJECTIVE
**Scottish**

**B** MASC/FEM NOUN
   **un escocés**
   a Scotsman
   **una escocesa**
   a Scotswoman
   **los escoceses**
   Scottish people

**Escocia** FEM NOUN
**Scotland**

**escoger** VERB
**to choose**
   **Yo escogí el azul.**
   I chose the blue one.

**escolar** (FEM **escolar**) ADJECTIVE
**school**
   **el uniforme escolar**
   the school uniform

**esconder** VERB
**to hide**
   **Lo escondí en el cajón.**
   I hid it in the box.
   **Me escondí debajo de la
   cama.**
   I hid under the bed.

**escondidas** FEM PL NOUN
   **a escondidas**
   in secret
   **Se ven a escondidas.**
   They meet in secret.

el **escondite** NOUN
   **jugar al escondite**
   to play hide-and-seek

la **escopeta** NOUN
**shotgun**

### escribir VERB
**to write**

**Les escribí una carta.**
I wrote them a letter.
**Escribe pronto.**
Write soon.
**Nos escribimos de vez en cuando.**
We write to each other from time to time.
**¿Cómo se escribe tu nombre?**
How do you spell your name?

### escrito (FEM escrita) ADJECTIVE
**written**

**un examen escrito**
a written exam

### el escritor
### la escritora NOUN
**writer**

**Pablo es escritor.**
Pablo's a writer.

### escuchar VERB
**to listen**

**Juan escuchaba con atención.**
Juan was listening attentively.
**Me gusta escuchar música.**
I like listening to music.

### la escuela NOUN
**school**

**Hoy no tengo que ir a la escuela.**
I don't have to go to school today.
**la escuela primaria**
primary school

### escupir VERB
**to spit**

### ese (FEM esa, MASC PL esos)
ADJECTIVE
**that**

**Dame ese libro.**
Give me that book.
**Trae esas sillas aquí.**
Bring those chairs over here.

### ése (FEM ésa, MASC PL ésos)
PRONOUN

**that one**

**Ése es mío.**
That one is mine.
**Ésos de ahí son mejores.**
Those ones over there are better.
**¿Cuánto valen ésos?**
How much are those?

---

#### Language tip

*Traditionally, the pronouns **ése**, **ésa**, **ésos** and **ésas** were written with an accent to distinguish them from the unaccented adjective forms. Nowadays, you don't have to give the accents unless the sentence would be confusing otherwise.*

---

### esforzarse VERB
**to make an effort**

**Tienes que esforzarte si quieres ganar.**
You have to make an effort if you want to win.

### el esfuerzo NOUN
**effort**

**Tuve que hacer un esfuerzo para aprobar el examen.**
I had to make an effort to pass the exam.

### el esguince NOUN
**sprain**

**Me hice un esguince en el tobillo.**
I sprained my ankle.

### la ESO ABBREVIATION
(= **Enseñanza Secundaria obligatoria**)

---

#### Did you know...?

*ESO is the compulsory secondary education course done by 12 to 16 year-olds.*

---

### eso PRONOUN
**that**

**Eso es mentira.**
That's a lie.
**Por eso te lo dije.**
That's why I told you.
**¡Y eso que estaba lloviendo!**

And it was raining and everything!

**¡Eso es!**
That's it!

**esos** ADJECTIVE ▷ *see* **ese**
**Dame esos lápices.**
Give me those pencils.

**ésos** PRONOUN ▷ *see* **ése**
**Ésos son míos.**
Those ones are mine.

el **espacio** NOUN
1 **room**
El piano ocupa mucho espacio.
The piano takes up a lot of room.
2 **space**
Deja más espacio entre las líneas.
Leave more space between the lines.

la **espada**
NOUN
**sword**

> *Language tip*
> Be careful! **espada** does not mean **spade**.

la **espalda** NOUN
**back**
Estaba tumbada de espaldas.
She was lying on her back.

**España** FEM NOUN
**Spain**

**español**

> **español** *can be an adjective or a noun.*

A (FEM **española**) ADJECTIVE
**Spanish**
B MASC/FEM NOUN
**español/española**
**Spaniard**
**los españoles**
the Spanish
C MASC NOUN
**Spanish**

**¿Hablas español?**
Do you speak Spanish?

**especial** (FEM **especial**)
ADJECTIVE
**special**
Fue un día muy especial.
It was a very special day.

**especialmente** ADVERB
1 **especially**
Me gusta mucho el pan, especialmente el integral.
I love bread, especially wholemeal bread.
2 **specially**
un vestido diseñado especialmente para ella
a dress designed specially for her

la **especie** NOUN
**species**

el **espectador**
la **espectadora** NOUN
**spectator**
los espectadores
the audience

el **espejo** NOUN
**mirror**
Me miré en el espejo.
I looked at myself in the mirror.

**esperar** VERB
1 **to wait**
Espera en la puerta, ahora mismo voy.
Wait at the door. I'm just coming.
2 **to wait for**
No me esperéis.
Don't wait for me.
Me hizo esperar una hora.

He kept me waiting for an hour.
**Fuimos a esperarla a la estación.**
We went to the station to meet her.

**3 to expect**
**Llegaron antes de lo que yo esperaba.**
They arrived sooner than I expected.

**4 to hope**
**Espero que no sea nada grave.**
I hope it isn't anything serious.
**¿Vendrás a la fiesta? – Espero que sí.**
Are you coming to the party? – I hope so.
**¿Crees que Carmen se enfadará? – Espero que no.**
Do you think Carmen will be angry? – I hope not.

la **espina** NOUN
**1 thorn**
**2 bone**

la **esponja** NOUN
**sponge**

la **esposa** NOUN
**1 wife**
**2 las esposas**
handcuffs

el **esposo** NOUN
**husband**

la **espuma** NOUN
**foam**

el **esqueleto** NOUN
**skeleton**

el **esquiador**
la **esquiadora** NOUN
**skier**

**esquiar** VERB
**to ski**
**¿Sabes esquiar?**
Can you ski?

la **esquina** NOUN
**corner**

**esta** (FEM **esta**) ADJECTIVE ▷ see **este**
**Esta pelota es mía.**
This ball is mine.

**ésta** PRONOUN ▷ see **éste**
**Mi casa es ésta.**
My house is this one.

**está** VERB ▷ see **estar**
**Está frío.**
It's cold.

la **estación** (PL las **estaciones**) NOUN
**1 station**
**la estación de autobuses**
the bus station
**la estación de ferrocarril**
the railway station
**2 season**
**las cuatro estaciones del año**
the four seasons of the year

**estacionar** VERB
**to park**

el **estadio** NOUN
**stadium**

los **Estados Unidos** NOUN
**the United States**
**en Estados Unidos**
in the United States

**estadounidense** ADJECTIVE, MASC/FEM NOUN
**American**

**estallar** VERB
**to explode**

el **estanco** NOUN
**tobacconist's**

**Did you know...?**

*In Spain, an* **estanco** *is recognizable by the brown and yellow 'T' sign that hangs over the door. As well as tobacco, they sell stamps and coupons for the football pools.*

a b c d e f g h i j k l m n ñ o p q r s t u v w x y z

el **estanque** NOUN
pond

la **estantería** NOUN
1 shelves
2 bookshelves

**estar** VERB
1 **to be**
**Madrid está en el centro
de España.**
Madrid is in the centre of Spain.
**Papá está en la cocina.**
Dad's in the kitchen.
**¿Dónde estabas?**
Where were you?
**¿Está Mónica?**
Is Mónica there?
**¿Cómo estás?**
How are you?
**Estoy muy cansada.**
I'm very tired.
**Estamos de vacaciones.**
We're on holiday.
**Estamos a treinta de enero.**
It's the thirtieth of January.
**Estábamos a 30°C.**
The temperature was 30°C.
**Estamos esperando a Manolo.**
We're waiting for Manolo.
**María estaba sentada en
la arena.**
María was sitting on the sand.
2 **to look**
**Ese vestido te está muy bien.**
That dress looks very good on you.

la **estatua** NOUN
statue

**este**

*este can be an adjective or a noun.*

**A** (FEM **esta**, MASC PL **estos**)
ADJECTIVE
**this**
**este libro**
this book

**estas revistas**
these magazines
**B** MASC NOUN, ADJECTIVE
**east**
**el este del país**
the east of the country

*Language tip*
*When it means 'east', the adjective
**este** never changes its ending, no
matter what it describes.*

**en la costa este**
on the east coast

**éste** (FEM **ésta**, MASC PL **éstos**)
PRONOUN
**this one**
**Me gusta más éste.**
I prefer this one.
**Éstos son muy caros.**
These ones are very expensive.
**¿Cuánto valen éstos?**
How much are these?

*Language tip*
*Traditionally, the pronouns **éste**,
**ésta**, **éstos** and **éstas** were
written with an accent to distinguish
them from the unaccented adjective
forms. Nowadays, you don't have to
give the accents unless the sentence
would be confusing otherwise.*

**esté** VERB ▷ *see* estar
**Espero que no esté muy lejos.**
I hope it won't be too far.

**estimado** (FEM **estimada**)
ADJECTIVE
**Estimado Sr. Pérez:**
Dear Mr Pérez,

*Language tip*
*Did you notice that there's a colon
(:) at the end of the opening line of
a letter in Spanish, not a comma?*

**estirar** VERB
**to stretch**
**No quiero estirar el jersey.**
I don't want to stretch my
jumper.

a b c d e f g h i j k l m n ñ o p q r s t u v w x y z

**esto** PRONOUN
**this**
> ¿Para qué es esto?
> What's this for?

el **estómago** NOUN
**stomach**
> Me dolía el estómago.
> I had a stomachache.

**estorbar** VERB
**to be in the way**
> Las maletas estorban aquí.
> The cases are in the way here.

**estornudar** VERB
**to sneeze**

**estos** PL ADJECTIVE ▷ see **este**
> Estos libros son bastante baratos.
> These books are quite cheap.

**éstos** PL PRONOUN ▷ see **éste**
> Éstos son míos.
> These ones are mine.

**estoy** VERB ▷ see **estar**
> Estoy cansado.
> I'm tired.

**estrecho** (FEM **estrecha**)
ADJECTIVE
1 **narrow**
2 **tight**
> La falda me va muy estrecha.
> The skirt is very tight on me.

la **estrella** NOUN
**star**
> una estrella de cine
> a film star
> una estrella de mar
> a starfish

**estreñido** (FEM **estreñida**)
ADJECTIVE
**constipated**

**estropeado** (FEM **estropeada**)
ADJECTIVE
1 **broken**
2 **broken down**

**estropear** VERB
1 **to break**
2 **to ruin**
> La lluvia nos estropeó las vacaciones.
> The rain ruined our holidays.
■ **estropearse**
**to break**
> Se nos ha estropeado la tele.
> The TV's broken.

el **estuche** NOUN
**case**

el/la **estudiante** NOUN
**student**

**estudiar** VERB
1 **to study**
> Quiere estudiar medicina.
> She wants to study medicine.
2 **to learn**
> Tengo que estudiar cuatro lecciones para el examen.
> I have to learn four lessons for the exam.

el **estudio** NOUN
> Ha dejado los estudios.
> He's given up his studies.

la **estufa** NOUN
**heater**
> una estufa eléctrica
> an electric heater

**estupendo** (FEM **estupenda**)
ADJECTIVE
**great**
> Pasamos unas Navidades estupendas.
> We had a great Christmas.

**¡Estupendo!**
Great!

la **estupidez** (PL las **estupideces**) NOUN
**No dice más que estupideces.**
He just talks rubbish.
**Lo que hizo fue una estupidez.**
What he did was stupid.

**estúpido**
**estúpida**

> *estúpido can be an adjective or a noun.*

**A** ADJECTIVE
**stupid**
**B** MASC/FEM NOUN
**idiot**
**Ese tío es un estúpido.**
That guy's an idiot.

**estuve** VERB ▷*see* **estar**
**Estuve una semana de vacaciones.**
I was on holiday for a week.

la **etiqueta** NOUN
**label**

el **euro** NOUN
**euro**

**Europa** FEM NOUN
**Europe**

el **europeo**
(FEM la **europea**) ADJECTIVE, NOUN
**European**

**evitar** VERB
**1 to avoid**
**Quiero evitar ese riesgo.**
I want to avoid that risk.
**Intento evitar a Carmen.**
I'm trying to avoid Carmen.
**No pude evitarlo.**
I couldn't help it.

**2 to save**
**Esto nos evitará muchos problemas.**
This will save us a lot of problems.

**exacto** (FEM **exacta**) ADJECTIVE
**exact**
**el precio exacto**
the exact price

**exagerado** (FEM **exagerada**)
ADJECTIVE
**exaggerated**
**una descripción exagerada**
an exaggerated description
**¡No seas exagerado, el pez no era tan grande!**
Don't exaggerate. The fish wasn't that big.

**El precio me parece exagerado.**
The price seems far too high.

el **examen** (PL los **exámenes**)
NOUN
**exam**

**examinar** VERB
**to examine**
**El médico la examinó.**
The doctor examined her.
**Mañana me examino de inglés.**
Tomorrow I've got an English exam.

**excelente** (FEM **excelente**)
ADJECTIVE
**excellent**

**excepto** PREPOSITION
**except for**
**todos, excepto Juan**
everyone, except for Juan

Spanish English

a b c **d e** f g h i j k l m n ñ o p q r s t u v w x y z

**excluyendo** VERB ▷ see **excluir**
**Excluyendo a mis padres, somos tres.**
Not counting my parents, there are three of us.

la **excursión** (PL las **excursiones**) NOUN
**trip**
**Mañana vamos de excursión con el colegio.**
Tomorrow we're going on a school trip.

la **excusa** NOUN
**excuse**

**existir** VERB
**to exist**
**¿Existen los fantasmas?**
Do ghosts exist?

el **éxito** NOUN
**success**
**Esa novela será un gran éxito.**
That novel will be a great success.
**Su película tuvo mucho éxito.**
His film was very successful.
**Acabaron con éxito el proyecto.**
They completed the project successfully.

*Language tip*
*Be careful!* **éxito** *does not mean* **exit***.*

la **experiencia** NOUN
**experience**

el **experimento** NOUN
**experiment**

el **experto**
la **experta** NOUN
**expert**
**Es un experto en informática.**
He's a computer expert.

la **explicación** (PL las **explicaciones**) NOUN
**explanation**

**explicar** VERB
**to explain**
**¿Quieres que te explique cómo hacerlo?**
Do you want me to explain to you how to do it?

la **explosión** (PL las **explosiones**) NOUN
**explosion**

la **exposición** (PL las **exposiciones**) NOUN
**exhibition**
**montar una exposición**
to put on an exhibition

**expresar** VERB
**to express**
**No sabe expresarse.**
He doesn't know how to express himself.

la **expresión** (PL las **expresiones**) NOUN
**expression**

**extender** VERB
**to spread**
**Extendí la toalla sobre la arena.**
I spread the towel out on the sand.
**El fuego se extendió rápidamente.**
The fire spread quickly.

**exterior** (FEM **exterior**)
ADJECTIVE
**outside**

**extinto** (FEM **extinta**) ADJECTIVE
**extinct**

**extra** (FEM **extra**) ADJECTIVE
**extra**
**una manta extra**
an extra blanket

**extraescolar**
(FEM **extraescolara**) ADJECTIVE
**actividades extraescolares**
extracurricular activities

**extranjero**
**extranjera**

> **extranjero** *can be an adjective or a noun.*

**A** ADJECTIVE
**foreign**
**B** MASC/FEM NOUN
**foreigner**

> **viajar al extranjero**
> to travel abroad

**extrañar** VERB
**to miss**
**Extraña mucho a sus padres.**
He misses his parents a lot.
**Me extraña que no haya llegado.**
I'm surprised he hasn't arrived.
**¡Ya me extrañaba a mí!**
I thought it was strange!

**extraño** (FEM **extraña**) ADJECTIVE
**strange**
**¡Qué extraño!**
How strange!

**extraordinario**
(FEM **extraordinaria**) ADJECTIVE
**extraordinary**

el **extremo** NOUN
**end**
**Cogí la cuerda por un extremo.**
I took hold of one end of the rope.
**pasar de un extremo a otro**
to go from one extreme to the
other

Spanish English

a
b
c
d
e
f
g
h
i
j
k
l
m
n
ñ
o
p
q
r
s
t
u
v
w
x
y
z

# F f

la **fábrica** NOUN
**factory**

> **Language tip**
> Be careful! **fábrica** does not mean
> **fabric**.

**fácil** (FEM **fácil**) ADJECTIVE
**easy**
> un ejercicio fácil
> an easy exercise

la **falda** NOUN
**skirt**

el **fallo** NOUN
1 **fault**
2 **mistake**
> ¡Qué fallo!
> What a stupid mistake!

**falso** (FEM **falsa**) ADJECTIVE
1 **false**
2 **forged**

la **falta** NOUN
1 **lack**
> la falta de dinero
> lack of money
2 **mistake**
> una falta de ortografía
> a spelling mistake

> **Me hace falta un ordenador.**
> I need a computer.
> **No hace falta que vengáis.**
> You don't need to come.

**faltar** VERB
1 **to be missing**
> Me falta un bolígrafo.
> One of my pens is missing.
> No podemos irnos. Falta
> Manolo.
> We can't go. Manolo isn't here
> yet.
> A la sopa le falta sal.
> There isn't enough salt in the soup.

**faltar al colegio**
to miss school
> **You mustn't miss school.**
> No debes faltar al colegio.
2 **Falta media hora para comer.**
> There's half an hour to go before
> lunch.
> **¿Te falta mucho?**
> Will you be long?

la **fama** NOUN
1 **fame**
2 **reputation**
> tener fama de
> to have a reputation for
> **Tiene fama de mandona.**
> She has a reputation for being
> bossy.

la **familia** NOUN
**family**

**familiar** (FEM **familiar**)
ADJECTIVE
1 **family**
> la vida familiar
> family life
2 **familiar**
> Su cara me es familiar.
> His face is familiar.

**famoso** (FEM **famosa**) ADJECTIVE
**famous**

el **fantasma** NOUN
**ghost**

la **farmacia** NOUN
**chemist's**
> Lo compré en la farmacia.
> I bought it at the chemist's.

> **Did you know…?**
> Spanish chemists are identifiable by
> a red or green cross outside the
> shop. Go to a **perfumería** instead
> if you want to buy cosmetics or
> toiletries.

el **faro** NOUN
1 **headlight**
2 **lighthouse**

**fastidiar**
VERB
**to annoy**
Lo que más me fastidia es tener que decírselo.
What annoys me most is having to tell him.

**fatal**

> **fatal** can be an adjective or an adverb.

A (FEM **fatal**) ADJECTIVE
**awful**
Me siento fatal.
I feel awful.
B ADVERB
Lo pasé fatal.
I had an awful time.
Lo hice fatal.
I made a mess of it.

el **favor** NOUN
**favour**
¿Puedes hacerme un favor?
Can you do me a favour?

**por favor**
please

**favorito** (FEM **favorita**)
ADJECTIVE
**favourite**
¿Cuál es tu color favorito?
What's your favourite colour?

**febrero** MASC NOUN
**February**

> **Language tip**
> Months are not spelled with a capital letter in Spanish.

Nació el veintiocho de febrero.

She was born on the twenty-eighth of February.

**en febrero**
in February
Nació el quince de febrero.
He was born on the fifteenth of February.

la **fecha** NOUN
**date**
¿En qué fecha estamos?
What's the date today?
su fecha de nacimiento
his date of birth

la **felicidad** NOUN
**happiness**
¡Felicidades!
Happy birthday!/
Congratulations!

> **Language tip**
> ¡Felicidades! has two meanings.

**felicitar** VERB
**to congratulate**
La felicité por sus notas.
I congratulated her on her exam results.
Felicítale por su cumpleaños.
Wish her a happy birthday.

**feliz** (FEM **feliz**, PL **felices**)
ADJECTIVE
**happy**
Se la ve muy feliz.
She looks very happy.

¡Feliz cumpleaños!
Happy birthday!
¡Feliz Año Nuevo!
Happy New Year!
¡Felices Navidades!
Happy Christmas!

**femenino** (FEM **femenina**)
ADJECTIVE
1 **feminine**
2 **female**
el sexo femenino
the female sex

**feo** (FEM **fea**) ADJECTIVE
**ugly**

**festivo** (FEM **festiva**) ADJECTIVE
**un día festivo**
a holiday

**fiar** VERB
**fiarse de alguien**
to trust somebody
**No me fío de él.**
I don't trust him.

la **ficha** NOUN
**counter**

los **fideos** NOUN
**noodles**

la **fiebre** NOUN
**temperature**
**Tiene fiebre.**
She has a temperature.
**fiebre de heno**
hay fever

la **fiesta** NOUN
1 **party**
**Voy a dar una fiesta para celebrarlo.**
I'm going to have a party to celebrate.
**El pueblo está en fiestas.**
There's a fiesta on in the town.
**una fiesta de cumpleaños**
a birthday party
2 **holiday**
**El lunes es fiesta.**
Monday is a holiday.

la **fila** NOUN
1 **row**

**Nos sentamos en la segunda fila.**
We sit in the second row.
2 **line**
**Los niños se pusieron en fila.**
The children got into line.

el **filete** NOUN
1 **steak**
**un filete con patatas fritas**
steak and chips
2 **fillet**
**un filete de merluza**
a hake fillet

el **fin** NOUN
**end**
**a fines de abril**
at the end of April
**En fin, ¿qué le vamos a hacer?**
Oh well, what can we do about it?
**por fin**
at last
**¡Por fin hemos llegado!**
We've got here at last!
**el fin de año**
New Year's Eve
**el fin de semana**
the weekend

## final

> **final** can be an adjective or a noun.

A (FEM **final**) ADJECTIVE
**final**
**el resultado final**
the final result
B MASC NOUN
**end**
**Al final de la calle hay un colegio.**
At the end of the street there's a school.
**a finales de mayo**
at the end of May
**al final**
in the end
**Al final tuve que darle la razón.**

In the end I had to admit that he was right.
**un final feliz**
a happy ending
**c** FEM NOUN
**final**
**la final de la copa**
the cup final

**fingir** VERB
**to pretend**
**Fingió no haberme oído.**
He pretended not to have heard me.
**Finge dormir.**
He's pretending to be asleep.

**fino** (FEM **fina**) ADJECTIVE
**1 thin**
**2 fine**

la **firma** NOUN
**signature**

**firmar** VERB
**to sign**

**firme** (FEM **firme**) ADJECTIVE
**steady**
**Mantén la escalera firme.**
Can you hold the ladder steady?

la **flauta** NOUN
**1 recorder**
**2 flute**

la **flecha** NOUN
**arrow**

el **flequillo**
NOUN
**fringe**

**flojo** (FEM **floja**) ADJECTIVE
**1 loose**
**2 weak**
**Todavía tengo las piernas muy flojas.**
My legs are still very weak.
**Está flojo en matemáticas.**
He's weak at maths.

la **flor** NOUN
**flower**

el **flotador** NOUN
**rubber ring**

el **folio** NOUN
**1 sheet of paper**
**2 page**

el **folleto** NOUN
**1 brochure**
**2 leaflet**

el **fondo** NOUN
**1 bottom**
**en el fondo del mar**
at the bottom of the sea
**2 end**
**Mi habitación está al fondo del pasillo.**
My room's at the end of the corridor.

el **fontanero**
la **fontanera** NOUN
**plumber**

la **forma** NOUN
**way**
**Me miraba de una forma extraña.**
She was looking at me in a strange way.
**de todas formas**
anyway
**De todas formas, debes ir a verlo.**
You should go to see him anyway.

**formal** (FEM **formal**) ADJECTIVE
**responsible**
**un chico muy formal**
a very responsible boy

**forrar** VERB
**to cover**

la **foto** NOUN
**photo**
> Les hice una foto a los niños.
> I took a photo of the children.

la **fotocopia** NOUN
**photocopy**

**fotocopiar** VERB
**to photocopy**

la **fotografía** NOUN
**photograph**
> una fotografía de mis padres
> a photograph of my parents

la **frambuesa** NOUN
**raspberry**

la **frase** NOUN
**sentence**

la **frecuencia** NOUN
**frequency**
> Nos vemos con frecuencia.
> We often see each other.

**frecuente** (FEM **frecuente**)
ADJECTIVE
**common**
> un error bastante frecuente
> a fairly common mistake

el **fregadero** NOUN
**sink**

**fregar** VERB
**to wash**
> Tengo que fregar la cazuela.
> I've got to wash the pan.
> Yo estaba en la cocina fregando.
> I was in the kitchen washing the dishes.
> Deberías fregar el suelo.
> You should mop the floor.

**freír** VERB
**to fry**

el **freno** NOUN
**brake**
> el freno de mano
> the handbrake

la **frente** NOUN
**forehead**
> Tiene una cicatriz en la frente.
> He has a scar on his forehead.

el **frente** NOUN
**front**
> frente a
> opposite
> Frente al hotel hay un banco.
> There's a bank opposite the hotel.

la **fresa** NOUN
**strawberry**

**fresco**

> **fresco** *can be an adjective or a noun.*

**A** (FEM **fresca**) ADJECTIVE
1 **cool**
2 **fresh**
**B** MASC NOUN
**fresh air**
> Salimos fuera a tomar el fresco.
> We went outside to get some fresh air.
> Hace fresco.
> It's chilly./It's cool.

> **Language tip**
> **hace fresco** *has two meanings. Look at the examples.*

> No quiero salir porque hace fresco.
> I don't want to go out because it's a bit chilly.
> En esta casa hace fresco en verano.
> This house is cool in summer.

**Hace más fresco dentro.**
It's cooler inside.

### friego
VERB
▷ see **fregar**
**Yo friego y tu seca.**
I'll wash and you dry.

### frío

> **frío** can be an adjective, noun or part of the verb **freír**.

**A** (FEM **fría**) ADJECTIVE
**cold**
**Tengo las manos frías.**
My hands are cold.

**B** MASC NOUN
**cold**
**Hace frío.**
It's cold.
**Tengo mucho frío.**
I'm very cold.

**C** VERB ▷ see **freír**
**¿Te frío un huevo?**
Shall I fry you an egg?

### frito

> **frito** can be an adjective or part of the verb **freír**.

**A** (FEM **frita**) ADJECTIVE
**fried**
**huevos fritos**
fried eggs

**B** VERB ▷ see **freír**
**He frito un huevo.**
I've fried an egg.

### la **frontera** NOUN
**border**
**Nos pararon en la frontera.**
We were stopped at the border.

### la **fruta** NOUN
**fruit**

**La fruta está muy cara.**
Fruit is very expensive.

### fue VERB ▷ see **ir**, **ser**
**Fue a la escuela en Barcelona.**
He went to school in Barcelona.
**Fue él.**
It was him.

### el **fuego** NOUN
**fire**
**Enciende el fuego.**
Light the fire.
**Puse la cazuela al fuego.**
I put the pot on to heat.
**¿Tiene fuego, por favor?**
Have you got a light, please?
**fuegos artificiales**
fireworks

### la **fuente** NOUN
**fountain**

### fuera

> **fuera** can be an adverb or a verb.

**A** ADVERB
**outside**
**Los niños estaban jugando fuera.**
The children were playing outside.
**Por fuera es blanco.**
It's white on the outside.
**¡Estamos aquí fuera!**
We are out here!
**Hoy vamos a cenar fuera.**
We're going out for dinner tonight.

**B** VERB ▷ see **ir**, **ser**
**Quería que fuera con ella.**
She wanted me to go with her.

**Si fuera yo, no se lo diría.**
If I were you, I wouldn't tell him.

## fuerte

fuerte *can be an adjective or an adverb.*

**A** (FEM **fuerte**) ADJECTIVE
1 **strong**
2 **loud**
3 **hard**
**B** ADVERB
**loudly**
**Siempre habla fuerte.**
He always talks loudly.
**Agárrate fuerte.**
Hold on tight.
**No le des tan fuerte.**
Don't hit it so hard.

la **fuerza** NOUN
**strength**
**No le quedaban fuerzas.**
He had no strength left.
**No te lo comas a la fuerza.**
Don't force yourself to eat it.
**la fuerza de la gravedad**
the force of gravity
**la fuerza de voluntad**
willpower

**fuerzo** VERB ▷ *see* forzar
**Solo se abrirá si la fuerzo.**
It will only open if I force it.

**fui** VERB ▷ *see* ir, ser
**Ayer fui al cine.**
I went to the cinema yesterday.
**Fui yo.**
It was me.

el **fumador**
la **fumadora** NOUN
**smoker**

**fumar** VERB
**to smoke**
**Mi padre quiere dejar de fumar.**
My dad wants to give up smoking.

**funcionar** VERB
**to work**
**El ascensor no funciona.**
The lift isn't working.
**Funciona con pilas.**
It runs on batteries.

el **funeral** NOUN
**funeral**

la **furgoneta** NOUN
**van**

**furioso** (FEM **furiosa**) ADJECTIVE
**furious**

el **fútbol** NOUN
**football**
**jugar al fútbol**
to play football

el **futbolín** (PL los **futbolines**)
NOUN
**table football**

el/la **futbolista** NOUN
**footballer**
**Quiere ser futbolista.**
He wants to be a footballer.

# G g

las **gafas** NOUN
1 **glasses**
**Lleva gafas.**
He wears glasses.
**Había unas gafas encima de la mesa.**
There was a pair of glasses on the table.
**gafas de sol**
sunglasses
2 **goggles**

**Gales** MASC NOUN
**Wales**
**el País de Gales**
Wales

la **galleta** NOUN
**biscuit**
**una galleta salada**
a cracker

**gallina** FEM NOUN
**hen**

el **gallo** NOUN
**cock**

el **gamberro**
la **gamberra** NOUN
**hooligan**

la **gana** NOUN
**Hazlo como te dé la gana.**
Do it however you like.
**Lo hizo de mala gana.**
She did it reluctantly.
**Tengo ganas de que llegue el sábado.**
I'm looking forward to Saturday.

**¡No me da la gana!**
I don't want to!

el **ganador**
la **ganadora** NOUN
**winner**

**ganar** VERB
1 **to win**
**Lo importante no es ganar.**
Winning isn't the most important thing.
**Con eso no ganas nada.**
You won't achieve anything by doing that.
2 **ganar a**
**to beat**
**Ganamos al Olimpic tres a cero.**
We beat Olimpic three-nil.
3 **to earn**
**Gana un buen sueldo.**
He earns a good wage.

el **garaje** NOUN
**garage**

la **garganta** NOUN
**throat**
**Me duele la garganta.**
I've got a sore throat.

el **gas** (PL los **gases**) NOUN
**gas**
**¿Te huele a gas?**
Can you smell gas?
**agua mineral sin gas**
still mineral water
**agua mineral con gas**
sparkling mineral water

la **gaseosa** NOUN

### Did you know…?
**Gaseosa** *is a sweet fizzy drink a bit like lemonade or soda.*

a b c d e f **g** h i j k l m n ñ o p q r s t u v w x y z

la **gasolina** NOUN
petrol

la **gasolinera** NOUN
petrol station

**gastado** (FEM **gastada**)
ADJECTIVE
worn

**gastar** VERB
1 **to spend**
2 **to use**
**Gastamos mucha electricidad.**
We use a lot of electricity.
**Se han gastado las pilas.**
The batteries have run out.
**Le gastamos una broma a Juan.**
We played a joke on Juan.

la **gata** NOUN
cat

**andar a gatas**
to crawl
**El niño todavía anda a gatas.**
The baby is still crawling.

el **gato** NOUN
cat

la **gaviota** NOUN
seagull

el **gemelo**
la **gemela**
NOUN
identical twin

los **gemelos**
NOUN
binoculars

**general** (FEM **general**) ADJECTIVE
general

**por lo general**
generally

**genial** (FEM **genial**) ADJECTIVE
brilliant

el **genio** NOUN
1 **temper**
**¡Menudo genio tiene tu padre!**
Your father has got such a temper!
**Tiene mal genio.**
He has a bad temper
2 **genius**
**¡Eres un genio!**
You're a genius!

la **gente** NOUN
people
**Había poca gente en la sala.**
There weren't many people in the room.

la **geografía** NOUN
geography

el **gesto** NOUN
**Hizo un gesto de alivio.**
He looked relieved.
**Me hizo un gesto para que me sentara.**
He signalled for me to sit down.

la **gimnasia** NOUN
gymnastics
**Mi madre hace gimnasia todas las mañanas.**
My mother does some exercise every morning.

el **gimnasio** NOUN
gym

**girar** VERB
**to turn**
**Giré la cabeza para ver quién era.**
I turned my head to see who it was.

**global** (FEM **global**) ADJECTIVE
global

el **globo** NOUN
balloon

el **gobierno** NOUN
government

el **gol** NOUN
goal
> **Metió un gol.**
> He scored a goal.

la **golosina** NOUN
sweet

**goloso** (FEM **golosa**) ADJECTIVE
> **Soy muy golosa.**
> I've got a very sweet tooth.

el **golpe** NOUN
knock
> **Oímos un golpe en la puerta.**
> We heard a knock at the door.
> **Me he dado un golpe en el codo.**
> I banged my elbow.
> **Se dio un golpe contra la pared.**
> He hit the wall.
> **de golpe**
> suddenly
> **De golpe decidió marcharse.**
> He suddenly decided to leave.

**golpear** VERB
1 **to hit**
> **Me golpeó en la cara con su raqueta.**
> He hit me in the face with his racquet.
2 **to bang**
> **El maestro golpeó el pupitre con la mano.**

The teacher banged the desk with his hand.

la **goma** NOUN
1 **rubber**
> **¿Me prestas la goma?**
> Can you lend me your rubber?
2 **elastic band**
> **Necesito una goma para el pelo.**
> I need an elastic band for my hair.

**gordo** (FEM **gorda**) ADJECTIVE
fat
> **Estoy muy gordo.**
> I'm very fat.

la **gorra** NOUN
cap

> **de gorra**
> for free
> **Entramos de gorra.**
> We got in for free.

el **gorro** NOUN
hat
> **Llevaba un gorro de lana.**
> He wore a woolly hat.
> **un gorro de baño**
> a swimming cap

la **gota** NOUN
drop
> **Solo bebí una gota de zumo.**
> I only had a drop of juice.
> **Están cayendo cuatro gotas.**
> It's spitting.

**grabar** VERB
1 **to record**
> **Lo grabaron en directo.**
> It was recorded live.
2 **to tape**
> **Quiero grabar esta película.**
> I want to tape this film.

**3** to engrave

**la gracia** NOUN

> **Sus chistes tienen mucha gracia.**
> His jokes are very funny.
> **Yo no le veo la gracia.**
> I don't see what's so funny.
> **Me hizo mucha gracia.**
> It was so funny.
> **No me hace gracia tener que salir con este tiempo.**
> I'm not too pleased about having to go out in this weather.

---

**gracias a**
thanks to
**¡Gracias!**
Thank you!
**¡Muchas gracias!**
Thanks very much!
**dar las gracias a alguien**
to thank somebody

---

**gracioso** (FEM **graciosa**) ADJECTIVE

**funny**

> **¡Qué gracioso!**
> How funny!

**el grado** NOUN

**degree**

> **Estaban a diez grados bajo cero.**
> It was ten degrees below zero.

**la gramática** NOUN

**grammar**

**el gramo** NOUN

**gram**

**gran** ADJECTIVE ▷ *see* **grande**

**un gran artista**
a great artist
**un gran número de gente**
a large number of people

**Gran Bretaña** FEM NOUN

**Great Britain**

**grande** (FEM **grande**) ADJECTIVE

*Language tip*

**grande** *becomes* **gran** *before a singular noun.*

**1** big

> **¿Cómo es de grande?**
> How big is it?
> **La camisa me está grande.**
> The shirt is too big for me.
> **unos grandes almacenes**
> a department store

**2** large

> **un gran número de visitantes**
> a large number of visitors

**el granizo** NOUN

**hail**

**la granja** NOUN

**farm**

**el grano** NOUN

**1** spot

> **Me ha salido un grano en la frente.**
> I've got a spot on my forehead.

**2** grain

**gratis**

*gratis can be an adjective or an adverb.*

**A** (FEM, PL **gratis**) ADJECTIVE

**free**

> **La entrada es gratis.**
> Entry is free.

**B** ADVERB

**for free**

> **Te lo arreglan gratis.**
> They'll fix it for free.

**grave** (FEM **grave**) ADJECTIVE

**serious**

> **Tenemos un problema grave.**
> We've got a serious problem.

**el grifo** NOUN

**tap**

> **Abre el grifo.**
> Turn on the tap.

**Cierra el grifo.**
Turn off the tap.

la **gripe** NOUN
**flu**
**Tengo la gripe**
I've got flu.

**gris** ADJECTIVE, MASC NOUN
**grey**

**gritar** VERB
1 **to shout**
**Niños, no gritéis tanto.**
Children, stop shouting so much.
2 **to scream**
**El enfermo no podía dejar de gritar.**
The patient couldn't stop screaming.

el **grito** NOUN
1 **shout**
**¡No des esos gritos!**
Stop shouting like that!
2 **scream**
**Oímos un grito en la calle.**
We heard a scream outside.

**grosero** (FEM **grosera**) ADJECTIVE
**rude**

la **grúa** NOUN
**crane**

el **grupo** NOUN
1 **group**
**Los alumnos trabajan en grupo.**
The students work in groups.
2 **band**
**un grupo de rock**
a rock band

el **guante** NOUN
**glove**
**unos guantes**
a pair of gloves

**guapo** (FEM **guapa**) ADJECTIVE
1 **handsome**
2 **pretty**

**guardar** VERB
1 **to put away**
**Los niños guardaron los juguetes.**
The children put away their toys.
2 **to keep**
**No sabe guardar un secreto.**
He can't keep a secret.
3 **to save**
**Debes guardar el fichero.**
You must save the file.

la **guardería** NOUN
**nursery**

el/la **guardia** NOUN
**police officer**

el **guarro**
la **guarra** NOUN
**¡Eres un guarro!**
You're disgusting!

**guay** (FEM **guay**) ADJECTIVE
**cool**
**¡Qué moto más guay!**
What a cool bike!

la **guerra** NOUN
**war**

**guía**
A MASC/FEM NOUN
**guide**
B FEM NOUN
**guidebook**
**Compré una guía turística de Londres.**
I bought a tourist guidebook to London.

**guiñar** VERB
**to wink**
**Me guiñó el ojo.**
He winked at me.

la **guitarra** NOUN
guitar

el **gusano** NOUN
worm

**gustar** VERB
**Me gustan las uvas.**
I like grapes.

**¿Te gusta viajar?**
Do you like travelling?
**Me gusta su hermana.**
I fancy his sister.
**Le gusta más llevar pantalones.**
She prefers to wear trousers.

# H h

**ha** VERB ▷see **haber**
**Me ha comprado un libro.**
He has bought me a book.

**haber** VERB
**to have**

> **Language tip**
>
> **haber** *is used to make the past tense of verbs.*

**He comido.**
I've eaten.
**¿Habéis comido?**
Have you eaten?
**Había comido.**
I'd eaten.
**Se ha sentado.**
She's sat down.
**hay**
there is/there are

> **Language tip**
>
> **hay** *has two meanings:* **there is** *and* **there are**. *Look at the examples.*

**Hay una iglesia en la esquina.**
There's a church on the corner.
**Hay treinta alumnos en mi clase.**
There are thirty pupils in my class.
**¿Hay entradas?**
Are there any tickets?
**hay que**
you must
**Hay que ser respetuoso.**
You must be respectful.

la **habitación** (PL las habitaciones) NOUN
**1 bedroom**
**Ésta es la habitación de mi hermana.**
This is my sister's bedroom.

**2 room**
**una habitación doble**
a double room
**una habitación individual**
a single room

el/la **habitante** NOUN
**inhabitant**
**los habitantes de la zona**
people living in the area

**hablar** VERB
**1 to speak**
**¿Hablas español?**
Do you speak Spanish?
**2 to talk**
**Estuvimos hablando toda la tarde.**
We were talking all afternoon.
**¿Has hablado con el profesor?**
Have you spoken to the teacher?
**Solo hablan de fútbol.**
They only talk about football.
**¡Ni hablar!**
No way!

**habré** VERB ▷see **haber**
**¿Dónde habré puesto las llaves?**
Where did I put my keys?

**hacer** VERB
**1 to make**
**Tengo que hacer la cama.**
I've got to make the bed.
**Estáis haciendo mucho ruido.**
You're making a lot of noise.
**2 to do**
**¿Qué haces?**
What are you doing?
**Tengo que hacer los deberes.**
I have to do my homework.
**Hace mucho deporte.**
She does a lot of sport.
**hacer clic en algo**
to click on something

**3 to be**
**Hace calor.**
It's hot.
**hace**
ago/for

### Language tip

*When talking about time,* **hace** *can mean* **ago** *or* **for**. *Look at the examples.*

**Terminé hace una hora.**
I finished an hour ago.
**Hace un mes que voy.**
I've been going for a month.
**¿Hace mucho que esperas?**
Have you been waiting long?
■ **hacerse**
**to become**
**Quiere hacerse famoso.**
He wants to become famous.

## hacia PREPOSITION
**towards**
**Venía hacia mí.**
He was coming towards me.
**hacia adelante**
forwards
**hacia atrás**
backwards
**hacia dentro**
inside
**hacia fuera**
outside
**hacia abajo**
down
**hacia arriba**
up

## hago VERB ▷ see hacer
**Y ahora, ¿qué hago?**
And now, what do I do?

## el hambre NOUN
**hunger**
**tener hambre**
to be hungry
**No tengo mucha hambre.**
I'm not
very hungry.

la **hamburguesa** NOUN
**hamburger**

## haré VERB ▷ see hacer
**Lo haré mañana.**
I'll do it tomorrow.

## hartar VERB
**hartarse de algo**
to get fed up with something
**Me harté de estudiar.**
I got fed up with studying.

## harto (FEM harta) ADJECTIVE
**fed up**
**Estoy harto de repetirlo.**
I'm fed up with repeating it.
**¡Me tienes harto!**
I'm fed up with you!

## hasta

**hasta** *can be a preposition, conjunction or adverb.*

**A** PREPOSITION, CONJUNCTION
**till**
**Está abierto hasta las cuatro.**
It's open till four o'clock.
**¿Hasta cuándo?**
How long?
**¿Hasta cuándo te quedas? – Hasta la semana que viene.**
How long are you staying? –
Till next week.
**hasta que**
until
**Espera aquí hasta que te llamen.**
Wait here until you're called.

**¡Hasta luego!**
See you!
**¡Hasta mañana!**
See you tomorrow!
**¡Hasta el sábado!**
See you on Saturday!

**B** ADVERB
**even**
**Estudia hasta cuando está de vacaciones.**

He even studies when he's on holiday.

**hay** VERB ▷ *see* **haber**
**Hay tres casas.**
There are three houses.

**haz** VERB ▷ *see* **hacer**
**Haz lo que quieras.**
Do whatever you like.

**he** VERB ▷ *see* **haber**
**No he estado nunca en Londres.**
I've never been to London.

**hecho**

> **hecho** *can be an adjective or part of the verb* **hacer**.

**A** (FEM **hecha**) ADJECTIVE
**made**
**¿De qué está hecho?**
What's it made of?
**hecho a mano**
handmade
**¡Bien hecho!**
Well done!
**B** VERB ▷ *see* **hacer**
**Ya lo he hecho.**
I've done it already.

**helado**

> **helado** *can be a noun or an adjective.*

**A** MASC NOUN
**ice cream**
**un helado de chocolate**
a chocolate ice cream
**B** (FEM **helada**) ADJECTIVE
**1 frozen**
**El lago está helado.**
The lake's frozen over.
**2 freezing**
**¡Estoy helado!**
I'm freezing!

el **helicóptero** NOUN
**helicopter**

**hemos** VERB ▷ *see* **haber**
**Ya hemos llegado.**
We've arrived.

la **herida** NOUN
**wound**

**herido** (FEM **herida**) ADJECTIVE
**1 wounded**
**2 injured**

**herir** VERB
**to wound**
**Lo hirieron en el pecho.**
He was wounded in the chest.

la **hermana** NOUN
**sister**

la **hermanastra** NOUN
**stepsister**

el **hermanastro** NOUN
**stepbrother**
**mis hermanastros**
my stepbrothers/my stepbrothers and sisters

> **Language tip**
>
> **mis hermanastros** *has two meanings. It can be translated as* **my stepbrothers** *or* **my stepbrothers and sisters**.

el **hermano** NOUN
brother
**mis hermanos**
my brothers/my brothers and sisters

> **Language tip**
>
> **mis hermanos** *has two meanings. It can be translated as* **my brothers** *or* **my brothers and sisters**.

el **héroe** NOUN
hero

la **herramienta** NOUN
**tool**

**hervir** VERB
**to boil**
**El agua está hirviendo.**
The water's boiling.

Spanish | English

a
b
c
d
e
f
g
**h**
i
j
k
l
m
n
ñ
o
p
q
r
s
t
u
v
w
x
y
z

**hice** VERB ▷see **hacer**
**Lo hice yo solo.**
I did it on my own.

el **hielo** NOUN
ice

la **hierba** NOUN
grass

el **hierro** NOUN
iron

la **higiene** NOUN
hygiene

**higiénico** (FEM **higiénica**)
ADJECTIVE
hygienic
**poco higiénico**
unhygienic

la **hija** NOUN
daughter
**Soy hija única.**
I'm an only child.

la **hijastra** NOUN
stepdaughter

el **hijastro** NOUN
stepson
**mis hijastros**
my stepsons/my stepchildren

> **Language tip**
> **mis hijastros** *has two meanings.*
> *It can be translated as* **my**
> **stepsons** *or* **my stepchildren**.

el **hijo** NOUN
son
**su hijo mayor**
his oldest son
**Soy hijo único.**
I'm an only child.
**mis hijos**
my sons/my children

> **Language tip**
> **mis hijos** *has two meanings. It can*
> *be translated as* **my sons** *or* **my**
> **children**.

**hinchado** (FEM **hinchada**)
ADJECTIVE
swollen

el **hipo** NOUN
hiccups
**Tengo hipo.**
I've got hiccups.

**hirviendo** VERB ▷see **hervir**
**La leche está hirviendo.**
The milk is boiling.

la **historia** NOUN
history
**mi profesor de historia**
my history teacher

**hizo** VERB ▷see **hacer**
**Lo hizo mi hermana.**
My sister did it.

el **hobby** NOUN
hobby
**Lo hago por hobby.**
I do it as a hobby.

el **hogar** NOUN
home

la **hoja** NOUN
**1** leaf

**2** sheet
**una hoja de papel**
a sheet of paper
**3** page
**las hojas de un libro**
the pages of a book

**hola** EXCLAMATION
hello!

**holgazán** (FEM **holgazana**, MASC
PL **holgazanes**) ADJECTIVE
lazy

el **hombre** NOUN
man
   **un hombre de negocios**
   a businessman

el **hombro** NOUN
shoulder

**hondo** (FEM **honda**) ADJECTIVE
deep
   **la parte honda de la piscina**
   the deep end of the pool

la **hora** NOUN
1 hour
   **El viaje dura una hora.**
   The journey lasts an hour.
2 time
   **¿A qué hora te levantas?**
   What time do you get up?
   **¿Tienes hora?**
   Have you got the time?
   **la hora de cenar**
   dinner time
   **a última hora**
   at the last minute

**¿Qué hora es?**
What's the time?

el **horario** NOUN
timetable

**horizontal** (FEM **horizontal**)
ADJECTIVE
horizontal

el **horizonte** NOUN
horizon

la **hormiga** NOUN
ant

el **horno** NOUN
oven
   **pollo al horno**
   roast chicken

el **horóscopo** NOUN
horoscope

la **horquilla** NOUN
hairgrip

**horrible** (FEM **horrible**)
ADJECTIVE
awful
   **Ha hecho un tiempo horrible.**
   The weather has been awful.

el **hospital** NOUN
hospital
   **La llevaron al hospital.**
   She was taken to hospital.

el **hotel** NOUN
hotel

**hoy** ADVERB
today
   **¿Qué día es hoy?**
   What's the date today?
   **de hoy en adelante**
   from now on
   **hoy por la mañana**
   this morning

la **hucha** NOUN
moneybox

**hueco**

**hueco** can be an adjective or a noun.

**A** (FEM **hueca**) ADJECTIVE
hollow

**B** MASC NOUN
space
   **Deja un hueco para la respuesta.**
   Leave a space for the answer.

la **huella** NOUN
footprint

   **las huellas del ladrón**
   the thief's footprints
   **huella digital**
   fingerprint

**huelo** VERB ▷*see* **oler**
**Lo huelo desde aquí.**
I can smell it from here.

el **hueso** NOUN
1 **bone**
2 **stone**

el **huevo** NOUN
**egg**
**un huevo duro**
a hard-boiled egg
**un huevo frito**
a fried egg
**huevos revueltos**
scrambled eggs
**un huevo pasado por agua**
a soft-boiled egg

**humano** (FEM **humana**)
ADJECTIVE
**human**
**el cuerpo humano**
the human body
**los seres humanos**
human beings

**húmedo** (FEM **húmeda**)
ADJECTIVE
1 **damp**
**Mi camiseta está húmeda todavía.**
My t-shirt is still damp.
2 **humid**

el **humo** NOUN
**smoke**
**Salía humo de la chimenea.**
Smoke was coming out of the chimney.

el **humor** NOUN
**mood**
**No está de humor para bromas.**
He's not in the mood for jokes.

**estar de buen humor**
to be in a good mood
**estar de mal humor**
to be in a bad mood

**hundirse** VERB
**to sink**
**El barco se hundió durante la tormenta.**
The boat sank during the storm.

**huyendo** VERB ▷*see* **huir**
**Estaban huyendo de un perro.**
They were running away from a dog.

# I i

**iba** VERB ▷see **ir**
**Iba por la calle.**
He was walking down the street.

la **ida** NOUN
**single**
**¿Cuánto cuesta la ida?**
How much does a single cost?
**El viaje de ida duró dos horas.**
The journey there took two hours.
**un billete de ida y vuelta**
a return ticket

la **idea** NOUN
**idea**
**¡Qué buena idea!**
What a good idea!
**Ya me voy haciendo a la idea.**
I'm beginning to get used to the idea.
**cambiar de idea**
to change one's mind
**He cambiado de idea.**
I've changed my mind.

> **No tengo ni idea.**
> I haven't the faintest idea.

**ideal** (FEM **ideal**) ADJECTIVE
**ideal**
**Es el lugar ideal para las vacaciones.**
It's the ideal place for a holiday.

**idéntico** (FEM **idéntica**)
ADJECTIVE
**identical**
**Tiene una falda idéntica a la mía.**
She has an identical skirt to mine.
**Es idéntica a su padre.**
She's the spitting image of her father.

el **idioma** NOUN
**language**
**Habla tres idiomas.**
He speaks three languages.

**idiota**

> **idiota** can be an adjective or a noun.

**A** (FEM **idiota**) ADJECTIVE
**stupid**
**¡No seas tan idiota!**
Don't be so stupid!
**B** MASC/FEM NOUN
**idiot**

la **iglesia** NOUN
**church**

**Voy a la iglesia todos los domingos.**
I go to church every Sunday.
**la Iglesia católica**
the Catholic Church

**ignorante** (FEM **ignorante**)
ADJECTIVE
**ignorant**

**igual**

> **igual** can be an adjective or an adverb.

**A** (FEM **igual**) ADJECTIVE
**1 equal**
**Se repartieron el dinero en partes iguales.**
They divided the money into equal shares.

**X es igual a Y.**
X is equal to Y.
**2 the same**
**Todas las casas son iguales.**
All the houses are the same.
**Es igual a su madre.**
She looks just like her mother./
She's just like her mother.

> **Language tip**
> **ser igual a** *has two meanings. It can be translated as* **to look just like** *and* **to be just like**.

**Tengo una falda igual que la tuya.**
I've got a skirt just like yours.

> **Me da igual.**
> I don't mind.

**B** ADVERB
**1 the same**
**Se visten igual.**
They dress the same.
**2 maybe**
**Igual no lo saben todavía.**
Maybe they don't know yet.
**3 anyway**
**No hizo nada pero la castigaron igual.**
She didn't do anything but they punished her anyway.

**igualmente** ADVERB
**the same to you**
**¡Feliz Navidad! - Gracias, igualmente.**
Happy Christmas! - Thanks, the same to you.

**ilegal** (FEM **ilegal**) ADJECTIVE
**illegal**

la **ilusión** (PL las **ilusiones**) NOUN
**dream**
**Mi mayor ilusión es llegar a ser médico.**
My dream is to become a doctor.
**Le hace mucha ilusión que vengas.**

He's really looking forward to you coming.
**Tu regalo me hizo mucha ilusión.**
I was really pleased with your present.

la **imagen** (PL las **imágenes**)
NOUN
**image**
**Han decidido cambiar de imagen.**
They've decided to change their image.
**Es la viva imagen de su madre.**
She's the spitting image of her mother.

la **imaginación** (PL las **imaginaciones**) NOUN
**imagination**
**Tiene mucha imaginación.**
He has a vivid imagination.
**Ni se me pasó por la imaginación.**
It never even occurred to me.

**imaginarse** VERB
**to imagine**
**Me imagino que seguirá en Madrid.**
I imagine that he's still in Madrid.
**¿Se enfadó mucho? - ¡Imagínate!**
Was he very angry? - What do you think!

**imbécil** (FEM **imbécil**)
ADJECTIVE
**stupid**
**¡No seas imbécil!**
Don't be stupid!

**imitar** VERB
1 **to copy**
**Imita todo lo que hace su hermano.**
He copies everything his brother does.
2 **to do an impression of**
**Imita muy bien a la directora.**
She does a very good impression of the headmistress.

**impar**

> **impar** *can be an adjective or a noun.*

**A** (FEM **impar**) ADJECTIVE
**odd**
**un número impar**
an odd number
**B** MASC NOUN
**odd number**

el **imperdible** NOUN
**safety pin**

la **importancia** NOUN
**importance**
**tener importancia**
to be important
**La educación tiene mucha importancia.**
Education is very important.

**importante** (FEM **importante**)
ADJECTIVE
**important**
**lo importante**
the important thing
**Lo importante es que vengas.**
The important thing is that you come.

**importar** VERB
**to matter**
**¿Y eso qué importa?**
And what does that matter?
**no importa**
it doesn't matter/never mind

> *Language tip*
> **no importa** *has two meanings. Look at the examples.*

**No importa lo que piensen los demás.**
It doesn't matter what other people think.
**No importa, podemos hacerlo mañana.**
Never mind, we can do it tomorrow.
**No me importa levantarme temprano.**
I don't mind getting up early.
**¿Le importa que abra la ventana?**
Do you mind if I open the window?

**imposible** (FEM **imposible**)
ADJECTIVE
**impossible**
**Es imposible predecir quién ganará.**
It's impossible to predict who will win.
**Es imposible que lo sepan.**
They can't possibly know.

**imprescindible**
(FEM **imprescindible**) ADJECTIVE
**essential**

la **impresión** (PL las
**impresiones**) NOUN
**impression**
**Le causó muy buena impresión a mis padres.**
He made a very good impression on my parents.
**Tengo la impresión de que no va a venir.**
I have a feeling that he won't come.

**impresionante**
(FEM **impresionante**) ADJECTIVE
1 **impressive**
**una colección de sellos impresionante**
an impressive stamp collection
2 **amazing**
**una cantidad impresionante de videojuegos**

117

a
b
c
d
e
f
g
h
i
j
k
l
m
n
ñ
o
p
q
r
s
t
u
v
w
x
y
z

an amazing number of videogames

**imprimir** VERB
**to print**

**inaceptable**
(FEM **inaceptable**) ADJECTIVE
**unacceptable**

**incapaz** (FEM **incapaz**,
PL **incapaces**) ADJECTIVE
**incapable**
> **Es incapaz de estarse callado.**
> He is incapable of keeping quiet.
> **Hoy soy incapaz de concentrarme.**
> I can't concentrate today.

el **incendio** NOUN
**fire**
> **Se declaró un incendio en el hotel.**
> A fire broke out in the hotel.

el **incidente** NOUN
**incident**

**inclinarse** VERB
**to lean**
> **inclinarse hacia delante**
> to lean forward
> **inclinarse hacia atrás**
> to lean back

**incluido** (FEM **incluida**)
ADJECTIVE
**included**
> **El servicio no está incluido en el precio.**
> Service is not included.

**incluir** VERB
**to include**
> **El precio incluye las comidas.**
> The price includes meals.

**incluso** ADVERB
**even**
> **He tenido que estudiar incluso los domingos.**
> I've even had to study on Sundays.

**incluyendo** VERB ▷ *see* **incluir**
> **Somos cinco, incluyendo a mi abuela.**
> It's five of us, including my grandmother.

**incómodo** (FEM **incómoda**)
ADJECTIVE
**uncomfortable**
> **Este asiento es muy incómodo.**
> This seat is very uncomfortable.

**inconsciente**
(FEM **inconsciente**) ADJECTIVE
**unconscious**
> **Quedó inconsciente con el golpe.**
> The force of the blow left him unconscious.

**inconveniente**

> **inconveniente** *can be an adjective or a noun.*

**A** (FEM **inconveniente**) ADJECTIVE
**inconvenient**
> **a una hora inconveniente**
> at an inconvenient time
**B** MASC NOUN
**problem**
> **Ha surgido un inconveniente.**
> A problem has come up.

**incorrecto** (FEM **incorrecta**)
ADJECTIVE
**incorrect**
> **una respuesta incorrecta**
> an incorrect answer

**increíble** (FEM increíble)
ADJECTIVE
incredible

**indicar** VERB
to indicate
El termómetro indicaba treinta grados.
The thermometer indicated thirty degrees.

el **índice** NOUN
1 index
un índice alfabético
an alphabetical index
el índice de materias
the table of contents
2 index finger

la **indirecta** NOUN
hint

**individual** (FEM individual)
ADJECTIVE
1 individual
Los venden en paquetes individuales.
They're sold in individual packets.
2 single
Quisiera una habitación individual.
I'd like a single room.

la **industria** NOUN
industry

**inesperado** (FEM inesperada)
ADJECTIVE
unexpected
una visita inesperada
an unexpected visit

**infantil** (FEM infantil) ADJECTIVE
1 children's
un programa infantil
a children's programme
2 childish
¡No seas tan infantil!
Don't be so childish!

el **infarto** NOUN
heart attack

Le dio un infarto.
He had a heart attack.

la **infección** (PL las infecciones)
NOUN
infection
tener una infección
to have an infection
Tiene una infección de oídos.
He has got an ear infection.

el **infierno** NOUN
hell

el **infinitivo** NOUN
infinitive

**inflar** VERB
1 to blow up
2 to inflate

la **información** (PL las informaciones) NOUN
information
Quisiera información sobre cursos de inglés.
I'd like some information on English courses.
una información muy importante
a very important piece of information

**informal** (FEM informal)
ADJECTIVE
1 informal
un ambiente muy informal
a very informal atmosphere
Prefiero la ropa informal.
I prefer casual clothes.
2 unreliable
Es una persona muy informal.
He's a very unreliable person.

a
b
c
d
e
f
g
h
i
j
k
l
m
n
ñ
o
p
q
r
s
t
u
v
w
x
y
z

**informar** VERB
**to inform**
> **Nos informaron de que venía con retraso.**
> They informed us that it was going to be late.
> **¿Me podría informar sobre los cursos de inglés?**
> Could you give me some information about English courses?

la **informática** NOUN
1 **computing**
> **los avances de la informática**
> advances in computing
> **Quiere estudiar informática.**
> He wants to study computer science.

2 **computer expert**

**informático**

> informático *can be an adjective or a noun.*

A (FEM **informática**) ADJECTIVE
**computer**
> **un programa informático**
> a computer program
B MASC NOUN
**computer expert**

el **informe** NOUN
**report**
> **Presentó un informe detallado sobre lo ocurrido.**
> He gave a detailed report about what had happened.

**Inglaterra** FEM NOUN
**England**
**inglés**

> inglés *can be an adjective or a noun.*

A (FEM **inglesa**, MASC PL **ingleses**)
ADJECTIVE
**English**
> **la comida inglesa**
> English food

B MASC/FEM NOUN
**un inglés**
an Englishman
**una inglesa**
an Englishwoman
**los ingleses**
English people
C MASC NOUN
**English**
> **Estudio inglés.**
> I'm studying English.

el **ingrediente** NOUN
**ingredient**

**ingresar** VERB
> **ingresar en el hospital**
> to go into hospital
> **ingresar en un club**
> to join a club

el **inhalador** NOUN
**inhaler**

la **inicial** NOUN
**initial**

**injusto** (FEM **injusta**) ADJECTIVE
**unfair**

**inmediato** (FEM **inmediata**)
ADJECTIVE
**immediate**

> **de inmediato**
> immediately

el/la **inmigrante** NOUN
**immigrant**

**inocente** (FEM **inocente**)
ADJECTIVE
**innocent**
> **Soy inocente.**
> I'm innocent.

**inolvidable** (FEM inolvidable)
ADJECTIVE
**unforgettable**

**inquietante** (FEM inquietante)
ADJECTIVE
**worrying**

**inquieto** (FEM inquieta)
ADJECTIVE
**worried**
**Estaba inquieta porque su hijo no había llegado a casa.**
She was worried because her son hadn't come home.

**insatisfecho**
(FEM insatisfecha) ADJECTIVE
**dissatisfied**

**inscribirse** VERB
**to enrol**
**Se inscribió en un curso de idiomas.**
He enrolled on a language course.

**inscrito** VERB ▷see inscribirse
**Estoy inscrito en un curso de informática.**
I've enrolled on a computing course.

el **insecto** NOUN
**insect**

**inseguro** (FEM insegura)
ADJECTIVE
1 **insecure**
2 **unsafe**

**insistir** VERB
**to insist**
**Insistió en hablar conmigo.**
He insisted on talking to me.

**insolente** (FEM insolente)
ADJECTIVE
**insolent**

**insoportable**
(FEM insoportable) ADJECTIVE
**unbearable**

el **inspector**

la **inspectora** NOUN
**inspector**

el **instante** NOUN
**moment**
**A cada instante suena el teléfono.**
The phone rings all the time.

el **instinto** NOUN
**instinct**

el **instituto** NOUN
**institute**
**un instituto de enseñanza secundaria**
a secondary school
**un instituto de bachillerato**
a secondary school

**Did you know...?**
In Spain the **institutos de bachillerato** are state secondary schools for 12- to 18-year-olds.

las **instrucciones** NOUN
**instructions**

el **instructor**
la **instructora** NOUN
**instructor**
**un instructor de esquí**
a ski instructor
**un instructor de autoescuela**
a driving instructor

el **instrumento** NOUN
**instrument**

**insuficiente**

**insuficiente** can be an adjective or a noun.

**A** (FEM insuficiente) ADJECTIVE
**insufficient**
**una cantidad insuficiente de dinero**
an insufficient amount of money
**B** MASC NOUN
**Sacó un insuficiente en francés.**
He got an F in French.

**insultar** VERB
to insult

el **insulto** NOUN
insult

la **inteligencia** NOUN
intelligence

**inteligente** (FEM **inteligente**)
ADJECTIVE
intelligent

la **intención** (PL las
intenciones) NOUN
intention
> No tengo la más mínima
> intención de hacerlo.
> I haven't got the slightest
> intention of doing it.
> **tener intención de hacer algo**
> to intend to do something
> **Tenía intención de descansar
> un rato.**
> He intended to rest for a while.

**intensivo** (FEM **intensiva**)
ADJECTIVE
intensive
> **un curso intensivo de inglés**
> an intensive English course

**intenso** (FEM **intensa**) ADJECTIVE
intense

**intentar** VERB
to try

> **¿Por qué no lo intentas
> otra vez?**
> Why don't you try again?
> **intentar hacer algo**
> to try to do something

> Voy a intentar llamarle esta
> noche.
> I'm going to try to call him
> tonight.

el **intento** NOUN
attempt
> **Aprobó al primer intento.**
> He passed at the first attempt.

el **intercambio** NOUN
exchange

el **interés** (PL los **intereses**)
NOUN
interest
> **Tienes que poner más interés
> en tus estudios.**
> You must take more cf an
> interest in your studies.

**interesante** (FEM **interesante**)
ADJECTIVE
interesting

**interesar** VERB
to interest
> **Eso es algo que siempre me
> ha interesado.**
> That's something that has
> always interested me.
> **Me interesa mucho la física.**
> I'm very interested in physics.

**interior**

> interior *can be an adject.ve or a
> noun.*

**A** (FEM **interior**) ADJECTIVE
inside
**B** MASC NOUN
inside
> **el interior del túnel**
> the inside of the tunnel

el **intermedio** NOUN
interval

el **intermitente** NOUN
indicator

**internacional**
(FEM **internacional**) ADJECTIVE
international

el/la **internauta** NOUN
internet user

el/la **Internet** NOUN
the internet
en Internet
on the internet

**interno**
interna

interno *can be an adjective or a noun.*

A ADJECTIVE
estar interno en un colegio
to be at boarding school
B MASC/FEM NOUN
boarder

**interpretar** VERB
to play
Interpreta el papel de Victoria.
She plays the part of Victoria.

el/la **intérprete** NOUN
interpreter
Quiere ser intérprete.
She wants to be an interpreter.

**interrogar** VERB
to question
Fue interrogado por la
policía.
He was questioned by the police.

**interrumpir** VERB
to interrupt

la **interrupción** (PL las
interrupciones) NOUN
interruption

el **interruptor** NOUN
switch

**intervenir** VERB
1 to take part
No intervino en el debate.
He did not take part in the
debate.
2 to intervene
La policía intervino para
separarlos.
The police intervened to
separate them.

**intimidar** VERB
to intimidate

**íntimo** (FEM **íntima**) ADJECTIVE
intimate
mis secretos íntimos
my intimate secrets
Es un amigo íntimo.
He's a close friend.

la **introducción** (PL las
introducciones) NOUN
introduction

**introducir** VERB
1 to introduce
2 to insert
Introdujo la moneda en
la ranura.
He inserted the coin in the
slot.

la **inundación** (PL las
inundaciones) NOUN
flood

**inundar** VERB
to flood
El río inundó el pueblo.
The river flooded the village.
■ inundarse
to be flooded
Se nos inundó el baño.
Our bathroom was flooded.

**inútil** (FEM **inútil**)

inútil *can be an adjective or a
noun.*

A ADJECTIVE
useless
La oficina está llena de
trastos inútiles.
The office is full of useless
rubbish.
Es inútil tratar de hacerle
entender.
It's useless trying to make him
understand.
B MASC/FEM NOUN
¡Es un inútil!
He's useless!

**Spanish English**

a b c d e f g h i j k l m n ñ o p q r s t u v w x y z

**invadir** VERB
to invade

la **inválida** NOUN
disabled woman

el **inválido** NOUN
disabled man
   los inválidos
   the disabled

**inventar** VERB
   1 **to invent**
   Inventaron un nuevo sistema.
   They invented a new system.
   2 **to make up**
   Inventó toda la historia.
   He made up the whole story.

el **invento** NOUN
invention

el **inventor**
la **inventora** NOUN
inventor

el **invernadero** NOUN
greenhouse
   el efecto invernadero
   the greenhouse effect

**invernar** VERB
to hibernate

**invertir** VERB
to invest
   Hemos invertido muchas
   horas en el proyecto.
   We've invested a lot of
   time in the project.

el **invierno** NOUN
winter

**en invierno**
n winter

**invisible** (FEM **invisible**)
ADJECTIVE
invisible

la **invitación** (PL las
invitaciones) NOUN
invitation

el **invitado**
la **invitada** NOUN
guest
   Es el invitado de honor.
   He's the guest of honour.

**invitar** VERB
to invite
   Me invitó a una fiesta.
   He invited me to a party.
   Me gustaría invitarla a
   cenar.
   I'd like to invite her to dinner.
   Te invito a una Coca-Cola.
   I'll buy you a Coke.
   Esta vez invito yo.
   This time it's on me.

el **iPod**® NOUN
**iPod**®

**ir** VERB
   1 **to go**
   ¿A qué colegio vas?
   What school do you go to?
   Anoche fuimos al cine.
   We went to the cinema last
   night.
   **ir a por**
   to go and get
   Voy a por el paraguas.
   I'll go and get the umbrella.
   Voy a hacerlo mañana.
   I'm going to do it tomorrow.
   **vamos**
   let's go

124

**Vamos a casa.**
Let's go home.
**¡Vamos!**
Come on!
**¡Vamos! ¡Di algo!**
Come on! Say something!

**2 to come**
**¡Ahora voy!**
I'm just coming!
**¿Puedo ir contigo?**
Can I come with you?

**3 to be**
**Va muy bien vestido.**
He's very well dressed.
**Iba con su madre.**
He was with his mother.
**Va a ser difícil.**
It's going to be difficult.

**ir a pie**
to walk
**ir en avión**
to fly
**ir de vacaciones**
to go on holiday
**¡Qué va!**
No way!

■ **irse** VERB
**to leave**
**Acaba de irse.**
He has just left.
**Vete a hacer los deberes.**
Go and do your homework.
**¡Vámonos!**
Let's go!
**¡Vete!**
Go away!

**Irlanda** FEM NOUN
**Ireland**

**irlandés**
**irlandesa**
(MASC PL **irlandeses**)

**irlandés** *can be an adjective or a noun.*

**A** ADJECTIVE
**Irish**
**un café irlandés**

an Irish coffee
**B** MASC/FEM NOUN
**un irlandés**
an Irishman
**una irlandesa**
an Irishwoman
**los irlandeses**
Irish people

**irónico** (FEM **irónica**) ADJECTIVE
**ironic**

**irresistible** (FEM **irresistible**)
ADJECTIVE
**irresistible**

**irresponsable**
(FEM **irresponsable**) ADJECTIVE
**irresponsible**

**irritar** VERB
**to irritate**

la **isla** NOUN
**island**
**una isla desierta**
a desert island

el **Islam** NOUN
**Islam**

la **izquierda** NOUN
**1 left hand**
**Escribo con la izquierda.**
I write with my left hand.
**2 left**
**doblar a la izquierda**
to turn left
**a la izquierda**
on the left
**la segunda calle a la izquierda**
the second turning on the left
**a la izquierda del edificio**
to the left of the building

**izquierdo** (FEM **izquierda**)
ADJECTIVE
**left**
**Levanta la mano izquierda.**
Raise your left hand.
**Escribo con la mano izquierda.**
I write with my left hand.

# izquierdo

### Language tip

*In Spanish you usually use an article like* **el**, **la**, **los** *with parts of the body.*

**el lado izquierdo**
the left side
**a mano izquierda**
on the left-hand side

# J j

el **jabón** (PL los **jabones**) NOUN
**soap**

**jamás** ADVERB
**never**
> **Jamás he visto nada parecido.**
> I've never seen anything like it.

el **jamón** (PL los **jamones**) NOUN
**ham**
> **un bocadillo de jamón**
> a ham sandwich
> **jamón serrano**
> cured ham
> **jamón de York**
> cooked ham

el **jarabe** NOUN
**syrup**
> **un jarabe para la tos**
> a cough syrup

el **jardín** (PL los **jardines**) NOUN
**garden**
> **Tienen una piscina en el jardín.**
> They have a swimming pool in the garden.
> **jardín de infancia**
> nursery school

la **jarra** NOUN
**jug**
> **una jarra de agua**
> a jug of water

el **jarrón** (PL los **jarrones**) NOUN
**vase**

el **jefe**
la **jefa** NOUN
**boss**
> **Carlos es el jefe.**
> Carlos is the boss.

el **jersey** (PL los **jerséis**) NOUN
**jumper**

**Jesús** EXCLAMATION
**Bless you!**

**joven** (FEM **joven**, PL **jóvenes**)

> **joven** *can be an adjective or a noun.*

**A** ADJECTIVE
**young**
> **una chica joven**
> a young girl

**B** MASC/FEM NOUN
> **un joven**
> a young man
> **una joven**
> a young woman
> **los jóvenes**
> young people

la **joya** NOUN
**jewel**
> **Me han robado las joyas.**
> My jewellery has been stolen.

**jubilado**
**jubilada**

> **jubilado** *can be an adjective or a noun.*

**A** ADJECTIVE
**retired**
> **estar jubilado**
> to be retired

**B** MASC/FEM NOUN
**pensioner**

**jubilarse** VERB
to retire

la **judía** NOUN
1 Jew
2 bean
   **judía verde**
   green bean

el **judío** NOUN
Jew

el **judo** NOUN
judo

**juego**

> juego *can be a noun or part of the verb* **jugar**.

**A** MASC NOUN
**game**
   **un juego de ordenador**
   a computer game
   **juegos de cartas**
   card games
   **un juego de café**
   a coffee set
   **No hace juego con la falda.**
   It doesn't go with the skirt.
**B** VERB ▷*see* **jugar**
   **Juego al tenis todos los días.**
   I play tennis every day.

la **juerga** NOUN
   **irse de juerga**
   to go out on the town

el **jueves** (PL los **jueves**) NOUN
**Thursday**

> *Language tip*
> Days of the week are not spelled with a capital letter in Spanish.

   **La vi el jueves.**
   I saw her on Thursday.

> **el jueves que viene**
> next Thursday
> **el jueves pasado**
> last Thursday
> **todos los jueves**
> every Thursday

el **jugador**
la **jugadora** NOUN
player

**jugar** VERB
to play
   **Los domingos jugamos al fútbol.**
   We play football on Sundays.
   **jugar una partida de dominó**
   to have a game of dominoes

el **juguete** NOUN
toy
   **un avión de juguete**
   a toy plane

**julio** MASC NOUN
July

> *Language tip*
> Months are not spelled with a capital letter in Spanish.

> **en julio**
> in July
> **Nació el cuatro de julio.**
> He was born on the fourth of July.

**junio** MASC NOUN
June

> *Language tip*
> Months are not written with a capital letter in Spanish.

> **en junio**
> in June
> **Nació el veinte de junio.**
> He was born on the twentieth of June.

**juntar** VERB
to put together
   **Vamos a juntar los pupitres.**
   Let's put the desks together.
■ **juntarse**
   to move closer together/to get together

> *Language tip*
> **juntarse** *has two meanings. Look at the examples.*

**Si os juntáis más, cabremos todos.**
If you move closer together, we'll all fit in.
**Nos juntamos para ver el partido.**
We got together to watch the match.

## junto (FEM junta)

*junto can be an adjective or an adverb.*

**A** ADJECTIVE
**together**
**Cuando estamos juntos lo pasamos muy bien.**
We have a good time when we're together.
**todo junto**
all together
**Ponlo todo junto en una bolsa.**
Put it all together in one bag.
**Los muebles están muy juntos.**
The furniture is too close together.
**B** ADVERB
**junto a**
by
**Hay una mesa junto a la ventana.**
There's a table by the window.
**Mi apellido se escribe todo junto.**
My surname is all one word.

## jurar VERB
**to swear**

## la justicia NOUN
**justice**

## justo (FEM justa)

*justo can be an adjective or an adverb.*

**A** ADJECTIVE
**1 fair**
**No es justo.**
It's not fair.

**2 tight**
**Me están muy justos estos pantalones.**
These trousers are tight on me.
**3 just enough**
**Tengo el dinero justo para un bocadillo.**
I have just enough money for a sandwich.
**en el momento justo**
at the right time
**B** ADVERB
**just**
**Está justo al doblar la esquina.**
It's just round the corner.
**Me dio un golpe justo en la nariz.**
He hit me right on the nose.

## juvenil (FEM juvenil) ADJECTIVE
**young**
**la moda juvenil**
young people's fashion
**el equipo juvenil**
the youth team

## la juventud NOUN
**youth**
**Fue soldado en su juventud.**
He was a soldier in his youth.

Spanish English

a
b
c
d
e
f
g
h
i
j
k
l
m
n
ñ
o
p
q
r
s
t
u
v
w
x
y
z

# K k

el **kárate** NOUN
karate

el **kilo** NOUN
kilo
**un kilo de tomates**
a kilo of tomatoes

el **kilogramo** NOUN
kilogramme

el **kilómetro** NOUN
kilometre
**Está a tres kilómetros de aquí.**
It's three kilometres from here.
**a noventa kilómetros por hora**
at ninety kilometres an hour

el **kiosco** NOUN
news stand

---

**Did you know...?**

In Spain you'll come across **kioscos**, newsstands on the street which sell newspapers, magazines and other items.

---

# L l

## la

*la can be an article or a pronoun.*

**A** ARTICLE

**the**
**la pared**
the wall
**la del sombrero rojo**
the girl in the red hat
**Yo fui la que te desperté.**
I was the one who woke you up.
**Ayer me lavé la cabeza.**
I washed my hair yesterday.
**Abróchate la camisa.**
Do your shirt up.
**No me gusta la fruta.**
I don't like fruit.
**Vendrá la semana que viene.**
He'll come next week.
**Me he encontrado a la Sra. Sendra.**
I bumped into Mrs Sendra.

**B** PRONOUN

**1 her**
**La quiero.**
I love her.
**La han despedido.**
She has been sacked.

**2 you**
**La acompaño hasta la puerta.**
I'll see you out.

**3 it**
**No la toques.**
Don't touch it.

el **labio** NOUN
**lip**

el **lado** NOUN
**side**
**a los dos lados de la carretera**
on both sides of the road
**Hay gente por todos lados.**
There are people everywhere.

**Tiene que estar en otro lado.**
It must be somewhere else.
**Mi casa está aquí al lado.**
My house is right nearby.
**al lado de**
beside
**la silla que está al lado del armario**
the chair beside the wardrobe
**Felipe se sentó a mi lado.**
Felipe sat beside me.

**ladrar** VERB
**to bark**
**El perro les ladró.**
The dog barked at them.

el **ladrillo** NOUN
**brick**

el **ladrón**
la **ladrona** NOUN

**1 thief**
**Un ladrón me quitó el bolso.**
A thief took my bag.

**2 burglar**
**Los ladrones entraron en la casa.**
The burglars broke into the house.

**3 robber**
**Tres ladrones atracaron el banco.**
Three robbers raided the bank.

el **lago** NOUN
**lake**

la **lágrima** NOUN
**tear**

a b c d e f g h i j k l m n ñ o p q r s t u v w x y z

## lamentar VERB
**Lamento lo ocurrido.**
I am sorry about what happened.
■ **lamentarse**
**to complain**
**De nada vale lamentarse.**
There's no use complaining.

la **lámpara** NOUN
**lamp**

la **lancha** NOUN
**motorboat**

**una lancha de salvamento**
a lifeboat

## lanzar VERB
**to throw**
**Lanzó una piedra al río.**
He threw a stone into the river.
■ **lanzarse**
**to dive**
**Los niños se lanzaron a la piscina.**
The children dived into the swimming pool.

el **lápiz** (PL los **lápices**) NOUN
**pencil**
**Escríbelo a lápiz.**
Write it in pencil.
**los lápices de colores**
crayons

## largo

*largo can be an adjective or a noun.*

**A** (FEM **larga**) ADJECTIVE
**long**
**Esta cuerda es demasiado larga.**
This piece of string is too long.

**B** MASC NOUN
**length**
**Nadé cuatro largos de la piscina.**
I swam four lengths of the pool.
**¿Cuánto mide de largo?**
How long is it?
**Tiene nueve metros de largo.**
It's nine metres long.
**a lo largo del río**
along the river
**a lo largo de la semana**
throughout the week
**Pasó de largo sin saludar.**
He passed by without saying hello.

> ### Language tip
> Be careful! **largo** does not mean **large**.

## las

*las can be an article or a pronoun.*

**A** ARTICLE
**the**
**las paredes**
the walls
**las del estante de arriba**
the ones on the top shelf
**Me duelen las piernas.**
My legs hurt.
**Poneos las bufandas.**
Put on your scarves.
**No me gustan las arañas.**
I don't like spiders.
**Vino a las seis de la tarde.**
He came at six in the evening.
**B** PRONOUN
**1 them**
**Las vi por la calle.**
I saw them in the street.
**Las han despedido.**
They've been sacked.
**2 you**
**Las acompañaré hasta la puerta, señoras.**
I'll see you out, ladies.

la **lata** NOUN
**1 tin**

**2 can**
**Deja de dar la lata.**
Stop being a pain.

el **latido** NOUN
**beat**

el **lavabo** NOUN
**1 sink**
**Llené el lavabo de agua.**
I filled the sink with water.
**2 toilet**
**Voy al lavabo.**
I'm going to the toilet.

la **lavadora** NOUN
**washing machine**

**lavar** VERB
**to wash**
**Lava estos vasos.**
Wash these glasses.
**lavar la ropa**
to do the washing
■ **lavarse**
**to wash**
**Me lavo todos los días.**
I wash every day.
**Ayer me lavé la cabeza.**
I washed my hair yesterday.
**Lávate los dientes.**
Brush your teeth.

el **lazo** NOUN
**1 bow**
**2 ribbon**

**le** PRONOUN
**1 him**
**Le mandé una carta.**
I sent him a letter.
**Le miré con atención.**
I watched him carefully.

**Le abrí la puerta.**
I opened the door for him.
**Le huelen los pies.**
His feet smell.

**2 her**
**Le mandé una carta.**
I sent her a letter.
**No le hablé de ti.**
I didn't speak to her about you.
**Le busqué el libro.**
I looked for the book for her.

**3 you**
**Le presento a la Sra.**
**Gutiérrez.**
Let me introduce you to
Mrs Gutiérrez.
**Le he arreglado el**
**ordenador.**
I've fixed the computer for
you.

la **lección** (PL las **lecciones**)
NOUN
**lesson**

la **leche** NOUN
**milk**
**la leche desnatada**
skimmed milk

**leer** VERB
**to read**

**lejos** ADVERB
**far**
**¿Está lejos?**
Is it far?
**No está lejos de aquí.**
It's not far from here.
**De lejos parecía un avión.**
From a distance it looked like a
plane.

la **lengua** NOUN
**tongue**
**Me he mordido la lengua.**
I've bitten my tongue.
**mi lengua materna**
my mother tongue

el **lenguaje** NOUN
**language**

la **lente** NOUN
**lense**
  **las lentes de contacto**
  contact lenses

la **lentilla** NOUN
  **contact lens**

**lento**

> **lento** *can be an adjective or an adverb.*

  **A** (FEM **lenta**) ADJECTIVE
  **slow**
    **un proceso lento**
    a slow progress
  **B** ADVERB
  **slowly**
    **Vas un poco lento.**
    You're going a bit slowly.

el **león** (PL los **leones**) NOUN
**lion**

la **leona** NOUN
**lioness**

**les** PRONOUN
  **1 them**
    **Les mandé una carta.**
    I sent them a letter.
    **Les miré con atención.**
    I watched them carefully.
    **Les abrí la puerta.**
    I opened the door for them.
    **Les eché de comer a los gatos.**
    I gave the cats something to eat.
  **2 you**
    **Les presento a la Sra. Gutiérrez.**
    Let me introduce you to Mrs Gutiérrez.

    **Les he arreglado el ordenador.**
    I've fixed the computer for you.

la **lesión** (PL las **lesiones**) NOUN
**injury**

la **letra** NOUN
  **1 letter**
    **la letra 'a'**
    the letter 'a'
  **2 handwriting**
    **Tengo muy mala letra.**
    My handwriting's very poor.

el **letrero** NOUN
**sign**

**levantar** VERB
**to lift**
    **Levanta la tapa.**
    Lift the lid.
    **Levantad la mano si tenéis alguna duda.**
    Raise your hand if you are unclear.
  ▪ **levantarse**
    **to get up**
    **Hoy me he levantado temprano.**
    I got up early this morning.
    **Me levanté y seguí caminando.**
    I got up and carried on walking.

la **ley** (PL las **leyes**) NOUN
**law**
    **la ley de la gravedad**
    the law of gravity

**leyendo** VERB ▷*see* **leer**
    **Estaba leyendo el periódico.**
    I was reading the newspaper.

**liar** VERB
**to confuse**
    **Me liaron con tantas explicaciones.**
    They confused me with all their explanations.
    **A mí no me líes en esto.**
    Don't get me mixed up in this.

**Spanish English**

- **liarse**
  **to get muddled up**
  **Me estoy liando, empezaré otra vez.**
  I'm getting muddled up, I'll start again.

la **libra** NOUN
**pound**
  **libra esterlina**
  pound sterling

**librarse** VERB
  **librarse de**
  **to get out of/to get rid of**

*Language tip*
**librarse de** *has two meanings. Look at the examples.*

  **¡No te librarás de fregar los platos!**
  You're not going to get out of doing the washing-up!
  **Logré librarme de mi hermana.**
  I managed to get rid of my sister.

**libre** (FEM **libre**) ADJECTIVE
**free**
  **¿Está libre este asiento?**
  Is this seat free?
  **El martes estoy libre.**
  I'm free on Tuesday.

la **librería** NOUN
**bookshop**

*Language tip*
*Be careful!* **librería** *does not mean* **library.**

la **libreta** NOUN
**notebook**

el **libro** NOUN
**book**
  **un libro de texto**
  a text book

**ligero** (FEM **ligera**) ADJECTIVE
1 **light**
  **Me gusta llevar ropa ligera.**
  I like to wear light clothing.

  **Comimos algo ligero.**
  We ate something light.
2 **slight**
  **Tengo un ligero dolor de cabeza.**
  I have a slight headache.
  **Andaba a paso ligero.**
  He walked quickly.

el **límite** NOUN
**limit**
  **el límite de velocidad**
  the speed limit
  **fecha límite**
  deadline

el **limón** (PL los **limones**) NOUN
**lemon**

**limpiar** VERB
1 **to clean**
  **El sábado voy a limpiar mi habitación.**
  I'm going to clean my room on Saturday.
2 **to wipe**
  **¿Has limpiado la mesa?**
  Have you wiped the table?
  **Límpiate la nariz.**
  Wipe your nose.

la **limpieza** NOUN
**cleaning**
  **Mi madre hace la limpieza los sábados.**
  My mum does the cleaning on Saturdays.

**limpio** (FEM **limpia**) ADJECTIVE
**clean**
  **El baño está muy limpio.**
  The bathroom's very clean.
  **Voy a pasar esto a limpio.**

Spanish English

a b c d e f g h i j k l m n ñ o p q r s t u v w x y z

I'm going to write this out in neat.

la **línea** NOUN
**line**
**Dibujó una línea recta.**
He drew a straight line.
**una línea aérea**
an airline
**estar en línea**
to be online

el **lío** NOUN
**muddle**
**hacerse un lío**
to get muddled up
**Se hizo un lío con tantos nombres.**
He got muddled up with all the names.

el **líquido** NOUN
**liquid**

**liso** (FEM **lisa**) ADJECTIVE
1 **smooth**
2 **straight**

la **lista** NOUN
**list**
**la lista de espera**
the waiting list
**pasar lista**
to call the register

**listo** (FEM **lista**) ADJECTIVE
1 **clever**
**Es una chica muy lista.**
She's a very clever girl.
2 **ready**
**¿Estás listo?**
Are you ready?

la **litera** NOUN
**bunk bed**

la **literatura** NOUN
**literature**

el **litro** NOUN
**litre**

la **llama** NOUN
**flame**

la **llamada** NOUN
**call**
**hacer una llamada telefónica**
to make a phone call

**llamar** VERB
1 **to call**
**Me llamaron mentiroso.**
They called me a liar.
**llamar a la policía**
to call the police
**llamar por teléfono a alguien**
to phone somebody
**Te llamaré por teléfono mañana.**
I will phone you tomorrow.
2 **to ring**
3 **to knock**
**llamar a la puerta**
to knock at the door

**¿Cómo te llamas?**
What's your name?
**Me llamo Adela.**
My name's Adela.

**llano** (FEM **llana**) ADJECTIVE
**flat**

la **llave** NOUN
**key**
**las llaves del coche**
the car keys

el **llavero** NOUN
**keyring**

la **llegada** NOUN
1 **arrival**
2 **finish**

**llegar** VERB
1 **to arrive**

**El avión llega a las dos.**
The plane arrives at two o'clock.
**Acabamos de llegar.**
We've just arrived.
**Llegamos tarde.**
We were late.

**2 llegar a**
**to get to**
**Llegamos a Granada a las cinco.**
We got to Granada at five o'clock.
**¿A qué hora llegaste a casa?**
What time did you get home?

**3 to reach**
**No llego al estante de arriba.**
I can't reach the top shelf.
**El agua me llegaba hasta las rodillas.**
The water came up to my knees.

## llenar VERB
**to fill**
**Llena la jarra de agua.**
Fill the jug with water.

## lleno (FEM llena) ADJECTIVE
**full**
**Todos los hoteles están llenos.**
All the hotels are full.
**El restaurante estaba lleno de gente.**
The restaurant was full of people.

## llevar VERB
**1 to take**
**¿Llevas los vasos a la cocina?**
Can you take the glasses to the kitchen?
**No llevará mucho tiempo.**
It won't take long.

**2 to wear**
**María llevaba un abrigo muy bonito.**
María was wearing a nice coat.

**3 to give a lift**
**Sofía nos llevó a casa.**
Sofía gave us a lift home.

**4 to carry**
**Yo te llevo la maleta.**
I'll carry your case.
**¿Cuánto tiempo llevas aquí?**
How long have you been here?
**Llevo horas esperando aquí.**
I've been waiting here for hours.

**Mi hermana mayor me lleva ocho años.**
My elder sister is eight years older than me.
**llevarse algo**
to take something
**Llévatelo.**
Take it with you.
**¿Le gusta? – Sí, me lo llevo.**
Do you like it? – Yes, I'll take it.
**Me llevo bien con mi hermano.**
I get on well with my brother.
**Nos llevamos muy mal.**
We don't get on at all.

## llorar VERB
**to cry**

## llover VERB
**to rain**

## llueve VERB >see llover
**Llueve mucho.**
It's raining hard.

## la lluvia NOUN
**rain**
   **bajo la lluvia**
   in the rain

## lluvioso (FEM lluviosa)
ADJECTIVE
**rainy**

a
b
c
d
e
f
g
h
i
j
k
**l**
m
n
ñ
o
p
q
r
s
t
u
v
w
x
y
z

## lo

lo *can be an article or a pronoun.*

**A** ARTICLE

**Lo peor fue que no pudimos entrar.**
The worst thing was we couldn't get in.

**Pon en mi habitación lo de Pedro.**
Put Pedro's things in my room.

**Lo mío son las matemáticas.**
Maths is my thing.

**Olvida lo de ayer.**
Forget what happened yesterday.

**¡No sabes lo aburrido que es!**
You don't know how boring he is!

**lo que**
what/whatever

### Language tip

lo que *has two meanings. Look at the examples.*

**Lo que más me gusta es nadar.**
What I like most is swimming.

**Ponte lo que quieras.**
Wear whatever you like.

**más de lo que**
more than

**Cuesta más de lo que crees.**
It costs more than you think.

**B** PRONOUN

**1 him**

**No lo conozco.**
I don't know him.

**Lo han despedido.**
He's been sacked.

**2 you**

**Yo a usted lo conozco.**
I know you.

**3 it**

**No lo veo.**
I can't see it.

**Voy a pensarlo.**
I'll think about it.

**No lo sabía.**
I didn't know.

**No parece lista pero lo es.**
She doesn't seem clever but she is.

**local** (FEM **local**) ADJECTIVE
**local**

**un producto local**
a local product

## loco
### loca

loco *can be an adjective or a noun.*

**A** ADJECTIVE
**mad**

**volver loco a alguien**
to drive somebody mad

**Me estás volviendo loco.**
You're driving me mad.

**volverse loco**
to go mad

**¿Estás loco?**
Are you mad?

**Está loco con su moto nueva.**
He's mad about his new motorbike.

**Me vuelve loco el marisco.**
I'm mad about seafood.

**B** MASC/FEM NOUN

**un loco**
a madman

**una loca**
a madwoman

la **locura** NOUN
**madness**

**Es una locura ir solo.**
It's madness to go on your own.

**lógico** (FEM **lógica**) ADJECTIVE
**natural**

**Es lógico que no quiera venir.**
It's only natural he doesn't want to come.

**lograr** VERB
**to manage**

**Logré escaparme de ellos.**
I managed to get away from them.

la **longitud** NOUN
**length**
> Tiene tres metros de longitud.
> It's three metres long.

**los**

> los *can be an article or a pronoun.*

**A** ARTICLE
**the**
**los barcos**
the boats
**los de las bufandas rojas**
the people in the red scarves
**Se lavaron los pies en el río.**
They washed their feet in the river.
**Abrochaos los abrigos.**
Button up your coats.
**Me gustan sus cuadros, pero prefiero los de Ana.**
I like his paintings, but I prefer Ana's.
**No me gustan los melocotones.**
I don't like peaches.
**Solo vienen los lunes.**
They only come on Mondays.

**B** PRONOUN
**1 them**
**Los vi por la calle.**
I saw them in the street.
**Los han despedido.**
They've been sacked.
**2 you**
**Los acompaño hasta la puerta, señores.**
I'll see you to the door, gentlemen.

la **lotería** NOUN
**lottery**
> Le tocó la lotería.
> He won the lottery.

la **lucha** NOUN
**fight**
> lucha libre
> wrestling

**luchar** VERB
**to fight**

**luego** ADVERB
**1 then**
> Primero se puso de pie y luego habló.
> First he stood up and then he spoke.
**2 later**
> Mi hermana viene luego.
> My sister's coming later.
> **desde luego**
> of course
> **¡Desde luego que me gusta!**
> Of course I like it!

> **¡Hasta luego!**
> See you!

el **lugar** NOUN
**place**
> Este lugar es muy bonito.
> This is a lovely place.
> **Llegó en último lugar.**
> He came last.

el **lujo** NOUN
**luxury**
> un apartamento de lujo
> a luxury apartment

la **luna** NOUN
**moon**
> la luna de miel
> honeymoon

el **lunar** NOUN
**mole**

el **lunes** (PL los **lunes**) NOUN
**Monday**

> **Language tip**
> *The days of the week are not spelled with a capital letter in Spanish.*

> La vi el lunes.
> I saw her on Monday.

> **todos los lunes**
> every Monday
> **el lunes pasado**
> last Monday
> **el lunes que viene**
> next Monday

a
b
c
d
e
f
g
h
i
j
k
l
m
n
ñ
o
p
q
r
s
t
u
v
w
x
y
z

a b c d e f g h i j k l m n ñ o p q r s t u v w x y z

la **lupa** NOUN
**magnifying glass**

la **luz** (PL las **luces**) NOUN
**light**
Enciende la luz, por favor.
Put on the light please.

# M m

los **macarrones** NOUN
**macaroni**
> **Me gustan los macarrones.**
> I like macaroni.

la **maceta** NOUN
**flowerpot**

**macho** ADJECTIVE, MASC NOUN
**male**
> **una rata macho**
> a male rat

la **madera** NOUN
**wood**
> **Está hecho de madera.**
> It's made of wood.
> **un juguete de madera**
> a wooden toy

la **madre** NOUN
**mother**

la **madrugada** NOUN
**early morning**
> **a las cuatro de la madrugada**
> at four o'clock in the morning

**madrugar** VERB
**to get up early**

**maduro** (FEM **madura**)
ADJECTIVE
1 **ripe**
2 **mature**

el **maestro**
la **maestra** NOUN
**teacher**
> **Mi tía es maestra.**
> My aunt's a teacher.

la **magia** NOUN
**magic**

**mágico**
(FEM **mágica**)
ADJECTIVE
**magic**

> **una varita mágica**
> a magic wand

**majo** (FEM **maja**) ADJECTIVE
1 **nice**
2 **pretty**

**mal**

> **mal** can be an adverb, a noun or an adjective.

**A** ADVERB
1 **badly**
> **Toca la guitarra muy mal.**
> He plays the guitar very badly.
> **Esta habitación huele mal.**
> This room smells bad.
> **Lo pasé muy mal.**
> I had a terrible time.
> **Me entendió mal.**
> He misunderstood me.
2 **wrong**
> **Han escrito mal mi apellido.**
> They've spelt my surname wrong.
> **Está mal mentir.**
> It's wrong to tell lies.

**B** MASC NOUN
**evil**

**C** ADJECTIVE ▷ see **malo**

**maleducado**
(FEM **maleducada**) ADJECTIVE
**bad-mannered**

la **maleta** NOUN
**suitcase**

> **hacer la maleta**
> to pack

a
b
c
d
e
f
g
h
i
j
k
l
**m**
n
ñ
o
p
q
r
s
t
u
v
w
x
y
z

**142**

el **maletero** NOUN
**boot**

**malo**
**mala**

*malo can be a noun or an adjective.*

**A** MASC/FEM NOUN
**el malo de la película**
the villain in the film
**B** ADJECTIVE

*Language tip*
*Use* **mal** *before a masculine noun.*

1 **bad**
**un mal día**
a bad day
**Este programa es muy malo.**
This is a very bad programme.
**Soy muy mala para las matemáticas.**
I'm very bad at maths.
**Lo malo es que ...**
The trouble is that ...

2 **naughty**
**¿Por qué eres tan malo?**
Why are you so naughty?

3 **ill**
**Mi hija está mala.**
My daughter's ill.
**Se puso malo después de comer.**
He started to feel ill after lunch.

la **mamá** (PL las **mamás**) NOUN
**mum**
**¡Hola, mamá!**
Hi Mum!

la **mancha** NOUN
**stain**

**manchar** VERB
**to stain**

**El agua no mancha.**
Water doesn't stain.

■ **mancharse**
**to get dirty**
**No te manches la camisa.**
Don't get your shirt dirty.
**Me he manchado el vestido de tinta.**
I've got ink stains on my dress.

*Language tip*
*In Spanish, the person is the direct subject of the action.*

**mandar** VERB
1 **to tell**
**¿Qué te mandaron hacer?**
What did they tell you to do?
**Nos mandó callar.**
He told us to be quiet.
**Aquí mando yo.**
I'm the boss here.
2 **to send**
**Se lo mandaremos por correo.**
We'll send it to you by post.
**Me mandaron a hacer un recado.**
They sent me on an errand.

el **mando** NOUN
**el mando a distancia**
the remote control
**los mandos**
the controls

**manejar** VERB
**to operate**

la **manera** NOUN
**way**
**Lo hice a mi manera.**
I did it my way.
**No hay manera de convencerla.**
There's nothing one can do to convince her.

la **manga** NOUN
**sleeve**
**Súbete las mangas.**
Roll your sleeves up.

**de manga corta**
short-sleeved
**de manga larga**
long-sleeved

la **manía** NOUN
**Tiene la manía de repetir todo lo que digo.**
He has an irritating habit of repeating everything I say.
**El profesor me tiene manía.**
The teacher has it in for me.

la **mano** NOUN
**hand**
**Dame la mano.**
Give me your hand.
**tener algo a mano**
to have something to hand
**Ahora no tengo ese libro a mano.**
I don't have that book to hand right now.
**hecho a mano**
handmade
**de segunda mano**
secondhand

**echar una mano**
to lend a hand

la **manta** NOUN
**blanket**

el **mantel** NOUN
**tablecloth**

**mantener** VERB
**to keep**
**Les mantendremos informados.**
We'll keep you informed.
**mantener la calma**
to keep calm
**mantenerse en forma**
to keep fit
**mantenerse en pie**
to remain standing

la **mantequilla** NOUN
**butter**

**mantuve** VERB ▷ see **mantener**

**Mantuve la calma.**
I stayed calm.

la **manzana** NOUN
**apple**

**mañana**

**mañana** *can be a noun or an adverb.*

**A** FEM NOUN
**morning**
**Llegó a las nueve de la mañana.**
He arrived at nine o'clock in the morning.
**Por la mañana voy al gimnasio.**
In the mornings I go to the gym.
**a media mañana**
mid-morning
**B** ADVERB
**tomorrow**

**¡Hasta mañana!**
See you tomorrow!
**pasado mañana**
the day after tomorrow
**mañana por la mañana**
tomorrow morning
**mañana por la noche**
tomorrow night

el **mapa** NOUN
**map**
**El pueblo no está en el mapa.**
The village isn't on the map.

el **maquillaje** NOUN
**make-up**

**maquillarse** VERB
**to put one's make-up on**
**Está maquillándose.**
She's putting her make-up on.

la **máquina** NOUN
**machine**
**una máquina de coser**
a sewing machine

**una máquina de afeitar**
an electric razor
**una máquina fotográfica**
a camera

la **maquinilla** NOUN
**razor**
**una maquinilla eléctrica**
an electric razor

el **mar** NOUN
**sea**
**por mar**
by sea

> **Language tip**
> Note that in some set phrases, **mar** is feminine.

**Lo hizo la mar de bien.**
He did it really well.

la **maravilla** NOUN
**¡Qué maravilla de casa!**
What a wonderful house!
**ser una maravilla**
to be wonderful
**Se llevan de maravilla.**
They get on wonderfully well together.

**maravilloso** (FEM maravillosa)
ADJECTIVE
**marvellous**

la **marca** NOUN
1 **mark**
**Había marcas de neumático en la arena.**
There were tyre marks in the sand.
2 **make**
**¿De qué marca es tu tele?**
What make's your TV?
3 **brand**
**una conocida marca de chocolate**
a well-known brand of chocolate
**la ropa de marca**
designer clothes

el **marcador** NOUN
1 **scoreboard**

2 **bookmark**

**marcar** VERB
1 **to dial**
2 **to score**

**marcharse** VERB
**to leave**

la **marea** NOUN
**tide**
**una marea negra**
an oil slick

**mareado** (FEM **mareada**)
ADJECTIVE
**Estoy mareado.**
I feel dizzy./I feel sick.

> **Language tip**
> **estoy mareado** has two meanings. It can be translated as I **feel dizzy** and I **feel sick**.

**marear** VERB
to make ... feel sick
**Ese olor me marea.**
That smell makes me feel sick.

**marearse** VERB
1 **to get dizzy**
**Te marearás si das tantas vueltas.**
You'll get dizzy going round and round like that.
**¡No me marees!**
Stop going on!
2 **to get sick**
**¿Te mareas cuando vas en barco?**
Do you get seasick when you travel by boat?
**Siempre me mareo en coche.**
I always get carsick.

el **mareo** NOUN
1 **sea sickness**
2 **car sickness**

la **margarina** NOUN
**margarine**

el **margen** (PL los **márgenes**) NOUN
**margin**
> **Escribe las notas al margen.**
> Write your notes in the margin.

el **marido** NOUN
**husband**

la **mariposa** NOUN
**butterfly**

el **martes** (PL los **martes**) NOUN
**Tuesday**

---

**Language tip**

*The days of the week are not spelled with a capital letter in Spanish.*

---

> **La vi el martes.**
> I saw her on Tuesday.

**todos los martes**
every Tuesday
**el martes pasado**
last Tuesday
**el martes que viene**
next Tuesday
**Martes de Carnaval**
Shrove Tuesday

---

**Did you know…?**

*During the week before Lent, all over Spain and Latin America there are fiestas and fancy-dress parades, with the main celebrations taking place on* **Martes de Carnaval** *(literally Carnival Tuesday).*

---

**marzo** MASC NOUN
**March**

---

**Language tip**

*Months are not spelled with a capital letter in Spanish.*

---

**en marzo**
in March
**Nació el diecisiete de marzo.**
He was born on the seventeenth of March.

**más** ADJECTIVE, ADVERB
**more**
> **Ahora salgo más.**
> I go out more these days.
> **Últimamente nos vemos más.**
> We've been seeing more of each other lately.
> **¿Quieres más?**
> Would you like some more?
> **No tengo más dinero.**
> I haven't got any more money.
> **deprisa - más deprisa**
> quickly - more quickly
> **barato - más barato**
> cheap - cheaper
> **lejos - más lejos**
> far - further
> **grande - más grande**
> big - bigger
> **temprano - más temprano**
> early - earlier
> **caro - más caro**
> expensive - more expensive
> **Es más grande que el tuyo.**
> It's bigger than yours.
> **Corre más rápido que yo.**
> He runs faster than I do.
> **más de mil libros**
> more than a thousand books
> **más de lo que yo creía**
> more than I thought
> **el niño más joven**
> the youngest child
> **el coche más grande**
> the biggest car
> **el punto más lejano**
> the furthest point
> **el más inteligente de todos**
> the most intelligent of all of them
> **Paco es el que come más.**
> Paco's the one who eats the most.

**Fue el que más trabajó.**
He was the one who worked the hardest.
**¿Qué más?**
What else?
**¡Qué perro más sucio!**
What a filthy dog!

**Tenemos uno de más.**
We have one too many.
**Por más que estudio no apruebo.**
However hard I study I don't pass.
**Dos más dos son cuatro.**
Two plus two is four.

**masculino** (FEM **masculina**)
ADJECTIVE
1 **male**
   **el sexo masculino**
   the male sex
2 **men's**
   **la ropa masculina**
   men's clothing
3 **masculine**

**masticar** VERB
**to chew**

**matar** VERB
**to kill**
   **Mi padre me va a matar.**
   My dad will kill me.

las **matemáticas** NOUN
**mathematics**

la **materia** NOUN
**subject**
   **Es un experto en la materia.**
   He's an expert on the subject.

**material** ADJECTIVE, MASC NOUN
**material**

**matricularse** VERB
**to enrol**

**máximo**

> **máximo** *can be a noun or an adjective.*

A MASC NOUN
**maximum**
   **un máximo de cincuenta euros**
   a maximum of fifty euros
   **como máximo**
   at the most/at the latest

*Language tip*
**como máximo** *has two meanings. Look at the examples.*

   **Te costará cinco libras como máximo.**
   It'll cost you five pounds at the most.
   **Llegaré a las diez como máximo.**
   I'll be there by ten o'clock at the latest.
B (FEM **máxima**) ADJECTIVE
**maximum**
   **la velocidad máxima**
   the maximum speed

**mayo** MASC NOUN
**May**

*Language tip*
*Months are not spelled with a capital letter in Spanish.*

   **en mayo**
   in May
   **Nació el veintiocho de mayo.**
   He was born on the twenty-eighth of May.

la **mayonesa** NOUN
**mayonnaise**

**mayor** (FEM **mayor**)

> **mayor** *can be an adjective, pronoun or noun.*

A ADJECTIVE, PRONOUN
**older**

**Paco es mayor que Nacho.**
Paco is older than Nacho.
**Es tres años mayor que yo.**
He is three years older than me.
**el hermano mayor**
the older brother/the oldest brother

### Language tip

**el hermano mayor** *has two meanings. It can be translated as* **the older brother** *and* **the oldest brother**.

**Soy el mayor.**
I'm the older./I'm the oldest.

### Language tip

**Soy el mayor** *has two meanings. It can be translated as* **I'm the older (of the two)** *and* **I'm the oldest**.

**Sus hijos ya son mayores.**
Their children are grown-up now.
**la gente mayor**
the elderly
**B** MASC/FEM NOUN
**un mayor de edad**
an adult
**los mayores**
grown-ups

la **mayúscula** NOUN
**capital letter**
**Empieza cada frase con mayúscula.**
Start each sentence with a capital letter.
**Escríbelo con mayúsculas.**
Write it in capitals.
**una M mayúscula**
a capital M

**me** PRONOUN
**1 me**
**Me quiere.**
He loves me.
**Me regaló una pulsera.**
He gave me a bracelet.
**Me lo dio.**
He gave it to me.

**¿Me echas esta carta?**
Will you post this letter for me?

**2 myself**
**No me hice daño.**
I didn't hurt myself.
**me dije a mí mismo**
I said to myself
**Me duelen los pies.**
My feet hurt.
**Me puse el abrigo.**
I put my coat on

la **medalla** NOUN
**medal**

la **media** NOUN
**average**
**la media de edad**
the average age
**medias**
stockings/tights

### Language tip

**medias** *has two meanings. It can be translated either as* **stockings** *or* **tights**.

**mediados** PL NOUN
**a mediados de**
around the middle of

la **medianoche** NOUN
**midnight**
**a medianoche**
at midnight

el **medicamento** NOUN
**medicine**

la **medicina** NOUN

a
b
c
d
e
f
g
h
i
j
k
l
**m**
n
ñ
o
p
q
r
s
t
u
v
w
x
y
z

**147**

**medicine**
> **Mi hermano estudia medicina en la universidad.**
> My brother's studying medicine at university.
> **¿Te has tomado ya la medicina?**
> Have you taken your medicine yet?

el **médico**
la **médica** NOUN
**doctor**
> **Quiere ser médica.**
> She wants to be a doctor.
> **el médico de cabecera**
> the family doctor

la **medida** NOUN
**measure**
> **medidas de seguridad**
> security measures
> **a medida que ...**
> as ...
> **Saludaba a los invitados a medida que iban llegando.**
> He greeted the guests as they arrived.

## medio

> **medio** *can be an adjective, an adverb or a noun.*

**A** (FEM **media**) ADJECTIVE
**1 half**
> **medio litro**
> half a litre
> **Nos queda media botella de leche.**
> We've got half a bottle of milk left.
> **media hora**
> half an hour
> **una hora y media**
> an hour and a half
> **Son las ocho y media.**
> It's half past eight.

**2 average**
> **la temperatura media**
> the average temperature

**B** ADVERB
**half**

> **Estaba medio dormido.**
> He was half asleep.

**C** MASC NOUN
**1 middle**
> **Está en el medio.**
> It's in the middle.

**2 means**
> **un medio de transporte**
> a means of transport
> **los medios de comunicación**
> the media
> **el medio ambiente**
> the environment

el **mediodía** NOUN
> **al mediodía**
> at midday/at lunchtime

> *Language tip*
>
> **al mediodía** *has two meanings. It can be translated as* **at midday** *and* **at lunchtime**.

**medir** VERB
**to measure**
> **¿Has medido la ventana?**
> Have you measured the window?
> **¿Cuánto mides? –**
> **Mido un metro cincuenta.**
> How tall are you? –
> I'm one metre fifty.
> **¿Cuánto mide esta habitación? – Mide tres metros por cuatro.**
> How big is this room? – It measures three metres by four.

la **mejilla** NOUN
**cheek**

**mejor** (FEM **mejor**)

> **mejor** *can be an adjective or an adverb.*

**A** ADJECTIVE
**1 better**
> **Éste es mejor que el otro.**
> This one is better than the other one.
> **Es el mejor de los dos.**
> He's the better of the two.

**2 best**
mi mejor amiga
my best friend

el mejor de la clase
the best in the class
**Es el mejor de todos.**
He's the best of the lot.

**B** ADVERB
**1 better**
**La conozco mejor que tú.**
I know her better than you do.
**2 best**
**¿Quién lo hace mejor?**
Who does it best?
**Mejor nos vamos.**
We had better go.

**a lo mejor**
probably

**mejorar** VERB
**to improve**
**El tiempo está mejorando.**
The weather's improving.
**Han mejorado el servicio.**
They have improved the service.

**¡Que te mejores!**
Get well soon!

la **melena** NOUN
**long hair**
**Lleva una melena rubia.**
She has long blond hair.

el **mellizo** (FEM la **melliza**)
ADJECTIVE, NOUN
**twin**
**Son mellizos.**
They're twins.

el **melocotón** (PL los
**melocotones**) NOUN
**peach**

el **melón** (PL los melones) NOUN
**melon**

la **memoria** NOUN
**memory**
**tener mala memoria**
to have a bad memory
**aprender algo de memoria**
to learn something by heart

**menor** (FEM menor)

menor *can be an adjective, a
pronoun or a noun.*

**A** ADJECTIVE, PRONOUN
**1 younger**
**Es tres años menor que yo.**
He's three years younger than
me.
**Juanito es menor que Pepe.**
Juanito is younger than Pepe.
**el hermano menor**
the younger brother/the
youngest brother

*Language tip*
el hermano menor *has two
meanings. It can be translated as*
**the younger brother** *and* **the
youngest brother**.

**Yo soy el menor.**
I'm the younger./I'm the
youngest.

*Language tip*
yo soy el menor *has two
meanings. It can be translated as*
**I'm the younger** *and* **I'm the
youngest**.

**2 smaller**
**una talla menor**
a smaller size
**No tiene la menor
importancia.**
It's not in the least important.
**B** MASC/FEM NOUN
**un menor de edad**
a minor
**los menores**
the under-18s

## menos

> **menos** *can be an adjective, an adverb or a preposition.*

**A** ADJECTIVE, ADVERB

**1 less**
**Ahora salgo menos.**
I go out less these days.
**Últimamente nos vemos menos.**
We've been seeing less of each other recently.
**menos caro**
less expensive
**menos harina**
less flour
**menos gatos**
fewer cats
**menos gente**
fewer people
**menos ... que**
less ... than
**Me gusta menos que el otro.**
I like it less than the other one.
**Trabaja menos que yo.**
He doesn't work as hard as I do.
**Es menos nerviosa que antes.**
She's less nervous than she was.
**menos de cincuenta cajas**
fewer than fifty boxes

**2 least**
**el chico menos desobediente de la clase**
the least disobedient boy in the class
**Fue el que menos trabajó.**
He was the one who worked the least hard.
**el examen con menos errores**
the exam paper with the fewest mistakes
**No quiero verle y menos visitarle.**
I don't want to see him, let alone visit him.

**¡Menos mal!**
Thank goodness!

**B** PREPOSITION
**except**
**todos menos él**
everyone except him
**Cinco menos dos son tres.**
Five minus two is three.
**a menos que**
unless

el **mensaje** NOUN
**message**
**un mensaje de texto**
a text message

**mentir** VERB
**to lie**
**No me mientas.**
Don't lie to me.

la **mentira** NOUN
**lie**
**No digas mentiras.**
Don't tell lies.
**Parece mentira que aún no te haya pagado.**
It's incredible that he still hasn't paid you.
**una pistola de mentira**
a toy pistol

el **mentiroso**
la **mentirosa** NOUN
**liar**

el **menú** (PL los **menús**) NOUN
**menu**
**el menú del día**
the set menu

**menudo** (FEM **menuda**)
ADJECTIVE
**¡Menudo lío!**
What a mess!

**a menudo**
often

el **meñique** NOUN
**little finger**

el **mercado** NOUN
**market**

**merecer** VERB

**to deserve**
**Mereces que te castiguen.**
You deserve to be punished.

**merece la pena**
it's worthwhile

**merendar** VERB
**to have tea**

la **merienda** NOUN
**tea**

el **mes** (PL los **meses**) NOUN
**month**

**el mes que viene**
next month

la **mesa** NOUN
**table**

**poner la mesa**
to lay the table

el **metal** NOUN
**metal**

**meter** VERB
**to put**
**¿Dónde has metido las llaves?**
Where have you put the keys?
**meterse en**
to go into
**Se metió en la cueva.**
He went into the cave.
**No te metas donde no te llaman.**
Don't poke your nose in where it doesn't belong.
**meterse con alguien**
to pick on somebody
**No te metas con tu hermano.**
Don't pick on your brother.

el **metro** NOUN
**1 underground**
**coger el metro**
to take the underground
**2 metre**
**Mide tres metros de largo.**
It's three metres long.

la **mezcla** NOUN
**mixture**

**mezclar** VERB
**to mix**
**Hay que mezclar el azúcar y la harina.**
You have to mix the sugar and the flour.

**mi** (FEM **mi**, PL **mis**) ADJECTIVE
**my**
**mis hermanas**
my sisters

**mí** PRONOUN
**me**
**para mí**
for me
**Para mí que ...**
I think that ...
**Por mí no hay problema.**
There's no problem as far as I'm concerned.

el **micrófono** NOUN
**microphone**

el **microondas** (PL los **microondas**) NOUN
**microwave**
**un horno microondas**
a microwave oven

el **microscopio** NOUN
**microscope**

**midiendo** VERB ▷ see medir
**Estaba midiendo la habitación.**
I was measuring the room.

el **miedo** NOUN
**fear**

**el miedo a la oscuridad**
fear of the dark

**tener miedo**
to be afraid
**Le tenía miedo a su padre.**
He was afraid of his father.
**Tengo miedo a caerme.**
I'm afraid of falling over.
**dar miedo a**
to scare
**Me daba miedo hacerlo.**
I was scared of doing it.

la **miel** NOUN
**honey**

el/la **miembro** NOUN
**member**

**mientras** ADVERB, CONJUNCTION
**while**
**Lava tú mientras yo seco.**
You wash while I dry.
**Seguiré jugando al fútbol mientras pueda.**
I'll carry on playing football for as long as I can.

**mientras tanto**
meanwhile

el **miércoles** (PL los **miércoles**)
NOUN
**Wednesday**

*Language tip*
*The days of the week are not spelled with a capital letter in Spanish.*

**La vi el miércoles.**
I saw her on Wednesday.

**todos los miércoles**
every Wednesday
**el miércoles pasado**
last Wednesday
**el miércoles que viene**
next Wednesday

**mil** (FEM **mil**) ADJECTIVE, PRONOUN
**thousand**
**miles de personas**
thousands of people
**dos mil euros**
two thousand euros

el **milagro** NOUN
**miracle**
**No nos hemos matado de milagro.**
It was a miracle we weren't killed.

el **milímetro** NOUN
**millimetre**

el **millón** (PL los **millones**) NOUN
**million**
**millones de personas**
millions of people
**mil millones**
a billion

el **millonario**
la **millonaria** NOUN
**millionaire**

**mimado** (FEM **mimada**)
ADJECTIVE
**spoiled**

**mineral** ADJECTIVE, MASC NOUN
**mineral**

**mínimo**

*mínimo can be a noun or an adjective.*

**A** MASC NOUN
**minimum**
**un mínimo de diez euros**
a minimum of ten euros
**lo mínimo que puede hacer**
the least he can do
**Como mínimo podrías haber llamado.**
You could at least have called.

**B** (FEM **mínima**) ADJECTIVE
**minimum**
> **la puntuación mínima**
> the minimum score
> **No tienes ni la más mínima idea.**
> You haven't the faintest idea.

la **minoría** NOUN
**minority**
> **las minorías étnicas**
> ethnic minorities

la **minúscula** NOUN
**small letter**

la **minusválida** NOUN
**disabled woman**

el **minusválido** NOUN
**disabled man**
> **los minusválidos**
> the disabled

el **minuto** NOUN
**minute**
> **Espera un minuto.**
> Wait a minute.

**mío** (FEM **mía**) ADJECTIVE, PRONOUN
**mine**
> **Estos caballos son míos.**
> Those horses are mine.
> **¿De quién es esta bufanda? – Es mía.**
> Whose scarf is this? – It's mine.
> **El mío está en el armario.**
> Mine's in the cupboard.
> **Éste es el mío.**
> This one's mine.
> **un amigo mío**
> a friend of mine

la **mirada** NOUN
**look**
> **con una mirada de odio**
> with a look of hatred
> **echar una mirada a algo**
> to have a look at something
> **¿Le has echado una mirada a mi informe?**

Have you had a look at my report?

**mirar** VERB
**to look**
> **¡Mira! Un ratón.**
> Look! A mouse.
> **Mira a ver si está ahí.**
> Look and see if he is there.
> **mirar algo**
> to look at something
> **Mira esta foto.**
> Look at this photo.
> **mirar por la ventana**
> to look out of the window
> **mirar algo fijamente**
> to stare at something
> **¡Mira que es tonto!**
> What an idiot!
> **mirarse al espejo**
> to look at oneself in the mirror

> **Se miraron asombrados.**
> They looked at each other in amazement.

la **misa** NOUN
**mass**

**mismo**

> mismo *can be an adjective, an adverb or a pronoun.*

**A** (FEM **misma**) ADJECTIVE
**same**
> **Nos gustan los mismos libros.**
> We like the same books.
> **Vivo en su misma calle.**
> I live in the same street as him.
> **yo mismo**
> myself

**Lo hice yo mismo.**
I did it myself.

**B** ADVERB

**Hoy mismo le escribiré.**
I'll write to him today.

**Nos podemos encontrar aquí mismo.**
We can meet right here.

**C** PRONOUN

**lo mismo**
the same

**Yo tomaré lo mismo.**
I'll have the same.

**Da lo mismo.**
It doesn't matter.

**No ha llamado pero lo mismo viene.**
He hasn't phoned but he may well come.

el **misterio** NOUN
**mystery**

la **mitad** NOUN
**half**

**Se comió la mitad del pastel.**
He ate half the cake.

**más de la mitad de los alumnos**
more than half the pupils

**La mitad son chicas.**
Half of them are girls.

**a mitad de precio**
half-price

**a mitad de camino**
halfway there

**Corta el pan por la mitad.**
Cut the loaf in half.

**mixto** (FEM **mixta**) ADJECTIVE
**mixed**

**una escuela mixta**
a mixed school

la **mochila** NOUN
**rucksack**

el **moco** NOUN

**Límpiate los mocos.**
Wipe your nose.

**tener mocos**
to have a runny nose

la **moda** NOUN
**fashion**

**estar de moda**
to be in fashion

**pasado de moda**
old-fashioned

los **modales** NOUN
**manners**

**buenos modales**
good manners

el/la **modelo** ADJECTIVE, NOUN
**model**

**una niña modelo**
a model child

**Quiero ser modelo.**
I want to be a model.

**moderno** (FEM **moderna**)
ADJECTIVE
**modern**

**modesto** (FEM **modesta**)
ADJECTIVE
**modest**

el **modo** NOUN
**way**

**Le gusta hacerlo todo a su modo.**
She likes to do everything her own way.

**de modo que**
so/so that

*Language tip*

**de modo que** *has two meanings.
Look at the examples.*

**No has hecho los deberes, de modo que no puedes salir.**
You haven't done your homework so you can t go out.

**Mueve la tele de modo que todos la podamos ver.**
Move the TV so that we can all see it.

**'modo de empleo'**
'instructions for use'

**de todos modos**
anyway

**mojado** (FEM **mojada**) ADJECTIVE
**wet**

**mojar** VERB
**to get ... wet**
¡No mojes la alfombra!
Don't get the carpet wet!
Me he mojado las mangas.
I got my sleeves wet.
Moja el pan en la salsa.
Dip the bread in the sauce.

- **mojarse**
**to get wet**

**molestar** VERB
1 **to bother**
¿Te molesta la radio?
Is the radio bothering you?
Siento molestarle.
I'm sorry to bother you.
2 **to disturb**
No me molestes, que estoy
trabajando.
Don't disturb me, I'm working.

- **molestarse**
**to get upset**
Se molestó por algo que
dije.
She got upset because of
something I said.

el **momento** NOUN
**moment**
Espera un momento.
Wait a moment.
en este momento
at the moment
Tenemos mucho trabajo en
este momento.
We've got a lot of work at the
moment.

de un momento a otro
any moment now
Llegarán de un momento
a otro.
They'll be here any moment
now.
Llegó el momento de irnos.
The time came for us to go.

la **moneda** NOUN
**coin**
una moneda de dos euros
a two-euro coin

el **monedero** NOUN
**purse**

**mono**

**mono** can be an adjective or a
noun.

A (FEM **mona**) ADJECTIVE
**pretty**
¡Qué piso tan mono!
What a pretty flat!
¡Qué niña tan mona!
What a sweet little girl!
B MASC NOUN
**monkey**

el **monopatín** (PL los
monopatines) NOUN
**skateboard**

el **monstruo** NOUN
**monster**

la **montaña** NOUN
**mountain**
Fuimos de vacaciones a la
montaña.
We went to the mountains on
holiday.

**la montaña rusa**
the roller coaster

## montar VERB
**to assemble**
- **montarse**
**to get on**
**Se montó en el autobús.**
He got on the bus.

**montar en bici**
to ride a bike

### el **montón** (PL los **montones**)
NOUN
**pile**
**Puso el montón de libros sobre la mesa.**
He put the pile of books on the table.
**un montón de ...**
loads of ...
**un montón de gente**
loads of people
**un montón de dinero**
loads of money

### la **moral** NOUN
**morale**
**levantar la moral a alguien**
to cheer somebody up

## morder VERB
**to bite**
**morderse las uñas**
to bite one's nails
**No te muerdas las uñas.**
Don't bite your nails.

### el **mordisco** NOUN
**bite**
**Dame un mordisco de tu bocadillo.**
Let me have a bite of your sandwich.
**dar un mordisco**
to bite
**Me dio un mordisco.**
He bit me.

## moreno (FEM morena) ADJECTIVE
**dark**
**Es moreno.**

### *Language tip*
**Es moreno** *has two meanings. It can be translated as* **he has dark hair** *and* **he is dark-skinned**.

**ponerse moreno**
to get brown

## morir VERB
**to die**
**¿Cuándo murió?**
When did he die?
**¡Me muero de hambre!**
I'm starving!
**Me muero de vergüenza.**
I'm so embarrassed.
**Me muero de ganas de ir a nadar.**
I'm dying to go for a swim.

### la **mosca** NOUN
**fly**

### el **mosquito**
NOUN
**mosquito**

### el **mostrador**
NOUN
**counter**

## mostrar VERB
**to show**
**Nos mostró el camino.**
He showed us the way.

### el **mote** NOUN
**nickname**

### el **motivo** NOUN
**reason**
**Dejó el trabajo por motivos personales.**
He left the job for personal reasons.

### la **moto** NOUN
**motorbike**

### el **motor** NOUN
**engine**

### el/la **motorista** NOUN
**motorcyclist**

**mover** VERB
  **to move**
  **Mueve un poco las cajas para que podamos pasar.**
  Move the boxes a bit so that we can get past.
  ▪ **moverse**
  **to move**
  **¡No te muevas!**
  Don't move!

**el móvil** NOUN
  **mobile**
  **un móvil con cámara**
  a camera phone

**el movimiento** NOUN
  **movement**

**el MP3** NOUN
  **MP3**
  **un reproductor de MP3**
  an MP3 player

**la muchacha** NOUN
  **girl**

**el muchacho** NOUN
  **boy**

**mucho** (FEM **mucha**)

> **mucho** can be an adjective, a pronoun or an adverb.

  **A** ADJECTIVE
  1 **a lot of**
  **Había mucha gente.**
  There were a lot of people.
  **Tiene muchas plantas.**
  He has got a lot of plants.
  2 **much**
  **No tenemos mucho tiempo.**
  We haven't got much time.
  **¿Conoces a mucha gente?**
  Do you know many people?
  **Muchas personas creen que ...**
  Many people think that ...
  **no hace mucho tiempo**
  not long ago
  **Hace mucho calor.**
  It's very hot.

**Tengo mucho frío.**
I'm very cold.

**Tengo mucha hambre.**
I'm very hungry.
**Tengo mucha sed.**
I'm very thirsty.

**B** PRONOUN
1 **a lot**
  **Tengo mucho que hacer.**
  I've got a lot to do.
  **¿Cuántos había? – Muchos.**
  How many were there? – A lot.
2 **much**
  **No tengo mucho que hacer.**
  I haven't got much to do.
  **¿Hay manzanas? –**
  **Sí, pero no muchas.**
  Are there any apples? –
  Yes, but not many.
  **¿Vinieron muchos?**
  Did many people come?
  **Muchos dicen que ...**
  Many people say that ...

**C** ADVERB
1 **very much**
  **Te quiero mucho.**
  I love you very much.
  **No me gusta mucho la carne.**
  I don't like meat very much.
  **Me gusta mucho el jazz.**
  I really like jazz.
2 **a lot**
  **Come mucho.**
  He eats a lot.
  **mucho más**
  a lot more
  **mucho antes**
  long before
  **No tardes mucho.**
  Don't be long.

**mudarse** VERB
  **to move**

**mudarse de casa**
to move house

el **mueble** NOUN
**un mueble**
a piece of furniture
**seis muebles**
six pieces of furniture
**los muebles**
furniture

la **muela** NOUN
**tooth**
**una muela del juicio**
a wisdom tooth

el **muelle** NOUN
1 spring
2 quay

**muerdo** VERB ▷ see **morder**
**Me duele cuando muerdo.**
It hurts when I bite.

la **muerte** NOUN
**death**
**Nos dio un susto de muerte.**
He nearly frightened us to death.

**muerto**
**muerta**

**muerto** *can be an adjective or a noun.*

A ADJECTIVE
**dead**
**Está muerto de cansancio.**
He's dead tired.

B MASC/FEM NOUN
**un muerto**
a dead man

**una muerta**
a dead woman
**los muertos**
the dead
**Hubo tres muertos.**
Three people were killed.

la **muestra** NOUN
**sign**
**dar muestras de**
to show signs of

**muestro** VERB ▷ see **mostrar**
**Ahora te muestro cómo se hace.**
I'll show you now how it's done.

**muevo** VERB ▷ see **mover**
**Yo no me muevo de aquí.**
I'm not moving from here.

la **mujer** NOUN
1 **woman**
**Vino a verte una mujer.**
A woman came to see you.
2 **wife**
**la mujer del médico**
the doctor's wife

la **multa** NOUN
**fine**
**una multa de cincuenta euros**
a fifty-euro fine

**multiplicar** VERB
**to multiply**
**Hay que multiplicarlo por cinco.**
You have to multiply it by five.
**la tabla de multiplicar**
the times tables

**mundial**

**mundial** *can be an adjective or a noun.*

A (FEM **mundial**) ADJECTIVE
1 **world**
**la copa mundial**
the world cup
2 **worldwide**
B MASC NOUN
**world championship**

el **mundo** NOUN
**world**
> **todo el mundo**
> everybody
> **Se lo ha dicho a todo el mundo.**
> He has told everybody.
> **No lo cambiaría por nada del mundo.**
> I wouldn't change it for anything in the world.

la **muñeca** NOUN
**1 wrist**
**2 doll**

el **muñeco** NOUN
**doll**
> **un muñeco de peluche**
> a soft toy
> **un muñeco de nieve**
> a snowman

el **museo** NOUN
**museum**
> **un museo de arte**
> an art gallery

la **música** NOUN
**music**

> **la música pop**
> pop music

**muy** ADVERB
**very**
> **muy bonito**
> very pretty

# N n

**nacer** VERB
**to be born**
Nació en 1964.
He was born in 1964.

**nacional** (FEM **nacional**)
ADJECTIVE
**national**
vuelos nacionales
domestic flights

**nada**

> **nada** can be a pronoun or an adverb.

A PRONOUN
1 **nothing**
¿Qué has comprado? – Nada.
What have you bought? – Nothing.
**No hace nada.**
He does nothing.
2 **anything**
**No quiero nada.**
I don't want anything.
**No dijo nada más.**
He didn't say anything else.
**Encendió la tele nada más llegar.**
He turned on the TV as soon as he came in.
**No sabe nada de español.**
He knows no Spanish at all.

> ¡Gracias! – De nada.
> Thanks! – You're welcome!

B ADVERB
**at all**
Esto no me gusta nada.
I don't like this at all.

el **nadador**
la **nadadora** NOUN
**swimmer**

**nadar** VERB
**to swim**

**nadie** PRONOUN
1 **nobody**
Nadie habló.
Nobody spoke.
**No había nadie.**
There was nobody there.
2 **anybody**
**No quiere ver a nadie.**
He doesn't want to see anybody.

**naranja**

> **naranja** can be an adjective or a noun.

A ADJECTIVE
**orange**

> **Language tip**
> The colour **naranja** never changes its ending no matter what it describes.

un anorak naranja
an orange anorak
B FEM NOUN
**orange** (fruit)
C MASC NOUN
**orange** (colour)

la **nariz** (PL las **narices**) NOUN
**nose**

la **nata** NOUN
**cream**

la **natación** NOUN
swimming

**natural** (FEM **natural**) ADJECTIVE
natural

la **naturaleza** NOUN
nature

las **náuseas** NOUN
tener náuseas
to feel sick

la **navaja** NOUN
penknife

la **nave** NOUN
ship
una nave espacial
a spaceship

**navegar** VERB
to sail

> navegar por
> Internet
> to surf
> the Net

la **Navidad**
NOUN
Christmas

> ¡Feliz Navidad!
> Happy Christmas!

**necesario** (FEM **necesaria**)
ADJECTIVE
necessary
No es necesario.
It isn't necessary.
Ya tengo el dinero necesario
para el billete.
I've now got the money I need
for the ticket.
No es necesario que vengas.
You don't have to come.

la **necesidad** NOUN
need
No hay necesidad de hacerlo.
There is no need to do it.

**necesitar** VERB
to need

Necesito cien euros.
I need a hundred euros.
Necesito sacar un notable en
el examen.
I need to get a good mark in the
exam.
Necesito que me ayudes.
I need you to help me.
'Se necesita camarero'
'Waiter wanted'

**negar** VERB
1 to deny
No lo puedes negar.
You can't deny it.
Negó con la cabeza.
He shook his head.

2 to refuse
Se negó a hacer las compras.
He refused to do the shopping.

**negativo** (FEM **negativa**)
ADJECTIVE
negative

**negro**

> negro can be an adjective or a
> noun.

A (FEM **negra**) ADJECTIVE
black
B MASC/FEM NOUN
un negro
a black man
una negra
a black woman
los negros
black people
C MASC NOUN
black (colour)

el **nervio** NOUN
nerve
Me pone de los nervios.
She gets on my nerves.

**nervioso** (FEM **nerviosa**)
ADJECTIVE

**nervous**
**Me pongo muy nervioso en los exámenes.**
I get very nervous during exams.
**¡Me pone nervioso!**
He gets on my nerves!

**nevar** VERB
**to snow**

la **nevera** NOUN
**refrigerator**

**ni** CONJUNCTION
**neither**
**Ella no fue, ni yo tampoco.**
She didn't go and neither did I.
**ni ... ni**
neither ... nor
**No vinieron ni Carlos ni Sofía.**
Neither Carlos nor Sofía came.
**No me gustan ni el bacalao ni el hígado.**
I don't like either cod or liver.
**No compré ni uno ni otro.**
I didn't buy either of them.
**Ni siquiera me saludó.**
He didn't even say hello.

el **nido** NOUN
**nest**

la **niebla** NOUN
**fog**
**Hay niebla.**
It's foggy.

**niego** VERB ▷ see **negar**
**No niego que esté enfadado.**
I'm not denying I'm angry.

la **nieta** NOUN
**granddaughter**

el **nieto** NOUN
**grandson**
**mis nietos**
my grandsons/my grandchildren

*Language tip*

**mis nietos** *has two meanings. It can be translated as* my **grandsons** *or* my **grandchildren**.

**nieva** VERB ▷ see **nevar**
**Nieva.**
It's snowing.

la **nieve** NOUN
**snow**

**ningún** PRONOUN ▷ see **ninguno**
**No tengo ningún caramelo.**
I don't have any sweets.

**ninguno** (FEM **ninguna**)
ADJECTIVE, PRONOUN
**1 no**
**No hay ninguna prisa.**
There's no hurry.
**2 any**
**No vimos a ningún amigo en las vacaciones.**
We didn't see any friends in the holidays.
**3 none**
**¿Cuál eliges? – Ninguno.**
Which one do you want? – None of them.
**No me queda ninguno.**
I have none left.
**Ninguno de nosotros va a ir a la fiesta.**
None of us is going to the party.
**No lo encuentro por ningún sitio.**
I can't find it anywhere.
**ninguno de los dos**
neither of them/either of them

*Language tip*

**ninguno de los dos** *has two meanings. Look at the examples.*

**A ninguna de las dos les gusta el café.**

Neither of them likes coffee.
**No me gusta ninguno de los dos.**
I don't like either of them.

la **niña** NOUN
**girl**

el **niño** NOUN
**boy**
**los niños**
the boys/the children

> **Language tip**
>
> **los niños** *has two meanings. It can be translated as* **the boys** *or* **the children**.

el **nivel** NOUN
1 **level**
**el nivel del agua**
the water level

2 **standard**
**el nivel de vida**
the standard of living

**no** ADVERB
**no**
**¿Quieres venir? – No.**
Do you want to come? – No.
**¿Te gusta? – No mucho.**
Do you like it? – Not really.
**No me gusta.**
I don't like it.
**María no habla inglés.**
María doesn't speak English.
**No puedo venir esta noche.**
I can't come tonight.
**No tengo tiempo.**
I haven't got time.

**No debes preocuparte**.
You mustn't worry.
**No hace frío.**
It isn't cold.
**No conozco a nadie.**
I don't know anyone.
**Esto es tuyo, ¿no?**
This is yours, isn't it?
**Fueron al cine, ¿no?**
They went to the cinema, didn't they?
**¿Puedo salir esta noche? – ¡Que no!**
Can I go out tonight? – I said no!
**los no fumadores**
non-smokers

la **noche** NOUN
**night**
**Pasó la noche sin dormir.**
He had a sleepless night.

**¡Buenas noches!**
Good evening!/Good night!

> **Language tip**
>
> **¡buenas noches!** *has two meanings. It can be translated as* **good evening!** *and* **good night!**

**Era de noche cuando llegamos a casa.**
It was night time when we got home.

**el sábado por la noche**
on Saturday night
**esta noche**
tonight
**por la noche**
at night

la **Nochebuena** NOUN
**Christmas Eve**

a
b
c
d
e
f
g
h
i
j
k
l
m
**n**
ñ
o
p
q
r
s
t
u
v
w
x
y
z

la **Nochevieja** NOUN
**New Year's Eve**

**nombrar** VERB
**to mention**
**Me nombró en su discurso.**
He mentioned me in his speech.

el **nombre** NOUN
**1 name**
**nombre de pila**
first name
**nombre y apellidos**
full name
**2 noun**

**noreste** MASC NOUN, ADJECTIVE
**northeast**

### Language tip
*The adjective **noreste** never changes its ending, no matter what it describes.*

la **noria** NOUN
**big wheel**

la **norma** NOUN
**rule**

**normal** (FEM **normal**) ADJECTIVE
**normal**
**una persona normal**
a normal person
**Es normal que quiera divertirse.**
It's natural that he should want to enjoy himself.

**noroeste** MASC NOUN, ADJECTIVE
**northwest**

### Language tip
*The adjective **noroeste** never changes its ending, no matter what it describes.*

**norte** MASC NOUN, ADJECTIVE
**north**
**el norte del país**
the north of the country

### Language tip
*The adjective **norte** never changes its ending, no matter what it describes.*

**en la costa norte**
on the north coast

el **norteamericano** (FEM la **norteamericana**) ADJECTIVE, NOUN
**American**

**nos** PRONOUN
**1 us**
**Nos vinieron a ver.**
They came to see us.
**Nos dio un consejo.**
He gave us some advice.
**Nos lo dio.**
He gave it to us.
**Nos tienen que arreglar el ordenador.**
They have to fix the computer for us.
**2 ourselves**
**Tenemos que defendernos.**
We must defend ourselves.
**Nos levantamos a las ocho.**
We got up at eight o'clock.
**Nos dolían los pies.**
Our feet were hurting.
**Nos pusimos los abrigos.**
We put our coats on.
**3 each other**
**No nos hablamos desde hace tiempo.**
We haven't spoken to each other for a long time.

la **nota** NOUN
**1 mark**
**Saca muy malas notas.**
He gets very bad marks.
**2 note**
**Tomó muchas notas en la conferencia.**
He took a lot of notes during the lecture.

**notar** VERB
**1 to notice**
**Notó que le seguían.**
He noticed they were following him.
**2 to feel**

**Con este abrigo no noto el frío.**
I don't feel the cold with this coat on.

**Se nota que has estudiado mucho este trimestre.**
You can tell that you've studied a lot this term.

la **noticia** NOUN
**news**
**Tengo una buena noticia que darte.**
I've got some good news for you.
**Fue una noticia excelente para la escuela.**
It was an excellent piece of news for the school.
**Vi las noticias de las nueve.**
I watched the nine o'clock news.

> **Language tip**
> Be careful! **noticia** does not mean notice.

el **novato**
la **novata** NOUN
**beginner**

**novecientos**
(FEM **novecientas**) ADJECTIVE,
PRONOUN
**nine hundred**

la **novedad** NOUN
**Las últimas novedades en moda infantil.**
The latest in children's fashions.

la **novela** NOUN
**novel**

**noveno** (FEM **novena**) ADJECTIVE,
PRONOUN
**ninth**
**Vivo en el noveno.**
I live on the ninth floor.

**noventa** (FEM **noventa**)
ADJECTIVE, PRONOUN
**ninety**
**el noventa aniversario**
the ninetieth anniversary

la **novia** NOUN
**girlfriend**

**noviembre** MASC NOUN
**November**

> **Language tip**
> Months are not spelled with a capital letter in Spanish.

> **en noviembre**
> in November
> **Nació el treinta de noviembre.**
> He was born on the thirtieth of November.

los **novillos** NOUN
**hacer novillos**
to play truant

el **novio** NOUN
**boyfriend**
**los novios**
the bride and groom

la **nube** NOUN
**cloud**

**nublado** (FEM **nublada**)
ADJECTIVE
**cloudy**

**nublarse** VERB
**to cloud over**

la **nuca** NOUN
nape

**nuclear** ADJECTIVE
nuclear
**una central nuclear**
a nuclear power station

el **nudo** NOUN
knot

**nuestro** (FEM **nuestra**)
ADJECTIVE, PRONOUN
1 **our**
**nuestro perro**
our dog
**nuestras bicicletas**
our bicycles
2 **ours**
**¿De quién es esto? –
Es nuestro.**
Whose is this? – It's ours.
**La nuestra es blanca.**
Ours is white.
**un amigo nuestro**
a friend of ours

**nueve** (FEM **nueve**) ADJECTIVE,
PRONOUN
**nine**
**Son las nueve.**
It's nine o'clock.

**el nueve de marzo**
the ninth of March
**Nació el nueve de marzo.**
He was born on the ninth of
March.

**nuevo** (FEM **nueva**) ADJECTIVE
**new**
**Necesito un ordenador
nuevo.**
I need a new computer.

**Tuve que leer el libro de
nuevo.**
I had to read the book again.

la **nuez** (PL las **nueces**) NOUN
**walnut**

el **número** NOUN
1 **number**
**Calle Aribau, sin número.**
Aribau street, no number.
**número de teléfono**
telephone number
2 **size**
(*of shoe*)

**nunca** ADVERB
1 **never**
**No viene nunca.**
He never comes.
**No la veré nunca más.**
I'll never see her again.
2 **ever**
**Ninguno de nosotros había
esquiado nunca.**
Neither of us had ever skied
before.
**Casi nunca me escribe.**
He hardly ever writes to me.

*Language tip*
*The Spanish alphabet has an extra
letter in it:* ñ. *Not many words begin
with it but you will see it in lots of
common words e.g.* **niño**, **cariño**.

**Spanish** **English**

a b c d e f g h i j k l m n ñ o p q r s t u v w x y z

# Ñ ñ

## ñoño
### ñoña

ñoño *can be an adjective or a noun.*

**A** ADJECTIVE
**wet**

**Me parece algo ñoña.**
I think she's a bit wet.

**B** MASC/FEM NOUN
**drip**
**Tu hermano es un ñoño.**
Your brother's a drip.

# O o

**o** CONJUNCTION
**or**
> **¿Quieres té o café?**
> Would you like tea or coffee?
> **¿Vas a ayudarme o no?**
> Are you going to help me or not?
> **o ... o ...**
> either ... or ...
> **O ha salido o no coge el teléfono.**
> Either he's out or he's not answering the phone.

**obedecer** VERB
**to obey**

**obediente** (FEM **obediente**)
ADJECTIVE
**obedient**

el **objeto** NOUN
**object**
> **un objeto metálico**
> a metal object

**obligar** VERB
**to force**
> **Nadie te obliga a ir a clases de karate.**
> Nobody's forcing you to do karate.

**obligatorio** (FEM **obligatoria**)
ADJECTIVE
**compulsory**

la **obra** NOUN

1 **work**
> **una obra de arte**
> a work of art

> **una obra de teatro**
> a play
2 **building site**
> **'obras'**
> 'roadworks'

**observar** VERB
**to observe**

el **obstáculo** NOUN
**obstacle**

**obtener** VERB
**to obtain**

**obvio** (FEM **obvia**) ADJECTIVE
**obvious**

la **ocasión** (PL las **ocasiones**)
NOUN
**opportunity**
> **Ésta es la ocasión que esperábamos.**
> This is the opportunity we've been waiting for.

el **océano** NOUN
**ocean**
> **el océano Atlántico**
> the Atlantic Ocean

**ochenta** (FEM **ochenta**)
ADJECTIVE, PRONOUN

**eighty**
**Tiene ochenta años.**
He's eighty.
**el ochenta aniversario**
the eightieth anniversary

**ocho** (FEM **ocho**) ADJECTIVE,
PRONOUN
**eight**
**Son las ocho.**
It's eight o'clock.

**el ocho de agosto**
the eighth of August
**Nació el ocho de agosto.**
He was born on the eighth of
August.

**ochocientos**
(FEM **ochocientas**) ADJECTIVE,
PRONOUN
**eight hundred**

**octavo** (FEM **octava**) ADJECTIVE,
PRONOUN
**eighth**
**Vivo en el octavo.**
I live on the eighth floor.

**octubre** MASC NOUN
**October**

*Language tip*
*Months are not spelled with a
capital letter in Spanish.*

**en octubre**
in October
**Nació el tres de octubre.**
He was born on the third of
October.

**ocupado** (FEM **ocupada**)
ADJECTIVE
**1 busy**
**Estoy muy ocupado.**
I'm very busy.
**2 engaged**
**La línea está ocupada.**
The line's engaged.
**'ocupado'**
'engaged'

**¿Está ocupado este asiento?**
Is this seat taken?

**ocupar** VERB
**to take up**
**Ocupa casi todo mi tiempo.**
It takes up almost all my time.
**Los espectadores ocuparon
sus asientos.**
The spectators took their seats.
**ocuparse de algo**
to look after something
**Juan se ocupa de las ventas.**
Juan looks after sales.

**ocurrir** VERB
**to happen**
**¿Qué ocurrió?**
What happened?
**¿Qué te ocurre?**
What's the matter?
**Se nos ocurrió una idea
brillante.**
We had a brilliant idea.

**odiar** VERB
**to hate**
**Odio tener que levantarme
pronto.**
I hate having to get up early.

**oeste** MASC NOUN, ADJECTIVE
**west**
**el oeste del país**
the west of the country

*Language tip*
*The adjective **oeste** never changes
its ending, no matter what it
describes.*

**en la costa oeste**
on the west coast

la **oferta** NOUN
offer

> **estar de oferta**
> to be on special offer

la **oficina** NOUN
office
> **la oficina de turismo**
> the tourist office
> **la oficina de correos**
> the post office
> **la oficina de objetos perdidos**
> the lost property office

**ofrecer** VERB
to offer
> **Nos ofrecieron un refresco.**
> They offered us something to drink.
> **Me ofrecí para ayudar.**
> I offered to help.

el **oído** NOUN
1 ear
2 hearing

**oír** VERB
1 **to hear**
> **He oído un ruido.**
> I heard a noise.
> **¿Me oyes bien desde ahí?**
> Can you hear me all right from there?
2 **to listen to**
> **Óyeme bien.**
> Listen to me.
> **oír la radio**
> to listen to the radio
> **¡Oye!**
> Hey!
> **¡Oiga, por favor!**
> Excuse me!

**ojalá** EXCLAMATION
I hope
> **¡Ojalá Toni venga hoy!**
> I hope Toni comes today!

el **ojo** NOUN
eye
> **Tengo algo en el ojo.**
> I've got something in my eye.

> **¡Ojo! Es muy mentiroso.**
> Watch out! He's a real liar.

la **ola** NOUN
wave

**oler** VERB
to smell
> **Huele a tabaco.**
> It smells of cigarette smoke.
> **Esta salsa huele muy bien.**
> This sauce smells very good.
> **¡Qué mal huelen estos zapatos!**
> These shoes smell awful!

el **olfato** NOUN
sense of smell

la **oliva** NOUN
olive
> **el aceite de oliva**
> olive oil

la **olla** NOUN
pot
> **una olla a presión**
> a pressure cooker

el **olor** NOUN
smell
> **un olor a tabaco**
> a smell of cigarette smoke
> **¡Qué mal olor!**
> What a horrible smell!

**olvidar** VERB
1 **to forget**
> **No olvides comprar el pan.**
> Don't forget to buy the bread.
> **Se me olvidó por completo.**
> I completely forgot.
2 **to leave**
> **Olvidé las llaves en la mesa.**
> I left the keys on the table.

**once** (FEM **once**) ADJECTIVE, PRONOUN
**eleven**

> **Tengo once años.**
> I'm eleven.
> **Son las once.**
> It's eleven o'clock.
> **el once de agosto**
> the eleventh of August
> **Nació el once de agosto.**
> He was born on the eleventh of August.

la **onda** NOUN
**wave**

la **operación** (PL **operaciones**) NOUN
**operation**
> **una operación de estómago**
> a stomach operation

**operar** VERB
> **Lo tienen que operar.**
> He has to have an operation.
- **operarse**
> **to have an operation**
> **Me tengo que operar de la rodilla.**
> I have to have a knee operation.

**opinar** VERB
**to think**
> **¿Y tú qué opinas del nuevo gimnasio?**
> So what do you think about the new gym?

la **opinión** (PL **las opiniones**) NOUN
**opinion**

la **oportunidad** NOUN
**chance**
> **No tuvo la oportunidad de hacerlo.**
> He didn't have a chance to do it.

**opuesto** (FEM **opuesta**) ADJECTIVE
**opposite**

**oral** (FEM **oral**) ADJECTIVE
**oral**
> **un examen oral**
> an oral exam

**orden**

> **orden** can be a masculine or a feminine noun.

**A** MASC NOUN
**order**

> **en orden alfabético**
> in alphabetical order

**B** (PL **las órdenes**) FEM NOUN
**order**

el **ordenador** NOUN
**computer**
> **un ordenador portátil**
> a laptop

**ordenar** VERB
**1 to tidy**
> **¿Por qué no ordenas tu habitación?**
> Why don't you tidy your room?

**2 to order**
> **El policía nos ordenó que saliéramos del edificio.**
> The policeman ordered us to leave the building.

**ordinario** (FEM **ordinaria**) ADJECTIVE
**ordinary**
> **los acontecimientos ordinarios**
> ordinary events

la **oreja** NOUN
**ear**

**organizar** VERB
**to organize**
Te tienes que organizar mejor.
You need to organize yourself better.

**orgulloso** (FEM orgullosa) ADJECTIVE
**proud**

el **origen** (PL los orígenes) NOUN
**origin**

**original** (FEM original) ADJECTIVE
**original**

la **orilla** NOUN
1 **shore**
un paseo a la orilla del mar
a walk along the seashore

2 **bank**
a orillas de
on the shores of/on the banks of

*Language tip*
a orillas de *has two meanings. It can be translated as* **on the shores of** *and* **on the banks of**.

el **oro** NOUN
**gold**
un collar de oro
a gold necklace

la **orquesta** NOUN
**orchestra**
una orquesta de jazz
a jazz band

la **ortografía** NOUN
**spelling**

**os** PRONOUN
1 **you**
No os oigo.
I can't hear you.

Os he comprado un libro a cada uno.
I've bought each of you a book.
Os lo doy.
I'll give it to you.
¿Os han arreglado ya el ordenador?
Have they fixed your computer yet?

2 **yourselves**
¿Os habéis hecho daño?
Did you hurt yourselves?
Os tenéis que levantar antes de las ocho.
You have to get up before eight.
Lavaos las manos.
Wash your hands.

3 **each other**
Quiero que os pidáis perdón.
I want you to say sorry to each other.

**oscurecer** VERB
**to get dark**

la **oscuridad** NOUN
**dark**
Estaban hablando en la oscuridad.
They were talking in the dark.

**oscuro** (FEM oscura) ADJECTIVE
**dark**
una habitación muy oscura
a very dark room
azul oscuro
dark blue

a oscuras
in the dark

el **oso**
la **osa** NOUN
**bear**
un oso de peluche
a teddy bear

el **otoño** NOUN
**autumn**

**en otoño**
in autumn

**otro** (FEM **otra**)

*otro can be an adjective or a
pronoun.*

**A** ADJECTIVE
**1 another**
otro coche
another car
**¿Me das otra manzana, por
favor?**
Can I have another apple,
please?
**¿Hay alguna otra manera de
hacerlo?**
Is there any other way of doing
it?

**otra vez**
again

**2 other**
**Tengo otros planes.**
I have other plans.

**B** PRONOUN
**1 another one**
**¿Has perdido el lápiz? –
No importa, tengo otro.**
Have you lost your pencil? –
It doesn't matter I've got
another one.
**el otro/la otra**
the other one
**No quiero éste, quiero el
otro.**
I don't want this one, I want the
other one.
**2 other**
**Tengo otros planes.**
I have other plans.

la **oveja** NOUN
**sheep**

el **oxígeno** NOUN
**oxygen**

**oyendo** VERB ▷*see* **oír**
**¿Estás oyendo lo que te dice?**
Are you listening to what she's
saying?

# P p

la **paciencia** NOUN
patience

**paciente** ADJECTIVE, MASC/FEM
NOUN
patient

**pacífico** (FEM pacífica)
ADJECTIVE
peaceful

el **padre** NOUN
father
mis padres
my parents

el **padrino** NOUN
godfather
mis padrinos
my godparents

**Did you know…?**
At a wedding, the **padrino** is the
person who escorts the bride down
the aisle and gives her away, usually
her father.

la **paga** NOUN
pocket money
Me dan la paga los
domingos.
I get my pocket money on
Sundays.

**pagar** VERB
to pay for
Tengo que pagar las
entradas.
I have to pay for the tickets.
¿Dónde pago?
Where do I pay?

la **página** NOUN
page
Está en la página diez.
It's on page ten.
una página web
a Web page

el **país** (PL los **países**) NOUN
country
el País Vasco
the Basque Country

el **paisaje** NOUN
landscape
el paisaje de Castilla
the Castilian landscape

la **paja** NOUN
straw
un sombrero de paja
a straw hat

el **pájaro** NOUN
bird

la **pajita** NOUN
straw

la **pala** NOUN
1 spade
2 shovel

la **palabra** NOUN
word

**pálido** (FEM pálida) ADJECTIVE
pale
Se puso pálida.
She turned pale.

la **palma** NOUN
palm

el **palo** NOUN
stick
Le pegó con un palo.
He hit him with a stick.
una cuchara de palo
a wooden spoon

la **paloma** NOUN
pigeon

las **palomitas** NOUN
las palomitas de maíz
popcorn

el **pan** NOUN
  1 **bread**
     **pan integral**
     wholemeal bread
     **pan de molde**
     sliced bread
     **una barra de pan**
     a loaf of bread
  2 **loaf**
     **Compré dos panes.**
     I bought two loaves.

la **panadería** NOUN
  **bakery**

la **pandilla** NOUN
  **gang**

el **pánico** NOUN
  **panic**
     **en un momento de pánico**
     in a moment of panic
     **Me entró pánico.**
     I panicked.

     **Les tengo pánico a las arañas.**
     I'm terrified of spiders.

la **pantalla** NOUN
  **screen**
     **una pantalla plana**
     a flat screen

los **pantalones** NOUN
  **trousers**
     **unos pantalones**
     a pair of trousers
     **pantalones cortos**
     shorts
     **pantalones vaqueros**
     jeans

el **pañal** NOUN
  **nappy**

el **paño** NOUN
  **cloth**
     **un paño de cocina**
     a dishcloth

el **pañuelo** NOUN
  **handkerchief**

el **papa** NOUN
  **pope**
     **el Papa**
     the Pope

el **papá** (PL los **papás**) NOUN
  **dad**
     **mis papás**
     my mum and dad
     **Papá Noel**
     Father Christmas

el **papel** NOUN
  1 **paper**
     **una bolsa de papel**
     a paper bag
     **papel de aluminio**
     foil
     **papel higiénico**
     toilet paper
  2 **piece of paper**
     **Lo escribí en un papel.**
     I wrote it on a piece of paper.

la **papelera** NOUN
  1 **wastepaper bin**
  2 **litter bin**

el **paquete** NOUN
  1 **packet**
  2 **parcel**
     **Me mandaron un paquete por correo.**
     I got a parcel in the post.

**par**

*par can be a noun or an adjective.*

175

**Spanish English**

**A** MASC NOUN

**1 couple**
**un par de horas al día**
a couple of hours a day

**2 pair**
**un par de calcetines**
a pair of socks
**Abrió la ventana de par en par.**
He opened the window wide.

**B** (FEM **par**) ADJECTIVE
**un número par**
an even number

**para** PREPOSITION
**for**
**Es para ti.**
It's for you.
**Tengo muchos deberes para mañana.**
I have a lot of homework to do for tomorrow.
**¿Para qué lo quieres?**
What do you want it for?
**¿Para qué sirve?**
What's it for?
**Estoy ahorrando para comprarme una moto.**
I'm saving up to buy a motorbike.
**para que te acuerdes de mí**
so that you remember me

la **parada** NOUN
**stop**
**una parada de autobús**
a bus stop
**una parada de taxis**
a taxi rank

**parado** (FEM **parada**) ADJECTIVE
**out of work**
**Hace seis meses que está parada.**
She's been out of work for six months.
**No te quedes ahí parado.**
Don't just stand there.

el **paraguas** (PL los **paraguas**)
NOUN
**umbrella**

**parar** VERB
**to stop**
**Paramos a poner gasolina.**
We stopped to get some petrol.
**No paró de llover en toda la noche.**
It didn't stop raining all night.

■ **pararse**
**to stop**
**El reloj se ha parado.**
The clock has stopped.

el **parasol** NOUN
**umbrella**

**parecer** VERB

**1 to seem**
**Parece muy simpática.**
She seems very nice.

**2 to look**
**Esos zapatos no parecen muy cómodos.**
Those shoes don't look very comfortable.
**Parece una modelo.**
She looks like a model.
**Parece que va a llover.**
It looks as if it's going to rain.

**3 to think**
**¿Qué te pareció la película?**
What did you think of the film?

**Me parece que sí.**
I think so.
**Me parece que no.**
I don't think so.

■ **parecerse**
**to look alike**
**María y Ana se parecen mucho.**
María and Ana look very much alike.

**176**

**parecerse a**
to look like
**Te pareces mucho a tu madre.**
You look very like your mother.

**parecido** (FEM **parecida**)
ADJECTIVE
**similar**
**Tu blusa es parecida a la mía.**
Your blouse is similar to mine.

la **pared** NOUN
**wall**

la **pareja** NOUN
 1 **couple**
**Había varias parejas bailando.**
There were several couples dancing.
 2 **pair**
**En este juego hay que formar parejas.**
For this game you have to get into pairs.

el **paréntesis** (PL los **paréntesis**) NOUN
**bracket**

**entre paréntesis**
in brackets

el/la **pariente** NOUN
**relative**
**Es pariente mío.**
He's a relative of mine.

*Language tip*
*Be careful!* **pariente** *does not mean* **parent.**

el **parking** (PL los **parkings**)
NOUN
**car park**

*Language tip*
*Be careful!* **parking** *does not mean* **parking.**

el **parque** NOUN
**park**
**un parque de atracciones**
an amusement park

**un parque zoológico**
a zoo

el **párrafo** NOUN
**paragraph**

la **parrilla** NOUN
**grill**
**carne a la parrilla**
grilled meat

la **parte** NOUN
**part**
**¿De qué parte de Inglaterra eres?**
What part of England are you from?
**la mayor parte de los españoles**
most Spanish people
**la parte delantera**
the front
**la parte de atrás**
the back
**la parte de arriba**
the top
**la parte de abajo**
the bottom
**alguna parte**
somewhere
**Tengo que haberlo dejado en alguna parte.**
I must have left it somewhere.
**por todas partes**
everywhere
**¡Hay gatos por todas partes!**
There are cats everywhere!

**¿De parte de quién?**
Who's calling please?

**participar** VERB
**to take part**
> **Voy a participar en un concurso.**
> I'm going to take part in a competition.

el **participio** NOUN
**participle**

**particular** (FEM **particular**)
ADJECTIVE
**private**
> **clases particulares**
> private classes

la **partida** NOUN
**game**
> **echar una partida de cartas**
> to have a game of cards

el **partido** NOUN
1 **match**
2 **party**

**partir** VERB
1 **to cut**
2 **to crack**
3 **to break off**

**a partir de ahora**
from now on

■ **partirse**
**to break**
> **El remo se partió en dos.**
> The oar broke in two.

la **pasada** NOUN
> **¡Ese coche es una pasada!**
> This car is amazing!

**pasado**

**pasado** *can be an adjective or a noun.*

**A** (FEM **pasada**) ADJECTIVE
1 **last**
> **el verano pasado**
> last summer
2 **after**

> **Pasado el semáforo, verás un cine.**
> After the traffic lights you'll see a cinema.

**pasado mañana**
the day after tomorrow

**B** NOUN
**past**
> **en el pasado**
> in the past

el **pasajero**
la **pasajera** NOUN
**passenger**

el **pasaporte** NOUN
**passport**

**pasar** VERB
1 **to pass**
> **¿Me pasas la sal, por favor?**
> Can you pass me the salt, please?
> **Cuando termines pásasela a Isabel.**
> When you've finished pass it on to Isabel.
> **Un momento, te paso con Pedro.**
> Just a moment, I'll put you on to Pedro.
2 **to go past**
> **Pasaron varios coches.**
> Several cars went past.
> **Pasaron cinco años.**
> Five years went by.
3 **to spend**
> **Voy a pasar unos días con ella.**
> I'm going to spend a few days with her.
> **Me pasé el fin de semana estudiando.**
> I spent the weekend studying.

4 **to happen**
> **Por suerte no le pasó nada.**
> Luckily nothing happened to him.

**¿Qué pasa?**
What's the matter?
**¿Qué le pasa a Juan?**
What's the matter with Juan?
**Hemos pasado mucho frío.**
We were very cold.

**¡Pase, por favor!**
Please come in.
**pasarlo bien**
to have a good time

el **pasatiempo** NOUN
hobby

la **Pascua** NOUN
Easter

**¡Felices Pascuas!**
Happy Christmas!

**pasear** VERB
to walk
**ir a pasear**
to go for a walk

el **paseo**
NOUN
walk
Salimos a
dar un paseo.
We went out
for a walk.
**un paseo en barco**
a boat trip

**un paseo en bicicleta**
a bike ride

**dar un paseo**
to go for a walk

el **pasillo** NOUN
1 corridor
2 aisle

**pasmado** (FEM pasmada)
ADJECTIVE

amazed
**Cuando me enteré, me
quedé pasmado.**
I was amazed when I found
out.

el **paso** NOUN
1 step
**Dio un paso hacia atrás.**
He took a step backwards.
**He oído pasos.**
I heard footsteps.
2 way
**Han cerrado el paso.**
They've blocked the way.
**El banco me pilla de paso.**
The bank is on my way.
**un paso de peatones**
a pedestrian crossing
**un paso de cebra**
a zebra crossing

la **pasta** NOUN
pasta
**pasta de dientes**
toothpaste

el **pastel** NOUN
cake

la **pastelería** NOUN
cake shop

la **pastilla** NOUN
pill
**pastillas para la tos**
cough sweets

la **pata** NOUN
leg
**saltar a la pata coja**
to hop

la **patada** NOUN
**Me dio una patada.**
He kicked me.

la **patata** NOUN
potato
**un filete con patatas fritas**
steak and chips
**una bolsa de patatas fritas**
a bag of crisps

a b c d e f g h i j k l m n ñ o **p** q r s t u v w x y z

el **patín** (PL los **patines**) NOUN
1 **roller skate**
   los patines en línea
   Rollerblades
2 **skate**

el **patinaje** NOUN
1 **roller skating**
2 **ice skating**

**patinar** VERB
1 **to roller-skate**
2 **to skate**

el **patinete** NOUN
**scooter**

el **patio** NOUN
**playground**
   el patio de recreo
   the playground

el **pato** NOUN
**duck**

el **payaso**
la **payasa** NOUN
**clown**
   Deja de hacer el payaso.
   Stop clowning around.

la **paz** (PL las **paces**) NOUN
**peace**

   ¡Déjame en paz!
   Leave me alone!

el **PC** ABBREVIATION
**PC**

el **peatón** (PL los **peatones**)
NOUN
**pedestrian**

la **peca** NOUN
**freckle**

el **pecho** NOUN
**chest**

**pedalear** VERB
**to pedal**

el **pedazo** NOUN
**piece**
   un pedazo de pan

a piece of bread
   hacer pedazos
   to smash

**pedir** VERB
**to ask for**
   Le pedí dinero a mi padre.
   I asked my father for some money.
   He pedido hora para el
   médico.
   I've asked for a doctor's
   appointment.
   ¿Te puedo pedir un favor?
   Can I ask you a favour?
   pedir disculpas a alguien
   to apologize to somebody
   Le pedí disculpas.
   I apologized to him.
   Tuve que pedir dinero
   prestado.
   I had to borrow some money.

el **pegamento** NOUN
**glue**

**pegar** VERB
1 **to hit**
   Andrés me ha pegado.
   Andrés hit me.
   La pelota pegó en el árbol.
   The ball hit the tree.
2 **to stick**
   Lo puedes pegar con celo.
   You stick it on with sellotape.
   Tengo que pegar las fotos en
   el álbum.
   I have to stick the photos in the
   album.
3 **to give**
   Le pegó una bofetada.
   She gave him a slap.
   ¡Qué susto me has pegado!
   What a fright you gave me!
   Pegó un grito.
   He shouted.

la **pegatina** NOUN
**sticker**

**peinar** VERB
   peinar a alguien
   to comb somebody's hair

**Péinate antes de salir.**
Comb your hair before you
go out.

el **peine** NOUN
**comb**

**p.ej.** ABBREVIATION
(= por ejemplo)
**e.g.**

**pelar** VERB
**to peel**
**Se me está pelando la
espalda.**
My back is peeling.

la **pelea** NOUN
**1 fight**
**Hubo una pelea en la
discoteca.**
There was a fight at the disco.
**2 argument**
**Tuvo una pelea con su
novio.**
She had an argument with her
boyfriend.

**pelear** VERB
**1 to fight**
**¡Deja de pelear con tu
hermano!**
Stop fighting with your brother!
**2 to argue**
**Pelean por cualquier
tontería.**
They argue over the slightest
thing.

la **película** NOUN
**film**
**A las ocho ponen una
película.**
There's a film on at eight.

el **peligro** NOUN
**danger**

**peligroso** (FEM **peligrosa**)
ADJECTIVE
**dangerous**

**pelirrojo** (FEM **pelirroja**)
ADJECTIVE
**Es pelirrojo.**
He has red hair.

**pellizcar** VERB
**to pinch**
**Me pellizcó el brazo.**
He pinched my arm.

el **pellizco** NOUN
**pinch**
**un pellizco de sal**
a pinch of salt

el **pelo** NOUN
**hair**
**Tiene el pelo rizado.**
He has curly hair.
**No perdí el avión por un pelo.**
I only just caught the plane.
**Se me pusieron los pelos de
punta.**
It made my hair stand on end.
**Me estás tomando el pelo.**
You're pulling my leg.

la **pelota** NOUN
**ball**
**jugar a la pelota**
to play ball

**peludo** (FEM **peluda**) ADJECTIVE
**hairy**

la **peluquería** NOUN
**hairdresser's**

el **peluquero**
la **peluquera** NOUN
**hairdresser**

la **pena** NOUN
**shame**

> **Es una pena que no puedas venir.**
> It's a shame you can't come.
> **Me dio tanta pena el pobre animal.**
> I felt so sorry for the poor animal.
> **Me da pena tener que marcharme.**
> I'm so sad to have to go away.

> **Vale la pena.**
> It's worth it.
> **¡Qué pena!**
> What a shame!

el **penalty** (PL los **penaltys**)
NOUN
**penalty**

el **pendiente** NOUN
**earring**

la **pendiente** NOUN
**slope**

**pensar** VERB
**to think**

> **Piénsalo bien antes de contestar.**
> Think carefully before you answer.
> **¿Piensas que vale la pena?**
> Do you think it's worth it?
> **¿Qué piensas de Manolo?**
> What do you think of Manolo?
> **Tengo que pensarlo.**
> I'll have to think about it.

la **pensión** (PL las **pensiones**)
NOUN
**pension**

> **pensión completa**
> full board
> **media pensión**
> half board

**penúltimo**
**penúltima**

**A** ADJECTIVE
> **la penúltima estación**
> the last station but one

**B** MASC/FEM NOUN
> **Soy el penúltimo.**
> I'm second to last.

**peor** (FEM **peor**) ADJECTIVE, ADVERB
**1 worse**

> **Su situación es peor que la nuestra.**
> Their situation is worse than ours.
> **Hoy me siento peor.**
> I feel worse today.

**2 worst**

> **el peor día de mi vida**
> the worst day of my life
> **Sacó la peor nota de toda la clase.**
> He got the worst mark in the whole class.

el **pepino** NOUN
**cucumber**

> **Me importa un pepino lo que piense.**
> I couldn't care less what he thinks.

la **pepita** NOUN
**pip**

**pequeño** (FEM **pequeña**)
ADJECTIVE
**small**

> **un niño pequeño**
> a small child
> **Estos zapatos me quedan pequeños.**
> These shoes are too small for me.
> **¿Cuál prefieres? –**
> **El pequeño.**
> Which would you prefer? –
> The small one.

mi hermana **pequeña**
my younger sister

la **pera** NOUN
pear

el **perdedor**
la **perdedora** NOUN
loser
**Eres mal perdedor.**
You're a bad loser.

**perder** VERB
1 **to lose**
**He perdido el monedero.**
I've lost my purse.
**Está intentando perder peso.**
He's trying to lose weight.
**perder el conocimiento**
to lose consciousness
**Perdimos dos a cero.**
We lost two nil.
2 **to miss**
**Date prisa o perderás el tren.**
Hurry up or you'll miss the
train.
**No quiero perder esta
oportunidad.**
I don't want to miss this
opportunity.
**Tenía miedo de perderme.**
I was afraid of getting lost.

la **pérdida** NOUN
loss
**Fue una pérdida de tiempo.**
It was a waste of time.

**perdido** (FEM **perdida**)
ADJECTIVE
lost

el **perdón** NOUN
**Le pedí perdón.**
I apologized to him.
**¡Perdón!**
Sorry!/Excuse me!

**perdonar** VERB
to forgive
**¿Me perdonas?**
Will you forgive me?
**¡Perdona! ¿Tienes hora?**
Excuse me, do you have the time?
**¡Perdona! ¿Te he hecho daño?**
I'm so sorry! Did I hurt you?

la **pereza** NOUN
laziness
**¡Qué pereza tengo!**
I feel so lazy!
**Me da pereza levantarme.**
I can't be bothered to get up.

**perezoso** (FEM **perezosa**)
ADJECTIVE
lazy

**perfecto** (FEM **perfecta**)
ADJECTIVE
perfect

el **periódico**
NOUN
newspaper

el **periodo** NOUN
period
**un periodo de tres meses**
a three-month period

el **permiso** NOUN
permission
**Tengo que pedirles permiso
a mis padres.**
I have to ask my parents'
permission.

**permitir** VERB
to allow
**No nos permiten llevar
zapatillas de deporte.**
We're not allowed to wear
trainers.
**No me lo puedo permitir.**
I can't afford it.

**pero** CONJUNCTION
**but**
> **Me gustaría, pero no puedo.**
> I'd like to, but I can't.

el **perro**
la **perra** NOUN
**dog**
> **un perro callejero**
> a stray dog
> **Es una perra muy buena.**
> She's a very good dog.
> **¿Es perra o perro?**
> Is it a bitch or a dog?
> **un perro pastor**
> a sheepdog

**perseguir** VERB
**to chase**
> **Mi perro persigue a los gatos.**
> My dog chases cats.
> **Me persigue la policía.**
> The police are after me.

**persiguiendo** VERB ▷see
perseguir
> **Me venían persiguiendo por la calle.**
> They were chasing me down the street.

la **persona** NOUN
**person**
> **Es una persona encantadora.**
> He's a really nice person.
> **personas**
> people
> **Había unas diez personas en la sala.**
> There were about ten people in the hall.

el **personaje** NOUN
**character**
> **los personajes de la novela**
> the characters in the novel

**personal** (FEM **personal**)
ADJECTIVE
**personal**

**pertenecer** VERB
> **pertenecer a**
> to belong to
> **Este reloj perteneció a su abuelo.**
> This watch belonged to his grandfather.
> **Esto me pertenece a mí.**
> This belongs to me.

la **pesa** NOUN
**weight**

la **pesadilla** NOUN
**nightmare**

**pesado**
**pesada**

> **pesado** can be an adjective or a noun.

**A** ADJECTIVE
**heavy**
> **¡No seas pesado!**
> Don't be a pain!
**B** MASC/FEM NOUN
> **Mi primo es un pesado.**
> My cousin is a pain.
> **Mi hermana es una pesada.**
> My sister is a pain.

**pesar** VERB
**1 to weigh**
> **El paquete pesaba dos kilos.**
> The parcel weighed two kilos.
> **¿Cuánto pesas?**
> How much do you weigh?
> **Tengo que pesarme.**
> I must weigh myself.

Spanish English

a b c d e f g h i j k l m n ñ o p q r s t u v w x y z

**2 to be heavy**
**Esta maleta pesa mucho.**
This suitcase is very heavy.
**¡No pesa nada!**
It isn't heavy at all!
**a pesar del mal tiempo**
in spite of the bad weather
**a pesar de que la quiero**
even though I love her

la **pesca** NOUN
**fishing**

la **pescadería** NOUN
**fishmonger's**

el **pescado** NOUN
**fish**
**Quiero comprar pescado.**
I want to buy some fish.

el **pescador** NOUN
**fisherman**
**Mi tío es**
**pescador.**
My uncle is
a fisherman.

**pescar** VERB
**1 to fish**
**Los domingos íbamos a**
**pescar.**
On Sundays we used to go fishing.
**2 to catch**
**Pescamos varias truchas.**
We caught several trout.

el **peso** NOUN
**weight**
**ganar peso**
to put on weight
**Ha perdido mucho peso.**
He's lost a lot of weight.

la **pestaña** NOUN
**eyelash**

la **peste** NOUN
**stink**

**¡Qué peste hay aquí!**
There's a real stink in here!

el **pestillo** NOUN
**1 bolt**
**2 latch**

el **petardo** NOUN
**banger**

la **petición** (PL las **peticiones**)
NOUN
**request**

el **petróleo** NOUN
**oil**

el **pez** (PL los **peces**) NOUN
**fish**

**Cogimos tres peces.**
We caught three fish.
**un pez de colores**
a goldfish

el **piano** NOUN
**piano**

la **picadura** NOUN
**1 bite**
**2 sting**

**picante** (FEM **picante**) ADJECTIVE
**hot**

**picar** VERB
**1 to bite**
**Me ha picado algo.**
I've been bitten by something.
**2 to sting**
**3 to chop up**
**Luego picas un poquito de**
**jamón.**
Then you chop up a bit of ham.
**La salsa pica bastante.**
The sauce is quite hot.
**Saqué algunas cosas para**
**picar.**
I put out some nibbles.

**Me pica la espalda.**
I've got an itchy back.

el **pico** NOUN
**Eran las tres y pico.**
It was just after three.
**doscientos y pico euros**
just over two hundred euros

**pidiendo** VERB ▷ see pedir
**Siempre anda pidiendo algo.**
She's always asking for something.

el **pie** NOUN
**foot**
**Fuimos a pie.**
We went on foot.
**Estaba de pie junto a mi cama.**
She was standing next to my bed.

**ponerse de pie**
to stand up

la **piedra** NOUN
**stone**
**Nos tiraban piedras.**
They were throwing stones at us.

la **piel** NOUN
1 **skin**
**Tengo la piel grasa.**
I have greasy skin.
2 **peel**
3 **fur**
**un abrigo de pieles**
a fur coat
4 **leather**
**un bolso de piel**
a leather bag

**pienso** VERB ▷ see pensar
**Pienso que sí.**
I think so.

**pierdo** VERB ▷ see perder
**Siempre pierdo.**
I always lose.

la **pierna** NOUN
**leg**

la **pieza** NOUN
**piece**
**una pieza del rompecabezas**
a piece of the jigsaw puzzle

el **pijama** NOUN
**pyjamas**
**un pijama**
a pair of pyjamas

la **pila** NOUN
1 **battery**
**Funciona con pilas.**
It goes on batteries.
2 **pile**
**una pila de revistas**
a pile of magazines

**pillar** VERB
**to catch**
**Pillaron al ladrón.**
They caught the thief.
**Lo pillé haciendo trampa.**
I caught him cheating.

**pillo** (FEM **pilla**) ADJECTIVE
1 **crafty**
2 **naughty**

el/la **piloto** NOUN
**pilot**

la **pimienta** NOUN
**pepper**
**pimienta negra**
black pepper

el **pimiento** NOUN
**pepper**

el **pincel** NOUN
**paintbrush**

el/la **pinchadiscos** (PL los/las pinchadiscos) NOUN
**disc jockey**

**pinchar** VERB
1 **to prick**
**Me pinché con un alfiler.**
I pricked myself on a pin.
**Me pincharon en el brazo.**
They gave me an injection in the arm.

**2 to burst**
El clavo pinchó la pelota.
The nail burst the ball.
**Se me pinchó una rueda.**
I had a puncture.

el **pinchazo** NOUN
**puncture**
Tuvimos un pinchazo en la autopista.
We got a puncture on the motorway.

el **ping-pong** NOUN
**table tennis**
jugar al ping-pong
to play table tennis

el **pino** NOUN
**pine tree**

hacer el pino
to do a headstand

la **pinta** NOUN
tener buena pinta
to look good
**La paella tiene muy buena pinta.**
The paella looks delicious.
**Con esas gafas tienes pinta de maestra.**
You look like a teacher with those glasses on.

el **pintalabios** NOUN (PL los pintalabios)
**lipstick**

**pintar** VERB
**1 to paint**
Quiero pintar la habitación de azul.
I want to paint the room blue.
**2 to colour in**
Dibujó un árbol y lo pintó.
He drew a tree and coloured it in.
**Me estoy pintando las uñas.**
I'm painting my nails.

el **pintor**
la **pintora** NOUN

**painter**
Soy pintor.
I'm a painter.

la **pintura** NOUN
**1 paint**
Tengo que comprar más pintura.
I've got to buy some more paint.
**2 painting**
varias pinturas al óleo
several oil paintings

la **pinza** NOUN
**1 clothes peg**
**2 hairgrip**

la **piña** NOUN
**pineapple**

la **pipa** NOUN
**1 pipe**
Fuma en pipa.
He smokes a pipe.
**2 seed**
comer pipas
to eat sunflower seeds

*Did you know...?*

**pipas** *are a common snack which both children and adults enjoy.*

el/la **pirata** NOUN
**pirate**
un pirata informático
a hacker
un DVD pirata
a pirate DVD

la **pisada** NOUN
**1 footprint**
**2 footstep**

**pisar** VERB
**1 to walk on**
¿Se puede pisar el suelo de la cocina?
Can I walk on the kitchen floor?

**2 to tread on**
Perdona, te he pisado.
Sorry, I trod on your toe.

la **piscina** NOUN
**swimming pool**

el **piso** NOUN
**1 flat**
Vivimos en un piso céntrico.
We live in a flat in the town centre.
**2 floor**
Su oficina está en el segundo piso.
His office is on the second floor.

la **pista** NOUN
**1 clue**
¿Te doy una pista?
Shall I give you a clue?
**2 court**
la pista de aterrizaje
the runway
la pista de esquí
the ski slope
la pista de patinaje
the ice rink

la **pistola** NOUN
**pistol**

**pitar** VERB
**to blow one's whistle**
El policía nos pitó.
The policeman blew his whistle at us.

el **pito** NOUN
**whistle**

la **pizarra** NOUN
**board**
una pizarra interactiva
an interactive whiteboard

la **pizca** NOUN
**pinch**
una pizca de sal
a pinch of salt

el **plan** NOUN
**plan**

¿Qué planes tienes para este verano?
What are your plans for the summer?
Lo dije en plan de broma.
I said it as a joke.

la **plancha** NOUN
**iron**
pescado a la plancha
grilled fish

**planchar** VERB
**1 to iron**
Tengo que planchar esta camisa.
I've got to iron this shirt.

**2 to do the ironing**
¿Quieres que planche?
Do you want me to do the ironing?

el **planeta** NOUN
**planet**

el **plano** NOUN
**street plan**
en primer plano
in close-up

la **planta** NOUN
**1 plant**
Tengo que regar las plantas.
I have to water the plants.
**2 floor**
El edificio tiene tres plantas.
The building has three floors.
la planta baja
the ground floor

**plantar** VERB
**to plant**

Spanish English

a
b
c
d
e
f
g
h
i
j
k
l
m
n
ñ
o
p
q
r
s
t
u
v
w
x
y
z

el **plástico** NOUN
**plastic**
  **cubiertos de plástico**
  plastic cutlery

la **plata** NOUN
**silver**

el **plátano** NOUN
**banana**

el **plato** NOUN
1 **plate**
  **¿Me pasas un plato?**
  Could you pass me a plate?
2 **dish**
  **un plato típico de Galicia**
  a typical Galician dish
  **el plato del día**
  the dish of the day
3 **course**
  **¿Qué hay de segundo plato?**
  What's for the main course?

la **playa** NOUN
1 **beach**
  **Los niños jugaban en la playa.**
  The children were playing on the beach.
2 **seaside**
  **Prefiero la playa a la montaña.**
  I prefer the seaside to the mountains.

la **plaza** NOUN
**square**
  **la plaza del pueblo**
  the town square
  **la plaza mayor**
  the main square
  **una plaza de toros**
  a bullring

el **plazo** NOUN
**period**
  **en un plazo de diez días**
  within a period of ten days
  **El viernes se cumple el plazo.**
  Friday is the deadline.

**pleno** (FEM **plena**) ADJECTIVE
  **en pleno verano**
  in the middle of summer
  **a plena luz del día**
  in broad daylight

el **pliegue** NOUN
**fold**

el **plomo** NOUN
1 **lead**
  **gasolina sin plomo**
  unleaded petrol
2 **fuse**
  **Se han fundido los plomos.**
  The fuses have blown.

la **pluma** NOUN
1 **feather**

2 **pen**
  **una pluma estilográfica**
  a fountain pen

**plural** ADJECTIVE, MASC NOUN
**plural**

la **población** (PL las **poblaciones**) NOUN
1 **population**
2 **town**

**pobre** (FEM **pobre**) ADJECTIVE
**poor**
  **Somos pobres.**
  We're poor.
  **los pobres**
  the poor

la **pobreza** NOUN
**poverty**

**poco** (FEM **poca**)

poco can be an adjective, adverb or pronoun.

A ADJECTIVE
**not much**
  **Hay poca leche.**
  There isn't much milk.

**Tenemos muy poco tiempo.**
We haven't got much time.
**pocos**
not many
**Tiene pocos amigos.**
He hasn't got many friends.
**B** ADVERB
**Sus libros son poco conocidos aquí.**
His books are not very well known here.
**por poco**
nearly
**Por poco me caigo.**
I nearly fell.
**C** PRONOUN
**unos pocos**
a few
**Me llevé unos pocos.**
I took a few with me.
**un poco**
a bit
**¿Tienes frío? – Un poco.**
Are you cold? – A bit.
**¿Me das un poco?**
Can I have a bit?
**Tomé un poco de zumo.**
I had a bit of juice.

**dentro de poco**
soon
**hace poco**
not long ago

**poder** VERB
**1 can**
**Yo puedo ayudarte.**
I can help you.
**¿Puedo usar tu teléfono?**
Can I use your phone?
**Aquí no se puede jugar.**
You can't play here.
**¡Me lo podías haber dicho!**
You could have told me!
**¡No puede ser!**
That's impossible!
**2 to be able to**
**Creo que mañana no voy a poder ir.**
I don't think I'll be able to

come tomorrow.
**Puede que llegue mañana.**
He may arrive tomorrow.

**poderoso** (FEM **poderosa**)
ADJECTIVE
**powerful**

**podrido** (FEM **podrida**)
ADJECTIVE
**rotten**

la **poesía** NOUN
**1 poetry**
**Me gusta la poesía.**
I like poetry.
**2 poem**
**una poesía de Machado**
a poem by Machado

el/la **poeta** NOUN
**poet**

**policía**

policía can be a masculine or a feminine noun.

**A** MASC NOUN
**policeman**
**Es policía.**
He's a policeman.
**B** FEM NOUN
**1 police**
**Llamamos a la policía.**
We called the police.
**2 policewoman**
**Soy policía.**
I'm a policewoman.

el **polideportivo** NOUN
**sports centre**

la **política** NOUN
**1 politics**
**Hablaban de política.**
They were talking about politics.
**2 politician**

**político**

político can be an adjective or a noun.

**A** (FEM **política**) ADJECTIVE
**political**

**B** NOUN
**politician**
**Soy político.**
I'm a politician.

el **pollo** NOUN
**chicken**
**pollo asado**
roast chicken

el **polo** NOUN
**1 ice lolly**

**2 polo shirt**

el **polvo** NOUN
**dust**
**quitar el polvo**
to do the dusting
**quitar el polvo a algo**
to dust something
**polvos de talco**
talcum powder
**Estoy hecho polvo.**
I'm shattered.

**pondrá** VERB ▷ see **poner**
**Ya lo pondrá en su sitio cuando acabe.**
He'll put it back when he's finished.

**poner** VERB
**1 to put**
**¿Dónde pongo mis cosas?**
Where shall I put my things?
**Se puso a mi lado en clase.**
He sat down beside me in class.
**2 to put on**
**Me puse el abrigo.**
I put my coat on.
**¿Pongo música?**
Shall I put some music on?
**Pon el radiador.**
Put the heater on.
**No sé que ponerme.**
I don't know what to wear.

**¿Ponen alguna película esta noche?**
Is there a film on tonight?
**3 to set**
**La maestra nos puso un examen.**
Our teacher set us an exam.
**Puse el despertador para las siete.**
I set the alarm for seven o'clock.
**poner la mesa**
to lay the table
**¿Me pone con el Sr. García, por favor?**
Could you put me through to Mr García, please?
**¿Qué te pongo?**
What can I get you?
**Cuando se lo dije se puso muy triste.**
He was very sad when I told him.
**ponerse a hacer algo**
to start doing something
**Se puso a llorar.**
He started crying.

**pongo** VERB ▷ see **poner**
**¿Lo pongo aquí?**
Shall I put it here?

**por** PREPOSITION
**1 for**
**Lo hice por mis padres.**
I did it for my parents.
**Lo vendió por cien euros.**
He sold it for a hundred euros.
**Me castigaron por mentir.**
I was punished for lying.
**2 through**
**Pasamos por Valencia.**
We went through Valencia.
**3 by**
**Fueron apresados por la policía.**
They were captured by the police.
**Me agarró por el brazo.**
He grabbed me by the arm.

**4 along**
**Paseábamos por la playa.**
We were walking along the beach.

**5 per**
**cien kilómetros por hora**
a hundred kilometres per hour
**diez euros por persona**
ten euros per person

**por la mañana**
in the morning
**por la noche**
at night
**¿Por qué?**
Why?

la **porción** (PL las **porciones**) NOUN
**portion**

**porque** CONJUNCTION
**because**
**No fuimos porque llovía.**
We didn't go because it was raining.

la **porquería** NOUN
**Este CD es una porquería.**
This CD's rubbish.

la **portada** NOUN
1 **front page**
2 **cover**

el **portal** NOUN
1 **hallway**
**Los buzones están en el portal.**
The letterboxes are in the hallway.
**el portal de Belén**
the nativity scene

2 **portal**

**portarse** VERB
**to behave**
**Se está portando muy mal.**
He's behaving very badly.

**¡Pórtate bien!**
Behave yourself!

**portátil** (FEM **portátil**) ADJECTIVE
**portable**

el **portazo** NOUN
**Dio un portazo.**
He slammed the door.

la **portería** NOUN
**goal**
**El balón entró en la portería.**
The ball went into the goal.

el **portero**
la **portera** NOUN
1 **caretaker**
2 **goalkeeper**
**un portero automático**
an entryphone

**poseer** VERB
**to possess**

la **posibilidad** NOUN
1 **possibility**
**Es una posibilidad.**
It's a possibility.
2 **chance**
**Tendrás la posibilidad de viajar.**
You'll have the chance to travel.
**Tiene muchas posibilidades de ganar.**
He has a good chance of winning.

**posible** (FEM **posible**) ADJECTIVE
**possible**
>**Es posible.**
>It's possible.
>**Haremos todo lo posible.**
>We'll do everything we can.
>**Es posible que ganen.**
>They might win.

la **posición** (PL las **posiciones**)
NOUN
**position**
>**una posición estratégica**
>a strategic position
>**Está en primera posición.**
>He's in first place.

**positivo** (FEM **positiva**)
ADJECTIVE
**positive**
>**El test dio positivo.**
>The test was positive.

la **postal** NOUN
**postcard**

el **poste** NOUN
**post**

el **póster** (PL los **pósters**) NOUN
**poster**

el **postre** NOUN
**dessert**
>**De postre tomé un helado.**
>I had ice cream for dessert.
>**¿Qué hay de postre?**
>What's for dessert?

**potable** (FEM **potable**) ADJECTIVE
**agua potable**
>drinking water

**potente** (FEM **potente**)
ADJECTIVE
**powerful**

el **pozo** NOUN
**well**

la **práctica** NOUN
**practice**
>**No tengo mucha práctica.**
>I haven't had much practice.

**practicar** VERB
**to practise**
>**Tengo que practicar un poco más.**
>I need to practise a bit more.
>**No practico ningún deporte.**
>I don't do any sports.

**práctico** (FEM **práctica**)
ADJECTIVE
**practical**

el **precio** NOUN
**price**
>**Han subido los precios.**
>Prices have gone up.

**precioso** (FEM **preciosa**)
ADJECTIVE
**beautiful**
>**¡Es precioso!**
>It's beautiful!

**preciso** (FEM **precisa**) ADJECTIVE
1 **precise**
>**en ese preciso momento**
>at that precise moment
2 **accurate**
>**un reloj muy preciso**
>a very accurate watch
>**No es preciso que vengas.**
>There's no need for you to come.

**preferido** (FEM **preferida**)
ADJECTIVE
**favourite**

**preferir** VERB
**to prefer**
>**Prefiero un buen libro a una película.**
>I prefer a good book to a film.
>**Prefiero ir mañana.**
>I'd rather go tomorrow.

**prefiero** VERB ▷see **preferir**
>**Prefiero el verde.**
>I prefer the green one.

la **pregunta** NOUN
**question**
>**hacer una pregunta**
>to ask a question

**preguntar** VERB
**to ask**
> **Siempre me preguntas lo mismo.**
> You're always asking me the same question.
> **Me preguntó por ti.**
> He asked after you.
> **Me pregunto si estará enterado.**
> I wonder if he's heard yet.

el **premio** NOUN
**prize**
> **llevarse un premio**
> to get a prize

**preocupado**
(FEM **preocupada**) ADJECTIVE
**worried**
> **Estoy preocupado por el examen.**
> I'm worried about the exam.

**preocupar** VERB
**to worry**
> **No te preocupes.**
> Don't worry.
> **preocuparse por algo**
> to worry about something
> **Se preocupa por sus gatitos.**
> She worries about her kittens.
> **Si llego un poco tarde se preocupa.**
> If I arrive a bit late he gets worried.

**preparar** VERB
1 **to prepare**
> **No he preparado el discurso.**
> I haven't prepared my talk.
2 **to prepare for**
> **¿Te has preparado el examen?**
> Have you prepared for the exam?
3 **to cook**
> **Mi madre estaba preparando la cena.**
> My mother was cooking dinner.
> **Me estaba preparando para salir.**
> I was getting ready to go out.

el **presentador**
la **presentadora** NOUN
**presenter**

**presentar** VERB
1 **to introduce**
> **Me presentó a sus padres.**
> He introduced me to his parents.
2 **to hand in**
> **Mañana tengo que presentar un trabajo.**
> I have to hand in an essay tomorrow.

**presentarse** VERB
1 **to turn up**
> **Se presentó en mi casa sin avisar.**
> He turned up at my house without warning.
2 **to introduce oneself**
> **Me voy a presentar.**
> Let me introduce myself.
> **presentarse a un examen**
> to sit an exam

el **presente** ADJECTIVE, NOUN
**present**
> **Juan no estaba presente en la reunión.**
> Juan was not present at the meeting.
> **el presente**
> the present
> **los presentes**
> those present

> **¡Presente!**
> Here!

el **presidente**
la **presidenta** NOUN
**president**

el **preso**
la **presa**
NOUN
**prisoner**

**prestado** (FEM **prestada**)
ADJECTIVE
> **La cinta no es mía, es prestada.**
> It's not my tape, somebody lent it to me.
> **Le pedí prestada la bicicleta.**
> I asked if I could borrow his bicycle.
> **Me dejó el coche prestado.**
> He lent me his car.

**prestar** VERB
**to lend**
> **Un amigo me prestó el diccionario.**
> A friend lent me the dictionary.
> **¿Me prestas el boli?**
> Can I borrow your pen?
> **Tienes que prestar atención.**
> You must pay attention.

**presumido** (FEM **presumida**)
ADJECTIVE
**vain**

**presumir** VERB
**to show off**
> **Lleva ropa cara para presumir.**
> He wears expensive clothes just to show off.

**pretender** VERB
1 **to intend**
> **Pretendo sacar al menos un notable.**
> I intend to get at least a B.
2 **to expect**
> **¡No pretenderás que te pague la comida!**
> You're not expecting me to pay for your meal, are you?
> **¿Qué pretendes decir con eso?**
> What do you mean by that?

*Language tip*
*Be careful!* **pretender** *does not mean* **to pretend**.

**prevenir** VERB
**to prevent**

**prevenir un accidente**
to prevent an accident

**previsto** (FEM **prevista**)
ADJECTIVE
> **Tengo previsto volver mañana.**
> I plan to return tomorrow.
> **El avión tiene prevista su llegada a las dos.**
> The plane is due in at two o'clock.
> **Como estaba previsto, ganó él.**
> As expected, he won.

la **primavera** NOUN
**spring**
> **en primavera**
> in spring

**primero** (FEM **primera**)
ADJECTIVE, PRONOUN
**first**

*Language tip*
**primero** *becomes* **primer** *before a masculine singular noun.*

> **el primer día**
> the first day
> **la primera planta**
> the first floor
> **Primero vamos a comer.**
> Let's eat first.
> **en primera fila**
> in the front row
> **En primer lugar, veamos los datos.**
> Firstly, let's look at the facts.
> **Vivo en el primero.**
> I live on the first floor.
> **Fui la primera en llegar.**
> I was the first to arrive.
> **Juan es el primero de la clase.**
> Juan is top of the class.
> **El examen será a primeros de mayo.**
> The exam will be at the beginning of May.

el **primo**
la **prima** NOUN
**cousin**

la **princesa** NOUN
princess

**principal** (FEM **principal**)
ADJECTIVE
**main**
**el personaje principal**
the main character
**Lo principal es que estás mejor.**
The main thing is that you're
better.

**principalmente** ADVERB
**mainly**

el **príncipe** NOUN
prince

el/la **principiante** NOUN
beginner

el **principio** NOUN
beginning
**El principio me gustó.**
I liked the beginning.
**Al principio parecía fácil.**
It seemed easy at first.

la **prisa** NOUN
rush
**Con las prisas me olvidé el**
**paraguas.**
In the rush I forgot my umbrella.

> **¡Date prisa!**
> Hurry up!
> **Tengo prisa.**
> I'm in a hurry.

la **prisión** (PL las **prisiones**)
NOUN
prison

el **prisionero**
la **prisionera** NOUN
prisoner

los **prismáticos**
NOUN
binoculars

**privado** (FEM **privada**) ADJECTIVE
private
**un colegio privado**
a private school

**probable** (FEM **probable**)
ADJECTIVE
**likely**
**Es muy probable.**
It's very likely.
**Es probable que llegue tarde.**
He'll probably arrive late.

**probablemente** ADVERB
**probably**

el **probador** NOUN
changing room

**probar** VERB
1 **to prove**
**La policía no pudo probarlo.**
The police could not prove it.
2 **to taste**
**Probé la sopa para ver si le**
**faltaba sal.**
I tasted the soup to see if it
needed more salt.
3 **to try**
**Prueba estas patatas a ver si**
**te gustan.**
Try these potatoes and see if you
like them.
**Me probé un vestido.**
I tried on a dress.

el **problema** NOUN
problem

la **procesión** (PL las
**procesiones**) NOUN
procession

el **proceso** NOUN
process

**procurar** VERB
to try

**Procura terminarlo mañana.**
Try to finish it tomorrow.

la **producción** (PL las producciones) NOUN
production

**producir** VERB
to produce
**No producimos lo suficiente.**
We are not producing enough.
**¿Cómo se produjo el accidente?**
How did the accident happen?

el **producto** NOUN
product
**productos de limpieza**
cleaning products
**productos lácteos**
dairy products

la **profesión** (PL las profesiones) NOUN
profession

**profesional** ADJECTIVE, MASC/FEM NOUN
professional

el **profesor**
la **profesora** NOUN
teacher
**Amelia es profesora de inglés.**
Amelia is an English teacher.
**mi profesor particular**
my private tutor

**Language tip**
Be careful! **profesor** does not mean **professor**.

la **profundidad** NOUN
depth
**la profundidad de la piscina**
the depth of the pool
**Tiene dos metros de profundidad.**
It's two metres deep.

**profundo** (FEM **profunda**)
ADJECTIVE
deep

**una piscina poco profunda**
a shallow pool

el **programa** NOUN
1 programme
**un programa de televisión**
a television programme
**un programa-concurso**
a quiz show
2 program
**un programa informático**
a computer program

el **progreso** NOUN
progress
**Carmen ha hecho muchos progresos este trimestre.**
Carmen has made great progress this term.

**prohibir** VERB
to ban
**Le prohibieron la entrada en el edificio.**
He was banned from entering the building.
**terminantemente prohibido**
strictly forbidden

el **promedio** NOUN
average

la **promesa** NOUN
promise

**prometer** VERB
to promise
**Prometió llevarnos al cine.**
He promised to take us to the cinema.

la **promoción** (PL **promociones**) NOUN
promotion
**Está en promoción.**
It's on offer.

el **pronombre** NOUN
pronoun

el **pronóstico** NOUN
**el pronóstico del tiempo**
the weather forecast

197

a
b
c
d
e
f
g
h
i
j
k
l
m
n
ñ
o
**p**
q
r
s
t
u
v
w
x
y
z

**pronto** ADVERB
1 **soon**
**Los invitados llegarán pronto.**
The guests will be here soon.

2 **early**
**¿Por qué has llegado tan pronto?**
Why are you so early?
**Hoy me he levantado muy pronto.**
I got up very early this morning.

**De pronto, empezó a nevar.**
All of a sudden it began to snow.

**¡Hasta pronto!**
See you soon!

**pronunciar** VERB
**to pronounce**
**¿Cómo se pronuncia esta palabra?**
How do you pronounce this word?

la **propina** NOUN
**tip**
**¿Vamos a dejar propina?**
Shall we leave a tip?

**propio** (FEM **propia**) ADJECTIVE
1 **own**
**Tengo mi propia habitación.**
I have my own room.

2 **himself**
**Lo anunció el propio ministro.**
It was announced by the minister himself.
**un nombre propio**
a proper noun

**proponer** VERB
**to suggest**

**Nos propuso pagar la cena a medias.**
He suggested that we should go halves on the cost of the meal.
**Se ha propuesto adelgazar.**
He's decided to lose some weight.

el **propósito** NOUN
**purpose**
**¿Cuál es el propósito de su visita?**
What is the purpose of your visit?
**A propósito, ya tengo los billetes.**
By the way, I've got the tickets.
**Lo hizo a propósito.**
He did it deliberately.

**propuesto** VERB ▷ *see* proponer
**He propuesto ayudarles.**
I've suggested helping them.

el/la **protagonista** NOUN
**main character**
**El protagonista no muere en la película.**
The main character doesn't die in the film.
**El protagonista es Tom Cruise.**
Tom Cruise plays the lead.

**proteger** VERB
**to protect**
**El muro le protegió de las balas.**
The wall protected him from the bullets.
**Nos protegimos de la lluvia en la cabaña.**
We sheltered from the rain in the hut.

**protestar** VERB
1 **to protest**
**Protestaron contra la subida de la gasolina.**
They protested against the rise in petrol prices.

**2 to complain**
**Cómete la verdura y no protestes.**
Eat your vegetables and don't complain.

el **provecho** NOUN
**¡Buen provecho!**
Enjoy your meal!

**Sacó mucho provecho del curso.**
He got a lot out of the course.

**provocar** VERB
**1 to provoke**
**No quería pegarle pero me provocó.**
I didn't mean to hit him but he provoked me.
**2 to cause**
**La lluvia ha provocado graves inundaciones.**
The rain caused serious flooding.
**El incendio fue provocado.**
The fire was started deliberately.

**próximo** (FEM **próxima**)
ADJECTIVE
**next**
**Lo haremos la próxima semana.**
We'll do it next week.
**la próxima calle a la izquierda**
the next street on the left

**la próxima vez**
next time

el **proyecto** NOUN
**project**

**prueba**

**prueba** *can be a noun or part of the verb* **probar**.

**A** FEM NOUN
**1 test**

**El médico me hizo más pruebas.**
The doctor did some more tests.
**2 proof**
**Eso es la prueba de que lo hizo él.**
This is the proof that he did it.
**B** VERB ▷ *see* **probar**
**Prueba esto.**
Try this.

**pruebo** VERB ▷ *see* **probar**
**A ver que pruebo yo.**
Let me try.

la **publicidad** NOUN
**advertising**
**una campaña de publicidad**
an advertising campaign

**público**

**público** *can be an adjective or a noun.*

**A** (FEM **pública**) ADJECTIVE
**public**
**B** MASC NOUN
**1 public**
**cerrado al público**
closed to the public
**2 spectators**

**pude** VERB ▷ *see* **poder**
**No pude hacerlo.**
I couldn't do it.

el **pueblo** NOUN
**1 village**
**2 town**

**puedo** VERB ▷ *see* **poder**
**Yo puedo ayudarte.**
I can help you.

el **puente** NOUN
**bridge**

hacer puente
to make a long weekend of it

**Did you know...?**
*When a public holiday falls on a Tuesday or Thursday people often take off Monday or Friday as well to give themselves a long weekend.*

la **puerta** NOUN
**door**
**Llaman a la puerta.**
There's somebody at the door.
**Susana me acompañó a la puerta.**
Susana saw me out.

el **puerto** NOUN
**port**
**un puerto pesquero**
a fishing port
**un puerto de montaña**
a mountain pass

**pues** CONJUNCTION
1 **then**
**Tengo sueño. – ¡Pues vete a la cama!**
I'm tired. – Then go to bed!
2 **well**
**Pues, como te iba contando ...**
Well, as I was saying ...
**¡Pues no lo sabía!**
Well I didn't know!

**¡Pues claro!**
Yes, of course!

**puesto**

**puesto** *can be a noun or part of the verb* **poner**.

**A** MASC NOUN
**place**
**Acabé en primer puesto.**
I finished in first place.
**un puesto de trabajo**
a job
**B** VERB ▷*see* **poner**
**Han puesto un cartel en la ventana.**

They've put a sign in the window.

el **pulgar** NOUN
**thumb**

el **pulmón** (PL los **pulmones**) NOUN
**lung**

**pulsar** VERB
**to press**

la **pulsera** NOUN
**bracelet**
**un reloj de pulsera**
a wrist watch

el **pulso** NOUN
**pulse**
**El doctor le tomó el pulso.**
The doctor took his pulse.
**Tengo muy mal pulso.**
My hand is very unsteady.
**Echamos un pulso y le gané.**
We had an arm-wrestling match and I won.

la **punta** NOUN
1 **tip**
2 **point**
**Sácale punta al lápiz.**
Sharpen your pencil.
**la hora punta**
the rush hour

la **puntería** NOUN
**tener buena puntería**
to be a good shot

la **puntilla** NOUN
**andar de puntillas**
to tiptoe
**ponerse de puntillas**
to stand on tiptoe

el **punto** NOUN
1 **point**
**Perdieron por tres puntos.**
They lost by three points.
**Ése es un punto importante.**
That's an important point.

**2 dot**
**Mi e-mail es loveday arroba collins punto E-S (loveday@collins.es).**
My email address is loveday at collins dot E-S (loveday@collins.es).

**3 full stop**
**punto y seguido**
full stop, new sentence
**punto y aparte**
full stop, new paragraph
**punto y coma**
semi-colon
**dos puntos**
colon
**puntos suspensivos**
dot, dot, dot
**Estábamos a punto de salir cuando llamaste.**
We were about to go out when you phoned.
**Estuve a punto de perder el tren.**
I very nearly missed the train.

**a la una en punto**
at one o'clock sharp

la **puntuación** (PL las puntuaciones) NOUN
**1 punctuation**
**los signos de puntuación**
punctuation marks

**2 score**
**Recibió una alta puntuación.**
He got a high score.

el **puñado** NOUN
**handful**
**un puñado de arena**
a handful of sand

el **puñetazo** NOUN
**punch**
**un puñetazo en la cara**
a punch in the face
**Le pegó un puñetazo.**
He punched him.

el **puño** NOUN
**fist**

el **puré** (PL los **purés**) NOUN
**puré de verduras**
vegetable soup
**puré de patatas**
mashed potato

**puro** (FEM **pura**) ADJECTIVE
**pure**
**pura lana**
pure wool
**Es la pura verdad.**
That's the absolute truth.

**puse** VERB ▷ see **poner**
**Yo lo puse allí.**
I put it there.

## Q q

a
b
c
d
e
f
g
h
i
j
k
l
m
n
ñ
o
p
**q**
r
s
t
u
v
w
x
y
z

el **quad** NOUN
quad bike

**que**

*que can be a conjunction or a pronoun.*

**A** CONJUNCTION
1 **than**
Es más alto que tú.
He's taller than you.
2 **that**
José sabe que estás aquí.
José knows that you're here.
Dijo que vendría.
He said he'd come.
Dile que me llame.
Ask her to call me.
¡Que te mejores!
Get well soon!
**B** PRONOUN
1 **which**
la película que ganó el premio
the film which won the award
el juego que te compraste ayer
the game you bought yesterday
2 **who**
el hombre que vino ayer
the man who came yesterday
la chica que conocí
the girl I met

**qué** ADJECTIVE, ADVERB, PRONOUN
1 **what**
¿Qué haces?
What are you doing?
¿Qué hora es?
What's the time?
2 **which**
¿Qué película quieres ver?
Which film do you want to see?
¿Qué tal?
How are things?

No lo he hecho. ¿Y qué?
I haven't done it. So what?
¡Qué asco!
How revolting!

**quedar** VERB
1 **to be left**
Quedan dos manzanas.
There are two apples left.
Me quedan diez euros.
I've got ten euros left.
2 **to be**
Eso queda muy lejos de aquí.
That's a long way from here.
3 **to suit**
No te queda bien ese vestido.
That dress doesn't suit you.
4 **to arrange to meet**
Hemos quedado en el cine.
We've arranged to meet at the cinema.
■ **quedarse**
**to stay**
Ve tú, yo me quedo.
You go, I'll stay.
quedarse con algo
to keep something
Quédese con el cambio.
Keep the change.

la **queja** NOUN
complaint

**quejarse** VERB
**to complain**
quejarse de algo
to complain about something
Se quejan de la comida.
They complain about the food.

**quejarse de que ...**
to complain that ...
**Pablo se queja de que nadie lo escucha.**
Pablo complains that nobody listens to him.

**quemado** (FEM **quemada**)
ADJECTIVE
**burnt**
**El arroz estaba quemado.**
The rice was burnt.
**quemado por el sol**
sunburnt

**quemar** VERB
**to burn**
**He quemado la camisa con la plancha.**
I burned my shirt with the iron.
**Esta sopa quema.**
This soup's boiling hot.
- **quemarse**
**to burn oneself**
**Me quemé con una cerilla.**
I burned myself with a match.

**quepa** VERB ▷ see **caber**
**No creo que quepa ahí.**
I don't think it will fit in there.

**querer** VERB
1 **to want**
**No quiero jugar.**
I don't want to play.
**¿Quieres un bocadillo?**
Would you like a sandwich?
2 **to love**
**Te quiero.**
I love you.
3 **to mean**
**No quería hacerte daño.**
I didn't mean to hurt you.
**Lo hice sin querer.**
It was an accident.
**querer decir**
to mean
**¿Qué quieres decir?**
What do you mean?

**querido** (FEM **querida**)
ADJECTIVE
**dear**
**Querido Sr. Lobos**
Dear Mr Lobos

**querré** VERB ▷ see **querer**
**Jamás querré ir allí.**
I'll never want to go there.

el **queso** NOUN
**cheese**
**un bocadillo de queso**
a cheese sandwich

**quien** PRONOUN
**who**
**Fue Juan quien nos lo dijo.**
It was Juan who told us.
**Vi al chico con quien sales.**
I saw the boy you're going out with.

**quién** PRONOUN
**who**
**¿Quién es ésa?**
Who's that?
**¿A quién viste?**
Who did you see?
**¿De quién es ... ?**
Whose is...?
**¿De quién es este libro?**
Whose is this book?
**¿Quién es?**
Who's there?/Who's calling?

### Language tip
**¿Quién es?** has two meanings. It can be translated as **Who's there?** when there's somebody at the door and **Who's calling?** when you answer the phone.

**quiero** VERB ▷ see **querer**
**Quiero un bocadillo.**
I want a sandwich.

**quieto** (FEM **quieta**) ADJECTIVE
**still**
**¡Estáte quieto!**
Keep still!

la **química** NOUN

a b c d e f g h i j k l m n ñ o p q r s t u v w x y z

1 **chemistry**
clase de química
chemistry class
2 **chemist**
Es química.
She's a chemist.

el **químico** NOUN
**chemist**
Es químico.
He's a chemist.

**quince** (FEM **quince**) ADJECTIVE,
PRONOUN
**fifteen**
quince euros
fifteen euros
**Mi hermano tiene quince años.**
My brother's fifteen.

**el quince de enero**
the fifteenth of January
**Nació el quince de enero.**
He was born on the fifteenth of January.

**quinientos** (FEM **quinientas**)
ADJECTIVE, PRONOUN
**five hundred**

**quinto** (FEM **quinta**) ADJECTIVE,
PRONOUN
**fifth**
**Vivo en el quinto.**
I live on the fifth floor.

el **quiosco** NOUN
un quiosco de periódicos
a news stand

*Did you know...?*
*In Spain, people traditionally buy their newspapers, lottery tickets etc from the **quioscos** that are dotted around a town.*

**quise** VERB ▷see **querer**
No quise ir al cine con él.
I didn't want to go to the cinema with him.

**quisquilloso**
(FEM **quisquillosa**) ADJECTIVE
**fussy**
**No soy quisquillosa con la comida.**
I'm not fussy about what I eat.

**quitar** VERB
**to take away**
Su hermana le quitó la pelota.
His sister took the ball away from him.
**Me han quitado la cartera.**
I've had my wallet stolen.
■ **quitarse**
**to take off**
Juan se quitó la chaqueta.
Juan took his jacket off.
**¡Quítate de en medio!**
Get out of the way!

**quizás** ADVERB
**perhaps**

# R r

la **rabia** NOUN
Me da mucha rabia.
It's really annoying.

la **rabieta** NOUN
tantrum
agarrarse una rabieta
to throw a tantrum

el **rabo** NOUN
tail
Ese perro tiene un rabo muy corto.
That dog has a very short tail.

la **racha** NOUN
una racha de buen tiempo
a spell of good weather
pasar una mala racha
to go through a bad patch

el **racimo** NOUN
bunch
un racimo de uvas
a bunch of grapes

la **ración** (PL las **raciones**)
NOUN
portion
una ración de patatas fritas
a portion of chips

la **radio** NOUN
radio
El abuelo escucha la radio.
Granddad listens to the radio.
Lo oí por la radio.
I heard it on the radio.
la radio digital
digital radio

el **radio** NOUN
radius
en un radio de cincuenta kilómetros
within a fifty-kilometre radius

la **radiografía** NOUN
X-ray
Tengo que hacerme una radiografía.
I've got to have an X-ray.

la **raíz** (PL las **raíces**) NOUN
root
a raíz de
as a result of

**rallar** VERB
to grate
Primero rallas el queso.
First you grate the cheese.

la **rama** NOUN
branch

el **ramo** NOUN
bunch
un ramo de rosas
a bunch of roses

**rápidamente** ADVERB
quickly

**rápido**

rápido *can be an adjective or an adverb.*

A (FEM **rápida**) ADJECTIVE
fast
un coche muy rápido
a very fast car
Fue una visita muy rápida.
It was a very quick visit.
B ADVERB
fast
Conduces demasiado rápido.
You drive too fast.

**Lo hice tan rápido como pude.**
I did it as quickly as I could.
**¡Rápido!**
Hurry up!

la **raqueta** NOUN
1 racket

2 bat

**raro** (FEM **rara**) ADJECTIVE
strange
**Es una cosa muy rara.**
It's a very strange thing.
**¡Qué raro!**
How strange!
**Sabe un poco raro.**
It tastes a bit funny.
**Es raro que haga tan buen tiempo.**
It's unusual to have such good weather.

**rascar** VERB
to scratch
**¿Me rascas la espalda?**
Could you scratch my back for me?
■ **rascarse**
to scratch
**No deja de rascarse.**
He can't stop scratching.

el **rastro** NOUN
trail
**seguir el rastro de alguien**
to follow somebody's trail

la **rata** NOUN
rat

el **rato** NOUN
while

**después de un rato**
after a while
**hace un rato**
a little while ago
**al poco rato**
shortly after
**Pasamos un buen rato.**
We had a good time.
**Pasamos un mal rato.**
We had a dreadful time.
**en mis ratos libres**
in my free time
**Tengo para rato con los deberes.**
My homework's going to take me quite a while.

el **ratón** (PL los **ratones**) NOUN
mouse
**dos ratones blancos**
two white mice

la **raya** NOUN
1 line
**trazar una raya**
to draw a line
**pasarse de la raya**
to overstep the mark
**un jersey a rayas**
a striped jumper
2 parting
**Me hago la raya en medio.**
I have a middle parting.

**rayar** VERB
to scratch

el **rayo** NOUN
lightning

**Cayó un rayo en la iglesia.**
The church was struck by
lightning.
**los rayos del sol**
the sun's rays

la **raza** NOUN
**race**
**la raza humana**
the human race
**¿De qué raza es tu perro?**
What breed's your dog?

la **razón** (PL las **razones**) NOUN
**reason**
**la razón de su visita**
the reason for his visit
**Pedro tiene razón.**
Pedro's right.
**no tener razón**
to be wrong

la **reacción** (PL las **reacciones**)
NOUN
**reaction**

**reaccionar** VERB
**to react**

**real** (FEM **real**) ADJECTIVE
**real**
**en la vida real**
in real life
**la familia real**
the royal family

la **realidad** NOUN
**reality**
**en realidad**
actually
**Parece mayor, pero en
realidad es menor que yo.**
He looks older but actually he's
younger than I am.
**Mi sueño se hizo realidad.**
My dream came true.

**realista** (FEM **realista**)
ADJECTIVE
**realistic**

el **reality** (PL los **realitys**) NOUN
**reality show**

**realmente** ADVERB
**really**
**un problema realmente
difícil**
a really difficult problem

la **rebaja** NOUN
**discount**
**Me hizo una rebaja.**
He gave me a discount.
**las rebajas**
the sales
**Las tiendas están de rebajas.**
The sales are on.

**rebajar** VERB
**to reduce**
**Han rebajado los abrigos.**
Coats have been reduced.

la **rebanada** NOUN
**slice**
**una rebanada de pan**
a slice of bread

**rebelde** (FEM **rebelde**) ADJECTIVE
**rebellious**

**rebotar** VERB
**to bounce**
**La pelota rebotó en el poste.**
The ball bounced off the post.

el **recado** NOUN
**errand**
**Ha ido a hacer unos recados.**
She's gone to do some errands.

el **recambio** NOUN
**refill**

la **receta** NOUN
1 **recipe**
**Me dió la receta de los
raviolis.**

**Spanish English**

a b c d e f g h i j k l m n ñ o p q r s t u v w x y z

He gave me the recipe for the ravioli.

**2 prescription**

> **Language tip**
> *Ee careful!* **receta** *does not mean* receipt.

**recetar** VERB
**to prescribe**

**rechazar** VERB
**to reject**
> **Rechazaron mi sugerencia.**
> They rejected my suggestion.

**recibir** VERB
**to receive**
> **No he recibido tu carta.**
> I haven't received your letter.
> **Recibí muchos regalos.**
> I got a lot of presents.

el **recibo** NOUN
**receipt**
> **No te lo devuelven sin recibo.**
> They won't give you a refund without a receipt.

**reciclar** VERB
**to recycle**

**recién** ADVERB
**just**
> **El comedor está recién pintado.**
> The dining room has just been painted.
> **un recién nacido**
> a newborn baby

**reciente** (FEM **reciente**)
ADJECTIVE
**recent**

**recientemente** ADVERB
**recently**

el **recipiente** NOUN
**container**

la **reclamación** (PL las reclamaciones) NOUN
**complaint**
> **hacer una reclamación**
> to make a complaint

**reclamar** VERB
**to complain**
> **Fuimos a reclamar al director.**
> We went and complained to the manager.

**recoger** VERB
**to pick up**
> **Me agaché para recoger la cuchara.**
> I bent down to pick up the spoon.
> **Me recogen en la estación.**
> They pick me up at the station.
> **Recógelo todo antes de marcharte.**
> Clear up everything before you leave.
> **recoger la mesa**
> to clear the table

**recomendar** VERB
**to recommend**
> **¿Qué nos recomienda?**
> What do you recommend?

la **recompensa** NOUN
**reward**

MISSING

€1000

**reconocer** VERB
**to recognize**
> No lo reconocí con ese traje.
> I didn't recognize him in that suit.

el **récord** (PL los **récords**) NOUN
**record**
> el récord mundial de salto de altura
> the world record in the high jump
> batir el récord
> to break the record

**recordar** VERB
**to remember**
> No recuerdo dónde lo puse.
> I can't remember where I put it.
> Me recuerda a su padre.
> He reminds me of his father.

*Language tip*

Be careful! **recordar** *does not mean* **to record**.

**recorrer** VERB
**to travel around**
> Recorrimos toda Francia.
> We travelled all around France.

**recortar** VERB
**to cut out**
> Lo recorté de una revista.
> I cut it out from a magazine.

el **recreo** NOUN
**break**
> Tenemos veinte minutos de recreo.
> We have a twenty-minute break
> Salimos al recreo a las once.
> We have a break at eleven o'clock.
> a la hora del recreo
> at playtime

**rectangular** (FEM **rectangular**) ADJECTIVE
**rectangular**

el **rectángulo** NOUN
**rectangle**

**recto** (FEM **recta**) ADJECTIVE, ADVERB
**straight**
> una línea recta
> a straight line
> Siga todo recto.
> Go straight on.

el **recuadro** NOUN
**box**

**recuerdo**

**recuerdo** *can be a noun or part of the verb* **recordar**.

**A** MASC NOUN
1 **memory**
> Me trae buenos recuerdos.
> It brings back happy memories.
2 **souvenir**
> una tienda de recuerdos
> a souvenir shop
> Dale recuerdos de mi parte.
> Give him my regards.

**B** VERB ▷ *see* **recordar**
> No recuerdo su nombre.
> I can't remember his name.

**recuperar** VERB
**to get back**
> Nunca recuperó la maleta.
> She never got her suitcase back.
> recuperar fuerzas
> to get one's strength back
> Se está recuperando de la operación.
> He's recovering from the operation.

la **red** NOUN
1 **net**
> La pelota dio contra la red.
> The ball went into the net.
2 **la Red**
> **the Net**

**redondo** (FEM **redonda**)
ADJECTIVE
**round**
> una mesa redonda
> a round table

a b c d e f g h i j k l m n ñ o p q r s t u v w x y z

**Todo salió redondo.**
Everything worked out perfectly.

**reducir** VERB
**to reduce**
**Reduzca la velocidad.**
Reduce speed.

**referirse** VERB
**referirse a**
to refer to
**¿Te refieres a mí?**
Are you referring to me?
**¿A qué te refieres con eso?**
What exactly do you mean by that?

**reflejar** VERB
**to reflect**

el **refresco** NOUN
**soft drink**

el **refugio** NOUN
**refuge**
**un refugio de montaña**
a mountain refuge

la **regadera** NOUN
**watering can**

**regalar** VERB
**to give**
**¿Y si le regalamos un libro?**
What about giving him a book?
**Me lo regalaron para mi cumpleaños.**
I got it for my birthday.

el **regalo** NOUN
**present**
**un regalo de Navidad**
a Christmas present

**hacer un regalo a alguien**
to give somebody a present
**papel de regalo**
wrapping paper
**de regalo**
free
**Te dan un CD de regalo.**
They give you a free CD.

**regañar** VERB
**to tell off**
**Me regañó por llegar tarde.**
He told me off for being late.

**regar** VERB
**to water**

el **régimen** (PL los **regímenes**)
NOUN
**diet**
**estar a régimen**
to be on a diet
**ponerse a régimen**
to go on a diet

la **región** (PL las **regiones**) NOUN
**region**

la **regla** NOUN
1 **ruler**
**Trazó la línea con una regla.**
He drew the line with a ruler.
2 **rule**
**saltarse las reglas**
to break the rules

**regresar** VERB
**to go back**
**Regresó a casa por el paraguas.**
He went back home for his umbrella.
**Regresamos tarde.**
We got back late.

el **regreso** NOUN
**return**
**el viaje de regreso**
the return journey
**de regreso**
on the way back
**De regreso paramos en Ávila.**
On the way back we stopped in Ávila.

# regular

*regular can be an adjective or an adverb.*

**A** (FEM **regular**) ADJECTIVE
**regular**
**un verbo regular**
a regular verb

**B** ADVERB
**El examen me fue regular.**
My exam didn't go brilliantly.
**Me encuentro regular.**
I'm not too bad.

la **reina** NOUN
**queen**

el **Reino Unido** NOUN
**the United Kingdom**

**reír** VERB
**to laugh**
**No te rías.**
Don't laugh.
**echarse a reír**
to burst out laughing
**Siempre nos reímos con él.**
We always have a good laugh with him.
**reírse de**
to laugh at
**¿De qué te ríes?**
What are you laughing at?

la **relación** (PL las **relaciones**)
NOUN
**1 link**
**la relación entre los dos casos**
the link between the two cases
**2 relationship**
**una relación de amistad**
a friendly relationship
**con relación a**
in relation to

**relajar** VERB
**to relax**

**¡Relájate!**
Relax!

**La música clásica la relaja mucho.**
She finds classical music really relaxing.

el **relámpago** NOUN
**flash of lightning**
**Vimos un relámpago.**
We saw a flash of lightning.
**No me gustan los relámpagos.**
I don't like lightning.

**relativo** (FEM **relativa**)
ADJECTIVE
**relative**
**un pronombre relativo**
a relative pronoun
**Eso es muy relativo.**
That's all relative

**religión** (PL **religiones**) NOUN
**religion**

**rellenar** VERB
**to fill in**
**Tienes que rellenar un impreso.**
You have to fill in a form.

**relleno** (FEM **rellena**) ADJECTIVE
**stuffed**
**aceitunas rellenas**
stuffed olives

el **reloj** NOUN
**1 clock**
**El reloj de la cocina va atrasado.**
The kitchen clock's slow.
**un reloj despertador**
an alarm clock

**contra reloj**
against the clock

**2 watch**
**Se me ha parado el reloj.**
My watch has stopped.
**un reloj sumergible**
a waterproof watch

**remar** VERB
**to row**

el **remedio** NOUN
**remedy**
**un remedio contra la tos**
a cough remedy
**No tuve otro remedio.**
I had no other choice.

el **remolque** NOUN
**trailer**

**remover** VERB
**to stir**
**Remueve la leche con una cuchara.**
Stir the milk with a spoon.

**rendirse** VERB
**1 to give up**
**No sé la respuesta; me rindo.**
I don't know the answer; I give up.
**2 to surrender**
**El enemigo se rindió.**
The enemy surrendered.

el **renglón** (PL los **renglones**)
NOUN
**line**

**reñir** VERB
**1 to tell somebody off**
**Mis padres me riñeron.**
My parents told me off.
**2 to quarrel**
**Mi hermana y yo siempre estamos riñendo.**
My sister and I are always quarrelling.

**repartir** VERB
**1 to hand out**
**El profesor repartió los**

**exámenes.**
The teacher handed out the exam papers.
**2 to share out**
**Nos repartimos el dinero.**
We shared out the money between us.

**repasar** VERB
**1 to check**
**Repasa la ortografía.**
Check the spelling.
**2 to revise**
**repasar para un examen**
to revise for an exam

el **repaso** NOUN
**revision**
**Tengo que darle un repaso a los apuntes.**
I have to revise my notes.

**repente** ADVERB
**de repente**
suddenly

**repetir** VERB
**1 to repeat**
**¿Podría repetirlo, por favor?**
Could you repeat that, please?
**2 to have seconds**
**Todavía tengo hambre. Voy a repetir.**
I'm still hungry. I'm going to have seconds.

**repitiendo** VERB ▷see **repetir**
**Repitiendo las tablas se aprenden.**
Repeating your tables helps you learn them.

**representar** VERB
**1 to represent**
**Van a representar a España.**
They will be representing Spain.
**2 to put on**
**Vamos a representar una obra de teatro.**
We're going to put on a play.

**reproducirse** VERB
**to reproduce**

el **reproductor** NOUN
**player**
> un reproductor de CD
> a CD player
> un reproductor de MP3
> an MP3 player

el **reptil** NOUN
**reptile**

**repugnante** (FEM **repugnante**)
ADJECTIVE
**revolting**

la **reputación** (PL las
reputaciones) NOUN
**reputation**
> tener buena reputación
> to have a good reputation

**resbalar** VERB
**to be slippery**
> Este suelo resbala.
> This floor's slippery.
- **resbalarse**
  **to slip**
  > Me resbalé y me caí.
  > I slipped and fell down.

**rescatar** VERB
**to rescue**

el/la **reserva** NOUN
**reserve**

**reservar** VERB
**to reserve**

**resfriado**

> resfriado *can be an adjective or a*
> *noun.*

**A** (FEM **resfriada**) ADJECTIVE
**estar resfriado**
to have a cold
**Estaba muy resfriado.**
I had a bad cold.
**B** MASC NOUN
**cold**

> agarrarse un resfriado
> to catch a cold

**resfriarse** VERB
**to catch a cold**

la **residencia** NOUN
**residence**
> la residencia del primer
> ministro
> the prime minister's residence

**resistir** VERB
**1 to resist**
> No pude resistir la
> tentación.
> I couldn't resist the temptation.

**2 to stand**
> No puedo resistir
> este frío.
> I can't stand
> this cold.

**resolver** VERB
**to solve**

**respetar** VERB
**to respect**
> Hay que respetar a los
> ancianos.
> We should respect old people.

el **respeto** NOUN
**respect**
> tener respeto a alguien
> to respect somebody
> No le faltes al respeto.
> Don't be disrespectful to him.

la **respiración** NOUN
> quedarse sin respiración
> to be out of breath
> la respiración boca a boca
> the kiss of life
> Le hicieron la respiración
> boca a boca.
> They gave him the kiss of life.

**respirar** VERB
**to breathe**

**responder** VERB
1 **to answer**
   **Tienes que responder sí o no.**
   You have to answer yes or no.
2 **to reply**
   **No han respondido a mi carta.**
   They haven't replied to my letter.

la **responsabilidad** NOUN
**responsibility**

**responsable**

> **responsable** *can be an adjective or a noun.*

A (FEM **responsable**) ADJECTIVE
   **responsible**
   **No parece muy responsable.**
   She doesn't seem very responsible.
   **Todos somos responsables de nuestros actos.**
   We are all responsible for our actions.
   **hacerse responsable de algo**
   to take responsibility for something
B MASC/FEM NOUN
   **Tú eres la responsable de lo ocurrido.**
   You're responsible for what happened.
   **Juan es el responsable de la cocina.**
   Juan is in charge of the kitchen.

la **respuesta** NOUN
**answer**

la **resta** NOUN
**subtraction**

**restar** VERB
**to subtract**
   **Está aprendiendo a restar.**
   He's learning to subtract.

   **Tienes que restar tres de ocho.**
   You have to take three away from eight.

el **restaurante** NOUN
**restaurant**

el **resto** NOUN
**rest**
   **Yo haré el resto.**
   I'll do the rest.
   **Juan se comió los restos.**
   Juan ate the leftovers.

**resuelto** VERB ▷*see* **resolver**
   **El problema ha quedado resuelto.**
   The problem has been solved.

**resuelvo** VERB ▷*see* **resolver**
   **Yo te resuelvo el problema.**
   I'll solve the problem for you.

el **resultado** NOUN
**result**
   **el resultado de los exámenes**
   the exam results

**resultar** VERB
**to turn out**
   **Al final resultó que él tenía razón.**
   In the end it turned out that he was right.

el **resumen** (PL los **resúmenes**)
NOUN
**summary**
   **un resumen de las noticias**
   a news summary
   **hacer un resumen de algo**
   to summarize something

**en resumen**
in short

**retirarse** VERB
**to retire**
Mi abuelo se retira el año que viene.
My granddad will be retiring next year.

**retorcer** VERB
**to twist**
Me retorció el brazo.
He twisted my arm.

**retrasado** (FEM **retrasada**)
ADJECTIVE
1 **slow**
Este reloj va retrasado.
This clock is slow.
2 **delayed**
Todos los vuelos iban retrasados.
All flights were delayed.

**retrasar** VERB
**to postpone**
Retrasaron el viaje.
They postponed the trip.
■ **retrasarse**
**to be late**
El tren de las nueve se retrasó.
The nine o'clock train was late.

el **retraso** NOUN
Date prisa que vamos con retraso.
Hurry up, we're running late.
El autobús lleva una hora de retraso.
The bus is an hour late.

**retuerzo** VERB ▷ see **retorcer**
Suéltame o te retuerzo el brazo.
Let go of me or I'll twist your arm.

**reunir** VERB
**to gather together**
Reunió a los niños en su despacho.
She gathered the children together in her office.
Estamos reuniendo dinero para el viaje.
We're raising money for the trip.

**reunirse** VERB
1 **to get together**
En Navidad nos reunimos toda la familia.
The whole family gets together at Christmas.
2 **to meet**
Los profesores se reúnen una vez a la semana.
The teachers meet once a week.

**revelar** VERB
**to develop**
Luis revela sus propias fotos.
Luis develops his own photos.

**reventar** VERB
**to burst**
No revientes los globos.
Don't burst the balloons.

el **revés** NOUN
**al revés**
the wrong way round
Lo tienes puesto al revés.
You've got it on the wrong way round.
El dibujo está al revés.
The picture's upside down.

**reviento** VERB ▷ see **reventar**
Reviento con las ganas de decírselo.
I'm bursting to tell him.

**revisar** VERB
**to check**

**Spanish English**

a b c d e f g h i j k l m n ñ o p q **r** s t u v w x y z

216

**Revisa que esté bien la cuenta.**
Check the sum is right.

la **revista** NOUN
**magazine**
   **una revista de modas**
   a fashion magazine

## revuelto

> *revuelto can be an adjective or part of the verb* **revolver**.

**A** (FEM **revuelta**) ADJECTIVE
**in a mess**
   **Todo estaba revuelto.**
   Everything was in a mess.

   **Tengo el estómago revuelto.**
   I've got an upset stomach.
**B** VERB ▷*see* **revolver**
   **Eso me ha revuelto el estómago.**
   That's turned my stomach.

el **rey** (PL los **reyes**) NOUN
**king**
   **Los reyes visitaron China.**
   The King and Queen visited China.
   **los Reyes Magos**
   the Three Wise Men

### Did you know...?

*As part of the Christmas festivities, the Spanish celebrate* **el día de Reyes** *(Epiphany) on the 6th of January, when the Three Wise Men bring presents for children.*

**rezar** VERB
**to pray**
   **rezar por algo**
   to pray for something

## rico
rica

> *rico can be an adjective or a noun.*

**A** ADJECTIVE
**rich**
   **Son muy ricos.**
   They're very rich.
   **¡Esto está muy rico!**
   This is delicious!
**B** MASC/FEM NOUN
   **un rico**
   a rich man
   **una rica**
   a rich woman
   **los ricos**
   the rich

**ridículo** (FEM **ridícula**)
ADJECTIVE
**ridiculous**
   **¿A que suena ridículo?**
   Doesn't it sound ridiculous?
   **hacer el ridículo**
   to make a fool of oneself
   **poner a alguien en ridículo**
   to make a fool of somebody

**riendo** VERB ▷*see* **reír**
   **Se estaba riendo de mí.**
   He was laughing at me.

el **riesgo** NOUN
**risk**
   **correr riesgos**
   to take risks
   **No quiero correr ese riesgo.**
   I don't want to take that risk.

la **rifa** NOUN
**raffle**

el **rincón** (PL los **rincones**) NOUN
**corner**
   **Pon la silla en ese rincón.**
   Put the chair in that corner.

**riñendo** VERB ▷*see* **reñir**
   **La profesora le estaba riñendo.**
   The teacher was telling him off.

## río

> *río can be a noun or part of the verb* **reír**.

**A** MASC NOUN
**river**
**el río Támesis**
the River Thames
**B** VERB ▷*see* **reír**
**No me río.**
I'm not laughing.

la **risa** NOUN
**laugh**
**una risa contagiosa**
an infectious laugh
**Me da risa.**
It makes me laugh.
**Daba risa cómo lo explicaba.**
It was so funny the way he told it.
**¡Qué risa!**
What a laugh!

el **ritmo** NOUN
**rhythm**

el/la **rival** ADJECTIVE, NOUN
**rival**

**rizado** (FEM **rizada**) ADJECTIVE
**curly**
**Tiene el pelo rizado.**
He has curly hair.

**rizar** VERB
**to curl**
**Se riza el pelo.**
She curls her hair.

**robar** VERB
**to steal**
**Le robaba dinero a su amigo.**
He was stealing money from his friend.
**¡Nos han robado!**
We've been robbed!

el **robo** NOUN
**theft**
**un robo de banco**
a bank robbery

la **roca** NOUN
**rock**

la **rodaja** NOUN
**slice**

**cortar algo en rodajas**
to cut something into slices

**rodar** VERB
**to roll**
**La pelota rodó por la calle.**
The ball rolled down the street.
**rodar una película**
to shoot a film

**rodear** VERB
**to surround**
**El bosque rodea el palacio.**
The forest surrounds the palace.
**rodeado de**
surrounded by

la **rodilla** NOUN
**knee**
**ponerse de rodillas**
to kneel down

**rojo** (FEM **roja**) ADJECTIVE, MASC
NOUN
**red**
**Va vestida de rojo.**
She's wearing red.
**ponerse rojo de vergüenza**
to go red with embarrassment

el **rollo** NOUN
**roll**
**un rollo de papel higiénico**
a roll of toilet paper
**¡Qué rollo de película!**
What a boring film!
**Nos soltó el rollo de siempre.**
He gave us the same old lecture.

el **romántico** (FEM la
**romántica**) ADJECTIVE, NOUN
**romantic**

el **rompecabezas**
(FL los **rompecabezas**)
NOUN
**jigsaw**

**romper** VERB
1 **to break**
   **Me rompí el brazo.**
   I broke my arm.
2 **to tear up**
   **Rompió la carta en pedazos.**
   He tore the letter up.
   **Se me han roto los pantalones.**
   I've torn my trousers.

**roncar** VERB
**to snore**

la **ropa** NOUN
**clothes**
   **Voy a cambiarme de ropa.**
   I'm going to change my clothes.
   **la ropa interior**
   underwear
   **ropa de deporte**
   sportswear

**rosa**

> *rosa can be an adjective or a noun.*

A ADJECTIVE
**pink**

> **Language tip**
>
> *The colour **rosa** never changes its ending no matter what it describes.*

   **Llevaba unos calcetines rosa.**
   She was wearing pink socks.
B FEM NOUN
   **rose**
   **una rosa amarilla**
   a yellow rose
C MASC NOUN
   **pink**
   **Va vestida de rosa.**
   She's wearing pink.

el **roscón** (PL los **roscones**)
NOUN
**cake**

> **Did you know...?**
>
> *In Spain it's traditional to eat **el roscón de Reyes** on 6th January. Hidden in this fruit-studded ring-shaped cake is a little figure or other surprise that is meant to bring good luck to the person that finds it.*

**roto**

> *roto can be an adjective or part of the verb **romper**.*

A (FEM **rota**) ADJECTIVE
**broken**
   **un vaso roto**
   a broken glass
   **Llevas la camisa rota.**
   Your shirt is torn.
B VERB ▷ *see* **romper**
   **Se ha roto.**
   It's broken.

el **rotulador** NOUN
**felt-tip pen**

**rubio** (FEM **rubia**) ADJECTIVE
**fair**
   **Luis tiene el pelo rubio.**
   Luis has got fair hair.
   **Es rubia con los ojos azules.**
   She has got fair hair and blue eyes.
   **Quiero teñirme el pelo de rubio.**
   I want to dye my hair blond.

la **rueda** NOUN
**wheel**
   **la rueda delantera**
   the front wheel
   **Se nos pinchó la rueda.**
   We got a puncture.

**ruego** VERB ▷ *see* **rogar**
**Te lo ruego.**
I'm begging you.

el **ruido** NOUN
**noise**
> **Hacen mucho ruido.**
> They make a lot of noise.

**ruidoso** (FEM **ruidosa**) ADJECTIVE
**noisy**

la **ruina** NOUN
> **las ruinas**
> the ruins

**El castillo está en ruinas.**
The castle is in ruins.

la **ruta** NOUN
**route**

la **rutina** NOUN
**routine**
> **la rutina diaria**
> the daily routine

# S s

el **sábado** NOUN
**Saturday**

> **Language tip**
> Days are not spelled with a capital letter in Spanish.

**Jugamos los sábados.**
We play on Saturdays.

**todos los sábados**
every Saturday
**el sábado pasado**
last Saturday
**el sábado que viene**
next Saturday

la **sábana** NOUN
**sheet**

**saber** VERB
1 **to know**
**No lo sé.**
I don't know.
**Sabe mucho de ordenadores.**
He knows a lot about computers.
**No sabe nadar.**
She can't swim.
**¿Sabes inglés?**
Can you speak English?
**Se sabe la lista de memoria.**
He knows the list off by heart.
2 **to taste**
**Sabe a pescado.**
It tastes of fish.

el **sabor** NOUN
1 **taste**
**Tiene un sabor muy raro.**
It's got a very strange taste.
2 **flavour**
**¿De qué sabor lo quieres?**
What flavour do you want?

**sabré** VERB ▷see saber
**Pronto lo sabré.**
I'll soon know.

**sabroso** (FEM **sabrosa**)
ADJECTIVE
**tasty**

el **sacapuntas** (PL los sacapuntas) NOUN
**pencil sharpener**

**sacar** VERB
1 **to take out**
**Se sacó las llaves del bolsillo.**
He took the keys out of his pocket.
**sacar la basura**
to take the rubbish out
**sacar al perro a pasear**
to take the dog out for a walk
2 **to get**
**Hoy sacaremos las entradas.**
We'll get the tickets today.
**sacar buenas notas**
to get good marks
**Le sacamos una foto a Jaime.**
We took a photo of Jaime.
**sacarse las botas**
to take off one's boots

el **saco** NOUN
**sack**
**un saco de patatas**
a sack of potatoes
**un saco de dormir**
a sleeping bag

**sacudir** VERB
**to shake**
**Hay que sacudir la alfombra.**
The carpet needs shaking.

la **sal** NOUN
**salt**

la **sala** NOUN
**room**
**sala de estar**
living room

**sala de espera**
waiting room

**sala de profesores**
staffroom

**salado** (FEM **salada**) ADJECTIVE
**salty**

la **salchicha** NOUN
**sausage**

el **salchichón** (PL los salchichones) NOUN
**spiced salami sausage**

**saldré** VERB ▷see **salir**
**Saldré después de almorzar.**
I'm going out after lunch.

**salgo** VERB ▷see **salir**
**Siempre salgo los sábados por la tarde.**
I always go out on Saturday afternoons.

la **salida** NOUN
**exit**
**salida de emergencia**
emergency exit

**salir** VERB
1 **to come out**
**Salió a jugar con nosotros.**
She came out to play with us.
**Sal del coche.**
Get out of the car.
2 **to go out**
**Ha salido a la tienda.**
He's gone out to the shop.
**Mi hermana está saliendo con Juan.**
Mi sister's going out with Juan.

3 **to leave**
**El autocar sale a las ocho.**
The coach leaves at eight.
**Sale a quince euros por persona.**
It works out at fifteen euros each.
**Todo salió bien.**
Everything worked out well.

el **salón** (PL los **salones**) NOUN
**living room**

**salpicar** VERB
**to splash**

la **salsa** NOUN
**sauce**
**salsa de tomate**
tomato sauce

**saltar** VERB
**to jump**
**saltar por la ventana**
to jump out of the window
**Te has saltado una página.**
You've skipped a page.

el **salto** NOUN
**jump**
**salto de altura**
high jump
**salto de longitud**
long jump
**dar un salto**
to jump

**salud**

**salud** *can be a noun or an exclamation.*

**A** FEM NOUN
**health**
**B** EXCLAMATION
**bless you!**

**saludable** (FEM **saludable**)
ADJECTIVE
**healthy**

**saludar** VERB
**to say hello**
**Entramos a saludarla.**
We went in to say hello to her.

el **saludo** NOUN
**greeting**

**saludos**
best wishes

**salvaje** (FEM **salvaje**) ADJECTIVE
**wild**

**salvar** VERB
**to save**
**Me has salvado la vida.**
You saved my life.
**He salvado el archivo.**
I've saved the file.

la **sandalia** NOUN
**sandal**
**unas sandalias**
a pair of sandals

la **sandía** NOUN
**watermelon**

el **sándwich** (PL los
**sándwiches**) NOUN
**sandwich**
**un sándwich de queso**
a cheese sandwich

la **sangre** NOUN
**blood**

**sano** (FEM **sana**) ADJECTIVE
**healthy**

**una dieta sana**
a healthy diet

**santo**
**santa**

*santo can be a noun or an
adjective.*

**A** MASC/FEM NOUN
**saint**
**Santa Clara**
Saint Clara
**Mañana es mi santo.**
Tomorrow is my saint's day.

*Did you know...?*
*Besides birthdays, some Spaniards
also celebrate the feast day of the
saint they are named after.*

**B** ADJECTIVE
**holy**
**un lugar santo**
a holy place

el **sapo** NOUN
**toad**

la **sartén** (PL las **sartenes**) NOUN
**frying pan**

**satisfecho** (FEM **satisfecha**)
ADJECTIVE
**satisfied**

**se** PRONOUN

*Language tip*
*When **se** is an indirect object and
appears in a sentence with another
pronoun, it means **him**, **her**, **them**
or **you**, when it refers to **él**, **ella**,
**ellos**, **ellas** and **usted** or **ustedes**.*

**Pedro necesitaba la
calculadora y se la dejé.**
Pedro needed the calculator and
I lent it to him.

**Rosa no lo sabe. No se lo digas.**
Rosa doesn't know. Don't tell her.

*Language tip*

*When the object is repeated, **se** isn't translated.*

**No se lo digas a Susana.**
Don't tell Susana.
**¿Se lo has preguntado a tus padres?**
Have you asked your parents?

*Language tip*

*When **se** is reflexive, it means* **himself, herself, itself, themselves, yourself** *o* **yourselves** *when it refers to* **él, ella, ellos, ellas** *and* **usted** *or* **ustedes.**

**Se ha cortado con un cristal.**
She cut himself on a piece of broken glass.
**¿Se ha hecho usted daño?**
Have you hurt yourself?

*Language tip*

*When it refers to parts of the body or clothes you wear, **se** isn't translated.*

**Pablo se lavó los dientes.**
Pablo brushed his teeth.
**Me puse los guantes.**
I put my gloves on.

*Language tip*

*When **se** is reciprocal, it is translated by* **each other.**

**Se dieron un beso.**
They gave each other a kiss.

*Language tip*

*When **se** is impersonal it is usually translated by* **it** *or* **you.**

**Eso pasa cuando se come tan deprisa.**
That's what happens when you eat so fast.

**sé** VERB ▷*see* **saber**
**No sé.**
I don't know.

**sea** VERB ▷*see* **ser**
**siempre que sea razonable**
as long as it's reasonable

el **secador** NOUN
**hair dryer**

**secar** VERB
**to dry**
**Voy a secarme el pelo.**
I'm going to dry my hair.
▪ **secarse**
**to dry oneself**
**Sécate con la toalla.**
Dry yourself with the towel.

la **sección** NOUN
1 **section**
**Lo leí en la sección de deportes.**
I read it in the sports section.
2 **department**
**la sección de zapatos**
the shoes department

**seco** (FEM **seca**) ADJECTIVE
**dry**
**La pintura ya está seca.**
The paint's dry already.
**flores secas**
dried flowers

el **secretario**
la **secretaria** NOUN
**secretary**
**Es secretaria.**
She's a secretary.

**secreto**

**secreto** *can be a noun or an adjective.*

**A** MASC NOUN
**secret**
**Te voy a contar un secreto.**
I'm going to tell you a secret.

**en secreto**
in secret

**B** (FEM **secreta**) ADJECTIVE
**secret**
**un agente secreto**
a secret agent

la **sed** NOUN
**thirst**
**apagar la sed**
to quench one's thirst
**Tengo sed.**
I'm thirsty.

la **seda** NOUN
**silk**
**una camisa de seda**
a silk shirt

**seguido** (FEM **seguida**)
ADJECTIVE
**in a row**
**tres días seguidos**
three days in a row
**en seguida**
straight away
**Vino en seguida.**
He came straight away.
**todo seguido**
straight on
**Vaya todo seguido hasta la plaza.**
Go straight on until the square.

**seguir** VERB
1 **to carry on**
**¡Sigue, no pares!**
Carry on, don't stop!
**Siguió hablando.**
She carried on talking.
**Sigue lloviendo.**
It's still raining.
2 **to follow**
**Tú ve primero que yo te sigo.**
You go first and I'll follow you.

**seguir adelante**
to go ahead
**Siguieron adelante con su plan.**
They went ahead with their plan.

**según** PREPOSITION
1 **according to**
**Según el testigo, el coche no paró.**
According to the witness, the car didn't stop.
2 **depending on**
**Iremos o no, según esté el tiempo.**
We might go, depending on the weather.

**segundo**

> **segundo** *can be an adjective, pronoun or noun.*

**A** (FEM **segunda**) ADJECTIVE, PRONOUN
**second**
**el segundo plato**
the second course
**la segunda planta**
the second floor
**Vive en el segundo.**
He lives on the second floor.

**B** MASC NOUN
**second**
**Es un segundo nada más.**
It'll only take a second.

**seguramente** ADVERB
**probably**
**Seguramente llegarán mañana.**
They'll probably arrive tomorrow.

**seguro** (FEM **segura**) ADJECTIVE
1 **safe**
**Aquí estaremos seguros.**
We'll be safe here.
2 **sure**
**¿Estás seguro?**
Are you sure?
**seguro que**
it's bound to

Seguro que llueve.
It's bound to rain.

**seis** (FEM **seis**) ADJECTIVE,
PRONOUN
**six**
Tiene seis años.
She's six.

Son las seis.
It's six o'clock.
**el seis de enero**
the sixth of January

**seiscientos** (FEM **seiscientas**)
ADJECTIVE, PRONOUN
**six hundred**

la **selección** (PL las
**selecciones**) NOUN
**1 selection**
una selección de juguetes
a selection of toys
**2 team**
**la selección nacional**
the national team

el **sello** NOUN
**stamp**
Colecciono sellos.
I collect stamps.

la **selva** NOUN
**jungle**

el **semáforo** NOUN
**traffic lights**
El semáforo está en rojo.
The lights are red.

la **semana** NOUN
**week**
dentro de una semana
in a week's time
**una vez a la semana**
once a week

la **semilla** NOUN
**seed**

**sencillo** (FEM **sencilla**) ADJECTIVE
**simple**
Es muy sencillo.
It's really simple.

**sensible** (FEM **sensible**)
ADJECTIVE
**sensitive**
Es un chico muy sensible.
He's a very sensitive boy.

*Language tip*
*Be careful!* **sensible** *does not mean*
**sensible**.

**sentar** VERB
**1 to suit**
Ese vestido te sienta muy bien.
That dress really suits you.
**2 to agree with**
El arroz no me sentó bien.
The rice didn't agree with me.
**Le sentó mal lo que dije.**
He didn't like what I said.
■ **sentarse**
**to sit down**
Me senté en el banco.
I sat down on the bench.

el **sentido** NOUN
**sense**
Eso no tiene sentido.
That doesn't make sense.
**sentido común**
common sense
**Eso es de sentido común.**
That's common sense.
**sentido del humor**
sense of humour
**No tiene sentido del humor.**
He doesn't have a sense of
humour.

el **sentimiento** NOUN
**feeling**

**sentir** VERB
**1 to feel**
Sentí un dolor en la pierna.
I felt a pain in my leg.
**2 to be sorry**
Lo siento mucho.
I'm very sorry.

a
b
c
d
e
f
g
h
i
j
k
l
m
n
ñ
o
p
q
r
**s**
t
u
v
w
x
y
z

**Siento llegar tarde.**
I'm sorry I'm late.
■ **sentirse**
**to feel**
**No me siento bien.**
I don't feel well.

la **seña** NOUN
**sign**
**Nos comunicamos por señas.**
We communicate by signs.

la **señal** NOUN
**1 sign**
**Eso es mala señal.**
That's a bad sign.
**una señal de tráfico**
a road sign
**2 signal**
**Yo daré la señal.**
I'll give the signal.

**señalar** VERB
**to mark**
**Señálalo con un bolígrafo rojo.**
Mark it with a red pen.
**señalar con el dedo**
to point

el **señor** NOUN
**1 man**
**¿Quién es ese señor?**
Who's that man?
**¿Qué le pongo, señor?**
What would you like, sir?

### Language tip
**Señor** is a handy way of attracting somebody's attention. Look at the example.

**¡Señor! ¡Se le ha caído el billete!**
Excuse me! You've dropped your ticket!
**2 Mr**
**el señor Delgado**
Mr Delgado
**Muy señor mío: ...**
Dear Sir, ...

la **señora** NOUN
**1 lady**
**Deja pasar a esta señora.**
Let the lady past.
**¿Qué le pongo, señora?**
What would you like, madam?

### Language tip
**Señora** is a handy way of attracting somebody's attention. Look at the example.

**¡Señora! ¡Se ha dejado las gafas!**
Excuse me! You've forgotten your glasses!
**2 Mrs**
**la señora Delgado**
Mrs Delgado
**3 wife**
**Vino con su señora.**
He came with his wife.

la **señorita** NOUN
**1 young lady**
**Hay una señorita esperando.**
There's a young lady waiting.
**2 Miss**
**la señorita Delgado**
Miss Delgado

**sepa** VERB ▷see **saber**
**Que yo sepa no.**
Not as far as I know.

**separado** (FEM **separada**)
ADJECTIVE
**separate**
**Ponlos en dos montones separados.**
Put them in two separate piles.
**Sus padres están separados.**
His parents are separated.

**separar** VERB
**to separate**

**septiembre** NOUN
**September**

### Language tip
Months are not spelled with a capital letter in Spanish.

**en septiembre**
in September
**Nació el once de septiembre.**
He was born on the eleventh of
September.

**séptimo** (FEM **séptima**)
ADJECTIVE, PRONOUN
**seventh**
Vivo en el séptimo.
I live on the seventh floor.

**ser**

> **ser** *can be a verb or a noun.*

**A** VERB
**to be**
Juan es muy alto.
Juan is very tall.
Es médico.
He's a doctor.
Era de noche.
It was night.

Soy Lucía.
It's Lucía.
Son las seis y media.
It's half past six.
Éramos cinco en el coche.
There were five of us in the car.
Es de Joaquín.
It's Joaquín's.
¿De dónde eres?
Where are you from?
Soy de Barcelona
I'm from Barcelona
Es de plástico.
It's made of plastic.
a no ser que ...
unless ...

a no ser que vayamos
mañana
unless we go tomorrow
**B** MASC NOUN
**being**
Son seres humanos.
They're human beings.

**serio** (FEM **seria**) ADJECTIVE
**serious**
No te pongas tan serio.
Don't look so serious.
No hablaba en serio.
I didn't mean it.

> **en serio**
> seriously

la **serpiente** NOUN
**snake**

el **servicio** NOUN
**1 service**
**2 toilet**
Está en el servicio.
He's in the toilet.
el servicio de
caballeros
the gents'
el servicio
de señoras
the ladies'

la **servilleta** NOUN
**napkin**

**servir** VERB
**to be useful for**
Estas cajas sirven para
muchas cosas.
These boxes are useful for a lot
of things.
¿Para qué sirve esto?
What's this for?
no servir para nada
to be useless
Este mapa no sirve para
nada.
This map is useless.

a b c d e f g h i j k l m n ñ o p q r s t u v w x y z

**sesenta** (FEM **sesenta**)
ADJECTIVE, PRONOUN
**sixty**
> Tiene sesenta años.
> He's sixty.

la **seta** NOUN
**mushroom**

**setecientos**
(FEM **setecientas**) ADJECTIVE,
PRONOUN
**seven hundred**

**setenta** (FEM **setenta**)
ADJECTIVE, PRONOUN
**seventy**
> Tiene setenta años.
> He's seventy.

**sexto** (FEM **sexta**) ADJECTIVE,
PRONOUN
**sixth**
> Vivo en el sexto.
> I live on the sixth floor.

**si** CONJUNCTION
**1 if**
> Si quieres te dejo mi bici.
> I'll lend you my bike if you like.
> ¿Y si llueve?
> And what if it rains?

**2 whether**
> No sé si ir o no.
> I don't know whether to go or not.
> **si no**
> otherwise/if not

### Language tip
**si no** *has two meanings. Look at the examples.*

> Ponte crema. Si no, te quemarás.
> Put some cream on, otherwise you'll get sunburned.
> Avísame si no puedes venir.
> Let me know if you can't come.

**sí**

*sí can be an adverb or a pronoun.*

**A** ADVERB
**yes**
> ¿Quieres un helado? –
> Sí, gracias.
> Do you want an ice-cream? –
> Yes, please.
> ¿Te gusta? – Sí.
> Do you like it? – Yes, I do.
> Creo que sí.
> I think so.
> Él no quiere pero yo sí.
> He doesn't want to but I do.

**B** PRONOUN
> Solo piensa en sí misma.
> She only thinks about herself.
> Hablaban entre sí.
> They were talking among themselves.
> Es mejor aprender las cosas por sí mismo.
> It's better to learn things by yourself.

**siempre** ADVERB
**always**
> Siempre llega tarde.
> She always arrives late.

**para siempre**
forever

**siendo** VERB ▷ *see* **ser**
> Sigue siendo feliz.
> She's still happy.

**siento** VERB ▷ *see* **sentir**
> Siento pena por ellos.
> I feel sorry for them.

**Lo siento.**
I'm sorry.

la **siesta** NOUN
**nap**

**echarse la siesta**
to have a nap

**A mi abuela le gusta echarse la siesta.**
My grandma likes to have an afternoon nap.

**siete** (FEM **siete**) ADJECTIVE, PRONOUN
**seven**
**Tiene siete años.**
She's seven.

**Son las siete.**
It's seven o'clock.
**el siete de marzo**
the seventh of March
**Nació el siete de marzo.**
He was born on the seventh of March.

el **siglo** NOUN
**century**
**el siglo veintiuno**
the twenty-first century

el **significado** NOUN
**meaning**

**significar** VERB
**to mean**
**¿Qué significa 'wild'?**
What does 'wild' mean?
**No sé lo que significa.**
I don't know what it means.

el **signo** NOUN
**sign**
**Eso es signo de buena salud.**
That's a sign of good health.
**¿De qué signo eres?**
What star sign are you?
**signo de admiración**
exclamation mark
**signo de interrogación**
question mark

*Did you know…?*
Don't forget that in Spanish you also need an upside-down exclamation mark or question mark at the beginning of your phrase or question.

**siguiendo** VERB ▷see seguir
**Nos están siguiendo.**
We're being followed.

**siguiente** (FEM **siguiente**)
ADJECTIVE
**next**
**Al día siguiente visitamos Toledo.**
The next day we visited Toledo.
**¡Que pase el siguiente, por favor!**
Next please!

**silbar** VERB
**to whistle**

el **silencio** NOUN
**silence**
**guardar silencio**
to keep quiet
**En la biblioteca hay que guardar silencio.**
You need to keep quiet in the library.

**¡Silencio!**
Quiet!

la **silla** NOUN
**chair**
**silla de paseo**
pushchair
**silla de ruedas**
wheelchair

el **sillón** (PL los **sillones**) NOUN
**armchair**

el **símbolo** NOUN
**symbol**

**simpático** (FEM **simpática**)
ADJECTIVE
**nice**
**Luisa es muy simpática.**
Luisa is very nice.
**Me cae simpático.**
I think he's really nice.

*Language tip*
Be careful! **simpático** does not mean **sympathetic**.

a
b
c
d
e
f
g
h
i
j
k
l
m
n
ñ
o
p
q
r
s
t
u
v
w
x
y
z

**simple** (FEM **simple**) ADJECTIVE
**simple**

**simplemente** ADVERB
**simply**

**sin** PREPOSITION
**without**
**Salió sin abrigo.**
She went out without a coat.
**sin hacer ruido**
without making a noise

**singular** ADJECTIVE, MASC NOUN
**singular**
**en singular**
in the singular

**sino** CONJUNCTION
**but**
**No son ingleses sino galeses.**
They're not English, but Welsh.

**sintiendo** VERB ▷ see **sentir**
**¿Te sigues sintiendo mal?**
Do you still feel ill?

**siquiera** ADVERB
**ni siquiera**
not even
**Ni siquiera se despidió.**
She didn't even say goodbye.

**sirviendo** VERB ▷ see **servir**
**Estas clases no me están
sirviendo para nada.**
I'm not finding these classes at all
useful.

el **sitio** NOUN
**1 place**
**Es un sitio tranquilo.**
It's a quiet place.
**¿Me puedo cambiar de sitio?**
Can I change places?

**en cualquier sitio**
anywhere
**en algún sitio**
somewhere

**2 room**
**Hay sitio de sobra.**
There's room to spare.

**Hacedme sitio.**
Can you make some room
for me?

**un sitio web**
a website

la **situación** (PL las **situaciones**)
NOUN
**situation**

el **SMS** NOUN
**text message**
**enviar un SMS**
to send a text
**enviarle un SMS a alguien**
to text somebody

**sobra** FEM NOUN
**Tenemos comida de sobra.**
We've got more than enough
food.

**sobrar** VERB
**to be left over**
**Ha sobrado mucha comida.**
There's plenty of food left over.
**Con diez euros sobrará.**
Ten euros will be more than
enough.

**sobre**

**sobre** can be a preposition or a
noun.

**A** PREPOSITION
**1 on**
**Deja el dinero sobre la mesa.**
Leave the money on the table.
**2 about**
**información sobre hoteles**
information about hotels

**sobre las seis**
at about six o'clock
**sobre todo**
above all

**Me gustan los deportes, sobre todo la natación.**
I like sport, especially swimming.

**B** MASC NOUN
**envelope**

el **sobresaliente** NOUN
**distinction**
**He sacado sobresaliente en matemáticas.**
I got top marks in maths.

**sobrevivir** VERB
**to survive**

la **sobrina** NOUN
**niece**

el **sobrino** NOUN
**nephew**
**mis sobrinos**
my nephews/my nieces and nephews

**Language tip**
**mis sobrinos** *has two meanings. It can be translated as* **my nephews** *or* **my nephews and nieces.**

la **sociedad** NOUN
**society**

el **socio**
la **socia** NOUN
**1 partner**
**2 member**

el/la **socorrista** NOUN
**lifeguard**

el **socorro** NOUN
**help**
**pedir socorro**
to ask for help
**La mujer pedía socorro.**
The woman was asking for help.

**¡Socorro!**
Help!

el **sofá**
(PL los **sofás**)
NOUN
**sofa**

**un sofá-cama**
a sofa bed

**sois** VERB ▷ see **ser**
**¿Sois hermanas?**
Are you sisters?

el **sol** NOUN
**sun**
**estar al sol**
to be in the sun
**Hace sol.**
It's sunny.
**tomar el sol**
to sunbathe

**solamente** ADVERB
**only**

el **soldado** NOUN
**soldier**

**soler** VERB

**Language tip**
*In the present, English normally uses the adverb* **usually** *to translate* **soler.**

**Suele salir a las ocho.**
He usually leaves at eight.

**Language tip**
*In the past, English normally uses the structure* **used to** *to translate* **soler.**

**Solíamos ir a la playa.**
We used to go to the beach.

**solo**

**solo** *can be an adjective or an adverb.*

**A** (FEM **sola**) ADJECTIVE
**1 alone**
**Me quedé solo.**
I was left alone.
**¿Estás solo?**
Are you on your own?
**Lo hice yo solo.**
I did it on my own.
**Había un solo problema.**
There was just one problem.

**Spanish English**

**2 lonely**
**A veces me siento solo.**
Sometimes I feel lonely.
**B** ADVERB
**only**
**Solo cuesta diez libras.**
It only costs ten pounds.
**no solo ... sino ...**
not only ... but ...
**No solo es bonito, sino barato.**
It's not only nice, but cheap.

> **Language tip**
> You may sometimes see **sólo** written
> with an accent when it is an adverb.

**soltar** VERB
**to let go of**
**No sueltes la cuerda.**
Don't let go of the rope.
**¡Suéltame!**
Let go of me!

**soltero** (FEM **soltera**) ADJECTIVE
**single**
**Es soltero.**
He's single.

la **solución** (PL las **soluciones**)
NOUN
**solution**

**solucionar** VERB
**to solve**

la **sombra** NOUN
**1 shade**
**Prefiero quedarme a la sombra.**
I prefer to stay in the shade.
**2 shadow**
**Solo vi una sombra.**
I only saw a shadow.
**sombra de ojos**
eye shadow

el **sombrero**
NOUN
**hat**

la **sombrilla** NOUN
**sunshade**

**sonar** VERB
**1 to sound**
**Sonaba un poco triste.**
She sounded a bit sad.
**Se escribe tal y como suena.**
It's written as it sounds.
**2 to ring**
**Sonó el timbre.**
The bell rang.
**sonarse la nariz**
to blow one's nose

el **sonido** NOUN
**sound**

**sonreír** VERB
**to smile**
**Me sonrió.**
She smiled at me.

la **sonrisa** NOUN
**smile**

**soñar** VERB
**to dream**
**Ayer soñé con él.**
I dreamed about him yesterday.

la **sopa** NOUN
**soup**

**soplar** VERB
**to blow**
**¡Sopla con fuerza!**
Blow hard!
**Soplaba un viento fuerte.**
A strong wind was blowing.

**soportar** VERB
**to stand**
**No la soporto.**
I can't stand her.

> **Language tip**
> Be careful! **soportar** does not mean
> **to support**.

**sordo** (FEM **sorda**) ADJECTIVE
**deaf**

**sorprender** VERB
**to surprise**

**No me sorprende.**
It doesn't surprise me.
**Me sorprendí al verlos.**
I was surprised to see them.

la **sorpresa** NOUN
 **surprise**
 **¡Qué sorpresa!**
 What a surprise!
 **Me pilló de sorpresa.**
 It took me by surprise.

el **sorteo** NOUN
 **draw**

**soso** (FEM **sosa**) ADJECTIVE
 1 **dull**
 **Es un poco soso.**
 He's a bit dull.
 2 **bland**
 **estar soso**
 to need more salt
 **Estas patatas fritas están
 sosas.**
 These chips need more salt.

**sospechar** VERB
 **to suspect**
 **Sospechan de Luisa.**
 They suspect Luisa.

**sospechoso** (FEM **sospechosa**)
 ADJECTIVE
 **suspicious**

**sostener** VERB
 1 **to support**
 **Está sostenido por dos
 columnas.**
 It is supported by two columns.
 2 **to hold**
 **Sostenían la caja entre los dos.**
 They held the box between the
 two of them.

**soy** VERB ▷ see **ser**
 **Soy española.**
 I'm Spanish.

**Sr.** ABBREVIATION
 **Mr**

**Sra.** ABBREVIATION
 **Mrs**

**Sres.** ABBREVIATION
 **Messrs**

**Srta.** ABBREVIATION
 **Miss**

**su** ADJECTIVE
 1 **his**
 **su mochila**
 his backpack
 **Antonio y sus padres**
 Antonio and his parents
 2 **her**
 **su falda**
 her skirt
 **Marta y sus amigas**
 Marta and her friends
 3 **its**
 **un oso y su cachorro**
 a bear and its cub
 4 **their**
 **mis padres y sus amigos**
 my parents and their friends
 5 **your**
 **No olviden sus paraguas.**
 Don't forget your umbrellas.

**suave** (FEM **suave**) ADJECTIVE
 1 **gentle**
 2 **soft**

**subir** VERB
 1 **to go up**
 **Subimos las escaleras.**
 We went up the stairs.
 **La gasolina ha subido.**
 Petrol's gone up.
 2 **to come up**
 **Sube, que te voy a enseñar
 una cosa.**
 Come up, I've got something to
 show you.
 3 **to take up**
 **Ayúdame a subir las maletas.**
 Help me take the cases up.
 4 **to turn up**
 **Sube la tele, que no se oye.**
 Turn the TV up. I can't hear it.

*Language tip*

**subirse a** *has several meanings.
Look at the examples.*

a b c d e f g h i j k l m n ñ o p q r s t u v w x y z

**subirse al coche**
to get into the car

**subirse al tren**
to get on the train
**subirse a la bici**
to get onto the bike
**subirse a un árbol**
to climb a tree

## subrayar VERB
**to underline**

el **suceso** NOUN
**incident**
    **El suceso ocurrió sobre las tres de la tarde.**
    The incident happened at around three in the afternoon.

> **Language tip**
> Be careful! **suceso** does not mean **success**.

**sucio** (FEM **sucia**) ADJECTIVE
**dirty**
    **Tienes las manos sucias.**
    You've got dirty hands.

**sudamericano**
**sudamericana** ADJECTIVE, MASC/FEM NOUN
**South American**

**sudar** VERB
**to sweat**

**sudeste** MASC NOUN, ADJECTIVE
**southeast**

> **Language tip**
> The adjective **sudeste** never changes its ending, no matter what it describes.

**sudoeste** MASC NOUN, ADJECTIVE
**southwest**

> **Language tip**
> The adjective **sudoeste** never changes its ending, no matter what it describes.

el **sudor** NOUN
**sweat**

la **suegra** NOUN
**mother-in-law**

el **suegro** NOUN
**father-in-law**

los **suegros** PL NOUN
**in-laws**

el **sueldo** NOUN
**salary**

## suelo

> **suelo** can be a noun or part of the verb **soler**.

**A** MASC NOUN
**1 floor**
    **un suelo de madera**
    a wooden floor
**2 ground**
    **El suelo está mojado.**
    The ground is wet.
    **Me caí al suelo.**
    I fell over.
**B** VERB ▷ see **soler**
    **Suelo ir al cine los domingos.**
    I usually go to the cinema on Sundays.

## suelto

> **suelto** can be an adjectivo, a noun or part of the verb **soltar**.

**A** (FEM **suelta**) ADJECTIVE
**loose**
    **Tiene varias hojas sueltas.**
    Some of the pages are loose.
    **Lleva el pelo suelto.**
    She wears her hair loose.
**B** MASC NOUN
**change**
    **No llevo suelto.**
    I don't have any change on me.

**c** VERB ▷ see **soltar**
**Si lo suelto, se cae.**
If I let go, it will fall.

**sueno** VERB ▷ see **sonar**
**Sueno rara cuando hablo inglés.**
I sound strange when I speak English.

## sueño

**sueño** *can be a noun or part of the verb* **soñar.**

**A** MASC NOUN
**dream**
**Anoche tuve un mal sueño.**
I had a bad dream last night.

**Tengo sueño.**
I'm sleepy.

**B** VERB ▷ see **soñar**
**Siempre sueño.**
I always dream.

la **suerte** NOUN
**luck**
**No tiene mucha suerte.**
She doesn't have much luck.
**Tuvo suerte.**
She was lucky.
**por suerte**
luckily

**¡Buena suerte!**
Good luck!
**¡Qué suerte!**
How lucky!

**suficiente** (FEM **suficiente**)
ADJECTIVE
**enough**
**No tenía dinero suficiente.**
I didn't have enough money.

**sufrir** VERB
**to suffer**
**Sufre de artritis.**
He suffers from arthritis.

la **sugerencia** NOUN
**suggestion**
**hacer una sugerencia**
to make a suggestion

**sugerir** VERB
**to suggest**
**Sugirió que fuéramos al cine.**
She suggested going to the cinema.

**sugiero** VERB ▷ see **sugerir**
**Sugiero que lo dejemos para mañana.**
I suggest we leave it until tomorrow.

**sujetar** VERB
**to hold**
**Sujeta la escalera.**
Hold the ladder.
**Sujeta al perro, que no se escape.**
Hold on to the dog so it doesn't get away.

la **suma** NOUN
**sum**
**hacer una suma**
to do a sum

**sumar** VERB
**to add up**

**supe** VERB ▷ see **saber**
**Siempre lo supe.**
I always knew it.

el **supermercado** NOUN
**supermarket**

el/la **superviviente** NOUN
**survivor**

**suponer** VERB
**to suppose**
**Supongo que vendrá.**
I suppose she'll come.

**Supongo que sí.**
I suppose so.
**Supongo que no.**
I suppose not.

a
b
c
d
e
f
g
h
i
j
k
l
m
n
ñ
o
p
q
r
s
t
u
v
w
x
y
z

**supuesto** VERB ▷*see* **suponer**

**por supuesto**
of course

**supuse** VERB ▷*see* **suponer**
**Ya supuse que no vendría.**
I thought he wouldn't come.

**sur** MASC NOUN, ADJECTIVE
**south**
**el sur del país**
the south of the country

*Language tip*
*The adjective **sur** never changes its ending, no matter what it describes.*

**sureste** MASC NOUN, ADJECTIVE
**southeast**

*Language tip*
*The adjective **sureste** never changes its ending, no matter what it describes.*

el **surf** NOUN
**surfing**
**surf a vela**
windsurfing
**practicar el surf**
to surf

**surgir** VERB
**to come up**
**Ha surgido un problema.**
A problem has come up.

**suroeste** MASC NOUN, ADJECTIVE
**southwest**

*Language tip*
*The adjective **suroeste** never changes its ending, no matter what it describes.*

la **suscripción** (PL las suscripciones) NOUN
**subscription**

**suspender** VERB
1 **to fail**
**He suspendido Matemáticas.**
I've failed maths.
2 **to call off**
**Suspendieron el partido.**
They called off the match.

**suspirar** VERB
**to sigh**

el **sustantivo** NOUN
**noun**

el **susto** NOUN
**fright**
**dar un susto a alguien**
to give somebody a fright
**Me has dado un susto.**
You gave me a fright.

# Tt

el **tabaco** NOUN
1 tobacco
2 cigarettes

la **tabla** NOUN
plank
> **El agujero estaba cubierto con tablas.**
> The hole was covered with planks.
> **la tabla de multiplicar**
> the multiplication table
> **una tabla de cocina**
> a chopping board
> **la tabla de surf**
> the surfboard

el **tablero** NOUN
board
> **el tablero de ajedrez**
> the chessboard

la **tableta** NOUN
1 bar
2 tablet

**tachar** VERB
to cross out
> **No lo taches, bórralo.**
> Don't cross it out, rub it out.

el **taco** NOUN
1 stud
2 cube
3 swearword
> **soltar tacos**
> to swear

el **tacón** (PL los **tacones**) NOUN
heel
> **zapatos de tacón**
> high-heeled shoes

**tal** (FEM **tal**) ADJECTIVE, PRONOUN
such
> **En tales casos es mejor consultar con un médico.**
> In such cases it's better to see a doctor.
> **Lo dejé tal como estaba.**
> I left it just as it was.
> **con tal de que**
> as long as
> **con tal de que regreséis antes de las once**
> as long as you get back before eleven
> **¿Qué tal has dormido?**
> How did you sleep?

> **¿Qué tal?**
> How are things?
> **tal vez**
> perhaps

la **talla** NOUN
size
> **¿Tienen esta camisa en la talla cuatro?**
> Do you have this shirt in a size four?

el **taller** NOUN
garage
> **Tenemos el coche en el taller.**
> Our car is in the garage.

el **tamaño** NOUN
size
> **¿Qué tamaño tiene?**
> What size is it?

**también** ADVERB
also
> **Canta flamenco y también baila.**
> He sings flamenco and a so dances.
> **Tengo hambre. –**
> **Yo también.**
> I'm hungry. – So am I.
> **Yo estoy de acuerdo. –**
> **Nosotros también.**
> I agree. – So do we.

a b c d e f g h i j k l m n ñ o p q r **s t** u v w x y z

el **tambor** NOUN
drum

**tampoco** ADVERB
1 **either**
 **Yo tampoco lo compré.**
 I didn't buy it either.
2 **neither**
 **Yo no la vi. – Yo tampoco.**
 I didn't see her. – Neither did I.
 **Nunca he estado en París. –
 Yo tampoco.**
 I've never been to Paris. –
 Neither have I.

**tan** ADVERB
**so**
 **No creí que fueras a venir tan
 pronto.**
 I didn't think you'd come so soon.
 **¡No es tan difícil!**
 It's not so difficult!
 **¡Qué hombre tan amable!**
 What a kind man!
 **tan ... como ...**
 as ... as ...
 **No es tan guapa como su
 madre.**
 She's not as pretty as her
 mother.
 **Vine tan pronto como pude.**
 I came as soon as I could.
 **tan ... que ...**
 so ... that ...
 **Habla tan deprisa que no la
 entiendo.**
 She talks so fast I can't
 understand her.

**tanto**

> **tanto** *can be an adjective, adverb,
> pronoun or noun.*

**A** (FEM **tanta**) ADJECTIVE, PRONOUN
**so much**

**Ahora no bebo tanta leche.**
I don't drink so much milk now.
**¡Tengo tantos ejercicios que
hacer hoy!**
I have so many exercises to do
today!
**Vinieron tantos que no
cabían en la sala.**
So many people came that they
couldn't fit into the room.

**B** ADVERB
1 **so much**
 **Se preocupa tanto que no
 puede dormir.**
 He worries so much that he
 can't sleep.
 **¡No corras tanto!**
 Don't run so fast!
 **tanto tú como yo**
 both you and I
2 **so often**
 **Ahora no la veo tanto.**
 I don't see her so often these days.

**C** MASC NOUN
**goal**
 **Juárez marcó el segundo
 tanto.**
 Juárez scored the second goal.
 **un tanto por ciento**
 a percentage
 **Había cuarenta y tantos
 invitados.**
 There were forty-odd guests.

la **tapa** NOUN
1 **lid**
2 **top**
3 **cover**
4 **tapa**
 **Pedimos unas tapas en el
 bar.**
 We ordered some tapas in the
 bar.

**tapar** VERB
**to cover**
 **La tapé con una manta.**
 I covered her with a blanket.
 **Tapa la olla.**
 Put the lid on the pan.

**Tápate bien que hace frío.**
Wrap up well as it's cold.

el **tapón** (PL los **tapones**) NOUN
1 plug
2 top

la **taquilla** NOUN
1 box office
2 ticket office

**tardar** VERB
to be late
**Te espero a las ocho. No tardes.**
I expect you at eight. Don't be late.
**Tardaron una semana en contestar.**
They took a week to reply.
**En avión se tarda dos horas.**
The plane takes two hours.

**tarde**

**tarde** *can be a noun or an adverb.*

A FEM NOUN
1 **afternoon**
**a las tres de la tarde**
at three in the afternoon
**¡Buenas tardes!**
Good afternoon!
**por la tarde**
in the afternoon
**hoy por la tarde**
this afternoon
2 **evening**
**a las ocho de la tarde**
at eight in the evening
**¡Buenas tardes!**
Good evening!
**por la tarde**
in the evening
**hoy por la tarde**
this evening
B ADVERB
**late**
**Se está haciendo tarde.**
It's getting late.
**más tarde**
later

**Llegaré a las nueve como muy tarde.**
I'll arrive at nine at the latest.

**tarde o temprano**
sooner or later

la **tarea** NOUN
task
**Una de sus tareas es repartir la correspondencia.**
One of his tasks is to hand out the mail.
**las tareas domésticas**
housework

la **tarjeta** NOUN
card
**Me mandó una tarjeta de Navidad.**
He sent me a Christmas card.
**una tarjeta de crédito**
a credit card
**una tarjeta telefónica**
a phonecard
**una tarjeta de embarque**
a boarding card

el **tarro** NOUN
jar

la **tarta** NOUN
1 cake
**una tarta de cumpleaños**
a birthday cake

2 tart

el **tatuaje** NOUN
tattoo

el **taxi** NOUN
taxi
**Cogimos un taxi.**
We got a taxi.

el/la **taxista** NOUN
taxi driver

la **taza** NOUN
1 **cup**
**Mis padres tomaron una taza de café.**
My parents had a cup of coffee.
2 **cupful**
**una taza de arroz**
a cupful of rice
3 **bowl**

el **tazón** (PL los **tazones**) NOUN
**bowl**

**te** PRONOUN
1 **you**
**Te quiero.**
I love you.
**Te voy a dar un consejo.**
I'm going to give you some advice.
**Me gustaría comprártelo.**
I'd like to buy it for you.
2 **yourself**
**¿Te has hecho daño?**
Have you hurt yourself?
**¿Te duelen los pies?**
Do your feet hurt?
**Te tienes que poner el abrigo.**
You should put your coat on.

el **té** (PL los **tés**) NOUN
**tea**
**Me hice un té.**
I made myself a cup of tea.

*Did you know...?*
People don't tend to drink as much tea in Spain as in England and tea with lemon or herbal teas are more common than the tea we are used to in Britain.

el **teatro** NOUN
**theatre**
**Por la noche fuimos al teatro.**
At night we went to the theatre.
**una obra de teatro**
a play

el **tebeo** NOUN
**comic**

el **techo** NOUN
**ceiling**
**El techo está pintado de blanco.**
The ceiling is painted white.

la **tecla** NOUN
**key**
**pulsar una tecla**
to press a key

el **teclado** NOUN
**keyboard**

**teclear** VERB
**to type**

la **técnica** NOUN
1 **technique**
2 **technology**
3 **technician**
**Mi hermana es técnica de laboratorio.**
My sister is a laboratory technician.

**técnico**

*técnico can be a noun or an adjective.*

A MASC NOUN
1 **technician**
**Es técnico de laboratorio.**
He is a laboratory technician.
2 **repairman**
**El técnico me arregló la lavadora.**
The repairman fixed my washing machine.
B (FEM **técnica**) ADJECTIVE
**technical**

la **tecnología** NOUN
**technology**
**tecnología punta**
state-of-the-art technology

el **tejado** NOUN
**roof**

la **tela** NOUN
**fabric**

la **telaraña** NOUN
**cobweb**

la **tele** NOUN
**TV**
Estábamos viendo la tele.
We were watching TV.

el **telediario** NOUN
**news**
el telediario de las nueve
the nine o'clock news

el **teléfono** NOUN
**telephone**
No tengo teléfono.
I don't have a telephone.
Está hablando por teléfono.
He's on the phone.
un teléfono móvil
a mobile phone

la **telenovela** NOUN
**soap opera**

el **telesilla** NOUN
**chairlift**

la **televisión** (PL las televisiones) NOUN
**television**
Dieron la noticia por la televisión.
They gave the news on the television.
¿Qué ponen en la televisión esta noche?
What's on the television tonight?
la televisión por cable
cable television
la televisión digital
digital TV

el **televisor** NOUN
**television set**

el **tema** NOUN
**1 topic**
El tema de la redacción era 'Las vacaciones'.

The topic of the essay was 'The holidays'.
**2 subject**
Luego hablaremos de ese tema.
We'll talk about that subject later.

**temblar** VERB
**to tremble**
Me temblaban las manos.
My hands were trembling.
temblar de miedo
to tremble with fear
temblar de frío
to shiver

**temer** VERB
**1 to be afraid**
No temas.
Don't be afraid.

**2 to be afraid of**
Le teme al profesor.
He's afraid of the teacher.

el **temor** NOUN
**fear**
por temor a equivocarme
for fear of making a mistake

la **temperatura** NOUN
**temperature**
El médico le tomó la temperatura.
The doctor took his temperature.

la **temporada** NOUN
**season**
la temporada alta
the high season

**la temporada baja**
the low season

**el temporal** NOUN
**storm**

**temprano** ADVERB
**early**
　　**por la mañana temprano**
　　early in the morning

**ten** VERB ▷*see* **tener**
**Ten el mío si quieres.**
Have mine if you like.

**tender** VERB
**to hang out**
　　**Marta estaba tendiendo la ropa.**
　　Marta was hanging out the
　　washing.
　　**tenderse en el sofá**
　　to lie down on the sofa

**tendrá** VERB ▷*see* **tener**
**Tendrá que hacerlo.**
She'll have to do it.

**el tenedor** NOUN
**fork**

**tener** VERB
**to have**
　　**Tengo dos hermanas.**
　　I have two sisters.
　　**¿Tienes dinero?**
　　Do you have any money?
　　**Tiene el pelo rubio.**
　　He has blond hair.
　　**Mi tía va a tener un niño.**
　　My aunt's going to have a baby.
　　**¿Cuántos años tienes?**
　　How old are you?
　　**Tiene cinco metros de largo.**
　　It's five metres long.
　　**Ten cuidado.**
　　Be careful.
　　**tener que hacer algo**
　　to have to do something
　　**Tengo que llamar a mi padre.**
　　I have to call my father.

**tenga** VERB ▷*see* **tener**

**No creo que tenga tiempo.**
I don't think I'll have time.

**el tenis** NOUN
**tennis**
　　**¿Juegas al tenis?**
　　Do you play tennis?
　　**tenis de mesa**
　　table tennis

**el/la tenista** NOUN
**tennis player**

**la tentación** (PL las
tentaciones) NOUN
**temptation**

**el tentempié** (PL los
tentempiés) NOUN
**snack**

**teñir** VERB
**to dye**
　　**Se ha teñido el pelo.**
　　He's dyed his hair.

**la teoría** NOUN
**theory**
　　**En teoría es fácil.**
　　In theory it's easy.

**tercero** (FEM **tercera**) ADJECTIVE,
PRONOUN
**third**
　　**la tercera vez**
　　the third time
　　**la tercera planta**
　　the third floor
　　**Llegué el tercero.**
　　I arrived third.
　　**una tercera parte de la población**
　　a third of the population
　　**Vivo en el tercero.**
　　I live on the third floor.

***Language tip***

**tercero** *becomes* **tercer** *before a masculine singular noun.*

el **tercio** NOUN
  third

**terco** (FEM **terca**) ADJECTIVE
  obstinate

**terminar** VERB
  **1 to finish**
  He terminado el libro.
  I've finished the book.
  cuando terminó de hablar
  when he finished talking
  **2 to end**
  ¿A qué hora termina la clase?
  At what time does the class end?
  Terminaron peleándose.
  They ended up fighting.
  Se nos ha terminado la leche.
  We've run out of milk.
  He terminado con Andrés.
  I've broken up with Andrés.

la **ternera** NOUN
  veal

la **terraza** NOUN
  **1 balcony**
  **2 roof terrace**

el **terremoto** NOUN
  earthquake

el **terreno** NOUN
  **1 land**
  una granja con mucho terreno
  a farm with a lot of land
  **2 un terreno**
  a plot of land
  Mis padres han comprado un terreno.
  My parents have bought a plot of land.
  **3 field**
  terrenos plantados de naranjos
  fields planted with orange trees
  el terreno de juego
  the pitch

**terrestre** (FEM **terrestre**)
  ADJECTIVE
  land
  los animales terrestres
  land animals

**terrible** (FEM **terrible**) ADJECTIVE
  terrible
  Fue una experiencia terrible.
  It was a terrible experience.

el **texto** NOUN
  text
  un libro de texto
  a textbook

**ti** PRONOUN
  you
  una llamada para ti
  a call for you
  Solo piensas en ti mismo.
  You only think of yourself.

la **tía** NOUN
  **1 aunt**
  mi tía
  my aunt
  **2 girl**
  Es una tía majísima.
  She's a really nice girl.

**tiemblo** VERB ▷see **temblar**
  Tiemblo de miedo.
  I'm shaking with fear
  Tiemblo de frío.
  I'm shivering.

el **tiempo** NOUN
  **1 time**
  No tengo tiempo.
  I don't have time.
  ¿Qué haces en tu tiempo libre?
  What do you do in your spare time?
  Me llevó bastante tiempo.
  It took me quite a long time.
  ¿Cuánto tiempo hace que vives aquí?
  How long have you been living here?
  Hace mucho tiempo que no la veo.

I haven't seen her for a long time.
**al mismo tiempo**
at the same time
**a tiempo**
in time
**Llegamos a tiempo de ver la película.**
We got there in time to see the film.

**2 weather**
**¿Qué tiempo hace ahí?**

What's the weather like there?
**Hizo buen tiempo.**
The weather was fine.
**Hace mal tiempo.**
The weather's bad.

**3 half**
**Metieron el gol durante el segundo tiempo.**
They scored the goal during the second half.

**perder el tiempo**
to waste time

la **tienda** NOUN
**shop**
**una tienda de comestibles**
a grocer's
**una tienda de discos**
a record shop
**una tienda de campaña**
a tent

**ir de tiendas**
to go shopping

**tiendo** VERB ▷see tender
**En el verano tiendo la ropa fuera.**
I hang out the washing outside in the summer.

**tiene** VERB ▷see tener
**Tiene dos hermanas.**
She has two sisters.

la **tierra** NOUN
**land**
**la Tierra**
the Earth

**tieso** (FEM **tiesa**) ADJECTIVE
**1 stiff**
**quedarse tieso de frío**
to be frozen stiff
**2 straight**
**Ponte tiesa.**
Stand up straight.

el **tigre** NOUN
**tiger**

las **tijeras** NOUN
**scissors**
**Es más fácil cortarlo con las tijeras.**
It's easier to cut it with scissors.
**¿Tienes unas tijeras?**
Do you have a pair of scissors?

el **timbre** NOUN
**bell**
**Ya ha sonado el timbre.**
The bell has already gone.

**llamar al timbre**
to ring the bell

**tímido** (FEM **tímida**) ADJECTIVE
**shy**

el **timo** NOUN
**1 con**
**2 rip off**
**¡Vaya timo!**
What a rip-off!

la **tinta** NOUN
**ink**

el **tinto** NOUN
**red wine**

**tiñendo** VERB ▷see teñir
**Mamá se está tiñendo el pelo.**
Mum is dyeing her hair.

el **tío** NOUN
 1 **uncle**
 **mis tíos**
 my uncle and aunt
 2 **guy**
 **Es un tío muy simpático.**
 He's a really nice guy.
 **Oye, tío, me alegro de verte.**
 Hey, man, nice to see you.

el **tiovivo** NOUN
 **merry-go-round**

**típico** (FEM **típica**) ADJECTIVE
 **typical**
 **Eso es muy típico de ella.**
 That's very typical of her.

el **tipo** NOUN
 1 **kind**
 **No me gusta este tipo de fiestas.**
 I don't like this kind of party.
 **todo tipo de ...**
 all sorts of ...
 2 **figure**
 **Marisa tiene un tipo muy bonito.**
 Marisa has a lovely figure.

la **tira** NOUN
 **strip**
 **una tira de papel**
 a strip of paper
 **una tira cómica**
 a comic strip
 **Hace la tira de tiempo que no la veo.**
 I haven't seen her for ages.

**tirado** (FEM **tirada**) ADJECTIVE
 1 **dirt-cheap**
 2 **dead easy**

**tirar** VERB
 1 **to throw**
 **Tírame la pelota.**
 Throw me the ball.
 **Se tiró al suelo.**
 He threw himself to the ground.
 2 **to throw away**
 **No tires la comida.**

Don't throw away the food.
 **tirar algo a la basura**
 to throw something out
 3 **to knock down**
 **Queremos tirar esta pared.**
 We want to knock this wall down.
 **tirar de la cadena**
 to pull the chain
 **tirarse al agua**
 to plunge into the water
 **tirarse de cabeza**
 to dive in head first
 **Se tiró toda la mañana estudiando.**
 He spent the whole morning studying.

la **tirita** NOUN
 **plaster**

el **tiro** NOUN
 **shot**
 **Oímos un tiro.**
 We heard a shot
 **un tiro libre**
 a free kick

**titular** VERB
 **to call**
 **La novela se titula 'Marcianos'.**
 The novel is called 'Marcianos'.

el **título** NOUN
 **title**
 **Necesito un título para el poema.**
 I need a title for the poem.

la **tiza** NOUN
 **chalk**
 **una tiza**
 a piece of chalk

la **toalla** NOUN
 **towel**
 **una toalla de baño**
 a bath towel

a
b
c
d
e
f
g
h
i
j
k
l
m
n
ñ
o
p
q
r
s
t
u
v
w
x
y
z

el **tobillo** NOUN
**ankle**
> **Me he torcido el tobillo.**
> I've twisted my ankle.

el **tobogán** (PL los **toboganes**)
NOUN
**slide**

**tocar** VERB
1 **to touch**
> **Si lo tocas te quemarás.**
> If you touch it you'll burn yourself.
2 **to play**
> **Toca el violín.**
> He plays the violin.
3 **Te toca fregar los platos.**
> It's your turn to do the dishes.
> **Le tocó la lotería.**
> He won the lottery.

**todavía** ADVERB
1 **still**
> **¿Todavía estás en la cama?**
> Are you still in bed?
> **¡Y todavía se queja!**
> And he still complains!
2 **yet**
> **Todavía no han llegado.**
> They haven't arrived yet.
> **¿Todavía no has comido?**
> Haven't you eaten yet?
> **Todavía no.**
> Not yet.

**todo** (FEM **toda**) ADJECTIVE,
PRONOUN
1 **all**
> **todos los niños**
> all the children
> **Todos son caros.**
> They're all expensive.
> **toda la noche**
> all night
> **todos vosotros**
> all of you
2 **every**
> **todos los días**
> every day
3 **the whole**

> **Me he aprendido toda la canción.**
> I've learnt the whole song.
4 **everything**
> **Lo sabemos todo.**
> We know everything.
5 **everybody**
> **Todos estaban de acuerdo.**
> Everybody agreed.
> **Todo el mundo lo sabe.**
> Everybody knows.

**tomar** VERB
1 **to take**
> **En clase tomamos apuntes.**
> We take notes in class.
2 **to have**
> **¿Qué quieres tomar?**
> What are you going to have?
> **De postre tomé un helado.**
> I had an ice cream for dessert.
> **Toma, esto es tuyo.**
> Here, this is yours.
> **tomar el pelo a alguien**
> to pull somebody's leg
> **¡Me estás tomando el pelo!**
> You're pulling my leg!

> **tomar el sol**
> to sunbathe

el **tomate** NOUN
**tomato**

el **tono** NOUN
1 **tone**
> **Lo dijo en tono cariñoso.**
> He said it in an affectionate tone.
> **un tono de llamada**
> a ringtone
2 **shade**
> **un tono un poco más oscuro**
> a slightly darker shade

la **tontería** NOUN
**silly thing**
  **Se pelearon por una tontería.**
  They fell out over a silly thing.
  **tonterías**
  nonsense
  **¡Eso son tonterías!**
  That's nonsense!
  **¡No digas tonterías!**
  Don't talk nonsense!

**tonto**
**tonta**

**tonto** *can be an adjective or a noun.*

**A** ADJECTIVE
  **silly**
  **¡Qué error más tonto!**
  What a silly mistake!
**B** MASC/FEM NOUN
  **fool**

**hacer el tonto**
to mess around

el **tope** NOUN
  **El autobús iba a tope.**
  The bus was packed.

el **toque** NOUN
  **dar los últimos toques a algo**
  to put the finishing touches to something

**torcer** VERB
**1 to twist**
  **¡Me estás torciendo el brazo!**
  You're twisting my arm!
  **Se torció el tobillo.**
  He sprained his ankle.
**2 to turn**
  **torcer a la derecha**
  to turn right
  **torcer la esquina**
  to turn the corner

la **tormenta**
NOUN
**storm**
  **Hubo tormenta.**

There was a storm.
  **un día de tormenta**
  a stormy day

el **torneo** NOUN
**tournament**

el **tornillo** NOUN
**screw**

el **toro** NOUN
**bull**
  **los toros**
  bullfighting

**torpe** (FEM **torpe**) ADJECTIVE
**1 clumsy**
**2 dim**

la **torre** NOUN
**tower**
  **la torre de control**
  the control tower

la **torta** NOUN
**small flat cake**

la **tortilla** NOUN
**omelette**
  **una tortilla de patatas**
  a Spanish omelette

la **tos** (PL las **toses**) NOUN
**cough**
  **Tengo mucha tos.**
  I have a bad cough.

**toser** VERB
**to cough**

la **tostada** NOUN
**piece of toast**
  **¿Quieres una tostada?**
  Do you want a piece of toast?
  **tostadas**
  toast
  **Tomé café con tostadas.**
  I had coffee and toast.

**tostar** VERB
**to toast**

a
b
c
d
e
f
g
h
i
j
k
l
m
n
ñ
o
p
q
r
s
t
u
v
w
x
y
z

## total

> **total** *can be an adjective, noun or adverb.*

**A** (FEM **total**) ADJECTIVE
**total**

**B** MASC NOUN
**El total son cuarenta y cinco euros con cincuenta.**
The total is forty-five euros fifty.
**En total éramos catorce.**
There were fourteen of us altogether.

**C** ADVERB
**Total, que perdimos.**
So, anyway, we lost.

## totalmente ADVERB
**totally**
**Mario es totalmente distinto a Carlos.**
Mario is totally different from Carlos.
**Estoy totalmente de acuerdo.**
I completely agree.
**¿Estás seguro? – Totalmente.**
Are you sure? – Absolutely.

**tóxico** (FEM **tóxica**) ADJECTIVE
**toxic**

el **trabajador**
la **trabajadora** NOUN
**worker**

**trabajar** VERB
**to work**
**No trabajes tanto.**
Don't work so hard.
**¿En qué trabajas?**
What's your job?
**Trabajo de camarero.**
I work as a waiter.

el **trabajo** NOUN
**1 work**
**Tengo mucho trabajo.**
I have a lot of work.
**2 job**
**Mi hermano no encuentra trabajo.**
My brother can't find a job.

la **tradición** (PL las **tradiciones**)
NOUN
**tradition**

**tradicional** (FEM **tradicional**)
ADJECTIVE
**traditional**

la **traducción** (PL las **traducciones**) NOUN
**translation**
**Una traducción del español al inglés.**
A translation from Spanish into English.

**traducir** VERB
**to translate**
**traducir del inglés al español**
to translate from English into Spanish

**traer** VERB
**to bring**
**He traído el paraguas por si acaso.**
I've brought the umbrella just in case.

el **tráfico** NOUN
**traffic**
**un accidente de tráfico**
a road accident

**tragar** VERB
**1 to swallow**
**Traga esta pastilla.**
Swallow this tablet.
**2 to stand**
**No la trago.**
I can't stand her.

la **tragedia** NOUN
**tragedy**

el **traidor**
la **traidora** NOUN
**traitor**

**traigo** VERB ▷see **traer**
¿Te traigo un vaso de leche?
Shall I bring you a glass of milk?

el **traje** NOUN
**suit**
Pedro llevaba un traje gris.
Pedro was wearing a grey suit.
**un traje de baño**
a pair of swimming trunks/a
swimsuit

> **Language tip**
>
> **un traje de baño** *can mean either*
> **a pair of swimming trunks** *or a*
> **swimsuit**.

la **trampa** NOUN
**trap**
caer en la trampa
to fall into the trap

> **hacer trampa**
> to cheat

el **tramposo**
la **tramposa** NOUN
**cheat**

**tranquilamente** ADVERB
**calmly**
Háblale tranquilamente.
Speak to him calmly.

la **tranquilidad** NOUN
**peace and quiet**
Necesito un poco de
tranquilidad.
I need a little peace and quiet.

**tranquilizar** VERB
**to calm down**
¡Tranquilízate!
Calm down!

**tranquilo** (FEM **tranquila**)
ADJECTIVE
**1 calm**
El día del examen estaba
bastante tranquilo.
On the day of the exam I was
quite calm.
**2 peaceful**

**transgénico**
(FEM **transgénica**) ADJECTIVE
**genetically modified**

la **transmisión** (PL las
transmisiones) NOUN
**broadcast**
una transmisión en directo
a live broadcast

**transmitir** VERB
**to transmit**

**transparente**
(FEM **transparente**) ADJECTIVE
**transparent**

el **transporte** NOUN
**transport**
el transporte público
public transport

el **trapo** NOUN
**cloth**
Lo limpié con un trapo.
I wiped it with a cloth.
**un trapo de cocina**
a dishcloth
**Pásale un trapo al espejo.**
Give the mirror a wipe.
**el trapo del polvo**
the duster

**tras** PREPOSITION
**after**
Salimos corriendo tras ella.
We ran out after her.
**semana tras semana**
week after week

el **trasero** NOUN
**bum**

el **trasto** NOUN
**piece of junk**

a
b
c
d
e
f
g
h
i
j
k
l
m
n
ñ
o
p
q
r
s
t
u
v
w
x
y
z

**El desván está lleno de trastos.**
The loft is full of junk.

**trastornado**
(FEM **trastornada**) ADJECTIVE
**disturbed**

**tratar** VERB
**to treat**
> **Su padrastro los trata muy bien.**
> Their stepfather treats them really well.

> **¿De qué se trata?**
> What's it about?

el **trato** NOUN
**deal**
> **hacer un trato**
> to make a deal

> **¡Trato hecho!**
> It's a deal!

**través** PREPOSITION
**a través de**
**across/through**

*Language tip*
**a través de** *has two meanings. Look at the examples.*

> **Nadó a través del río.**
> He swam across the river.
> **Se enteraron a través de un amigo.**
> They found out through a friend.

**travieso** (FEM **traviesa**)
ADJECTIVE
**naughty**

el **trayecto** NOUN
**1 journey**
**2 way**

**¿Qué trayecto hace ese autobús?**
What way does that bus go?

el **trébol** NOUN
**clover**

**trece** (FEM **trece**) ADJECTIVE,
PRONOUN
**thirteen**
> **Tengo trece años.**
> I'm thirteen.

**el trece de enero**
the thirteenth of January
**Nació el trece de enero.**
He was born on the thirteenth of January.

**treinta** (FEM **treinta**) ADJECTIVE,
PRONOUN
**thirty**
> **Tiene treinta años.**
> He's thirty.
> **el treinta de enero**
> the thirtieth of January
> **Nació el treinta de enero.**
> He was born on the thirtieth of January.

**tremendo** (FEM **tremenda**)
ADJECTIVE
**1 terrible**
> **Tenía un tremendo dolor de cabeza.**
> I had a terrible headache.
> **Hacía un frío tremendo.**
> It was terribly cold.
**2 tremendous**
> **La película tuvo un éxito tremendo.**
> The film was a tremendous success.

el **tren** NOUN
**train**
> **viajar en tren**
> to travel by train

la **trenza** NOUN
**plait**
> **Le hice una trenza.**
> I put her hair up in a plait.

**tres** (FEM **tres**) ADJECTIVE, PRONOUN
**three**

> **Son las tres.**
> It's three o'clock.
> **el tres de febrero**
> the third of February
> **Nació el tres de febrero.**
> He was born on the third of February.

**trescientos** (FEM **trescientas**) ADJECTIVE, PRONOUN
**three hundred**

el **triángulo** NOUN
**triangle**

el **trimestre** NOUN
**term**

el **trineo** NOUN
**1 sledge**
**2 sleigh**

el **trío** NOUN
**trio**

la **tripa** NOUN
**gut**

el **triple** NOUN
> **Esta habitación es el triple de grande.**
> This room is three times as big.
> **Gastan el triple que nosotros.**
> They spend three times as much as we do.

la **tripulación** (PL las tripulaciones) NOUN
**crew**

**triste** (FEM **triste**) ADJECTIVE
**sad**
> **Me puse muy triste cuando me enteré.**
> I was very sad when I heard.

la **tristeza** NOUN
**sadness**

**triunfar** VERB
**to triumph**

el **triunfo** NOUN
**triumph**

el **trofeo** NOUN
**trophy**

la **trompeta** NCUN
**trumpet**

**tronar** VERB
**to thunder**
> **Ha estado tronando toda la noche.**
> It has been thundering all night.

**troncharse** VERB
> **Yo me tronchaba de risa.**
> I was killing myself laughing.

el **tronco** NOUN
**1 trunk**
**2 log**

el **trono** NOUN
**throne**

**tropezar** VERB
**to trip**
> **Tropecé y me caí.**
> I tripped and fell.
> **tropezar contra un árbol**
> to bump into a tree

el **tropezón** (PL los **tropezones**) NOUN
**trip**

**tropical** (FEM **tropical**) ADJECTIVE
**tropical**

**tropiece** VERB ▷ see **tropezar**
> **Mira que no tropiece con la puerta.**
> Make sure it doesn't bang into the door.

el **trozo** NOUN
**piece**
**un trozo de madera**
a piece of wood
**Dame un trocito solo.**
Just give me a small piece.

la **trucha** NOUN
**trout**

el **truco** NOUN
**trick**
**Ya le he cogido el truco.**
I've got the hang of it already.

**truena** VERB ▷see **tronar**
**Truena.**
It's thundering.

el **trueno** NOUN
**Oímos un trueno.**
We heard a clap of thunder.
**Me despertaron los truenos.**
The thunder woke me up.

**tu** ADJECTIVE
**your**
**tu bicicleta**
your bicycle
**tus familiares**
your relations

**tú** PRONOUN
**you**
**Cuando tú quieras.**
Whenever you like.

la **tubería** NOUN
**pipe**
**Ha reventado una tubería.**
A pipe has burst.

el **tubo** NOUN
**1 pipe**
**2 tube**
**un tubo de crema para las manos**
a tube of hand cream

**tuerzo** VERB ▷see **torcer**
**Si no me sueltas, te tuerzo el brazo.**
Let go or I'll twist your arm.

la **tumba** NOUN
**grave**

**tumbar** VERB
**to knock down**
**El perro me tumbó.**
The dog knocked me down.
■ **tumbarse**
**to lie down**
**Me tumbé en el sofá.**
I lay down on the sofa.

el **túnel** NOUN
**tunnel**

el **turismo** NOUN
**tourism**
**El turismo es importante para nuestra economía.**
Tourism is important for our economy.
**turismo rural**
tourism in rural areas

el/la **turista** NOUN
**tourist**

**turístico** (FEM **turística**)
ADJECTIVE
**tourist**

**turnarse** VERB
**to take it in turns**
**Nos turnamos para fregar los platos.**
We take it in turns to do the washing-up.

el **turno** NOUN
**turn**
**cuando me tocó el turno**
when it was my turn

el **turrón** (PL los **turrones**)
NOUN
**nougat**

**Did you know...?**
*There is a wide range of **turrones** in Spain which people traditionally eat at Christmas.*

**tutear** VERB

**Did you know...?**
*In Spanish there are two ways of addressing people. You can use the familiar **tú** form to talk to friends and people you know, and this is known as **tutear**. You should use the more formal **usted** form to talk to people you don't know, especially if they are adults.*

**Se tutean con el profesor.**
They address their teacher in familiar terms.

el **tutor**
la **tutora** NOUN
tutor

**tuve** VERB ▷*see* tener
**Tuve fiebre.**
I had a temperature.

**tuyo** (FEM **tuya**) ADJECTIVE,
PRONOUN
**yours**
**¿Es tuyo este abrigo?**
Is this coat yours?
**La tuya está en el armario.**
Yours is in the cupboard.
**mis amigos y los tuyos**
my friends and yours
**un amigo tuyo**
a friend of yours

a b c d e f g h i j k l m n ñ o p q r s t u v w x y z

# U u

**u** CONJUNCTION
**or**

> **Language tip**
> **u** is used instead of **o** before words
> starting with **o-** or **ho-**.

> **¿Minutos u horas?**
> Minutes or hours?

**Ud.** ABBREVIATION = **usted**

**Uds.** ABBREVIATION = **ustedes**

la **UE** ABBREVIATION
= **Unión Europea**
**EU**

**uf** EXCLAMATION
1 **phew!**
2 **ugh!**

**últimamente** ADVERB
**recently**

**último**
**última**

> **último** can be an adjective or a
> noun.

**A** ADJECTIVE
1 **last**
   **la última vez que hablé con
   ella**
   the last time I spoke to her
2 **top**
   **No llego al último estante.**
   I can't reach the top shelf.
3 **back**
   **Nos sentamos en la última
   fila.**
   We sat in the back row.

**la última moda**
the latest fashion
**llegar en último lugar**
to come last

**a última hora**
at the last minute

**B** MASC/FEM NOUN
**the last one**
**a últimos de mes**
towards the end of the month
**por último**
lastly

**un**
**una** ARTICLE
1 **a**
   **una silla**
   a chair
2 **an**
   **un paraguas**
   an umbrella
3 **some**
   **Fui con unos amigos.**
   I went with some friends.
   **Había unas veinte personas.**
   There were about twenty people.
   **Me he comprado unos
   zapatos de tacón.**
   I have bought a pair of high-heels.

**undécimo** (FEM **undécima**)
ADJECTIVE, PRONOUN
**eleventh**
**Vivo en el undécimo piso.**
I live on the eleventh floor.

**único**
**única**

> **único** can be an adjective or a
> noun.

**A** ADJECTIVE
**only**
**el único día que tengo libre**
the only day I have free

**Soy hija única.**
I'm an only child.
**Lo único que no me gusta ...**
The only thing I don't like ...
**B** MASC/FEM NOUN
**el único/la única**
**the only one**
**el único que me queda**
the only one I've got left

la **unidad** NOUN
**unit**
**una unidad de peso**
a unit of weight

**unido** (FEM **unida**) ADJECTIVE
**close**
**una familia muy unida**
a very close family

el **uniforme** NOUN
**uniform**
**Llevaba el uniforme del colegio.**
He was wearing his school uniform.

la **unión** (PL las **uniones**) NOUN
**union**
**la Unión Europea**
the European Union

**unir** VERB
**1 to link**
**Este pasaje une los dos edificios.**
This passage links the two buildings.
**2 to join**
**Unió los dos extremos con una cuerda.**
He joined the two ends with some string.
**unirse a algo**
to join something
**Andrés se unió a la expedición.**
Andrés joined the expedition.

la **universidad** NOUN
**university**
**Mi hermana va a la universidad.**
My sister's at university.

el **universo** NOUN
**universe**

**uno** (FEM **una**) ADJECTIVE,
PRONOUN
**one**
**Vivo en el número uno.**
I live at number one.
**Uno de ellos era mío.**
One of them was mine.
**Entraron uno a uno.**
They came in one by one.
**unas diez personas**
about ten people

**el uno de abril**
the first of April
**Es la una.**
It's one o'clock.

**untar** VERB
**untar algo con algo**
to spread something on something
**Primero hay que untar el pan con mantequilla.**
First you have to spread the butter on the bread.
**Te has untado las manos de chocolate.**
You've got chocolate all over your hands.

la **uña** NOUN
**nail**

la **urbanización** (PL las
**urbanizaciones**) NOUN
**housing estate**

la **urgencia** NOUN
**emergency**
**los servicios de urgencia**
the emergency services
**urgencias**
accident and emergency department

**urgente** (FEM **urgente**)
ADJECTIVE
**urgent**

Spanish English

a
b
c
d
e
f
g
h
i
j
k
l
m
n
ñ
o
p
q
r
s
t
u
v
w
x
y
z

**usado** (FEM **usada**) ADJECTIVE
**1 secondhand**
**una tienda de ropa usada**
a secondhand clothes shop
**2 worn**
**Estas zapatillas**
**están ya muy**
**usadas.**
These slippers
are very worn
now.

**usar** VERB
**1 to use**
**¿Usaste el grande o el**
**pequeño?**
Did you use the small one or the
big one?
**2 to wear**
**Esta falda está sin usar.**
This skirt has never been worn.
**¿Qué número de zapato**
**usas?**
What size shoe do you take?

el **uso** NOUN
**use**
**instrucciones de uso**
instructions for use

**usted** PRONOUN
**you**
**Quisiera hablar con usted en**
**privado.**
I'd like to speak to you in private.

**útil** (FEM **útil**) ADJECTIVE
**useful**

**utilizar** VERB
**to use**

la **uva** NOUN
**grape**

### Did you know...?
*in Spain, people celebrate the start*
*of the New Year by eating twelve*
*grapes, one with each of the twelve*
*chimes, representing a month's luck*
*for each grape that is eaten.*

**va** VERB ▷ *see* **ir**
**Va a la escuela del barrio.**
He goes to the local school.

la **vaca** NOUN
1 **cow**
2 **beef**
**No como carne de vaca.**
I don't eat beef.

las **vacaciones** NOUN
**holidays**
**las vacaciones de Navidad**
the Christmas holidays
**La secretaria está de vacaciones.**
The secretary is on holiday.
**En agosto me voy de vacaciones.**
I'm going on holiday in August.

**vaciar** VERB
**to empty**
**Ayúdame a vaciar este cajón.**
Help me empty this drawer.

**vacío** (FEM **vacía**) ADJECTIVE
**empty**

el **vagabundo**
la **vagabunda** NOUN
**tramp**

**vago** (FEM **vaga**) ADJECTIVE
**lazy**

el **vagón** (PL los **vagones**) NOUN
**carriage**

la **vainilla** NOUN
**vanilla**
**un helado de vainilla**
a vanilla ice cream

el **vale** NOUN
**voucher**
**un vale de regalo**
a gift voucher

**valer** VERB
1 **to cost**
**¿Cuánto vale?**
How much does it cost?
2 **to be worth**
**El terreno vale más que la casa.**
The land is worth more than the house.
**vale la pena**
it's worth it
**no vale la pena**
it's not worth it
**No vale la pena gastar tanto dinero.**
It's not worth spending that much money.
**Este cuchillo no vale para nada.**
This knife is useless.
**¿Vamos a tomar algo? – ¡Vale!**
Shall we go for a drink? – OK!

**¡Eso no vale!**
That's not fair!
**¿Vale?**
OK?

**válido** (FEM **válida**) ADJECTIVE
**valid**

**valiente** (FEM **valiente**) ADJECTIVE
**brave**

la **valla** NOUN
**fence**

el **valle** NOUN
**valley**

el **valor** NOUN
1 **value**
**valor sentimental**
sentimental value
**objetos de valor**
valuables
2 **courage**
**armarse de valor**
to pluck up courage

el **vapor** NOUN
**steam**
**al vapor**
steamed

el **vaquero** NOUN
**cowboy**
**una película de vaqueros**
a western
**vaqueros**
jeans
**Llevaba unos vaqueros negros.**
He was wearing black jeans.

**variado** (FEM **variada**) ADJECTIVE
**varied**
**Tenemos un programa muy variado.**
Our timetable is really varied.

**variar** VERB
**to vary**
**Los precios varían según las tallas.**
Prices vary according to size.
**Decidí ir en tren, para variar.**
I decided to go by train for a change.

la **variedad** NOUN
**variety**

**varios** (FEM **varias**) ADJECTIVE, PRONOUN
**several**
**Estuve enfermo varios días.**
I was ill for several days.
**Le hicimos un regalo entre varios.**

Several of us clubbed together to get him a present.

**varón** (PL **varones**)

**varón** *can be an adjective or a noun.*

A ADJECTIVE
**male**
B MASC NOUN
**Tiene dos hembras y un varón.**
She has two girls and a boy.
**Sexo: varón.**
Sex: male.

**vasco**

**vasco** *can be an adjective or a noun.*

A (FEM **vasca**) ADJECTIVE
**Basque**
**el País Vasco**
the Basque Country
B MASC/FEM NOUN
**vasco/vasca**
**Basque**
C MASC NOUN
**Basque**
**Hablamos vasco.**
We speak Basque.

el **vaso** NOUN
**glass**
**Bebí un vaso de leche.**
I drank a glass of milk.
**un vaso de plástico**
a plastic cup

**vaya** VERB ▷*see* **ir**
**¿Quieres que vaya contigo?**
Do you want me to go with you?

**Vd.** ABBREVIATION = **usted**

**Vds.** ABBREVIATION = **ustedes**

**ve** VERB ▷*see* **ir, ver**
**Ve con él.**
Go with him.
**Mi perro no ve bien.**
My dog can't see very well.

el **vecindario** NOUN
neighbourhood

el **vecino**
la **vecina** NOUN
neighbour
**los vecinos de al lado**
the next door neighbours

**vegetal** ADJECTIVE, MASC NOUN
vegetable
**aceite vegetal**
vegetable oil

el **vehículo** NOUN
vehicle

**veinte** (FEM **veinte**) ADJECTIVE,
PRONOUN
twenty

**Tiene veinte años.**
He's twenty.
**el veinte de enero**
the twentieth of January
**Nació el veinte de enero.**
He was born on the twentieth of
January.
**el siglo veinte**
the twentieth century

la **vejez** NOUN
old age

la **vela** NOUN
1 candle
**Encendimos una vela.**
We lit a candle.

2 sail

la **velocidad** NOUN
speed

**Pasó una moto a toda
velocidad.**
A motorbike went past at full
speed.
**¿A qué velocidad ibas?**
How fast were you going?

**veloz** (FEM **veloz**, PL **veloces**)
ADJECTIVE
swift

**ven** VERB ▷see **ir**, **ver**
**Ven conmigo.**
Come with me.
**Sus padres no ven el problema.**
Her parents can't see the problem.

la **vena** NOUN
vein

**vencer** VERB
1 to defeat
2 to overcome

la **venda** NOUN
bandage
**Me pusieron una venda en
el brazo.**
They bandaged my arm.

**vendar** VERB
to bandage
**Me vendaron el codo.**
They bandaged my elbow.
**vendar los ojos a alguien**
to blindfold somebody

**vender** VERB
to sell
**He vendido la bici.**
I've sold my bike.

**'se vende'**
'for sale'

**vendré** VERB ▷see **venir**
**Mañana vendré de nuevo.**
I'll come again tomorrow.

el **veneno** NOUN
poison

**venenoso** (FEM **venenosa**)
ADJECTIVE
poisonous

Spanish English

a
b
c
d
e
f
g
h
i
j
k
l
m
n
ñ
o
p
q
r
s
t
u
v
w
x
y
z

**vengo** VERB ▷ *see* **venir**
**No vengo aquí mucho.**
I don't come here much.

**venir** VERB
**1 to come**
**Vino en taxi.**
He came by taxi.
**Vinieron a verme al hospital.**
They came to see me in hospital.
**¡Ven aquí!**
Come here!
**2 to be**
**La noticia venía en el periódico.**
The news was in the paper.
**¿Te viene bien el sábado?**
Is Saturday all right for you?

**el año que viene**
next year
**¡Venga, vámonos!**
Come on, let's go!
**¡Venga ya!**
Come off it!

la **ventaja** NOUN
**advantage**
**Tiene la ventaja de que está cerca de casa.**
It has the advantage of being close to home.

la **ventana** NOUN
**window**

la **ventanilla** NOUN
**window**
**Baja la ventanilla.**
Open the window.

**ver** VERB
**1 to see**
**Te vi en el parque.**
I saw you in the park.
**¡Cuánto tiempo sin verte!**
I haven't seen you for ages!
**No he visto esa película.**
I haven't seen that film.
**¿Ves? Ya te lo dije.**
See? I told you so.
**Eso no tiene nada que ver.**
That has nothing to do with it.
**¡No la puede ver!**
He can't stand her!
**Se ve que no tiene idea de informática.**
It's clear he's got no idea about computers.
**2 to watch**
**¿Te apetece ver la tele?**
Do you feel like watching TV?

**A ver ...**
Let's see ...

el **verano** NOUN
**summer**
**En verano hace mucho calor.**
It's very hot in summer.
**las vacaciones de verano**
the summer holidays

**en verano**
in summer

el **verbo** NOUN
**verb**

la **verdad** NOUN
**truth**
**Les dije la verdad.**
I told them the truth.
**La verdad es que no tengo ganas.**
I don't really feel like it.
**De verdad que yo no dije eso.**
I didn't say that, honestly.
**Es bonito, ¿verdad?**
It's pretty, isn't it?
**No te gusta, ¿verdad?**
You don't like it, do you?

**¿De verdad?**
Really?

**verdadero** (FEM **verdadera**)
ADJECTIVE
**real**
Su apellido verdadero es Rodríguez.
His real surname is Rodríguez.

**verde**

**verde** *can be an adjective or a noun.*

**A** (FEM **verde**) ADJECTIVE
**green**
Tiene los ojos verdes.
She has green eyes.
Estos plátanos están todavía verdes.
These bananas are still green.
**B** MASC NOUN
**green**

la **verdura** NOUN
**vegetables**
Comemos mucha verdura.
We eat a lot of vegetables.

**vergonzoso** (FEM **vergonzosa**)
ADJECTIVE
1 **shy**
Es muy vergonzosa.
She is very shy.
2 **disgraceful**
Es vergonzoso cómo los trataron.
It's disgraceful the way they were treated.

la **vergüenza** NOUN
1 **embarrassment**
Casi me muero de vergüenza.
I almost died of embarrassment.

¡Qué vergüenza!
How embarrassing!
**Le da vergüenza pedirle ayuda.**
He's embarrassed to ask her for help.
2 **shame**
No tienen vergüenza.
They have no shame.
¡Es una vergüenza!
It's disgraceful!

la **versión** (PL las **versiones**)
NOUN
**version**

**vertical** (FEM **vertical**) ADJECTIVE
**vertical**
Ponlo vertical.
Put it upright.

**vestido**

**vestido** *can be a noun or an adjective.*

**A** NOUN
**dress**
**B** (FEM **vestida**) ADJECTIVE
Iba vestida de negro.
She was dressed in black
Yo iba vestido de payaso.
I was dressed as a clown.

**vestir** VERB
**to wear**
Vestía pantalones vaqueros y una camiseta.
He was wearing jeans and a T-shirt.
■ **vestirse**
**to get dressed**
Se está vistiendo.
He's getting dressed.
Se vistió de princesa.
She dressed up as a princess.

el **veterinario**
la **veterinaria**
NOUN
**vet**

la **vez** (PL las **veces**) NOUN
**time**
¿Cuántas veces al año?
How many times a year?
¿La has visto alguna vez?
Have you ever seen her?
una vez
once
La veo una vez a la semana.
I see her once a week.
dos veces
twice

a veces
sometimes
algunas veces
sometimes
de vez en cuando
from time to time
en vez de
instead of
otra vez
again
tal vez
maybe

**vi** VERB ▷see **ver**
Lo vi ayer.
I saw him yesterday.

**viajar** VERB
**to travel**
viajar en autocar
to travel by coach

el **viaje** NOUN
1 **trip**
¡Buen viaje!
Have a good trip!
2 **journey**
Es un viaje muy largo.
It's a very long journey.

estar de viaje
to be away

el **viajero**
la **viajera** NOUN
**passenger**

la **vida** NOUN
**life**

He vivido aquí toda mi vida.
I've lived here all my life.

el **vídeo** NOUN
**video**

la **videocámara** NOUN
**video camera**

el **videojuego** NOUN
**video game**

el **vidrio** NOUN
**glass**
botellas de vidrio
glass bottles
Me corté el dedo con un
vidrio.
I cut my finger on a piece of
glass.

**viejo**
**vieja**

viejo *can be an adjective or a noun.*

**A** ADJECTIVE
**old**
un viejo amigo mío
an old friend of mine
Estos zapatos ya están muy
viejos.
These shoes are very old now.
**B** MASC/FEM NOUN
un viejo
an old man
una vieja
an old woman
los viejos
old people

**viene** VERB ▷see **venir**
¿Viene o no?
Is she coming or not?

el **viento** NOUN
**wind**

el **vientre** NOUN
**stomach**

**Spanish English**

el **viernes** (PL los **viernes**) NOUN
**Friday**

> *Language tip*
> *Days are not spelled with a capital letter in Spanish.*

**La vi el viernes.**
I saw her on Friday.
**Viernes Santo**
Good Friday

**todos los viernes**
every Friday
**el viernes pasado**
last Friday
**el viernes que viene**
next Friday

**vigilar** VERB
1 **to guard**
**Un policía vigilaba al preso.**
A policeman was guarding the prisoner.
2 **to watch**
**Nos vigilan.**
They're watching us.

el **vinagre** NOUN
**vinegar**

**vine** VERB ▷ *see* **venir**
**Vine sola.**
I came on my own.

**viniendo** VERB ▷ *see* **venir**
**¿Nos veías viniendo por la montaña?**
Could you see us coming down the mountain?

el **vino** NOUN
**wine**
**vino blanco**
white wine
**vino tinto**
red wine

la **violencia** NOUN
**violence**

**violento** (FEM **violenta**)
ADJECTIVE
**violent**
**La película contiene algunas escenas violentas.**
The film contains some violent scenes.

el **violín** (PL los **violines**) NOUN
**violin**

el/la **violinista** NOUN
**violinist**

el **virus** (PL los **virus**) NOUN
**virus**

**visible** (FEM **visible**) ADJECTIVE
**visible**

la **visión** (PL las **visiones**) NOUN
**vision**
**la visión nocturna**
night vision

la **visita** NOUN
1 **visit**
**hacer una visita a alguien**
to visit somebody
**Hice una visita a mi abuela.**
I visited my grandmother.
2 **visitor**
**Tienes visita.**
You've got visitors.
**horario de visita**
visiting hours

**visitar** VERB
**to visit**
**Miles de personas han visitado ya la exposición.**
Thousands of people have already visited the exhibition.

la **víspera** NOUN
**the day before**
**la víspera del partido**
the day before the match

la **vista** NOUN
1 **sight**

a b c d e f g h i j k l m n ñ o p q r s t u v w x y z

**conocer a alguien de vista**
to know somebody by sight
**La conozco de vista.**
I know her by sight.
**2 view**
**una habitación con vistas al mar**
a room with a sea view

**¡Hasta la vista!**
See you!

el **vistazo** NOUN
**echar un vistazo a algo**
to have a look at something
**Échale un vistazo a esta revista.**
Have a look at this magazine.

**vistiendo** VERB ▷ see **vestir**
**Se está vistiendo.**
She's getting dressed.

**visto** (FEM **vista**)

**visto** can be an adjective or part of the verb **ver**.

**A** ADJECTIVE
**Está visto que ...**
It's clear that ...

**por lo visto**
apparently

**B** VERB ▷ see **ver**
**¿Has visto a Elena?**
Have you seen Elena?

**viuda**

**viuda** can be an adjective or a noun.

**A** ADJECTIVE
**Es viuda.**
She's a widow.
**B** FEM NOUN
**widow**

**viudo**

**viudo** can be an adjective or a noun.

**A** ADJECTIVE
**Es viudo.**

He's a widower.
**B** MASC NOUN
**widower**

**vivir** VERB
**1 to live**
**¿Dónde vives?**
Where do you live?
**2 to be alive**
**¿Todavía vive?**
Is he still alive?

**¡Viva!**
Hurray!

**vivo** (FEM **viva**) ADJECTIVE
**1 alive**
**Estaba vivo.**
He was alive.
**en vivo**
live
**una retransmisión en vivo**
a live broadcast
**2 bright**

el **vocabulario** NOUN
**vocabulary**

la **vocal** NOUN
**vowel**

el **volante** NOUN
**steering wheel**

**volar** VERB
**to fly**
**El helicóptero volaba muy bajo.**
The helicopter was flying very low.
**Se me pasó la semana volando.**
The week just flew by.
**Tuvimos que ir volando al hospital.**
We had to rush to the hospital.

el **voleibol** NOUN
**volleyball**

la **voltereta** NOUN
**somersault**
**dar una voltereta**
to do a somersault

el **volumen** (PL los **volúmenes**)
  NOUN
  **volume**
    **bajar el volumen**
    to turn the volume down
    **subir el volumen**
    to turn the volume up

la **voluntad** NOUN
  1 **will**
    **Lo hizo contra mi voluntad.**
    He did it against my will.
  2 **willpower**
    **Le cuesta, pero tiene mucha
    voluntad.**
    It's difficult for him, but he has
    a lot of willpower.

**voluntario**
**voluntaria**

> **voluntario** can be an adjective or a noun.

  **A** ADJECTIVE
    **voluntary**
  **B** MASC/FEM NOUN
    **volunteer**

**volver** VERB
  1 **to come back**
  2 **to go back**
  3 **to turn**
    **Me volvió la espalda.**
    He turned away from me.
    **Me volví para ver quién era.**
    I turned round to see who it was.
  4 **to become**
    **Se ha vuelto muy
    cariñoso.**
    He's become
    very
    affectionate.

**volver a hacer algo**
to do something again

**Volví a abrir la puerta.**
I opened the door again.

**vomitar** VERB
  **to be sick**
    **Ha vomitado dos veces.**
    He's been sick twice.
    **Vomitó todo lo que había
    comido.**
    He threw up everything he'd
    eaten.

**votar** VERB
  **to vote**
    **Voté por Alcántara.**
    I voted for Alcántara.

**voy** VERB ▷ see **ir**
    **Voy al parque.**
    I'm going to the park.

la **voz** (PL las **voces**) NOUN
  **voice**
    **No tengo buena voz.**
    I don't have a very good voice.

**vuelo**

> **vuelo** can be a noun or part of the verb **volar**.

  **A** MASC NOUN
    **flight**
  **B** VERB ▷ see **volar**
    **Esta vez vuelo en primera
    clase.**
    I'm flying first class this time.

la **vuelta** NOUN
  1 **return**
    **un billete de ida y vuelta**
    a return ticket
  2 **lap**
    **Di tres vueltas a la pista.**
    I did three laps of the track.
  3 **change**
    **Quédese con la vuelta.**
    Keep the change.
    **Vive a la vuelta de la esquina.**
    He lives round the corner.
    **dar una vuelta**
    to go for a walk/to go for a drive

Spanish English

a b c d e f g h i j k l m n ñ o p q r s t u v w x y z

### Language tip
**dar una vuelta** *has two meanings. It can be translated as* **to go for a walk** *and* **to go for a drive**.

**vuelto** VERB ▷*see* **volver**
**Ya ha vuelto del viaje.**
He's back from his trip already.

**vuelvo** VERB ▷*see* **volver**
**Mañana vuelvo.**
I'll be back tomorrow.

**vuestro** (FEM **vuestra**)

**vuestro** *can be an adjective or a pronoun.*

**A** ADJECTIVE
**your**
**vuestra casa**
your house
**vuestros amigos**
your friends
**un amigo vuestro**
a friend of yours

**B** PRONOUN
**yours**
**¿Son vuestros?**
Are they yours?
**¿Es ésta la vuestra?**
Is this one yours?
**¿Y los bocadillos? –
Los vuestros están aquí.**
Where are the sandwiches? –
Yours are over here.

# W w

el **walkman®**
(PL los **walkmans**) NOUN
**Walkman®**

el **wáter** NOUN
**loo**

*Language tip*
*Be careful!* **wáter** *does not mean*
**water**.

la **web** NOUN
1 **website**
2 **(World Wide) Web**

la **webcam** NOUN
**webcam**

el **windsurf** NOUN
**windsurfing**

**WWW** ABBREVIATION
(= World Wide Web)
**WWW**

a
b
c
d
e
f
g
h
i
j
k
l
m
n
ñ
o
p
q
r
s
t
u
v
w
x
y
z

# X x

el **xilófono** NOUN
xylophone

# Y y

**y** CONJUNCTION
**and**
>**Andrés y su novia.**
>Andrés and his girlfriend.
>**Yo quiero una ensalada.**
>**¿Y tú?**
>I'd like a salad. What about you?
>**Son las tres y cinco.**
>It's five minutes past three.

**ya** ADVERB
**already**
>**Ya se han ido.**
>They've already left.
>**¿Ya has terminado?**
>Have you finished already?
>**ya no**
>not ... any more
>**Ya no salimos juntos.**
>We aren't going out together
>any more.

>**ya que**
>since
>**Ya lo sé.**
>I know.
>**¡Ya voy!**
>I'm coming!

**el yate** NOUN
**yacht**

**la yema** NOUN
**1 yolk**
**2 fingertip**

**yendo** VERB ▷see ir
>**Llevo todo el día yendo y**
>**viniendo.**
>I've spent all day coming and going.

**el yeso** NOUN
**plaster**

**yo** PRONOUN
**1 I**
>**Carlos y yo no fuimos.**
>Carlos and I didn't go.

**2 me**
>**¿Quién ha visto la película? –**
>**Ana y yo.**
>Who's seen the film? –
>Ana and me.
>**Es más alta que yo.**
>She's taller than me.
>**Soy yo, María.**
>It's me, María.
>**yo mismo**
>myself
>**Lo hice yo misma.**
>I did it myself.

>**¡Yo también!**
>Me too!
>**yo que tú**
>if I were you

**el yoga** NOUN
**yoga**

**el yogur** NOUN
**yoghurt**

# Z z

**zamparse** VERB
**to wolf down**
> **Se zampó todas las galletas.**
> He wolfed down all the biscuits.

la **zanahoria** NOUN
**carrot**

la **zancadilla** NOUN
> **Me puso la zancadilla.**
> He tripped me up.

la **zanja** NOUN
**ditch**

la **zapatería** NOUN
**shoe shop**

la **zapatilla** NOUN
**slipper**
> **Tráeme las zapatillas.**
> Bring me my slippers.
> **zapatillas de ballet**
> ballet shoes
> **zapatillas de deporte**
> trainers

el **zapato** NOUN
**shoe**
> **zapatos cómodos**
> comfortable shoes

> **zapatos de tacón**
> high-heeled shoes

el **zapping** NOUN
**channel hopping**
> **hacer zapping**
> to channel-hop

la **zona** NOUN
**area**
> **Viven en una zona muy tranquila.**
> They live in a very quiet area.
> **una zona peatonal**
> a pedestrian precinct
> **una zona verde**
> a green space

el **zoo** NOUN
**zoo**

el **zoológico** NOUN
**zoo**

el **zorro** NOUN
**fox**

**zumbar** VERB
**to buzz**
> **Me zumban los oídos.**
> My ears are buzzing.

el **zumo** NOUN
**juice**
> **zumo de naranja**
> orange juice

**zurdo** (FEM **zurda**) ADJECTIVE
1 **left-handed**
2 **left-footed**

**zurrar** VERB
**to thrash**

# Language plus

# Language plus

### • Pets – Los animales domésticos

**budgie** N el periquito

**canary** N el canario

**cat** N el gato

**dog** N el perro

**goldfish** N el pez de colores
(PL los peces de colores)

**guinea pig** N el conejillo de Indias

**hamster** N el hámster
(PL los hámsters)

**kitten** N el gatito

**mouse** N el ratón
(PL los ratones)

**parrot** N el loro

**poodle** N el caniche

**puppy** N el cachorro

**rabbit** N el conejo

**tortoise** N la tortuga

### • Farm animals – Los animales de la granja

**bull** N el toro

**calf** N el ternero

**chick** N el polluelo

**chicken** N el pollo

**cock** N el gallo

**cow** N la vaca

**donkey** N el burro

**goat** N la cabra

**goose** N la oca

**hen** N la gallina

**horse** N el caballo

**lamb** N el cordero

**mare** N la yegua

**peacock** N el pavo real

**pheasant** N el faisán
(PL los faisanes)

**pig** N el cerdo

**pony** N el poney (PL los poneys)

**ram** N el carnero

**sheep** N la oveja

**sheepdog** N el perro pastor

**turkey** N el pavo

### • Wild animals – Los animales salvajes

**ant** N la hormiga

**ape** N el simio

**bat** N el murciélago

**bear** N el oso

**bee** N la abeja

**beetle** N el escarabajo

**bird** N el pájaro

**butterfly** N la mariposa

**camel** N el camello *(two humps)*

**camel** N el dromedario
*(one hump)*

**cheetah** N el guepardo
**crab** N el cangrejo
**crocodile** N el cocodrilo
**cub** N el cachorro
**deer** N el ciervo
**dolphin** N el delfín
  (PL los **delfines**)
**duck** N el pato
**elephant** N el elefante
**fish** N el pez (PL los **peces**)
**fly** N la mosca
**fox** N el zorro
**frog** N la rana
**giraffe** N la jirafa
**gorilla** N el gorila
**hare** N la liebre
**hedgehog** N el erizo
**hippo** N el hipopótamo
**insect** N el insecto
**jellyfish** N la medusa
**kangaroo** N el canguro
**koala** N el koala
**ladybird** N la mariquita
**leopard** N el leopardo

**lion** N el **león** (PL los **leones**)
**lioness** N la leona
**lizard** N el lagarto
**mammoth** N el mamut
**mole** N el topo
**monkey** N el mono
**mosquito** N el mosquito
**moth** N la polilla
**octopus** N el pulpo
**ostrich** N el avestruz
  (PL los **avestruces**)
**owl** N el búho
**panther** N la pantera
**penguin** N el pingüino

**pigeon** N la paloma
**polar bear** N el oso polar
**rat** N la rata
**raven** N el cuervo
**reindeer** N el reno
**reptile** N el reptil
**rhino** N el rinoceronte
**robin** N el petirrojo
**seagull** N la gaviota
**seal** N la foca

**shark** N el **tiburón**
(PL los **tiburones**)

**slug** N la **babosa**

**snail** N el **caracol**

**snake** N la **serpiente**

**sparrow** N el **gorrión**
(PL los **gorriones**)

**spider** N la **araña**

**squirrel** N la **ardilla**

**swallow** N la **golondrina**

**swan** N el **cisne**

**tadpole** N el **renacuajo**

**tiger** N el **tigre**

**toad** N el **sapo**

**turtle** N la **tortuga de mar**

**wasp** N la **avispa**

**whale** N la **ballena**

**wolf** N el **lobo**

**worm** N el **gusano**

**zebra** N la **cebra**

**ankle** N el tobillo

**arm** N el brazo

**back** N la espalda

**beard** N la barba

**blood** N la sangre

**body** N el cuerpo

**brain** N el cerebro

**cheek** N la mejilla

**chest** N el pecho

**chin** N la barbilla

**ear** N la oreja

**elbow** N el codo

**eye** N el ojo

**eyebrow** N la ceja

**eyelash** N la pestaña

**eyelid** N el párpado

**face** N la cara

**finger** N el dedo (de la mano)

**fist** N el puño

**foot** N el pie

**forehead** N la frente

**freckles** N las pecas

**fringe** N el flequillo

**hair** N el pelo

**hand** N la mano

**head** N la cabeza

**heart** N el corazón (PL los corazones)

**heel** N el talón (PL los talones)

**hip** N la cadera

**jaw** N la mandíbula

**kidney** N el riñón (PL los riñones)

**knee** N la rodilla

**leg** N la pierna

**lip** N el labio

**liver** N el hígado

**lung** N el pulmón (PL los pulmones)

**moustache** N el bigote

**mouth** N la boca

**muscle** N el músculo

**nail** N la uña

**neck** N el cuello

**nerve** N el nervio

**nose** N la nariz (PL las narices)

**organ** N el órgano

**palm** N la palma

**rib** N la costilla

**shoulder** N el hombro

**skeleton** N el esqueleto

**skin** N la piel

**skull** N el cráneo

**spine** N la columna vertebral

**stomach** N el estómago

**thigh** N el muslo

**throat** N la garganta

**thumb** N el pulgar

**toe** N el dedo (del pie)

**tongue** N la **lengua**

**tonsils** N PL las **amígdalas**
**tooth** N el **diente**
**tummy** N la **barriga**
**waist** N la **cintura**
**wrist** N la **muñeca**

**anorak** N  el anorak

**apron** N  el delantal

**ballet shoes** N PL
las zapatillas de ballet

**baseball cap** N  la gorra
de béisbol

**belt** N  el cinturón
(PL los **cinturones**)

**beret** N  la boina

**bikini** N  el bikini

**blouse** N  la blusa

**boots** N PL  las botas

**bow tie** N  la pajarita

**boxer shorts** N  el boxer

**bra** N  el sujetador

**cagoule** N  el chubasquero

**cap** N  la gorra

**cardigan** N  la rebeca

**clothes** N  la ropa

**coat** N  el abrigo

**dress** N  el vestido

**dressing gown** N  la bata

**dungarees** N  el peto

**fleece** N  el forro polar

**flippers** N PL  las aletas

**football boots** N PL
las botas de fútbol

**football shirt** N
la camiseta de fútbol

**glasses** N PL  las gafas

**glove** N  el guante

**goggles** N PL  las gafas
de piscina

**hat** N  el sombrero

**helmet** N  el casco

**hood** N  la capucha

**hoodie** N  el jersey con
capucha

**jacket** N  la chaqueta

**jeans** N PL  los vaqueros

**jumper** N  el jersey

**kilt** N  la falda escocesa

**knickers** N PL  las bragas

**leather jacket** N
la chaqueta de cuero

**leggings** N PL  las mallas

**miniskirt** N PL  la minifalda

**nightdress** N  el camisón
(PL los **camisones**)

**overall** N  la bata

**polo shirt** N  el polo

**polo-necked sweater** N
el jersey de cuello alto

**pyjamas** N  el pijama

**raincoat** N  el impermeable

**sandals** N PL  las sandalias

**scarf** N la **bufanda**

**shirt** N la **camisa**

**shoes** N PL los **zapatos**

**shorts** N PL los **pantalones cortos**

**ski boots** N PL las **botas de esquí**

**skirt** N la **falda**

**slippers** N PL las **zapatillas**

**sock** N el **calcetín** (PL los **calcetines**)

**suit** N el **traje**

**sunglasses** NPL las **gafas de sol**

**sweatshirt** N la **sudadera**

**swimming costume** N el **bañador**

**tie** N la **corbata**

**tights** N las **medias**

**top** N el **top**

**tracksuit** N el **chándal** (PL los **chándals**)

**trainers** N PL las **zapatillas de deporte**

**trousers** N PL los **pantalones**

**trunks** N el **bañador**

**T-shirt** N la **camiseta**

**underpants** N PL los **calzoncillos**

**underwear** N la **ropa interior**

**uniform** N el **uniforme**

**vest** N la **camiseta**

**waistcoat** N el **chaleco**

**wellingtons** N PL las **botas de agua**

**wetsuit** N el **traje de neopreno**

**beige** ADJ beige
(FEM, PL beige)

**black** ADJ negro (FEM negra)

**blonde** ADJ rubio
(FEM rubia)

**blue** ADJ azul (FEM azul)

**brown** ADJ marrón
(FEM marrón)

**cream** ADJ crema
(FEM, PL crema)

**green** ADJ verde (FEM verde)

**grey** ADJ gris (FEM gris)

**maroon** ADJ burdeos
(FEM, PL burdeos)

**navy blue** ADJ azul
marino (FEM, PL azul marino)

**orange** ADJ naranja
(FEM, PL naranja)

**pink** ADJ rosa (FEM, PL rosa)

**purple** ADJ morado
(FEM morada)

**red** ADJ rojo (FEM roja)

**turquoise** ADJ turquesa
(FEM, PL turquesa)

**white** ADJ blanco
(FEM blanca)

**yellow** ADJ amarillo
(FEM amarilla)

**aunt** N la **tía**
**baby** N el **bebé**
**brother** N el **hermano**
**brother-in-law** N el **cuñado**
**child** N la **niña**
**child** N el **niño**
**cousin** N la **prima**
**cousin** N el **primo**
**dad** N el **papá**
**daughter** N la **hija**
**daughter-in-law** N
  la **nuera**
**family** N la **familia**
**father** N el **padre**
**father-in-law** N el **suegro**
**fiancé** N el **prometido**
**fiancée** N la **prometida**

**grandchildren** N PL
  los **nietos**
**granddad** N el **abuelo**

**granddaughter** N la **nieta**
**grandparents** N PL
  los **abuelos**
**grandson** N el **nieto**
**granny** N la **abuela**
**half-brother** N
  el **hermanastro**
**half-sister** N
  la **hermanastra**
**husband** N el **marido**
**in-laws** N PL los **suegros**
**mother** N la **madre**
**mother-in-law** N la **suegra**
**mum** N la **mamá**
**nephew** N el **sobrino**
**niece** N la **sobrina**
**parents** N los **padres**
**sister** N la **hermana**
**sister-in-law** N la **cuñada**
**son** N el **hijo**
**son-in-law** N el **yerno**
**stepdaughter** N la **hijastra**
**stepfather** N el **padastro**
**stepmother** N la **madrastra**
**stepson** N el **hijastro**
**uncle** N el **tío**
**wife** N la **mujer**

## • Days of the week - Los días de la semana

**Monday** el lunes

**Tuesday** el martes

**Wednesday** el miércoles

**Thursday** el jueves

**Friday** el viernes

**Saturday** el sábado

**Sunday** el domingo

## • Months of the year - Los meses del año

**January** enero

**February** febrero

**March** marzo

**April** abril

**May** mayo

**June** junio

**July** julio

**August** agosto

**September** septiembre

**October** octubre

**November** noviembre

**December** diciembre

## • Special days - Fiestas señaladas

**New Year's Day** N el **Día de Año Nuevo**

**Mother's Day** N el **Día de la Madre**

**Father's Day** N el **Día del Padre**

**Valentine's Day** N el **Día de San Valentín**

**Christmas** N la **Navidad**

**Christmas Eve** N la **Nochebuena**

**New Year's Eve** N la **Nochevieja**

**Easter** N la **Semana Santa**

**It's chilly.** Hace fresco.

**It's cloudy.** Está nublado.

**It's cold.** Hace frío.

**It's foggy.** Hay niebla.

**It's freezing.** Hace mucho frío.

**It's frosty.** Hay escarcha.

**It's hot.** Hace calor.

**It's icy.** Hay hielo.

**It's misty.** Hay niebla.

**It's nice.** Hace buen tiempo.

**It's overcast.** El cielo está nublado.

**It's raining.** Llueve.

**It's snowing.** Nieva.

**It's stormy.** Hay tormenta.

**It's sunny.** Hace sol.

**It's windy.** Hace viento.

**• Seasons - Las estaciones del año**

**spring** N la **primavera**

**summer** N el **verano**

**autumn** N el **otoño**

**winter** N el **invierno**

**Africa** N África

**Albania** N Albania

**Algeria** N Argelia

**America** N América

**Asia** N Asia

**Australia** N Australia

**Austria** N Austria

**Belgium** N Bélgica

**Brazil** N Brasil

**Brussels** N Bruselas

**Bulgaria** N Bulgaria

**Canada** N Canadá

**China** N China

**Cornwall** N Cornualles

**Corsica** N Córcega

**Croatia** N Croacia

**Cyprus** N Chipre

**Denmark** N Dinamarca

**Dublin** N Dublín

**Edinburgh** N Edimburgo

**Egypt** N Egipto

**Eire** N la República de Irlanda

**England** N Inglaterra

**Estonia** N Estonia

**Ethiopia** N Etiopia

**Europe** N Europa

**Far East** N Extremo Oriente

**Finland** N Finlandia

**Francia** N France

**Germany** N Alemania

**Great Britain** N Gran Bretaña

**Greece** N Grecia

**Holland** N Holanda

**Hungary** N Hungría

**Iceland** N Islandia

**India** N India

**Iran** N Irán

**Iraq** N Irak

**Ireland** N Irlanda

**Israel** N Israel

**Italy** N Italia

**Japan** N Japón

**Jordan** N Jordania

**Korea** N Corea

**Latin America** N América Latina

**Latvia** N Letonia

**Lebanon** N Líbano

**Libya** N Libia

**Lithuania** N Lituania

**London** N Londres

**Luxembourg** N Luxemburgo

**Majorca** N Mallorca

**Malaysia** N Malasia

**Malta** N Malta

**Mexico** N México

**Middle East** N Oriente Medio

**Milan** N Milán

**Monaco** N Mónaco

**Morocco** N Marruecos

**Naples** N Nápoles

**New Zealand** N Nueva Zelanda

**North America** N
América del Norte

**Northern Ireland** N
Irlanda del Norte

**Norway** N Noruega

**Orkneys** N Órcadas

**Pakistan** N Paquistán

**Palestine** N Palestina

**Paris** N París

**Poland** N Polonia

**Portugal** N Portugal

**Romania** N Rumania

**Rome** N Roma

**Russia** N Rusia

**Sardinia** N Cerdeña

**Saudi Arabia** N Arabia
Saudí

**Scandinavia** N los países
escandinavos

**Scotland** N Escocia

**Shetland Islands** N PL
las Islas Shetland

**Sicily** N Sicilia

**Slovakia** N Eslovaquia

**Slovenia** N Eslovenia

**South Africa** N Sudáfrica

**South America** N
Sudamérica

**Spain** N España

**Sweden** N Suecia

**Switzerland** N Suiza

**the Alps** N PL los Alpes

**the Atlantic** N el Atántico

**the British Isles** las Islas
Británicas

**the Caribbean** N
el Caribe

**the Czech Republic** N
la República Checa

**the English Channel** N
el Canal de la Mancha

**the Mediterranean** N
el Mediterráneo

**the Netherlands** N PL
los Países Bajos

**the North Pole** N el Polo
Norte

**the North Sea** N el Mar
del Norte

**the South Pole** N el Polo
Sur

**the Thames** N el Támesis

**the United Kingdom** N
el Reino Unido

**the United States** N PL
los Estados Unidos

**the US** N los EE. UU.

**the West Indies** N PL
las Antillas

**Tunisia** N Túnez

**Turkey** N Turquía

**Vietnam** N Vietnam

**Wales** N Gales

- **Savoury - Alimentos salados**

**bacon** N la panceta

**baked potato** N la patata asada

**beans** N PL las alubias

**beef** N la carne de vaca

**beefburguer** N la hamburguesa

**biscuit** N la galleta

**bread** N el pan

**butter** N la mantequilla

**cereal** N los cereales

**cheese** N el queso

**chicken** N el pollo

**chips** N la patatas fritas

**chop** N la chuleta

**cod** N el bacalao

**corn on the cob** N la mazorca de maíz

**cracker** N la galleta salada

**cream** N la nata

**cream cheese** N el queso para untar

**crisps** N las patatas fritas

**egg** N el huevo

**fish** N el pescado

**fried egg** N el huevo frito

**garlic** N el ajo

**gravy** N el jugo de carne

**ham** N el jamón

**hard-boiled egg** N el huevo cocido

**herbs** N PL las hierbas aromáticas

**hot dog** N el perrito caliente

**ketchup** N el ketchup

**kidney** N el riñón (PL los riñones)

**lamb** N el cordero

**lamb chop** N la chuleta de cordero

**lentil** N la lenteja

**liver** N el hígado

**loaf of bread** N el pan

**lobster** N la langosta

**macaroni** N los macarrones

**mackerel** N la caballa

**margarine** N la margarina

**mashed potatoes** N el puré de patatas

**mayonnaise** N la mayonesa

**meat** N la carne

**mince** N la carne picada

**muesli** N el muesli

**mushroom** N el champiñón (PL los champiñones) (button mushrooms)

**mushroom** N la seta (open-cup)

**mussel** N el mejillón (PL los mejillones)

**mustard** N la mostaza

287

**noodles** N PL los **fideos**

**oats** N la **avena**

**oil** N el **aceite**

**olive** N la **aceituna**

**olive oil** N el **aceite de oliva**

**omelette** N la **tortilla**

**oyster** N la **ostra**

**parsley** N el **perejil**

**pasta** N la **pasta**

**pâté** N el **paté**

**pepper** N la **pimienta**

**pizza** N la **pizza**

**pork** N la **carne de cerdo**

**potato** N la **patata**

**prawn** N la **gamba**

**rice** N el **arroz**

**roast potatoes** N las **patatas asadas**

**roll** N el **bollo**

**rye** N el **centeno**

**rye bread** N el **pan de centeno**

**salad** N la **ensalada**

**salad dressing** N el **aliño**

**salami** N el **salami**

**salmon** N el **salmón**

**salt** N la **sal**

**sandwich** N el **bocadillo**

**sardine** N la **sardina**

**sauce** N la **salsa**

**sausage** N la **salchicha**

**scampi** N las **gambas rebozadas**

**scrambled eggs** N PL los **huevos revueltos**

**seafood** N el **marisco**

**shellfish** N el **marisco**

**shrimps** N PL los **camarones**

**soft-boiled egg** N el **huevo pasado por agua**

**soup** N la **sopa**

**soy sauce** N la **salsa de soja**

**steak** N el **bistec**

**stew** N el **estofado**

**sweetcorn** N el **maíz**

**thyme** N el **tomillo**

**toast** N las **tostadas**

**toasted sandwich** N el **sándwich caliente**

**trout** N la **trucha**

**tuna** N el **atún**

**turkey** N el pavo

**veal** N la ternera

**vinegar** N el vinagre

**wheat** N el trigo

**wholemeal bread** N el pan integral

- **Sweet - Alimentos dulces**

**apple tart** N la tarta de manzana

**biscuit** N la galleta

**cake** N el pastel *(small)*

**cake** N la tarta *(big)*

**candyfloss** N el algodón de azúcar

**caramel** N el caramelo líquido

**caramel** N el flan

**chewing gum** N el chicle

**chocolate** N el chocolate

**chocolate mousse** N la mousse de chocolate

**cone** N el cucurucho

**cream** N la nata

**cream cake** N la tarta de nata

**custard** N las natillas

**dessert** N el postre

**fruit salad** N la macedonia

**honey** N la miel

**ice cream** N el helado

**ice lolly** N el polo

**jam** N la mermelada

**jelly** N la gelatina

**lollipop** N el pirulí

**marmalade** N la mermelada de naranja

**marzipan** N e mazapán

**meringue** N el merengue

**mint** N el caramelo de menta

**mousse** N la mousse

**pancake** N la tortita

**popcorn** N las palomitas

**rice pudding** N el arroz con leche

**sponge cake** N el bizcocho

**sugar** N el azúcar

**sweet** N el caramelo

**vanilla** N la vainilla

**whipped cream** N la nata montada

**yoghurt** N el yogur

**apple** N la **manzana**

**apricot** N el **albaricoque**

**aubergine** N la **berenjena**

**avocado** N el **aguacate**

**banana** N el **plátano**

**beetroot** N la **remolacha**

**blackberry** N la **mora**

**blackcurrant** N la **grosella negra**

**broccoli** N el **brécol**

**Brussels sprouts** N PL las **coles de Bruselas**

**cabbage** N la **col**

**carrot** N la **zanahoria**

**cauliflower** N la **coliflor**

**celery** N el **apio**

**cherry** N la **cereza**

**chestnut** N la **castaña**

**clementine** N la **clementina**

**coconut** N el **coco**

**courgette** N el **calabacín** (PL los **calabacines**)

**cress** N el **berro**

**cucumber** N el **pepino**

**French beans** N PL las **judías verdes**

**fruit** N la **fruta**

**fruit salad** N la **macedonia**

**gooseberry** N la **grosella espinosa**

**grapefruit** N el **pomelo**

**grapes** N PL las **uvas**

**hazelnut** N la **avellana**

**leek** N el **puerro**

**lemon** N el **limón** (PL los **limones**)

**lettuce** N la **lechuga**

**lime** N la **lima**

**mango** N el **mango**

**melón** N el **melón** (PL los **melones**)

**onion** N la **cebolla**

**orange** N la **naranja**

**pea** N el **guisante**

**peach** N el **melocotón** (PL los **melocotones**)

**peanut** N el **cacahuete**

**pear** N la **pera**

**pepper** N el **pimiento**

**pineapple** N la **piña**

**plum** N la **ciruela**

**pumpkin** N la **calabaza**

**radish** N el **rábano**

**raisin** N la **pasa**

**raspberry** N la **frambuesa**

**redcurrant** N la **grosella roja**

**spinach** N las **espinacas**

**strawberry** N la **fresa**

**sultana** N la **pasa sultana**

**tangerine** N la **mandarina**

**tomato** N el **tomate**

**turnip** N el **nabo**

**vegetables** N PL las **verduras**

**walnut** N la **nuez**

**watermelon** N la **sandía**

**apple juice** N el zumo
de manzana

**beer** N la cerveza

**black coffee** N el café solo

**champagne** N el champán

**cocoa** N el cacao

**coffee** N el café

**Coke**® N la Coca-Cola®

**decaffeinated coffee** N
el café descafeinado

**fruit juice** N el zumo de
fruta

**hot chocolate** N
el chocolate caliente

**juice** N el zumo

**latte** N el café con leche

**lemonade** N la gaseosa

**milk** N la leche

**milkshake** N el batido

**mineral water** N el agua
mineral

**orange juice** N el zumo
de naranja

**peach juice** N el zumo de
melocotón

**pineapple juice** N
el zumo de piña

**tea** N el té

**water** N el agua

**wine** N el vino

**armchair** N el **sillón**
(PL los **sillones**)

**bath tub** N la **bañera**

**bed** N la **cama**

**bench** N el **banco**

**bookcase** N la **librería**

**bookshelf** N la **estantería**

**bunk beds** N PL las **camas literas**

**chair** N la **silla**

**chest of drawers** N la **cómoda**

**coffee table** N la **mesa de centro**

**cooker** N la **cocina**

**couch** N el **sofá**

**cupboard** N el **armario**

**curtain** N la **cortina**

**cushion** N el **cojín**
(PL los **cojines**)

**deckchair** N la **tumbona**

**dishwasher** N el **lavavajillas**
(PL los **lavavajillas**)

**double bed** N la **cama de matrimonio**

**easy chair** N la **butaca**

**freezer** N el **congelador**

**fridge** N la **nevera**

**microwave** N el **microondas**
(PL los **microondas**)

**oven** N el **horno**

**refrigerator** N el **frigorífico**

**rug** N la **alfombra**

**sink** N el **fregadero**

**sink** N el **lavabo**

**table** N la **mesa**

**television** N la **televisión**

**tumble dryer** N la **secadora**

**washing machine** N la **lavadora**

All the jobs in the following list can be done by both men and women. For reasons of space, only the masculine forms have been given for nouns that end in **-o** in the masculine and **-a** in the feminine, so don't forget to change el to la and the **-o** ending to **-a** when referring to a woman.

Where the article is shown as el/la, it means that the same noun works for both males and females, eg el/la **juez** N **judge**. Where two translations are given, the one that starts with el is the masculine form while the one that starts with la is the feminine form.

**accountant** N el/la **contable**

**actor** N el **actor**

**actress** N la **actriz**

**air hostess** N la **azafata de vuelo**

**archaeologist** N el **arqueólogo**

**architect** N el **arquitecto**

**artist** N el/la **artista**

**athlete** N el/la **atleta**

**au pair** N el/la **au pair**

**baker** N el **panadero**

**barber** N el **barbero**

**boxer** N el **boxeador**, la **boxeadora**

**builder** N el **albañil**

**bus driver** N el **conductor de autobús**, la **conductora de autobús**

**butcher** N el **carnicero**

**captain** N el **capitán**, la **capitana**

**caretaker** N el **guardián**, la **guardiana**

**chef** N el **cocinero**

**chemist** N el **químico**

**child minder** N el/la **canguro**

**conductor** N el **director de orquesta**, la **directora de orquesta**

**dancer** N el **bailarín** (PL los **bailarines**), la **bailarina**

**dentist** N el/la **dentista**

**detective** N el/la **detective**

**director** N el **director**, la **directora**

**disc jockey** N el/la **disc jockey**

**doctor** N el **médico**

**drummer** N el/la **batería**

**dustman** N el **basurero**

**electrician** N el/la **electricista**

**engineer** N el **ingeniero**

**farmer** N el **agricultor**, la **agricultora**

**film star** N el/la **artista de cine**

**fireman** N el **bombero**

**fisherman** N el **pescador**

**flight attendant** N el/la auxiliar de vuelo

**florist** N el/la **florista**

**football player** N
el **jugador de fútbol**,
la **jugadora de fútbol**

**footballer** N el/la **futbolista**

**gardener** N el **jardinero**

**goalkeeper** N el **portero**

**hairdresser** N el **peluquero**

**head teacher** N
el **director de colegio**,
la **directora de colegio**

**housewife** N ama de casa
*(fem)*

**iman** N el **imán**

**instructor** N el **instructor**,
la **instructora**

**interior designer** N
el **diseñador de interiores**,
la **diseñadora de interiores**

**interpreter** N el/la intérprete

**interviewer** N
el **entrevistador**,
la **entrevistadora**

**inventor** N el **inventor**,
la **inventora**

**jeweller** N el **joyero**

**jockey** N el/la **jockey**

**joiner** N el **carpintero**

**journalist** N el/la **periodista**

**judge** N el/la **juez**

**labourer** N el **obrero**

**lawyer** N el **abogado**

**lecturer** N el **profesor universitario**, la **profesora universitaria**

**librarian** N el **bibliotecario**

**lorry driver** N el **camionero**

**magician** N el **mago**

**mayor** N el **alcalde**,
la **alcaldesa**

**mechanic** N el **mecánico**

**midwife** N la **comadrona**

**miner** N el **minero**

**minister** N el **ministro**

**model** N el/la **modelo**

**monk** N el **monje**

**MP** N el **diputado**

**musician** N el **músico**

**nanny** N la **niñera**

**nun** N la **monja**

**nurse** N la **enfermera**,
el **enfermero**

**operator** N el **teleoperador**,
la **teleoperadora**

**optician** N el **óptico**

**painter** N el **pintor**,
la **pintora**

**paperboy** N el **repartidor de periódicos**

**papergirl** N la repartidora de periódicos

**pharmacist** N el farmacéutico

**physicist** N el físico

**physiotherapist** N el/la fisioterapeuta

**pianist** N el/la pianista

**pilot** N el/la piloto

**plumber** N el fontanero

**policeman** N el policía

**policewoman** N la policía

**pop singer** N el/la cantante pop

**postman** N el cartero

**priest** N el sacerdote

**prison officer** N el/la guardia de prisiones

**professor** N el catedrático

**programmer** N el programador, la programadora

**psychiatrist** N el/la psiquiatra

**psychoanalyst** N el/la psicoanalista

**psychologist** N el psicólogo

**rabbi** N el rabino

**receptionist** N el/la recepcionista

**rep** N el/la representante

**reporter** N el reportero

**sailor** N el marinero

**salesman** N el comercial

**scientist** N el científico

**secretary** N el secretario

**shepherd** N el pastor, la pastora

**shop assistant** N el dependiente, la dependienta

**shopkeeper** N el/la comerciante

**social worker** N el/la asistente social

**soldier** N el/la soldado

**solicitor** N el notario

**supply teacher** N el maestro suplente, la maestra suplente (primary)

**supply teacher** N el profesor suplente, la profesora suplente (secondary)

**surgeon** N el cirujano

**surveyor** N el tasador, a tasadora

**taxi driver** N el/la taxista

**teacher** N el maestro (primary school)

**teacher** N el profesor, la profesora (secondary school)

**technician** N el técnico

**translator** N el traductor, la traductora

**vet** N el veterinario

**vicar** N el cura

**waiter** N el camarero

**waitress** N la camarera

**writer** N el escritor, la escritora

**atlas** N el **atlas**

**bell** N la **campana**

**Biro**® N el **bolígrafo**

**blackboard** N la **pizarra**

**book** N el **libro**

**break time** N el **recreo**

**calculator** N la **calculadora**

**canteen** N el **comedor**

**cassette player** N
el **casete**

**chair** N la **silla**

**chalk** N la **tiza**

**chart** N el **gráfico**

**class** N la **clase**

**classroom** N el **aula** (fem)

**clock** N el **reloj**

**computer** N el **ordenador**

**corridor** N el **pasillo**

**curriculum** N el **programa**

**deputy head** N
el **subdirector**,
la **subdirectora**

**desk** N la **mesa**

**diagram** N el **esquema**

**dictionary** N el **diccionario**

**door** N la **puerta**

**drawing** N el **dibujo**

**drawing pin** N
la **chincheta**

**essay** N la **redacción**
(PL las **redacciones**)

**exam** N el **examen**
(PL los **exámenes**)

**exercise** N el **ejercicio**

**exercise book** N
el **cuaderno**

**felt-tip pen** N el **rotulador**

**folder** N la **carpeta**

**general knowledge** N
la **cultura general**

**grammar** N la **gramática**

**gym** N el **gimnasio**

**gym kit** N la **ropa de
gimnasia**

**head teacher** N el **director**,
la **directora**

**homework** N los **deberes**

**ink** N la **tinta**

**jotter** N el **bloc de notas**

**language laboratory** N
el **laboratorio de idiomas**

**lesson** N la **lección** (PL las
**lecciones**)

**library** N la **biblioteca**

**mouse** N el **ratón** (PL los
**ratones**)

**mousemat** N la **alfombrilla
del ratón**

**page** N la **página**

**pen** N la **pluma**

**pencil** N el **lápiz** (PL los **lápices**)

**pencil case** N el lapicero

**pencil sharpener** N
el **sacapuntas** (PL los sacapuntas)

**photocopier** N
la **fotocopiadora**

**photocopy** N la fotocopia

**playground** N el patio de recreo

**printer** N la impresora

**pupil** N el alumno

**registration** N la inscripción

**rubber** N la goma

**ruler** N la regla

• **School subjects –
Las asignaturas**

**art** N el dibujo

**English** N el inglés

**French** N el francés

**geography** N la geografía

**gym** N la gimnasia

**history** N la historia

**ICT** N la informática

**literacy** N la lengua

**maths** N las matemáticas

**school** N el colegio

**schoolbag** N la cartera

**schoolboy** N el colegial

**secondary school** N
el **instituto de secundaria**

**teacher** N el maestro

**test** N la prueba

**textbook** N el libro de texto

**whiteboard** N la pizarra blanca

**window** N la ventana

**music** N la música

**numeracy** N las matemáticas

**PE** N la educación física

**RE** N la religión

**science** N las ciencias

**attic** N el ático
**basement** N el sótano
**bedroom** N el dormitorio

**canteen** N el comedor
**changing room** N
el vestuario
**classroom** N el aula

**cloakroom** N
el guardarropa
**garage** N el garaje
**hall** N la entrada
**kitchen** N la cocina
**library** N la biblioteca
**living room** N la sala
de estar
**lounge** N el salón
(PL los salones)
**office** N la oficina
**staircase** N la escalera
**study** N el despacho
**toilet** N el baño

| | | | | | | |
|---|---|---|---|---|---|---|
| **1** | uno | **14** | catorce | **70** | setenta |
| **2** | dos | **15** | quince | **80** | ochenta |
| **3** | tres | **16** | dieciséis | **90** | noventa |
| **4** | cuatro | **17** | diecisiete | **100** | cien |
| **5** | cinco | **18** | dieciocho | **101** | ciento uno |
| **6** | seis | **19** | diecinueve | **200** | doscientos |
| **7** | siete | **20** | veinte | **250** | doscientos |
| **8** | ocho | **21** | veintiuno | | cincuenta |
| **9** | nueve | **22** | veintidós | | |
| **10** | diez | **30** | treinta | **1,000** | mil |
| **11** | once | **40** | cuarenta | **2,000** | dos mil |
| **12** | doce | **50** | cincuenta | **1,000,000** | un millón |
| **13** | trece | **60** | sesenta | | |

| **What time is it?** | **It's ...** |
|---|---|
| ¿Qué hora es? | Es .../Son ... |

**one o'clock**
la una

**ten past one**
la una y diez

**quarter past one**
la una y cuarto

**half past one**
la una y media

**twenty to two**
las dos menos veinte

**quarter to two**
las dos menos cuarto

| **What time...?** | **¿A qué hora ... ?** |
|---|---|

**at midnight**
a medianoche

**at midday**
a mediodía

**at one o'clock**
(in the afternoon)
a la una (de la tarde)

**at eight o'clock**
(at night)
a las ocho
(de la noche)

**at quarter past
eleven**
(in the morning)
a las once y cuarto
(de la mañana)

**at quarter to nine**
(at night)
a las nueve menos cuarto
(de la noche)

The tables that follow show how the main Spanish verbs work in the present tense.

In Spanish the ending of the verb changes according to the person. This means that the form of the verb used for **yo** is different from the form used for **nosotros**, **ellos** etc.

The first three verbs given (**hablar**, **comer** and **vivir**) can be used as models for any other regular -**ar**, -**er** or -**ir** verb.

At the end of each table, there are some useful phrases which require other tenses. The examples throughout the dictionary use a variety of basic tenses that children and teachers alike will find useful.

### 1 hablar (to speak)

| (yo) | hablo | (nosotros/as) | hablamos |
|---|---|---|---|
| (tú) | hablas | (vosotros/as) | habláis |
| (él/ella/usted) | habla | (ellos/ellas/ustedes) | hablan |

**Hoy he hablado con mi hermana.** I've spoken to my sister today.
**No hables tan alto.** Don't talk so loud.
**No se hablan.** They don't talk to each other.

### 2 comer (to eat)

| (yo) | como | (nosotros/as) | comemos |
|---|---|---|---|
| (tú) | comes | (vosotros/as) | coméis |
| (él/ella/usted) | come | (ellos/ellas/ustedes) | comen |

**No come carne.** He doesn't eat meat.
**No comas tan deprisa.** Don't eat so fast.
**Se lo ha comido todo.** He's eaten it all.

### 3 vivir (to live)

| (yo) | vivo | (nosotros/as) | vivimos |
|---|---|---|---|
| (tú) | vives | (vosotros/as) | vivís |
| (él/ella/usted) | vive | (ellos/ellas/ustedes) | viven |

**¿Dónde vives?** Where do you live?
**Viven en Valencia.** They live in Valencia.
**Vivimos en Inglaterra dos años.** We lived in England for two years.

**4** **estar** (to be)

|  |  |  |  |
|---|---|---|---|
| (yo) | estoy | (nosotros/as) | estamos |
| (tú) | estás | (vosotros/as) | estáis |
| (él/ella/usted) | está | (ellos/ellas/ustedes) | están |

**Estoy cansado.** I'm tired.
**Estuvimos en casa de mi tía.** We went to my aunt's.
**¿A qué hora estarás en casa?** What time will you be home?

**5** **ser** (to be)

|  |  |  |  |
|---|---|---|---|
| (yo) | soy | (nosotros/as) | somos |
| (tú) | eres | (vosotros/as) | sois |
| (él/ella/usted) | es | (ellos/ellas/ustedes) | son |

**Soy español.** I'm Spanish.
**¿Fuiste tú el que llamó?** Was it you who phoned?
**Era de noche.** It was dark.

**6** **ir** (to go)

|  |  |  |  |
|---|---|---|---|
| (yo) | voy | (nosotros/as) | vamos |
| (tú) | vas | (vosotros/as) | vais |
| (él/ella/usted) | va | (ellos/ellas/ustedes) | van |

**Voy al colegio del barrio.** I go to the local school.
**Vamos al parque.** Let's go to the park.
**Ayer fuimos al cine.** We went to the cinema yesterday.

**7** **tener** (to have)

|  |  |  |  |
|---|---|---|---|
| (yo) | tengo | (nosotros/as) | tenemos |
| (tú) | tienes | (vosotros/as) | tenéis |
| (él/ella/usted) | tiene | (ellos/ellas/ustedes) | tienen |

**Tengo dos hermanos.** I have two brothers.
**¿Cuántos años tienes?** How old are you?
**Tengo que hacer los deberes.** I have to do my homework.

**8** **haber** (to have [auxiliary])

|  |  |  |  |
|---|---|---|---|
| (yo) | he | (nosotros/as) | hemos |
| (tú) | has | (vosotros/as) | habéis |
| (él/ella/usted) | ha | (ellos/ellas/ustedes) | han |

**¿Has visto eso?** Did you see that?
**Ya hemos ido a ver esa película.** We've already been to see that film.
**Ya te lo había dicho.** I'd already told you.

**9** **decir** (to say)

| | | | |
|---|---|---|---|
| (yo) | digo | (nosotros/as) | decimos |
| (tú) | dices | (vosotros/as) | decís |
| (él./ella/usted) | dice | (ellos/ellas/ustedes) | dicen |

**Pero ¿qué dices?** What are you saying?
**Me lo dijo ayer.** He told me yesterday.
**¿Te ha dicho lo del profesor?** Has he told you about the teacher?

**10** **dar** (to give)

| | | | |
|---|---|---|---|
| (yo) | doy | (nosotros/as) | damos |
| (tú) | das | (vosotros/as) | dais |
| (él/ella/usted) | da | (ellos/ellas/ustedes) | dan |

**Me da miedo la oscuridad.** I'm scared of the dark.
**Nos dieron un par de entradas gratis.** They gave us a couple of free tickets.
**Te daré el número de mi móvil.** I'll give you my mobile phone number.

mi villa

la estación

el hospital

el río

HOSPITAL

la oficina de correos

el puente

el museo

la farmacia

la plaza

la iglesia

el banco

el mercado

el cine · ODEON

la calle

el patio de recreo

la acera

la escuela

el supermercado

el semáforo

ESCUELA

303

en casa

el edificio

la tercera planta

la escalera

la segunda planta

el tejado

la primera planta

La planta baja

la ventana

el ascensor

la puerta

la entrada

el jardín

la llave

la planta

MI HABITACIÓN

el balcón

# mi habitación

el armario

la cortina

el ordenador

el libro

la mesa

el juguete

la silla

el cajón

el juego de ordenador

la librería

los cómics

el despertador

las zapatillas

la cama

el edredón

el pijama

la almohada

la guitarra

mi fiesta de cumpleaños

la vela

la tarta

el globo

el algodón de azúcar

la pajita

el tenedor

el vaso

la servilleta

el plato

la cuchara

el zumo

las patatas fritas

la limonada

la cámara

el regalo

los caramelos

en el parque

la cometa

el tiovivo

el tobogán

el columpio

el césped

el monopatín

el balón

la flor

los patines en línea

REFRESCOS

el helado

el estanque

el banco

el cisne

la bici

el pato

la mariposa

En la montaña

la pista de esquí

la nieve

el esquiador

el trineo

el telesilla

el patinaje
sobre hielo

la mochila

el muñeco
de nieve

la trucha

el lago

la cierva

las botas de
montaña

la vaca

la cabra

# En la playa

el sol

la gaviota

la ola

el pez

las aletas

la roca

la nadadora

el mar

el socorrista

el flotador

el parasol

la arena

el bañador

la estrella de mar

el cangrejo

las gafas de sol

la crema solar

el castillo de arena

el cubo y la pala

la concha

En el bosque

la ardilla
el búho
el árbol
el zorro
el abeto
la hoja
el ciervo
el conejo
el trébol
la seta
el arroyo
la castaña
la frambuesa
la hormiga
el erizo

# English - Spanish

# A a

**a** ARTICLE
**un** *masc*
**una** *fem*

> **Language tip**
> Use **un** for masculine nouns and
> **una** for feminine nouns.

> **a book**
> un libro
> **a girl**
> una chica

> **Language tip**
> **a** isn't always translated by **un** and
> **una**.

> **He's a mechanic.**
> Es mecánico.
> **It costs ten pence a packet.**
> Cuesta diez peniques el paquete.
> **a hundred pounds**
> cien libras

**able** ADJECTIVE
> **to be able to**
> poder
> **Will you be able to come?**
> ¿Podrás venir?
> **I won't be able to help you.**
> No podré ayudarte.

**about** ADVERB, PREPOSITION
1 **alrededor de** (*approximately*)
> **about fifty euros**
> alrededor de cincuenta euros
> **at about eleven o'clock**
> alrededor de las once
2 **sobre** (*concerning*)
> **a programme about lions**
> un programa sobre los leones
> **How about a game of cards?**
> ¿Por qué no jugamos a las cartas?
> **I'm hungry, how about you?**
> Yo tengo hambre, ¿y tú?
> **We're about to go out.**
> Estamos a punto de salir.

**above** PREPOSITION

> **Language tip**
> When something is located above
> something, use **encima de**. When
> there is movement involved, use **por
> encima de**.

1 **encima de**
> **There's a picture above the
> fireplace.**
> Hay un cuadro encima de a
> chimenea.
2 **por encima de**
> **Throw the ball above your
> head.**
> Lanza el balón por encima de la
> cabeza.

> **Language tip**
> In Spanish you usually use an article
> like **el**, **la**, **los** with parts of the
> body.

3 **más de** (*more than*)
> **above thirty degrees**
> más de treinta grados

**abroad** ADVERB
1 **en el extranjero** (*in a foreign
country*)
> **They live abroad.**
> Viven en el extranjero.
2 **al extranjero** (*to a foreign
country*)
> **We're going abroad this
> year.**
> Vamos al extranjero este año.

**absent** ADJECTIVE
> **Who's absent today?**
> ¿Quién no está hoy?
> **Tom's absent.**
> Tom no está.

**absurd** ADJECTIVE
> **absurdo** *masc*
> **absurda** *fem*

**That's absurd!**
¡Eso es absurdo!

**academy** NOUN
la **academia** *fem*

**accent** NOUN
el **acento** *masc*
**He's got a good accent.**
Tiene buen acento.

**accident** NOUN
el **accidente** *masc*
**It was an accident.**
Fue un accidente.
**a car accident**
un accidente de coche
**by accident**
por casualidad/sin querer

*Language tip*
**by accident** *has two translations.*
*Look at the examples.*

**They discovered it by accident.**
Lo descubrieron por casualidad.
**The player touched the ball by accident.**
El jugador tocó el balón sin querer.

**ace** NOUN
el **as** *masc*
**the ace of hearts**
el as
de corazones

to **ache** VERB
**My leg's aching.**
Me duele la pierna.

*Language tip*
*In Spanish you usually use an article like* **el**, **la**, **los** *with parts of the body.*

**across** PREPOSITION
**al otro lado de**
**It's across the road.**
Está al otro lado de la calle.
**You mustn't run across the road.**

No debes cruzar la calle
corriendo.

to **act** VERB
**actuar**
**He's acting in a play.**
Actúa en una obra de teatro.

**activity** NOUN
la **actividad** *fem*
**outdoor activities**
actividades al aire libre

**actor** NOUN
el **actor** *masc*
la **actriz** *fem* (PL las **actrices**)
**He's an actor.**
Es actor.

*Language tip*
*In Spanish, you do not use an article with people's jobs.*

**actress** NOUN
la **actriz** *fem* (PL las **actrices**)

**actually** ADVERB
**en realidad**
**Actually, it's good fun.**
En realidad, es bastante
divertido.

*Language tip*
*Be careful! The translation of*
**actually** *is not* **actualmente**.

**AD** ABBREVIATION
(= **Anno Domini**)
**d.C.** (= *después de Cristo*)
**in 800 AD**
en el 800 d.C.

to **add** VERB
**añadir**
**Add some sugar.**
Añade un poco de azúcar.

to **add up** VERB
**sumar**
**You have to add the figures up.**
Hay que sumar las cantidades.

**address** NOUN
la **dirección** *fem* (PL las
**direcciones**)

**What's your address, Emma?**
¿Cuál es tu dirección, Emma?

**adjective** NOUN
el **adjetivo** masc

**admission** NOUN
la **entrada** fem
'admission free'
'entrada libre'

**adopted** ADJECTIVE
I'm adopted.
Soy adoptado.

**adult** NOUN
el **adulto** masc
la **adulta** fem
two adults and one child
dos adultos y un menor

**advantage** NOUN
la **ventaja** fem
It's an advantage to be able to speak English.
Es una ventaja saber hablar inglés.

**adventure** NOUN
la **aventura** fem
Harry has lots of adventures.
A Harry le suceden muchas aventuras.

**adverb** NOUN
el **adverbio** masc

**advert** NOUN
el **anuncio** masc
They put an advert in the newspaper.
Pusieron un anuncio en el periódico.

**advice** NOUN
los **consejos** masc pl
Can you give me some advice?
¿Puedes darme algunos consejos?
That's good advice.
Es un buen consejo.
a piece of advice
un consejo

**Language tip**
Be careful! The translation of advice is not aviso.

**aerobics** NOUN
el **aerobic** masc

**aeroplane** NOUN
el **avión** masc (PL los **aviones**)
on an aeroplane
en un avión

**affectionate** ADJECTIVE
**cariñoso** masc
**cariñosa** fem
My cat is very affectionate.
Mi gato es muy cariñoso.

to **afford** VERB
**permitirse**
I can't afford a new pair of jeans.
No puedo permitirme comprar unos vaqueros nuevos.

**Language tip**
There isn't really a verb that translates afford in Spanish. You need to use a phrase with permitirse.

**afraid** ADJECTIVE
to be afraid
tener miedo
I'm afraid.
Tengo miedo.
I'm afraid of spiders.
Me dan miedo las arañas.
Are you afraid of the dark?
¿Te da miedo la oscuridad?

**after** PREPOSITION
**después de**
after break
después del recreo
after lunch
después de comer

**afternoon** NOUN
la **tarde** fem
In the morning or in the afternoon?

¿Por la mañana o por la tarde?
**at three o'clock in the afternoon**
a las tres de la tarde
**I'm playing football on Saturday afternoon.**
Voy a jugar al fútbol el sábado por la tarde.

**this afternoon**
esta tarde
**in the afternoon**
por la tarde
**Good afternoon!**
¡Buenas tardes!

**afters** PL NOUN
el **postre** *masc*
**What do you want for afters?**
¿Qué quieres de postre?

**again** ADVERB
**otra vez**
**I'd like to hear it again.**
Quiero escucharlo otra vez.
**Try again!**
¡Inténtalo otra vez!

**Language tip**
*You can also use* **volver a** *followed by the main verb to translate* **again.**

**Try again!**
¡Vuelve a intentarlo!

**against** PREPOSITION
**contra**
**You mustn't lean your chair against the wall.**
No debes apoyar la silla contra la pared.

**age** NOUN
la **edad** *fem*
**Write your name and age.**
Escribe tu nombre y tu edad.
**at the age of thirteen**
a la edad de trece años

**I am the same age as you.**
Tengo la misma edad que tú.

**Language tip**
*Note that in Spanish you use the verb* **tener** *to talk about somebody's age.*

**ago** ADVERB
**I bought it six months ago.**
Lo compré hace seis meses.

**a week ago**
hace una semana
**a long time ago**
hace mucho tiempo

to **agree** VERB
**estar de acuerdo**
**I agree.**
Estoy de acuerdo.
**I agree with Carol.**
Estoy de acuerdo con Carol.

**ahead** ADVERB
**Look straight ahead!**
¡Mira hacia adelante!
**The red team is five points ahead.**
El equipo rojo lleva cinco puntos de ventaja.
**There were a lot of people ahead of us in the queue.**
Había mucha gente delante de nosotros en la cola.

**air** NOUN
el **aire** *masc*
**Throw the ball into the air.**
Lanza el balón al aire.
**I prefer to travel by air.**
Prefiero viajar en avión.

**air-conditioned** ADJECTIVE
**climatizado** *masc*
**climatizada** *fem*

**airmail** NOUN
**by airmail**
por avión

**airport** NOUN
el **aeropuerto** *masc*

**alarm clock** NOUN
el **despertador** *masc*

**album** NOUN
el **álbum** *masc*

**alcohol** NOUN
el **alcohol** *masc*
**I don't drink alcohol.**
No bebo alcohol.

**A levels** PL NOUN
el **bachillerato** *masc*
**My brother is doing his A levels.**
Mi hermano está haciendo el bachillerato.

> **Did you know...?**
> The **bachillerato** is the Spanish equivalent of **A levels**.

**alive** ADJECTIVE
**vivo** *masc*
**viva** *fem*
**They're still alive.**
Todavía siguen vivos.

**all** ADJECTIVE, PRONOUN
**todo** *masc*
**toda** *fem*
**all the time**
todo el tiempo
**all night**
toda la noche
**all my friends**
todos mis amigos
**all the girls**
todas las chicas
**The score is five all.**
El marcador está empatado a cinco.

> **Is that all?**
> ¿Eso es todo?

**allergic** ADJECTIVE
**alérgico** *masc*
**alérgica** *fem*

**I'm allergic to cats.**
Soy alérgica a los gatos.

**allergy** NOUN
la **alergia** *fem*
**Have you got any allergies?**
¿Tienes alguna alergia?

**allowed** ADJECTIVE
**permitido** *masc*
**permitida** *fem*
**It's not allowed.**
No está permitido.
**We're not allowed to use calculators in the exam.**
No se nos permite usar calculadora en el examen.

**all right** ADVERB, ADJECTIVE
1 **bien** *(not bad)*
**Are you all right?**
¿Estás bien?
**Is that all right?**
¿Está bien así?
**Do you like school? – It's all right.**
¿Te gusta ir al colegio? – Regular.
2 **de acuerdo** *(when agreeing)*
**I'd like a coffee. – All right.**
Quiero un café. – De acuerdo.

**almost** ADVERB
**casi**
**Are you ready? – Almost.**
¿Estás lista? – Casi.

**alone** ADJECTIVE
1 **solo** *masc*
**sola** *fem*
**to be alone**
estar solo
**He was alone in the house.**
Estaba solo en la casa.
**She lives alone.**
Vive sola.
2 **tranquilo** *masc*
**tranquila** *fem* *(in peace)*
**Paul, leave Graham alone!**
¡Paul, deja tranquilo a Graham!
**Leave him alone!**
¡Déjalo tranquilo!

**Leave me alone!**
¡Déjame tranquilo!
**Leave my things alone!**
¡No toques mis cosas!

**along** PREPOSITION
**por**
   **a walk along the beach**
   un paseo por la playa

**aloud** ADVERB
**en voz alta**
   **Read the words aloud, children.**
   Leed las palabras en voz alta, niños.
   **Read the words aloud, Richard.**
   Lee las palabras en voz alta, Richard.

**alphabet** NOUN
   el **alfabeto** *masc*

**alphabetical order** NOUN
   **in alphabetical order**
   por orden alfabético

**already** ADVERB
**ya**
   **I've already done it.**
   Ya lo he hecho.
   **Have you finished already?**
   ¿Ya has terminado?

**also** ADVERB
**también**
   **I also play the flute.**
   También toco la flauta.

**alternate** ADJECTIVE
   **on alternate days**
   cada dos días

**alternative** NOUN
   la **alternativa** *fem*
   **You have no alternative.**
   No tienes alternativa.

**altogether** ADVERB
**en total**
   **That's twenty pounds altogether.**
   Son veinte libras en total.

**always** ADVERB
**siempre**
   **The bus is always late.**
   El autobús siempre llega tarde.

**am** VERB ▷ *see* **be**

**a.m.** ABBREVIATION
**de la mañana**
   **at four a.m.**
   a las cuatro de la mañana

**amazing** ADJECTIVE
**1 increíble** *masc & fem* (*surprising*)
   **That's amazing!**
   ¡Eso es increíble!
**2 excelente** *masc & fem* (*excellent*)
   **Vivian's an amazing cook.**
   Vivian es una cocinera excelente.

**ambulance** NOUN
   la **ambulancia** *fem*

**America** NOUN
   los **Estados Unidos** *masc pl*
   **We're going to America.**
   Vamos a Estados Unidos.

## American

American *can be an adjective or a noun.*

**A** ADJECTIVE
   **americano** *masc*
   **americana** *fem*
   **American food**
   la cocina americana

**He's American.**
Es americano.
**She's American.**
Es americana.

**B** NOUN
   el **americano** *masc*
   la **americana** *fem*
   **the Americans**
   los americanos

*Language tip*

**americano** *is not spelled with a capital letter in Spanish.*

**amount** NOUN
la **cantidad** *fem*
**a huge amount of rice**
una enorme cantidad de arroz
**a large amount of money**
una gran suma de dinero

**amusement arcade** NOUN
el **salón recreativo** *masc* (PL
los **salones recreativos**)

**an** ARTICLE
**un** *masc*
**una** *fem*

**Language tip**
Use **un** for masculine
nouns and **una** for
feminine nouns.

**an animal**
un animal
**an apple**
una manzana

**Language tip**
Sometimes the article **an** isn't
translated.

**He's an actor.**
Es actor.
**ten kilometres an hour**
diez kilómetros por hora

**and** CONJUNCTION
**y**
**my brother and me**
mi hermano y yo
**Two and two are four.**
Dos y dos son cuatro.

**Language tip**
Use **e** instead of **y** before words
beginning with **i-** or **hi-** but not
**hie-**.

**Miguel and Ignacio**
Miguel e Ignacio

**Language tip**
Don't translate **and** in numbers.

**two hundred and fifty**
doscientos cincuenta

**angel** NOUN
el **ángel** *masc*

**Language tip**
Even though **ángel** is a masculine
word, you can use it to refer to a
woman or girl.

**You're an angel!**
¡Eres un ángel!

**angry** ADJECTIVE
**enfadado** *masc*
**enfadada** *fem*
**He's very angry.**
Está muy enfadado.
**to get angry**
enfadarse
**Mum gets angry if I'm
late.**
Mi madre se enfada si llego
tarde.

**animal** NOUN
el **animal** *masc*

**anniversary** NOUN
el **aniversario** *masc*
**my parents' wedding
anniversary**
el aniversario de bodas de mis
padres

**Happy anniversary!**
¡Feliz aniversario!

**Language tip**
Have you noticed the upside-down
exclamation mark at the start of
Spanish exclamations?

**announcement** NOUN
el **anuncio** *masc*
**an important announcement**
un anuncio importante

**anorak** NOUN
el **anorak** *masc*
**my new anorak**
mi anorak nuevo

**another** ADJECTIVE, PRONOUN
**otro** *masc*
**otra** *fem*

**Would you like another sandwich?**
¿Quieres otro sandwich?
**There are plenty of apples. Would you like another one?**
Hay muchas manzanas. ¿Quieres otra?

## answer

> **answer** *can be a verb or a noun.*

**A** VERB
**to answer**
contestar
**Isabel, you have to answer yes or no.**
Isabel, tienes que contestar sí o no.
**Think before you answer.**
Piensa antes de contestar.
**to answer a question**
contestar a una pregunta
**Who can answer the question?**
¿Quién puede contestar a la pregunta?
**B** NOUN
la **respuesta** *fem*
**the right answer**
la respuesta correcta

## anthem NOUN
**the national anthem**
el himno nacional

## any

> **any** *can be an adjective or a pronoun.*

**A** ADJECTIVE

> *Language tip*
> *You usually don't translate **any** in questions.*

**Do you want any bread?**
¿Quieres pan?
**Have you got any brothers or sisters?**
¿Tienes hermanos?

> *Language tip*
> *However, you can use **algún** with a masculine singular noun and **alguna** with a feminine singular noun when the emphasis is on each individual person or thing.*

**Do you have any hobbies?**
¿Tienes algún pasatiempo?

> *Language tip*
> *Similarly, you usually don't translate **any** in negative sentences.*

**I don't want any bread.**
No quiero pan.
**There aren't any oranges.**
No hay naranjas.

> *Language tip*
> *However, you can use **ningún** with a masculine singular noun and **ninguna** with a feminine singular noun when **not ... any** is equivalent to **not a single**.*

**I haven't got any CDs left.**
No me queda ningún CD.
**I can't see any flowers.**
No veo ninguna flor.

**Have you got any money?**
¿Tienes dinero?
**Have you got any pets?**
¿Tienes alguna mascota?
**There isn't any milk.**
No hay leche.

**B** PRONOUN
**1** **alguno** *masc*
**alguna** *fem (in questions)*
**I need a stamp. Have you got any left?**
Necesito un sello. ¿Te queda alguno?

> *Language tip*
> *Only use **alguno/alguna** when you mean one or two of something. Otherwise, don't translate **any**.*

**I fancy some soup. Have we got any?**
Me apetece sopa. ¿Tenemos?

I need some oil. Is there any?
Necesito aceite. ¿Hay?
**2 ninguno** *masc*
**ninguna** *fem (in negatives)*
**I don't like any of them.**
No me gusta ninguno.
**A stamp? Sorry, I haven't got any.**
¿Un sello? Lo siento, no tengo ninguno.

### Language tip
*Only use **ninguno/ninguna** when **not any** means **not a single one**. Otherwise, don't translate **any**.*

**I prefer apple juice, but we haven't got any.**
Prefiero zumo de manzana, pero no tenemos.
**I don't want any more.**
No quiero más.

## anybody PRONOUN
**1 alguien** *(in questions)*
**Does anybody want a sweet?**
¿Alguien quiere un caramelo?
**2 nadie** *(in negatives)*
**I didn't see anybody.**
No vi a nadie.

## anyone PRONOUN
**1 alguien** *(in questions)*
**Does anyone want to try?**
¿Alguien quiere probar?
**2 nadie** *(in negatives)*
**I can't see anyone.**
No veo a nadie.

### Language tip
*Don't forget the personal **a** in examples like this one.*

## anything
PRONOUN
**1 algo** *(in questions)*
**Do you want anything to eat?**
¿Quieres comer algo?

**2 nada** *(in negatives)*
**I don't want anything.**
No quiero nada.

## anywhere PRONOUN
**1 en algún sitio** *(in questions)*
**Have you seen my pen anywhere?**
¿Has visto mi bolígrafo en algún sitio?
**Are you going anywhere?**
¿Vas a algún sitio?
**2 en ningún sitio** *(in negatives)*
**I can't find it anywhere.**
No lo encuentro en ningún sitio.
**I'm not going anywhere.**
No voy a ningún sitio.

## apart ADVERB
**Stand with your feet apart.**
Ponte de pie con los pies separados.

### Language tip
*In Spanish you usually use an article like **el**, **la**, **los** with parts of the body.*

**apart from**
aparte de
**Apart from that, everything's fine.**
Aparte de eso, todo va bien.

## apartment NOUN
el **piso** *masc*

## apostrophe NOUN
el **apóstrofo** *masc*
**Don't forget the apostrophe!**
¡Que no se te olvide el apóstrofo!

## apple NOUN
la **manzana** *fem*
**a big red apple**
una manzana grande y roja

## apple juice NOUN
el **zumo de manzana** *masc*

## apple pie NOUN
el **pastel de manzana** *masc*

**appointment** NOUN
la **cita** *fem*
**I've got a dental appointment.**
Tengo cita con el dentista.

**April** NOUN
**abril** *masc*
**My birthday's in April.**
Mi cumpleaños es en abril.
**It's the fifth of April today.**
Hoy es cinco de abril.

**in April**
en abril
**on the ninth of April**
el nueve de abril

*Language tip*
*Months are not spelled with a capital letter in Spanish.*

**April Fool** NOUN
**April Fool!**
¡Inocente!

**April Fools' Day** NOUN
el **día de los Santos Inocentes** *masc*

*Did you know...?*
*In Spanish-speaking countries the day people play practical jokes on each other is 28 December, which is called **el día de los Santos Inocentes**.*

**apron** NOUN
el **delantal** *masc*
**a white apron**
un delantal blanco

**are** VERB ▷ *see* **be**

**area** NOUN
la **zona** *fem*
**a mountainous area of Spain**
una zona montañosa de España

to **argue** VERB
**discutir**

**Stop arguing!**
¡Dejad de discutir!

**arm** NOUN
el **brazo** *masc*
**I've hurt my arm.**
Me he hecho daño en el brazo.

*Language tip*
*In Spanish you usually use an article like **el**, **la**, **los** with parts of the body.*

**armchair** NOUN
el **sillón** *masc* (PL los **sillones**)

**army** NOUN
el **ejército** *masc*
**He's in the army.**
Está en el ejército.

**around** PREPOSITION
1 **alrededor de**
**The pupils are sitting around the teacher.**
Los alumnos están sentados alrededor del profesor.
**I go to bed around ten o'clock.**
Me voy a la cama alrededor de las diez.
2 *(near)*
**around here**
por aquí
**Is there a chemist's around here?**
¿Hay una farmacia por aquí?

to **arrive** VERB
**llegar**
**What time does the train arrive?**
¿A qué hora llega el tren?

**arrow** NOUN
la **flecha** *fem*
**Follow the arrows.**
Siga las flechas.

**art** NOUN
1 el **dibujo** *masc* (at school)
**Art is my favourite subject.**
El dibujo es mi asignatura preferida.

**2** el **arte** *masc (artwork)*
**modern art**
el arte moderno

## art gallery NOUN
el **museo** *masc*
**The art gallery is closed.**
El museo está cerrado.

## artist NOUN
el/la **artista**
*masc/fem*

## as CONJUNCTION, PREPOSITION
**1** **como** *(since)*
**Alice, as it's your birthday you can choose.**
Alice, como es tu cumpleaños, puedes elegir.
**2** **de** *(in the role of)*
**He works as a waiter in the holidays.**
Trabaja de camarero en las vacaciones.
**as ... as**
tan ... como
**Edward's as tall as Stephen.**
Edward es tan alto como Stephen.
**Write to me as soon as possible.**
Escríbeme lo antes posible.

## ashamed ADJECTIVE
**avergonzado** *masc*
**avergonzada** *fem*
**He's ashamed.**
Está avergonzado.
**You should be ashamed of yourself!**
¡Debería darte vergüenza!

## ashtray NOUN
el **cenicero** *masc*

## to ask VERB
**1** **preguntar** *(make inquiry)*
**Ask his name.**
Pregúntale el nombre.

**Ask your friend.**
Pregúntale a tu amigo.

> **Language tip**
> *Don't forget the personal **a** in examples like this one.*

**Who wants to ask a question?**
¿Quién quiere hacer una pregunta?
**Ask the question.**
Haz la pregunta.
**2** **pedir** *(request)*
**If you need help, ask!**
Si necesitas ayuda, ¡pídela!
**3** **invitar** *(invite)*
**Are you going to ask Matthew to the party?**
¿Vas a invitar a Matthew a la fiesta?

> **Language tip**
> *Don't forget the personal **a** in examples like this one.*

## to ask for VERB
**pedir**
**Ask for some chips and a drink.**
Pide patatas fritas y una bebida.

## asleep ADJECTIVE
**dormido** *masc*
**dormida** *fem*
**to be asleep**
estar dormido
**Are you asleep?**
¿Estás dormido?

**assembly** NOUN
la **reunión de los profesores y alumnos** fem

> **Did you know…?**
> There is no **assembly** in Spanish schools.

**assistant** NOUN
1 el **dependiente** masc
la **dependienta** fem (shop assistant)
**Ask the assistant.**
Pregúntale a la dependienta.
2 el/la **ayudante** masc/fem (helper)
**my assistant**
mi ayudante

**asthma** NOUN
el **asma** fem
**I've got asthma.**
Tengo asma.

> **Language tip**
> Even though it's a feminine noun, remember that you use **el** with **asma**.

**astronomy** NOUN
la **astronomía** fem

**at** PREPOSITION
1 **en** (with place, festival)
**at the café**
en el café
**at Christmas**
en Navidad
2 **a** (with time, speed)
**at four o'clock**
a las cuatro
**at fifty kilometres an hour**
a cincuenta kilómetros por hora
**What time did you arrive at the station?**
¿A qué hora llegaste a la estación?

> **Language tip**
> **a** combines with **el** to form **al**.

**What time did you arrive at the airport?**
¿A qué hora llegaste al aeropuerto?
3 la **arroba** fem (at sign)

**My email address is loveday at collins dot co dot U-K (loveday@collins.co.uk).**
Mi e-mail es loveday arroba collins punto co punto U-K (loveday@collins.co.uk).

**at night**
por la noche
**What are you doing at the weekend?**
¿Qué vas a hacer el fin de semana?
**at school**
en el colegio
**at home**
en casa
**two at a time**
dos a la vez

**ate** VERB ▷see **eat**

**athlete** NOUN
el/la **atleta** masc/fem

**Atlantic** NOUN
el **Atlántico** masc

**atlas** NOUN
el **atlas** masc (PL los **atlas**)

**attention** NOUN
la **atención** fem
**Pay attention, everyone!**
¡Prestad atención todos!
**Pay attention, Mark!**
¡Presta atención, Mark!

**attic** NOUN
el **desván** masc (PL los desvanes)

**attractive** ADJECTIVE
**atractivo** masc
**atractiva** fem
**She's very attractive.**
Es muy atractiva.

**August** NOUN
**agosto** *masc*
> **My birthday's in August.**
> Mi cumpleaños es en agosto.
> **It's the tenth of August today.**
> Hoy es diez de agosto.

**in August**
en agosto
**on the fifth of August**
el cinco de agosto

*Language tip*
*Months are not spelled with a capital letter in Spanish.*

**aunt** NOUN
la **tía** *fem*
> **my aunt**
> mi tía
> **my aunt and uncle**
> mis tíos

**au pair** NOUN
el/la **au pair** *masc/fem* (PL los/las au pair)
> **She's working as an au pair in London.**
> Está de au pair en Londres.

**Australia** NOUN
**Australia** *fem*

**Australian**

*Australian can be an adjective or a noun.*

**A** ADJECTIVE
**australiano** *masc*
**australiana** *fem*

**He's Australian.**
Es australiano.
**She's Australian.**
Es australiana.

**B** NOUN
el **australiano** *masc*
la **australiana** *fem*

*Language tip*
*australiano is not spelled with a capital letter in Spanish.*

**author** NOUN
1 el **autor** *masc*
la **autora** *fem* (cf particular book)
> **the author of the book**
> el autor del libro
2 el **escritor** *masc*
la **escritora** *fem* (as a job)
> **a famous author**
> un escritor famoso

**autumn** NOUN
el **otoño** *masc*

**in autumn**
en otoño

**avenue** NOUN
la **avenida** *fem*

**average**

*average can be a noun or an adjective.*

**A** NOUN
la **media** *fem*
**on average**
de media
**above average**
por encima de la media
**B** ADJECTIVE
**medio** *masc*
**media** *fem*
**the average age**
la edad media
**I'm average height.**
Soy de estatura media

**away** ADVERB
**fuera**

**He's away on a business trip.**
Está fuera en viaje de negocios.
**He'll be away for a week.**
Estará fuera una semana.

**awful** ADJECTIVE
**horroroso** *masc*
**horrorosa** *fem*

**The food's awful.**
La comida está horrorosa.
**That's awful!**
¡Eso es horroroso!
**I feel awful.**
Me siento fatal.

# B b

**baby** NOUN
el **bebé** *masc*

> **Language tip**
> The masculine form **el bebé** applies
> to both boys and girls.

**The baby's asleep.**
El bebé está durmiendo.
**She's going to have a baby.**
Va a tener un niño.
**Don't be a baby!**
¡No seas crío!

to **babysit** VERB
hacer de canguro
**I babysit at the weekends.**
Hago de canguro los fines de
semana.

**babysitter** NOUN
el/la **canguro** *masc/fem*

> **Did you know...?**
> Did you know that **un canguro** is
> also a kangaroo?

## back

> **back** can be a noun or an adjective.

**A** NOUN
1 la **espalda** *fem (of person)*
**My back hurts.**
Me duele la espalda.

> **Language tip**
> In Spanish you usually use an article
> like **el**, **la**, **los** with parts of the
> body.

**Lie on your back!**
¡Túmbate de espaldas!
2 el **fondo** *masc (of room)*
**at the back**
al fondo
**Tony and I sit at the back.**
Tony y yo nos sentamos al
fondo.

**at the back of the house**
en la parte de atrás de la casa
3 el **final** *masc (of book)*
**The verb tables are at the
back of the book.**
Las conjugaciones verbales
están al final del libro.
**B** ADJECTIVE
**trasero** *masc*
**trasera** *fem*
**the back seat**
el asiento trasero
**He came in the back door.**
Entró por la puerta de atrás.

**backache** NOUN
**I've got backache.**
Me duele la espalda.

**background** NOUN
el **fondo** *masc*
**a house in the background**
una casa en el fondo

**backstroke** NOUN
la **espalda** *fem*
**I can do the backstroke.**
Sé nadar a espalda.

**backwards** ADVERB
hacia atrás
**Take a step backwards!**
¡Da un paso hacia atrás!

**bacon** NOUN
el **beicon** *masc*
**bacon and eggs**
huevos con beicon

**bad** ADJECTIVE
1 **malo** *masc*
**mala** *fem (awful)*
**a bad film**
una mala película
**Smoking is bad for you.**
Fumar es malo para la salud.

**Language tip**
*Shorten* **malo** *to* **mal** *before a masculine singular noun.*

**bad weather**
mal tiempo

**Language tip**
**mal** *is also used in some phrases.*

**That's not bad.**
No está mal.
**I'm bad at drawing.**
Se me da mal el dibujo.
2 **grave** *masc & fem (serious)*
**a bad accident**
un accidente grave
3 **travieso** *masc*
**traviesa** *fem (naughty)*
**You bad boy!**
¡Eres un chico travieso!

**Bad luck!**
¡Mala suerte!

**badge** NOUN
la **chapa** *fem*

**badly** ADVERB
**mal**
**He behaved badly.**
Se portó mal.

**badminton** NOUN
el **bádminton** *masc*
**I play badminton.**
Juego al bádminton.

**Language tip**
*In Spanish, you need to add* **al** *before the name of the sport or game.*

**bag** NOUN
1 la **bolsa** *fem*
**a plastic bag**
una bolsa de plástico
2 el **bolso** *masc (handbag)*

**bagpipes** PL NOUN
la **gaita** *fem*
**Jimmy plays the bagpipes.**
Jimmy toca la gaita.

**baked beans**
PL NOUN
las **alubias con tomate**
*fem pl*
**I like baked beans.**
Me gustan las alubias con tomate.

**baked potato** NOUN
la **patata asada** *fem*

**baker's** NOUN
la **panadería** *fem*

**bakery** NOUN
la **panadería** *fem*

**balcony** NOUN
el **balcón** *masc* (PL los **balcones**)

**bald** ADJECTIVE
**calvo** *masc*
**calva** *fem*
**My grandfather is bald.**
Mi abuelo es calvo.

**ball** NOUN
1 la **pelota** *fem (for tennis, golf, cricket)*
**Hit the ball!**
¡Dale a la pelota!
2 el **balón** *masc* (PL los **balones**)
*(for football, rugby)*
**Pass the ball!**
¡Pasa el balón!

**ballet** NOUN
el **ballet** *masc*
**I do ballet.**
Hago ballet.

**ballet dancer** NOUN
el **bailarín** *masc* (PL los bailarines)
la **bailarina** *fem*

**ballet shoes** PL NOUN
las **zapatillas de ballet** *fem pl*

**balloon** NOUN
el **globo** *masc*
**a red balloon**
un globo rojo

**banana** NOUN
el **plátano** *masc*

**band** NOUN
1 el **grupo de rock** *masc* (rock band)
2 la **banda de música** *fem* (brass band)

**bandage** NOUN
la **venda** *fem*
**He's got a bandage round his arm.**
Lleva una venda en el brazo.

*Language tip*

*In Spanish you usually use an article like* **el**, **la**, **los** *with parts of the body.*

**bang**

bang *can be a noun or a verb.*

**A** NOUN
el **golpe** *masc*
**I heard a bang.**
Oí un golpe.
**I got a nasty bang on my head.**
Me di un golpe fuerte en la cabeza.
**The door shut with a bang.**
La puerta se cerró de un portazo.
**B** VERB
**to bang**
golpear
**Mind you don't bang your head!**

¡Cuidado no te vayas a golpear la cabeza!
**Don't bang the door!**
¡No des un portazo!

**banger** NOUN
1 la **salchicha** *fem* (sausage)
**bangers and mash**
salchichas con puré de patatas
2 el **petardo** *masc* (firework)
**Peter is scared of bangers.**
A Peter le asustan los petardos.

**bank** NOUN
1 el **banco** *masc* (for money)
**She works in a bank.**
Trabaja en un banco.
2 la **orilla** *fem* (of river, lake)
**the banks of the Thames**
las orillas del Támesis

**bank holiday** NOUN
el **día festivo** *masc*
**It's a bank holiday today.**
Hoy es día festivo.

**bar** NOUN
1 (piece)
**a bar of chocolate**
una tableta de chocolate
**a bar of soap**
una pastilla de jabón

2 el **bar** *masc* (place)
**She works in a bar.**
Trabaja en un bar.

**barbecue** NOUN
la **barbacoa** *fem*

**barber's** NOUN
la **barbería** *fem*
**at the barber's**
en la barbería

# English Spanish

**bare** ADJECTIVE
**desnudo** *masc*
**desnuda** *fem*
**She had bare arms.**
Tenía los brazos desnudos.
**Don't run about in bare feet.**
No andes por ahí descalzo.

**bargain** NOUN
la **ganga** *fem*
**It's a bargain!**
¡Es una ganga!

to **bark** VERB
**ladrar**
**My dog barks a lot.**
Mi perro ladra mucho.

**baseball** NOUN
el **béisbol** *masc*
**I play baseball.**
Juego al béisbol.

**Language tip**

*In Spanish, you need to add **al** before the name of the sport or game.*

**baseball cap** NOUN
la **gorra de béisbol** *fem*

**basement** NOUN
el **sótano** *masc*

**basin** NOUN
el **lavabo** *masc* (washbasin)

**basket** NOUN
la **cesta** *fem*

**basketball** NOUN
el **baloncesto** *masc*
**Do you play basketball?**
¿Juegas al baloncesto?

**Language tip**

*In Spanish, you need to add **al** before the name of the sport or game.*

**bat** NOUN
1 el **bate** *masc* (for cricket, rounders)
2 la **raqueta** *fem* (for table tennis)

3 el **murciélago**
*masc (animal)*

**bath** NOUN
1 el **baño** *masc* (wash)
**a hot bath**
un baño caliente
**to have a bath**
bañarse
**I have a bath every night.**
Me baño todas las noches.
2 la **bañera** *fem* (tub)
**There's a spider in the bath!**
¡Hay una araña en la bañera!

**Language tip**

*Don't confuse **la bañera** (the bathtub) with **el baño** (the wash you have in it).*

**bathroom** NOUN
el **cuarto de baño** *masc*

**battery** NOUN
1 la **pila** *fem* (for torch, toy)
**I need a battery.**
Necesito una pila.
2 la **batería** *fem* (for car)
**The battery's flat.**
La batería está descargada.

**battle** NOUN
la **batalla** *fem*

**BC** ABBREVIATION (= **before Christ**)
**a.C.** (= *antes de Cristo*)
**in 200 BC**
en el 200 a.C.

to **be** VERB

**Language tip**

*There are two main verbs **ser** and **estar** for **to be** in Spanish.*

1 **ser**

**Language tip**

*Use **ser** to talk about size, shape, colour and characteristics which are generally permanent.*

**I'm quite tall.**
Soy bastante alto.
**She's blonde.**
Es rubia.
**It's green.**
Es verde.
**It isn't very big.**
No es muy grande.
**It's round.**
Es redondo.
**They're wooden.**
Son de madera.
**It's easy.**
Es fácil.

*Language tip*
Use **ser** to talk about where
someone's from.

**I'm English.**
Soy inglesa.
**I'm from Manchester.**
Soy de Manchester.

*Language tip*
Use **ser** with a following noun
(naming word) to say what someone
or something is.

**He's a teacher.**
Es profesor.
**It's a table.**
Es una mesa.
**It's the 28th of October
today.**
Hoy es 28 de octubre.

**It's me.**
Soy yo.

**2 estar**

*Language tip*
Use **estar** to talk about where
people, places and objects are.

**I'm at home.**
Estoy en casa.
**Lima is in Peru.**
Lima está en Perú.
**Where are the keys?**
¿Dónde están las llaves?

*Language tip*
Use **estar** with adjectives
(describing words) to talk about
passing or temporary states.

**I'm tired.**
Estoy cansado.
**Are you ready?**
¿Estás listo?
**The coffee's cold.**
El café está frío.
**He's ill today.**
Hoy está enfermo.

*Language tip*
Use **estar** when talking about what
someone is doing now.

**I'm writing a letter.**
Estoy escribiendo una carta.
**What are you doing?**
¿Qué estás haciendo?

**3 tener**

*Language tip*
Use **tener** when saying you're 'hot',
'cold', 'hungry', 'thirsty' or 'sleepy'.

**I'm hot.**
Tengo calor.
**I'm cold.**
Tengo frío.
**I'm hungry.**
Tengo hambre.
**I'm thirsty.**
Tengo sed.
**I'm sleepy.**
Tengo sueño.

*Language tip*
Use **tener** when talking about
somebody's age.

**I'm eleven.**
Tengo once años.
**My brother is thirteen.**
Mi hermano tiene trece años.

**4 hacer**

*Language tip*
Use **hacer** when talking about the
weather.

It's cold.
Hace frío.
It's hot.
Hace calor.
It's a nice day.
Hace buen día.

**beach** NOUN
la **playa** *fem*

**beans** PL NOUN

1 las **alubias con tomate** *fem pl (baked beans)*
**Would you like some beans?**
¿Quieres unas alubias con tomate?

2 las **judías verdes** *fem pl (green beans)*

**beard** NOUN
la **barba** *fem*
**Our teacher's got a beard.**
Nuestro profesor tiene barba.

to **beat** VERB
**ganar a** *(in game)*
**We're going to beat you!**
¡Os vamos a ganar!

**beautiful** ADJECTIVE

1 **precioso** *masc*
**preciosa** *fem (thing, place)*
**Your garden is beautiful.**
Tu jardín es precioso.

2 **guapo** *masc*
**guapa** *fem (person)*
**Emma is very beautiful.**
Emma es muy guapa.

**because** CONJUNCTION
**porque**
**We can't play outside because it's too cold.**
No podemos jugar fuera porque hace mucho frío.

### Language tip
*The Spanish translations for* **why** *and* **because** *are very similar. When it is used to ask a question,*

¿**por qué**? *is two separate words and has an accent on the* **qué**.

**Why don't you eat meat? – Because I don't like it.**
¿Por qué no comes carne? – Porque no me gusta.
**I can't sleep because of the noise.**
No puedo dormir por el ruido.
**because of the weather**
debido al mal tiempo
**because of you**
por ti

to **become** VERB
**hacerse**
**He became a footballer.**
Se hizo futbolista.

### Language tip
*In Spanish, you do not use an article with people's jobs.*

**bed** NOUN
la **cama** *fem*
**in bed**
en la cama
**to go to bed**
acostarse
**I go to bed at ten o'clock.**
Me acuesto a las diez.
**What time do you go to bed?**
¿A qué hora te acuestas?

**bed and breakfast** NOUN
la **pensión** *fem* (PL as pensiones)

**bedroom** NOUN
la **habitación** *fem* (PL las habitaciones)
**my bedroom**
mi habitación

**bedtime** NOUN
**Ten o'clock is my usual bedtime.**
Casi siempre me acuesto a las diez.
**Bedtime!**
¡A la cama!

**bee** NOUN
la **abeja** *fem*

**beef** NOUN
la **ternera** *fem*
**Would you like beef or chicken?**
¿Quieres ternera o pollo?
**roast beef**
el rosbif

**beefburger** NOUN
la **hamburguesa** *fem*

**been** VERB ▷ *see* **be**

**beer** NOUN
la **cerveza** *fem*
**a can of beer**
una lata de cerveza

## before

> **before** *can be a preposition, conjunction or adverb.*

**A** PREPOSITION
**antes de**
**before three o'clock**
antes de las tres
**B** CONJUNCTION
**Think before you answer, Rose!**
¡Piensa antes de contestar, Rose!
**C** ADVERB
**antes**
**Why didn't you say so before?**
¿Por qué no lo has dicho antes?
**I've never been to Scotland before.**
Nunca había estado en Escocia.

to **begin** VERB
**empezar**
**It begins with 'b'.**
Empieza por 'b'.
**It's beginning to get cold.**
Está empezando a hacer frío.

**beginner** NOUN
el/la **principiante** *masc/fem*

**I'm a beginner.**
Soy principiante.

**beginning** NOUN
el **principio** *masc*
**at the beginning**
al principio

**begun** VERB ▷ *see* **begin**

to **behave** VERB
**portarse**
**He behaves badly.**
Se porta mal.
**She's behaving like an idiot.**
Se está portando como una idiota.
**Behave!**
¡Pórtate bien!

**behind** PREPOSITION
**detrás de**
**It's behind the television.**
Está detrás del televisor.
**one behind the other**
uno detrás del otro

## beige

> **beige** *can be an adjective or a noun.*

**A** ADJECTIVE
**beige** *masc & fem*
**It's beige.**
Es beige.
**a beige skirt**
una falda beige

### Language tip
*Colour adjectives come after the noun in Spanish.*

**B** NOUN
el **beige** *masc*

to **believe** VERB
**creer**
**I don't believe you.**
No te creo.

**bell** NOUN
1 la **campana** *fem* (at school, in church)
**The bell rang.**

English Spanish
a b c d e f g h i j k l m n o p q r s t u v w x y z

Sonó la campana.
**2** el **timbre** masc (at door, on reception)
**Ring the bell.**
Llama al timbre.
**3** el **cascabel** masc (small bell)
**My cat has a bell on its collar.**
Mi gato lleva un cascabel en el collar.

to **belong** VERB
**to belong to somebody**
pertenecer a alguien
**That belongs to me.**
Eso me pertenece a mí.
**Does this belong to you?**
¿Es tuyo esto?
**Who does it belong to?**
¿De quién es?
**The ball belongs to Tony.**
El balón es de Tony.

**below** PREPOSITION
**bajo**
**below ground**
bajo tierra
**ten degrees below freezing**
diez grados bajo cero

**belt** NOUN
el **cinturón** masc (PL los cinturones)

**bench** NOUN
el **banco** masc

**bend**

> **bend** can be a noun or a verb.

**A** NOUN
la **curva** fem
**a dangerous bend**
una curva peligrosa
**B** VERB
**to bend**
doblar

**Bend your legs!**
¡Dobla las piernas!

> **Language tip**
> In Spanish you usually use an article like **el**, **la**, **los** with parts of the body.

**beneath** PREPOSITION
**debajo de**
**beneath the table**
debajo de la mesa

**bent** VERB ▷ see **bend**

**beside** PREPOSITION
**al lado de**
**beside the television**
al lado del televisor
**Sit beside me.**
Siéntate a mi lado.

**best**

> **best** can be an adjective, noun or adverb.

**A** ADJECTIVE
**mejor** masc & fem
**Francis is my best friend.**
Francis es mi mejor amigo.
**Mary and Olga are my best friends.**
Mary y Olga son mis mejores amigas.
**the best team in the world**
el mejor equipo del mundo
**B** NOUN
el/la **mejor** masc/fem
**He's the best in the class.**
Es el mejor de la clase.
**C** ADVERB
**mejor**
**Emily sings best.**
Emily es la que canta mejor.

**Best wishes!**
¡Saludos cordiales!

**Language tip**
*Have you noticed the upside-down exclamation mark at the start of Spanish exclamations?*

**best man** NOUN
el **padrino de boda** *masc*

**better**

**better** *can be an adjective or an adverb.*

**A** ADJECTIVE
**mejor** *masc & fem*
**The ice cream is better than the cake.**
El helado está mejor que el pastel.
**That's better!**
¡Eso está mejor!

**B** ADVERB
**mejor**
**I can sing better than you.**
Yo canto mejor que tú.

**Get better soon!**
¡Que te mejores pronto!

**Language tip**
*Have you noticed the upside-down exclamation mark at the start of Spanish exclamations?*

**between** PREPOSITION
**entre**
**Think of a number between one and twelve.**
Piensa en un número entre uno y doce.

**Bible** NOUN
la **Biblia** *fem*

**bicycle**
NOUN
la **bicicleta**
*fem*
**by bicycle**
en bicicleta

**big** ADJECTIVE
**grande** *masc & fem*
**a big garden**
un jardín grande
**a big house**
una casa grande
**Have you got it in a bigger size?**
¿Tiene una talla más grande?

**Language tip**
*Shorten* **grande** *to* **gran** *before a singular noun.*

**a big problem**
un gran problema
**my big brother**
mi hermano mayor
**her big sister**
su hermana mayor

**bike** NOUN
1 la **bici** *fem (bicycle)*
**by bike**
en bici
2 la **moto** *fem (motorbike)*

**Language tip**
*Even though it ends in* **-o**, **la moto** *is a feminine noun.*

**bikini** NOUN
el **bikini** *masc*

**bill** NOUN
la **cuenta** *fem (in restaurant, hotel)*
**Can we have the bill, please?**
¿Nos puede traer la cuenta, por favor?

**billion** NOUN
**mil millones** *masc pl*
**a billion dollars**
mil millones de dólares

**Language tip**
*Be careful! The translation of* **billion** *is not* **billón**.

**bin** NOUN
1 la **papelera** *fem (wastepaper basket)*

a
b
c
d
e
f
g
h
i
j
k
l
m
n
o
p
q
r
s
t
u
v
w
x
y
z

Put your chewing gum in the bin.
Tira el chicle a la papelera.
**2** el **cubo de la basura** *masc* (rubbish bin)
**The bin is in the kitchen.**
El cubo de la basura está en la cocina.

**bingo** NOUN
el **bingo** *masc*
**We're going to play bingo.**
Vamos a jugar al bingo.

**Language tip**

*In Spanish, you need to add **al** before the name of the sport or game.*

**biology** NOUN
la **biología** *fem*

**bird** NOUN
el **pájaro** *masc*

**Biro**® NOUN
el **boli** *masc*

**birthday** NOUN
el **cumpleaños**
*masc* (PL los **cumpleaños**)
**My birthday is the third of May.**
Mi cumpleaños es el tres de mayo.
**When's your birthday?**
¿Cuándo es tu cumpleaños?

**Happy Birthday!**
¡Feliz cumpleaños!

**Language tip**

*Have you noticed the upside-down exclamation mark at the start of Spanish exclamations?*

**birthday cake** NOUN
la **tarta de cumpleaños** *fem*

**birthday card** NOUN
la **tarjeta de cumpleaños** *fem*
**I got ten birthday cards.**
He recibido diez tarjetas de cumpleaños.

**birthday party** NOUN
la **fiesta de cumpleaños** *fem*
**Would you like to come to my birthday party?**
¿Quieres venir a mi fiesta de cumpleaños?

**biscuit** NOUN
la **galleta** *fem*
**Would you like a biscuit?**
¿Quieres una galleta?

**bit** NOUN
**a bit**
un poco
**I'm a bit tired.**
Estoy un poco cansado.

to **bite** VERB
**1 morder** (with teeth)
**My dog doesn't bite.**
Mi perro no muerde.
**Stop biting your nails!**
¡Deja de morderte las uñas!
**2 picar** (insect)
**I've been bitten by something.**
Me ha picado algo.

**black**

*black can be an adjective or a noun.*

**A** ADJECTIVE
**negro** *masc*
**negra** *fem*
**She's black.**
Es negra.
**a black jacket**
una chaqueta negra

**Language tip**

*Colour adjectives come after the noun in Spanish.*

**B** NOUN
el **negro** *masc*
**He's dressed in black.**
Va vestido de negro.

**blackberry** NOUN
la **mora** *fem*
**We picked blackberries.**
Cogimos moras.

**blackboard** NOUN
la **pizarra** *fem*
**Look at the blackboard!**
¡Mira la pizarra!

**black coffee** NOUN
1 el **café solo** *masc (small)*
2 el **café americano** *masc*
*(large)*

> **Did you know...?**
> un **café solo** *is a very small strong*
> *black coffee while* un **café**
> **americano** *is a mug of weaker*
> *black coffee.*

**blackcurrant** NOUN
la **grosella negra** *fem*
**blackcurrant jam**
mermelada de grosella negra

**blank**

> **blank** *can be an adjective or a*
> *noun.*

A ADJECTIVE
**en blanco**
**a blank sheet of paper**
un folio en blanco
B NOUN
el **espacio en blanco** *masc*
**Fill in the blanks.**
Rellena los espacios en blanco.

**blanket** NOUN
la **manta** *fem*

**blazer** NOUN
el **blazer** *masc*
**a navy blazer**
un blazer azul marino

to **bless** VERB
**Bless you!**
¡Salud!

> **Did you know...?**
> *People say* ¡salud! *when someone*
> *sneezes in Spain.*

**blew** VERB ▷*see* **blow**

**blind**

> **blind** *can be an adjective or a noun.*

A ADJECTIVE
**ciego** *masc*
**ciega** *fem*
**My grandfather is blind.**
Mi abuelo es ciego.
**a blind man**
un ciego
B NOUN
la **persiana** *fem*
**Open the blinds!**
¡Sube las persianas!

to **blindfold** VERB
**I'm going to blindfold you.**
Te voy a vendar los ojos.

**block** NOUN
**a block of flats**
un bloque de pisos

**blonde** ADJECTIVE
**rubio** *masc*
**rubia** *fem*
**She's got blonde hair.**
Tiene el pelo rubio.

**blood** NOUN
la **sangre** *fem*

**blouse** NOUN
la **blusa** *fem*
**a white blouse**
una blusa blanca

to **blow** VERB
**soplar**
**The wind is blowing.**
Está soplando el viento.

English Spanish

a
b
c
d
e
f
g
h
i
j
k
l
m
n
o
p
q
r
s
t
u
v
w
x
y
z

**Stop when I blow the whistle!**
¡Para cuando toque el silbato!
**Blow your nose!**
¡Suénate la nariz!

> **Language tip**
> In Spanish you usually use an article like **el**, **la**, **los** with parts of the body.

**Blow out the candles!**
¡Apaga las velas!

# blue

> **blue** can be an adjective or a noun.

**A** ADJECTIVE
**azul** *masc & fem*
**The sky is blue.**
El cielo es azul.
**a blue dress**
un vestido azul

> **Language tip**
> Colour adjectives come after the noun in Spanish.

**B** NOUN
el **azul** *masc*
**Blue is my favourite colour.**
El azul es mi color preferido.

## board NOUN
la **pizarra** *fem (blackboard, whiteboard)*
**on the board**
en la pizarra

## board game NOUN
el **juego de mesa** *masc*

## boarding school NOUN
el **internado** *masc*
**I go to boarding school.**
Voy a un internado.

## boat NOUN
1 el **barco** *masc (ferry, liner)*
**by boat**
en barco
2 el **bote** *masc (rowing boat, dinghy)*

## body NOUN
el **cuerpo** *masc*

## boiled ADJECTIVE
**cocido** *masc*
**cocida** *fem*
**boiled potatoes**
patatas cocidas
**a boiled egg**
un huevo pasado por agua

## bomb NOUN
la **bomba** *fem*

## bonfire NOUN
la **hoguera** *fem*

> **Did you know...?**
> The Spanish do not celebrate **Bonfire Night** though it is traditional in many places in Spain to celebrate **la noche de San Juan** (Saint John's Eve) with a public bonfire on the 23rd of June.

# book

> **book** can be a noun or a verb.

**A** NOUN
1 el **libro** *masc (printed)*
**Open your books at page ten.**
Abrid los libros por la página diez.
2 el **cuaderno** *masc (exercise book)*
**Write the words in your books.**
Escribid las palabras en los cuadernos.
**B** VERB
**to book**
reservar
**I want to book a seat.**
Quiero reservar un asiento.

## bookcase NOUN
la **librería** *fem*

> **Language tip**
> Did you know that **la librería** is also the word for **bookshop** in Spanish?

**booklet** NOUN
el **folleto** *masc*

**bookshelf** NOUN
la **estantería** *fem*
**on the bookshelves**
en las estanterías

**bookshop** NOUN
la **librería** *fem*

**boot** NOUN
1 la **bota** *fem*
**I like your boots!**
¡Me gustan tus botas!
**football boots**
botas de fútbol
2 el **maletero** *masc (of car)*
**It's in the boot.**
Está en el maletero.

**border** NOUN
la **frontera** *fem (of country)*

**bored** ADJECTIVE
**aburrido** *masc*
**aburrida** *fem*
**I'm bored.**
Estoy aburrido.

**boring** ADJECTIVE
**aburrido** *masc*
**aburrida** *fem*
**a boring programme**
un programa aburrido
**This game is pretty boring, isn't it?**
Este juego es bastante aburrido, ¿verdad?

**born** ADJECTIVE
**I was born in 2000.**
Nací en el 2000.

to **borrow** VERB
**Can I borrow your pen?**
¿Me dejas tu boli?

### Language tip
*Notice how the action is reversed in Spanish. You would normally use* **¿me dejas...?** *or* **¿me prestas...?** *when you want to borrow something.*

**boss** NOUN
el **jefe** *masc*
la **jefa** *fem*

**bossy** ADJECTIVE
**mandón** *masc* (PL **mandones**)
**mandona** *fem*

**both** PRONOUN, ADJECTIVE
los **dos** *masc pl*
las **dos** *fem pl*
**Adam and Daniel, you're both late!**
Adam y Daniel, ¡habéis llegado tarde los dos!
**Peter and Laura have both got a rabbit.**
Tanto Peter como Laura tienen un conejo.

to **bother** VERB
**molestar**
**I'm sorry to bother you.**
Siento molestarle.

**Don't bother!**
¡No te preocupes!

**bottle** NOUN
la **botella** *fem*
**a bottle of mineral water**
una botella de agua mineral

**bottom** NOUN
1 la **parte de abajo** fem
(of page, list)
**Look at the bottom of the page.**
Mira en la parte de abajo de la página.
2 el **fondo** masc (of container, bag, sea)
**My pen's at the bottom of my bag.**
Mi boli está en el fondo del bolso.
3 el **trasero** masc (bum)

**bought** VERB ▷ see **buy**

**bow**

> **bow** can be a noun or a verb.

**A** NOUN
1 el **lazo** masc (in ribbon, string)
**Tie a bow!**
¡Haz un lazo!
**She's wearing a pink bow in her hair.**
Lleva un lazo rosa en el pelo.
2 el **arco** masc (for archery)
**a bow and arrow**
un arco y una flecha
**B** VERB
**to bow**
hacer una reverencia

**bowl** NOUN
el **tazón** masc (PL los **tazones**)
**a bowl of soup**
un tazón de sopa

**bowling** NOUN
los **bolos** masc pl
**Do you want to come bowling?**
¿Quieres venir a jugar a los bolos?

### Language tip
In Spanish, you need to add **a** and the article before the name of the sport.

**box** NOUN
1 la **caja** fem (container)
**a box of matches**
una caja de cerillas
**a cardboard box**
una caja de cartón

2 la **casilla** fem (in questionnaire)
**Tick the boxes.**
Haz una señal en las casillas.

**boxer** NOUN
el **boxeador** masc

**boxer shorts** PL NOUN
los **bóxers** masc pl

**boxing** NOUN
el **boxeo** masc
**I don't like boxing.**
No me gusta el boxeo.

**Boxing Day** NOUN
el **día después de Navidad** masc
**on Boxing Day**
el día después de Navidad

### Did you know...?
**Boxing Day** is not celebrated in Spain.

**boy** NOUN
1 el **niño** masc (young)
**a boy of six**
un niño de seis años
2 el **chico** masc (older)
**Well done, boys!**
¡Muy bien, chicos!

**boyfriend** NOUN
el **novio** masc
**Have you got a boyfriend?**
¿Tienes novio?

**bra** NOUN
el **sujetador** *masc*

**brace** NOUN
el **aparato dental** *masc*
**She wears a brace.**
Lleva un aparato dental.

**bracelet** NOUN
la **pulsera** *fem*

**bracket** NOUN
el **paréntesis** *masc* (PL los paréntesis)
**in brackets**
entre paréntesis

**brain** NOUN
el **cerebro** *masc*

**brainy** ADJECTIVE
**listo** *masc*
**lista** *fem*
**Marina is very brainy.**
Marina es muy lista.

**branch** NOUN
la **rama** *fem (of tree)*

**brand-new** ADJECTIVE
**flamante** *masc & fem*
**It's brand-new.**
Es flamante.

**brass band** NOUN
la **banda de música** *fem*

**brave** ADJECTIVE
**valiente** *masc & fem*
**Be brave!**
¡Sé valiente!

**bread** NOUN
el **pan** *masc*
**Would you like some bread?**
¿Quieres pan?
**bread and butter**
pan con mantequilla

**break**

> **break** *can be a noun or a verb.*

**A** NOUN
1 el **descanso** *masc (in activity)*
2 el **recreo** *masc (at school)*

**during morning break**
durante el recreo de la mañana
**B** VERB
**to break**
**romper**
**You're going to break it.**
Lo vas a romper.
**Who broke the window?**
¿Quién rompió el cristal?
**Richard has broken his arm.**
Richard se ha roto el brazo.

> ### Language tip
> In Spanish you usually use an article like **el**, **la**, **los** with parts of the body.

to **break down** VERB
**averiarse**
**The bus has broken down.**
El autobús se ha averiado.
**Our car broke down.**
Se nos averió el coche.

to **break up** VERB
**We break up next Wednesday.**
Empezamos las vacaciones el miércoles que viene.

**breakfast** NOUN
el **desayuno** *masc*
**Breakfast is at eight o'clock.**
El desayuno es a las ocho.
**I have cereal for breakfast.**
Tomo cereales para el desayuno.
**to have breakfast**
desayunar
**When do you have breakfast?**
¿A qué hora desayunas?

**break time** NOUN
el **recreo** *masc*
**at break time**
en el recreo

**breaststroke** NOUN
la **braza** *fem*
**I can do the breaststroke.**
Sé nadar a braza.

**breath** NOUN
**Take a deep breath!**
¡Respira hondo!

**brick** NOUN
el **ladrillo** *masc*
**a brick wall**
una pared de ladrillo

**bride** NOUN
la **novia** *fem*
**the bride and groom**
los novios

**bridegroom** NOUN
el **novio** *masc*

**bridesmaid** NOUN
la **dama de honor** *fem*

**bridge** NOUN
el **puente** *masc*

**bright** ADJECTIVE
**vivo** *masc*
**viva** *fem*
**a bright colour**
un color vivo
**bright blue**
azul vivo
**a bright blue shirt**
una camisa azul vivo

*Language tip*
*When you describe something as* **bright blue**, **bright red** *and so on, neither the colour nor* **vivo** *changes its ending to agree with the noun.*

**brilliant** ADJECTIVE
**estupendo** *masc*
**estupenda** *fem*
**We're going to London. - Brilliant!**
Nos vamos a Londres. - ¡Estupendo!

to **bring** VERB
**traer**
**Could you bring me a glass of water?**
¿Me podrías traer un vaso de agua?

**Bring the money tomorrow.**
Trae el dinero mañana.

to **bring back** VERB
**devolver**
**You must bring them back tomorrow.**
Tienes que devolverlos mañana.

**Britain** NOUN
**Gran Bretaña** *fem*
**in Britain**
en Gran Bretaña

**British**

*British can be an adjective or a noun.*

**A** ADJECTIVE
**británico** *masc*
**británica** *fem*
**She's British.**
Es británica.
**B** NOUN
**the British**
los británicos

*Language tip*
**británico** *is not spelled with a capital letter in Spanish.*

**British Isles** PL NOUN
las **Islas Británicas** *fem pl*

**broccoli** NOUN
el **brécol** *masc*
**Would you like some broccoli?**
¿Quieres brécol?

**brochure** NOUN
el **folleto** *masc*

**broke** VERB ▷*see* **break**

**broken**
**A** ADJECTIVE
**roto** *masc*
**rota** *fem*
**It's broken.**
Está roto.
**He's got a broken arm.**
Tiene un brazo roto.
**B** VERB ▷*see* **break**

**bronze** NOUN
el **bronce** *masc*
**the bronze medal**
la medalla de bronce

**brother** NOUN
el **hermano** *masc*
**my big brother**
mi hermano mayor
**I've got one brother
and two sisters.**
Tengo un hermano y dos
hermanas.
**I haven't got any brothers
or sisters.**
No tengo hermanos.

**Have you got any brothers or
sisters?**
¿Tienes hermanos?

**brought** VERB ▷ *see* **bring**

**brown**

**brown** *can be an adjective or a noun.*

**A** ADJECTIVE
**1 marrón** *masc & fem*
(PL **marrones**)
**My shoes are brown.**
Mis zapatos son marrones.
**I've got brown eyes.**
Tengo los ojos marrones.

*Language tip*
*Colour adjectives come after the
noun in Spanish.*

**2 castaño** *masc*
**castaña** *fem (hair)*
**I've got brown hair.**
Tengo el pelo castaño.
**She's got light brown hair.**
Tiene el pelo castaño claro.
**3 moreno** *masc*
**morena** *fem (tanned)*
**Liz is very brown.**
Liz está muy morena.
**B** NOUN
el **marrón** *masc*

**Do you have these shoes
in brown?**
¿Tiene estos zapatos en marrón?

**brown bread** NOUN
el **pan integral** *masc*

**Brownie** NOUN
la **exploradora** *fem*
**I'm a Brownie.**
Soy exploradora.

**bruise** NOUN
el **moretón** *masc* (PL los
**moretones**)
**You've got a bruise.**
Tienes un moretón.

**brush**

**brush** *can be a noun or a verb.*

**A** NOUN
el **cepillo** *masc*
**a brush and comb**
un cepillo y un peine
**B** VERB
**to brush**
**cepillar**
**I brush my pony.**
Cepillo a mi pony.
**I brush my hair.**
Me cepillo el pelo.
**I brush my teeth every night.**
Me cepillo los dientes todas las
noches.

*Language tip*
*In Spanish you usually use an article
like* **el**, **la**, **los** *with parts of the
body.*

**bubble gum** NOUN
el **chicle** *masc*

**bucket** NOUN
el **cubo** *masc*
**my bucket and spade**
mi cubo y mi pala

**bug** NOUN
el **virus** *masc* (PL los **virus**)
**Amy's got a bug.**
Amy tiene un virus.

**buggy** NOUN
la **sillita de paseo** *fem*

to **build** VERB
**construir**
**My dad is building a garage.**
Mi padre está construyendo un garaje.

**building** NOUN
el **edificio** *masc*
**a tall building**
un edificio alto

**built** VERB ▷*see* **build**

**bull** NOUN

el **toro** *masc*
**There's a bull in the field.**
Hay un toro en el prado.

**bully** NOUN
el **abusón** *masc* (PL los **abusones**)
la **abusona** *fem*

**bum** NOUN
el **trasero** *masc*

**bun** NOUN
el **bollo** *masc*
**I'd like a bun.**
Quiero un bollo.

**bunch** NOUN
el **ramo** *masc*
**a bunch of flowers**
un ramo de flores

**bunches** PL NOUN
las **coletas** *fem pl*
**She has bunches.**
Lleva coletas.

**bunk beds** PL NOUN
las **literas** *fem pl*

**burger** NOUN
la **hamburguesa** *fem*
**a burger and chips**
una hamburguesa y patatas fritas

**burglar** NOUN
el **ladrón** *masc* (PL los **ladrones**)
la **ladrona** *fem*

**bus** NOUN
el **autobús** *masc* (PL los **autobuses**)
**I go to school by bus.**
Voy al colegio en autobús.
**the school bus**
el autobús escolar

**by bus**
en autobús

**bus driver** NOUN
el **conductor de autobús** *masc*
la **conductora de autobús** *fem*
**My uncle's a bus driver.**
Mi tío es conductor de autobús.

*Language tip*
*In Spanish, you do not use an article with people's jobs.*

**bus station** NOUN
la **estación de autobuses** *fem* (PL las **estaciones de autobuses**)

**bus stop** NOUN
la **parada de autobús** *fem*

**business** NOUN
1 los **negocios** *masc pl (activity)*
**He's away on business.**
Está en viaje de negocios.
**a business trip**
un viaje de negocios
2 la **empresa** *fem (company)*
**My mum has her own business.**
Mi madre tiene su propia empresa.

**busy** ADJECTIVE
**ocupado** *masc*
**ocupada** *fem*
**My mother is always busy.**
Mi madre siempre está ocupada.

**but** CONJUNCTION
**pero**
**Thanks, but I'm not hungry.**
Gracias, pero no tengo hambre.

**butcher's** NOUN
la **carnicería** *fem*

**butter** NOUN
la **mantequilla** *fem*

**butterfly** NOUN
la **mariposa** *fem*

**button** NOUN
el **botón** *masc* (PL los **botones**)

to **buy** VERB
**comprar**

**What are you going to buy?**
¿Qué vas a comprar?
**I'm going to buy a present for Tim.**
Voy a comprar un regalo para Tim.

**by** PREPOSITION
1 **por** *(person)*
**a meal prepared by Helen**
una comida preparada por Helen
2 **de** *(artist)*
**a painting by Picasso**
un cuadro de Picasso
**a book by J.K. Rowling**
un libro de J.K. Rowling
3 **al lado de** *(place)*
**Where's the library? –
It's by the post office.**
¿Dónde está la biblioteca? –
Está al lado de correos.
4 **en** *(transport)*
**We're going by car.**
Vamos en coche.

**by car**
en coche
**by train**
en tren
**by bus**
en autobús

**bye** EXCLAMATION
**¡adiós!**

# C c

### a b c d e f g h i j k l m n o p q r s t u v w x y z

**cab** NOUN
el **taxi** *masc*

**cabbage** NOUN
la **col** *fem*

**café** NOUN
la **cafetería** *fem*

> **Did you know...?**
> Spanish cafés are a bit different
> from the ones in Britain. They tend
> to stay open at night and can serve
> alcoholic drinks throughout the day.

**cafeteria** NOUN
el **restaurante autoservicio**
*masc* (PL los **restaurantes
autoservicio**)

**cage** NOUN
la **jaula** *fem*

**cagoule** NOUN
el **chubasquero** *masc*

**cake** NOUN
1 el **pastel** *masc (individual)*
2 la **tarta** *fem (bigger)*
**I'm going to bake a cake.**
Voy a hacer una tarta.
**a piece of cake**
un trozo de tarta

**calculator** NOUN
la **calculadora** *fem*

**calendar** NOUN
el **calendario** *masc*

**calf** NOUN
el **ternero** *masc*

**call**

> **call** *can be a verb or a noun.*

**A** VERB
**to call**
**llamar**

**Everyone calls her Fi.**
Todos la llaman Fi.
**Call this number.**
Llama a este número.
**Call the police!**
¡Llama a la policía!
**My cat is called Fluffy.**
Mi gato se llama Fluffy.

**What's your cat called?**
¿Cómo se llama tu gato?
**What are your brothers
called?**
¿Cómo se llaman tus hermanos?

> **What are you called?**
> ¿Cómo te llamas?
> **I'm called Helen.**
> Me llamo Helen.
> **I am going to call the register.**
> Voy a pasar lista.

**B** NOUN
la **llamada** *fem*
**Thanks for your call.**
Gracias por tu llamada.
**Give me a call.**
Llámame.

to **call back** VERB
**volver a llamar**
**I'll call you back later.**
Te volveré a llamar más tarde.

**call centre** NOUN
el **servicio de atención
telefónica** *masc*
**My sister works in a call
centre in London.**
Mi hermana trabaja en un
servicio de atención telefónica
de Londres.

**calm** ADJECTIVE
**tranquilo** *masc*
**tranquila** *fem*

to **calm down** VERB
**Calm down, Paul!**
¡Tranquilo, Paul!
**Calm down, Janet!**
¡Tranquila, Janet!
**Calm down, children!**
¡Tranquilos, niños!

**calves** PL NOUN
los **terneros** *masc pl* (young cattle)

**camcorder** NOUN
la **videocámara** *fem*

**came** VERB ▷see **come**

**camera** NOUN
la **cámara** *fem*
**I've got a new camera.**
Tengo una cámara nueva.

**camera phone** NOUN
el **móvil con cámara** *masc*

**camp** NOUN
el **campamento** *masc*

**camping** NOUN
**to go camping**
ir de camping
**We're going camping.**
Vamos a ir de camping.

### Language tip
*Note that in Spanish the word* **camping** *on its own means* **campsite**. *To talk about the activity, you need to say* **ir de camping**.

**campsite** NOUN
el **camping** *masc* (PL los campings)
**The campsite is next to the river.**
El camping está al lado del río.

**can**

### can *can be a noun or a verb.*

**A** NOUN
la **lata** *fem*
**a can of Coke**
una lata de Coca-Cola
**B** VERB
1 **poder** (be able to)
**I can't go.**
No puedo ir.
**Can I come in?**
¿Puedo entrar?
**Can you open the door?**
¿Puedes abrir la puerta?

### Language tip
*You don't always translate* **can**.

**I can't see it.**
No lo veo.
**Can you speak English? – No, I can't.**
¿Hablas inglés? – No.

**I can.**
Puedo.
**I can't.**
No puedo.
**Can you?**
¿Puedes?

2 **saber** (know how to)
**I can swim.**
Sé nadar.
**I can't ride a bike.**
No sé montar en bicicleta.

**Canada** NOUN
**Canadá** *masc*

**Canadian**

### Canadian *can be an adjective or a noun.*

**A** ADJECTIVE
**canadiense** *masc & fem*

**She's Canadian**
Es canadiense.

**B** NOUN
el/la **canadiense** *masc/fem*

*Language tip*
**canadiense** *is not spelled with a capital letter in Spanish.*

**canal** NOUN
el **canal** *masc*

to **cancel** VERB
**cancelar**
We've got to cancel our trip to London.
Tenemos que cancelar nuestro viaje a Londres.

**cancer** NOUN
el **cáncer** *masc*
He's got cancer.
Tiene cáncer.

**candle** NOUN
la **vela** *fem*

**canoe** NOUN
la **canoa** *fem*

**canoeing** NOUN
to go canoeing
hacer piragüismo
We're going canoeing.
Vamos a hacer piragüismo.

**can-opener** NOUN
el **abrelatas** *masc* (PL los abrelatas)

**can't** VERB ▷*see* can

**canteen** NOUN
la **cafetería** *fem*
I eat in the canteen.
Yo como en la cafetería.

**cap** NOUN
la **gorra** *fem*

**capital** NOUN
1 la **capital** *fem (city)*
Madrid is the capital of Spain.
Madrid es la capital de España.

2 la **mayúscula** *fem (letter)*
Write your address in capitals.
Escribe tu dirección en mayúsculas.

**capital letter** NOUN
la **mayúscula** *fem*

**captain** NOUN
el **capitán** *masc* (PL los capitanes)
la **capitana** *fem*
She's captain of the hockey team.
Es capitana del equipo de hockey.

**caption** NOUN
la **leyenda** *fem*

**car** NOUN
el **coche** *masc*
We've got a new car.
Tenemos un coche nuevo.
by car
en coche
We're going there by car.
Vamos allí en coche.

**caravan** NOUN
la **caravana** *fem*

**caravan site** NOUN
el **camping de caravanas** *masc*

**card** NOUN
1 la **carta** *fem (playing card)*
They are playing cards.
Están jugando a las cartas.

*Language tip*
*In Spanish, you need to give* **a las** *before* **cartas**.

2 la **tarjeta** *fem (for birthday, Christmas)*
I got lots of cards.
He recibido muchas tarjetas.

*Did you know...?*
*Spanish people don't generally send as many cards as we do in Britain.*

**cardboard** NOUN
el **cartón** *masc*

**card game** NOUN
el **juego de cartas** *masc*

**cardigan** NOUN
la **rebeca** *fem*
**a green cardigan**
una rebeca verde

**care**

> care *can be a noun or a verb.*

**A** NOUN
el **cuidado** *masc*
**with care**
con cuidado
**B** VERB
**to care: I don't care!**
¡No me importa!

**careful** ADJECTIVE
**to be careful**
tener cuidado
**Be careful, Gordon!**
¡Ten cuidado, Gordon!

**carefully** ADVERB
**con cuidado**
**Fold the paper carefully.**
Dobla el papel con cuidado.
**Think carefully, Hazel!**
¡Piénsatelo bien, Hazel!
**Listen carefully, children!**
¡Escuchad con atención, niños!

**careless** ADJECTIVE
**a careless mistake**
un error de descuido

**caretaker** NOUN
el **bedel** *masc*

---

> ### Language tip
> In Spanish, you do not use an article with people's jobs.

**carol** NOUN
**a Christmas carol**
un villancico

**car park** NOUN
el **parking** *masc* (PL los **parkings**)

**carpet** NOUN
la **moqueta** *fem* (fitted)
**My bedroom carpet is blue.**
La moqueta de mi habitación es azul.

**carriage** NOUN
el **vagón** *masc* (PL los **vagones**)

**carrier bag** NOUN
la **bolsa de asas** *fem*

**carrot** NOUN
la **zanahoria** *fem*

to **carry** VERB
**llevar**
**I'll carry your bag.**
Yo te llevo la bolsa.

to **carry on** VERB
**seguir**
**Carry on, Diane!**
¡Sigue, Diane!

**carton** NOUN
el **cartón** *masc* (PL los **cartones**)
**a carton of milk**
un cartón de leche

**cartoon** NOUN
**1** los **dibujos animados** *masc pl* (on television)
**I watch cartoons on Saturdays.**
Veo los dibujos animados los sábados.
**2** la **viñeta** *fem* (strip cartoon)

**case** NOUN
la **maleta** *fem* (suitcase)
**That's my case!**
¡Ésa es mi maleta!

**English Spanish**

a b c d e f g h i j k l m n o p q r s t u v w x y z

**casserole** NOUN
el **guiso** *masc*

**cassette** NOUN
la **cinta** *fem*

**castle** NOUN
el **castillo** *masc*
**Dover Castle**
el castillo de Dover

**casual** ADJECTIVE
**informal** *masc & fem*
**I prefer casual clothes.**
Prefiero la ropa informal.

**cat** NOUN
el **gato** *masc*
la **gata** *fem*
**Have you got a cat?**
¿Tienes gato?

to **catch** VERB
**coger**
**Catch!**
¡Cógelo!
**Which bus do you catch?**
¿Qué autobús coges tú?
**My cat catches birds.**
Mi gato atrapa pájaros.

**cathedral** NOUN
la **catedral** *fem*

## Catholic

*Catholic can be an adjective or a noun.*

**A** ADJECTIVE
**católico** *masc*
**católica** *fem*
**B** NOUN

el **católico** *masc*
la **católica** *fem*
**I'm a Catholic.**
Soy católico.

*Language tip*

**católico** *is not spelled with a capital letter in Spanish.*

**cauliflower** NOUN
la **coliflor** *fem*

**cave** NOUN
la **cueva** *fem*

**CD** NOUN
el **CD** *masc* (PL los **CDs**)

**CD player** NOUN
el **reproductor de CDs** *masc*

**ceiling** NOUN
el **techo** *masc*

*Did you know...?*

*Did you know that* **el techo** *is also the word for* **roof**?

to **celebrate** VERB
**celebrar**
**Let's celebrate!**
¡Vamos a celebrarlo!

**celery** NOUN
el **apio** *masc*

**cellar** NOUN
el **sótano** *masc*
**The cellar is damp.**
El sótano está húmedo.
**a wine cellar**
una bodega

**cello** NOUN
el **violonchelo** *masc*
**I play the cello.**
Toco el violonchelo.

**cemetery** NOUN
el **cementerio** *masc*

**cent** NOUN
el **céntimo** *masc* (division of euro)
**two euros and twenty cents**
dos euros y veinte céntimos

**centigrade** ADJECTIVE
**centígrado** *masc*
**centígrada** *fem*
**twenty degrees centigrade**
veinte grados centígrados

**centimetre** NOUN
el **centímetro** *masc*

**central heating** NOUN
la **calefacción central** *fem*

**centre** NOUN
el **centro** *masc*
**in the centre**
en el centro
**The office is in the centre of town.**
La oficina está en el centro de la ciudad.
**a sports centre**
un polideportivo

**century** NOUN
el **siglo** *masc*
**the twenty-first century**
el siglo veintiuno

**cereal** NOUN
los **cereales** *masc pl*
**I have cereal for breakfast.**
Desayuno cereales.

**certain** ADJECTIVE
1 **cierto** *masc*
**cierta** *fem*
**a certain person**
una cierta persona
2 **seguro** *masc*
**segura** *fem (sure)*
**I'm not certain.**
No estoy seguro.

**certainly** ADVERB
**Certainly!**
¡Por supuesto!
**Certainly not!**
¡Por supuesto que no!

**certificate** NOUN
el **certificado** *masc*

**chain** NOUN
la **cadena** *fem*

**a silver chain**
una cadena de plata

**chair** NOUN
1 la **silla** *fem*
**There's a table and four chairs in the kitchen.**
Hay una mesa y cuatro sillas en la cocina.
2 el **sillón** *masc* (PL los **sillones**) *(armchair)*
**There are two chairs and a sofa in the lounge.**
Hay dos sillones y un sofá en el salón.

**chalk** NOUN
la **tiza** *fem*
**a piece of chalk**
una tiza

**champagne** NOUN
el **champán** *masc*
**a glass of champagne**
una copa de champán

**champion** NOUN
el **campeón** *masc* (PL los **campeones**)
la **campeona** *fem*
**Mike is the champion!**
¡Mike es el campeón!

**championship** NOUN
el **campeonato** *masc*

**chance** NOUN
la **oportunidad** *fem*
**I'll give you another chance.**
Te daré otra oportunidad.
**No chance!**
¡Ni en broma!

English Spanish

a b c d e f g h i j k l m n o p q r s t u v w x y z

You're taking a chance!
¡Te estás arriesgando!

## change

*change can be a verb or a noun.*

**A** VERB
**to change**
1 **cambiar**
**I'd like to change fifty pounds.**
Quiero cambiar cincuenta libras.
**How you've changed!**
¡Cuánto has cambiado!
2 **cambiar de** *(swap)*
**Change places!**
¡Cambiad de sitio!
**I want to change my cards.**
Quiero cambiar de cartas.
**I've changed my mind.**
He cambiado de idea.
3 **cambiarse** *(get changed)*
**I must go and change.**
Tengo que ir a cambiarme.
**B** NOUN
el **cambio** *masc*
**I haven't got any change.**
No tengo cambio.

## changeable

ADJECTIVE
**variable**
*masc & fem*
**The weather is changeable.**
El tiempo está variable.

## changing room NOUN

1 el **vestuario** *masc (in school)*
2 el **probador** *masc (in shop)*

## Channel NOUN

**the English Channel**
el Canal de la Mancha

## channel NOUN

la **cadena** *fem (on TV)*
**There's football on the other channel.**
Hay fútbol en la otra cadena.

## Channel Islands PL NOUN

**the Channel Islands**
las Islas del Canal de la Mancha

## Channel Tunnel NOUN

**the Channel Tunnel**
el túnel del Canal de la Mancha *masc*

## chapter NOUN

el **capítulo** *masc*

## character NOUN

el **personaje** *masc*
**Harriet is the main character.**
Harriet es el personaje principal.

> ### *Language tip*
> *Even though el personaje is a masculine noun, you can use it to refer to a woman or girl.*

## charge NOUN

**an extra charge**
un suplemento
**There's no charge.**
No hay que pagar nada.
**to be in charge**
ser el responsable
**Who is in charge?**
¿Quién es el responsable?

## charity NOUN

la **organización benéfica** *fem*
**We give the money to charity.**
Donamos el dinero a una organización benéfica.

## chart NOUN

el **gráfico** *masc*
**We're making a chart.**
Estamos haciendo un gráfico.

## charter flight NOUN

el **vuelo chárter** *masc*

## to chase VERB

**perseguir**
**My dog chases cats.**
Mi perro persigue a los gatos.

to **chat** VERB
**charlar**
> **Paul chats a lot.**
> Paul charla mucho.
> **Stop chatting.**
> Dejad de charlar.

**cheap** ADJECTIVE
**barato** *masc*
**barata** *fem*
> **It's cheaper by bus.**
> Es más barato en autobús.

**cheat**

> **cheat** *can be a verb or a noun.*

**A** VERB
**to cheat**
**hacer trampa**
> **You're cheating!**
> ¡Estás haciendo trampa!

**B** NOUN
el **tramposo** *masc*
la **tramposa** *fem*
> **Patrick, you're a cheat!**
> ¡Patrick, eres un tramposo!

to **check** VERB
**comprobar**
> **Check your spelling.**
> Comprobad la ortografía.

to **check in** VERB
**facturar** *(at airport)*
> **What time do I have to check in?**
> ¿A qué hora tengo que facturar?

**checked** ADJECTIVE
**de cuadros**
> **a checked shirt**
> una camisa de cuadros

**checkout** NOUN
la **caja** *fem*
> **at the checkout**
> en la caja

**cheek** NOUN
la **mejilla** *fem*
> **He kissed her on the cheek.**
> Le dio un beso en la mejilla.

**cheeky** ADJECTIVE
**descarado** *masc*
**descarada** *fem*
> **Don't be cheeky, Nigel!**
> ¡No seas descarado, Nigel!

**cheer**

> **cheer** *can be a noun or a verb.*

**A** NOUN
> **There was a loud cheer.**
> Hubo una fuerte ovación.
> **Three cheers for the captain!**
> ¡Viva el capitán!
> **Cheers!**
> ¡Salud!/¡Gracias!

> *Language tip*
> *Translate* **cheers!** *as* ¡**salud!** *when making a toast. Use* ¡**gracias!** *instead when thanking someone.*

> **Cheers, everyone!**
> ¡Salud, por todos!
> **Cheers, Tony! That's very kind of you.**
> Gracias, Tony! Eres muy amable.

**B** VERB
**to cheer**
**gritar entusiasmado**
> **The crowd was cheering.**
> La multitud estaba gritando entusiasmada.

**Cheer up!**
¡Anímate!

**cheerful** ADJECTIVE
**alegre** *masc & fem*

**cheerio** EXCLAMATION
¡**hasta luego!**

**cheese** NOUN
el **queso** *masc*
> **a cheese sandwich**
> un sandwich de queso

**chef** NOUN
el **chef** *masc*

**chemist** NOUN
**1** la **farmacia** *fem* (shop)

**You get it from the chemist.**
Lo compras en la farmacia.
**the chemist's**
la farmacia

### Did you know...?
*Spanish chemists are identifiable by a red or green cross outside the shop. Go to a* **perfumería** *instead if you want to buy cosmetics or toiletries.*

**2** el **farmacéutico** *masc*
la **farmacéutica** *fem*
*(pharmacist)*

**chemistry** NOUN
la **química** *fem*
**the chemistry teacher**
el profesor de química

**cherry** NOUN
la **cereza** *fem*
**I love cherries.**
Me encantan las cerezas.

**chess** NOUN
el **ajedrez** *masc*
**I can play chess.**
Sé jugar al ajedrez.

### Language tip
*In Spanish, you need to add* **al** *before the name of the game.*

**chest** NOUN
el **pecho** *masc*

**chest of drawers** NOUN
la **cómoda** *fem*

**chewing gum** NOUN
el **chicle** *masc*
**Put your chewing gum in the bin!**
¡Tira el chicle a la papelera!

**chick** NOUN
el **pollito** *masc*

**chicken** NOUN
el **pollo** *masc*
**Chicken and chips, please.**
Pollo con patatas fritas, por favor.

**chickenpox** NOUN
la **varicela** *fem*
**Paul has got chickenpox.**
Paul tiene varicela.

**child** NOUN
**1** el **niño** *masc (boy)*
la **niña** *fem (girl)*
**Goodbye children!**
¡Adiós, niños!
**2** el **hijo** *masc (son)*
la **hija** *fem (daughter)*
**They've got three children.**
Tienen tres hijos.

**child minder** NOUN
el **niñero** *masc*
la **niñera** *fem*

**children** PL NOUN
**1** los **niños** *masc pl (boys and girls)*
**Where are the children?**
¿Dónde están los niños?
**2** los **hijos** *masc pl (sons and daughters)*
**They've got three children.**
Tienen tres hijos.

**chilly** ADJECTIVE
**It's chilly today.**
Hace frío hoy.

**chip** NOUN
la **patata frita** *fem*
**I'd like some chips.**
Quiero patatas fritas.

**chocolate** NOUN
**1** el **chocolate** *masc*
**I love chocolate.**
Me encanta el chocolate.

a chocolate cake
una tarta de chocolate
a chocolate ice cream
un helado de chocolate
2 el **bombón** *masc* (PL los
bombones) *(sweet)*
a box of chocolates
una caja de bombones

**choice** NOUN
la **elección** *fem*
I had no choice.
No tenía elección.
You have to make a choice.
Tienes que elegir.

**choir** NOUN
el **coro** *masc*
I sing in the school choir.
Canto en el coro de la escuela.

to **choose** VERB
**elegir**
It's difficult to
choose.
Es difícil elegir.

**chop** NOUN
la **chuleta** *fem*
a pork chop
una chuleta de cerdo

**chose** VERB ▷ *see* **choose**

**chosen** VERB ▷ *see* **choose**

**christening** NOUN
el **bautizo** *masc*

**Christian name** NOUN
el **nombre de pila** *masc*

**Christmas** NOUN
la **Navidad** *fem*
at Christmas
en Navidad

**Happy Christmas!**
¡Feliz Navidad!

**Language tip**
Have you noticed the upside-down
exclamation mark at the start of
Spanish exclamations?

**Christmas cake** NOUN
el **pastel de Navidad** *masc*

**Did you know..?**
In Spain it's traditional to eat **el
roscón de Reyes** on 6th January.
Hidden in this fruit-studded ring-
shaped cake is a little figure or other
surprise that is meant to bring good
luck to the person that finds it.

**Christmas card** NOUN
la **tarjeta de Navidad** *fem*

**Christmas Day** NOUN
el **día de Navidad** *masc*

**Christmas dinner** NOUN
la **comida de Navidad** *fem*

**Did you know...?**
In Spain, people usually have their
special Christmas meal on
Christmas Eve.

**Christmas Eve** NOUN
la **Nochebuena** *fem*

**Did you know...?**
In Spain, it's often **los Reyes
Magos** *(the Three Kings)* rather
than **Papá Noel** *(Father Christmas)*
who bring children their presents.
They come on 5th January rather
than on 24th December.

**Christmas present** NOUN
el **regalo de Navidad** *masc*

**Christmas tree** NOUN
el **árbol de Navidad**
*masc*

**church** NOUN
la **iglesia** *fem*

**cider** NOUN
la **sidra** *fem*

**cigarette**
NOUN
el **cigarrillo**
*masc*

**cinema** NOUN
el **cine** *masc*

**I'm going to the cinema this evening.**
Voy a ir al cine esta noche.

## circle NOUN
el **círculo** masc
**Stand in a cicle.**
Poneos de pie formando un círculo.

## circus NOUN
el **circo** masc

## citizenship NOUN
la **ciudadanía** fem

## city NOUN
la **ciudad** fem
**I live in a city.**
Vivo en una ciudad.
**the city centre**
el centro de la ciudad
**It's in the city centre.**
Está en el centro de la ciudad.

## clap

clap can be a verb or a noun.

**A** VERB
**to clap**
**aplaudir**
**The audience was clapping.**
El público estaba aplaudiendo.
**Clap your hands!**
¡Haced palmas!
**B** NOUN
**Give Cordy a clap.**
Dadle un aplauso a Cordy.

## clarinet NOUN
el **clarinete** masc
**I play the clarinet.**
Toco el clarinete.

## class NOUN
la **clase** fem
**Martin is in my class.**
Martin está en mi clase.
**I go to dancing classes.**
Voy a clases de baile.

## classroom NOUN
el **aula** fem

### Language tip
*Even though it's a feminine noun, remember that you use **el** and **un** with **aula**.*

## classroom assistant
NOUN
el **profesor de apoyo** masc
la **profesora de apoyo** fem

## clean

clean can be an adjective or a verb.

**A** ADJECTIVE
**limpio** masc
**limpia** fem
**a clean shirt**
una camisa limpia
**The bath isn't very clean.**
La bañera no está muy limpia.
**B** VERB
**to clean**
**limpiar**
**I'm cleaning the cooker.**
Estoy limpiando la cocina.
**Clean the board please!**
¡Borrad la pizarra, por favor!
**I clean my teeth twice a day.**
Me lavo los dientes dos veces al día.

### Language tip
*In Spanish you usually use an article like **el**, **la**, **los** with parts of the body.*

## cleaner NOUN
el **señor de la limpieza** masc
la **señora de la limpieza** fem

## clear ADJECTIVE
**claro** masc
**clara** fem
**a clear explanation**
una explicación clara

## clementine NOUN
la **mandarina** fem

## clever ADJECTIVE
**listo** masc
**lista** fem
**Diane is very clever.**
Diane es muy lista.

English Spanish

a
b
c
d
e
f
g
h
i
j
k
l
m
n
o
p
q
r
s
t
u
v
w
x
y
z

to **click** VERB
**clicar**
**Click on the icon.**
Clica en el icono.

**climate** NOUN
el **clima** masc

> **Language tip**
> Even though it ends in **-a**, **el clima** is a masculine noun.

**We have a terrible climate.**
Tenemos un clima espantoso.

to **climb** VERB
1 **escalar** (mountain)
**I want to climb that mountain.**
Quiero escalar esa montaña.
2 **subirse a** (tree, wall)
**Can you climb that tree?**
¿Puedes subirte a ese árbol?

**cloakroom** NOUN
1 el **guardarropa** masc (for coats)

> **Language tip**
> Even though it ends in **-a**, **el guardarropa** is a masculine noun.

2 el **servicio** masc (toilet)

**clock** NOUN
el **reloj** masc

**Look at the clock.**
Mira al reloj.

> **Language tip**
> Did you know that **reloj** is also the word for a **watch**?

**close**

> **close** can be a verb or an adverb.

**A** VERB
**to close**
**cerrar**

**Please close the door.**
Por favor, cierra la puerta.
**Close your books, children.**
Cerrad los libros, niños.
**What time does the pool close?**
¿A qué hora cierra la piscina?
**B** ADVERB
**cerca**
**The shops are very close.**
Las tiendas están muy cerca.
**My house is close to the school.**
Mi casa está cerca del colegio.
**Come closer, Daniel.**
Acércate más, Daniel.

**closed** ADJECTIVE
**cerrado** masc
**cerrada** fem
**The door's closed.**
La puerta está cerrada.

**clothes** PL NOUN
la **ropa** fem
**I'd like to buy some new clothes.**
Quiero comprarme ropa nueva.

> **Language tip**
> Even though **clothes** is a plural word in English, you use **ropa** in the singular in Spanish.

**cloud** NOUN
la **nube** fem
**There are some black clouds.**
Hay nubes negras.

**cloudy** ADJECTIVE
**nublado** masc
**nublada** fem
**It's cloudy today.**
Está nublado hoy.

**clown** NOUN
el **payaso** masc
la **payasa** fem

357

## club NOUN
1 el **club** *masc (organization)*
**a football club**
un club de fútbol
2 *(in cards)*
**clubs**
los tréboles
*masc pl*
**the ace
of clubs**
el as de tréboles

## coach NOUN
1 el **autocar** *masc (vehicle)*
**by coach**
en autocar
**We're going by coach.**
Vamos en autocar.
2 el **entrenador** *masc*
la **entrenadora** *fem (person)*

## coach station NOUN
la **estación de autobuses**
*fem*

## coal NOUN
el **carbón** *masc*

## coast NOUN
la **costa** *fem*
**It's on the west coast of
Scotland.**
Está en la costa oeste de
Escocia.

## coat NOUN
el **abrigo** *masc*
**I'm wearing a blue coat.**
Llevo un abrigo azul.

## cocoa NOUN
el **cacao** *masc*

## coconut NOUN
el **coco** *masc*

## coffee NOUN
el **café** *masc*
**I like coffee.**
Me gusta el café.
**I'd like a white coffee.**
Quiero un café con leche.

## coin NOUN
la **moneda** *fem*
**a two-euro coin**
una moneda de dos euros

## Coke® NOUN
la **Coca-Cola®** *fem*
**a can of Coke**
una lata de Coca-Cola

## cold

cold can be an adjective or a noun.

**A** ADJECTIVE
**frío** *masc*
**fría** *fem*
**The water's
cold.**
El agua
está fría.

It's cold today.
Hace frío hoy.
**I'm cold.**
Tengo frío.
**I'm not cold.**
No tengo frío.
**Are you cold?**
¿Tienes frío?

**B** NOUN *(illness)*
**I've got a cold.**
Estoy resfriado.
**Julie's got a cold.**
Julie está resfriada.

## coleslaw NOUN
la **ensalada de col,
zanahoria, cebolla y
mayonesa**

## collar NOUN
1 el **cuello** *masc (on clothing)*
2 el **collar** *masc (for dog, cat)*

## to collect VERB
1 **recoger** *(pick up)*
**Collect the books please,
Ryan.**
Recoge los libros, por favor,
Ryan.
2 **coleccionar** *(as hobby)*

**I collect stamps.**
Colecciono sellos.

**collection** NOUN
la **colección** *fem* (PL las colecciones)

**college** NOUN
la **universidad** *fem* (university)
**Do you want to go to college?**
¿Quieres ir a la universidad?
**a technical college**
una escuela técnica

**colour**

*colour can be a noun or a verb.*

**A** NOUN
el **color** *masc*
**What colour are the curtains?**
¿De qué color son las cortinas?
**What colour eyes has he got?**
¿De qué color tiene los ojos?

**What colour is it?**
¿De qué color es?

**B** VERB
**to colour**
pintar
**I'm going to colour the house yellow.**
Voy a pintar la casa de amarillo.

**comb**

*comb can be a noun or a verb.*

**A** NOUN
el **peine** *masc*

**B** VERB
**to comb**
peinar
**to comb one's hair**
peinarse

**I comb my hair every day.**
Me peino todos los días.
**I'm combing my hair.**
Me estoy peinando.

**to come** VERB
**1 venir**
**Come with me, June.**
Ven conmigo, June.

*Language tip*
Use **ir** (**go**) rather than **venir** when you tell someone you're coming to join them.

**Can I come too?**
¿Puedo ir yo también?
**I'll come with you.**
Iré contigo.
**2 llegar** (arrive)
**The bus is coming.**
Ya llega el autobús.
**The letter came this morning.**
La carta llegó esta mañana.

**I'm coming!**
¡Ya voy!
**Come on!**
¡Vamos!

**to come back** VERB
**volver**
**Come back, Basil!**
¡Vuelve, Basil!

**to come from** VERB
**ser de**
**Where do you come from?**
¿De dónde eres?

**to come in** VERB
**entrar**
**Can I come in?**
¿Puedo entrar?

**Come in!**
¡Pasa!

**comfortable** ADJECTIVE
**cómodo** *masc*
**cómoda** *fem* (person, shoes, chair)
**Make yourself comfortable.**
Ponte cómodo.

English Spanish

a b c d e f g h i j k l m n o p q r s t u v w x y z

**comic** NOUN
el **cómic** masc (PL los **cómics**)
(magazine)

**comma** NOUN
la **coma** fem

**common** ADJECTIVE
**común** masc & fem (PL
**comunes**)
'Davies' is a very common
surname.
'Davies' es un apellido muy
común.

**compared** ADJECTIVE
**compared with**
en comparación con
**Oxford is small compared
with London.**
Oxford es pequeño en
comparación con Londres.

**competition**
NOUN
el **concurso**
masc

**competitor**
NOUN
el/la
**concursante**
masc/fem

**complete**

complete can be an adjective or a
verb.

A ADJECTIVE
**completo** masc
**completa** fem
B VERB
**to complete**
**completar**
**Complete the following
phrases.**
Completa las frases siguientes.

**completely** ADVERB
**completamente**

**complicated** ADJECTIVE
**complicado** masc

**complicada** fem

**comprehension** NOUN
el **ejercicio de comprensión**
masc

**comprehensive school**
NOUN
el **instituto de secundaria**
masc

**computer** NOUN
el **ordenador** masc

**computer game** NOUN
el **juego de ordenador** masc
**I like computer games.**
Me gustan los juegos de
ordenador.

**computer room** NOUN
la **sala de informática** fem

**concert** NOUN
el **concierto** masc

**cone** NOUN
el **cucurucho** masc
**an ice-cream cone**
un cucurucho de helado

**congratulations**
PL NOUN
la **enhorabuena** fem
**Congratulations!**
¡Enhorabuena!

**conservatory** NOUN
el **solárium cubierto** masc

**constant** ADJECTIVE
**constante** masc & fem

**contact lens** NOUN
la **lentilla** fem
**I wear contact lenses.**
Llevo lentillas.

**container** NOUN
el **recipiente** masc
**a plastic container**
un recipiente de plástico

**contest** NOUN
el **concurso** masc

**contestant** NOUN
el/la **concursante** *masc/fem*

**continent** NOUN
el **continente** *masc*
**How many continents are there?**
¿Cuántos continentes hay?
**the Continent**
Europa
**on the Continent**
en Europa

**continental breakfast** NOUN
el **desayuno europeo** *masc*

to **continue** VERB
**seguir**
**Continue with your work, children!**
¡Seguid con vuestro trabajo, niños!

**conversation** NOUN
la **conversación** *fem* (PL las conversaciones)

**cook**

cook *can be a verb or a noun.*

**A** VERB
**to cook**
1 **cocinar**
**I can cook.**
Sé cocinar.
**I can't cook.**
No sé cocinar.
2 **cocer** *(potatoes, rice etc)*
**Cook the pasta for ten minutes.**
Cocer la pasta durante diez minutos.
**B** NOUN
el **cocinero** *masc*

la **cocinera** *fem*
**Matthew's an excellent cook.**
Matthew es un excelente cocinero.

**cookbook** NOUN
el **libro de cocina** *masc*

**cooked** ADJECTIVE
**cocido** *masc*
**cocida** *fem*

**cooker** NOUN
la **cocina** *fem*
**a gas cooker**
una cocina de gas

**cooking** NOUN
la **cocina** *fem*
**I like cooking.**
Me gusta la cocina.

**cool** ADJECTIVE
1 **fresquito** *masc*
**fresquita** *fem* (*quite cold*)
**It's cooler in the shade.**
Hace más fresquito en la sombra.
2 **guay** (*super*)
**Cool!**
¡Guay!
**What a cool T-shirt!**
¡Qué camiseta más guay!

**copy**

copy *can be a noun or a verb.*

**A** NOUN
la **copia** *fem*
**I'll make a copy.**
Haré una copia.
**B** VERB
**to copy**
**copiar**
**Copy the words off the board.**
Copiad las palabras de la pizarra.

**cork** NOUN
el **corcho** *masc*

**corkscrew** NOUN
el **sacacorchos** *masc* (PL los sacacorchos)

English Spanish

a
b
c
d
e
f
g
h
i
j
k
l
m
n
o
p
q
r
s
t
u
v
w
x
y
z

**corner** NOUN
1 el **rincón** *masc* (PL los **rincones**) *(in room)*
**in a corner of the room**
en un rincón de la habitación

2 la **esquina** *fem (of street)*
**on a street corner**
en una esquina de la calle

**cornflakes** PL NOUN
los **copos de maíz** *masc pl*

**correct**

> *correct can be an adjective or a verb.*

**A** ADJECTIVE
**correcto** *masc*
**correcta** *fem*
**That's correct.**
Eso es correcto.
**the correct answer**
la respuesta correcta

**B** VERB
**to correct**
corregir
**I have to correct the spelling.**
Tengo que corregir la ortografía.

**correction** NOUN
la **corrección** *fem* (PL las **correcciones**)

**correctly** ADVERB
**correctamente**

**corridor** NOUN
el **pasillo** *masc*
**in the corridor**
en el pasillo

to **cost** VERB
**costar**
**It costs two euros.**
Cuesta dos euros.

> **How much does it cost?**
> ¿Cuánto cuesta?

**costume** NOUN
el **disfraz** *masc* (PL los **disfraces**) *(fancy-dress)*
**Mum's making me a clown costume.**
Mi madre me está haciendo un disfraz de payaso.

**cottage** NOUN
la **casa de campo** *fem*

**cotton** NOUN
el **algodón** *masc*
**a cotton shirt**
una camisa de algodón

**couch** NOUN
el **sofá** *masc*

**cough**

> *cough can be a noun or a verb.*

**A** NOUN
la **tos** *fem*
**I've got a cough.**
Tengo tos.

**B** VERB
**to cough**
toser
**I can't stop coughing.**
No dejo de toser.

**could** VERB
**Could I make a phone call?**
¿Puedo hacer una llamada?
**Could you open the door?**
¿Puedes abrir la puerta?
**Could I have a kilo of potatoes?**
¿Me da un kilo de patatas?
**Could I have an orange juice?**
¿Me pone un zumo de naranja?

**Could I...?**
¿Puedo...?
**Could you...?**
¿Puedes...?

to **count** VERB
contar
**Count from one to twenty.**
Cuenta del uno al veinte.

**counter** NOUN
1 el **mostrador** *masc (in shop)*
2 la **ficha** *fem (in game)*
**Take ten yellow counters.**
Coge diez fichas amarillas.

**country** NOUN
1 el **país** *masc (Spain, Britain etc)*
**Spain is a big country.**
España es un país grande.
**the border between the two countries**
la frontera entre los dos países
2 el **campo** *masc (countryside)*
**I live in the country.**
Vivo en el campo.

**countryside** NOUN
el **campo** *masc*

**in the countryside**
en el campo

**couple** NOUN
**a couple of**
un par de
**a couple of days**
un par de días
**a young couple**
una pareja joven

**courgette** NOUN
el **calabacín** *masc* (PL los calabacines)

**course** NOUN
1 el **plato** *masc (of meal)*
**the main course**
el plato principal
**the first course**
el primer plato
2 el **curso** *masc (lessons)*
**an English course**
un curso de inglés
**Do you love me? –**
**Of course I do!**
¿Me quieres? – ¡Claro que sí!
**Of course not!**
¡Claro que no!

**of course**
claro

**court** NOUN
la **pista** *fem*
**There are two tennis courts.**
Hay dos pistas de tenis.

**cousin** NOUN
el **primo** *masc*
la **prima** *fem*

**cover**

**cover** *can be a noun or a verb.*

A NOUN
1 la **funda** *fem (of duvet)*
2 la **tapa** *fem (of book)*
B VERB
**to cover**
cubrir
**The roof is covered with snow.**
El techo está cubierto de nieve.

**cow** NOUN
la **vaca** *fem*

**crab** NOUN
el **cangrejo** *masc*

**cracker** NOUN
la **galleta salada** *fem (biscuit)*

**Did you know...?**
*The Spanish don't pull crackers at Christmas.*

**crash** NOUN
el **accidente** *masc*
**a car crash**
un accidente de coche

**crawl** NOUN
el **crol** *masc*
**I can do the crawl.**
Sé nadar a crol.

**crazy** ADJECTIVE
**loco** *masc*
**loca** *fem*
**Are you crazy?**
¿Estás loco?

**cream**

> **cream** *can be a noun or an adjective.*

A NOUN
la **nata** *fem*
**strawberries and cream**
fresas con nata
B ADJECTIVE
**de color crema** *(cream-coloured)*
**a cream shirt**
una camisa de color crema

**cream cake** NOUN
el **pastel de nata** *masc*
**two cream cakes**
dos pasteles de nata

**credit card** NOUN
la **tarjeta de crédito** *fem*

**cress** NOUN
los **berros** *masc pl*
**I'm growing cress.**
Estoy cultivando berros.

**crew cut** NOUN
el **pelo rapado** *masc*
**He's got a crew cut.**
Lleva el pelo rapado.

**cricket** NOUN
el **críquet** *masc*
**I play cricket.**
Juego al críquet.

> ***Language tip***
> In Spanish, you need to add **al**
> before the name of the game or
> sport.

**cricket bat** NOUN
el **bate de críquet** *masc*

**crisps** PL NOUN
las **patatas fritas** *fem pl*
**a bag of crisps**
una bolsa de patatas fritas

**cross**

> **cross** *can be a verb, noun or adjective.*

A VERB
**to cross**
**cruzar**
**Cross the road at the lights.**
Cruza la calle por el semáforo.
B NOUN
la **cruz** *fem* (PL las **cruces**)
**Put a tick or a cross.**
Poned una señal o una cruz.
C ADJECTIVE
**enfadado** *masc*
**enfadada** *fem*
**She is cross.**
Está enfadada.

**crossing** NOUN
la **travesía** *fem*
**the crossing from Plymouth to Santander**
la travesía de Plymouth a Santander

**crossroads** NOUN
el **cruce** *masc*
**at the crossroads**
en el cruce

**crossword** NOUN
el **crucigrama** *masc*
**I like doing crosswords.**
Me gusta hacer crucigramas.

**crowd** NOUN
la **multitud** *fem*

**crowded** ADJECTIVE
**lleno de gente** *masc*
**llena de gente** *fem*
The pool is crowded on
Saturdays.
La piscina está llena
de gente los sábados.

**crown** NOUN
la **corona** *fem*

**crutch** NOUN
la **muleta** *fem*

to **cry** VERB
**llorar** *(weep)*
Why are you
crying?
¿Por qué lloras?

**cub** NOUN
1 el **cachorro**
*masc (young animal)*
a lion cub
un cachorro de león
2 el **lobato** *masc (scout)*

**cube** NOUN
el **cubo** *masc*

**cucumber** NOUN
el **pepino** *masc*

**cup** NOUN
la **taza** *fem*
a cup of tea
una taza de té
a paper cup
un vaso de papel

**cupboard** NOUN
el **armario** *masc*
What's in the cupboard?
¿Qué hay en el armario?

**curious** ADJECTIVE
**curioso** *masc*
**curiosa** *fem*

**curly** ADJECTIVE
**rizado** *masc*
**rizada** *fem*
She's got curly hair.
Tiene el pelo rizado.

**currant** NOUN
la **pasa** *fem*
I don't like currants.
No me gustan las pasas.

**curriculum** NOUN
el **programa de estudios**
*masc*

**curry** NOUN
el **curry** *masc*
chicken curry
el pollo al curry

**curtain** NOUN
la **cortina** *fem*
Draw the curtains, please.
Corre las cortinas, por favor.

**cushion** NOUN
el **cojín** *masc* (PL los **cojines**)

**custard** NOUN
las **natillas** *fem pl*

**custom** NOUN
la **costumbre** *fem*
It's an old custom.
Es una vieja costumbre.

**customer** NOUN
el **cliente** *masc*
la **clienta** *fem*

● ● ● ● ● ● ● ● ● ● ● ● ● ● ● ● ● ● ● ● ● ● ● ● ● ● ● ● ●

**English Spanish**

a
b
c
d
e
f
g
h
i
j
k
l
m
n
o
p
q
r
s
t
u
v
w
x
y
z

to **cut** VERB
**cortar**
**I'll cut the cake.**
Yo cortaré la tarta.
**Mind you don't cut yourself!**
¡Ten cuidado de no cortarte!

**cutlery** NOUN
los **cubiertos** *masc pl*

to **cycle** VERB
**montar en bici**
**I like cycling.**
Me gusta montar en bici.

**I cycle to school.**
Voy en bici al colegio.

**cycle lane** NOUN
el **carril-bici** *masc* (PL los
carriles-bici)

**cycling** NOUN
el **ciclismo** *masc*

**cyclist** NOUN
el/la **ciclista** *masc/fem*

# D d

## dad NOUN
1 el **padre** _masc_
**my dad**
mi padre
**my mum and dad**
mis padres
2 el **papá** _masc (used as a name)_
**Let's ask Dad.**
¡Vamos a preguntarle a papá!

## daddy NOUN
el **papá** _masc_
**Hello Daddy!**
¡Hola, papá!

## daffodil NOUN
el **narciso** _masc_

## daily ADVERB
**diariamente**
**The pool is open daily from nine a.m. to six p.m.**
La piscina está abierta diariamente de nueve de la mañana a seis de la tarde.

## damn EXCLAMATION
**¡maldita sea!**

## damp ADJECTIVE
**húmedo** _masc_
**húmeda** _fem_

## dance

> **dance** _can be a noun or a verb._

**A** NOUN
el **baile** _masc_

**It's a new dance.**
Es un nuevo baile.
**Are you going to the dance tonight, Tony?**
¿Vas a ir al baile esta noche, Tony?

**B** VERB
**to dance**
**bailar**
**Can you dance?**
¿Sabes bailar?
**I like dancing.**
Me gusta bailar.

## dancer NOUN
el **bailarín** _masc_ (PL los **bailarines**)
la **bailarina** _fem_

## danger NOUN
el **peligro** _masc_
**in danger**
en peligro
**His life is in danger.**
Su vida está en peligro.

## dangerous ADJECTIVE
**peligroso** _masc_
**peligrosa** _fem_

## dark

> **dark** _can be an adjective or a noun._

**A** ADJECTIVE
**oscuro** _masc_
**oscura** _fem_
**She's got dark hair.**
Tiene el pelo oscuro.
**We wear dark green skirts.**
Llevamos unas faldas verde oscuro.

### Language tip
_When you describe something as **dark green**, **dark blue** and so on, neither the colour nor **oscuro** changes its ending to agree with the noun._

a
b
c
d
e
f
g
h
i
j
k
l
m
n
o
p
q
r
s
t
u
v
w
x
y
z

**some dark blue curtains**
unas cortinas azul oscuro
**It's dark in here.**
Está oscuro aquí dentro.
**It's dark at six o'clock.**
Es de noche a las seis.
**It's getting dark.**
Se está haciendo de noche.
**B** NOUN
la **oscuridad** *fem*
**I'm afraid of the dark.**
Me da miedo la oscuridad.

**darling** NOUN
**cariño** *masc*
**Thank you, darling!**
¡Gracias, cariño!

*Language tip*

*Did you know that* **cariño** *still ends
in* **-o** *even when it refers to a woman
or girl?*

**dart** NOUN
el **dardo** *masc*
**Do you want to play darts?**
¿Quieres jugar a los dardos?

*Language tip*

*In Spanish, you need to add* **a los**
*before* **dardos**.

**date** NOUN
la **fecha** *fem (day)*
**What's the date on the
letter?**
¿Qué fecha pone en la carta?
**my date of birth**
mi fecha de nacimiento

**What's the date today?**
¿A cuántos estamos hoy?

**daughter** NOUN
la **hija** *fem*

**day** NOUN
el **día** *masc*
**I'm going to London for three
days.**
Voy a ir tres días a Londres.
**during the day**
durante el día
**It's Richard's birthday the
day after tomorrow.**
Pasado mañana es el
cumpleaños de Richard.
**It's my day off.**
Es mi día libre.

**the days of the week**
los días de la semana
**every day**
todos los días
**all day**
todo el día
**What day is it today?**
¿Qué día es hoy?
**the day after tomorrow**
pasado mañana
**the day before yesterday**
anteayer

*Language tip*

*Even though it ends in* **-a**, **el día** *is
a masculine noun.*

**dead** ADJECTIVE
**muerto** *masc*
**muerta** *fem*
**He's dead.**
Está muerto.

**deaf** ADJECTIVE
**sordo** *masc*
**sorda** *fem*
**She's deaf.**
Es sorda.

**deal**

**deal** *can be a noun or a verb.*

**A** NOUN
el **trato** *masc*
**It's a deal!**

¡Trato hecho!
**a great deal**
mucho
**a great deal of money**
mucho dinero
**B** VERB
**to deal**
**repartir** (cards)
**It's your turn to deal.**
Te toca repartir a ti.

**dear** ADJECTIVE
1 **querido** masc
**querida** fem (in letters to friends)
**Dear Julia, ...**
Querida Julia: ...
**Dear Mum and Dad, ...**
Queridos papás: ...
2 **estimado** masc
**estimada** fem (in formal letters)
**Dear Mrs Blanco, ...**
Estimada Sra. Blanco: ...

> **Language tip**
> Did you notice that there's a colon (:) at the end of the opening line of a letter in Spanish, not a comma?

**death** NOUN
la **muerte** fem

**December** NOUN
**diciembre** masc
**My birthday's in December.**
Mi cumpleaños es en diciembre.
**It's the sixth of December today.**
Hoy es seis de diciembre.

> **in December**
> en diciembre
> **on the fifth of December**
> el cinco de diciembre

> **Language tip**
> Months are not spelled with a capital letter in Spanish.

to **decide** VERB
**decidir**
**I have decided to go to the party.**
He decidido ir a la fiesta.
**I can't decide.**
No puedo decidirme.

**decision** NOUN
la **decisión** fem (PL las decisiones)
**We need to take a decision.**
Tenemos que tomar una decisión.

**deck** NOUN
la **cubierta** fem
**on deck**
en cubierta

**deckchair** NOUN
la **tumbona** fem

to **decorate** VERB
1 **decorar** (with decorations)
**We decorate the classroom for Christmas.**
Decoramos la clase para la Navidad.
2 **pintar** (paint)
**Mum's going to decorate my bedroom.**
Mi madre va a pintar mi habitación.
3 **empapelar** (paper)
**Mum's going to decorate my bedroom.**
Mi madre va a empapelar mi habitación.

> **Language tip**
> There's no single verb meaning both 'to paint' and 'to paper' in Spanish. Use one or the other or **pintar y empapelar** together if you mean both.

**decorations** PL NOUN
los **adornos** masc pl
**Christmas decorations**
adornos de Navidad

**deep** ADJECTIVE
1 **profundo** *masc*
**profunda** *fem (water, hole, cut)*
**Is it deep?**
¿Es profundo?
**Take a deep breath, girls!**
¡Respirad hondo, chicas!
2 **espeso** *masc*
**espesa** *fem (snow, mud)*
**a deep layer of snow**
una espesa capa de nieve

**deer** NOUN
el **ciervo** *masc*

**defence** NOUN
la **defensa** *fem*
**I play in defence.**
Juego en la defensa.

**defender** NOUN
el/la **defensa**
*masc/fem (in sport)*

**definite** ADJECTIVE
1 **definitivo** *masc*
**definitiva** *fem (fixed)*
**I haven't got any definite plans.**
No tengo ningún plan definitivo.
2 **seguro** *masc*
**segura** *fem (certain)*
**Maybe, it's not definite.**
Quizás, no es seguro.

**definitely** ADVERB
**sin duda**
**He's definitely the best player.**
Es sin duda el mejor jugador.
**Definitely!**
¡Claro que sí!

**degree** NOUN
1 el **grado** *masc (measurement)*
**a temperature of thirty degrees**
una temperatura de treinta grados
2 la **licenciatura** *fem (qualification)*
**a degree in maths**
una licenciatura en matemáticas

**delayed** ADJECTIVE
**retrasado** *masc*
**retrasada** *fem*
**All flights are delayed.**
Todos los vuelos están retrasados.

**delicatessen** NOUN
la **charcutería fina** *fem*

**delicious** ADJECTIVE
**buenísimo** *masc*
**buenísima** *fem*
**The chocolate mousse is delicious!**
¡La mousse de chocolate está buenísima!

to **deliver** VERB
1 **repartir** *(mail, newspapers)*
**I deliver newspapers.**
Yo reparto periódicos.
2 **entregar** *(order, goods)*
**They'll deliver my new bed on Friday.**
Me van a entregar la cama nueva el viernes.

**denim** NOUN
**a denim jacket**
una cazadora vaquera

**dentist** NOUN
el/la **dentista** *masc/fem*
**I'm going to the dentist.**
Voy a ir al dentista.
**Brian is a dentist.**
Brian es dentista.

**Language tip**

*Did you notice that* **dentista** *still ends in* **-a** *even when referring to a man? Remember that in Spanish, you do not use an article with people's jobs.*

**department** NOUN
1 la **sección** *fem* (PL las **secciones**) *(in shop)*

the shoe department
la sección de calzados

**2** el **departamento** *masc*
(of school, university)
**He works in the English department.**
Trabaja en el departamento de inglés.

**department store** NOUN
los **grandes almacenes** *masc pl*
**This is my favourite department store.**
Éstos son mis grandes almacenes favoritos.

**departure** NOUN
la **salida** *fem*

**departure lounge** NOUN
la **sala de embarque** *fem*

to **depend** VERB
**It depends.**
Depende.
**depending on the weather**
dependiendo del tiempo

> **Language tip**
> Even though we say **to depend on** in English, remember that in Spanish they say **depender de**.

**deposit** NOUN
**1** la **señal** *fem (part payment)*
**You have to pay a deposit when you book.**
Hay que dejar una señal para hacer la reserva.

**2** el **depósito** *masc (when hiring something)*
**You get the deposit back when you return the bike.**
Recuperas el depósito cuando devuelves la bici.

**depressed**
ADJECTIVE
**deprimido** *masc*
**deprimida** *fem*
**I feel depressed.**
Me encuentro deprimido.

**deputy head** NOUN
el **subdirector** *masc*
la **subdirectora** *fem*

to **describe** VERB
describir
**Can you describe the man you saw?**
¿Puedes describir al hombre que viste?

> **Language tip**
> Don't forget the personal **a** in examples like this last one.

**Describe yourself.**
Descríbete.

**description** NOUN
la **descripción** *fem* (PL las descripciones)

> **Language tip**
> Have you noticed that words ending in **-tion** in English often have Spanish counterparts ending in **-ción**?

**desert** NOUN
el **desierto** *masc*

**desert island** NOUN
la **isla desierta** *fem*

to **deserve** VERB
merecerse
**You deserve a prize, Beth.**
Te mereces un premio, Beth.

**design**

> **design** *can be a noun or a verb.*

**A** NOUN
el **modelo** *masc*
**a simple design**
un modelo simple

**B** VERB
**to design**
diseñar

**designer** NOUN
el **diseñador** *masc*
la **diseñadora** *fem*

**designer clothes** PL NOUN
la **ropa de diseñadores
famosos** *fem*

> **Language tip**
> *Even though we always talk about
> clothes in the plural in English, in
> Spanish they use* **la ropa** *in the
> singular.*

**desk** NOUN
**1** la **mesa** *fem (in school, office)*
**my desk**
mi mesa
**2** el **mostrador** *masc (in hotel,
at airport)*

**dessert** NOUN
el **postre** *masc*
**for dessert**
de postre

**destination** NOUN
el **destino** *masc*

**detached house** NOUN
la **casa independiente** *fem*

**detail** NOUN
el **detalle** *masc*
**in detail**
con detalle

**detective** NOUN
el/la **detective** *masc/fem*

**detective story** NOUN
la **novela policíaca** *fem*

**detention** NOUN
**You'll get a detention!**
¡Te vas a quedar castigado
después de clase!

to **develop** VERB
revelar
**I want to have this film
developed.**
Quiero revelar este carrete.

**diabetic** NOUN
el **diabético** *masc*
la **diabética** *fem*
**I'm a diabetic.**
Soy diabética.

**diagonal** ADJECTIVE
**diagonal** *masc & fem*

**diagram** NOUN
el **diagrama** *masc*

> **Language tip**
> *Even though it ends in* -a, **el
> diagrama** *is a masculine noun.*

to **dial** VERB
marcar
**Dial the number.**
Marca el número.

**dialogue** NOUN
el **diálogo** *masc*

**diamond** NOUN
el **diamante** *masc*
**a diamond ring**
un anillo de diamantes
**the ace of diamonds**
el as de diamantes

**diary** NOUN
**1** la **agenda** *fem (for
appointments)*
**I've got her phone number in
my diary.**
Tengo su número de teléfono en
mi agenda.
**2** el **diario** *masc (personal record)*
**I keep a diary.**
Estoy escribiendo un diario.

**dice** NOUN
el **dado** *masc*

**Throw the dice, Sonia.**
Tira los dados, Sonia.

**dictionary** NOUN
el **diccionario** *masc*
**Look in the dictionary.**
Mira en el diccionario.

**did** VERB ▷*see* **do**

**didn't** (= did not) ▷*see* **do**

to **die** VERB
**morir**
**He died last year.**
Murió el año pasado.
**She's dying.**
Se está muriendo.

**diesel** NOUN
el **gasoil** *masc*

**diet**

> **diet** *can be a noun or a verb.*

**A** NOUN
**1** la **dieta** *fem*
**a healthy diet**
una dieta sana
**2** el **régimen** *masc* (PL los
**regímenes**) *(for slimming)*
**My dad's on a diet.**
Mi padre está a régimen.
**Are you on a diet?**
¿Estás a régimen?
**B** VERB
**to diet**
**hacer régimen**
**My mum's dieting.**
Mi madre está haciendo
régimen.

**difference** NOUN
la **diferencia** *fem*

**What's the difference?**
¿Cuál es la diferencia?
**the difference between
Barcelona and Madrid**
la diferencia entre Barcelona
y Madrid

**different** ADJECTIVE
**diferente** *masc & fem*
**We are very different.**
Somos muy diferentes.
**Dublin is different from
London.**
Dublín es diferente de Londres.

> *Language tip*
> *Don't forget that there's only one* **f**
> *in the Spanish word* **diferente**.

**difficult** ADJECTIVE
**difícil** *masc & fem*
**It's difficult.**
Es difícil.
**a difficult question**
una pregunta difícil

> *Language tip*
> *Don't forget that there's only one* **f**
> *in the Spanish word* **difícil**.

**difficulty** NOUN
la **dificultad** *fem*
**without difficulty**
sin dificultad

to **dig** VERB
**cavar**
**My dog digs lots of holes.**
Mi perro cava muchos
hoyos.

**The children are digging in
the sand.**
Los niños están haciendo hoyos
en la arena.

**digital** ADJECTIVE
**digital** *masc & fem*
  **a digital camera**
  una cámara digital
  **digital radio**
  la radio digital
  **digital television**
  la televisión digital

**dinghy** NOUN
  **a rubber dinghy**
  una lancha neumática

**dining room** NOUN
  el **comedor** *masc*

**dinner** NOUN
  1 la **comida** *fem (midday meal)*
  **Dinner's ready!**
  ¡La comida está lista!
  **We always go home for dinner.**
  Siempre vamos a comer a casa.
  **We usually have dinner at one o'clock.**
  Normalmente comemos a la una.

### Language tip
*Only use* **la comida** *and the verb* **comer** *when talking about a midday meal.*

  2 la **cena** *fem (evening meal)*
  **There's a good film on after dinner.**
  Echan una película buena después de la cena.
  **What are we having for dinner tonight?**
  ¿Qué hay para cenar esta noche?
  **We usually have dinner at seven o'clock.**
  Normalmente cenamos a las siete.

### Language tip
*Only use* **la cena** *and the verb* **cenar** *when talking about an evening meal.*

**dinner lady** NOUN
  la **señora que ayuda en el comedor** *fem*

**dinner time** NOUN
  1 la **hora de comer** *fem (for midday meal)*
  2 la **hora de cenar** *fem (for evening meal)*

### Did you know...?
*The Spanish tend to have their meals much later than in Britain, with the lunchtime meal around 2pm and the evening meal around 9pm or 10pm.*

**dinosaur** NOUN
  el **dinosaurio** *masc*

**direct** ADJECTIVE
  **directo** *masc*
  **directa** *fem*
  **the most direct route**
  la ruta más directa

**direction** NOUN
  la **dirección** *fem* (PL las **direcciones**)
  **We're going in the wrong direction.**
  Vamos en la dirección equivocada.
  **Let's ask somebody for directions.**
  Vamos a pedirle a alguien que nos indique el camino.

### Language tip
*Have you noticed that words ending in* **-tion** *in English often have Spanish counterparts ending in* **-ción**?

**dirty** ADJECTIVE
  **sucio** *masc*
  **sucia** *fem*
  **The house is very dirty.**
  La casa está muy sucia.

**disabled** ADJECTIVE
  **discapacitado** *masc*
  **discapacitada** *fem*
  **disabled people**
  gente discapacitada

to **disagree** VERB
**I disagree!**
¡No estoy de acuerdo!
**He disagrees with me.**
No está de acuerdo conmigo.

**disappointed** ADJECTIVE
**decepcionado** *masc*
**decepcionada** *fem*
**We are very disappointed.**
Estamos muy decepcionados.

**disappointment** NOUN
la **decepción** *fem* (PL las **decepciones**)

**disaster** NOUN
el **desastre** *masc*
**It's a disaster!**
¡Es un desastre!

**discipline** NOUN
la **disciplina** *fem*

**disc jockey** NOUN
el/la **disc-jockey** *masc/fem* (PL los/las **disc-jockeys**)

**disco** NOUN
el **baile** *masc*
**There's a disco at school tonight.**
Hay un baile en el colegio esta noche.
**disco music**
la música disco

**discussion** NOUN
la **discusión** *fem* (PL las **discusiones**)

to **disguise** VERB
**disfrazar**
**He was disguised as a policeman.**
Iba disfrazado de policía.

**disgusting** ADJECTIVE
**asqueroso** *masc*
**asquerosa** *fem*
**It looks disgusting.**
Tiene un aspecto asqueroso.

**dish** NOUN
el **plato** *masc* (*meal, plate*)
**a vegetarian dish**
un plato vegetariano
**to wash the dishes**
fregar los platos
**I always wash the dishes.**
Yo siempre friego los platos.

**dishwasher** NOUN
el **lavaplatos** *masc* (PL los **lavaplatos**)

**disk** NOUN
el **disco** *masc*

**dislike** NOUN
**my likes and dislikes**
lo que me gusta y lo que no

**distance** NOUN
la **distancia** *fem*
**a distance of ten kilometres**
una distancia de diez kilómetros
**in the distance**
a lo lejos

to **distract** VERB
**distraer**
**Don't distract him, Poppy.**
No lo distraigas, Poppy.

**district** NOUN
1 el **barrio** *masc* (*of town*)
2 la **región** *fem* (PL las **regiones**) (*of country*)

to **disturb** VERB
**molestar**
**I'm sorry to disturb you.**
Siento molestarte.
**'Do not disturb'**
'No molestar'

to **dive** VERB
**tirarse de cabeza**
**I like diving.**
Me gusta tirarme de cabeza.
**He dived into the water.**
Se tiró al agua de cabeza.

to **divide** VERB
  **dividir**
    **Divide the pastry in half.**
    Divide la masa en dos.
    **Twelve divided by three is four.**
    Doce dividido entre tres son cuatro.
    **Divide into two groups!**
    ¡Dividíos en dos grupos!

**diving board** NOUN
  el **trampolín** masc (PL los trampolines)

**divorced** ADJECTIVE
  **divorciado** masc
  **divorciada** fem
    **My parents are divorced.**
    Mis padres están divorciados.

**DIY** NOUN
  el **bricolaje** masc
    **He likes doing DIY.**
    Le gusta hacer bricolaje.

**dizzy** ADJECTIVE
  **mareado** masc
  **mareada** fem
    **I feel dizzy.**
    Estoy mareada.

**DJ** NOUN
  el/la **disc-jockey** masc/fem (PL los/las **disc-jockeys**)

to **do** VERB
  **hacer**
    **What are you going to do this evening?**
    ¿Qué vas a hacer esta noche?
    **My brother does judo.**
    Mi hermano hace yudo.
    **I haven't done my homework.**

No he hecho mis deberes.
    **Who did that?**
    ¿Quién hizo eso?
    **That'll do, thanks.**
    Así está bien, gracias.

> **Language tip**
> You often use **do** to form questions in English. Don't use **hacer** like this in Spanish. Just use the normal form of the verb and make your voice go up at the end. Don't forget the opening and closing question marks in written Spanish.

    **Do you speak English? – Yes, I do.**
    ¿Hablas inglés? – Sí.
    **Do you like horses? – No, I don't.**
    ¿Te gustan los caballos? – No.
    **Where does he live?**
    ¿Dónde vive?
    **What do you do in your free time?**
    ¿Qué haces en tu tiempo libre?

> **Language tip**
> Just use **no** to make sentences negative.

    **I don't understand.**
    No entiendo.
    **She doesn't like dogs.**
    No le gustan los perros.

> **Language tip**
> Use **¿no?** to check information where in English we'd say **don't you?**, **doesn't he?** and so on.

    **You go swimming on Fridays, don't you?**
    Tú vas a nadar los viernes, ¿no?

> **Language tip**
> You can also use **¿verdad?** to check information.

    **It doesn't matter, does it?**
    No importa, ¿verdad?

  **What are you doing?**
  ¿Qué estás haciendo?

**I'm not doing anything.**
No estoy haciendo nada.
**... don't you?**
... ¿no?
**... do you?**
... ¿verdad?

to **do up** VERB
**1 atarse** *(tie)*
**Do up your shoes!**
¡Átate los cordones!
**2 abrocharse** *(fasten)*
**Do up your coat!**
¡Abróchate el abrigo!
**Do up your zip!**
¡Súbete la cremallera!

> **Language tip**
> In Spanish you usually use an article
> like **el**, **la**, **los** with clothes you are
> wearing.

**doctor** NOUN
el **médico** *masc*
la **médica** *fem*
**I'd like to be a doctor.**
Me gustaría ser médico.

> **Language tip**
> In Spanish, you do not use an article
> with people's jobs.

**She's a doctor.**
Es médica.
**I need to see a doctor.**
Tengo que ver a un médico.

> **Language tip**
> Don't forget the personal **a** in
> examples like this one.

**dodgems** PL NOUN
los **coches de choque** *masc pl*

**does** VERB ▷ *see* **do**

**doesn't** (= does not) ▷ *see* **do**

**dog** NOUN
el **perro** *masc*
**Have you got a dog?**
¿Tienes perro?

**doll** NOUN
la **muñeca** *fem*

**dollar** NOUN
el **dólar** *masc*

**dolphin** NOUN
el **delfín** *masc*
(PL los **delfines**)

**dominoes** PL NOUN
**Let's have a game of
dominoes.**
Vamos a echar una partida al
dominó.

**done** VERB ▷ *see* **do**

**donkey** NOUN
el **burro** *masc*
la **burra** *fem*

**don't** (= do not) ▷ *see* **do**

**door** NOUN
la **puerta** *fem*
**the first door on the right**
la primera puerta a la derecha

**dormitory** NOUN
el **dormitorio** *masc*

**dot** NOUN
el **punto** *masc*
**My email address is loveday
at collins dot co dot U-K
(loveday@collins.co.uk).**
Mi e-mail es loveday arroba
collins punto co punto U-K
(loveday@collins.co.uk).

**double** ADJECTIVE
**doble** *masc & fem*
**a double helping**
una ración doble

**double bed** NOUN
la **cama de matrimonio** *fem*

**English Spanish**

a b c **d** e f g h i j k l m n o p q r s t u v w x y z

**double room** NOUN
la **habitación doble** *fem* (PL las **habitaciones dobles**)

**double-decker bus** NOUN
el **autobús de dos pisos** *masc* (PL los **autobuses de dos pisos**)

to **doubt** VERB
**dudar**
**I doubt it.**
Lo dudo.

**doughnut** NOUN
el **donut** (PL los **donuts**)

**down**

> **down** *can be an adverb, preposition or adjective.*

**A** ADVERB
**abajo**
**It's down in the cellar.**
Está abajo en el sótano.
**It's down there.**
Está ahí abajo.
**Don't look down!**
¡No mires hacia abajo!
**B** PREPOSITION
**He ran down the road.**
Corrió calle abajo.
**I live just down the road.**
Vivo aquí cerca en esta calle.
**C** ADJECTIVE
**I'm feeling a bit down.**
Me siento un poco deprimido.
**The computer's down.**
El ordenador no funciona.

to **download** VERB
**descargar**
**You can download the file.**
Puedes descargar el archivo.

**downstairs** ADVERB
**abajo**
**The bathroom's downstairs.**
El baño está abajo.
**I'm downstairs!**
¡Estoy abajo!

**dozen** NOUN
la **docena** *fem*

**two dozen**
dos docenas
**a dozen eggs**
una docena de huevos

**dragon** NOUN
el **dragón** *masc* (PL los **dragones**)

**drama** NOUN
el **teatro** *masc*
**Drama is my favourite subject.**
Teatro es mi asignatura favorita.

**drank** VERB ▷*see* **drink**

**draughts** NOUN
las **damas** *fem pl*
**Do you want to play draughts?**
¿Quieres jugar a las damas?

> ### Language tip
> *In Spanish, you need to add* **a las** *before* **damas**.

**draw**

> **draw** *can be a verb or a noun.*

**A** VERB
**to draw**
1 **dibujar** *(with pencil, pen)*
**I can't draw.**
No sé dibujar.
**Draw a house, everyone.**
Dibujad todos una casa.
**I'm drawing a picture.**
Estoy haciendo un dibujo.
2 **empatar** *(in game)*
**We drew two all.**
Empatamos a dos.
**B** NOUN
el **empate** *masc (in game)*
**It's a draw between the boys and the girls.**
Es un empate entre los niños y las niñas.

**drawer** NOUN
el **cajón** *masc* (PL los **cajones**)

**drawing** NOUN
1 el **dibujo** *masc* (picture)
2 (activity)
**I like drawing.**
Me gusta dibujar.

**drawing pin** NOUN
la **chincheta** *fem*

**dream** NOUN
el **sueño** *masc*
**Sweet dreams, darling!**
¡Felices sueños, cariño!
**a bad dream**
un mal sueño

**dress**

> **dress** *can be a noun or a verb.*

**A** NOUN
el **vestido** *masc*
**Laura is wearing a white dress.**
Laura lleva un vestido blanco.
**B** VERB
**to get dressed**
**vestirse**
**I'm getting dressed.**
Me estoy vistiendo.
**Go and get dressed.**
Ve a vestirte.

to **dress up** VERB
**disfrazarse**
**I'm going to dress up as a princess.**
Voy a disfrazarme de princesa.

**dressed** ADJECTIVE
**vestido** *masc*
**vestida** *fem*
**I'm not dressed yet.**
Todavía no estoy vestido.
**How was he dressed?**
¿Cómo iba vestido?

**She was dressed in a green sweater and jeans.**
Iba vestida con un jersey verde y unos vaqueros.

**drew** VERB > see **draw**

**drink**

> **drink** *can be a verb or a noun.*

**A** VERB
**to drink**
**beber**
**What would you like to drink?**
¿Qué quieres beber?
**B** NOUN
la **bebida** *fem*
**a cold drink**
una bebida fría
**a hot drink**
una bebida caliente
**Would you like a drink?**
¿Quieres beber algo?

**drive**

> **drive** *can be a noun or a verb.*

**A** NOUN
1 (in car)
**Let's go for a drive.**
Vamos a dar una vuelta en el coche.
**It's a twenty-minute drive to school.**
El colegio está a veinte minutos en coche.
2 (of house)
**You can park your car in the drive.**
Puedes aparcar en la entrada de la casa.
**B** VERB
**to drive**
1 **conducir** (as skill)
**She's learning to drive.**
Está aprendiendo a conducir.
**Can you drive?**
¿Sabes conducir?
2 **ir en coche** (go by car)
**Are you going by train? – No, we're driving.**

¿Vais en tren? – No, vamos en coche.
**3 llevar en coche** (take by car)
**My mother drives me to school.**
Mi madre me lleva en coche al colegio.

## driver NOUN
el **conductor** masc
la **conductora** fem
**She's an excellent driver.**
Es una conductora excelente.

## driving licence NOUN
el **carnet de conducir** masc
(PL los **carnets de conducir**)

## drop

drop can be a noun or a verb.

**A** NOUN
la **gota** fem
**a drop of water**
una gota de agua
**B** VERB
**to drop**
**dejar caer**
**Don't drop that glass, will you!**
No dejes caer ese vaso, ¿vale?

## drove VERB ▷see drive

## drug NOUN
**1** la **medicina** fem (medicine)
**They need food and drugs.**
Necesitan alimentos y medicinas.
**2** la **droga** fem (illegal)
**hard drugs**
drogas duras
**It's crazy to take drugs.**
Es una locura drogarse.

## drum NOUN
el **tambor** masc
**an African drum**
un tambor africano
**I play drums.**
Toco la batería.

## drum kit NOUN
la **batería** fem

## drummer NOUN
el/la **batería** masc/fem

## drunk ADJECTIVE
**borracho** masc
**borracha** fem

## dry

dry can be an adjective or a verb.

**A** ADJECTIVE
**1 seco** masc
**seca** fem (not wet)
**The paint isn't dry yet.**
La pintura no está seca todavía.
**2 sin lluvias** (without rain)
**a long dry period**
una larga temporada sin lluvias
**B** VERB
**to dry**
**1 secar**

### Language tip
Use **secar** to talk about drying objects, animals and babies.

**Can you dry the dishes?**
¿Puedes secar los platos?
**2 secarse**

### Language tip
Use **secarse** when something dries.

**Let the glue dry.**
Deja que se seque el pegamento.

### Language tip
Use **secarse** when someone dries themselves or their own hair, hands, feet, etc.

**Dry yourself on this towel.**
Sécate con esta toalla.
**I need to dry my hair.**
Tengo que secarme el pelo.
**Have you dried your hands?**
¿Te has secado las manos?

## duck NOUN
el **pato** masc

**due** ADJECTIVE
**The plane is due in half an hour.**
El avión llegará dentro de media hora.
**When's the baby due?**
¿Para cuándo nacerá el niño?
**due to**
debido a
**We can't go out due to the bad weather.**
No podemos salir debido al mal tiempo.

**dug** VERB ▷ see **dig**

**dull** ADJECTIVE
**It's dull today.**
Hace un día gris hoy.

**dummy** NOUN
el **chupete** *masc (for baby)*

**dungeon** NOUN
la **mazmorra** *fem*

**during** PREPOSITION
**durante**
**during the day**
durante el día

**dustbin** NOUN
el **cubo de la basura** *masc*

**duty-free shop** NOUN
la **tienda libre de impuestos** *fem*

**duvet** NOUN
el **edredón nórdico** *masc* (PL los **edredones nórdicos**)

**DVD** NOUN
el **DVD** *masc* (PL los **DVDs**)
**I've got that film on DVD.**
Tengo esa película en DVD.

**DVD player** NOUN
el **reproductor de DVD** *masc*

**dwarf** NOUN
el **enano** *masc*

# E e

## each

*each can be an adjective or a pronoun.*

**A** ADJECTIVE
**cada** *masc & fem*
**each day**
cada día

### Language tip
*Even though **cada** ends in **-a**, you can use it with a masculine noun.*

**B** PRONOUN
**cada uno** *masc*
**cada una** *fem*
**They have ten points each.**
Tienen diez puntos cada uno.
**The towels cost five pounds each.**
Las toallas cuestan cinco libras cada una.
**Take one card each.**
Coged una carta cada uno.
**We write to each other.**
Nos escribimos.

## ear NOUN
1 la **oreja** *fem (outer part)*
**I want to have my ears pierced.**
Quiero hacerme agujeros en las orejas.
2 el **oído** *masc (inner part)*
**My ears are aching.**
Me duelen los oídos.

## earache NOUN
**I've got earache.**
Me duele el oído.

## early ADVERB
1 **temprano** *(early in the day)*
**I get up early.**
Me levanto temprano.
**I go to bed early.**
Me acuesto temprano.
2 **pronto** *(ahead of time)*
**Come early to get a good seat.**
Llega pronto para conseguir un buen sitio.

## to earn VERB
**ganar**
**She earns ten pounds an hour.**
Gana diez libras a la hora.

## earring NOUN
el **pendiente** *masc*
**diamond earrings**
pendientes de diamantes
**a pair of earrings**
unos pendientes

## earth NOUN
la **tierra** *fem*

## east

*east can be an adjective or a noun.*

**A** ADJECTIVE
**este**

### Language tip
*When it means 'east', **este** never changes its ending no matter what it describes. Did you know that adjectives that behave like this are called 'invariable adjectives'?*

**the east coast**
la costa este
**B** NOUN
el **este** *masc*
**in the east**
en el este

**Easter** NOUN
la **Semana Santa** *fem*
**at Easter**
en Semana Santa
**the Easter holidays**
las vacaciones de Semana Santa
**Easter Saturday**
el Sábado Santo
**Easter Sunday**
el Domingo de Resurrección

**Happy Easter!**
¡Felices Pascuas!

***Did you know...?***
*Many places in Spain have festivals
during* **Semana Santa** *(Easter
week). These usually involve
religious floats and processions of
people wearing white robes and
hoods which cover their faces.*

**Easter egg** NOUN
el **huevo de Pascua** *masc*
**a big Easter egg**
un gran huevo de Pascua

**easy** ADJECTIVE
**fácil** *masc & fem*
**It's easy!**
¡Es fácil!

to **eat** VERB
**comer**
**I eat a lot of sweets.**
Como muchos caramelos.
**Would you like
something to
eat?**
¿Quieres comer
algo?

**edge** NOUN
el **borde**
*masc*
**on the edge of the table**
en el borde de la mesa

**Edinburgh** NOUN
**Edimburgo** *masc*
**Andrew lives in Edinburgh.**
Andrew vive en Edimburgo.

**education** NOUN
la **educación** *fem*

**effect** NOUN
el **efecto** *masc*

**effort** NOUN
el **esfuerzo** *masc*
**You have to make an effort.**
Tienes que hacer un esfuerzo.

**e.g.** ABBREVIATION
**p.ej.** (= *por ejemplo*)

**egg** NOUN
el **huevo** *masc*
**a boiled egg**
un huevo pasado por agua
**a hard-boiled egg**
un huevo cocido
**scrambled eggs**
huevos revueltos
**a fried egg**
un huevo frito

**eight** NUMBER
**ocho**
**eight euros**
ocho euros

**She's eight.**
Tiene ocho años.

***Language tip***
*In English you can say* **she's eight**
*or* **she's eight years old**. *In
Spanish you can only say* **tiene
ocho años**. *Have you noticed that
in Spanish you need to use the verb*
**tener** *to talk about somebody's
age?*

**eighteen** NUMBER
**dieciocho**
**eighteen euros**
dieciocho euros

**He's eighteen.**
Tiene dieciocho años.

***Language tip***
*In English you can say* **he's
eighteen** *or* **he's eighteen years**

**English   Spanish**

a b c d **e** f g h i j k l m n o p q r s t u v w x y z

old. *In Spanish you can only say* **tiene dieciocho años.** *Have you noticed that in Spanish you need to use the verb* **tener** *to talk about somebody's age?*

## eighteenth NUMBER
**dieciocho**
> **on the eighteenth floor**
> en el piso dieciocho
> **It's my brother's eighteenth birthday on Saturday.**
> Mi hermano cumple dieciocho años el sábado.
> **My birthday's the eighteenth of August.**
> Mi cumpleaños es el dieciocho de agosto.
> **Today's the eighteenth of May.**
> Hoy es dieciocho de mayo.

**on the eighteenth of June**
el dieciocho de junio

### Language tip
*Use the same set of numbers that you use for counting (**uno**, **dos**, **tres** and so on) when giving Spanish dates.*

## eighth NUMBER
**octavo** *masc*
**octava** *fem*
> **on the eighth floor**
> en el octavo piso
> **My birthday's the eighth of May.**
> Mi cumpleaños es el ocho de mayo.
> **It's the eighth of June today.**
> Hoy es ocho de junio.

**on the eighth of Abril**
el ocho de abril

### Language tip
*Use the same set of numbers that you use for counting (**uno**, **dos**, **tres** and so on) when giving Spanish dates.*

## eighty NUMBER
**ochenta**
> **My grandmother is eighty.**
> Mi abuela tiene ochenta años.

### Language tip
*In English you can say **she's eighty** or **she's eighty years old.** In Spanish you can only say **tiene ochenta años.** Have you noticed that in Spanish you need to use the verb **tener** to talk about somebody's age?*

## Eire NOUN
la **República de Irlanda** *fem*

## either ADVERB, CONJUNCTION, PRONOUN
**tampoco**
> **I don't like milk, and I don't like eggs either.**
> No me gusta la leche ni tampoco me gustan os huevos.
> **I haven't got any money. – I haven't either.**
> No tengo dinero. – Ni yo tampoco.
> **I don't like either of them.**
> No me gusta ninguno de los dos.

**either ... or ...**
o ... o ...
> **You can have either ice cream or yoghurt.**
> Puedes tomar o he ado o yogur.

## elastic band NOUN
la **goma elástica** *fem*

**elbow** NOUN
el **codo** *masc*
**I've hurt my elbow.**
Me he hecho daño en el codo.

> **Language tip**
> In Spanish you usually use an article like **el**, **la**, **los** with parts of the body.

**elder** ADJECTIVE
**mayor** *masc & fem*
**my elder sister**
mi hermana mayor

**elderly** ADJECTIVE
**mayor** *masc & fem*
**an elderly gentleman**
un señor mayor
**the elderly**
los ancianos

**eldest** ADJECTIVE
**mayor** *masc & fem*
**my eldest brother**
mi hermano mayor
**He's the eldest.**
Él es el mayor.

**election** NOUN
la **elección** *fem* (PL las elecciones)
**the election of the new mayor**
la elección del nuevo alcalde
**The elections will be in May.**
Las elecciones serán en mayo.

**electric** ADJECTIVE
**eléctrico** *masc*
**eléctrica** *fem*
**an electric guitar**
una guitarra eléctrica

**electrician** NOUN
el/la **electricista** *masc/fem*
**He's an electrician.**
Es electricista.

> **Language tip**
> In Spanish, you do not use an article with people's jobs.

**electricity** NOUN
la **electricidad** *fem*

**electronic** ADJECTIVE
**electrónico** *masc*
**electrónica** *fem*

**elegant** ADJECTIVE
**elegante** *masc & fem*

**elephant** NOUN
el **elefante** *masc*

**eleven** NUMBER
**once**
**eleven euros**
once euros

**I'm eleven.**
Tengo once años.

> **Language tip**
> In English you can say **I'm eleven** or **I'm eleven years old.** In Spanish you can only say **tengo once años.** Have you noticed that in Spanish you need to use the verb **tener** to talk about somebody's age?

**eleventh** NUMBER
**undécimo** *masc*
**undécima** *fem*
**on the eleventh floor**
en el undécimo piso
**My birthday's the eleventh of June.**
Mi cumpleaños es el once de junio.
**It's the eleventh of December today.**
Hoy es once de diciembre.

**on the eleventh of January**
el once de enero

*Language tip*
*Use the same set of numbers that you use for counting (uno, dos, tres and so on) when giving Spanish dates.*

**else** ADVERB
**más**
   **nobody else**
   nadie más
   **nothing else**
   nada más
   **Would you like anything else?**
   ¿Quieres algo más?
   **I don't want anything else.**
   No quiero nada más.
   **somebody else**
   otra persona

## email

*email can be a noun or a verb.*

**A** NOUN
   el **e-mail** *masc* (PL los **e-mails**)
   **by email**
   por e-mail
   **Send your friend an email.**
   Envíale un e-mail a tu amigo.
**B** VERB
   **to email**
   mandar un e-mail a
   **I'll email you.**
   Te mandaré un e-mail.

**email address** NOUN
   el **e-mail** *masc* (PL los **e-mails**)
   **My email address is loveday at collins dot co dot U-K (loveday@collins.co.uk).**
   Mi e-mail es loveday arroba collins punto co punto U-K (loveday@collins.co.uk).

**embarrassed** ADJECTIVE
   **I was really embarrassed.**
   Me dio mucha vergüenza.

**embarrassing**
ADJECTIVE
**incómodo** *masc*
**incómoda** *fem*
   **an embarrassing situation**
   una situación incómoda

**emergency** NOUN
   la **emergencia** *fem*
   **This is an emergency!**
   ¡Es una emergencia!
   **in an emergency**
   en caso de emergencia

**emergency exit** NOUN
   la **salida de emergencia** *fem*

## empty

*empty can be an adjective or a verb.*

**A** ADJECTIVE
   **vacío** *masc*
   **vacía** *fem*
   **The cage is empty.**
   La jaula está vacía.
**B** VERB
   **to empty**
   vaciar
   **Can you empty the wastepaper basket?**
   ¿Podrías vaciar la papelera?

to **encourage** VERB
**animar**
   **Encourage your team!**
   ¡Anima a tu equipo!

**encyclopedia** NOUN
   la **enciclopedia** *fem*

## end

*end can be a noun or a verb.*

**A** NOUN
   el **final** *masc*
   **the end of the lesson**
   el final de la clase
   **at the end of the street**
   al final de la calle

**in the end**
al final

**B** VERB
**to end**
terminar
**What time does the lesson end?**
¿A qué hora termina la clase?

**ending** NOUN
el **final** *masc*
**It's a great film, especially the ending.**
Es una película estupenda, sobre todo el final.

**enemy** NOUN
el **enemigo** *masc*
la **enemiga** *fem*

**energetic** ADJECTIVE
**lleno de energía** *masc*
**llena de energía** *fem*

**energy** NOUN
la **energía** *fem*

**engaged** ADJECTIVE
1 **ocupado** *masc*
**ocupada** *fem (busy)*
**The toilet is engaged.**
El baño está ocupado.
**Her phone is always engaged.**
Su teléfono está siempre comunicando.
2 **prometido** *masc*
**prometida** *fem (to be married)*
**My brother is engaged.**
Mi hermano está prometido.
**She's engaged to Rob.**
Está prometida con Rob.

**engagement**
NOUN
el **compromiso** *masc (to be married)*

**engagement ring** NOUN
el **anillo de compromiso** *masc*

**engine** NOUN
1 el **motor** *masc (of car, machine)*
2 la **locomotora** *fem (train)*

**engineer** NOUN
el **ingeniero** *masc*
la **ingeniera** *fem*
**He's an engineer.**
Es ingeniero.

*Language tip*
*In Spanish, you do not use an article with people's jobs.*

**England** NOUN
**Inglaterra** *fem*
**I live in England.**
Vivo en Inglaterra.
**Are you coming to England?**
¿Vienes a Inglaterra?

**English**

**English** *can be an adjective or a noun.*

**A** ADJECTIVE
**inglés** *masc* (PL **ingleses**)
**inglesa** *fem*
**I'm English.**
Soy inglés.
**English food is different.**
La comida inglesa es diferente.
**English people**
los ingleses

**He's English.**
Es inglés.
**She's English.**
Es inglesa.

**B** NOUN
el **inglés** *masc*
**Do you speak English?**
¿Hablas inglés?
**the English**
los ingleses

*Language tip*
**inglés** *is not spelled with a capital letter in Spanish.*

a
b
c
d
e
f
g
h
i
j
k
l
m
n
o
p
q
r
s
t
u
v
w
x
y
z

**Englishman** NOUN
el **inglés** *masc* (PL los **ingleses**)
**an Englishman**
un inglés

*Language tip*
**inglés** *is not spelled with a capital letter in Spanish.*

**Englishwoman** NOUN
la **inglesa** *fem* (PL las **inglesas**)
**an Englishwoman**
una inglesa

*Language tip*
**inglesa** *is not spelled with a capital letter in Spanish.*

to **enjoy** VERB
**I enjoy learning English.**
Me gusta aprender inglés.
**Did you enjoy the film?**
¿Te gustó la película?
**to enjoy oneself**
divertirse
**Did you enjoy yourself?**
¿Te divertiste?

**enjoyable** ADJECTIVE
**agradable** *masc & fem*

**enormous** ADJECTIVE
**enorme** *masc & fem*

**enough**

*enough can be an adjective, pronoun or adverb.*

**A** ADJECTIVE
**suficiente** *masc & fem*
**enough time**
tiempo suficiente
**I haven't got enough money.**
No tengo dinero suficiente.

*Language tip*
*You can also use* **bastante**, *which goes before the noun.*

**I haven't got enough money.**
No tengo bastante dinero.
**B** PRONOUN
**bastante** *masc & fem*

**Have you got enough?**
¿Tienes bastante?
**I've had enough!**
¡Ya está bien!

**That's enough.**
Ya basta.

**C** ADVERB
**This hat isn't big enough.**
Este sombrero no es lo suficientemente grande.
**Is your coffee hot enough?**
¿Tu café está lo suficientemente caliente?

to **enter** VERB
**I'm going to enter the competition.**
Voy a participar en el concurso.

**enthusiasm** NOUN
el **entusiasmo** *masc*

**enthusiastic** ADJECTIVE
**entusiasta** *masc & fem*

**entrance** NOUN
la **entrada** *fem*
**I'll wait for you by the entrance.**
Te esperaré en la entrada.

**entrance exam** NOUN
la **prueba de acceso** *fem*

**entry** NOUN
la **entrada** *fem*
**'no entry'**
'prohibida la entrada'

**entry phone** NOUN
el **portero automático** *masc*

**envelope** NOUN
el **sobre** *masc*

**envious** ADJECTIVE
**envidioso** *masc*
**envidiosa** *fem*

**environment** NOUN
el **medio ambiente** masc

**episode** NOUN
el **capítulo** masc

**equal**

> equal can be an adjective or a verb.

**A** ADJECTIVE
**igual** masc & fem
**Cut the pizza into six equal pieces.**
Corta la pizza en seis trozos iguales.
**B** VERB
**to equal**
**ser igual a**
**Two times three equals six.**
Dos por tres es igual a seis.

to **equalize** VERB
**empatar**
**Henry has equalized.**
Henry ha empatado.

**equipment** NOUN
el **equipo** masc
**lots of equipment**
mucho equipo

**error** NOUN
el **error** masc
**a small error**
un pequeño error

**escalator** NOUN
la **escalera mecánica** fem
**Is there an escalator?**
¿Hay escalera mecánica?

to **escape** VERB
**escaparse**
**A lion has escaped.**
Se ha escapado un león.

**especially** ADVERB
**sobre todo**
**It's very hot, especially in summer.**
Hace mucho calor, sobre todo en verano.

**essay** NOUN
el **trabajo** masc
**a history essay**
un trabajo de historia

**essential** ADJECTIVE
**esencial** masc & fem
**It's essential to bring warm clothes.**
Es esencial traer ropa de abrigo.

**euro** NOUN
el **euro** masc

**Europe** NOUN
**Europa** fem

**European** ADJECTIVE
**europeo** masc
**europea** fem

> **Language tip**
> **europeo** is not spelled with a capital letter in Spanish.

**even**

> even can be an adverb or an adjective.

**A** ADVERB
**incluso**
**I like all animals, even snakes.**
Me gustan todos los animales, incluso las serpientes.
**B** ADJECTIVE
**an even number**
un número par

**evening** NOUN
**1** la **tarde** fem (early evening)

> **Language tip**
> Use **la tarde** in the early evening while it's still light.

**at six o'clock in the evening**
a las seis de la tarde

**this evening at about six thirty**
esta tarde, a eso de las seis y media
**2** la **noche** *fem (after dark)*

***Language tip***
*Use* **la noche** *for later in the evening, particularly after dark.*

**at nine o'clock in the evening**
a las nueve de la noche
**tomorrow evening**
mañana por la noche
**yesterday evening**
ayer por la noche
**Good evening!**
¡Buenas noches!

***Language tip***
*Change* **noche** *and* **noches** *to* **tarde** *and* **tardes** *if it's very early in the evening.*

**evening class** NOUN
la **clase nocturna** *fem*
**My mother goes to an evening class.**
Mi madre va a una clase nocturna.

**event** NOUN
el **acontecimiento** *masc*
**an important event**
un acontecimiento importante

**ever** ADVERB
**alguna vez** *(in questions)*
**Have you ever been to France?**
¿Has estado alguna vez en Francia?
**for the first time ever**
por primera vez
**Nothing ever happens.**
Nunca pasa nada.

**every** ADJECTIVE
**every pupil**
todos los alumnos
**I talk to her every day.**
Hablo con ella todos los días.
**I do judo every week.**
Hago yudo todas las semanas.

**every time**
cada vez

**every day**
todos los días
**every night**
todas las noches
**every week**
todas las semanas

**everybody** PRONOUN
**todos** *masc pl*
**todas** *fem pl*
**Good morning everybody!**
¡Buenos días a todos!
**Is everybody here?**
¿Están todos?
**Everybody likes sweets.**
A todo el mundo le gustan los caramelos.

**everyone** PRONOUN
**todos** *masc pl*
**todas** *fem pl*
**Good morning everyone!**
¡Buenos días a todos!
**Is everyone here?**
¿Están todos?
**Everyone likes sweets.**
A todo el mundo le gustan los caramelos.

**everything** PRONOUN
**todo** *masc*
**Everything's fine!**
¡Todo está bien!
**Is that everything?**
¿Eso es todo?

**everywhere** ADVERB
**por todas partes**

English Spanish

a b c d e f g h i j k l m n o p q r s t u v w x y z

I looked everywhere, but I couldn't find it.
Miré por todas partes, pero no lo encontré.
**There are cats everywhere!**
¡Hay gatos por todas partes!

**exact** ADJECTIVE
**exacto** *masc*
**exacta** *fem*

**exactly** ADVERB
**exactamente**
Our trainers are exactly the same.
Nuestras zapatillas de deporte son exactamente iguales.
**not exactly**
no exactamente
**It's exactly ten o'clock.**
Son las diez en punto.

**Language tip**

*Have you noticed that the Spanish equivalent of the English -ly ending is -mente? It's added to the feminine form of the adjective.*

**exam** NOUN
el **examen** *masc* (PL los exámenes)
**an English exam**
un examen de inglés

**example** NOUN
el **ejemplo** *masc*
**for example**
por ejemplo

**excellent** ADJECTIVE
**excelente** *masc & fem*
**Excellent!**
¡Excelente!

**except** PREPOSITION
**excepto**
**everyone except me**
todos menos yo

to **exchange** VERB
**cambiar**
I want to exchange the book for a video.

Quiero cambiar el libro por un vídeo.

**exchange rate** NOUN
el **tipo de cambio** *masc*

**excited** ADJECTIVE
**entusiasmado** *masc*
**entusiasmada** *fem*

**exciting** ADJECTIVE
**emocionante** *masc & fem*
**an exciting film**
una película emocionante

**exclamation mark** NOUN
el **signo de admiración** *masc*

to **excuse** VERB

**Excuse me!**
¡Perdón!

**exercise** NOUN
el **ejercicio** *masc*

**exercise book** NOUN
el **cuaderno** *masc*

**exhausted** ADJECTIVE
**agotado** *masc*
**agotada** *fem*
**Clare is exhausted.**
Clare está agotada.

**exhibition** NOUN
la **exposición** *fem* (PL las exposiciones)

**exit** NOUN
la **salida** *fem*
**Where is the exit?**
¿Dónde está la salida?

to **expect** VERB
1 **esperar** *(wait for)*
**I'm expecting a phone call.**
Estoy esperando una llamada.
**She's expecting a baby.**
Está esperando un hijo.
2 **imaginarse** *(imagine)*
**I expect he'll be late.**
Me imagino que llegará tarde.

**expedition** NOUN
la **expedición** *fem* (PL las
expediciones)

**expensive** ADJECTIVE
**caro** *masc*
**cara** *fem*
**It's too expensive.**
Es demasiado caro.

**experience** NOUN
la **experiencia** *fem*
**an interesting experience**
una experiencia interesante

**experiment** NOUN
el **experimento** *masc*

**expert** NOUN
el **experto** *masc*
la **experta** *fem*
**She's a computer expert.**
Es una experta en informática.
**Matthew is an expert cook.**
Matthew es un experto cocinero.

to **explain** VERB
**explicar**
**I'll explain it in English.**
Te lo explicaré en inglés.

**explanation** NOUN
la **explicación** *fem* (PL las
explicaciones)
**a clear explanation**
una explicación clara

to **explode** VERB
**explotar**
**It's going to
explode!**
¡Va a explotar!

**explosion** NOUN
la **explosión** *fem*
(PL las
explosiones)

**extension** NOUN
1 la **extensión** *fem* (P_ las
extensiones) *(phone)*
**Extension 3137, please.**
Con la extensión 3137, por favor.
2 *(of building)*
**We're having an extension
built.**
Nos están construyendo una
ampliación de la casa.

**extra**

**extra** *can be an adjective or an
adverb.*

**A** ADJECTIVE
1 *(additional)*
**an extra blanket**
una manta más
2 *(not included)*
**Breakfast is extra.**
El desayuno no está incluido.
**B** ADVERB
**to pay extra**
pagar más
**You have to pay extra for a
room with a sea view.**
Si quieres una habitación con
vistas al mar tienes que pagar
más.
**It costs extra.**
Lleva un suplemento aparte.

**extremely** ADVERB
**sumamente**

**eye** NOUN
el **ojo** *masc*
**I've got blue eyes.**
Tengo los ojos azules.
**What colour eyes has he got?**
¿De qué color tiene los ojos?
**She opened her eyes.**
Abrió los ojos.

**eyebrow** NOUN
la **ceja** *fem*

**eyelash** NOUN
la **pestaña** *fem*

She's got very long eyelashes.
Tiene las pestañas muy largas.

**eyelid** NOUN
el **párpado** *masc*

**eyesight** NOUN
la **vista** *fem*

English Spanish

a b c d e f g h i j k l m n o p q r s t u v w x y z

393

# F f

**fabulous** ADJECTIVE
**fantástico** masc
**fantástica** fem

**face** NOUN
la **cara** fem
His face is red.
Tiene la cara roja.

*Language tip*

In Spanish you usually use an article like **el**, **la**, **los** with parts of the body.

**face cloth** NOUN
la **toallita** fem

**facilities** PL NOUN
las **instalaciones** fem pl

**fact** NOUN
el **hecho** masc
an interesting fact
un hecho interesante
in fact
en realidad

**factory** NOUN
la **fábrica** fem
My mum works in a factory.
Mi madre trabaja en una fábrica.

to **fail** VERB
**suspender**
She's going to fail her exams.
Va a suspender los exámenes.

**fair**

**fair** *can be an adjective or a noun.*

**A** ADJECTIVE
**1 justo** masc
**justa** fem (right)
That's not fair.
Eso no es justo.

**2 rubio** masc
**rubia** fem (blonde)
He's got fair hair.
Tiene el pelo rubio.
**B** NOUN
la **feria** fem
Are you going to the fair?
¿Vas a ir a la feria?

**fair-haired** ADJECTIVE
Nina is fair-haired.
Nina tiene el pelo rubio.

**fairly** ADVERB
**bastante**
That's fairly good.
Eso está bastante bien.

**fairy** NOUN
la **hada** fem

**fairy tale** NOUN
el **cuento de hadas** masc

to **fall** VERB
**caerse**
Mind you don't fall!
¡Ten cuidado de no caerte!
to fall asleep
quedarse dormido
I'm falling asleep.
Me estoy quedando dormido.

to **fall off** VERB
caerse de

He's going to fall off the wall.
Se va a caer del muro.

**false** ADJECTIVE
**falso** masc

394

**falsa** *fem*
**True or false?**
¿Verdadero o falso?

**family** NOUN
la **familia** *fem*
**my family**
mi familia
**the whole family**
toda la familia
**the Crooks family**
la familia Crooks

**famous** ADJECTIVE
**famoso** *masc*
**famosa** *fem*

**fan** NOUN
1 el **ventilador** *masc (electric)*
2 el **abanico** *masc (hand-held)*
3 el/la **hincha** *masc/fem*
(enthusiast)
**football fans**
los hinchas de fútbol

to **fancy** VERB
**Do you fancy an ice cream?**
¿Te apetece un helado?
**I fancy watching a film.**
Me apetece ver una película.
**I fancy that girl.**
Me gusta esa chica.

**fantastic** ADJECTIVE
**fantástico** *masc*
**fantástica** *fem*

**far** ADVERB
1 **lejos** *(distant)*
**It isn't very far.**
No está muy lejos.
**far from**
lejos de
**It isn't far from here.**
No está lejos de aquí.

**Is it far?**
¿Está lejos?
**No, it isn't far.**
No, no está lejos.
**It's too far.**
Está demasiado lejos.

2 **mucho** *(much)*
**That's far better!**
¡Eso está mucho mejor!

**farm** NOUN
la **granja** *fem*

**farmer** NOUN
el **agricultor** *masc*
la **agricultora** *fem*
**He's a farmer.**
Es agricultor.

*Language tip*

*In Spanish, you do not use an article with people's jobs.*

**farmhouse** NOUN
la **granja** *fem*

**fashion** NOUN
la **moda** *fem*
**These shoes are in fashion.**
Estos zapatos están de moda.

**fashionable** ADJECTIVE
**de moda**
**This style is very fashionable.**
Este estilo está muy de moda.
**Jane wears fashionable
clothes.**
Jane se viste a la moda.

**fashion show** NOUN
el **desfile de moda** *masc*

**fast**

**fast** *can be an adverb or an
adjective.*

**A** ADVERB
**rápido**
**You walk fast.**
Andas rápido.
**B** ADJECTIVE
**rápido** *masc*

a
b
c
d
e
f
g
h
i
j
k
l
m
n
o
p
q
r
s
t
u
v
w
x
y
z

**rápida** *fem*
**a fast car**
un coche rápido
**fast food**
la comida rápida

to **fasten** VERB
**abrocharse**
**Fasten your seat belts, please.**
Abróchense los cinturones de seguridad, por favor.

**fat** ADJECTIVE
**gordo** *masc*

**gorda** *fem*
**They're both fat.**
Los dos están gordos.

**father** NOUN
el **padre** *masc*
**my father**
mi padre
**my mother and father**
mis padres

**Father Christmas** NOUN
**Papá Noel** *masc*

**Did you know…?**

*In Spain it's often* **los Reyes Magos** *(the Three Kings) who bring children their presents. And instead of Christmas Eve they come on the night of the fifth of January, so children open their presents on the sixth.*

**Father's Day** NOUN
el **día del Padre** *masc*

**fault** NOUN
la **culpa** *fem*
**It's your fault!**
¡Es culpa tuya!
**It wasn't my fault.**
No fue culpa mía.

**favour** NOUN
el **favor** *masc*
**Could you do me a favour?**
¿Me podrías hacer un favor?

**favourite** ADJECTIVE
**favorito** *masc*
**favorita** *fem*
**Blue's my favourite colour.**
El azul es mi color favorito.

**feather** NOUN
la **pluma** *fem*

**February** NOUN
**febrero** *masc*
**My birthday's the fourteenth of February.**
Mi cumpleaños es el catorce de febrero.
**It's the eighth of February today.**
Hoy es ocho de febrero.

**in February**
en febrero
**on the fifth of February**
el cinco de febrero

**Language tip**
*Months are not spelled with a capital letter in Spanish.*

to **feed** VERB
**dar de comer a**
**I'm going to feed the cat.**
Voy a darle de comer al gato.

to **feel** VERB
**encontrarse**
**I don't feel well.**
No me encuentro bien.
**I feel like …**
Me apetece …
**I feel like going for a walk.**
Me apetece dar un paseo.
**Do you feel like an ice cream?**
¿Te apetece un helado?

**feet** PL NOUN
los **pies** *masc pl*
**My feet are cold.**
Tengo los pies fríos.

**Language tip**
In Spanish you usually use an article like **el**, **la**, **los** with parts of the body.

**fell** VERB ▷ see **fall**

**felt-tip pen** NOUN
 el **rotulador** masc
  Can I borrow your felt-tip pens?
  ¿Me dejas tus rotuladores?

**female** NOUN
 la **hembra** fem
  Is it a male or a female?
  ¿Es macho o hembra?

**feminine**
 ADJECTIVE
 **femenino** masc
 **femenina** fem

**fence** NOUN
 la **valla** fem

**ferret** NOUN
 el **hurón** masc (PL los hurones)

**ferry** NOUN
 el **ferry** masc (PL los **ferrys**)

to **fetch** VERB
 **ir a buscar**
  Can you fetch my bag?
  ¿Puedes ir a buscar mi bolso?
  Mum always fetches us from school.
  Mamá siempre nos va a buscar al colegio.

**few** ADJECTIVE, PRONOUN
 **a few**
 **unos pocos**

**Language tip**
Remember to change **unos pocos** to **unas pocas** when describing or referring to a feminine noun.

  **a few hours**
  unas pocas horas
  **How many potatoes do you want? – Just a few.**
  ¿Cuántas patatas quieres? – Solo unas pocas.
  **quite a few people**
  bastante gente
  **I've got fewer sweets than Jim.**
  Tengo menos caramelos que Jim.
  **Who's got the fewest cards?**
  ¿Quién tiene menos cartas?

**fiancé** NOUN
 el **prometido** masc
  He's her fiancé.
  Es su prometido.

**fiancée** NOUN
 la **prometida** fem
  She's his fiancée.
  Es su prometida.

**field** NOUN
 el **campo** masc
  **a football field**
  un campo de fútbol
  **a field of wheat**
  un campo de trigo

**fifteen** NUMBER
 **quince**
  **fifteen euros**
  quince euros

  **I'm fifteen.**
  Tengo quince años.

**Language tip**
In English you can say I**'m fifteen** or I**'m fifteen years old**. In Spanish you can only say **tengo quince años**. Have you noticed that in Spanish you need to use the verb **tener** to talk about somebody's age?

**fifteenth** NUMBER
 **quince**
  **on the fifteenth floor**
  en el piso quince
  **Today's the fifteenth of July.**
  Hoy es quince de julio.

**My birthday's the fifteenth of August.**
Mi cumpleaños es el quince de agosto.

**on the fifteenth of November**
el quince de noviembre

*Language tip*
*Use the same set of numbers that you use for counting (uno, dos, tres and so on) when giving Spanish dates.*

**fifth** NUMBER
**quinto** *masc*
**quinta** *fem*
**on the fifth floor**
en el quinto piso
**Today's the fifth of April.**
Hoy es cinco de abril.
**My birthday's the fifth of March.**
Mi cumpleaños es el cinco de marzo.

**on the fifth of August**
el cinco de agosto

*Language tip*
*Use the same set of numbers that you use for counting (uno, dos, tres and so on) when giving Spanish dates.*

**fifty** NUMBER
**cincuenta**
**My aunt is fifty.**
Mi tía tiene cincuenta años.

*Language tip*
*In English you can say she's fifty or she's fifty years old. In Spanish you can only say tiene cincuenta años. Have you noticed that in Spanish you need to use the verb tener to talk about somebody's age?*

**fight**

*fight can be a noun or a verb.*

**A** NOUN
la **pelea** *fem*
**B** VERB
**to fight**
**pelearse**
**Two boys are fighting.**
Dos niños se están peleando.

**figure** NOUN
la **cifra** *fem*
**Shall I write it in figures or in words?**
¿Lo escribo en cifras o en palabras?

**file** NOUN
**1** la **carpeta** *fem (folder)*
**Keep the leaflets in your file.**
Guarda los folletos en tu carpeta.
**2** el **archivo** *masc (on computer)*

to **fill** VERB
**llenar**
**Can you fill the glasses?**
¿Puedes llenar las copas?

to **fill in** VERB
**rellenar**
**You have to fill in the gaps in the sentences.**
Hay que rellenar los huecos de las frases.

**filling** NOUN
el **empaste** *masc (in tooth)*

**film** NOUN
**1** la **película** *fem (movie)*
**Is it a good film?**
¿Es una buena película?

**2** el **carrete** *masc (for camera)*
**I'd like to have this film developed.**
Quiero revelar este carrete.

**film star** NOUN
la **estrella de cine** *fem*
**Eddie Murphy is a film star.**
Eddie Murphy es una estrella de cine.

**final**

**A** ADJECTIVE
**último** *masc*
**última** *fem*
**the final minutes**
los últimos minutos
**B** NOUN
la **final** *fem*
**The final is tomorrow.**
La final es mañana.

**finally** ADVERB
**finalmente**

to **find** VERB
**encontrar**
**My brother wants to find a job.**
Mi hermano quiere encontrar trabajo.

**fine** ADJECTIVE
**bien**

**That's fine, thanks.**
Eso está bien, gracias.
**How are you? – I'm fine.**
¿Qué tal estás? – Estoy bien.

**finger** NOUN
el **dedo** *masc*
**my little finger**
mi dedo meñique
**My finger is hurting.**
Me duele el dedo.

**fingernail** NOUN
la **uña** *fem*

to **finish** VERB
**terminar**
**I've got to finish my homework.**
Tengo que terminar los deberes.
**I've finished!**
¡He terminado!
**Is it finished?**
¿Está terminado?

**fire** NOUN
1 el **fuego** *masc*
**You mustn't play with fire.**
No hay que jugar con el fuego.
2 el **incendio** *masc* (accidental)
**There's a fire in the wood.**
Hay un incendio en el bosque.

**fire engine** NOUN
el **coche de bomberos** *masc*

**fire extinguisher** NOUN
el **extintor** *masc*

**fire fighter** NOUN
el **bombero** *masc*
la **bombera** *fem*
**He's a fire fighter.**
Es bombero.

**fireplace** NOUN
la **chimenea** *fem*

**fire station** NOUN
el **parque de bomberos** *masc*

## fireworks PL NOUN
los **fuegos artificiales** *masc pl*
**There are fireworks this evening.**
Hay fuegos artificiales esta noche.

## first

> **first** *can be an adjective, noun or adverb.*

**A** ADJECTIVE
**primero** *masc*
**primera** *fem*
**the first time**
la primera vez

> ### Language tip
> Shorten **primero** to **primer** before a masculine singular noun.

**the first day**
el primer día
**to come first**
quedar primero
**Rachel came first in the race.**
Rachel quedó primera en la carrera.
**Who's first?**
¿Quién va primero?
**Me first!**
¡Yo primero!
**B** NOUN
**at first**
al principio
**It's easy at first.**
Es fácil al principio.
**My birthday's the first of October.**
Mi cumpleaños es el uno de octubre.
**Today's the first of June.**
Hoy es uno de junio.

> **on the first of September**
> el uno de septiembre

> ### Language tip
> Use the same set of numbers that you use for counting (**uno**, **dos**, **tres** and so on) when giving Spanish dates.

**C** ADVERB
**primero**
**First write your names.**
Primero escribid vuestros nombres.
**first of all**
en primer lugar

## first aid NOUN
los **primeros auxilios** *masc pl*

## first name NOUN
el **nombre de pila** *masc*

## fish

> **fish** *can be a noun or a verb.*

**A** NOUN
**1** el **pescado** *masc (as food)*
**I don't like fish.**
No me gusta el pescado.
**2** el **pez** *masc (PL los **peces**)* *(animal)*
**I caught three fish.**
Pesqué tres peces.
**B** VERB
**to go fishing**
ir a pescar
**Let's go fishing.**
Vamos a pescar.

## fish fingers PL NOUN
las **varitas de merluza** *fem pl*

## fishing NOUN
la **pesca** *fem*
**I like fishing.**
Me gusta la pesca.

## fishing boat NOUN
la **barca de pesca** *fem*

## fishing rod NOUN
la **caña de pescar** *fem*

## fish tank NOUN
el **acuario** *masc*

## fit

> **fit** *can be a verb or an adjective.*

**A** VERB

to fit
**caber**
**It doesn't fit in the kitchen.**
No cabe en la cocina.
**These trousers don't fit me.**
Estos pantalones no me están
bien.
**B** ADJECTIVE
**en forma** (healthy)
**He's fit.**
Está en forma.

**five** NUMBER
**cinco**
**five euros**
cinco euros

**She's five.**
Tiene cinco años.

*Language tip*

*In English you can say **she's five** or
**she's five years old.** In Spanish
you can only say **tiene cinco años.**
Have you noticed that in Spanish
you need to use the verb **tener** to
talk about somebody's age?*

to **fix** VERB
**arreglar**
**Can you fix my bike?**
¿Me puedes arreglar la bici?

**fizzy** ADJECTIVE
**con gas**
**I don't like fizzy drinks.**
No me gustan las bebidas con
gas.

**flag** NOUN
la **bandera** *fem*

**flame** NOUN
la **llama** *fem*

**flan** NOUN
**1** la **tarta** *fem (sweet)*
**a raspberry flan**
una tarta de frambuesa

*Language tip*

*Be careful! The translation of **flan** is
not **flan.***

**2** el **pastel** *masc (savoury)*
**a cheese and onion flan**
un pastel de queso y cebolla

**flannel** NOUN
la **toallita** *fem*

**flash** NOUN
**a flash of lightning**
un relámpago

**flask** NOUN
el **termo** *masc*

**flat**

*flat can be an adjective or a noun.*

**A** ADJECTIVE
**1** **plano** *masc*
**plana** *fem (level)*
**a flat roof**
un tejado plano
**flat shoes**
zapatos planos
**2** **pinchado** *masc*
**pinchada** *fem (tyre)*
**I've got a flat tyre.**
Tengo una rueda pinchada.
**B** NOUN
el **piso** *masc*
**She lives in a flat.**
Vive en un piso.

**flavour** NOUN
el **sabor** *masc*
**Which flavour of ice cream
would you like?**
¿De qué sabor quieres el
helado?

**fleece** NOUN
el **forro polar** masc

**flew** VERB ▷ see **fly**

**flight** NOUN
el **vuelo** masc
**What time is the flight to London?**
¿A qué hora es el vuelo a Londres?

**floor** NOUN
1 el **suelo** masc (of room)
**on the floor**
en el suelo
**Sit on the floor, Jenny.**
Siéntate en el suelo, Jenny.
2 la **planta** fem (storey)
**the ground floor**
la planta baja
**the first floor**
la primera planta
**on the third floor**
en la tercera planta

**florist** NOUN
el/la **florista** masc/fem
**He's a florist.**
Es florista.
**a florist's**
una floristería

**flour** NOUN
la **harina** fem

**flower** NOUN
la **flor** fem

**flu** NOUN
la **gripe** fem
**Nathan has got flu.**
Nathan tiene gripe.

**fluent** ADJECTIVE
**My sister speaks fluent Spanish.**
Mi hermana habla español con fluidez.

**flute** NOUN
la **flauta** fem
**I play the flute.**
Toco la flauta.

to **flush** VERB
**to flush the toilet**
tirar de la cadena

**fly**

**fly** can be a verb or a noun.

**A** VERB
**to fly**
1 **ir en avión** (go by plane)
**I'm going to fly to Florida.**
Voy a ir a Florida en avión.
2 **volar** (with wings)
**A bee was flying around the room.**
Había una abeja volando por la habitación.
**B** NOUN
la **mosca** fem

**fog** NOUN
la **niebla** fem

**foggy** ADJECTIVE
**a foggy day**
un día de niebla

**It's foggy.**
Hay niebla.

to **fold** VERB
**doblar**
**Fold the paper in half.**
Dobla el papel por la mitad.

**folder** NOUN
la **carpeta** fem

to **follow** VERB
**seguir**
**Follow me, Kevin.**
Sígueme, Kevin.

**following** ADJECTIVE
**siguiente** masc & fem
**the following day**
el día siguiente

**food** NOUN
la **comida** fem
**I like Spanish food.**
Me gusta la comida española.
**We need to buy some food.**
Necesitamos comprar comida.

**food processor** NOUN
el **robot de cocina** *masc*

**foot** NOUN
el **pie** *masc*
**My feet are hurting.**
Me duelen los pies.

> *Language tip*
> In Spanish you usually use an article like **el**, **la**, **los** with parts of the body.

**on foot**
a pie
**Richard is six foot tall.**
Richard mide seis pies de altura.

**football** NOUN
1 el **fútbol** *masc (game)*
**I like playing football.**
Me gusta jugar al fútbol.
**Do you want to play football, boys?**
¿Queréis jugar al fútbol, niños?

> *Language tip*
> In Spanish, you need to add **al** before the name of the sport.

2 el **balón** *masc* (PL los **balones**) *(ball)*
**Jason's got a new football.**
Jason tiene un balón nuevo.

**football boots** PL NOUN
las **botas de fútbol** *fem pl*

**footballer** NOUN
el/la **futbolista** *masc/fem*
**He's a footballer.**
Es futbolista.

> *Language tip*
> In Spanish, you do not use an article with people's jobs.

**football player** NOUN
el **jugador de fútbol** *masc*
la **jugadora de fútbol** *fem*
**David Beckham is a famous football player.**
David Beckham es un jugador de fútbol famoso.

**football shirt** NOUN
la **camiseta de fútbol** *fem*

**footpath** NOUN
el **sendero** *masc*

**footstep** NOUN
el **paso** *masc*

**for** PREPOSITION
1 **para** *(intended for, destined for)*
**a present for me**
un regalo para mí
**the train for London**
el tren para Londres
**I'll do it for you.**
Yo te lo haré.
**What's the Spanish for 'lion'?**
¿Cómo se dice 'lion' en español?
**It's time for lunch.**
Es la hora de comer.

> **What's it for?**
> ¿Para qué es?
> **B for Barcelona**
> B de Barcelona

2 **por** *(in exchange for)*
**I'll give it to you for five pounds.**
Te lo doy por cinco libras.
**He bought it for ten euros.**
Lo compró por diez euros.
3 *(for a period of)*
**We're going there for three weeks.**
Vamos a pasar ahí tres semanas.

> *Language tip*
> You can often use the verb **llevar** to talk about how long you've been doing something.

**I have been learning Spanish for six months.**
Llevo seis meses aprendiendo español.

> *Language tip*
> But there are other ways of saying how long you've been doing something.

**I haven't seen her for two years.**
No la veo desde hace dos años.

**forbidden** ADJECTIVE
**prohibido** *masc*
**prohibida** *fem*
　**Smoking is forbidden.**
　Está prohibido fumar.

**forecast** NOUN
　**the weather forecast**
　el pronóstico del tiempo
　**What's the forecast for today?**
　¿Cuál es el pronóstico para hoy?

**forehead** NOUN
　la **frente** *fem*

**foreign** ADJECTIVE
**extranjero** *masc*
**extranjera** *fem*

**foreigner** NOUN
　el **extranjero** *masc*
　la **extranjera** *fem*
　**He's a foreigner.**
　Es extranjero.

**forest** NOUN
　**1** el **bosque** *masc (wood)*
　**2** la **selva** *fem (tropical)*

to **forget** VERB
**olvidarse**

> **Language tip**
>
> To say **I've forgotten** ... *use* **se me ha olvidado** *when you've forgotten one thing and* **se me han olvidado** *when you've forgotten two or more things.*

　**I've forgotten his name.**
　Se me ha olvidado su nombre.
　**I've forgotten my keys.**
　Se me han olvidado las llaves.
　**Don't forget!**
　¡Que no se te olvide!
　**to forget to do something**

olvidarse de hacer algo
　**I forgot to post the letter.**
　Me olvidé de echar la carta.

**fork** NOUN
　el **tenedor** *masc*

**form** NOUN
　el **impreso** *masc*
　**You have to fill in the form.**
　Tienes que rellenar el impreso.

**fortnight** NOUN
　**a fortnight**
　dos semanas
　**I'm going on holiday for a fortnight.**
　Me voy dos semanas de vacaciones.

**fortunately** ADVERB
**afortunadamente**

**forty** NUMBER
**cuarenta**
　**My father is forty.**
　Mi padre tiene cuarenta años.

> **Language tip**
>
> *In English you can say* **he's forty** *or* **he's forty years old**. *In Spanish you can only say* **tiene cuarenta años**. *Have you noticed that in Spanish you need to use the verb* **tener** *to talk about somebody's age?*

**forward** ADVERB
**hacia adelante**
　**a step forward**
　un paso hacia adelante
　**to move forward**
　avanzar
　**Move forward two spaces.**
　Avanza dos casillas.

**fought** VERB ▷ *see* **fight**

**found** VERB ▷ *see* **find**

**fountain** NOUN
　la **fuente** *fem*

**fountain pen** NOUN
　la **pluma estilográfica** *fem*

**four** NUMBER
**cuatro**
  **four euros**
  cuatro euros

**He's four.**
Tiene cuatro años.

**Language tip**
*In English you can say* **he's four** *or* **he's four years old**. *In Spanish you can only say* **tiene cuatro años**. *Have you noticed that in Spanish you need to use the verb* **tener** *to talk about somebody's age?*

**fourteen** NUMBER
**catorce**
  **fourteen euros**
  catorce euros

**I'm fourteen.**
Tengo catorce años.

**Language tip**
*In English you can say* **I'm fourteen** *or* **I'm fourteen years old**. *In Spanish you can only say* **tengo catorce años**. *Have you noticed that in Spanish you need to use the verb* **tener** *to talk about somebody's age?*

**fourteenth** NUMBER
**catorce**
  **on the fourteenth floor**
  en el piso catorce
  **My birthday's the fourteenth of January.**
  Mi cumpleaños es el catorce de enero.
  **Today's the fourteenth of July.**
  Hoy es catorce de julio.

**on the fourteenth of August**
el catorce de agosto

**Language tip**
*Use the same set of numbers that you use for counting (***uno**, **dos**, **tres** *and so on) when giving Spanish dates.*

**fourth** NUMBER
**cuarto** *masc*
**cuarta** *fem*
  **on the fourth floor**
  en el cuarto piso
  **My birthday's the fourth of December.**
  Mi cumpleaños es el cuatro de diciembre.
  **Today's the fourth of October.**
  Hoy es cuatro de octubre.

**on the fourth of June**
el cuatro de junio

**Language tip**
*Use the same set of numbers that you use for counting (***uno**, **dos**, **tres**, **cuatro** *and so on) when giving Spanish dates.*

**fox** NOUN
el **zorro** *masc*

**frame** NOUN
el **marco** *masc*
  **a photo frame**
  un marco de fotos

**freckles** PL NOUN
las **pecas** *fem pl*

**free** ADJECTIVE
**1 gratis** *(free of charge)*

**Language tip**
**gratis** *never changes its ending no matter what it describes.*

  **a free brochure**
  un folleto gratis
**2 libre** *masc & fem (not taken)*
  **Excuse me, is this seat free?**
  Perdón, ¿está libre este asiento?

**freezer** NOUN
el **congelador** *masc*

**freezing** ADJECTIVE
**helado** *masc*
**helada** *fem*
  **I'm freezing!**
  ¡Estoy helado!

It's absolutely freezing!
¡Hace un frío que pela!

**French beans** PL NOUN
las **judías verdes** *fem pl*

**French fries** PL NOUN
las **patatas fritas** *fem pl*

**fresh** ADJECTIVE
**fresco** *masc*
**fresca** *fem*
I need some fresh air.
Necesito un poco de aire fresco.

**Friday** NOUN
el **viernes** *masc*
It's Friday today.
Hoy es viernes.

**on Friday**
el viernes
**on Fridays**
os viernes
**every Friday**
todos los viernes
**last Friday**
el viernes pasado
**next Friday**
el viernes que viene

*Language tip*

*Days are not spelled with a capital letter in Spanish.*

**fridge** NOUN
la **nevera** *fem*

**fried** ADJECTIVE
**frito** *masc*
**frita** *fem*
a fried egg
un huevo frito

**friend** NOUN
el **amigo** *masc*
la **amiga** *fem*
my friend George
mi amigo George
my friend Natasha
mi amiga Natasha

**friendly** ADJECTIVE
**simpático** *masc*

**simpática** *fem*
She's very friendly.
Es muy simpática.

**frightened** ADJECTIVE
to be frightened
tener miedo
I'm not frightened.
No tengo miedo.
Alison is frightened of spiders.
A Alison le dan miedo las arañas.

I'm frightened!
¡Tengo miedo!

**fringe** NOUN
el **flequillo** *masc*
She's got a fringe.
Lleva flequillo.

**Frisbee®**
NOUN
el **disco volador** *masc*

**from** PREPOSITION
**de**
She comes from Bristol.
Es de Bristol.
a letter from my friend
una carta de mi amiga

*Language tip*
*de combines with el to form del.*

We aren't very far from the centre.
No estamos muy lejos del centro.
from ... to ...
desde ... hasta ...
from London to New York
desde Londres hasta Nueva York
the numbers from one to ten
los números del uno al diez

Where are you from?
¿De dónde eres?
I'm from Birmingham.
Soy de Birmingham.

## front

*front can be a noun or an adjective.*

English Spanish

a b c d e **f** g h i j k l m n o p q r s t u v w x y z

**A** NOUN
la **parte delantera** *fem*
**the front of the house**
la parte delantera de la casa
**in front of**
delante de
**in front of the house**
delante de la casa
**B** ADJECTIVE
**de delante**
**the front row**
la fila de delante

**front door** NOUN
la **puerta principal** *fem*

**frontier** NOUN
la **frontera** *fem*

**frost** NOUN
la **helada** *fem*

**frosty** ADJECTIVE
**a frosty morning**
una mañana de helada

> **It's frosty today.**
> Ha helado hoy.

**frozen** ADJECTIVE
1 **congelado** *masc*
**congelada** *fem (food)*
**frozen peas**
guisantes congelados
2 **helado** *masc*
**helada** *fem (lake, fingers)*
**I'm frozen.**
Estoy helado.

**fruit** NOUN
la **fruta** *fem*
**I like fruit.**
Me gusta la fruta.
**a piece of fruit**
una fruta

**fruit juice** NOUN
el **zumo de frutas** *masc*

**fruit salad** NOUN
la **macedonia** *fem*

to **fry** NOUN
**freír**

**frying pan** NOUN
la **sartén** *fem* (PL las **sartenes**)

**full** ADJECTIVE
**lleno** *masc*
**llena** *fem*
**The bottle's full.**
La botella está llena.
**I'm full.**
Estoy lleno.

**full stop** NOUN
el **punto** *masc*

**fun** NOUN
**to have fun**
pasárselo bien
**Are you having fun?**
¿Te lo estás pasando bien?

> **It's fun!**
> ¡Es divertido!
> **Have fun!**
> ¡Que te diviertas!

**funfair** NOUN
la **feria** *fem*

**funny** ADJECTIVE
**divertido** *masc*
**divertida** *fem*
**It was very funny.**
Fue muy divertido.

**fur** NOUN
1 la **piel** *fem (used in clothing)*
**a fur coat**
un abrigo de piel
2 el **pelo** *masc (of animal)*
**the dog's fur**
el pelo del perro

**furious** ADJECTIVE
**furioso** *masc*
**furiosa** *fem*

Dad is furious with me.
Papá está furioso conmigo.

## furniture NOUN
los **muebles** *masc pl*
We've got new furniture.
Tenemos muebles nuevos.
**a piece of furniture**
un mueble

### Language tip
*Use **un mueble** to refer to one piece of furniture and **muebles** in the plural to talk about **furniture** in general.*

## future NOUN
el **futuro** *masc*
What are your plans for the future?
¿Qué planes tienes para el futuro?
**Be more careful in future.**
De ahora en adelante ten más cuidado.

# G g

**game** NOUN
1 el **juego** *masc*
Let's play a game.
Vamos a jugar a algún juego.
a game of chess
una partida de ajedrez
2 el **partido** *masc* (match)
The game is tomorrow.
El partido es mañana.
a game of football
un partido de fútbol

**games** PL NOUN
la **educación física** *fem* (at school)
I like games.
Me gusta la educación física.

**gang** NOUN
1 la **banda** *fem* (of thieves, troublemakers, bullies)
2 la **pandilla** *fem* (of friends)

**gap** NOUN
el **hueco** *masc*
You have to fill in the gaps in the sentences.
Hay que rellenar los huecos de las frases.

**garage** NOUN
el **garaje** *masc*

**garden** NOUN
el **jardín** *masc* (PL los **jardines**)
We haven't got a garden.
No tenemos jardín.

**gardener** NOUN
el **jardinero** *masc*
la **jardinera** *fem*

**gardening** NOUN
la **jardinería** *fem*

**garlic** NOUN
el **ajo** *masc*
I don't like garlic.
No me gusta el ajo.
a clove of garlic
un diente de ajo

**gas** NOUN
el **gas** *masc*

**gas cooker** NOUN
la **cocina de gas** *fem*

**gate** NOUN
1 el **portón** *masc* (PL los **portones**) (wooden)
Please close the gate.
Por favor, cierre el portón.
2 la **verja** *fem* (metal)
There's a cow by the gate.
Hay una vaca al lado de la verja.
3 la **puerta** *fem* (at airport)
Please go to gate seven.
Diríjanse a la puerta siete.

**gave** VERB ▷ see **give**

**GCSE** NOUN
el **Título de Graduado en Educación Secundaria** *masc*

### Did you know...?
*Exams in Spain are different from British ones. There, the qualification you can get at sixteen is the **Título de Graduado en Educación Secundaria**.*

**general knowledge** NOUN
la **cultura general** *fem*
a general knowledge quiz
un concurso de cultura general

**generous** ADJECTIVE
**generoso** *masc*

**generosa** *fem*
> **That's very generous of you.**
> Eso es muy generoso de tu parte.

## genius NOUN
el **genio** *masc*
> **She's a genius!**
> ¡Es un genio!

> **Language tip**
> Did you notice that you still use the masculine **un genio** even when referring to a woman or girl?

## gentleman NOUN
el **caballero** *masc*

## gents NOUN
el **baño de caballeros** *masc*
> **Where is the 'gents', please?**
> ¿Dónde está el baño de caballeros, por favor?

## geography NOUN
la **geografía** *fem*
> **I like geography.**
> Me gusta la geografía.

## gerbil NOUN
el **gerbo** *masc*

## German measles NOUN
la **rubeola** *fem*
> **He's got German measles.**
> Tiene rubeola.

## to get VERB
1 **recibir** *(receive)*
> **He always gets lots of presents.**
> Siempre recibe muchos regalos.
> **What did you get for your birthday?**
> ¿Qué te regalaron para tu cumpleaños?

> **How much pocket money do you get?**
> ¿Cuánto te dan de paga?
> **I get five pounds a week.**
> Me dan cinco libras a la semana.

2 **comprar** *(buy)*
> **Can you get me a smoothie?**
> ¿Me puedes comprar un batido?
> **Mum's getting me a PlayStation.**
> Mamá me va a comprar una play.

3 **conseguir** *(obtain)*
> **We couldn't get any tickets for the match.**
> No logramos conseguir entradas para el partido.

4 **ir a buscar** *(fetch)*
> **I'll get my coat.**
> Voy a buscar el abrigo.

5 **llegar** *(arrive)*
> **How do you get to the castle, please?**
> ¿Cómo se llega al castillo, por favor?
> **What time do we get there?**
> ¿A qué hora llegamos allí?

6 **to have got** ▷ *see* got

## to get away VERB
**escaparse**
> **Quick! He's getting away!**
> ¡Rápido! ¡Que se escapa!

## to get back VERB
**volver**
> **What time will you get back?**
> ¿A qué hora volverás?

## to get in VERB
**entrar**
> **Get in, boys!**
> ¡Entrad, chicos!
> **Get in the car, Ruth.**
> Entra en el coche, Ruth.

## to get off VERB
**bajarse de**
> **Where do we get off the train?**
> ¿Dónde nos bajamos del tren?

to **get on** VERB
**1 subirse a** *(bus, train)*
**I get on the bus at the station.**
Me subo al autobús en la estación.
**2 montarse en** *(bike)*
**I got on my bike.**
Me monté en mi bici.

**How are you getting on?**
¿Cómo te va?

to **get out** VERB
**1 salir** *(of room, building, car)*
**Get out!**
¡Salid!
**2 sacar** *(book, object)*
**Get your book out, Darren.**
Saca tu libro, Darren.

to **get up** VERB
**levantarse**
**What time do you get up?**
¿A qué hora te levantas?
**I get up early.**
Me levanto temprano.

**ghost** NOUN
el **fantasma** *masc*

**Language tip**
*Even though it ends in* **-a**, *el* **fantasma** *is a masculine noun.*

**giant** NOUN
el **gigante** *masc*
la **giganta** *fem*

**gift** NOUN
el **regalo** *masc*
**Christmas gifts**
regalos de Navidad

**gift shop** NOUN
la **tienda de regalos** *fem*

**gigantic** ADJECTIVE
**gigantesco** *masc*
**gigantesca** *fem*

**ginger** ADJECTIVE
**I've got ginger hair.**
Soy pelirrojo.

**Language tip**
*If you're a girl, say* **soy pelirroja** *instead.*

**giraffe** NOUN
la **jirafa** *fem*

**girl** NOUN
**1** la **niña** *fem (young)*
**a five-year-old girl**
una niña de cinco años
**2** la **chica** *fem (older)*
**a sixteen-year-old girl**
una chica de dieciséis años

**girlfriend** NOUN
la **novia** *fem*
**She's his girlfriend.**
Es su novia.

to **give** VERB
**1 dar**
**Give me the book, please.**
Dame el libro, por favor.
**Give the books to Lisa.**
Dale los libros a Lisa.
**2 regalar** *(as gift)*
**What are you giving Charlie?**
¿Qué le vas a regalar a Charlie?
**My parents gave me a bike.**
Mis padres me regalaron una bici.

to **give out** VERB
**repartir**
**Will you give out the books, please, Mike?**
¿Quieres repartir los libros, por favor, Mike?

**given** VERB ▷ *see* **give**

English Spanish

a b c d e f **g** h i j k l m n o p q r s t u v w x y z

**glad** ADJECTIVE
**contento** *masc*
**contenta** *fem*
>   **She's glad she's won.**
>   Está contenta de haber ganado.

**glass** NOUN
1  el **vaso** *masc (beaker)*
>   **I'd like a glass of milk.**
>   Quiero un vaso de leche.
2  la **copa** *fem (with stem)*
>   **a glass of wine**
>   una copa de vino
3  el **vidrio** *masc (material)*

**glasses** PL NOUN
las **gafas** *fem pl*
>   **I wear glasses.**
>   Llevo gafas.

**globe** NOUN
el **globo
terráqueo** *masc*
>   **We've got a globe
>   in the classroom.**
>   Tenemos un globo terráqueo en
>   la clase.

**glove** NOUN
el **guante** *masc*
>   **a pair of gloves**
>   unos guantes

**glue** NOUN
el **pegamento** *masc*

**go**

*go can be a noun or a verb.*

A  NOUN
>   **It's my go.**
>   Me toca a mí.
>   **Whose go is it?**
>   ¿A quién le toca?
B  VERB
**to go**
**ir**
>   **I don't want to go to school.**
>   No quiero ir al colegio.
>   **I don't go to school on
>   Saturdays.**
>   No voy al colegio los sábados.

**Where are you going?**
¿Adónde vas?
**I went to London.**
Fui a Londres.
**Where did you go yesterday?**
¿Dónde fuiste ayer?
**He's gone.**
Se ha ido.

> *Language tip*
>
> *In the same way that we say **I'm
> going to** and **we're going to** and
> so on to talk about the future, in
> Spanish they use **voy a** and **vamos
> a** and so on.*

>   **I'm going to win.**
>   Voy a ganar.
>   **We're going to visit our
>   cousins on Friday.**
>   Vamos a visitar a nuestros
>   primos el viernes.
>   **I'm not going to play.**
>   No voy a jugar.

to **go away** VERB
**irse**
>   **Go away!**
>   ¡Vete!

to **go back** VERB
1  **retroceder** *(in game)*
>   **Go back three spaces.**
>   Retrocede tres casillas.
2  **volver** *(return)*
>   **Go back to your seats, boys!**
>   ¡Volved a vuestro sitio, chicos!
>   **Let's go back to the beginning.**
>   Volvamos al principio.

to **go down** VERB
**bajar**
>   **Let's go down to the cellar.**
>   Vamos a bajar al sótano.

to **go forward** VERB
**avanzar**
>   **Go forward three spaces,
>   James.**
>   Avanza tres casillas, James.

to **go in** VERB
**entrar**

Let's go in.
Vamos a entrar.

to **go on** VERB
  1 **seguir** (continue)
    **Shall I go on?**
    ¿Sigo?
    **Go on, don't stop.**
    Sigue, no pares.
  2 **pasar** (happen)
    **What's going on?**
    ¿Qué está pasando?

to **go out** VERB
  **salir**
    **Are you going out tonight?**
    ¿Vas a salir esta noche?
    **Peter's going out with Kim.**
    Peter está saliendo con Kim.

to **go past** VERB
  **pasar por**
    **We're going past the cathedral.**
    Estamos pasando por la catedral.
    **Go past the station and turn right.**
    Pasa la estación y gira a la derecha.

to **go up** VERB
  **subir**
    **I'm going up to my room.**
    Voy a subir a mi habitación.

**goal** NOUN
  el **gol** masc
    **It's a goal!**
    ¡Es un gol!
    **He's scored a goal!**
    ¡Ha marcado un gol!

**goalkeeper** NOUN
  el **portero** masc
  la **portera** fem
    **He's the goalkeeper.**
    Es el portero.

**goat** NOUN
  la **cabra** fem

**God** NOUN
  **Dios** masc

**godfather** NOUN
  el **padrino** masc
    **my godfather**
    mi padrino

**godmother** NOUN
  la **madrina** fem
    **my godmother**
    mi madrina

**goggles** PL NOUN
  las **gafas de natación** fem pl (for swimming)
    **I've got new goggles.**
    Tengo unas gafas de natación nuevas.

**gold**

gold can be a noun or an adjective.

  **A** NOUN
    el **oro** masc
  **B** ADJECTIVE
    **de oro**
      **a gold necklace**
      un collar de oro

**goldfish** NOUN
  el **pez de colores** masc (PL los peces de colores)
    **I've got five goldfish.**
    Tengo cinco peces de colores.

**golf** NOUN
  el **golf** masc
    **My dad plays golf.**
    Mi padre juega al golf.

**golf club** NOUN
  1 el **palo de golf** masc (stick)
  2 el **club de golf** masc (place)

**golf course** NOUN
  el **campo de golf** masc

**gone** VERB ▷ see **go**

**good** ADJECTIVE
**bueno** *masc*
**buena** *fem*

**That's a good idea.**
Ésa es una buena idea.
**It's a very good film.**
Es una película muy buena.

> ### Language tip
> Shorten **bueno** to **buen** before a masculine singular noun.

**We've got a good teacher.**
Tenemos un buen profesor.
**Pablo's very good at English.**
Pablo es muy bueno en inglés.
**Be good, Andrew!**
¡Pórtate bien, Andrew!

> **It's good.**
> Es bueno.
> **Good morning!**
> ¡Buenos días!
> **Good morning everyone!**
> ¡Buenos días a todos!
> **Good afternoon!**
> ¡Buenas tardes!
> **Good evening!**
> ¡Buenas tardes!/¡Buenas noches!
> **Good night!**
> ¡Buenas noches!
> **Good luck!**
> ¡Buena suerte!

> ### Language tip
> If you want to wish someone a **good evening** in the early evening, use **¡buenas tardes!** instead of **¡buenas noches!**

**goodbye** EXCLAMATION
**¡adiós!**

**Good Friday** NOUN
el **Viernes Santo** *masc*

**good-looking** ADJECTIVE
**guapo** *masc*
**guapa** *fem*

**Wayne is very good-looking.**
Wayne es muy guapo.

**gorgeous** ADJECTIVE
1 **guapísimo** *masc*
**guapísima** *fem (person)*
**Isn't she gorgeous!**
¿Verdad que es guapísima?
2 **excelente** *masc & fem*
*(weather)*
**The weather's gorgeous.**
El tiempo es excelente.

**got** VERB
1 **to have got**
**tener**
**I've got a dog**
**and two cats.**
Tengo un perro
y dos gatos.

**I haven't got a mobile phone.**
No tengo móvil.
**Elaine has got fair hair.**
Elaine tiene el pelo rubio.
**How many have you got?**
¿Cuántos tienes?

> **I've got a cat.**
> Tengo un gato.
> **I haven't got a dog.**
> No tengo perro.
> **Have you got a sister?**
> ¿Tienes una hermana?
> **She's got long hair.**
> Tiene el pelo largo.

2 **to have got to**
**tener que**
**I've got to go to the dentist.**
Tengo que ir al dentista.
**You've got to take a card,**
**Christine.**
Tienes que coger una carta,
Christine.
**You've got to be careful,**
**children.**
Tenéis que tener cuidado, niños.
3 ▷ *see* **get**

**government** NOUN
el **gobierno** *masc*

**grade** NOUN
la **nota** *fem*
  **very good grades**
  muy buenas notas

**gradually** ADVERB
  **poco a poco**

**graffiti** NOUN
las **pintadas** *fem pl*
  **There's a lot of graffiti.**
  Hay muchas pintadas.

**gram** NOUN
el **gramo** *masc*
  **two hundred grams of cheese**
  doscientos gramos de queso

**grammar** NOUN
la **gramática** *fem*

**grandchild** NOUN
el **nieto** *masc*
la **nieta** *fem*
  **her grandchildren**
  sus nietos

**granddad** NOUN
el **abuelo** *masc*
  **my granddad**
  mi abuelo

**granddaughter** NOUN
la **nieta** *fem*
  **He has two granddaughters.**
  Tiene dos nietas.

**grandfather** NOUN
el **abuelo** *masc*
  **my grandfather**
  mi abuelo

**grandma** NOUN
la **abuela** *fem*
  **her grandma**
  su abuela

**grandmother** NOUN
la **abuela** *fem*
  **his grandmother**
  su abuela

**grandpa** NOUN
el **abuelo** *masc*
  **my grandpa**
  mi abuelo

**grandparents** P_ NOUN
los **abuelos** *masc p.*
  **my grandparents**
  mis abuelos

**grandson** NOUN
el **nieto** *masc*
  **her grandsons**
  sus nietos

**granny** NOUN
la **abuela** *fem*
  **my granny**
  mi abuela

**grapefruit** NOUN
el **pomelo** *masc*
  **I don't like grapefruit.**
  No me gusta el pomelo.

**grapefruit juice** NOUN
el **zumo de pomelo** *masc*

**grapes** PL NOUN
las **uvas** *fem pl*
  **a kilo of grapes**
  un kilo de uvas

**grass** NOUN
  1 la **hierba** *fem (plant)*
  2 el **césped** *masc (lawn)*
  **The children are playing on the grass.**
  Los niños están jugando en el césped.

**grated** ADJECTIVE
**rallado** *masc*
**rallada** *fem*

grated cheese
queso rallado

**grateful** ADJECTIVE
**agradecido** *masc*
**agradecida** *fem*
We're very grateful.
Le estamos muy agradecidos.

**gravy** NOUN
I'd like some gravy.
Quiero un poco de jugo de carne.

**great** ADJECTIVE
**estupendo** *masc*
**estupenda** *fem*
We're going to New York. - Great!
Vamos a ir a Nueva York. - ¡Estupendo!

> **That's great!**
> ¡Eso es estupendo!

**Great Britain** NOUN
**Gran Bretaña** *fem*
We live in Great Britain.
Vivimos en Gran Bretaña.

**greedy** ADJECTIVE
**glotón** *masc* (PL **glotones**)
**glotona** *fem*
Don't be so greedy, Tina.
No seas tan glotona, Tina.

**green**

> **green** *can be an adjective or a noun.*

**A** ADJECTIVE
**verde** *masc & fem*
It's green.
Es verde.
I've got green eyes.
Tengo los ojos verdes.

> *Language tip*
> *Colour adjectives come after the noun in Spanish.*

**B** NOUN
el **verde** *masc*
Green is my favourite colour.
El verde es mi color favorito.

**green beans** PL NOUN
las **judías verdes** *fem pl*

**greengrocer's** NOUN
la **verdulería** *fem*
at the greengrocer's
en la verdulería

**greenhouse** NOUN
el **invernadero** *masc*

**grew** VERB ▷see **grow**

**grey**

> **grey** *can be an adjective or a noun.*

**A** ADJECTIVE
**gris** *masc & fem*
It's grey.
Es gris.
a grey skirt
una falda gris
She's got grey hair.
Tiene el pelo gris.

> *Language tip*
> *Colour adjectives come after the noun in Spanish.*

**B** NOUN
el **gris** *masc*
He's dressed in grey.
Va vestido de gris.

to **grin** VERB
**sonreír**
Why are you grinning like that?
¿Por qué estás sonriendo de esa manera?

**grocer's** NOUN
la **tienda de comestibles** *fem*
I'm going to the grocer's.
Voy a la tienda de comestibles.

**groom** NOUN
el **novio** masc

**ground** NOUN
1 el **suelo** masc
We sat on the ground.
Nos sentamos en el suelo.
2 la **tierra** fem (earth)
The ground is wet.
La tierra está mojada.
3 el **campo** masc (sports ground)
Where's the football ground?
¿Dónde está el campo de fútbol?

on the ground
en el suelo

**ground floor** NOUN
la **planta baja** fem
This is the ground floor.
Ésta es la planta baja.
The toilets are on the ground
floor.
Los baños están en la planta baja.

on the ground floor
en la planta baja

**group** NOUN
el **grupo** masc
Get into groups of four.
Formad grupos de cuatro.

to **grow** VERB
1 **crecer** (get bigger)
Grass grows fast.
La hierba crece rápido.
2 **cultivar** (gardiner)
I'm growing a sunflower.
Estoy cultivando un girasol.

to **grow up** VERB
What do you want to be
when you grow up, Sandra?
¿Qué quieres ser cuando seas
mayor, Sandra?

to **growl** VERB
**gruñir**
My dog growls a lot.
Mi perro gruñe
mucho.

**grown** VERB ▷see **grow**

**grown-up** NOUN
el **adulto** masc
la **adulta** fem
the grown-ups
los adultos

**guard dog** NOUN
el **perro guardián** masc (PL los
perros guardianes)

**guarantee** NOUN
la **garantía** fem

to **guess** VERB
**adivinar**
Guess what this is!
¡Adivina lo que es esto!

**guest** NOUN
el **invitado** masc
la **invitada** fem
our Spanish guests
nuestros invitados españoles

**guide** NOUN
1 el/la **guía** masc/fem (tourist
guide)
He works as a guide at the
castle.
Trabaja de guía en el castillo.
2 la **exploradora** fem (girl guide)

**guidebook** NOUN
la **guía** fem

**guide dog** NOUN
el **perro guía** masc

**guinea pig** NOUN
el **conejillo de Indias** masc
I've got a guinea pig.
Tengo un conejillo
de Indias.

**guitar** NOUN
la **guitarra** fem

I play the guitar.
Toco la guitarra.

**gun** NOUN
la **pistola** fem

**guy** NOUN
**you guys**
vosotros
**What do you guys think?**
¿Vosotros qué pensáis?
**Hurry up you guys!**
¡Vamos chicos, daos prisa!

**gym** NOUN
1 la **gimnasia** *fem (school subject)*
**We've got gym today.**
Hoy tenemos gimnasia.

2 el **gimnasio** *masc (place)*
**My mum goes to the gym.**
Mi madre va al gimnasio.

**gymnastics** NOUN
la **gimnasia** *fem*
**I like gymnastics.**
Me gusta la gimnasia.
**I do gymnastics.**
Hago gimnasia.

# H h

## had VERB ▷ see have
## hadn't (= had not) ▷ see have
## hail

*hail can be a noun or a verb.*

**A** NOUN
el **granizo** *masc*
**B** VERB
**to hail**
granizar
**It's hailing.**
Está granizando.

## hair NOUN
el **pelo** *masc*
**He's got black hair.**
Tiene el pelo negro.
**My cat has long hair.**
Mi gato tiene el pelo largo.
**You've had your hair cut!**
¡Te has cortado el pelo!
**I want to wash my hair.**
Quiero lavarme la cabeza.

### Language tip
*In Spanish you usually use an article like el, la, los with parts of the body.*

## hairbrush NOUN
el **cepillo** *masc*

## haircut NOUN
el **corte de pelo** *masc*
**That's a nice haircut!**
¡Qué corte de pelo tan bonito!
**to have a haircut**
cortarse el pelo
**I need to have a haircut.**
Tengo que cortarme el pelo.

## hairdresser NOUN
el **peluquero** *masc*
la **peluquera** *fem*
**He's a hairdresser.**
Es peluquero.

### Language tip
*In Spanish, you do not use an article with people's jobs.*

**the hairdresser's**
la peluquería
**at the hairdresser's**
en la peluquería

## hairstyle NOUN
el **peinado** *masc*
**You've got a new hairstyle.**
Llevas un nuevo peinado.

## half

*half can be a noun, adjective or adverb.*

**A** NOUN
**1** la **mitad** *fem (fraction)*
**half of the class**
la mitad de la clase
**to cut something in half**
cortar algo por la mitad

**two and a half**
dos y medio
**half an hour**
media hora
**half past ten**
las diez y media
**half a kilo**
medio kilo

**2** el **billete para niños** *masc (ticket)*
**A half to the town centre, please.**
Un billete para niños para el centro, por favor.
**B** ADJECTIVE
**medio** *masc*
**media** *fem*
**a half portion**
media ración
**C** ADVERB
**medio**

**I'm half Scottish.**
Soy medio escocés.

### Language tip
*When you use* **medio** *before an adjective its ending never changes.*

**half-brother** NOUN
el **hermanastro** *masc*
   **my half-brother**
   mi hermanastro

**half-sister** NOUN
la **hermanastra** *fem*
   **my half-sister**
   mi hermanastra

**half-term** NOUN
las **vacaciones de mitad de trimestre** *fem*

### Did you know...?
*Spanish students don't have half-term as such. However in winter some schools have* **la semana blanca**, *or 'white week' – the perfect opportunity for many to take off for the ski slopes.*

**half-time** NOUN
el **descanso** *masc*

**hall** NOUN
  **1** el **salón de actos** *masc*
    (assembly hall)
  **2** la **entrada** *fem* (entrance hall)

**Hallowe'en** NOUN
la **víspera de Todos los Santos** *fem*

### Did you know...?
**Hallowe'en** *is not celebrated in Spain, but All Saints' Day (1st November) is a public holiday and the day when people often visit family graves. In Latin America 1st/2nd November often means colourful and fun fiestas with skulls, skeletons and symbols of death everywhere in honour of* **el Día de los Muertos** (**The Day of the Dead** *or* **All Souls' Day**)*.*

**ham** NOUN
el **jamón** *masc* (PL los **jamones**)
   **a ham sandwich**
   un sandwich de jamón de York

### Did you know...?
*In Spain you'll come across two main types of ham:* **jamón serrano**, *which is the more expensive cured ham, and the softer* **jamón de York**, *also known as* **jamón dulce**, *which is boiled and similar to British ham.*

**hamburger** NOUN
la **hamburguesa** *fem*
   **I'd like a hamburger.**
   Yo quiero una hamburguesa.

**hammer** NOUN
el **martillo** *masc*

**hamster** NOUN
el **hámster** *masc* (PL los **hámsters**)

**hand** NOUN
  **1** la **mano** *fem*
    (of person)

### Language tip
*Even though it ends in* **-o**, **la mano** *is a feminine noun.*

   **Put up your hand if you know the answer.**
   Levantad la mano si sabéis la respuesta.

### Language tip
*In Spanish you usually use an article like* **el**, **la**, **los** *with parts of the body.*

   **Can you give me a hand?**
   ¿Me puedes echar una mano?
  **2** la **aguja** *fem* (of clock)

to **hand in** VERB
**entregar**
   **Hand in your books.**
   Entregad vuestros libros.

to **hand out** VERB
**repartir**

Hand out the books, Ahmed.
Reparte los libros, Ahmed.

**handbag** NOUN
el **bolso** *masc*

**handball** NOUN
el **balonmano** *masc*
Can we play handball?
¿Podemos jugar al balonmano?

*Language tip*
*In Spanish, you need to add **al** before the name of the sport.*

**handkerchief** NOUN
el **pañuelo** *masc*
Have you got a handkerchief?
¿Tienes un pañuelo?

**handle** NOUN
1 el **asa** *fem (of cup, briefcase)*

*Language tip*
*Even though it's a feminine noun, remember that you use **el** and **un** with **asa**.*

the handles
las asas
2 el **picaporte** *masc (of door)*

**handsome** ADJECTIVE
**guapo** *masc*
**guapa** *fem*
Paul is very handsome.
Paul es muy guapo.

**handwriting** NOUN
la **letra** *fem*
He has nice handwriting.
Tiene una letra bonita.

to **hang** VERB
colgar

to **hang on** VERB
esperar
Hang on a minute please.
Espera un minuto, por favor.

**hangman** NOUN
el **ahorcado** *masc (game)*
to play hangman
jugar al ahorcado

*Language tip*
*In Spanish, you need to add **al** before the name of the game.*

to **happen** VERB
pasar
What's happening?
¿Qué está pasando?

**happy** ADJECTIVE
**contento** *masc*
**contenta** *fem*
Beatrice is happy.
Beatrice está contenta.
The children are happy.
Los niños están contentos.

Happy birthday!
¡Feliz cumpleaños!
Happy Mother's Day!
¡Feliz día de la madre!
Happy Christmas!
¡Feliz Navidad!
Happy New Year!
¡Feliz Año Nuevo!

*Language tip*
*Have you noticed the upside-down exclamation mark at the start of Spanish exclamations?*

**harbour** NOUN
el **puerto** *masc*

**hard**

*hard can be an adjective or an adverb.*

**A** ADJECTIVE
1 **difícil** *masc & fem (difficult)*
This question's too hard for me.
Esta pregunta es demasiado difícil para mí.

**2 duro** *masc*
**dura** *fem (not soft)*
**This chair is very hard.**
Esta silla es muy dura.
**B** ADVERB
**mucho**
**Diane works hard.**
Diane trabaja mucho.

## hard disk NOUN
el **disco duro** *masc*

## hardly ADVERB
**casi**
**hardly ever**
casi nunca
**hardly anything**
casi nada

## has VERB ▷see **have**

## hasn't (= has not) ▷see **have**

## hat NOUN
**1** el **sombrero** *masc*
**2** el **gorro** *masc (knitted)*
**a woolly hat**
un gorro
de lana

## to **hate** VERB
**odiar**
**I hate maths.**
Odio las
matemáticas.

## to **have** VERB
**1 tener**
**I have a bike.**
Tengo una bici.
**He has blue eyes.**
Tiene los ojos azules.

### Language tip
*You also use* **tener** *to translate* **have got**.

**I've got a bike.**
Tengo una bici.
**He has got blue eyes.**
Tiene los ojos azules.
**I haven't got any pets.**
No tengo mascota.

**Have you got a sister? –
Yes, I have.**
¿Tienes una hermana? – Sí.
**Have you got any sweets? –
No, I haven't.**
¿Tienes caramelos? – No.

**I've got …**
Tengo …
**I haven't got**
No tengo …
**Have you got…?**
¿Tienes…?
**Yes, I have.**
Sí.
**No, I haven't.**
No.

### Language tip
*Just use* **sí** *and* **no** *to translate* **yes,
I have** *and* **no, I haven't**.

**2 haber** *(used to form tenses)*
**I have done the shopping.**
He hecho las compras.
**He hasn't seen it.**
No lo ha visto.
**They've arrived.**
Han llegado.
**Have you done your
homework? – Yes, I have.**
¿Has hecho los deberes? – Sí.

### Language tip
*Just use* **sí** *and* **no** *to translate* **yes,
I have** *and* **no, I haven't**.

**3 tomar** *(eat, drink)*
**What are you going to have?**
¿Qué vas a tomar?
**I'll have a white coffee.**
Voy a tomar un café con leche.
**What time do you have
breakfast?**
¿A qué hora desayunas?
**4 to have a shower**
**ducharse**
**I have a shower every day.**
Me ducho todos los días.
**5 to have a bath**
**bañarse**

I'll have a bath.
Me voy a bañar.
6 to have to
tener que
You have to be careful.
Tienes que tener cuidado.
She has to do her homework.
Tiene que hacer los deberes.
Do I have to?
¿Tengo que hacerlo?
You have to ...
Tienes que ...
You have got to ...
Tienes que ...

**haven't** (= have not) ▷see have

**hay fever** NOUN
la **alergia al polen** fem

**hazelnut** NOUN
la **avellana** fem

**he** PRONOUN
**él**
He's got a radio but I haven't.
Él tiene una radio pero yo no.

**Language tip**
he isn't usually translated unless it's
emphatic.

He works in a bank.
Trabaja en un banco.

**head** NOUN
1 la **cabeza** fem (of person)
Mind your head!
¡Cuidado con la cabeza!

**Language tip**
In Spanish you usually use an article
like el, la, los with parts of the body.

Heads or tails? – Heads.
¿Cara o cruz? – Cara.
2 el **director** masc
la **directora** fem (headteacher)

**headache** NOUN
I've got a headache.
Me duele la cabeza.

**headmaster** NOUN
el **director** masc

**headmistress** NOUN
la **directora** fem

**head teacher** NOUN
el **director** masc
la **directora** fem

**health** NOUN
la **salud** fem

**healthy** ADJECTIVE
**sano** masc
**sana** fem
a healthy diet
una dieta sana

to **hear** VERB
**oír**
I can't hear.
No oigo.
I can't hear you.
No te oigo.
Can you hear the difference?
¿Notas la diferencia al oírlo?

**heart** NOUN
el **corazón** masc (PL los
corazones)
the ace
of hearts
el as de
corazones

**heat** NOUN
el **calor** masc

**heater** NOUN
la **estufa** fem
an electric heater
una estufa eléctrica

**heavy** ADJECTIVE
**pesado** masc
**pesada** fem
This bag's very heavy.
Esta bolsa es muy pesada.

**he'd**
1 (= he had) ▷see have
2 (= he would) ▷see would

**hedgehog** NOUN
el **erizo** masc

## heel NOUN
1 el **tacón** *masc* (PL los **tacones**)
   (*of shoe*)
   **high heels**
   tacones altos
2 el **talón** *masc* (PL los **talones**)
   (*of foot, sock*)

## height NOUN
1 la **estatura** *fem* (*of person*)
2 la **altura** *fem* (*of object, person*)

## held VERB ▷ *see* hold

## helicopter NOUN
el **helicóptero** *masc*

## he'll (= he will) ▷ *see* will

## hello EXCLAMATION
¡**hola**!

### Did you know...?
*If you ring a Spanish person up, they'll probably answer the phone with* **idígame!** *or* **idiga!** *They won't say* **¡hola!**

## helmet NOUN
el **casco** *masc*

## help

*help can be a verb or a noun.*

**A** VERB
   **to help**
   **ayudar**
   **Can you help me?**
   ¿Me puedes ayudar?
   **Help yourself!**
   ¡Sírvete!

### Help!
¡Socorro!

**B** NOUN
   la **ayuda** *fem*
   **Do you need
   any help?**
   ¿Necesitas
   ayuda?

## hen NOUN
la **gallina** *fem*

## her

**her** *can be an adjective or a pronoun.*

**A** ADJECTIVE
   **su** *masc & fem* (PL **sus**)

### Language tip
*Remember to use* **su** *before a singular noun and* **sus** *before a plural one.*

   **her name**
   su nombre
   **her house**
   su casa
   **her cats**
   sus gatos
   **her aunts**
   sus tías

### Language tip
*You usually translate* **her** *using* **el**, **la**, *etc before parts of the body or clothes, particularly when using a reflexive verb.*

   **She took off her coat.**
   Se quitó el abrigo.
**B** PRONOUN
1 **la** (*direct object*)
   **I love her.**
   La quiero.
   **Do you know her?**
   ¿La conoces?
   **Look at her!**
   ¡Mírala!
2 **le** (*indirect object*)

### Language tip
*Use* **le** *when* **her** *means* **to her**.

   **I gave her a book.**
   Le di un libro.
   **What did you say to her?**
   ¿Qué le dijiste?

### Language tip
*Change* **le** *to* **se** *when combining it with a direct object pronoun like* **lo**.

   **I'll tell her.**
   Se lo diré.

We've already handed it over to her.
Ya se lo hemos entregado.

*Language tip*
*Because* **se** *can mean* **to him, to them** *and* **to you** *as well as* **to her,** *you can add* **a ella** *(to her) after the verb for clarity.*

I'm going to give it to her.
Voy a dárselo a ella.

**3 ella** *(after prepositions)*
It's for her.
Es para ella.
He's next to her.
Está al lado de ella.

*Language tip*
*Use* **ella** *in comparisons.*

I'm older than her.
Soy mayor que ella.

*Language tip*
*Use* **ella** *after the verb* **ser.**

It must be her.
Debe de ser ella.
It's her.
Es ella.

## here ADVERB
**aquí**
I live here.
Yo vivo aquí.
Here he is!
¡Aquí está!
Here's Helen.
Aquí está Helen.
Here are the books.
Aquí tienes los libros.

## hers PRONOUN
el **suyo** *masc*
la **suya** *fem*

*Language tip*
*Remember that the choice of* **el suyo, la suya, los suyos** *or* **las suyas** *depends entirely on the thing or things referred to.*

That's not Mandy's coat. Hers is here.
Aquél no es el abrigo de Mandy. El suyo está aquí.
Those aren't Marian's boots. Hers are here.
Aquéllas no son las botas de Marian. Las suyas están aquí.

*Language tip*
*After* **ser** *you can usually just use* **suyo, suya, suyos** *or* **suyas** *to agree with the noun referred to.*

Is this hers?
¿Es suyo esto?
These boots are hers.
Estas botas son suyas.
Whose is this? - It's hers.
¿De quién es esto? – Es suyo.

*Language tip*
*Because* **suyo** *can also mean* **his, theirs** *and* **yours,** *you can avoid confusion by using* **de ella** *instead.*

Whose is this? - It's hers.
¿De quién es esto? - Es de ella.

**a friend of hers**
un amigo suyo

## herself PRONOUN
**1 se** *(reflexive use)*
She's hurt herself.
Se ha hecho daño.
My cat washes herself a lot.
Mi gata se lava mucho.
**2 sí misma** *(after preposition)*
She talked about herself.
Habló de sí misma.
**3 ella misma** *(for emphasis)*
She did it herself.
Lo hizo ella misma.
She lives by herself.
Ella vive sola.

**by herself**
sola

## he's
**1** (= **he is**) ▷*see* **be**
**2** (= **he has**) ▷*see* **have**

**hi** EXCLAMATION
¡hola!

**hiccups** NOUN
el **hipo** masc
**I've got hiccups.**
Tengo hipo.

to **hide** VERB
1 **esconder**
**Mum hides the biscuits.**
Mamá esconde las galletas.
2 **esconderse** (hide oneself)
**Hide!**
¡Escóndete!
**Daniel is hiding under the bed.**
Daniel está escondido debajo de la cama.

**hide-and-seek** NOUN
el **escondite** masc
**Let's play hide-and-seek!**
¡Vamos a jugar al escondite!

**Language tip**

In Spanish, you need to add **al** before the name of the game.

**high** ADJECTIVE
**alto** masc
**alta** fem
**It's too high.**
Es demasiado alto.
**How high is Mount Everest?**
¿Cuál es la altura del Everest?
**The wall is two metres high.**
El muro tiene dos metros de altura.

**high jump** NOUN
el **salto de altura** masc

**high-rise** NOUN
la **torre de pisos** fem
**I live in a high-rise.**
Vivo en una torre de pisos.

**high school** NOUN
el **instituto** masc

**high street** NOUN
la **calle principal** fem

**hiking** NOUN
**We're going to go hiking.**
Vamos a ir de excursión al campo.

**hill** NOUN
la **colina** fem

**him** PRONOUN
1 **lo** (direct object)
**I love him.**
Lo quiero.
**Do you know him?**
¿Lo conoces?
**Look at him!**
Míralo.

**Language tip**

In some parts of Spain you'll hear people using **le** instead of **lo**.

2 **le** (indirect object)

**Language tip**

Use **le** when **him** means **to him**.

**I gave him a book.**
Le di un libro.
**What did you say to him?**
¿Qué le dijiste?

**Language tip**

Change **le** to **se** when combining it with a direct object pronoun like **lo**.

**I'll tell him.**
Se lo diré.
**We've already handed it over to him.**
Ya se lo hemos entregado.

**Language tip**

Because **se** can mean **to her, to them** and **to you** as well as **to him**, you can add **a él** (to him) after the verb for clarity.

**I'm going to give it to him.**
Voy a dárselo a él.
3 **él**

**Language tip**

Use **él** after a preposition.

**It's for him.**
Es para él.

**She's next to him.**
Ella está al lado de él.

*Language tip*
*Use **él** in comparisons.*

**I'm older than him.**
Soy mayor que él.

*Language tip*
*Use **él** after the verb **ser**.*

**It must be him.**
Debe de ser él.
**It's him.**
Es él.

# himself PRONOUN
1 **se** *(reflexive use)*
**He's hurt himself.**
Se ha hecho daño.
**The cat is washing himself.**
El gato está lavándose.
2 **sí mismo** *(after preposition)*
**He talked about himself.**
Habló de sí mismo.
3 **él mismo** *(for emphasis)*
**He did it himself.**
Lo hizo él mismo.
**He lives by himself.**
Vive solo.

**by himself**
solo

# hip NOUN
la **cadera** *fem*

# hippo NOUN
el **hipopótamo** *masc*

# to hire VERB
**alquilar**
**You can hire bikes.**
Se pueden alquilar bicis.

# his

*his can be an adjective or a
pronoun.*

**A** ADJECTIVE
**su** *masc & fem* (PL **sus**)

*Language tip*
*Remember to use **su** with singular
nouns and **sus** with plural ones.*

**his name**
su nombre
**his house**
su casa
**his cats**
sus gatos
**his aunts**
sus tías

*Language tip*
*You usually translate **his** using **el**,
**la**, etc before parts of the body or
clothes, particularly when using a
reflexive verb.*

**He took off his coat.**
Se quitó el abrigo.
**B** PRONOUN
el **suyo** *masc*
la **suya** *fem*

*Language tip*
*Remember that the choice of **el
suyo**, **la suya**, **los suyos** or **las
suyas** depends entirely on the thing
or things referred to.*

**That's not Mike's coat. His is
here.**
Aquél no es el abrigo de Mike.
El suyo está aquí.
**Those aren't Martin's boots.
His are here.**
Aquéllas no son las botas de
Martin. Las suyas están aquí.

*Language tip*
*After **ser** you can usually just use
**suyo**, **suya**, **suyos** or **suyas** to
agree with the noun referred to.*

**Is this his?**
¿Esto es suyo?
**These boots are his.**
Estas botas son suyas.
**Whose is this? – It's his.**
¿De quién es esto? – Es suyo.

### Language tip
*Because* **suyo** *can also mean* **hers**, **theirs** *and* **yours**, *you can avoid confusion by using* **de él** *instead.*

**Whose is this? – It's his.**
¿De quién es esto? – Es de él.

**a friend of his**
un amigo suyo

## history NOUN
la **historia** *fem*
**History is my favourite subject.**
La historia es mi asignatura favorita.

## hit

**hit** *can be a verb or a noun.*

**A** VERB
**to hit**
**pegar**
**Don't hit me!**
¡No me pegues!
**He's hitting his brother.**
Le está pegando a su hermano.

### Language tip
*Don't forget the personal* **a** *in examples like this one.*

**B** NOUN
**1** el **éxito** *masc (success)*
**Take That's latest hit**
el último éxito de Take That
**2** el **acierto** *masc (on internet)*
**I got a lot of hits.**
Tuve muchos aciertos.

## hobby NOUN
la **afición** *fem* (PL las **aficiones**)
**What are your hobbies?**
¿Cuáles son tus aficiones?

## hockey NOUN
el **hockey** *masc*
**I play hockey.**
Juego al hockey.

### Language tip
*In Spanish, you need to add* **al** *before the name of the sport.*

## to hold VERB
**1** **sostener** *(hold on to)*
**Can you hold the baby?**
¿Puedes sostener al niño?
**2** **sujetar** *(keep in position)*
**Can you hold the ladder?**
¿Puedes sujetar la escalera?
**3** **llevar en la mano** *(carry)*
**He's holding a gun.**
Lleva una pistola en la mano.
**Hold hands!**
¡Cogeos de la mano!

## to hold on VERB
**esperar**
**Hold on a minute!**
¡Espera un momento!

## to hold up VERB
**Hold up your hands.**
Levantad las manos.

### Language tip
*In Spanish you usually use an article like* **el**, **la**, **los** *with parts of the body.*

## hole NOUN
el **agujero** *masc*

## holiday NOUN
**1** las **vacaciones** *fem pl*
**our holiday in France**
nuestras vacaciones en Francia
**When are you going on holiday?**
¿Cuándo te vas de vacaciones?
**We are on holiday.**
Estamos de vacaciones.
**in the school holidays**
durante las vacaciones escolares

**on holiday**
de vacaciones
**the school holidays**
las vacaciones escolares

**2** la **fiesta** *fem (public holiday)*
**Monday is a holiday.**
El lunes es fiesta.

## holly NOUN
el **acebo** *masc*

**home** NOUN
la **casa** *fem*
**Is Chris at home?**
¿Está Chris en casa?
**What time do you get home?**
¿A qué hora llegas a casa?
**I get home at five o'clock.**
Llego a casa a las cinco.
**to go home**
irse a casa
**I've got to go home.**
Tengo que irme a casa.

**at home**
en casa
**Let's go home.**
Vámonos a casa.

**homesick** ADJECTIVE
**I'm homesick.**
Echo de menos mi casa.

**homework** NOUN
los **deberes** *masc pl*
**We have too much homework.**
Tenemos demasiados deberes.
**my geography homework**
mis deberes de geografía

**honey** NOUN
la **miel** *fem*

**honeymoon** NOUN
la **luna de miel** *fem*

**hood** NOUN
la **capucha** *fem*

**hook** NOUN
el **gancho** *masc*

**hooray** EXCLAMATION
¡hurra!

to **hop** VERB
**saltar a la pata coja**
**Hop!**
¡Salta a la pata coja!
**children hopping on one leg**
niños saltando a la pata coja

to **hope** VERB
**esperar**

**I'm hoping to go to Spain.**
Espero ir a España.
**I hope that's okay.**
Espero que eso esté bien.

**I hope so.**
Espero que sí.
**I hope not.**
Espero que no.

**hopeless** ADJECTIVE
**I'm hopeless at maths.**
Soy un negado para las matemáticas.
**She's hopeless at biology.**
Es una negada para la biología.
**You're hopeless, Louise!**
¡No tienes remedio, Louise!

**horrible** ADJECTIVE
**horrible** *masc & fem*

**horror film** NOUN
la **película de terror** *fem*

**horse** NOUN
el **caballo** *masc*
**I can ride a horse.**
Sé montar a caballo.

**hospital** NOUN
el **hospital** *masc*
**My grandmother is in hospital.**
Mi abuela está en el hospital.

**hot** ADJECTIVE
1 **caliente** *masc & fem*
**a hot bath**
un baño caliente
**I'm too hot.**
Tengo mucho calor.

**It's very hot today.**
Hace mucho calor hoy.
**The weather is hotter in Spain.**
En España hace más calor.

**I'm hot.**
Tengo calor.
**It's hot.**
Hace calor.

**2 picante** *(spicy)*
**a very hot curry**
un curry muy picante

**hot chocolate** NOUN
el **chocolate caliente** *masc*

**hot dog** NOUN
el **perrito caliente** *masc*

**hotel** NOUN
el **hotel** *masc*
**We're staying at a hotel near the beach.**
Nos alojamos en un hotel cerca de la playa.

**hour** NOUN
la **hora** *fem*
**an hour and ten minutes**
una hora y diez minutos
**an hour and a half**
una hora y media

**a quarter of an hour**
un cuarto de hora
**half an hour**
media hora
**two and a half hours**
dos horas y media

**house** NOUN
la **casa** *fem (building)*
**You've got a nice house.**
Tienes una casa bonita.
**Do you want to play at my house?**
¿Quieres jugar en mi casa?

**at my house**
en mi casa

**housewife** NOUN
el **ama de casa** *fem* (PL las **amas de casa**)

### Language tip
*Even though it's a feminine noun, remember that you use* **el** *and* **un** *with* **ama de casa**.

**how** ADVERB
**cómo**
**How do you say 'apple' in Spanish?**
¿Cómo se dice 'apple' en español?
**How do you spell your name?**
¿Cómo se escribe tu nombre?
**How many...?**
¿Cuántos...?
**How many pupils are there in the class?**
¿Cuántos alumnos hay en la clase?
**How many apples are there?**
¿Cuántas manzanas hay?
**How much...?**
¿Cuánto...?
**How much sugar would you like?**
¿Cuánto azúcar quieres?
**How much is it?**
¿Cuánto es?
**How old is your brother?**
¿Cuántos años tiene tu hermano?

**How are you?**
¿Cómo estás?
**How old are you?**
¿Cuántos años tienes?
**How many?**
¿Cuántos?
**How much?**
¿Cuánto?

### Language tip
*Don't forget the accent on question words like* **cómo** *and* **cuántos** *nor the upside-down question mark at the start of questions.*

## hug

*hug can be a noun or a verb.*

**A** NOUN
el **abrazo** *masc*
**a big hug**
un fuerte abrazo
**Give me a hug.**
Dame un abrazo.

### Did you know...?
*Did you know that Spanish speakers sometimes end letters, postcards and emails to friends with* **un abrazo** *(a hug) or* **un fuerte abrazo** *(a big hug)?*

**B** VERB
**to hug**
abrazar

**huge** ADJECTIVE
**enorme** *masc & fem*

**human** ADJECTIVE
**humano** *masc*
**humana** *fem*
**a human being**
un ser humano

**hundred** NOUN
**a hundred**
cien

### Language tip
*When translating* **a hundred** *or* **one hundred** *use* **cien** *before words for things and people.*

**a hundred euros**
cien euros
**a hundred students**
cien estudiantes

### Language tip
*Use* **cien** *before* **mil** *(thousand).*

**one hundred thousand**
cien mil

### Language tip
*When translating* **a hundred and** *use* **ciento**.

**one hundred and one**
ciento uno
**one hundred and twenty-five**
ciento veinticinco

### Language tip
*There are special words for two hundred, three hundred and so on.*

**two hundred**
doscientos
**three hundred and fifty people**
trescientas cincuenta personas
**five hundred and one**
quinientos uno
**hundreds of people**
cientos de personas

**hung** VERB ▷*see* **hang**

**hungry** ADJECTIVE
**to be hungry**
tener hambre
**Are you hungry?**
¿Tienes hambre?

**I'm hungry.**
Tengo hambre.
**I'm not hungry.**
No tengo hambre.

**hunting** NOUN
la **caza** *fem*
**I'm against hunting.**
Estoy en contra de la caza.

**hurry** NOUN
**to be in a hurry**
tener prisa
**I'm in a hurry!**
¡Tengo prisa!

to **hurry up** VERB
**Hurry up, Paul!**
¡Date prisa, Paul!
**Hurry up, children!**
¡Daos prisa, niños!

to **hurt** VERB
**You're hurting me!**
¡Me estás haciendo daño!
**Have you hurt yourself?**
¿Te has hecho daño?

**My leg hurts.**
Me duele la pierna.

### Language tip

*In Spanish you usually use an article like* **el**, **la**, **los** *with parts of the body.*

**That hurts.**
Eso duele.

**husband** NOUN
el **marido** *masc*

**hut** NOUN
la **cabaña** *fem*

**hymn** NOUN
el **himno** *masc*

**hyphen** NOUN
el **guión** *masc* (PL los **guiones**)

# I i

**I** PRONOUN
**yo**
> He's got a bike but I haven't.
> Él tiene una bici pero yo no.
> Ann and I
> Ann y yo

**Language tip**

I *isn't usually translated before a verb unless it's emphatic.*

> I speak English.
> Hablo inglés.
> I play the flute.
> Toco la flauta.

**ice** NOUN
el **hielo** *masc*

**ice cream** NOUN
el **helado** *masc*
> Would you like an ice cream?
> ¿Quieres un helado?
> vanilla ice cream
> helado de vainilla

**ice cube** NOUN
el **cubito de hielo** *masc*

**ice lolly** NOUN
el **polo** *masc*

**ice rink** NOUN
la **pista de patinaje** *fem*

**ice-skating** NOUN
el **patinaje sobre hielo** *masc*
> an ice-skating championship
> un campeonato de patinaje sobre hielo
> I like ice-skating.
> Me gusta patinar sobre hielo.

**ICT** NOUN
la **informática** *fem*

**icy** ADJECTIVE
> The roads are icy.

> Las carreteras están cubiertas de hielo.

**I'd**
1 (= I had) ▷ *see* **have**
2 (= I would) ▷ *see* **would**

**idea** NOUN
la **idea** *fem*
> Good idea!
> ¡Buena idea!
> I have no idea.
> No tengo ni idea.

**identical** ADJECTIVE
**idéntico** *masc*
**idéntica** *fem*
> They're identical.
> Son idénticos.

**idiot** NOUN
el/la **idiota** *masc/fem*

**if** CONJUNCTION
**si**
> You can have it if you like.
> Te lo puedes quedar si quieres.
> Do you know if he's there?
> ¿Sabes si él está allí?
> if I were you
> yo que tú

**I'll** (= I will) ▷ *see* **will**

**ill** ADJECTIVE
**enfermo** *masc*
**enferma** *fem*
> Melissa is ill.
> Melissa está enferma.

**I'm** (= I am) ▷ *see* **be**

**imagination** NOUN
la **imaginación** *fem*

to **imagine** VERB
**imaginar**

**Imagine you have lots of money.**
Imagina que tienes mucho dinero.

to **imitate** VERB
**imitar**
**Imitate the sound.**
Imita el sonido.

**immediately** ADVERB
**inmediatamente**
**I'll do it immediately.**
Lo haré inmediatamente.

**immigrant** NOUN
el/la **inmigrante** *masc/fem*

**impatient** ADJECTIVE
**impaciente** *masc & fem*
**Don't be so impatient, Sasha.**
No seas tan impaciente, Sasha.

**important** ADJECTIVE
**importante** *masc & fem*
**Today's an important day.**
Hoy es un día importante.

**impossible** ADJECTIVE
**imposible** *masc & fem*
**Sorry, it's impossible.**
Lo siento, es imposible.

> **Language tip**
> Don't forget that there's only one **s** in the Spanish word **imposible**.

to **improve** VERB
**mejorar**
**You need to improve your work.**
Tienes que mejorar tu trabajo.

## in

> **in** can be a preposition or an adverb.

**A** PREPOSITION
**1 en**
**in the house**
en la casa
**What can you see in the picture?**
¿Qué ves en la foto?
**in England**
en Inglaterra
**in hospital**
en el hospital
**in 2007**
en el 2007

> **in London**
> en Londres
> **in Spain**
> en España
> **in English**
> en inglés
> **in Spanish**
> en español

**2 de**
**the tallest person in the family**
la persona más alta de la familia
**She's the oldest in the class.**
Ella es la mayor de la clase.
**at six o'clock in the morning**
a las seis de la mañana
**the boy in the blue shirt**
el chico de la camisa azul
**B** ADVERB
**He isn't in.**
No está.

**inch** NOUN
la **pulgada** *fem*
**six inches**
seis pulgadas

> **Did you know...?**
> **Inches**, **feet** and **yards** aren't used in Spain. Use **centímetros** (centimetres) and **metros** (metres) instead.

**included** ADJECTIVE
**incluido** *masc*
**incluida** *fem*
> **Service is not included.**
> La propina no está incluida.

**including** PREPOSITION

> *Language tip*
>
> **including** *is often translated by* **incluido**, *which, as it's an adjective, changes to* **incluida**, **incluidos** *or* **incluidas** *to agree with the noun that goes with it.*

> **Everybody came, including Jack.**
> Vinieron todos, incluido Jack.
> **Everybody came, including Sophie.**
> Vinieron todos, incluida Sophie.
> **There are fifteen people, not including me.**
> Hay quince personas, sin incluirme a mí.

**incredible** ADJECTIVE
**increíble** *masc & fem*
> **That's incredible!**
> ¡Eso es increíble!

**indeed** ADVERB
> **Thank you very much indeed!**
> ¡Muchísimas gracias!

**indoor** ADJECTIVE
> **an indoor swimming pool**
> una piscina cubierta

**indoors** ADVERB
**dentro**
> **They're indoors.**
> Están dentro.

**inexpensive** ADJECTIVE
**barato** *masc*
**barata** *fem*
> **an inexpensive hotel**
> un hotel barato

**infant school** NOUN
**la primaria** *fem*

> **He's going to start infant school.**
> Va a empezar primaria.

**infection** NOUN
**la infección** *fem* (PL las infecciones)
> **an ear infection**
> una infección de oído

**information** NOUN
**la información** *fem*
> **I need some information.**
> Necesito información.
> **information about Ireland**
> información sobre Irlanda

**ingredient** NOUN
**el ingrediente** *masc*
> **a list of ingredients**
> una lista de ingredientes

**inhabitant** NOUN
**el/la habitante** *masc/fem*

**inhaler** NOUN
**el inhalador** *masc*

**initials** PL NOUN
**las iniciales** *fem pl*
> **My initials are G-A-C.**
> Mis iniciales son G-A-C.

**injection** NOUN
**la inyección** *fem* (PL las inyecciones)

to **injure** VERB
**herir**
> **Was anyone injured?**
> ¿Resultó alguien herido?

**injury** NOUN
**la herida** *fem*
> **a serious injury**
> una herida grave

**ink** NOUN
**la tinta** *fem*

to **inquire** VERB
**to inquire about something**
informarse acerca de algo
**I'm going to inquire about train times.**
Voy a informarme acerca del horario de los trenes.

**inquisitive** ADJECTIVE
**curioso** *masc*
**curiosa** *fem*

**insect** NOUN
el **insecto** *masc*

**inside**

inside *can be an adverb or a preposition.*

**A** ADVERB
**dentro**
**They're inside.**
Están dentro.
**B** PREPOSITION
**dentro de**
**inside the house**
dentro de la casa

**inspector** NOUN
el **inspector** *masc*
la **inspectora** *fem*

**instance** NOUN
**for instance**
por ejemplo

**instantly** ADVERB
**al instante**

**instead** ADVERB
**instead of**
en vez de
**Eat fruit instead of sweets.**
Come fruta en vez de caramelos.
**instead of me**
en vez de yo

*Language tip*
When **instead** is not followed by **of** it isn't always translated.

**The pool was closed so we played tennis instead.**

La piscina estaba cerrada así que jugamos al tenis.
**There's no apple juice. Do you want orange juice instead?**
No hay zumo de manzana. ¿Quieres de naranja?

**instructions** PL NOUN
las **instrucciones** *fem pl*
**Follow the instructions.**
Sigue las instrucciones.

**instructor** NOUN
el **monitor** *masc*
la **monitora** *fem (swimming, skiing)*
**She's a skiing instructor.**
Es monitora de esquí.
**He's a driving instructor.**
Es profesor de autoescuela.

*Language tip*
In Spanish, you do not use an article with people's jobs.

**instrument** NOUN
el **instrumento** *masc*
**Do you play an instrument?**
¿Tocas algún instrumento?

**intelligent** ADJECTIVE
**inteligente** *masc & fem*
**You're very intelligent.**
Eres muy inteligente.

*Language tip*
Don't forget that there's only one **l** in the Spanish word **inteligente**.

**interest** NOUN
**1** el **interés** *masc* (PL los intereses)

436

**to lose interest in something**
perder el interés por algo
**She shows interest in languages.**
Se interesa por los idiomas.
2 la **afición** *fem* (PL las aficiones)
**My main interest is music.**
Mi mayor afición es la música.

**interested** ADJECTIVE
**I'm not interested.**
No me interesa.
**I'm not interested in football.**
No me interesa el fútbol.
**Are you interested?**
¿Te interesa?

**interesting** ADJECTIVE
**interesante** *masc & fem*
**It's a very interesting story.**
Es una historia muy interesante.

**international** ADJECTIVE
**internacional** *masc & fem*
**an international school**
un colegio internacional

**internet** NOUN
**the internet**
Internet
**on the internet**
en Internet

**internet café** NOUN
el **cibercafé** *masc*

**to interrupt** VERB
**interrumpir**
**Don't interrupt, Anthony!**
¡No interrumpas, Anthony!

**interval** NOUN
el **descanso** *masc*
**during the interval**
durante el descanso

**interview** NOUN
la **entrevista** *fem*

**interviewer** NOUN
el **entrevistador** *masc*
la **entrevistadora** *fem*

**into** PREPOSITION
1 **a** *(to)*
**I'm going into town.**
Voy a la ciudad.
**Translate it into English.**
Tradúcelo al inglés.
2 **en** *(in)*
**He got into the car.**
Se metió en el coche.

**Divide into two groups.**
Dividíos en dos grupos.

**to introduce** VERB
**presentarse**
**I'd like to introduce you to Julia.**
Quiero presentarte a Julia.
**Can you introduce yourselves?**
¿Podéis presentaros vosotros mismos?

**inventor** NOUN
el **inventor** *masc*
la **inventora** *fem*

**invisible** ADJECTIVE
**invisible** *masc & fem*

**invitation** NOUN
la **invitación** *fem* (PL las invitaciones)
**Thank you for the invitation.**
Gracias por la invitación.

**to invite** VERB
**invitar**
**Thank you for inviting me.**
Gracias por invitarme.
**I'm going to invite Graham to my party.**
Voy a invitar a Graham a mi fiesta.

> **Language tip**
> Don't forget the personal **a** in examples like this one.

**iPod**® NOUN
el **iPod**® *masc*

**Ireland** NOUN
**Irlanda** *fem*
**I live in Ireland.**
Vivo en Irlanda.
**I'm from Ireland.**
Soy de Irlanda.

**in Ireland**
en Irlanda
**I'm going to Ireland.**
Voy a Irlanda.

**Irish**

> **Irish** *can be an adjective or a noun.*

**A** ADJECTIVE
**irlandés** *masc* (PL **irlandeses**)
**irlandesa** *fem*
**I'm Irish.**
Soy irlandés.
**I like Irish music.**
Me gusta la música irlandesa.
**Irish people**
los irlandeses

**He's Irish.**
Es irlandés.
**She's Irish.**
Es irlandesa.

**B** NOUN
el **irlandés** *masc* (language)
**Do you speak Irish?**
¿Hablas irlandés?
**the Irish**
los irlandeses

> **Language tip**
> **irlandés** *is not spelled with a capital letter in Spanish.*

**Irishman** NOUN
el **irlandés** *masc* (PL los irlandeses)

> **Language tip**
> **irlandés** *is not spelled with a capital letter in Spanish.*

**Irishwoman** NOUN
la **irlandesa** *fem*

> **Language tip**
> **irlandesa** *is not spelled with a capital letter in Spanish.*

**iron**

> **iron** *can be a noun or a verb.*

**A** NOUN
1 el **hierro** *masc* (metal)
**an iron gate**
un portón de hierro
2 la **plancha** *fem* (for clothes)
**B** VERB
**to iron**
planchar
**I can iron a shirt.**
Sé planchar una camisa.

**ironing** NOUN
**to do the ironing**
planchar

**irritating** ADJECTIVE
**irritante** *masc & fem*

**is** VERB ▷ *see* **be**

**Islam** NOUN
el **Islam** *masc*

**island** NOUN
la **isla** *fem*

**isle** NOUN
**the Isle of Man**
la Isla de Man

English Spanish

the Isle of Wight
la Isla de Wight

**isn't** (= is not) ▷ see **be**

**it** PRONOUN
1 *(subject)*

**Language tip**

*When* **it** *is the subject of a verb, it isn't translated into Spanish.*

**Where's my book? - It's on the table.**
¿Dónde está mi libro? – Está en la mesa.
**Where's my notebook? - It's in your bag.**
¿Dónde está mi libreta? – Está en tu bolsa.
**It's easy.**
Es fácil.
**It's incredible!**
¡Es increíble!

**It's expensive.**
Es caro.
**It's one o'clock.**
Es la una.
**It's two o'clock.**
Son las dos.
**It's me.**
Soy yo.
**It's hot.**
Hace calor.

2 **lo** *masc*
**la** *fem (direct object)*

**Language tip**

*Remember to use* **lo** *to refer to a masculine noun and* **la** *to refer to a feminine one.*

**There's one cake left. Do you want it?**
Queda un pastel. ¿Lo quieres?
**It's a good film. Have you seen it?**
Es una buena película. ¿La has visto?
**This is my new jumper. Do you like it?**

Éste es mi jersey nuevo.
¿Te gusta?

**itch** VERB
**picar**
**My arm itches.**
Me pica el brazo.

**Language tip**

*In Spanish you usually use an article like* **el**, **la**, **los** *with parts of the body.*

**it'd**
1 (= it had) ▷ see **have**
2 (= it would) ▷ see **would**

**item** NOUN
el **artículo** *masc*

**it'll** (= it will) ▷ see **will**

**it's**
1 (= it is) ▷ see **be**
2 (= it has) ▷ see **have**

**its** ADJECTIVE
**su** *masc & fem* (PL **sus**)

**Language tip**

*Remember to use* **su** *with singular nouns and* **sus** *with plural ones.*

**Everything is in its place.**
Cada cosa está en su sitio.
**This model has its disadvantages.**
Este modelo tiene sus desventajas.
**What's its name?**
¿Cómo se llama?

**itself** PRONOUN
**by itself**
solo
**She left the cat by itself.**
Dejó al gato solo.

**Language tip**

*Don't forget the personal* **a** *in examples like this one.*

**I've** (= I have) ▷ see **have**

# J j

**jab** NOUN
la **inyección** *fem* (PL las inyecciones)

**jack** NOUN
la **jota** *fem*
**the jack of hearts**
la jota de corazones

**jacket** NOUN
la **chaqueta** *fem*
**a white jacket**
una chaqueta blanca

**jacket potato** NOUN
la **patata asada con piel** *fem*

**jail** NOUN
la **cárcel** *fem*
**in jail**
en la cárcel

**jam** NOUN
la **mermelada** *fem*
**strawberry jam**
mermelada de fresa

**jam jar** NOUN
el **tarro de mermelada** *masc*

**janitor** NOUN
el/la **conserje** *masc/fem*
**He's a janitor.**
Es conserje.

### Language tip
*In Spanish, you do not use an article with people's jobs.*

**January** NOUN
**enero** *masc*
**My birthday's in January.**
Mi cumpleaños es en enero.
**It's the sixth of January today.**
Hoy es seis de enero.

**in January**
en enero
**on the fifth of January**
el cinco de enero

### Language tip
*Months are not spelled with a capital letter in Spanish.*

**jealous** ADJECTIVE
**celoso** *masc*
**celosa** *fem*
**Anne is jealous.**
Anne está celosa.
**She's jealous of Kate.**
Le tiene envidia a Kate.

**jeans** PL NOUN
los **vaqueros** *masc pl*
**I've got some new jeans.**
Tengo unos vaqueros nuevos.
**a pair of jeans**
unos vaqueros

**jelly** NOUN
la **gelatina** *fem*

**jersey** NOUN
el **jersey** *masc* (PL los jerseys)

**Jew** NOUN
el **judío** *masc*
la **judía** *fem*

**jewel** NOUN
la **joya** *fem*

**jewellery** NOUN
las **joyas** *fem pl*

**Jewish** ADJECTIVE
**judío** *masc*
**judía** *fem*

**He's Jewish.**
Es judío.
**She's Jewish.**
Es judía.

**Language tip**
judío isn't spelled with a capital letter in Spanish.

**jigsaw** NOUN
el **rompecabezas** *masc* (PL los rompecabezas)
**I like doing jigsaws.**
Me gusta hacer rompecabezas.

**job** NOUN
el **trabajo** *masc*
**He's got an interesting job.**
Tiene un trabajo interesante.
**She's looking for a job.**
Está buscando trabajo.

**jogging** NOUN
el **footing** *masc*
**She goes jogging.**
Hace footing.

**joke** NOUN
1 el **chiste** *masc* (funny story)
**He told me a joke.**
Me contó un chiste.
2 la **broma** *fem* (trick)
**It was only a joke.**
Era solo una broma.

**jotter** NOUN
el **bloc** *masc* (MASC PL los **blocs**)

**journalist** NOUN
el/la **periodista** *masc/fem*
**He's a journalist.**
Es periodista.

**Language tip**
Did you notice that **periodista** still ends in **-a** even when referring to a man? Remember that in Spanish, you do not use an article with people's jobs.

**journey** NOUN
el **viaje** *masc*
**I don't like long journeys.**
No me gustan los viajes largos.

**judge**

judge can be a noun or a verb.

**A** NOUN
el **juez** *masc*
la **jueza** *fem*
**B** VERB
**to judge**
hacer de juez en
**Who's going to judge the competition?**
¿Quién va a hacer de juez en el concurso?

**judo** NOUN
el **yudo** *masc*
**I do judo.**
Hago yudo.

**juggler** NOUN
el/la **malabarista** *masc/fem*

**juice** NOUN
el **zumo** *masc*
**I'd like some orange juice.**
Quiero zumo de naranja.

**July** NOUN
**julio** *masc*
**My birthday is in July.**
Mi cumpleaños es en julio.
**It's the fourth of July today.**
Hoy es cuatro de julio.

**in July**
en julio
**on the fourteenth of July**
el catorce de julio

a b c d e f g h i j k l m n o p q r s t u v w x y z

### Language tip
*Months are not spelled with a capital letter in Spanish.*

to **jump** VERB
**saltar**
**Jump!**
¡Salta!

**jumper** NOUN
el **jersey** *masc* (PL los **jerseys**)
**a dark green jumper**
un jersey verde oscuro

## June NOUN
**junio** *masc*
**My birthday is in June.**
Mi cumpleaños es en junio.
**It's the eighteenth of June today.**
Hoy es dieciocho de junio.

**in June**
en junio
**on the fourth of June**
el cuatro de junio

### Language tip
*Months are not spelled with a capital letter in Spanish.*

## junior NOUN
**the juniors**
los alumnos de los primeros cursos

**junior school** NOUN
el **colegio de primaria** *masc*

**junk food** NOUN
la **comida basura** *fem*

**just** ADVERB
**1 justo**
**just after Christmas**
justo después de Navidad
**just now**
en este momento
**I'm busy just now.**
Estoy ocupada en este momento.
**I'm just coming!**
¡Ya voy!
**2 sólo** (only)
**It's just a suggestion.**
Es sólo una sugerencia.

### Language tip
*Traditionally, the adverb **sólo** was written with an accent to distinguish it from the unaccented adjective **solo**, meaning 'alone'. Nowadays, you don't have to give the accent unless the sentence would be confusing otherwise.*

**Just a moment, please.**
Un momento, por favor.
**3 to have just done something**
**acabar de hacer algo**
**I've just done it.**
Acabo de hacerlo.
**He's just arrived.**
Acaba de llegar.

# K k

**kangaroo** NOUN
el **canguro** *masc*

**karaoke** NOUN
el **karaoke** *masc*

**karate** NOUN
el **karate** *masc*
I do karate.
Hago karate.

**keen** ADJECTIVE
**entusiasmado** *masc*
**entusiasmada** *fem*
He's not very keen.
No está muy entusiasmado.
I'm very keen on football.
Me gusta mucho el fútbol.
I'm not very keen on spinach.
No me gustan mucho las espinacas.

---
**Language tip**

Remember that you use **me gusta...** to say that you're keen on one thing and **me gustan...** to say that you're keen on two or more things.

---

to **keep** VERB
1 **quedarse con** (have)
You can keep it.
Puedes quedarte con él.
Keep the receipt.
Quédate con el recibo.
2 **quedarse** (stay)
Keep still!
¡Quédate quieto!
Keep quiet!
¡Estaros callados!

to **keep on** VERB
**seguir**
Keep on singing.
Seguid cantando.

**keep-fit** NOUN
la **gimnasia** *fem*

The keep-fit class is on Tuesday.
La clase de gimnasia es el martes.

**kept** VERB ▷see **keep**

**kettle** NOUN
el **hervidor** *masc*

**key** NOUN
la **llave** *fem*
Where are my keys?
¿Dónde están mis llaves?

**keyboard** NOUN
el **teclado** *masc*

**kick**

> **kick** can be a noun or a verb.

A NOUN
la **patada** *fem*
B VERB
to kick
**dar una patada a**
He kicked me!
¡Me dio una patada!
Kick the ball.
Dale una patada al balón.

**kid** NOUN
el **niño** *masc*
la **niña** *fem* (child)
the kids
los niños

to **kill** VERB
**matar**
My cat kills birds.
Mi gato mata pájaros.

**kilo** NOUN
el **kilo** *masc*
   **two euros a kilo**
   dos euros el kilo

**kilometre** NOUN
el **kilómetro** *masc*

**kilt** NOUN
la **falda escocesa** *fem*

**kind**

*kind can be an adjective or a noun.*

**A** ADJECTIVE
**amable** *masc & fem*
   **She's a kind lady.**
   Es una señora amable.
   **That's very kind of you.**
   Es muy amable de tu parte.
**B** NOUN
el **tipo** *masc*
   **It's a kind of sausage.**
   Es un tipo de salchicha.

**kindergarten** NOUN
el **jardín de infancia** *masc* (PL
   los **jardines de infancia**)

**king** NOUN
el **rey** *masc*
   **the king of hearts**
   el rey de corazones
   **the king and queen**
   los reyes

**kiss**

*kiss can be a noun or a verb.*

**A** NOUN
el **beso** *masc*
   **Give me a kiss.**
   Dame un beso.

**Did you know...?**
*Did you know that Spanish speakers sometimes end e-mails, postcards and letters to friends with **un beso** (a kiss) or **besos** (kisses)?*

**B** VERB
**to kiss**
**besar**

**Kiss me.**
Bésame.

**kit** NOUN
el **equipo** *masc*
   **Don't forget your gym kit.**
   Que no se te olvide el equipo de gimnasia.

**kitchen** NOUN
la **cocina** *fem*
   **She's in the kitchen.**
   Está en la cocina.

**kite** NOUN
la **cometa** *fem*

**kitten** NOUN
el **gatito** *masc*
la **gatita** *fem*

**knee** NOUN
la **rodilla** *fem*

to **kneel** VERB
**arrodillarse**

**knew** VERB ▷see **know**

**knickers** PL NOUN
las **bragas** *fem pl*
   **Your knickers are showing!**
   ¡Se te ven las bragas!
   **a pair of knickers**
   unas bragas

**knife** NOUN
el **cuchillo** *masc*

to **knit** VERB
**hacer punto**
   **I can knit.**
   Sé hacer punto.
   **She's knitting a scarf.**
   Se está haciendo una bufanda de punto.

**knives** PL NOUN
los **cuchillos** *masc pl*
   **knives, forks and spoons**
   cuchillos, tenedores y cucharas

**knob** NOUN
1 el **pomo** *masc* (on door)

**2** el **botón** masc (PL los **botones**)
(on radio, TV)

to **knock** VERB
**llamar**
Someone's knocking at the door.
Alguien está llamando a la puerta.

to **know** VERB

*Language tip*
Use **saber** for knowing facts and **conocer** for knowing people and places.

**1 saber** (fact)
It's a long way. – Yes, I know.
Está lejos. – Sí, ya lo sé.
Who knows the answer?
¿Quién sabe la respuesta?

I don't know.
No lo sé.

**2 conocer** (person, place)
I know her.
La conozco.
I don't know him.
No lo conozco.

*Language tip*
Don't forget the personal **a** when you name the person.

Do you know Tom?
¿Conoces a Tom?
I know Madrid well.
Conozco bien Madrid.

**knowledge** NOUN
el **conocimiento** masc

**Koran** NOUN
el **Corán** masc

English Spanish

a
b
c
d
e
f
g
h
i
j
**k**
l
m
n
o
p
q
r
s
t
u
v
w
x
y
z

# L l

**label** NOUN
la **etiqueta** *fem*

**lace** NOUN
el **cordón** *masc* (PL los **cordones**)
(*of shoe*)
**Tie your laces.**
Átate los cordones.

### Language tip
*In Spanish you usually use an article
like* **el**, **la**, **los** *with clothes you are
wearing.*

**ladder** NOUN
la **escalera de mano** *fem*

**lady** NOUN
la **señora** *fem*
**an old lady**
una señora mayor
**a young lady**
una joven
**Ladies and gentlemen ...**
Señoras y caballeros ...
**Where is the 'ladies'?**
¿Dónde está
el baño de
señoras?

**laid** VERB
▷ *see* **lay**

**lain** VERB
▷ *see* **lie**

**lake** NOUN
el **lago** *masc*

**lamb** NOUN
el **cordero** *masc*
**a lamb chop**
una chuleta de cordero

**lamp** NOUN
la **lámpara** *fem*

**land**

### land *can be a noun or a verb.*

**A** NOUN
la **tierra** *fem*
**on land**
en tierra
**B** VERB
**to land**
aterrizar
**The plane lands at nine
o'clock.**
El avión aterriza a las nueve.

**lane** NOUN
el **camino** *masc*
**a country lane**
un camino de campo
**the fast lane**
el carril de adelantamiento

**language** NOUN
el **idioma** *masc*
**Spanish isn't a difficult
language.**
El español no es un idioma
difícil.

### Language tip
*Even though it ends in* -a, **el
idioma** *is a masculine noun.*

**language laboratory**
NOUN
el **laboratorio de idiomas**
*masc*

**lap** NOUN
**on my lap**
en mi regazo

**laptop** NOUN
el **ordenador portátil** *masc*

**large** ADJECTIVE
**grande** *masc & fem*
**a large house**
una casa grande
**a large dog**
un perro grande

**English Spanish**

*Language tip*
grande *normally follows the noun when it means 'large'. However, when it does go before a singular noun, it is shortened to* gran.

a large number of people
un gran número de personas

*Language tip*
*Be careful! The translation of* large *is not* largo.

## last

last *can be an adjective or an adverb.*

**A** ADJECTIVE
**último** *masc*
**última** *fem*
**the last time**
la última vez
**He arrived last night.**
Llegó anoche.
**We've got here at last!**
¡Por fin hemos llegado!

last Friday
el viernes pasado
last week
la semana pasada
last year
el año pasado
last night
anoche
at last
por fin

**B** ADVERB
**en último lugar** *(in last place)*
**He always comes last.**
Siempre llega en último lugar.
**I've lost my bag. – When did you last see it?**
He perdido el bolso. – ¿Cuándo lo viste por última vez?

## late ADVERB, ADJECTIVE
**tarde**
**I go to bed late.**
Me acuesto tarde.

**to be late**
llegar tarde
**You're going to be late!**
¡Vas a llegar tarde!
**Sorry I'm late!**
¡Siento llegar tarde!
**I'm late for school.**
Voy tarde para el colegio.

## later ADVERB
**más tarde**
**I'll do it later.**
Lo haré más tarde.

See you later!
¡Hasta luego!

## latest ADJECTIVE
**último** *masc*
**última** *fem*
**their latest album**
su último álbum

## Latin NOUN
el **latín** *masc*
**I do Latin.**
Hago latín.

## to laugh VERB
**reírse**
**Why are you laughing?**
¿Por qué os reís?

## lawn NOUN
el **césped** *masc*

## lawnmower NOUN
la **cortadora de césped** *fem*

## lawyer NOUN
el **abogado** *masc*
la **abogada** *fem*
**My mother's a lawyer.**
Mi madre es abogada.

*Language tip*
*In Spanish, you do not use an article with people's jobs.*

## to lay VERB
**1 poner**
**Lay your cards on the table.**
Pon tus cartas sobre la mesa.
**to lay the table**

poner la mesa
**It's Sylvia's turn to lay the table.**
Le toca a Sylvia poner la mesa.
**2** ▷*see* **lie**

## lazy ADJECTIVE
**vago** *masc*
**vaga** *fem*
**My sister is very lazy.**
Mi hermana es muy vaga.

## lead

**lead** *can be a noun or a verb.*

**A** NOUN
**1** **to be in the lead**
ir en cabeza
**Our team is in the lead.**
Nuestro equipo va en cabeza.
**2** el **cable** *masc (cable)*
**3** la **correa** *fem (of dog)*
**B** VERB
**to lead**
llevar
**This street leads to the station.**
Esta calle lleva a la estación.

## leaf NOUN
la **hoja** *fem*

## to lean out VERB
**asomarse**
**Don't lean out of the window.**
No te asomes a la ventana.

## to lean over VERB
**inclinarse**
**Don't lean over too far.**
No te inclines demasiado.

## leap year NOUN
el **año bisiesto** *masc*

## to learn VERB
**aprender**
**I'm learning Spanish.**
Estoy aprendiendo español.
**I'm learning to ski.**

Estoy aprendiendo a esquiar.

## least ADVERB, ADJECTIVE, PRONOUN
**menos**

*Language tip*
**menos** *never changes its ending.*

**the least expensive hotel**
el hotel menos caro
**the least expensive camera**
la cámara menos cara
**the least expensive hotels**
los hoteles menos caros
**Who's got the least money?**
¿Quién tiene menos dnero?
**It will cost at least two hundred pounds.**
Costará al menos doscientas libras.

**at least**
al menos

## leather NOUN
el **cuero** *masc*
**It's made of leather.**
Es de cuero.
**a black leather jacket**
una chaqueta de cuero negra

## to leave VERB
**1** **dejar** *(object)*
**Don't leave your bag in the car.**
No dejes el bolso en el coche.
**I've left my book at home.**
Me he dejado el libro en casa.
**2** **salir** *(depart)*
**The bus leaves at eight.**
El autobús sale a las ocho.
**3** **irse** *(go away)*
**He's already left.**
Ya se ha ido.

## leaves PL NOUN
las **hojas** *fem pl*

## led VERB ▷*see* **lead**

## leek NOUN
el **puerro** *masc*

## left

**left** *can be an adjective, adverb, noun or verb.*

**A** ADJECTIVE
**1** **izquierdo** *masc*
**izquierda** *fem (not right)*
**Stretch out your left arm.**
Estira el brazo izquierdo.
**on the left side of the road**
en el lado izquierdo de la calle

**2** *(remaining)*
**I've got fifteen euros left.**
Me quedan quince euros.
**How many cards have you got left?**
¿Cuántas cartas te quedan?
**I haven't got any money left.**
No me queda dinero.

**B** ADVERB
**a la izquierda**
**Turn left.**
Gira a la izquierda.
**Take the next left.**
Toma la siguiente a la izquierda.

**C** NOUN
la **izquierda** *fem*
**It's on the left.**
Está a la izquierda.
**the house on the left**
la casa de la izquierda

**D** VERB ▷ *see* **leave**

**left-hand** ADJECTIVE
**the left-hand side**
la izquierda
**It's on the left-hand side.**
Está a la izquierda.

**left-handed** ADJECTIVE
**zurdo** *masc*
**zurda** *fem*
**Tina is left-handed.**
Tina es zurda.

**left-luggage office** NOUN
la **consigna** *fem*

**leftovers** PL NOUN
las **sobras** *fem pl*

**leg** NOUN
**1** la **pierna** *fem (of person)*

**She has a broken leg.**
Tiene una pierna rota.
**I've hurt my leg.**
Me he hecho daño en la pierna.

### Language tip
*In Spanish you usually use an article like* **el**, **la**, **los** *with parts of the body.*

**2** la **pata** *fem (of animal, table)*
**It's got a wobbly leg.**
Tiene una pata que cojea.
**a chicken leg**
un muslo de pollo

**leggings** PL NOUN
las **mallas** *fem pl*

**leisure centre** NOUN
el **polideportivo** *masc*

**lemon** NOUN
el **limón** *masc*
(PL los **limones**)

**lemonade**
NOUN
la **gaseosa** *fem*

to **lend** VERB
**dejar**
**Can you lend me a pencil?**
¿Me puedes dejar un lápiz?

**less** ADJECTIVE, ADVERB, PRONOUN
**menos**

### Language tip
**menos** *never changes its ending.*

**Less noise, please!**
¡Menos ruido, por favor!
**A bit less, please.**
Un poco menos, por favor.

### Language tip
*You normally translate* **less than** *as* **menos que**.

**I've got less than him!**
¡Tengo menos que él!
**I'm less nervous than I was.**
Ahora estoy menos nervioso que antes.

*Language tip*
Use **menos de** instead before numbers.

**It costs less than ten euros.**
Cuesta menos de diez euros.

**lesson** NOUN
1 la **clase** *fem*
**una clase de inglés**
an English lesson
**Each lesson lasts forty minutes.**
Cada clase dura cuarenta minutos.
2 la **lección** *fem* (PL las **lecciones**) (in book)

to **let** VERB
1 **dejar** (allow)
**Let me see.**
Déjame ver.
**Let me go!**
¡Suéltame!
**I'll let you know.**
Ya te lo diré.
2 (in suggestions)

*Language tip*
**let's ...** is often translated by **vamos a ...** when making a suggestion.

**Let's send him an email!**
¡Vamos a enviarle un e-mail!

*Language tip*
**vamos** is also used to mean **let's go**.

**Let's go to the park!**
¡Vamos al parque!

*Language tip*
Alternatively you can make suggestions using **¿por qué no...?**, which literally means 'why not...?'.

**Let's send him an email!**
¿Por qué no le enviamos un e-mail?
**Let's go to the park!**
¿Por qué no vamos al parque?

**Let's go!**
¡Vamos!
**Let's start now!**
¡Vamos a empezar ahora!

**letter** NOUN
1 la **carta** *fem* (note)
**I'm writing a letter to my friend.**
Le estoy escribiendo una carta a mi amigo.
2 la **letra** *fem* (of alphabet)
**It's a five-letter word.**
Es una palabra de cinco letras.

**letterbox** NOUN
el **buzón** *masc* (PL los **buzones**)

*Did you know...?*
Spanish **letterboxes** tend to be metal boxes in which the postman leaves any mail rather than the hole in the door that is common in the UK.

**lettuce** NOUN
la **lechuga** *fem*

**level** NOUN
el **nivel** *masc*

**liar** NOUN
el **mentiroso** *masc*
la **mentirosa** *fem*

**library** NOUN
la **biblioteca** *fem*

*Language tip*
Be careful! The translation of **library** is not **librería**.

**licence** NOUN
el **permiso** *masc*
**a fishing licence**
un permiso de pesca
**a driving licence**
un carnet de conducir

to **lick** VERB
**lamer**
**The dog is licking me.**
El perro me está lamiendo.

**lid** NOUN
la **tapa** *fem*

## to **lie**

> **lie** *can be a verb or a noun.*

**A** VERB
1 **mentir** *(tell lies)*
**She's lying.**
Está mintiendo.
2 **estar tumbado** *(lie down)*
**He is lying on the sofa.**
Está tumbado en el sofá.

**B** NOUN
la **mentira** *fem*
**That's a lie!**
¡Eso es mentira!

## **life** NOUN
la **vida** *fem*

## **life jacket** NOUN
el **chaleco salvavidas** *masc*
(PL los **chalecos salvavidas**)

## **lift**

> **lift** *can be a verb or a noun.*

**A** VERB
**to lift**
**levantar**
**It's too heavy, I can't lift it.**
Pesa demasiado, no puedo
levantarlo.
**B** NOUN
1 el **ascensor** *masc* *(to another
floor)*
**The lift isn't working.**
El ascensor no funciona.
2 *(in car)*
**Can you give me a lift to the
station?**
¿Me puedes llevar a la estación?

## **light**

> **light** *can be an adjective, noun or
verb.*

**A** ADJECTIVE

1 **ligero** *masc*
**ligera** *fem (in weight)*
**as light as a feather**
tan ligero como una pluma
2 **claro** *masc*
**clara** *fem (in colour)*
**light blue socks**
calcetines azul claro

> ### *Language tip*
> When you describe something as
> **light blue**, **light green** and so on,
> neither the colour nor **claro** changes
> its ending to agree with the noun.

**some light green curtains**
unas cortinas verde claro
**B** NOUN
la **luz** *fem* (PL las **luces**)
**Switch on the light.**
Enciende la luz.
**Switch off the light.**
Apaga la luz.
**Turn right at the lights.**
Gira a la derecha al llegar al
semáforo.
**C** VERB
**to light**
**encender**
**Let's light the fire.**
Vamos a encender el fuego.

## **light bulb** NOUN
la **bombilla** *fem*

## **lighter** NOUN
el **mechero** *masc*

## **lighthouse** NOUN
el **faro** *masc*

## **lightning** NOUN
los **relámpagos** *masc pl*
**There was thunder and
lightning.**
Había
truenos y
relámpagos.
**a flash of
lightning**
un
relámpago

## like

*like can be a verb or a preposition.*

**A** VERB
**to like**
1 **I like ...**
   Me gusta .../Me gustan ...

### Language tip
*Remember that you use **me gusta** ... to say you like one thing and **me gustan** ... to say you like two or more things.*

**I like milk.**
Me gusta la leche.
**I don't like riding.**
No me gusta montar a caballo.
**I like cherries.**
Me gustan las cerezas.
**I don't like grapes.**
No me gustan las uvas.
**Do you like coffee?**
¿Te gusta el café?
**Do you like sweets?**
¿Te gustan los caramelos?
**I like Paul.**
Paul me cae bien.
2 **querer** *(want)*
**Yes, if you like.**
Sí, si quieres.
**I'd like an orange juice, please.**
Quiero un zumo de naranja, por favor.
**I'd like some chips.**
Quiero patatas fritas.
**What would you like for breakfast?**
¿Qué quieres desayunar?
**Would you like to go for a walk?**
¿Quieres ir a dar un paseo?
**What would you like, Madam?**
¿Qué desea, señora?

**I'd like ...**
Quiero ...

**B** PREPOSITION

**como**
**a city like London**
una ciudad como Londres
**I look like my brother.**
Me parezco a mi hermano.
**What's Madrid like?**
¿Cómo es Madrid?
**What's the weather like?**
¿Cómo está el tiempo?
**like this**
así

## likely ADJECTIVE
**probable** *masc & fem*
**That's not very likely.**
Eso no es muy probable.

## line NOUN
la **línea** *fem*
**a straight line**
una línea recta

## lion NOUN
el **león** *masc*
(PL los **leones**)

## lip NOUN
el **labio** *masc*

## lipstick NOUN
la **barra de labios** *fem*

## liquid NOUN
el **líquido** *masc*

## list

*list can be a noun or a verb.*

**A** NOUN
la **lista** *fem*
**a shopping list**
una lista de la compra
**B** VERB
**to list**
hacer una lista de
**List your hobbies.**
Haz una lista de tus aficiones.

## to listen VERB
**escuchar**
**Are you listening, Sonia?**
¿Estás escuchando, Sonia?

**to listen to something**
escuchar algo
**Listen to this, everybody!**
¡Escuchad esto, todos!

**Listen to me, children!**
¡Escuchadme, niños!

*Language tip*
*Have you noticed that in Spanish you don't need a preposition after the verb* **escuchar**?

**litre** NOUN
el **litro** *masc*

**litter** NOUN
la **basura** *fem*
**Don't leave litter.**
No dejéis basura.

**litter bin**
NOUN
la **papelera** *fem*

**little**

*little can be an adjective or a pronoun.*

**A** ADJECTIVE
1 **pequeño** *masc*
**pequeña** *fem (small)*
**a little girl**
una niña pequeña
2 **poco** *masc*
**poca** *fem (in quantity)*
**We've got very little time.**
Tenemos muy poco tiempo.
**B** PRONOUN
**a little**
un poco
**How much would you like? – Just a little.**
¿Cuánto quieres? –
Solo un poco.
**There's very little left.**
Queda muy poco.

to **live** VERB
vivir

**Where do you live?**
¿Dónde vives?
**I live here.**
Vivo aquí.
**I live in Edinburgh.**
Vivo en Edimburgo.
**I live with my grandmother.**
Vivo con mi abuela.
**My parents don't live together any more.**
Mis padres ya no viven juntos.

**living room** NOUN
la **sala de estar** *fem*

**lizard** NOUN
la **lagartija** *fem*

**load**

*load can be a noun or a verb.*

**A** NOUN
**loads of**
un montón de
**loads of people**
un montón de gente
**loads of money**
un montón de dinero
**B** VERB
**to load**
cargar

**loaf** NOUN
**a loaf of bread**
un pan
**two loaves of bread**
dos panes
**a French loaf**
una barra de pan

**lock**

*lock can be a noun or a verb.*

**A** NOUN
la **cerradura** *fem*
**The lock is broken.**
La cerradura está rota.
**B** VERB
**to lock**
cerrar con llave
**I must lock the door.**
Tengo que cerrar la puerta con llave.

English Spanish

a
b
c
d
e
f
g
h
i
j
k
**l**
m
n
o
p
q
r
s
t
u
v
w
x
y
z

**locker** NOUN
la **taquilla** *fem*
**Leave your books in your locker.**
Deja los libros en la taquilla.

**log** NOUN
el **tronco** *masc*

to **log in** VERB
**conectarse**
**I can't log in.**
No puedo conectarme.

to **log off** VERB
**desconectarse**
**I've forgotten how to log off.**
He olvidado cómo desconectarme.

to **log on** VERB
**conectarse**
**Have you logged on yet?**
¿Te has conectado ya?

to **log out** VERB
**desconectarse**
**Please log out now.**
Por favor, desconéctate ahora.

**lollipop** NOUN
el **pirulí** *masc* (PL los **pirulís**)

*Did you know…?*
Schools in Spain don't use a
**lollipop man** or **lollipop lady**.

**London** NOUN
**Londres** *masc*
**in London**
en Londres
**to London**
a Londres
**I'm from London.**
Soy de Londres.

**lonely** ADJECTIVE
**solo** *masc*
**sola** *fem*
**to feel lonely**
sentirse solo
**She feels lonely.**
Se siente sola.

**long** ADJECTIVE
**largo** *masc*
**larga** *fem*
**She's got long hair.**
Tiene el pelo largo.
**There's a long queue.**
Hay una larga cola.
**How long is the flight?**
¿Cuánto dura el vuelo?

**How long does it take?**
¿Cuánto tiempo se tarda?
**It takes a long time.**
Se tarda mucho tiempo.
**How long is it?**
¿Cuánto mide de largo?
**It's two hundred metres long.**
Mide doscientos metros de largo.

**loo** NOUN
el **baño** *masc*
**Where's the loo?**
¿Dónde está el baño?
**Can I go to the loo?**
¿Puedo ir al baño?

**look**

**look** *can be a noun or a verb.*

**A** NOUN
**to have a look**
echar un vistazo
**Have a look at this!**
¡Echa un vistazo a esto!
**B** VERB
**to look**
**1** mirar
**Look, children!**
¡Mirad, niños!
**to look at something**
mirar algo
**Look at the picture.**
Mira la foto.
**Look at me, Simon.**
Mírame, Simon.
**2** *(seem)*
**That cake looks nice.**
Esa tarta tiene buena pinta.

**Look!**
¡Mira!
**Look at the board.**
Mirad a la pizarra.
**Look out!**
¡Cuidado!

to **look after** VERB
cuidar
　　I look after my little sister.
　　Cuido a mi hermana pequeña.

**Language tip**

*Don't forget the personal **a** in examples like this one.*

to **look for** VERB
buscar
　　**What are you looking for?**
　　¿Qué estás buscando?
　　**I'm looking for my rubber.**
　　Estoy buscando mi goma de borrar.
　　**We're looking for Daniel.**
　　Estamos buscando a Daniel.

**Language tip**

*Don't forget the personal **a** in examples like this one.*

to **look up** VERB
consultar
　　**You'll need to look up the words in the dictionary.**
　　Tendrás que consultar las palabras en el diccionario.

**lorry** NOUN
el **camión** *masc* (PL los camiones)

**lorry driver** NOUN
el **camionero** *masc*
la **camionera** *fem*
　　**He's a lorry driver.**
　　Es camionero.

**Language tip**

*In Spanish, you do not use an article with people's jobs.*

to **lose** VERB
perder

**I've lost my purse.**
He perdido mi monedero.
**Our team always loses.**
Nuestro equipo siempre pierde.
**to get lost**
perderse
**We got lost in the wood.**
Nos perdimos en el bosque.

**loser** NOUN
el **perdedor** *masc*
la **perdedora** *fem*

**lost** VERB ▷see **lose**

**lot** NOUN
　　**a lot**
　　mucho
　　**She talks a lot.**
　　Habla mucho.
　　**Do you like football? – Not a lot.**
　　¿Te gusta el fútbol? – No mucho.
　　**How many friends have you got? – A lot.**
　　¿Cuántos amigos tienes? – Muchos.
　　**a lot of**
　　mucho
　　**We haven't got a lot of time.**
　　No tenemos mucho tiempo.

**Language tip**

*Remember to change the ending of **mucho** to agree with what it describes.*

　　**She's got a lot of books.**
　　Tiene muchos libros.
　　**He's got lots of experience.**
　　Tiene mucha experiencia.

**Thanks a lot.**
Muchas gracias.

**lottery** NOUN
la **lotería** *fem*
　　**I hope I win the lottery.**
　　Espero que me toque la lotería.
　　**a lottery ticket**
　　un billete de lotería

## loud ADJECTIVE
**alto** *masc*
**alta** *fem*
**The television is too loud.**
La televisión está demasiado alta.
**Speak louder!**
¡Habla más alto!

## lounge NOUN
el **salón** *masc* (PL los **salones**)

## love

**love** *can be a noun or a verb.*

**A** NOUN
el **amor** *masc*
**her love for animals**
su amor por los animales
**She's in love.**
Está enamorada.
**She's in love with Mike.**
Está enamorada de Mike.
**Give Emma my love.**
Dale recuerdos a Emma de mi parte.
**Love, Peter.**
Un abrazo, Peter.

**B** VERB
**to love**
1 **querer** *(person)*
**Do you love me?**
¿Me quieres?
**Everybody loves her.**
Todos la quieren.
**I love Roger.**
Quiero a Roger.

### Language tip
*Don't forget the personal **a** in examples like this one.*

2 *(thing)*
**I love chocolate.**
Me encanta el chocolate.
**I love skiing.**
Me encanta esquiar.
**I love roses.**
Me encantan las rosas.

### Language tip
*Remember that you use **me encanta** ... to say you love one thing and **me encantan** ... to say you love two or more things.*

**I love you.**
Te quiero.
**Love from ...**
Un abrazo de ...

## lovely ADJECTIVE
**bonito** *masc*
**bonita** *fem*
**They've got a lovely house.**
Tienen una casa bonita.
**It's a lovely day.**
Hace un día bonito.
**Have a lovely time!**
¡Que lo paséis bien!

## low ADJECTIVE
**bajo** *masc*
**baja** *fem*
**a low price**
un precio bajo

## luck NOUN
la **suerte** *fem*
**She doesn't have much luck.**
No tiene mucha suerte.

**Good luck!**
¡Buena suerte!
**Bad luck!**
¡Qué mala suerte!

### Language tip
*Have you noticed the upside-down exclamation mark at the start of Spanish exclamations?*

## luckily ADVERB
**afortunadamente**

## lucky ADJECTIVE
**to be lucky**
**tener suerte**
**You're lucky!**
¡Tienes suerte!
**Sarah is lucky, she's going to Ireland.**

Sarah tiene suerte, se va a Irlanda.
**Black cats are lucky.**
Los gatos negros traen suerte.

**a lucky horseshoe**
una herradura de la suerte

**luggage** NOUN
el **equipaje** masc
**Have you got any luggage?**
¿Tienes equipaje?

**lump** NOUN
1 el **trozo** masc (piece)
**a lump of cheese**
un trozo de queso
2 el **chichón** masc (PL los chichones) (bump)

**He's got a lump on his forehead.**
Tiene un chichón en la frente.

> **Language tip**
> In Spanish you usually use an article like **el**, **la**, **los** with parts of the body.

**lunch** NOUN
la **comida** fem
**Lunch is nearly ready.**
La comida está casi lista.
**I go home for lunch.**
Voy a casa a comer.
**It's time for lunch.**
Es hora de comer.
**to have lunch**
comer
**We have lunch at twelve thirty.**
Comemos a las doce y media.

**lying** VERB ▷ see **lie**

# M m

**machine** NOUN
la **máquina** *fem*

**mad** ADJECTIVE
1 **loco** *masc*
**loca** *fem (insane)*
**You're mad!**
¡Estás loco!
**He's mad about football.**
Está loco por el fútbol.
**She's mad about horses.**
Le encantan los caballos.
2 **furioso** *masc*
**furiosa** *fem*
*(angry)*
**He's mad at me for losing his watch.**
Está furioso conmigo por haber perdido su reloj.

**Madam** NOUN
la **señora** *fem*
**Excuse me, Madam.**
Perdone, señora.

**made** VERB ▷*see* **make**

**Madrid** NOUN
**Madrid** *masc*
**in Madrid**
en Madrid
**to Madrid**
a Madrid
**Luis is from Madrid.**
Luis es de Madrid.

**magazine** NOUN
la **revista** *fem*

**magic**

**magic** *can be an adjective or a noun.*

**A** ADJECTIVE

1 **mágico** *masc*
**mágica** *fem*
**a magic wand**
una varita mágica
**a magic trick**
un truco de magia
2 **fantástico** *masc*
**fantástica** *fem (brilliant)*
**It was magic!**
¡Fue fantástico!
**B** NOUN
la **magia** *fem*
**by magic**
por magia

**magician** NOUN
el **mago** *masc*
la **maga** *fem*

**magnifying glass** NOUN
la **lupa** *fem*

**mail**

**mail** *can be a noun or a verb.*

**A** NOUN
el **correo** *masc*
**You've got some mail.**
Tienes correo.
**by mail**
por correo
**B** VERB
**to mail**
enviar un e-mail a *(email)*
**I'll mail my friend.**
Voy a enviar un e-mail a mi amigo.

**main** ADJECTIVE
**principal** *masc & fem*
**the main problem**
el problema principa
**The hotel is on the main road.**
El hotel está en la carretera principal.

**major** ADJECTIVE
**muy importante**
   **a major change**
   un cambio muy importante
   **a major problem**
   un problema serio

**Majorca** NOUN
**Mallorca** *fem*

**make**

> **make** *can be a noun or a verb.*

**A** NOUN
   la **marca** *fem*
   **What make is that car?**
   ¿De qué marca es ese coche?
**B** VERB
   **to make**
1 **hacer**
   **I'm going to make a cake.**
   Voy a hacer un pastel.
   **They are making a lot of noise.**
   Están haciendo mucho ruido.
   **He made it himself.**
   Lo hizo él solo.
   **I make my bed every morning.**
   Me hago la cama todas las mañanas.
   **Two and two make four.**
   Dos y dos son cuatro.
   **Four take away two, what does that make?**
   Si a cuatro le quitamos dos, ¿cuánto queda?

> **made in Spain**
> fabricado en España
> **It's made of iron.**
> Es de hierro.

2 **ganar** *(earn)*
   **He makes a lot of money.**
   Gana mucho dinero.

to **make up** VERB
**inventar**
   **You're making it up!**
   ¡Te lo estás inventando!

**make-up** NOUN
   el **maquillaje** *masc*

**male** ADJECTIVE
1 **macho** *(animal)*

> **Language tip**
> **macho** *never changes its ending when it's used to describe a noun.*

   **a male tortoise**
   una tortuga macho
2 **varón** *masc (on forms)*
   **Sex: male.**
   Sexo: varón.

**man** NOUN
   el **hombre** *masc*
   **an old man**
   un hombre mayor

to **manage** VERB
**arreglárselas**
   **It's okay, I can manage.**
   Está bien, yo me
   las arreglo.

   **I can't manage all that.**
   No puedo acabar con todo eso.
   **to manage to do something**
   conseguir hacer algo
   **I managed to fix my bike.**
   Conseguí arreglar mi bicicleta.

**manager** NOUN
1 el **director** *masc*
   la **directora** *fem (of company)*
2 el **encargado** *masc*
   la **encargada** *fem (of shop, restaurant)*
   **I'd like to speak to the manager.**
   Quiero hablar con el encargado.
3 el/la **gerente** *masc/fem (of hotel)*
4 el **entrenador** *masc*
   la **entrenadora** *fem (of team)*

**manageress** NOUN
  1 la **encargada** fem (of shop, restaurant)
  2 la **gerente** fem (of hotel)

**manners** PL NOUN
  los **modales** masc pl
  **good manners**
  buenos modales
  **Her manners are appalling.**
  Tiene muy malos modales.
  **It's bad manners to speak with your mouth full.**
  Es de mala educación hablar con la boca llena.

**many** ADJECTIVE, PRONOUN
  **muchos** masc pl
  **muchas** fem pl
  **He hasn't got many friends.**
  No tiene muchos amigos.
  **I haven't bought many magazines.**
  No he comprado muchas revistas.
  **How many...?**
  ¿Cuántos...?

*Language tip*
Don't forget the accent on question words like **cuántos** nor the upside-down question mark at the start of questions.

  **How many sisters have you got?**
  ¿Cuántas hermanas tienes?
  **That's too many.**
  Ésos son demasiados.
  **You ask too many questions!**
  ¡Haces demasiadas preguntas!

**How many?**
¿Cuántos?
**Not many**
No muchos.
**too many**
demasiados

**map** NOUN
  1 el **mapa** masc (of country, area)
  **a map of Spain**
  un mapa de España

*Language tip*
Even though it ends in **-a**, **el mapa** is a masculine noun.

  2 el **plano** masc (of town)
  **a map of London**
  un plano de Londres

**marathon** NOUN
  el **maratón** masc (PL los maratones)
  **the London marathon**
  el maratón de Londres

**marbles** PL NOUN
  las **canicas** fem pl
  **Do you want to play marbles?**
  ¿Quieres jugar a las canicas?

*Language tip*
In Spanish, you need to add **a las** before **canicas**.

**March** NOUN
  **marzo** masc
  **My birthday's in March.**
  Mi cumpleaños es en marzo.
  **It's the twenty-ninth of March today.**
  Hoy es veintinueve de marzo.

**in March**
en marzo
**on the fifth of March**
el cinco de marzo

*Language tip*
Months are not spelled with a capital letter in Spanish.

**margarine** NOUN
  la **margarina** fem

**margin** NOUN
  el **margen** masc (PL los márgenes)
  **Write notes in the margin.**
  Escribid anotaciones en el margen.

## mark

> **mark** *can be a noun or a verb.*

**A** NOUN

1 la **nota** *fem (at school)*
   **I get good marks in English.**
   Saco buenas notas en inglés.
2 la **mancha** *fem (stain)*
   **You've got a mark on your shirt.**
   Tienes una mancha en la camisa.

> **On your marks, get set, go!**
> ¡Preparados, listos, ya!

**B** VERB
   **to mark**
   **corregir**
   **She's got books to mark.**
   Tiene cuadernos para corregir.

## market NOUN
el **mercado** *masc*

## marmalade NOUN
la **mermelada de naranja** *fem*

> ### Language tip
> *Don't forget to say* **de naranja** *if you mean 'orange marmalade'.* **La mermelada** *on its own just means 'jam'.*

## marriage NOUN
el **matrimonio** *masc*

## married ADJECTIVE
**casado** *masc*
**casada** *fem*
   **They are not married.**
   No están casados.
   **She's married to my cousin.**
   Está casada con mi primo.
   **to get married**
   casarse
   **They want to get married.**
   Quieren casarse.
   **My sister's getting married in June.**
   Mi hermana se va a casar en junio.

**a married couple**
un matrimonio

## to marry VERB
**casarse con**
   **He wants to marry her.**
   Quiere casarse con ella.

## marvellous ADJECTIVE
**estupendo** *masc*
**estupenda** *fem*
   **She's a marvellous cook.**
   Es una cocinera estupenda.
   **The weather was marvellous.**
   Hizo un tiempo estupendo.

## masculine ADJECTIVE
**masculino** *masc*
**masculina** *fem*

## mashed potatoes PL NOUN
el **puré de patatas** *masc*
   **sausages and mashed potatoes**
   salchichas con puré de patatas

## mask NOUN
la **máscara** *fem*

## mass NOUN

1 el **montón** *masc* (PL los montones)
   **a mass of books and papers**
   un montón de libros y papeles
   **We've got masses of homework today.**
   Hoy tenemos montones de deberes.
2 la **misa** *fem (in church)*
   **We go to mass on Sundays.**
   Vamos a misa los domingos.

**massive** ADJECTIVE
**enorme** *masc & fem*

**masterpiece** NOUN
la **obra maestra** *fem*

**mat** NOUN
el **felpudo** *masc (doormat)*
**Wipe your feet on the mat.**
Límpiate los pies en el felpudo.

### Language tip
*In Spanish you usually use an article like* **el**, **la**, **los** *with parts of the body.*

## match

**match** *can be a noun or a verb.*

**A** NOUN
1 la **cerilla** *fem (for striking)*
**a box of matches**
una caja de cerillas
2 el **partido** *masc (game)*
**a football match**
un partido de fútbol
**B** VERB
**to match**
1 **hacer juego con** *(go with)*
**The jacket matches the trousers.**
La chaqueta hace juego con los pantalones.
2 **hacer corresponder con** *(put with)*
**Match the words to the pictures.**
Haz corresponder las palabras con las imágenes.

**matching** ADJECTIVE
**a juego**
**My bedroom has matching wallpaper and curtains.**
Mi habitación tiene el papel y las cortinas a juego.

**mate** NOUN
el **amigo** *masc*
la **amiga** *fem (friend)*

**He's my mate.**
Es mi amigo.

**material** NOUN
la **tela** *fem (cloth)*
**It's made of red material.**
Está hecho de tela roja.

**maths** NOUN
las **matemáticas** *fem*

## matter

**matter** *can be a noun or a verb.*

**A** NOUN
**What's the matter? Why are you crying?**
¿Qué pasa? ¿Por qué estás llorando?
**What's the matter with him?**
¿Qué le pasa?
**B** VERB
**to matter**: **It doesn't matter.**
No importa.

**mattress** NOUN
el **colchón** *masc* (PL los colchones)

**maximum** ADJECTIVE
**máximo** *masc*
**máxima** *fem*

**May** NOUN
**mayo** *masc*
**My birthday's in May.**
Mi cumpleaños es en mayo.
**It's the eleventh of May today.**
Hoy es once de mayo.

**in May**
en mayo
**on the fifth of May**
el cinco de mayo

### Language tip
*Months are not spelled with a capital letter in Spanish.*

**may** VERB
**May I come in?**
¿Puedo entrar?
**She may not come.**
Puede que no venga.

**maybe** ADVERB
**a lo mejor**
**maybe not**
a lo mejor no
**Maybe she's at home.**
A lo mejor está en casa.

**mayonnaise** NOUN
la **mayonesa** *fem*

**mayor** NOUN
el **alcalde** *masc*
la **alcaldesa** *fem*

**maze** NOUN
el **laberinto** *masc*

**me** PRONOUN
**1 me**
**Do you love me?**
¿Me quieres?
**Can you help me?**
¿Me puedes ayudar?
**Wait for me!**
¡Espérame!
**Are you looking for me?**
¿Me estás buscando?
**Can you give it to me?**
¿Me lo puedes dar?
**He wants to talk to me.**
Quiere hablar conmigo.
**2 mí**

*Language tip*
*Use* **mí** *after a preposition.*

**Is it for me?**
¿Es para mí?
**You're after me.**
Tú vas detrás de mí.

*Language tip*
*Remember that* **with me** *translates as* **conmigo.**

**He was with me.**
Estaba conmigo.
**3 yo**

*Language tip*
*Use* **yo** *after the verb* **ser.**

**It's me.**
Soy yo.

*Language tip*
*Use* **yo** *in comparisons.*

**He's taller than me.**
Es más alto que yo.

**It's me.**
Soy yo.
**Me too.**
Yo también.
**Excuse me!**
¡Perdóname!

**meal** NOUN
la **comida** *fem*

**mean**

**mean** *can be a verb or an adjective.*

**A** VERB
**to mean**
**significar**
**What does 'complete' mean?**
¿Qué significa 'complete'?
**I don't know what it means.**
No sé lo que significa.
**What do you mean?**
¿Qué quieres decir?
**That's not what I mean.**
Eso no es lo que quiero decir.

**What does it mean?**
¿Qué significa?

**B** ADJECTIVE
**1 tacaño** *masc*
**tacaña** *fem (with money)*
**He's too mean to buy presents.**

463

Es demasiado tacaño para comprar regalos.
**2 mezquino** *masc*
**mezquina** *fem (unkind)*
**You're being mean to me.**
Estás siendo mezquina conmigo.

**meaning** NOUN
el **significado** *masc*

**measles** NOUN
el **sarampión** *masc*

to **measure** VERB
**medir**
**Measure the length.**
Medid la longitud.

**meat** NOUN
la **carne** *fem*
**I don't eat meat.**
No como carne.

**Mecca** NOUN
**La Meca** *fem*

**mechanic** NOUN
el **mecánico** *masc*
la **mecánica** *fem*
**He's a mechanic.**
Es mecánico.

---

*Language tip*

*In Spanish, you do not use an article with people's jobs.*

---

**medal** NOUN
la **medalla** *fem*
**the gold medal**
la medalla de oro

**medical**

---

**medical** *can be an adjective or a noun.*

---

**A** ADJECTIVE
**She's a medical student.**
Es estudiante de medicina.
**B** NOUN
**You have to have a medical.**
Necesitas hacerte una revisión médica.

**medicine** NOUN
la **medicina** *masc*
**What's this medicine for?**
¿Para qué es esta medicina?
**I want to study medicine.**
Quiero estudiar medicina.

**Mediterranean** NOUN
**the Mediterranean**
el Mediterráneo *masc*

**medium** ADJECTIVE
**mediano** *masc*
**mediana** *fem*
**a man of medium height**
un hombre de estatura mediana
**Small, medium or large?**
¿Pequeño, mediano o grande?

**medium-sized** ADJECTIVE
**de tamaño medio**
**a medium-sized town**
una ciudad de tamaño medio

to **meet** VERB
**1 encontrarse con** *(by chance)*
**I met Paul in town.**
Me encontré con Paul en el centro.
**2** *(by arrangement)*
**I'm meeting my friends at the swimming pool.**
He quedado con mis amigos en la piscina.
**Let's meet in front of the tourist office.**
¿Por qué no quedamos delante de la oficina de turismo?
**3 conocer** *(get to know)*
**He met Tim at a party.**
Conoció a Tim en una fiesta.

---

*Language tip*

*Don't forget the personal* **a** *after* **conocer** *when you name the person.*

---

**Have you met Amy?**
¿Conoces a Amy?
**Where did you two meet?**
¿Dónde os conocisteis vosotros dos?

**4 recoger** *(pick up)*
**I'll meet you at the station.**
Te recogeré en la estación.

**meeting** NOUN
la **reunión** *fem* (PL las reuniones)
**their first meeting**
su primera reunión

**melon** NOUN
el **melón** *masc* (PL los melones)

to **melt** VERB
**derretirse**
**The snow is melting.**
La nieve se está derritiendo.

**member**
NOUN
el **socio** *masc*
la **socia** *fem*
**a member of our club**
un socio de nuestro club

**memory** NOUN
1 la **memoria** *fem* (for facts, words)
**I haven't got a good memory.**
No tengo buena memoria.
2 el **recuerdo** *masc* (of past)
**some happy memories**
algunos recuerdos felices

**men** PL NOUN
los **hombres** *masc pl*

to **mend** VERB
**arreglar**
**Can you mend it?**
¿Puedes arreglarlo?

to **mention** VERB
**Thank you! - Don't mention it!**
¡Gracias! - ¡De nada!

**menu** NOUN
1 la **carta** *fem* (in restaurant)
**Could I have the menu please?**

¿Me trae la carta por favor?
2 el **menú** *masc* (on computer)

**merry** ADJECTIVE

**Merry Christmas!**
¡Feliz Navidad!

*Language tip*

Have you noticed the upside-down exclamation mark at the start of Spanish exclamations?

**merry-go-round** NOUN
el **tiovivo** *masc*

**mess** NOUN
el **desorden** *masc*
**What a mess!**
¡Qué desorden!
**My bedroom's in a mess.**
Mi habitación está desordenada.

**message** NOUN
el **mensaje** *masc*

**met** VERB ▷ see **meet**

**metal** NOUN
el **metal** *masc*

**method** NOUN
el **método** *masc*

**metre** NOUN
el **metro** *masc*
**I can swim two hundred metres.**
Puedo nadar doscientos metros.
**I'm one metre thirty tall.**
Mido un metro treinta.

**metric** ADJECTIVE
**métrico** *masc*
**métrica** *fem*

**mice** PL NOUN
los **ratones** *masc pl*

**microphone** NOUN
el **micrófono** *masc*

**microscope** NOUN
el **microscopio** *masc*

**microwave** NOUN
el **microondas** *masc* (PL los microondas)

**midday** NOUN
el **mediodía** *masc*
**It's midday.**
Es mediodía.

**at midday**
al mediodía

*Language tip*
*Even though it ends in* -a, **el mediodía**, *like* **día**, *is a masculine noun.*

**middle** NOUN
el **centro** *masc*
**Come into the middle, Andrew.**
Ven al centro, Andrew.
**in the middle of the road**
en medio de la carretera
**in the middle of the night**
en mitad de la noche

**middle-aged** ADJECTIVE
de mediana edad
**a middle-aged man**
un hombre de mediana edad

**middle name** NOUN
el **segundo nombre** *masc*
**It's my middle name.**
Es mi segundo nombre.

**midge** NOUN
el **mosquito** *masc*

**midnight** NOUN
la **medianoche** *fem*
**It's midnight.**
Es medianoche.

**at midnight**
a medianoche

**might** VERB
**I might, I might not.**
Puede que sí, puede que no.

*Language tip*
*Literally,* **puede que sí, puede que no** *means 'maybe, maybe not'.*

**It might rain.**
Puede que llueva.

**migraine** NOUN
la **jaqueca** *fem*
**I've got a migraine.**
Tengo jaqueca.

**mild** ADJECTIVE
**suave** *masc & fem*
**The winters are quite mild.**
Los inviernos son bastante suaves.
**It's mild today.**
No hace mucho frío hoy.

**mile** NOUN
la **milla** *fem*
**It's five miles from here.**
Está a cinco millas de aquí.
**We walked miles!**
¡Caminamos durante kilómetros!

*Did you know...?*
*In Spain distances are measured in kilometres. A mile is about 1.6 kilometres.*

**milk** NOUN
la **leche** *fem*
**tea with milk**
té con leche

**milkman**
NOUN
el **lechero** *masc*

*Language tip*
*In Spanish, you do not use an article with people's jobs.*

**milk shake** NOUN
el **batido** *masc*

**millimetre** NOUN
el **milímetro** *masc*

**million** NOUN
el **millón** *masc* (PL los **millones**)
  **a million times**
  un millón de veces
  **two million**
  dos millones

**millionaire** NOUN
el **millonario** *masc*
la **millonaria** *fem*

**mince** NOUN
la **carne picada** *fem*

> *Did you know...?*
> **Mince pies** *are not eaten in Spain.*

**mind**

> *mind can be a verb or a noun.*

**A** VERB
  **to mind: Do you mind if I**
  **open the window?**
  ¿Le importa si abro la ventana?
  **Mind the step!**
  ¡Cuidado con el escalón!

> **I don't mind.**
> No me importa.
> **Never mind!**
> ¡No importa!

**B** NOUN
  **I've changed my mind.**
  He cambiado de idea.
  **Make your mind up!**
  ¡Decídete ya!

**mine**

> *mine can be a pronoun or a noun.*

**A** PRONOUN
  el **mío** *masc*
  la **mía** *fem*

> *Language tip*
> *Remember that the choice of* **el**
> **mío, la mía, los míos** *or* **las mías**

depends entirely on the thing or
things referred to and not on the
person who owns it or them.

  **That's not my coat. Mine is**
  **here.**
  Ése no es mi abrigo. El mío está
  aquí.
  **Those aren't my boots. Mine**
  **are here.**
  Ésas no son mis botas. Las mías
  están aquí.

> *Language tip*
> *After* **ser**, *you can often just use*
> **mío, mía, míos** *or* **mías** *to agree*
> *with the noun referred to.*

  **This scarf is mine.**
  Esta bufanda es mía.
  **These books are mine.**
  Estos libros son míos.

**a friend of mine**
una amigo mío
**It's mine.**
Es mío.

**B** NOUN
  la **mina** *fem*
  **a coal mine**
  una mina de carbón

**mineral water** NOUN
el **agua mineral** *fem*
  **A mineral water for me,**
  **please.**
  Para mí un agua mineral.

> *Language tip*
> *Even though it's a feminine noun,*
> *remember that you use* **el** *and* **un**
> *with* **agua**.

**English Spanish**

a b c d e f g h i j k l **m** n o p q r s t u v w x y z

**minibus** NOUN
el **microbús** masc (PL los microbuses)

**minimum** ADJECTIVE
**mínimo** masc
**mínima** fem

**miniskirt** NOUN
la **minifalda** fem

**minister** NOUN
1 el **ministro** masc
la **ministra** fem (in government)
2 el **pastor** masc
la **pastora** fem (in church)

**minor** ADJECTIVE
**de poca importancia**
**a minor problem**
un problema de poca importancia
**a minor injury**
una herida leve

**mint** NOUN
1 el **caramelo de menta** masc (sweet)

2 la **hierbabuena** fem (plant)
**mint sauce**
salsa con hierbabuena

**minus** PREPOSITION
**menos**
**Seventeen minus three is fourteen.**
Diecisiete menos tres son catorce.
**It's minus two degrees outside.**
Fuera hace dos grados bajo cero.

**minute** NOUN
el **minuto** masc
**Wait a minute!**
¡Espera un minuto!

**mirror** NOUN
el **espejo** masc

to **misbehave** VERB
**portarse mal**
**She's misbehaving.**
Se está portando mal.
**Don't misbehave, Patrick!**
¡No te portes mal, Patrick!

**mischief** NOUN
las **travesuras** fem pl
**My little sister's always up to mischief.**
Mi hermana pequeña siempre está haciendo travesuras.

**miserable** ADJECTIVE
1 **muy triste** masc & fem (person)
**You're looking miserable.**
Pareces muy triste.
2 **deprimente** masc & fem (weather)
**The weather was miserable.**
El tiempo fue deprimente.

**Miss** NOUN
1 la **señorita** fem
**Yes, Miss.**
Sí, señorita.
2 **Srta.** (in addresses)
**Miss Jones**
Srta. Jones

**Language tip**
*Don't forget the dot at the end of Spanish abbreviations.*

to **miss** VERB
1 **perder**
**Hurry or you'll miss the bus.**
Date prisa o perderás el autobús.
**Miss a turn.**
Pierde un turno.
2 **echar de menos** (long for)
**I miss you.**

Te echo de menos.
**He misses his family.**
Echa de menos a su familia.

> **Language tip**
>
> *Don't forget the personal **a** in examples like this one.*

**missing** ADJECTIVE
**perdido** *masc*
**perdida** *fem*
**the missing piece**
la pieza perdida *fem*
**to be missing**
faltar
**My rucksack is missing.**
Falta mi mochila.
**Two children are missing.**
Faltan dos niños.

**mist** NOUN
la **neblina** *fem*

**mistake** NOUN
el **error** *masc*
**She only made two mistakes.**
Solo cometió dos errores.
**a spelling mistake**
una falta de ortografía
**by mistake**
por error
**I took his bag by mistake.**
Cogí su bolso por error.

**mistletoe** NOUN
el **muérdago** *masc*

**misty** ADJECTIVE
**de neblina**
**a misty morning**
una mañana de neblina

> **It's misty.**
> Hay neblina.

to **mix** VERB
**mezclar**
**Mix the flour with the sugar.**
Mezclar la harina con el azúcar.

to **mix up** VERB
**confundir**
**He always mixes me up with my sister.**
Siempre me confunde con mi hermana.

**mixed** ADJECTIVE
**mixto** *masc*
**mixta** *fem*
**a mixed school**
un colegio mixto

**mixture** NOUN
la **mezcla** *fem*

**mix-up** NOUN
el **lío** *masc*

**mobile** NOUN
el **móvil** *masc*
**I haven't got a mobile.**
No tengo móvil.

**mobile phone** NOUN
el **teléfono móvil** *masc*
**Have you got a mobile phone?**
¿Tienes teléfono móvil?

## model

> **model** *can be a noun or an adjective.*

**A** NOUN
**1** la **maqueta** *fem (small version)*
**I'm making a model of the castle.**
Estoy haciendo una maqueta del castillo.
**2** el/la **modelo** *masc/fem (person)*
**She's a famous model.**
Es una modelo famosa.
**B** ADJECTIVE
**a model plane**
una maqueta de avión

**a model railway**
una vía férrea en miniatura

**modern** ADJECTIVE
**moderno** *masc*
**moderna** *fem*

**moment** NOUN
el **momento** *masc*
**Wait a moment, Mike.**
Espera un momento, Mike.
**Could you wait a moment?**
¿Puedes esperar un momento?
**in a moment**
dentro de un momento
**I'm a bit busy at the moment.**
Estoy algo ocupado en este momento.

**Just a moment!**
¡Un momento!
**at the moment**
en este momento

**Monday** NOUN
el **lunes** *masc*
**It's Monday today.**
Hoy es lunes.

**on Monday**
el lunes
**on Mondays**
los lunes
**every Monday**
cada lunes
**last Monday**
el lunes pasado
**next Monday**
el lunes que viene

*Language tip*
*Days are not spelled with a capital letter in Spanish.*

**money** NOUN
el **dinero** *masc*
**I haven't got enough money.**
No tengo suficiente dinero.
**I need to change some money.**
Necesito cambiar dinero.

**monk** NOUN
el **monje** *masc*

**monkey** NOUN
el **mono** *masc*

**monster** NOUN
el **monstruo** *masc*

**month** NOUN
el **mes** *masc*
**two months**
dos meses
**at the end of the month**
a final de mes

**this month**
este mes
**next month**
el mes que viene
**last month**
el mes pasado
**every month**
cada mes
**What month is it?**
¿Qué mes es?

**monument** NOUN
el **monumento** *masc*

**mood** NOUN
el **humor** *masc*
**She's in a bad mood.**
Está de mal humor.
**He's in a good mood.**
Está de buen humor.

**moon** NOUN
la **luna** *fem*
**the moon and the stars**
la luna y las estrellas

**English Spanish**

**moped** NOUN
el **ciclomotor** *masc*

**more** ADVERB, ADJECTIVE, PRONOUN
**más**
  **more difficult**
  más difícil
  **Could you speak more slowly?**
  ¿Puedes hablar más despacio?
  **There are more girls in the class.**
  Hay más chicas en la clase.
  **Do you want some more tea?**
  ¿Quieres más té?
  **Would you like some more, Luke?**
  ¿Quieres más, Luke?
  **There isn't any more.**
  Ya no queda más.
  **Two more minutes!**
  ¡Dos minutos más!

*Language tip*
*You normally translate* **more than** *using* **más que**.

  **more than me**
  más que yo
  **He's more intelligent than me.**
  Es más inteligente que yo.
  **more than that**
  más que eso

*Language tip*
*Use* **más de** *instead before numbers.*

  **I've got more than fifty euros.**
  Tengo más de cincuenta euros.

**a bit more**
un poco más
**more ... than**
más ... que

**morning** NOUN
la **mañana** *fem*
  **on Saturday morning**
  el sábado por la mañana

**all morning**
toda la mañana
**Are they staying all morning?**
¿Se quedan toda la mañana?

**this morning**
esta mañana
**tomorrow morning**
mañana por la mañana
**yesterday morning**
ayer por la mañana
**every morning**
todas las mañanas
**at seven o'clock in the morning**
a las siete de la mañana

**mosque** NOUN
la **mezquita** *fem*

**mosquito** NOUN
el **mosquito** *masc*
  **a mosquito bite**
  una picadura de mosquito

**most** ADVERB, ADJECTIVE, PRONOUN

*Language tip*
*When* **most** *goes with an adjective or verb, it usually translates as* **más**.

  **the most expensive restaurant**
  el restaurante más caro
  **the most expensive restaurants**
  los restaurantes más caros
  **Stephen talks the most.**
  Stephen es el que más habla.
  **He got the most votes.**
  Fue él que sacó más votos.

*Language tip*
*You can usually use* **la mayoría de** *to translate* **most of** *with a plural noun.*

  **most of my friends**
  la mayoría de mis amigos
  **most of them**
  la mayoría
  **most Spanish people**
  la mayoría de los españoles

a b c d e f g h i j k l **m** n o p q r s t u v w x y z

**471**

**Language tip**

*Use* **la mayor parte de** *to translate* **most of** *with a singular noun.*

**most of the time**
la mayor parte del tiempo
**most of the class**
la mayor parte de la clase
**at the most**
como máximo
**two hours at the most**
dos horas como máximo

**motel** NOUN
el **motel** *masc*

**moth** NOUN
la **mariposa nocturna** *fem*

**mother** NOUN
la **madre** *fem*
**my mother**
mi madre
**your mother**
tu madre
**my mother and father**
mis padres

**Mother's Day** NOUN
el **día de la Madre**
**It's Mother's Day on Sunday.**
El domingo es el día de la Madre.

**Happy Mother's Day!**
¡Feliz día de la Madre!

**Language tip**

*Have you noticed the upside-down exclamation mark at the start of Spanish exclamations?*

**motor** NOUN
el **motor** *masc*

**motorbike** NOUN
la **moto** *fem*

**Language tip**

*Even though it ends in* **-o**, **la moto** *is a feminine noun.*

**motorboat** NOUN
la **lancha motora** *fem*

**motorcycle** NOUN
la **motocicleta** *fem*

**motorcyclist** NOUN
el/la **motociclista** *masc/fem*

**motorist** NOUN
el/la **automovilista** *masc/fem*

**motorway** NOUN
la **autopista** *fem*
**on the motorway**
en la autopista

**mountain** NOUN
la **montaña** *fem*

**mountain bike** NOUN
la **bicicleta de montaña** *fem*

**mouse** NOUN
el **ratón** *masc* (PL los **ratones**)

**mouse mat** NOUN
la **alfombrilla del ratón** *fem*

**mousse** NOUN
la **mousse** *fem*
**chocolate mousse**
la mousse de chocolate

**moustache** NOUN
el **bigote** *masc*
**He's got a moustache.**
Tiene bigote.

**mouth** NOUN
la **boca** *fem*
**Open your mouth.**
Abre la boca.

> **Language tip**
> In Spanish you usually use an article like **el**, **la**, **los** with parts of the body.

**move**

> **move** *can be a noun or a verb.*

**A** NOUN
el **turno** *masc*
**It's your move.**
Es tu turno.
**Get a move on, Sebastian!**
¡Muévete, Sebastian!
**B** VERB
to move
**1** **mover** *(object)*
**Could you move your stuff please?**
¿Puedes mover tus cosas, por favor?
**2** **moverse** *(change position)*
**Don't move!**
¡No te muevas!
**You moved!**
¡Te has movido!
**Move forward two spaces!**
¡Adelanta dos casillas!

to **move over** VERB
**correrse**
**Could you move over a bit?**
¿Puedes correrte un poco?

**movement** NOUN
el **movimiento** *masc*

**MP** NOUN
el **diputado** *masc*
la **diputada** *fem*

**She's an MP.**
Es diputada.

> **Language tip**
> In Spanish, you do not use an article with people's jobs.

**MP3** NOUN
el **MP3**
**an MP3 player**
un reproductor de MP3

**Mr** NOUN
**1** el **señor** *masc*
**Good morning, Mr Jones.**
¡Buenos días, señor Jones!
**Mr Jones wants to see you.**
El señor Jones quiere verte.
**Mr and Mrs Carrasco are here.**
Los señores Carrasco están aquí.
**2** **Sr.** *(in addresses)*
**Mr Silvestre**
Sr. Silvestre
**Mr and Mrs Ruiz**
Srs. Ruiz

> **Language tip**
> Don't forget the dot at the end of Spanish abbreviations.

**Mrs** NOUN
**1** la **señora** *fem*
**Good morning, Mrs Jones.**
¡Buenos días, señora Jones!
**Mrs Jones wants to see you.**
La señora Jones quiere verte.
**2** **Sra.** *(in addresses)*
**Mrs Silvestre**
Sra. Silvestre

> **Language tip**
> Don't forget the dot at the end of Spanish abbreviations.

**Ms** NOUN
**1** la **señora** *fem*
**Ms Smith is here.**
La señora Smith está aquí.
**2** **Sra.** *(in addresses)*

> **Did you know..?**
> There isn't a specific word for **Ms** in Spanish. Just use **Sra.**

**English Spanish**

a
b
c
d
e
f
g
h
i
j
k
l
**m**
n
o
p
q
r
s
t
u
v
w
x
y
z

**much** ADJECTIVE, ADVERB, PRONOUN
**mucho** *masc*
**mucha** *fem*
  **not much**
  no mucho
  **I haven't got much money.**
  No tengo mucho dinero.
  **I don't want very much milk.**
  No quiero mucha leche.
  **I don't like sport much.**
  No me gusta mucho el deporte.
  **I don't want much.**
  No quiero mucho.
  **I like England very much.**
  Me gusta muchísimo Inglaterra.
  **How much?**
  ¿Cuánto?
  **How much money have you got?**
  ¿Cuánto dinero tienes?
  **How much jam is left?**
  ¿Cuánta mermelada queda?

### Language tip

*Don't forget the accent on question words like* **cuánto** *nor the upside-down question mark at the start of questions.*

  **How much does it cost?**
  ¿Cuánto cuesta?
  **How much do you want?**
  ¿Cuánto quieres?
  **How much is it all together?**
  ¿Cuánto es todo junto?
  **It costs too much.**
  Cuesta demasiado.
  **That's too much!**
  ¡Eso es demasiado!
  **too much butter**
  demasiada mantequilla

**How much?**
¿Cuánto?
**not much**
no mucho
**too much**
demasiado
**Thank you very much.**
Muchas gracias.

**mud** NOUN
el **barro** *masc*

**muddy** ADJECTIVE
**cubierto de barro** *masc*
**cubierta de barro** *fem*

**mug** NOUN
el **tazón** *masc* (PL los **tazones**)
  **Do you want a cup or a mug?**
  ¿Quieres una taza o un tazón?

to **multiply** VERB
**multiplicar**
  **Multiply six by three.**
  Multiplica seis por tres.
  **Two multiplied by three is six.**
  Dos multiplicado por tres son seis.

**mum** NOUN
1 la **madre** *fem*
  **my mum**
  mi madre
  **my mum and dad**
  mis padres
2 la **mamá** *fem* (used as name)
  **Hi, Mum.**
  Hola, mamá.
  **I'll ask Mum.**
  Se lo preguntaré a mamá.

**mummy** NOUN
la **mamá** *fem*
  **Hello, Mummy!**
  ¡Hola, mamá!

**mumps** NOUN
las **paperas** *fem pl*
  **Teresa has got mumps.**
  Teresa tiene paperas.

**murder** NOUN
el **asesinato** *masc*

**muscle** NOUN
el **músculo** *masc*

**museum** NOUN
el **museo** *masc*

**mushroom** NOUN
1 el **champiñón** *masc* (PL los
champiñones) *(button
mushroom)*

2 la **seta** *fem* *(open-cup
mushroom)*

**music** NOUN
la **música** *fem*
**I like listening to music.**
Me gusta escuchar música.

**musical instrument**
NOUN
el **instrumento musical** *masc*
**Can you play a musical
instrument?**
¿Sabes tocar algún instrumento
musical?

**musician** NOUN
el **músico** *masc*
la **música** *fem*

**Muslim** NOUN
el **musulmán** *masc* (PL los
musulmanes)
la **musulmana** *fem*
**He's a Muslim.**
Es musulmán.

### Language tip
*Remember that **musulmán** is not
spelled with a capital letter in
Spanish.*

**mussel** NOUN
el **mejillón** *masc* (PL los
mejillones)

**must** VERB
1 **tener que** *(have to)*
**You must be careful, Edward.**

Tienes que tener cuidado,
Edward.
**You must listen, children.**
Tenéis que escuchar, niños.
2 **deber de** *(in guesses)*
**You must be tired.**
Debes de estar cansado.

**mustard** NOUN
la **mostaza** *fem*

**mustn't** (= must not) ▷ *see*
must

**my** ADJECTIVE
**mi** *masc & fem* (PL **mis**)

### Language tip
*Remember to use **mi** before a
singular noun and **mis** before a
plural one.*

**my father**
mi padre
**my friend Alicia**
mi amiga Alicia
**my parents**
mis padres

### Language tip
*In Spanish you usually use an article
like **el**, **la**, **los** with parts of the body
and clothes.*

**I wash my face in the
morning.**
Me lavo la cara por las mañanas.
**I'm going to wear my shorts
today.**
Voy a llevar los pantalones
cortos hoy.

**myself** PRONOUN
1 **me** *(reflexive use)*
**I've hurt myself.**
Me he hecho daño.
**I like to look at myself in the
mirror.**
Me gusta
mirarme en
el espejo.

English Spanish

a
b
c
d
e
f
g
h
i
j
k
l
m
n
o
p
q
r
s
t
u
v
w
x
y
z

**I'm enjoying myself.**
Me estoy divirtiendo.
**2 mí** *(after preposition)*
**I'll tell you about myself.**
Te contaré sobre mí.
**3 yo mismo** *(for emphasis)*
**I made it myself.**
Lo hice yo mismo.
**by myself**
solo

**I don't like travelling by myself.**
No me gusta viajar solo.

**mysterious** ADJECTIVE
**misterioso** *masc*
**misteriosa** *fem*

**mystery** NOUN
el **misterio** *masc*

# N n

**nail** NOUN
  1 la **uña** *fem (fingernail)*
  **Don't bite your nails!**
  ¡No te muerdas las uñas!

### Language tip
*In Spanish you usually use an article like* **el**, **la**, **los** *with parts of the body.*

  2 el **clavo** *masc (for hammering)*

**nailfile** NOUN
  la **lima de uñas** *fem*

**nail varnish** NOUN
  el **esmalte de uñas** *masc*

**naked** ADJECTIVE
  **desnudo** *masc*
  **desnuda** *fem*

**name** NOUN
  el **nombre** *masc*
  **a pretty name**
  un nombre bonito
  **What's your dog's name?**
  ¿Cómo se llama tu perro?
  **His name's Max.**
  Se llama Max.

  **What's your name?**
  ¿Cómo te llamas?
  **My name is Ruth.**
  Me llamo Ruth.

**nanny** NOUN
  la **niñera** *fem*
  **She's a nanny.**
  Es niñera.

### Language tip
*In Spanish, you do not use an article with people's jobs.*

**napkin** NOUN
  la **servilleta** *fem*

**narrow** ADJECTIVE
  **estrecho** *masc*
  **estrecha** *fem*

**a narrow street**
una calle estrecha

**nasty** ADJECTIVE
  **malo** *masc*
  **mala** *fem*
  **Don't be nasty!**
  ¡No seas malo!

### Language tip
*Shorten* **malo** *to* **mal** *before a masculine singular noun.*

  **a nasty smell**
  un mal olor
  **a nasty cold**
  un resfriado terrible
  **He's a nasty man.**
  Es un hombre con mala idea.

**nationality** NOUN
  la **nacionalidad** *fem*

**natural** ADJECTIVE
  **natural** *masc & fem*

**nature** NOUN
  la **naturaleza** *fem*

**naughty** ADJECTIVE
  **travieso** *masc*
  **traviesa** *fem*
  **Naughty girl!**
  ¡Qué chica más traviesa!

**Don't be naughty!**
¡No seas malo!

**navy** NOUN
la **armada** fem
**He's in the navy.**
Está en la armada.

## navy-blue

**navy-blue** can be an adjective or a noun.

**A** ADJECTIVE
**azul marino**

*Language tip*
**azul marino** never changes its endings to agree with the noun it describes.

**a navy-blue skirt**
una falda azul marino
**B** NOUN
el **azul marino** masc

## near

**near** can be an adverb, adjective or preposition.

**A** ADVERB, ADJECTIVE
**1 cerca**

*Language tip*
Use **cerca** when saying that something or someone is near. As it's an adverb, it never changes its ending.

**It's fairly near.**
Está bastante cerca.
**2 cercano** masc
**cercana** fem

*Language tip*
Use the adjective **cercano**, **cercana**, etc in noun phrases.

**the nearest village**
el pueblo más cercano
**Where's the nearest service station?**
¿Dónde está la gasolinera más cercana?

**The nearest shops are three kilometres away.**
Las tiendas más cercanas están a tres kilómetros.
**B** PREPOSITION
**cerca de** (close to)
**I live near Liverpool.**
Vivo cerca de Liverpool.
**near my house**
cerca de mi casa
**near here**
cerca de aquí
**Is there a bank near here?**
¿Hay un banco cerca de aquí?

*Language tip*
Another way of saying **near here** is **por aquí cerca**.

**Is there a supermarket near here?**
¿Hay un supermercado por aquí cerca?

**nearby** ADVERB
**cerca**
**There's a supermarket nearby.**
Hay un supermercado cerca.

**nearly** ADVERB
**casi**
**Dinner's nearly ready.**
La cena está casi lista.
**I'm nearly ten.**
Tengo casi diez años.

**neat** ADJECTIVE
**1 ordenado** masc
**ordenada** fem (room, desk)
**a neat room**
una habitación ordenada
**2 claro** masc
**clara** fem (writing)
**She has very neat writing.**
Tiene una letra muy clara.

**necessary** ADJECTIVE
**necesario** masc
**necesaria** fem

**neck** NOUN
el **cuello** masc

I've hurt my neck.
Me he hecho daño en el cuello.

### Language tip
*In Spanish you usually use an article like* **el**, **la**, **los** *with parts of the body.*

**necklace** NOUN
el **collar** *masc*
**a diamond necklace**
un collar de diamantes

to **need** VERB
**necesitar**
**I need a rubber.**
Necesito una goma de borrar.
**to need to**
tener que
**I need to wash the dishes.**
Tengo que fregar los platos.

**needle** NOUN
la **aguja** *fem*

**neighbour** NOUN
el **vecino** *masc*
la **vecina** *fem*
**the neighbours' garden**
el jardín de los vecinos

**neighbourhood** NOUN
el **barrio** *masc*

**neither** PRONOUN, CONJUNCTION, ADVERB
**ni una cosa ni otra**
**Carrots or peas? – Neither, thanks.**
¿Zanahorias o guisantes? –
Ni una cosa ni otra, gracias.
**neither ... nor ...**
ni ... ni ...
**Neither Sarah nor Julia is coming to the party.**
Ni Sarah ni Julia vienen a la fiesta.

**Neither do I.**
Yo tampoco.
**Neither have I.**
Yo tampoco.

**nephew** NOUN
el **sobrino** *masc*
**her nephew**
su sobrino

**nerve** NOUN
el **nervio** *masc*
**She gets on my nerves.**
Me pone de los nervios.

**nervous** ADJECTIVE
**nervioso** *masc*
**nerviosa** *fem*
**I bite my nails when I'm nervous.**
Cuando estoy nervioso me muerdo las uñas.

**Net** NOUN
**the Net**
Internet
**I like to surf the Net.**
Me gusta navegar por Internet.

**netball** NOUN

### Did you know...?
**Netball** *is not played in Spain. The most similar game played there is* **el baloncesto** *or* **basketball**.

**never** ADVERB
**nunca**
**When are you going to phone him? – Never!**
¿Cuándo vas a te efonearle? –
¡Nunca!
**I never go to the cinema.**
Nunca voy al cine.
**We never see them.**
No los vemos nunca.

**Language tip**
*Don't forget to put **no** before the verb when putting **nunca** after it.*

**new** ADJECTIVE
**nuevo** *masc*
**nueva** *fem*

**Language tip**
*When **new** means **brand-new**, you usually put **nuevo** after the noun.*

    **a new skirt**
    una falda nueva

**Language tip**
*When **new** means **replacement** rather than **brand-new**, you usually put **nuevo** before the noun.*

    **her new boyfriend**
    su nuevo novio

**news** NOUN
**1** la **noticia** *fem*

**Language tip**
*Use **noticia** in the singular when you're referring to a single piece of news.*

    **That's wonderful news!**
    ¡Eso es una noticia estupenda!
**2** las **noticias** *fem pl*

**Language tip**
*Use **noticias** in the plural when you're referring to more than one piece of news or to a news bulletin.*

    **It was on the news.**
    Salió en las noticias.

**newsagent's** NOUN
la **tienda de periódicos**

**Did you know...?**
*In Spain you'll come across **kioscos**, newsstands on the street which sell newspapers, magazines and other items.*

**newspaper** NOUN
el **periódico** *masc*

**New Year** NOUN
    **New Year's Day**
    el Día de
    Año Nuevo
    **New Year's Eve**
    la Nochevieja

**Happy New Year!**
¡Feliz Año Nuevo!

**Did you know...?**
*In Spain, it's traditional to see the New Year in by eating **doce uvas** (twelve grapes) for good luck as the clock strikes midnight.*

## next

*next can be an adjective or adverb.*

**A** ADJECTIVE
**1** **próximo** *masc*
    **próxima** *fem (in sequence)*
    **the next time**
    la próxima vez
    **Who's next?**
    ¿A quién le toca?
    **I'm next.**
    Me toca a mí.
**2** **que viene** *(coming)*
    **next Saturday**
    el sábado que viene

**next year**
el año que viene
**next week**
la semana que viene
**next summer**
el verano que viene

**3** **They live next door.**
    Viven al lado.
    **the flat next door**
    el piso de al lado

**B** ADVERB

**1 después** *(afterwards)*
**What shall I do next?**
¿Qué hago después?

**2 next to**
**al lado de**
**It's next to the bank.**
Está al lado del banco.
**I sit next to my friend.**
Me siento al lado de mi amigo.

**next-door** ADJECTIVE
**de al lado**
**the next-door flat**
el piso de al lado

**nice** ADJECTIVE

**1 simpático** *masc*
**simpática** *fem (friendly)*
**Your parents are very nice.**
Tus padres son muy simpáticos.

**2 amable** *masc & fem (kind)*
**She was always very nice to me.**
Siempre fue muy amable conmigo.

**3 bonito** *(pretty)*
**Granada is a nice town.**
Granada es una ciudad bonita.
**What a nice dress!**
¡Qué vestido más bonito!

**4 bueno** *(good)*
**The soup is very nice.**
La sopa está muy buena.

**Language tip**

*Shorten* **bueno** *to* **buen** *before a masculine singular noun.*

**nice weather**
buen tiempo

**Have a nice time!**
Que te diviertas!
**It's a nice day.**
Hace buen día.

**niece** NOUN
a **sobrina** *fem*
**his niece**
su sobrina

**night** NOUN
la **noche** *fem*
**I want a room for two nights.**
Quiero una habitación para dos noches.
**We arrived last night.**
Llegamos anoche.

**last night**
anoche
**tomorrow night**
mañana por la noche

**nightie** NOUN
el **camisón** *masc* (PL los **camisones**)

**nightmare** NOUN
la **pesadilla** *fem*
**I have nightmares.**
Tengo pesadillas.

**nil** NOUN
el **cero** *masc*
**We won two-nil.**
Ganamos dos a cero.

**nine** NUMBER
**nueve**
**nine euros**
nueve euros

**She's nine.**
Tiene nueve años.

**Language tip**

*In English you can say* **she's nine** *or* **she's nine years old**. *In Spanish you can only say* **tiene nueve años**. *Have you noticed that in Spanish you need to use the verb* **tener** *to talk about somebody's age?*

### nineteen NUMBER
**diecinueve**
> **nineteen euros**
> diecinueve euros

> **She's nineteen.**
> Tiene diecinueve años.

#### Language tip
*In English you can say **she's nineteen** or **she's nineteen years old**. In Spanish you can only say **tiene diecinueve años**. Have you noticed that in Spanish you need to use the verb **tener** to talk about somebody's age?*

### nineteenth NUMBER
**diecinueve**
> **on the nineteenth floor**
> en la planta diecinueve
> **We break up on the nineteenth of December.**
> Empezamos las vacaciones el diecinueve de diciembre.
> **It's the nineteenth of February today.**
> Hoy es diecinueve de febrebro.

> **on the nineteenth of August**
> el diecinueve de agosto

#### Language tip
*Use the same set of numbers that you use for counting (**uno**, **dos**, **tres** and so on) when giving Spanish dates.*

### ninety NUMBER
**noventa**
> **My gran is ninety.**
> Mi abuela tiene noventa años.

#### Language tip
*In English you can say **he's ninety** or **he's ninety years old**. In Spanish you can only say **tiene noventa años**. Have you noticed that in Spanish you need to use the verb **tener** to talk about somebody's age?*

### ninth NUMBER
**noveno** *masc*
**novena** *fem*
> **on the ninth floor**
> en la planta novena
> **My birthday's the ninth of April.**
> Mi cumpleaños es el nueve de abril.
> **It's the ninth of July today.**
> Hoy es nueve de julio.

> **on the ninth of February**
> el nueve de febrero

#### Language tip
*Use the same set of numbers that you use for counting (**uno**, **dos**, **tres** and so on) when giving Spanish dates.*

### no

> *no can be an adverb or an adjective.*

**A** ADVERB
**no**
> **Are you coming? – No, I'm not.**
> ¿Vienes? – No.
> **Can you swim? – No, I can't.**
> ¿Sabes nadar? – No.

**B** ADJECTIVE
> **There are no trains on Sundays.**
> No hay trenes los domingos.
> **'no smoking'**
> 'prohibido fumar'

### nobody PRONOUN
**nadie**
> **Who's going with you? – Nobody.**
> ¿Quién va contigo? – Nadie.

**Nobody saw me.**
Nadie me vio.
**Nobody came.**
Nadie vino.

**There's nobody in the
classroom.**
No hay nadie en la clase.

to **nod** VERB
**decir que sí con la cabeza**

**noise** NOUN
el **ruido** *masc*
**Please make less noise.**
Por favor, haced menos ruido.

**noisy** ADJECTIVE
**ruidoso** *masc*
**ruidosa** *fem*
**the noisiest city in the world**
la ciudad más ruidosa del mundo

**none** PRONOUN
**1 ninguno** *masc*
**ninguna** *fem*

**How many girls? – None.**
¿Cuántas chicas? – Ninguna.
**None of these pens work.**
No funciona ninguno de estos
bolígrafos.
**There are none left.**
No queda ninguno.

**2 nada**

**milk**, *Spanish uses* **nada**, *which is
also singular. Don't forget to put* **no**
*before the verb when putting* **nada**
*after it.*

**There's none left.**
No queda nada.

**nonsense** NOUN
las **tonterías** *fem pl*
**She talks a lot of nonsense.**
Dice muchas tonterías.

**noodles** PL NOUN
los **fideos** *masc pl*

**noon** NOUN
las **doce del mediodía** *fem pl*
**It's noon.**
Son las doce del mediodía.

**no one** PRONOUN
**nadie**
**Who's going with you? –
No one.**
¿Quién va contigo? – Nadie.
**No one saw me.**
Nadie me vio.
**No one came.**
Nadie vino.

**There's no one in the
classroom.**
No hay nadie en la clase.

**nor** CONJUNCTION
**neither ... nor**
ni ... ni
**neither Jack nor Jimmy**
ni Jack ni Jimmy

**normal** ADJECTIVE
**normal** *masc & fem*
　**at the normal time**
　a la hora normal

## north

> **north** *can be an adjective or a noun.*

**A** ADJECTIVE
**norte**

### Language tip

**norte** *never changes its ending no matter what it describes. Did you know that adjectives that behave like this are called 'invariable adjectives'?*

　**the north coast**
　la costa norte
**B** NOUN
　el **norte** *masc*
　**in the north**
　en el norte

## Northern Ireland NOUN
**Irlanda del Norte** *fem*
　**in Northern Ireland**
　en Irlanda del Norte
　**to Northern Ireland**
　a Irlanda del Norte
　**I'm from Northern Ireland.**
　Soy de Irlanda del Norte.

## North Pole NOUN
el **Polo Norte** *masc*

## North Sea NOUN
el **mar del Norte** *masc*

**nose** NOUN
la **nariz** *fem*
　(PL las **narices**)
　**My nose is blocked.**
　Tengo la nariz tapada.

### Language tip

*In Spanish you usually use an article like* **el**, **la**, **los** *with parts of the body.*

**nosy** ADJECTIVE
**curioso** *masc*
**curiosa** *fem*

**not** ADVERB
**no**
　**Are you coming or not?**
　¿Vienes o no?
　**It's not raining.**
　No está lloviendo.
　**I don't like cheese.**
　No me gusta el queso.
　**He can't drive.**
　No sabe conducir.
　**Sit down everybody! Not you, June.**
　¡Sentaos todos! Tú no, June.
　**Have you finished? – Not yet.**
　¿Has terminado? – Todavía no.

> **not yet**
> todavía no
> **not you**
> tú no
> **Thank you! – Not at all!**
> ¡Gracias! – ¡De nada!

**note** NOUN
**1** la **nota** *fem (message)*
　**I'll write her a note.**
　Le escribiré una nota.
**2** el **billete** *masc (banknote)*

**notebook** NOUN
el **cuaderno** *masc*

**notepad** NOUN
el **bloc** *masc* (PL los **blocs**)

**notepaper** NOUN
el **papel de cartas** *masc*

**nothing** PRONOUN
**nada**
　**What's wrong? – Nothing.**
　¿Qué pasa? – Nada.

### Language tip

*Don't forget to put* **no** *before the verb when putting* **nada** *after it.*

　**Nothing's the matter.**
　No pasa nada.

He does nothing.
No hace nada.

## notice

notice *can be a noun or a verb.*

**A** NOUN
el **anuncio** *masc*

### Language tip
*Be careful! The translation of* **notice** *is not* **noticia**.

**B** VERB
**to notice**
**darse cuenta de**
**Don't worry, he won't notice anything.**
No te preocupes. No se dará cuenta de nada.

**notice board** NOUN
el **tablón de anuncios** *masc*
(PL los **tablones de anuncios**)

**noun** NOUN
el **sustantivo** *masc*

**novel** NOUN
la **novela** *fem*

**November** NOUN
**noviembre** *masc*
**My birthday's in November.**
Mi cumpleaños es en noviembre.
**It's the eleventh of November today.**
Hoy es once de noviembre.

**in November**
en noviembre
**on the fifth of November**
el cinco de noviembre

### Language tip
*Months are not spelled with a capital letter in Spanish.*

**now** ADVERB
**ahora**
**What are you doing now?**
¿Qué estás haciendo ahora?

I'm rather busy just now.
Estoy bastante ocupado en este momento.

**not now**
ahora no
**just now**
en este momento
**now and then**
de vez en cuando
**from now on**
de ahora en adelante

**nowhere** ADVERB
**a ningún sitio**
**Where did you go? - Nowhere.**
¿Dónde fuiste? - A ningún sitio.
**There's nowhere to go in the evenings.**
No hay ningún sitio adonde ir por la noche.

**number** NOUN
1 el **número** *masc* (of house, telephone)
**They live at number five.**
Viven en el número cinco.
**What's your phone number?**
¿Cuál es tu número de teléfono?
2 la **cantidad** *fem* (of people, things)
**a large number of people**
una gran cantidad de personas
3 la **cifra** *fem* (figure)
**the second number**
la segunda cifra

**nun** NOUN
la **monja** *fem*

**nurse** NOUN
el **enfermero** *masc*
la **enfermera** *fem*
**I want to be a nurse.**
Quiero ser enfermera.

### Language tip
*In Spanish, you do not use an article with people's jobs.*

**nursery** NOUN
   la **guardería** fem
      **My sister goes to nursery.**
      Mi hermana va a la guardería.

**nursery school** NOUN
   la **escuela infantil** fem
      **My little sister goes to
      nursery school.**
      Mi hermana pequeña va a la
      escuela infantil.

**nut** NOUN
   el **fruto seco** masc
      **I like nuts.**
      Me gustan los frutos secos.
      **a bowl of nuts**
      un cuenco de frutos secos

# O o

**oats** PL NOUN
la **avena** *fem*

> *Language tip*
> **avena** *is a singular word.*

**obedient** ADJECTIVE
**obediente** *masc & fem*

to **obey** VERB
**cumplir**
You must obey the rules of the game.
Tienes que cumplir las reglas del juego.

**object** NOUN
el **objeto** *masc*

**obstacle** NOUN
el **obstáculo** *masc*

**obvious** ADJECTIVE
**evidente** *masc & fem*
That's obvious!
¡Eso es evidente!

**occasion** NOUN
la **ocasión** *fem* (PL las ocasiones)
a special occasion
una ocasión especial
on several occasions
en varias ocasiones

**occasionally** ADVERB
**de vez en cuando**

**occupation** NOUN
la **ocupación** *fem* (PL las ocupaciones)

**ocean** NOUN
el **océano** *masc*
the Atlantic Ocean
el océano Atlántico
the Pacific Ocean
el océano Pacífico

> *Language tip*
> **océano** *is not spelled with a capital letter in names of oceans.*

**o'clock** ADVERB
at four o'clock
a las cuatro

It's one o'clock.
Es la una.
It's five o'clock.
Son las cinco.

**October** NOUN
**octubre** *masc*
My birthday's in October.
Mi cumpleaños es en octubre.
It's the eleventh of October today.
Hoy es once de octubre.

in October
en octubre
on the fifth of October
el cinco de octubre

> *Language tip*
> *Months are not spelled with a capital letter in Spanish.*

**odd** ADJECTIVE
1 **raro** *masc*
**rara** *fem* (strange)
That's odd!
¡Eso es raro!
2 **impar** *masc & fem* (not even)
an odd number
un número impar

**of** PREPOSITION
**de**
a bottle of water
una botella de agua
a kilo of oranges
un kilo de naranjas
a boy of ten
un niño de diez años

**the end of the film**
el final de la película

> **Language tip**
> de *combines with* el *to form* del.

**a photo of the school**
una foto del colegio
**Do you want some of them?**
¿Quieres algunos de ellos?
**a friend of mine**
un amigo mío
**That's very kind of you.**
Eso es muy amable de tu parte.
**There are three of us.**
Somos tres.
**There are seven of them.**
Son siete.

## off

> **off** *can be an adjective, preposition or adverb.*

**A** ADJECTIVE
1 **apagado** *masc*
  **apagada** *fem (switched off)*
  **The light is off.**
  La luz está apagada.
2 **cerrado** *masc*
  **cerrada** *fem (turned off)*
  **Is the tap off?**
  ¿Está cerrado el grifo?
3 *(cancelled)*
  **The match is off.**
  El partido se ha cancelado.
4 *(absent)*
  **He's off today.**
  Hoy no ha venido.
  **Dad's got the day off tomorrow.**
  Papá no trabaja mañana.
5 *(not available)*
  **The soup's off.**
  No hay sopa.
6 *(milk)*
  **The milk's off.**
  La leche está cortada.
**B** PREPOSITION
  **He's off school.**
  No ha ido al colegio./
  No ha venido al colegio.

> **Language tip**
> **he's off school** *has two translations depending on whether he hasn't gone to school or he hasn't come to school. Look at the examples.*

**David's upstairs, he's off school today.**
David está arriba, hoy no ha ido al colegio.
**Ryan isn't here, he's off school today.**
Ryan no está aquí, hoy no ha venido al colegio.
**C** ADVERB
  **Off you go, Jack!**
  ¡Hala Jack, vete!

## offer

> **offer** *can be a verb or a noun.*

**A** VERB
  **to offer**
  ofrecer
  **Can you offer Teresa something to drink?**
  ¿Puedes ofrecerle a Teresa algo de beber?
**B** NOUN
  la **oferta** *fem*
  **There's a special offer on dictionaries.**
  Hay una oferta especial de diccionarios.

## office NOUN
la **oficina** *fem*
  **She works in an office.**
  Trabaja en una oficina.

## often ADVERB
a menudo

**We often go to London.**
Vamos a menudo a Londres.
**It often rains.**
Llueve a menudo.

How often do you clean your teeth?
¿Con qué frecuencia te lavas los dientes?

**oil** NOUN
el **aceite** masc

**OK** EXCLAMATION, ADJECTIVE
= okay

## okay

okay can be an exclamation or an adjective.

A EXCLAMATION
**¡de acuerdo!**
**I'll go tomorrow. - Okay!**
Iré mañana. - ¡De acuerdo!
B ADJECTIVE
**bien**

*Language tip*
bien never changes its ending.

**I'm okay thanks.**
Estoy bien, gracias.
**Is everything okay?**
¿Está todo bien?
**Do you like school? - It's okay.**
¿Te gusta el colegio? - No está mal.
**Is that okay with you?**
¿Estás de acuerdo con eso?

**Okay!**
¡De acuerdo!
**Are you okay?**
¿Estás bien?

**old** ADJECTIVE
**viejo** masc
**vieja** fem
**an old dog**
un perro viejo
**an old house**
una casa vieja
**old shoes**
zapatos viejos

*Language tip*
It sounds more polite if you describe someone as **mayor** rather than **viejo**.

**an old man**
un hombre mayor
**an old lady**
una señora mayor
**old people**
los mayores

*Language tip*
**mayor** can also mean **older** or **oldest** while **mayor que** means **older than**.

**my older sister**
mi hermana mayor
**my oldest brother**
mi hermano mayor
**Damian's the oldest in the class.**
Damian es el mayor de la clase.
**I'm older than you.**
Soy mayor que tú.
**She's two years older than me.**
Ella tiene dos años más que yo.

**How old are you?**
¿Cuántos años tienes?
**He's ten years old.**
Tiene diez años.

**old age pensioner** NOUN
el **jubilado** masc
la **jubilada** fem
**She's an old age pensioner.**
Ella está jubilada.

**Olympic** ADJECTIVE
**olímpico** masc
**olímpica** fem
**the Olympic Games**
los Juegos Olímpicos

**omelette** NOUN
la **tortilla** fem

## on

on can be an adjective or a preposition.

A ADJECTIVE
1 **encendido** masc
**encendida** fem (switched on)
**The light is on.**
La luz está encendida.

**2 abierto**
**abierta** *(tap)*
**The tap is on.**
El grifo está abierto.

**B** PREPOSITION
**1 en**
**Your books are on the table.**
Tus libros están en la mesa.
**on the wall**
en la pared
**I go to school on my bike.**
Voy al colegio en bici.
**Is there anything on television?**
¿Hay algo en la televisión?
**I'm on the phone.**
Estoy hablando por teléfono.
**2 sobre** *(about)*
**a book on Ghandi**
un libro sobre Ghandi
**3** *(with days and dates)*

> *Language tip*
> *Just give* **el** *with a particular day or date.*

**on Monday**
el lunes
**on the fifteenth of June**
el quince de junio

> *Language tip*
> *To say* **on Sundays**, **on Tuesdays**, *and so on, use* **los**.

**on Sundays**
los domingos
**on Tuesdays**
los martes
**4** *(in expressions)*
**It's on the right.**
Está a la derecha.
**They're on holiday.**
Están de vacaciones.

**on Friday**
el viernes
**on Fridays**
los viernes
**on June 20th**
el 20 de junio
**on Christmas Day**
el día de Navidad
**on holiday**
de vacaciones
**on the left**
a la izquierda

**once** ADVERB
una **vez**
**once a week**
una vez por semana
**only once**
solo una vez
**Come here at once!**
¡Ven aquí enseguida!
**Everybody answered at once.**
Todo el mundo contestó a la vez.
**once more**
otra vez

**one** NUMBER, PRONOUN
**1 un** *masc (before noun)*
**una** *fem*

> *Language tip*
> *Use* **un** *before a masculine noun and* **una** *before a feminine noun.*

**one day**
un día
**one hour**
una hora
**I've got one brother and one sister.**
Tengo un hermano y una hermana.

> **She's one.**
> Tiene un año.

> *Language tip*
> *In English you can say* **she's one** *or* **she's one year old**. *In Spanish you can only say* **tiene un año**. *Have you noticed that in Spanish you need to use the verb* **tener** *to talk about somebody's age?*

English Spanish

a b c d e f g h i j k l m n o p q r s t u v w x y z

**2 uno** *masc (not before noun)*
**una** *fem*
**This sweater is too big, I need a smaller one.**
Este jersey es demasiado grande.
Necesito uno más pequeño.
**This T-shirt is too small, I need a bigger one.**
Esta camiseta es demasiado pequeña. Necesito una más grande.
**Which packet do you want? – The big one.**
¿Qué paquete quieres? – El grande.
**Which card do you want? – The red one.**
¿Qué carta quieres? – La roja.
**one, two, three, four, five ...**
uno, dos, tres, cuatro, cinco ...
**It's one o'clock.**
Es la una.

**onion** NOUN
la **cebolla** *fem*

## only

**only** *can be an adjective or an adverb.*

**A** ADJECTIVE
**único** *masc*
**única** *fem*
**my only dress**
mi único vestido
**my only clean T-shirt**
mi única camiseta limpia
**I'm an only child.**
Soy hijo único.
**Tracy is an only child.**
Tracy es hija única.
**B** ADVERB
**sólo**
**only ten euros**
sólo diez euros
**I've only got two cards.**

Sólo tengo dos cartas.
**He's only three.**
Sólo tiene tres años.

> ### Language tip
> Traditionally, the adverb **sólo** was written with an accent to distinguish it from the unaccented adjective **solo**, meaning 'alone'. Nowadays, you don't have to give the accent unless the sentence would be confusing otherwise

## open

**open** *can be an adjective or a verb.*

**A** ADJECTIVE
**abierto** *masc*
**abierta** *fem*
**The supermarket is open on Sunday mornings.**
El supermercado está abierto los domingos por la mañana.
**B** VERB
**to open**
**abrir**
**Can I open the window?**
¿Puedo abrir la ventana?
**Open your books.**
Abrid vuestros libros.
**What time does the bank open?**
¿A qué hora abre el banco?

## opening hours PL NOUN
el **horario de apertura** *masc*

## operation NOUN
la **operación** *fem* (PL las operaciones)
**He is recovering from an operation.**
Se está recuperando de una operación.
**My mum's going to have an operation.**
Van a operar a mi madre.

## opinion NOUN
la **opinión** *fem* (PL las opiniones)
**in my opinion**
en mi opinión

English Spanish

a b c d e f g h i j k l m n o p q r s t u v w x y z

491

**What's your opinion?**
¿Tú qué opinas?

**opponent** NOUN
el **adversario** *masc*
la **adversaria** *fem*

**opportunity** NOUN
la **oportunidad** *fem*
**It's a good opportunity.**
Es una buena oportunidad.

## opposite

> **opposite** *can be an adjective, noun, adverb or preposition.*

**A** ADJECTIVE
**contrario** *masc*
**contraria** *fem*
**It's in the opposite direction.**
Está en la dirección contraria.

**B** NOUN
**the opposite**
lo contrario
**the opposite of good**
lo contrario de bueno

**C** ADVERB
**enfrente**
**They live opposite.**
Viven enfrente.

**D** PREPOSITION
**enfrente de**
**the girl sitting opposite me**
la niña que está sentada
enfrente de mí

**or** CONJUNCTION
**1 o**
**Would you like tea or coffee?**
¿Quieres té o café?

**Hurry up or you'll miss the bus.**
Date prisa o perderás el autobús.

> ***Language tip***
> *Change* **o** *to* **u** *before words starting with* **o-** *or* **ho-**.

**seven or eight**
siete u ocho
**men or women**
mujeres u hombres
**2 ni** *(in negatives)*
**I don't eat meat or fish.**
No como carne ni pescado.

**oral** NOUN
el **examen oral** *masc* (PL los **exámenes orales**)
**I've got my Spanish oral soon.**
Tengo mi examen oral de español pronto.

## orange

> **orange** *can be a noun or an adjective.*

**A** NOUN
**1** la **naranja** *fem (fruit)*
**a big orange**
una naranja grande
**2** el **naranja** *masc (colour)*
**Orange is my favourite colour.**
El naranja es mi color favorito.

> ***Language tip***
> *When it means the colour* **orange**, **el naranja**, *like all colours in Spanish, is masculine.*

**B** ADJECTIVE
**naranja**

> ***Language tip***
> *The colour* **naranja** *never changes its ending no matter what it describes. Don't forget that colour adjectives come after the noun in Spanish.*

**orange curtains**
cortinas naranja

**orange juice** NOUN
el **zumo de naranja** masc

**orchestra** NOUN
la **orquesta** fem
**I play in the school orchestra.**
Toco en la orquesta del colegio.

**order**

> order can be a noun or a verb.

**A** NOUN
**1** el **orden** masc (sequence)
**Put the words in alphabetical order, children.**
Poned las palabras en orden alfabético, niños.
**The words are not in the right order.**
Las palabras no están en el orden correcto.
**2** (in restaurant)
**The waiter took our order.**
El camarero tomó nota de lo que queríamos.
**3** la **orden** fem (PL las **órdenes**) (command)

> **'out of order'**
> 'no funciona'

**B** VERB
**to order**
pedir
**Are you ready to order?**
¿Ya saben lo que van a pedir?

**ordinary** ADJECTIVE
**normal** masc & fem
**an ordinary day**
un día normal

to **organize** VERB
organizar
**We are organizing a trip to London.**
Estamos organizando un viaje a Londres.

**original** ADJECTIVE

**original** masc & fem
**It's a very original idea.**
Es una idea muy original.

**orphan** NOUN
el **huérfano** masc
la **huérfana** fem

**other**

> other can be an adjective or a pronoun.

**A** ADJECTIVE
**otro** masc
**otra** fem
**on the other side of the street**
al otro lado de la calle
**the other day**
el otro día

> **Language tip**
> The translation of **the other one** depends on whether you're referring to something masculine or feminine. Use **el otro** for something masculine and **la otra** for something feminine.

**This knife? – No, the other one.**
¿Este cuchillo? – No, el otro.
**This spoon? – No, the other one.**
¿Esta cuchara? – No, la otra.

**B** PRONOUN
el **otro** masc
la **otra** fem
**Get into twos, one behind the other.**
Poneos de dos en dos, uno detrás del otro.
**Where are the others?**
¿Dónde están los otros?

**ought** VERB

> **Language tip**
> To translate **ought to** you need to use the conditional tense of the verb **deber**.

**I ought to phone my parents.**
Debería llamar a mis padres.

**our** ADJECTIVE
**nuestro** *masc*
**nuestra** *fem*
  **our dog**
  nuestro perro
  **our house**
  nuestra casa
  **our friends**
  nuestros amigos
  **our plants**
  nuestras plantas

### Language tip
*You usually translate **our** using **el**, **la**, etc before parts of the body or clothes, particularly when using a reflexive verb.*

  **We took off our coats.**
  Nos quitamos los abrigos.

**ours** PRONOUN
el **nuestro** *masc*
la **nuestra** *fem*

### Language tip
*Remember that the choice of **el nuestro**, **la nuestra**, **los nuestros** or **las nuestras** depends entirely on the thing or things referred to.*

  **That's not our car. Ours is here.**
  Aquél no es nuestro coche. El nuestro está aquí.
  **Those aren't our backpacks. Ours are here.**
  Aquéllas no son nuestras mochilas. Las nuestras están aquí.

### Language tip
*After **ser** you can usually just use **nuestro**, **nuestra**, **nuestros** or **nuestras** to agree with the noun referred to.*

  **Is this ours?**
  ¿Es nuestro esto?
  **These cases are ours.**
  Estas maletas son nuestras.
  **Whose is this? – It's ours.**

¿De quién es esto? – Es nuestro.

**ourselves** PRONOUN
1 **nos** *(reflexive)*
  **We enjoyed ourselves.**
  Nos divertimos.
2 **nosotros mismos** *masc pl*
  **nosotras mismas** *fem pl*
  *(for emphasis)*
  **We did it ourselves!**
  ¡Lo hicimos nosotros mismos!
  **by ourselves**
  solos
  **We want to do it by ourselves.**
  Queremos hacerlo solos.

**out**

*out can be an adverb or an adjective.*

**A** ADVERB
1 **fuera** *(not at home)*
  **Derek's out.**
  Derek está fuera.
  **I'm going out.**
  Voy a salir.
  **He was coming out of the cinema.**
  Estaba saliendo del cine.
  **Can you get the paints out of the cupboard?**
  ¿Puedes sacar las pinturas del armario?
2 **eliminado** *masc*
  **eliminada** *fem (in game)*

### Language tip
**eliminado** *is an adjective, so remember that it needs to agree with the person it refers to.*

  **You're out, Lucy!**
  ¡Estás eliminada, Lucy!

### 'way out'
'salida'

**B** ADJECTIVE
**apagado** *masc*
**apagada** *fem (turned off)*

**All the lights are out.**
Todas las luces están apagadas.

**outdoor** ADJECTIVE
**al aire libre**
**outdoor activities**
actividades al aire libre
**an outdoor swimming pool**
una piscina exterior

**outdoors** ADVERB
**al aire libre**

**outer space** NOUN
el **espacio** masc
**a monster from outer space**
un monstruo del espacio

**outside**

> **outside** can be an adverb or a preposition.

**A** ADVERB
**fuera**
**It's very cold outside.**
Hace mucho
frío fuera.
**B** PREPOSITION
**fuera de**
**outside**
**the school**
fuera del
colegio

**oven** NOUN
el **horno** masc

**over**

> **over** can be a preposition or an adjective.

**A** PREPOSITION
**1 más de** (more than)
**There were over five hundred people at the concert.**
Había más de quinientas personas en el concierto.
**Are you over ten?**
¿Tienes más de diez años?
**The temperature is over thirty degrees.**
La temperatura supera los

treinta grados.
**2 durante** (during)
**over Christmas**
durante la Navidad
**3 al otro lado de** (across)
**The baker's is over the road.**
La panadería está al otro lado de la calle.
**4 encima de** (above)
**There's a mirror over the washbasin.**
Encima del lavabo hay un espejo.

> **Language tip**
> Use **por encima de** instead when there is movement **over** something.

**The ball went over the wall.**
La pelota pasó por encima del muro.
**a bridge over the river**
un puente sobre el río

> **over here**
> aquí
> **over there**
> allí
> **all over Scotland**
> por toda Escocia

**B** ADJECTIVE (finished)
**The match is over.**
Se ha terminado el partido.

**overcast** ADJECTIVE
**cubierto** masc
**cubierta** fem
**The sky was overcast.**
El cielo estaba cubierto.

**overhead projector** NOUN
el **retroproyector** masc

to **owe** VERB
**deber**
**He owes me five pounds.**
Me debe cinco libras.

**owl** NOUN
el **búho** masc

**own** ADJECTIVE
**propio** masc
**propia** fem

> **I've got my own bathroom.**
> Tengo mi propio cuarto de baño.
> **I'd like a room of my own.**
> Quiero una habitación para mí solo.
> **He lives on his own.**
> Vive solo.

**on his own**
solo
**on her own**
sola

**owner** NOUN
el **propietario** masc
la **propietaria** fem

# Pp

## pack

*pack can be a verb or a noun.*

**A** VERB
**to pack**
**hacer las maletas**
**I have to pack.**
Tengo que hacer las maletas.
**B** NOUN
1 el **pack** *masc (of goods)*
**a pack of six**
un pack de seis
2 el **paquete** *masc (packet)*
3 la **baraja** *fem (of cards)*
**a pack of cards**
una baraja de cartas

## packed lunch NOUN
**I take a packed lunch to school.**
Me llevo la comida al colegio.

## packet NOUN
el **paquete** *masc*
**a packet of crisps**
una bolsa de patatas fritas

## page NOUN
la **página** *fem*
**on page ten**
en la página diez
**Look at page six, everyone.**
Mirad todos en la página seis.

## paid VERB ▷*see* pay

## pain NOUN
1 el **dolor** *masc*
**a terrible pain**
un dolor horrible
2 **to be a pain**
ser un pesado
**He's a pain.**
Es un pesado.

### Language tip
*Change* **un pesado** *to* **una pesada** *if you're referring to a girl.*

**My little sister is a pain.**
Mi hermana pequeña es una pesada.

## paint

*paint can be a noun or a verb.*

**A** NOUN
la **pintura** *fem*
**red paint**
pintura roja
**'wet paint'**
'recién pintado'
**B** VERB
**to paint**
**pintar**
**I'm going to paint it green.**
Lo voy a pintar de verde.

## paintbrush NOUN
1 el **pincel** *masc (for artwork)*
2 la **brocha** *fem (for walls, ceiling)*

## painting NOUN
1 el **cuadro** *masc (picture)*
**a painting by Picasso**
un cuadro de Picasso
2 la **pintura** *fem (activity)*
**I like painting.**
Me gusta la pintura.

## pair NOUN
el **par** *masc*
**a pair of shoes**
un par de zapatos
**a pair of trousers**
unos pantalones
**two pairs of trousers**
dos pantalones
**a pair of jeans**
unos vaqueros
**in pairs**
por parejas
**We work in pairs.**
Trabajamos por parejas.

**Can you get into pairs?**
¿Podéis colocaros por parejas?

**pal** NOUN
el **amigo** masc
la **amiga** fem

**palace** NOUN
el **palacio** masc

**pale** ADJECTIVE
1 **pálido** masc
**pálida** fem
**She looks very pale.**
Está muy pálida.
2 **claro** masc
**clara** fem (in colour)
**pale blue**
azul claro
**a pale blue shirt**
una camisa azul claro

### Language tip
*When you describe something as* **pale blue**, **pale green** *and so on, neither the colour nor* **claro** *changes its ending to agree with the noun.*

**some pale green curtains**
unas cortinas verde claro

**pan** NOUN
1 la **cacerola** fem (saucepan)
2 la **sartén** fem (PL las **sartenes**)
(frying pan)

**pancake** NOUN
la **tortita** fem

**Pancake Day** NOUN
el **Martes de Carnaval** masc

### Did you know…?
*During the week before Lent, all over Spain and Latin America there are fiestas and fancy-dress parades,*

*with the main celebrations taking place on* **Martes de Carnaval** *(literally Carnival Tuesday).*

to **panic** VERB
**Don't panic!**
¡Tranquilo!

### Language tip
*Change* ¡**Tranquilo!** *to* ¡**Tranquila!** *if talking to a woman or girl.*

**pantomime** NOUN
la **pantomima navideña** fem

### Did you know…?
*There are no pantomime traditions in Spain.*

**pants** PL NOUN
1 los **calzoncillos** masc pl
(for men, boys)
**a pair of pants**
unos calzoncillos
2 las **braguitas** fem pl
(for women, girls)
**a pair of pants**
unas braguitas

**paper** NOUN
1 el **papel** masc
**Have you got a pencil and some paper?**
¿Tienes lápiz y papel?
**a paper towel**
una servilleta
de papel
**a piece of paper**
un papel
2 el **periódico**
masc (newspaper)

**paper boy**
NOUN
el **repartidor**
**de periódicos** masc

**paper girl** NOUN
la **repartidora de**
**periódicos** fem

**parade** NOUN
el **desfile** masc

**paragraph** NOUN
el **párrafo** *masc*

**parcel** NOUN
el **paquete** *masc*

**pardon** NOUN
**Pardon?**
¿Cómo?

**parents** PL NOUN
los **padres** *masc pl*
**my parents**
mis padres

> **Language tip**
> Be careful! The translation of
> **parents** is not **parientes**.

**park**

> **park** can be a noun or a verb.

**A** NOUN
el **parque** *masc*
**There's a nice park.**
Hay un parque bonito.
**B** VERB
**to park**
aparcar
**It's difficult to park.**
Es difícil aparcar.

**parking** NOUN
**'no parking'**
'prohibido
aparcar'

**parrot** NOUN
el **loro** *masc*

**part** NOUN
1 la **parte** *fem*
**The first part is easy.**
La primera parte es fácil.
2 **to take part in something**
participar en algo
**I'm taking part in the
competition.**
Participo en el concurso.

**partly** ADVERB
**en parte**

**partner** NOUN

1 el **compañero** *masc*
la **compañera** *fem* (in game,
role play)
2 la **pareja** *fem* (in dance,
relationship)

> **Language tip**
> Even though **la pareja** is a feminine
> word, you can use it to refer to a
> man.

**part-time** ADJECTIVE, ADVERB
**a tiempo parcial**
**a part-time job**
un trabajo a tiempo parcial
**She works part-time.**
Trabaja a tiempo parcial.

**party** NOUN
la **fiesta** *fem*
**I'm going to a party on
Saturday.**
Voy a una fiesta el sábado.
**a birthday party**
una fiesta de cumpleaños
**a Christmas party**
una fiesta de Navidad

to **pass** VERB
1 **pasar** (give)
**Pass the ball, Nina!**
¡Pasa la pelota, Nina!
**Could you pass me the salt?**
¿Me puedes pasar la sal?
2 **pasar por delante de**
(go past)
**You pass the post office.**
Pasas por delante de Correos.

**passenger** NOUN
el **pasajero** *masc*
la **pasajera** *fem*

**Passover** NOUN
la **Pascua Judía** *fem*
**at Passover**
en la Pascua Judía

**passport** NOUN
el **pasaporte** *masc*
**Have you got your passport?**
¿Llevas tu pasaporte?

English Spanish

a
b
c
d
e
f
g
h
i
j
k
l
m
n
o
**p**
q
r
s
t
u
v
w
x
y
z

**password** NOUN
la **contraseña** *fem*

**past**

> **past** *can be a preposition or a noun.*

**A** PREPOSITION
**1 después de** *(after)*
It's on the right, just past the station.
Está a la derecha, justo después de la estación.
**2** *(with times)*
It's quarter past one.
Es la una y cuarto.
It's half past ten.
Son las diez y media.
It's quarter past nine.
Son las nueve y cuarto.
It's ten past eight.
Son las ocho y diez.
at ten past five
a las cinco y diez

> **half past eight**
> las ocho y media
> **quarter past ten**
> las diez y cuarto

**B** NOUN
el **pasado** *masc*
in the past
en el pasado

**pasta** NOUN
la **pasta** *fem*
Pasta is easy to cook.
La pasta es fácil de cocinar.

**path** NOUN
**1** el **camino** *masc (in garden, town)*
Follow the path.
Sigue el camino.
**2** el **sendero** *masc (in woods)*

**patience** NOUN
la **paciencia** *fem*
He hasn't got much patience.
No tiene mucha paciencia.

**patient**

> **patient** *can be a noun or an adjective.*

**A** NOUN
el/la **paciente** *masc/fem*
**B** ADJECTIVE
**paciente** *masc & fem*
The teacher is very patient.
El maestro es muy paciente.
Be patient, Joshua.
Ten paciencia, Joshua.

**patio** NOUN
el **patio** *masc*

**pattern** NOUN
el **diseño** *masc*
a simple pattern
un diseño sencillo

**pause** NOUN
la **pausa** *fem*

**pavement**
NOUN
la **acera** *fem*
on the pavement
en la acera

**paw** NOUN
la **pata** *fem*

**pay**

> **pay** *can be a noun or a verb.*

**A** NOUN
la **paga** *fem*
What is the pay?
¿Cuánto es la paga?
**B** VERB
to pay
pagar
Who's going to pay?
¿Quién va a pagar?
Where do I pay?
¿Dónde pago?
to pay for something
pagar algo
I've paid for my ticket.
He pagado mi entrada.

**I paid ten euros for the book.**
Pagué diez euros por el libro.
**to pay attention**
prestar atención

**Pay attention, Hayley!**
¡Presta atención, Hayley!
**Pay attention, everybody!**
¡Prestad todos atención!

**PC** NOUN
el **PC** *masc*
**I have a PC at home.**
Tengo un PC en casa.

**PE** NOUN
la **educación física** *fem*
**We have PE twice a week.**
Tenemos educación física dos
veces por semana.

**pea** NOUN
el **guisante** *masc*
**a tin of peas**
una lata de guisantes

**peace** NOUN
la **paz** *fem*

**peach** NOUN
el **melocotón** *masc* (PL los
melocotones)
**a kilo of peaches**
un kilo de melocotones

**peanut** NOUN
el **cacahuete** *masc*
**a packet of peanuts**
un paquete de cacahuetes

**peanut butter** NOUN
la **mantequilla de
cacahuete** *fem*
**a peanut butter sandwich**
un bocadillo de mantequilla de
cacahuete

**pear** NOUN
la **pera** *fem*
**Which would you like, a pear
or an apple?**
¿Qué es lo que quieres: una pera
o una manzana?

**pebble** NOUN
el **guijarro** *masc*

**pedal** NOUN
el **pedal** *masc*

**peg** NOUN
1 el **gancho** *masc* (for coats)
2 la **pinza de la ropa** *fem*
(clothes peg)

**pen** NOUN
el **bolígrafo** *masc*
**Can I borrow your pen?**
¿Me dejas tu bolígrafo?

**pence** PL NOUN
los **peniques** *masc pl*

**pencil** NOUN
el **lápiz** *masc* (PL los **lápices**)
**in pencil**
a lápiz
**coloured pencils**
lápices de colores

**pencil case** NCUM
el **estuche** *masc*

**pencil sharpener** NOUN
el **sacapuntas** *masc* (PL los
sacapuntas)

**penfriend** NOUN
el **amigo por
correspondencia** *masc*
la **amiga por
correspondencia** *fem*
**I'm Emma, your English
penfriend.**
Soy Emma, tu amiga por
correspondencia inglesa.

**penknife** NOUN
la **navaja** *fem*

**penny** NOUN
el **penique** *masc*

**pensioner** NOUN
el/la **pensionista** *masc/fem*

**people** PL NOUN
1 la **gente** *fem*
**The people are nice.**

La gente es simpática.
**a lot of people**
mucha gente
**There are too many people here.**
Aquí hay demasiada gente.

*Language tip*

*Remember that **gente** is a singular word in Spanish.*

**2** las **personas** *fem pl (individuals)*
**Four people can play.**
Pueden jugar cuatro personas.
**How many people are there in your family?**
¿Cuántas personas forman tu familia?

*Language tip*

*In English you can say **tall people**, **rich people** etc. In Spanish you say the equivalent of **the tall**, **the rich** etc.*

**tall people**
los altos
**rich people**
los ricos
**Spanish people**
los españoles

**pepper** NOUN
**1** la **pimienta** *fem (spice)*
**Pass the pepper, please.**
Pásame la pimienta, por favor.
**2** el **pimiento** *masc (vegetable)*
**a red pepper**
un pimiento rojo

**per** PREPOSITION
por
**per day**
por día

**per cent** ADVERB
por ciento
**fifty per cent**
cincuenta por ciento

**perfect** ADJECTIVE
**perfecto** *masc*

**perfecta** *fem*
**Raquel speaks perfect English.**
Raquel habla un inglés perfecto.

**performance** NOUN
la **representación** *fem* (PL las representaciones)
**The performance starts at two o'clock.**
La representación empieza a las dos.

**perfume** NOUN
el **perfume** *masc*
**a bottle of perfume**
un frasco de perfume

**perhaps**
ADVERB
**a lo mejor**
**Perhaps he's ill.**
A lo mejor está enfermo.

**period** NOUN
el **periodo** *masc*
**the holiday period**
el periodo de vacaciones

**permission** NOUN
el **permiso** *masc*
**Have you got permission?**
¿Tienes permiso?

**person** NOUN
la **persona** *fem*
**She's a very nice person.**
Es una persona muy simpática.

**personality** NOUN
la **personalidad** *fem*

**pet** NOUN
la **mascota** *fem*
**Have you got a pet?**
¿Tienes alguna mascota?

**petrol** NOUN
la **gasolina** *fem*
**unleaded petrol**
gasolina sin plomo

**pet shop** NOUN
la **tienda de animales** *fem*

## phone

phone *can be a noun or a verb.*

**A** NOUN
el **teléfono** *masc*
**Where's the phone?**
¿Dónde está el teléfono?
**She's on the phone at the moment.**
Ahora mismo está al teléfono.
**Can I use the phone, please?**
¿Puedo llamar por teléfono, por favor?

**B** VERB
**to phone**
llamar
**I'll phone you tomorrow.**
Mañana te llamo.
**I have to phone my mum.**
Tengo que llamar a mi madre.
**Who are you phoning?**
¿A quién llamas?

**Language tip**
*Don't forget the personal **a** in examples like the last two.*

**phone box** NOUN
la **cabina telefónica** *fem*

**phone call** NOUN
la **llamada** *fem*
**She gets lots of phone calls.**
Recibe muchas llamadas.
**Can I make a phone call?**
¿Puedo hacer una llamada?

**phonecard** NOUN
la **tarjeta telefónica** *fem*

**phone number** NOUN
el **número de teléfono** *masc*
**What's your phone number?**
¿Cuál es tu número de teléfono?

**photo** NOUN
la **foto** *fem*
**This is a photo of my family.**
Ésta es una foto de mi familia.
**I want to take some photos.**
Quiero hacer unas fotos.
**I want to take a photo of you.**
Quiero hacerte una foto.

**Language tip**
*Even though it ends in -o, **la foto** is a feminine noun.*

**photocopier** NOUN
la **fotocopiadora** *fem*

## photocopy

photocopy *can be a noun or a verb.*

**A** NOUN
la **fotocopia** *fem*
**It's only a photocopy.**
Es solo una fotocopia.

**B** VERB
**to photocopy**
fotocopiar
**You can photocopy it.**
Puedes fotocopiarlo.

**photograph** NOUN
la **fotografía** *fem*

**physics** NOUN
la **física** *fem*
**She teaches physics.**
Ella da clases de física.

**pianist** NOUN
e /la **pianista** *masc/fem*

**piano** NOUN
el **piano** *masc*

**I play the piano.**
Toco el piano.
**I have piano lessons.**
Tomo clases de piano.

## pick

> pick *can be a noun or a verb.*

**A** NOUN
**Take your pick!**
¡Escoge el que quieras!
**B** VERB
**to pick**
**1 escoger** *(choose)*
**Pick a card, Murray!**
¡Escoge una carta, Murray!
**Pick three girls and three boys.**
Escoge a tres niños y tres niñas.

> **Language tip**
> Don't forget the personal **a** in examples like this one.

**2 coger** *(fruit, flowers)*
**I like picking strawberries.**
Me gusta coger fresas.

## to **pick up** VERB
**1 recoger** *(collect)*
**We can come to the airport to pick you up.**
Podemos ir al aeropuerto a recogerte.
**2 coger** *(take)*
**Pick up another card, William!**
¡Coge otra carta, William!

> **Language tip**
> Use **tomar** instead of **coger** if talking to someone from Latin America.

**3 aprender** *(learn)*
**I hope I'll pick up some Spanish.**
Espero aprender un poco de español.

## picnic NOUN
el **picnic** *masc*
**I like picnics.**

Me gustan los picnics.
**to have a picnic**
hacer un picnic
**We had a picnic on the beach.**
Hicimos un picnic en la playa.

## picture NOUN
**1** la **foto** *fem (photo)*
**This is a picture of my family.**
Ésta es una foto de mi familia.

> **Language tip**
> Even though it ends in **-o**, **la foto** is a feminine noun.

**2** el **cuadro** *masc (painting)*
**a famous picture**
un cuadro famoso
**3** el **dibujo** *masc (drawing)*
**I'll draw a picture.**
Haré un dibujo.
**Draw a picture of your pet, Lisa.**
Haz un dibujo de tu mascota, Lisa.
**4** la **ilustración** *fem* (PL las **ilustraciones**) *(illustration)*
**Look at the picture.**
Mira la ilustración.

## pie NOUN
la **tarta** *fem*
**an apple pie**
una tarta de manzana

## piece NOUN
el **trozo** *masc*
**A small piece, please.**
Un trozo pequeño, por favor.

## pierced ADJECTIVE
**I've got pierced ears.**
Tengo los agujeros hechos en las orejas.
**I want to get my ears pierced.**
Quiero hacerme los agujeros en las orejas.

> **Language tip**
> In Spanish you usually use an article like **el**, **la**, **los** with parts of the body.

**pig** NOUN
el **cerdo**
*masc*

**pigeon**
NOUN
la **paloma**
*fem*

**piggy bank** NOUN
la **hucha** *fem*

**pigtail** NOUN
la **trenza** *fem*
She's got pigtails.
Lleva trenzas.

**pile** NOUN
el **montón** *masc* (PL los montones)
a pile of books
un montón de libros

**pill** NOUN
la **píldora** *fem*

**pillow** NOUN
la **almohada** *fem*

**pilot** NOUN
el/la **piloto** *masc/fem*
She's a pilot.
Es piloto.

*Language tip*
*Even though* **piloto** *ends in* **-o**, *you can use it to refer to a woman. Remember that in Spanish, you do not use an article with people's jobs.*

**pineapple** NOUN
la **piña** *fem*

**pink**

pink *can be an adjective or a noun.*

**A** ADJECTIVE
**rosa**

*Language tip*
*The colour* **rosa** *never changes its ending no matter what it describes. Don't forget that colour adjectives come after the noun in Spanish.*

a pink dress
un vestido rosa
**B** NOUN
el **rosa** *masc*
Pink is my favourite colour.
El rosa es mi color favorito.

*Language tip*
*When it means the colour* **pink**, *el* **rosa**, *like all colours in Spanish, is masculine.*

**pint** NOUN
la **pinta** *fem*
a pint of milk
una pinta de leche

*Did you know...?*
*In Spain liquids are measured in litres and centilitres. A pint is about 0.6 litres.*

**pipe** NOUN
la **tubería** *fem* (for water)

**pirate** NOUN
el/la **pirata** *masc/fem*
a pirate DVD
un DVD pirata

**pitch** NOUN
el **campo** *masc*
a football pitch
un campo de fútbol

**pity** NOUN
What a pity she can't come!
¡Qué pena que no pueda venir!

What a pity!
¡Qué pena!

**pizza** NOUN
la **pizza** *fem*

**place** NOUN
el **sitio** *masc*
It's a quiet place.
Es un sitio tranquilo.
There are a lot of interesting places to visit.
Hay un montón de sitios interesantes que visitar.
Can I change places?

¿Puedo cambiarme de sitio?
**Carol, change places with Harry!**
¡Carol, cámbiate de sitio con Harry!

## plain ADJECTIVE
**liso** *masc*
**lisa** *fem (not patterned)*
**a plain grey fabric**
una tela gris lisa

## plain chocolate NOUN
el **chocolate amargo** *masc*

## plait NOUN
la **trenza** *fem*
**She wears her hair in a plait.**
Lleva el pelo recogido en una trenza.

### *Language tip*
*In Spanish you usually use an article like* **el**, **la**, **los** *with parts of the body.*

## plan

**plan** *can be a noun or a verb.*

**A** NOUN
1 el **plan** *masc*
**Have you got any plans for the holidays?**
¿Tienes planes para las vacaciones?
2 el **plano** *masc (map)*
**a plan of the school**
un plano del colegio
**B** VERB
**to plan**
**planear**
**We're planning a trip to the States.**
Estamos planeando hacer un viaje a Estados Unidos.

## plane NOUN
el **avión** *masc* (PL los **aviones**)
**by plane**
en avión

## plant NOUN
la **planta** *fem*

## plaster NOUN
la **tirita** *fem*

## plastic

**plastic** *can be a noun or an adjective.*

**A** NOUN
el **plástico** *masc*
**It's made of plastic.**
Es de plástico.
**B** ADJECTIVE
**de plástico**
**a plastic bag**
una bolsa de plástico

## plate NOUN
el **plato**
*masc*

## platform NOUN
el **andén** *masc* (PL los **andenes**)
**I'll wait for you on the platform, ok?**
Te espero en el andén, ¿vale?

### *Did you know...?*
*At railway stations in Spain, it is the track rather than the platform that's numbered.*

**on platform seven**
en la vía siete

## play

**play** *can be a verb or a noun.*

**A** VERB
**to play**
1 **jugar**
**He's playing with his friends.**
Está jugando con sus amigos.
2 **jugar a** *(sport, game)*
**I play football.**
Juego al fútbol.
**Can you play chess?**
¿Sabes jugar al ajedrez?

**3 tocar** *(instrument)*
**I play the guitar.**
Toco la guitarra.
**What sort of music do they play?**
¿Qué tipo de música tocan?
**4 poner** *(CD)*
**Why don't you play that CD that you like?**
¿Por qué no pones ese CD que te gusta?
**B** NOUN
la **obra** *fem*
**a play by Shakespeare**
una obra de Shakespeare

**player** NOUN
el **jugador** *masc*
la **jugadora** *fem*
**a football player**
un jugador de fútbol

**playground** NOUN
**1** el **patio de recreo** *masc* *(at school)*
**2** los **columpios** *masc pl* *(in park)*

**playgroup** NOUN
la **guardería** *fem*

**playing card** NOUN
la **carta** *fem*

**playing field** NOUN
el **campo de deportes** *masc*

**playtime** NOUN
el **recreo** *masc*
**at playtime**
en el recreo

**please** EXCLAMATION
por favor
**Two coffees, please.**
Dos cafés, por favor.

***Did you know...?***
*In Spanish you don't use* **por favor** *as often as you'd say* **please** *in English. Speakers often show politeness by phrasing requests as a question.*

**I'd like a lemonade, please.**
¿Me pone una gaseosa?
**Can we have the bill, please?**
¿Nos puede traer a cuenta?
**Can you open the door for me, please?**
¿Me puede abrir la puerta?

**Yes, please!**
¡Sí, por favor!

**pleased** ADJECTIVE
**contento** *masc*
**contenta** *fem*
**My mother isn't pleased.**
Mi madre no está contenta.

**pleasure** NOUN
el **gusto** *masc*
**with pleasure**
con mucho gusto

**plenty** NOUN
**I've got plenty.**
Tengo de sobra.
**You've got plenty of time.**
Tienes tiempo de sobra.

**That's plenty, thanks.**
Así está bien, gracias.

to **plug in** VERB
enchufar
**Is it plugged in?**
¿Está enchufado?
**It isn't plugged in.**
No está enchufado.

**plum** NOUN
la **ciruela** *fem*
**plum jam**
mermelada de ciruela

**plump** ADJECTIVE
**regordete** *masc & fem*

**plural** NOUN
el **plural** *masc*

**in the plural**
en plural

**plus** PREPOSITION
**más**
> **Four plus three equals seven.**
> Cuatro más tres son siete.

**p.m.** ABBREVIATION
1 **de la tarde** (in the afternoon or evening)
> **at two p.m.**
> a las dos de la tarde
2 **de la noche** (at night)
> **at ten p.m.**
> a las diez de la noche

### Language tip
Use **de la tarde** at times when it's still light and **de la noche** at times when it's dark.

**poached egg** NOUN
el **huevo escalfado** masc

**pocket** NOUN
el **bolsillo** masc
> **It's in my pocket.**
> Lo tengo en el bolsillo.

**pocket money** NOUN
la **paga** fem
> **I get two pounds a week pocket money.**
> Me dan dos libras a la semana de paga.

**poem** NOUN
el **poema** masc

### Language tip
Even though it ends in -a, **el poema** is a masculine noun.

**point**

### point can be a noun or a verb.

**A** NOUN
1 el **punto** masc
> **You've got five points.**
> Tienes cinco puntos.
> **What's the point?**
> ¿Para qué?

> **What's the point of leaving so early?**
> ¿Para qué vamos a salir tan pronto?
2 la **coma** fem (in decimals)
> **two point five (2.5)**
> dos coma cinco (2,5)

### Did you know...?
In Spanish you use a comma instead of a point in decimal numbers.

**B** VERB
> **to point: Which cake? Can you point to it?**
> ¿Qué pastel? ¿Puedes señalarlo?
> **The guide pointed out the Columbus monument to us.**
> El guía nos señaló dónde estaba el monumento a Colón.

**poison** NOUN
el **veneno** masc

**poisonous** ADJECTIVE
**venenoso** masc
**venenosa** fem
> **a poisonous snake**
> una serpiente venenosa

**police** PL NOUN
la **policía** fem
> **The police are usually very helpful.**
> La policía suele ser de mucha ayuda.

### Language tip
**policía** is a singular word in Spanish.

**police car** NOUN
el **coche de policía** masc

**policeman** NOUN
el **policía** masc
> **He's a policeman.**
> Es policía.

**Language tip**
In Spanish, you do not use an article with people's jobs.

**police station** NOUN
la **comisaría** fem

**policewoman** NOUN
la **policía** fem
  **She's a policewoman.**
  Es policía.

**Language tip**
In Spanish, you do not use an article with people's jobs.

**polite** ADJECTIVE
**educado** masc
**educada** fem
  **He's a very polite boy.**
  Es un chico muy educado.

**polluted** ADJECTIVE
**contaminado** masc
**contaminada** fem

**pollution** NOUN
la **contaminación** fem

**polo shirt** NOUN
el **polo** masc

**pond** NOUN
el **estanque** masc
  **There's a pond in our garden.**
  Hay un estanque en nuestro jardín.

**pony** NOUN
el **poney** masc (PL los **poneys**)

**ponytail** NOUN
la **cola de caballo** fem
  **I've got a ponytail.**
  Llevo una cola de caballo.

**pony trekking**
NOUN
  **I go pony trekking.**
  Voy de excursión en poney.

**pool** NOUN
1 la **piscina** fem (swimming pool)
  **There's a pool.**
  Hay una piscina.
2 el **billar** masc (game)
  **Can you play pool?**
  ¿Sabes jugar al billar?

**poor** ADJECTIVE
**pobre** masc & fem
  **They're very poor.**
  Son muy pobres.

**Language tip**
In noun phrases you put **pobre** before the noun when you mean **unlucky**.

  **Poor David, he's very unlucky!**
  ¡Pobre David, tiene muy mala suerte!

**Language tip**
You put **pobre** after the noun when you mean **not wealthy**.

  **a poor family**
  una familia pobre

**popcorn** NOUN
las **palomitas de maíz** fem

**Pope** NOUN
el **Papa** masc

**pop group** NOUN
el **grupo de pop** masc
  **What's your favourite pop group?**
  ¿Cuál es tu grupo de pop favorito?

**pop music** NOUN
la **música pop** fem

**poppy** NOUN
la **amapola** fem

**pop song** NOUN
la **canción pop** fem (PL las **canciones pop**)

**popular** ADJECTIVE
  **She's a very popular girl.**

Es una chica que gusta a todo
el mundo.

**porch** NOUN
el **porche** *masc*

**pork** NOUN
la **carne de cerdo** *fem*
**I don't eat pork.**
No como carne de cerdo.
**a pork chop**
una chuleta de cerdo

**port** NOUN
el **puerto** *masc*

**portable** ADJECTIVE
**portátil** *masc & fem*
**a portable TV**
un televisor portátil

**portion** NOUN
la **ración** *fem* (PL las **raciones**)
**a large portion of chips**
una ración grande de patatas fritas

**posh** ADJECTIVE
**de lujo**
**a posh hotel**
un hotel de lujo

**positive** ADJECTIVE
**seguro** *masc*
**segura** *fem*
**Are you positive, Geoffrey?**
¿Estás seguro, Geoffrey?

**possibility** NOUN
**It's a possibility.**
Es posible.

**possible** ADJECTIVE
**posible** *masc & fem*
**as soon as possible**
lo antes posible

> **Language tip**
> *Don't forget that there's only one **s**
> in the Spanish word **posible**.*

**post**

> **post** *can be a noun or a verb.*

**A** NOUN
el **correo** *masc*

**Is there any post for me?**
¿Hay correo para mí?

**B** VERB
**to post**
**enviar por correo**
**I've got some cards to post.**
Tengo que enviar por correo
algunas postales.
**Can you post this letter for
me?**
¿Me echas esta carta al correo?

**postbox** NOUN
el **buzón** *masc* (PL los **buzones**)

**postcard** NOUN
la **postal** *fem*
**Thank you for the postcard,
Jill.**
Gracias por la postal, Jill.

**postcode** NOUN
el **código postal** *masc*
**What is your postcode?**
¿Cuál es tu código postal?

**poster** NOUN
el **póster** *masc* (PL los **pósters**)
**I've got posters on my
bedroom walls.**
Tengo pósters en las paredes
de mi habitación.

**postman** NOUN
el **cartero** *masc*

**He's a postman.**
Es cartero.

> **Language tip**
> *In Spanish, you do not use an article
> with people's jobs.*

**post office** NOUN
  la **oficina de Correos** *fem*
    **Where's the post office, please?**
    ¿Dónde está la oficina de Correos, por favor?

**potato** NOUN
  la **patata** *fem*
    **mashed potatoes**
    el puré de patatas
    **boiled potatoes**
    patatas cocidas
    **a baked potato**
    una patata asada

**potato salad** NOUN
  la **ensaladilla de patatas** *fem*

**pottery** NOUN
  la **cerámica** *fem*

**pound** NOUN
  la **libra** *fem*
    **How many euros do you get for a pound?**
    ¿Cuántos euros equivalen a una libra?
    **a pound of tomatoes**
    una libra de tomates

> **Did you know…?**
> In Spain measurements are in grams and kilograms. One pound is about 450 grams.

to **pour** VERB
  1 **echar** *(pour out)*
    **She poured some water into the pan.**
    Echó un poco de agua en la olla.
  2 **diluviar** *(with rain)*
    **It's pouring.**
    Está diluviando.

**powerful** ADJECTIVE
  **poderoso** *masc*
  **poderosa** *fem*

**practically** ADVERB
  **prácticamente**
    **It's practically impossible.**
    Es prácticamente imposible.

**practice** NOUN
  el **entrenamiento** *masc*
    **football practice**
    entrenamiento de fútbol
    **I've got to do my piano practice.**
    Tengo que hacer mis ejercicios de piano.

to **practise** VERB
  1 **practicar** *(instrument, language)*
    **I ought to practise more.**
    Debería practicar más.
    **I practise my flute every evening.**
    Practico con la flauta todas las noches.
    **I like practising my Spanish.**
    Me gusta poner en práctica el español.
  2 **entrenar** *(do training)*
    **The team practises on Thursdays.**
    El equipo entrena los jueves.

**prawn** NOUN
  la **gamba** *fem*

to **pray** VERB
  **rezar**
    **Let's pray for them.**
    Rezemos por ellos.
    **Let us pray.**
    Oremos.

**prayer** NOUN
  la **oración** *fem* (PL as **oraciones**)

**precisely** ADVERB
    **at ten a.m. precisely**
    a las diez en punto de la mañana

to **prefer** VERB
  **preferir**
    **Which would you prefer?**
    ¿Cuál prefieres?
    **Which do you prefer, tennis or football?**
    ¿Qué prefieres, el tenis o el fútbol?
    **I prefer English to geography.**
    Prefiero el inglés a la geografía.

**English Spanish**

a b c d e f g h i j k l m n o **p** q r s t u v w x y z

**pregnant** ADJECTIVE
**embarazada** *fem*
> **She's six months pregnant.**
> Está embarazada de seis meses.

**prep** NOUN
los **deberes** *masc pl*
> **history prep**
> los deberes de historia

to **prepare** VERB
preparar
> **She's preparing dinner.**
> Está preparando la cena.

**prep school** NOUN
el **colegio privado** *masc*

**preposition** NOUN
la **preposición** *fem* (PL las preposiciones)

## present

> *present can be an adjective or a noun.*

**A** ADJECTIVE
**presente** *masc & fem*
> **Ten present, two absent.**
> Diez presentes, dos faltas.
> **He was present at the meeting.**
> Asistió a la reunión.
> **the present tense**
> el presente *masc*

**B** NOUN
1 el **regalo** *masc* (gift)
> **I'm going to give Julia a present.**
> Le voy a hacer un regalo a Julia.
> **I got lots of presents.**
> Me hicieron muchos regalos.

2 el **presente** *masc* (time)
> **the present and the future**
> el presente y el futuro

**president** NOUN
el **presidente** *masc*
la **presidenta** *fem*

to **pretend** VERB
> **Pretend you are in a café.**
> Haz como si estuvieras en una cafetería.

> *Language tip*
> *Be careful! The translation of* **pretend** *is not* **pretender**.

## pretty

> *pretty can be an adjective or an adverb.*

**A** ADJECTIVE
1 **guapo** *masc*
**guapa** *fem* (good-looking)
> **She's very pretty.**
> Es muy guapa.
> **Sarah is prettier than Irene.**
> Sarah es más guapa que Irene.
> **She's the prettiest girl in the class.**
> Es la chica más guapa de la clase.
2 **bonito** *masc*
**bonita** *fem* (lovely)
> **a pretty blouse**
> una blusa bonita

**B** ADVERB
**bastante**
> **It's pretty old.**
> Es bastante viejo.
> **The weather was pretty awful.**
> Hizo un tiempo bastante horrible.

**previous** ADJECTIVE
**anterior** *masc & fem*
> **the previous day**
> el día anterior

**price** NOUN
el **precio** *masc*

512

**priest** NOUN
el **sacerdote** *masc*

**primary school** NOUN
la **escuela primaria** *fem*
**I am at primary school.**
Estoy en la escuela primaria.

**prince** NOUN
el **príncipe** *masc*
**the Prince of Wales**
el Príncipe de Gales

**princess** NOUN
la **princesa** *fem*
**Princess Anne**
la princesa Ana

**Did you know…?**
In Spain a princess who is not the heir to the throne is called an **infanta** *rather than a* **princesa** *while a prince who is not the heir to the throne is an* **infante**.

to **print** VERB
1 **escribir en letra de imprenta** (write)
**Print your name.**
Escribe tu nombre en letra de imprenta.
2 **imprimir** (on machine)

**printer** NOUN
la **impresora** *fem*

**prison** NOUN
la **cárcel** *fem*
**in prison**
en la cárcel

**private** ADJECTIVE
**privado** *masc*
**privada** *fem*
**a private letter**
una carta privada
**I have private lessons.**
Tomo clases particulares.

**private school** NOUN
el **colegio privado** *masc*

**prize** NOUN
el **premio** *masc*

**The prize is one hundred euros.**
El premio son cien euros.
**You can win a prize.**
Puedes ganar un premio.

**prize-giving** NOUN
la **entrega de premios** *fem*

**prizewinner** NOUN
el **ganador** *masc*
la **ganadora** *fem*

**probably** ADVERB
**probablemente**
**probably not**
probablemente no

**problem** NOUN
el **problema** *masc*
**Is there a problem?**
¿Hay algún problema?

**Language tip**
Even though it ends in -a, el **problema** is a masculine noun.
**What's the problem?**
¿Qué pasa?

**No problem!**
¡No importa!

**procession** NOUN
la **procesión** *fem* (PL las procesiones)

**profession** NOUN
la **profesión** *fem* (PL las profesiones)

**professor** NOUN
el **catedrático** *masc*
la **catedrática** *fem*

**Language tip**
Be careful! The translation of **professor** is not **profesor**.

**profit** NOUN
el **beneficio** *masc*

**program** NOUN
el **programa** *masc*

**a computer program**
un programa informático

*Language tip*
*Even though it ends in* **-a**, **el**
**programa** *is a masculine noun.*

**programme** NOUN
el **programa** *masc*
**my favourite TV programme**
mi programa favorito de la tele
**Would you like a**
**programme?**
¿Quieres un programa?

*Language tip*
*Even though it ends in* **-a**, **el**
**programa** *is a masculine noun.*

**progress** NOUN
**You're making progress,**
**Edward!**
¡Estás progresando, Edward!

**projector** NOUN
el **proyector** *masc*

**promise**

**promise** *can be a noun or a verb.*

**A** NOUN
la **promesa** *fem*
**I'll make you a promise.**
Te haré una promesa.
**That's a promise!**
¡Es una promesa!
**B** VERB
**to promise**
**prometer**
**I promise!**
¡Lo prometo!
**I'll write, I promise!**
¡Escribiré, lo prometo!

**prompt**

**prompt** *can be an adjective or an*
*adverb.*

**A** ADJECTIVE
**rápido** *masc*
**rápida** *fem*
**a prompt reply**
una rápida respuesta

**B** ADVERB
**at eight o'clock prompt**
a las ocho en punto

**pronoun** NOUN
el **pronombre** *masc*

to **pronounce** VERB
**pronunciar**
**How do you pronounce that**
**word?**
¿Cómo se pronuncia esa
palabra?

**pronunciation** NOUN
la **pronunciación** *fem*
**Your pronunciation is good!**
¡Tienes una buena
pronunciación!

**proper** ADJECTIVE
**adecuado** *masc*
**adecuada** *fem (suitable)*
**the proper equipment**
el equipo adecuado
**You should eat a proper**
**breakfast.**
Deberías desayunar como Dios
manda.

**properly** ADVERB
**correctamente**
**I can't pronounce it properly.**
No puedo pronunciarlo
correctamente.

**Protestant**

**Protestant** *can be an adjective or*
*a noun.*

**A** ADJECTIVE
**protestante** *masc & fem*
**B** NOUN
el/la **protestante** *masc/fem*
**I'm a Protestant.**
Soy protestante.

*Language tip*
*In Spanish* **protestante** *is not*
*spelled with a capital letter.*
*Remember that you do not use an*
*article with people's religions in*
*Spanish.*

**proud** ADJECTIVE
**orgulloso** *masc*
**orgullosa** *fem*
> **Her parents are proud of her.**
> Sus padres están orgullosos de ella.

**prune** NOUN
la **ciruela pasa** *fem*

**PTO** ABBREVIATION
(= **please turn over**)
**sigue**

**pub** NOUN
el **pub** *masc*

**public**

> **public** *can be a noun or an adjective.*

**A** NOUN
el **público** *masc*
> **The castle is open to the public.**
> El castillo está abierto al público.

**B** ADJECTIVE
**público** *masc*
**pública** *fem*
> **a public swimming pool**
> una piscina pública

**publicity** NOUN
la **publicidad** *fem*

**public school** NOUN
el **colegio privado** *masc*

**public transport** NOUN
el **transporte público** *masc*
> **by public transport**
> en transporte público

**pudding** NOUN
el **postre** *masc*
> **Would you like a pudding?**
> ¿Quieres postre?
> **What's for pudding?**
> ¿Qué hay de postre?

to **pull** VERB
**tirar**
> **Pull!**
> ¡Tira!

**pullover** NOUN
el **jersey** *masc* (PL los **jerseys**)
> **What colour is your pullover?**
> ¿De qué color es tu jersey?

**pump** NOUN
**1** la **bomba** *fem (for pumping)*
> **a bicycle pump**
> una bomba de bicicleta
**2** la **zapatilla de deporte** *fem (shoe)*
> **Have you got your pumps?**
> ¿Tienes tus zapatillas de deporte?

to **pump up** VERB
**inflar**
> **Pump up your tyres!**
> ¡Infla tus ruedas!

**pumpkin** NOUN
la **calabaza** *fem*

to **punch** VERB
**dar un puñetazo a**
> **He punched me!**
> ¡Me dio un puñetazo!

**punctual** ADJECTIVE
**puntual** *masc & fem*
> **Be punctual!**
> ¡Sé puntual!

**punctuation** NOUN
la **puntuación** *fem*

**punishment** NOUN
el **castigo** *masc*

**pupil** NOUN
el **alumno** *masc*
la **alumna** *fem*

**There are twenty-two pupils in my class.**
Hay veintidós alumnos en mi clase.

**puppet** NOUN
la **marioneta** *fem*

**puppy** NOUN
el **cachorro** *masc*

**pure** ADJECTIVE
**puro** *masc*
**pura** *fem*
**It's pure orange juice.**
Es zumo de naranja puro.

## purple

*purple can be an adjective or a noun.*

**A** ADJECTIVE
**morado** *masc*
**morada** *fem*
**a purple skirt**
una falda morada

*Language tip*

*Colour adjectives come after the noun in Spanish.*

**B** NOUN
el **morado** *masc*
**Purple is my favourite colour.**
El morado es mi color favorito.

**purpose** NOUN
**on purpose**
a propósito
**You're doing it on purpose.**
Lo estás haciendo a propósito.

to **purr** VERB
**ronronear**
**The cat is purring.**
El gato está ronroneando.

**purse** NOUN
el **monedero** *masc*
**I've lost my purse.**
He perdido mi monedero.

to **push** VERB
**empujar**
**Push!**
¡Empuja!

**pushchair** NOUN
la **sillita de paseo** *fem*

to **put** VERB
**poner**
**Where shall I put my things?**
¿Dónde pongo mis cosas?
**Don't forget to put your name on the paper.**
No te olvides de poner tu nombre en la hoja.
**She's putting the baby to bed.**
Está acostando al niño.
**Put your chewing gum in the bin.**
Tira el chicle a la papelera.

to **put away** VERB
**guardar**
**Put your things away, children.**
Guardad vuestras cosas, niños.

to **put back** VERB
**poner en su sitio**
**Don't forget to put it back.**
No te olvides de ponerlo en su sitio.

to **put down** VERB
**soltar** *(stop holding)*
**Put the bags down for a moment.**
Suelta las bolsas un momento.
**Put down a card.**
Suelta una carta.
**Put your hands down.**
Bajad las manos.

*Language tip*

*In Spanish you usually use an article like **el**, **la**, **los** with parts of the body.*

to **put off** VERB
  1 **apagar** (switch off)
    **Shall I put the light off?**
    ¿Apago la luz?
  2 **distraer** (distract)
    **Stop putting me off!**
    ¡Deja de distraerme!

to **put on** VERB
  1 **ponerse** (clothes)
    **I'll put my coat on.**
    Me pondré el abrigo.

---

**Language tip**

In Spanish you usually use an article like **el**, **la**, **los** with clothes you are wearing.

---

  2 **encender** (switch on)
    **Shall I put the light on?**
    ¿Enciendo la luz?

to **put up** VERB
  1 **colgar** (hang)
    **I'll put the poster up on my wall.**
    Colgaré el póster en la pared.
  2 **subir** (raise)
    **They've put up the price.**
    Han subido el precio.
    **Put up your hand if you know the answer.**
    Que levante la mano el que sepa la respuesta.

**puzzle** NOUN
  el **rompecabezas** masc (PL los rompecabezas)

**puzzled** ADJECTIVE
  **perplejo** masc
  **perpleja** fem
    **You look puzzled.**
    Parece que te has quedado perplejo.

**pyjamas** PL NOUN
  el **pijama** masc
    **my pyjamas**
    mi pijama
    **I've got some new pyjamas.**
    Tengo un pijama nuevo.
    **a pair of pyjamas**
    un pijama

---

**Language tip**

In Spanish **el pijama** is a singular word.

---

a
b
c
d
e
f
g
h
i
j
k
l
m
n
o
**P**
q
r
s
t
u
v
w
x
y
z

# Q q

**quad bike** NOUN
el **quad** *masc*

**quality** NOUN
1 la **calidad** *fem (of work, product)*
**good quality towels**
toallas de buena calidad
2 la **cualidad** *fem (of person)*
**She's got lots of good qualities.**
Tiene un montón de buenas cualidades.

**quantity** NOUN
la **cantidad** *fem*

to **quarrel** VERB
**pelearse**
**They're always quarrelling.**
Siempre se están peleando.

**quarter** NOUN
la **cuarta parte** *fem*
**a quarter of the class**
una cuarta parte de la clase
**It's a quarter to one.**
Es la una menos cuarto.
**It's a quarter past six.**
Son las seis y cuarto.
**at a quarter to eight**
a las ocho menos cuarto

**three quarters**
tres cuartos
**a quarter of an hour**
un cuarto de hora
**three quarters of an hour**
tres cuartos de hora
**a quarter past ten**
las diez y cuarto
**a quarter to eleven**
las once menos cuarto

**queen** NOUN
la **reina** *fem*
**Queen Elizabeth**
la reina Isabel

*Did you know...?*
*Did you know that Spanish speakers translate the names of the British royal family into Spanish?*

**the queen of hearts**
la reina de corazones

**question** NOUN
1 la **pregunta** *fem (query)*
**Are there any questions?**
¿Hay alguna pregunta?
**Can I ask a question?**
¿Puedo hacer una pregunta?
2 la **cuestión** *fem* (PL las cuestiones) *(matter)*
**That's a difficult question.**
Ésa es una cuestión complicada.

**question mark** NOUN
el **signo de interrogación** *masc*

**questionnaire** NOUN
el **cuestionario** *masc*

**queue**

*queue can be a noun or a verb.*

A NOUN
la **cola** *fem*
**There's a very long queue.**
Hay una cola muy larga.
B VERB
**to queue**
**hacer cola**
**You have to queue.**
Tienes que hacer cola.

**quick** ADJECTIVE
**rápido** *masc*
**rápida** *fem*
**a quick lunch**
una comida rápida
**It's quicker by train.**
Es más rápido en tren.

**Be quick, Laura!**
¡Date prisa, Laura!
**Be quick, girls!**
¡Daos prisa, niñas!

**quickly** ADVERB
**rápido**
   **Am I speaking too quickly?**
   ¿Estoy hablando demasiado
   rápido?

**quiet** ADJECTIVE
1 **callado** *masc*
  **callada** *fem (not chatty)*
  **You're very quiet, Julia.**
  Estás muy callada, Julia.

> **Language tip**
> When **be quiet** means 'fall silent',
> you translate it using the verb
> **callarse**.

  **Be quiet all of you, I'm
  thinking!**
  ¡Callaos todos, que estoy
  pensando!

**Be quiet, Jeremy!**
¡Cállate, Jeremy!
**Quiet!**
¡Silencio!

2 **tranquilo** *masc*
  **tranquila** *fem (peaceful)*
  **a quiet place**
  un lugar tranquilo
  **a quiet weekend**
  un fin de semana tranquilo

**quietly** ADVERB
1 **en voz baja** *(in a low voice)*
  **Talk quietly.**
  Hablad en voz baja.
2 **sin hacer ruido** *(noiselessly)*
  **Shut the door quietly, Sophie.**
  Cierra la puerta sin hacer ruido,
  Sophie.

**quilt** NOUN
el **edredón** *masc*
(PL los **edredones**)

**quite** ADVERB
1 **bastante** *(rather)*
  **It's quite expensive.**
  Es bastante caro.
  **It's quite warm today.**
  Hace bastante calor hoy.
  **It's quite a long way.**
  Está bastante lejos.
  **quite a lot of money**
  bastante dinero
2 **totalmente** *(completely)*
  **I'm quite sure he's coming.**
  Estoy totalmente seguro de que
  viene.
  **Are you ready, Lorna? – Not
  quite.**
  ¿Estás lista, Lorna? – No del
  todo.

**quite good**
bastante bueno

**quiz** NOUN
el **concurso** *masc*

# R r

**rabbi** NOUN
  el **rabino** masc
  la **rabina** fem

**rabbit** NOUN
  el **conejo** masc

**race** NOUN
  la **carrera** fem
  **a cycle race**
  una carrera ciclista
  **Let's have a race!**
  ¡Vamos a echar una carrera!

**racing car** NOUN
  el **coche de carreras** masc

**racket** NOUN
  la **raqueta** fem
  **my tennis racket**
  mi raqueta de tenis

**radiator** NOUN
  el **radiador** masc

**radio** NOUN
  la **radio** fem
  **I heard it on the radio.**
  Lo escuché en la radio.

> **Language tip**
> *Even though it ends in* **-o**, *la radio is a feminine noun.*

**raffle** NOUN
  la **rifa** fem

**raffle ticket**
  NOUN
  la **papeleta para la rifa**
  *fem*
  **Do you want to buy a raffle ticket?**
  ¿Quieres comprar una papeleta para la rifa?

**rage** NOUN
  **to be in a rage**
  estar furioso

> **Language tip**
> *Change* **furioso** *to* **furiosa** *if it's a woman or girl who's in a rage.*

  **She's in a rage.**
  Está furiosa.

**rail** NOUN
  **by rail**
  en tren

**railway** NOUN
  el **ferrocarril** masc

**railway line** NOUN
  la **línea de ferrocarril** fem

**railway station** NOUN
  la **estación de trenes** fem (PL
  las **estaciones de trenes**)

**rain**

> **rain** *can be a noun or a verb.*

  **A** NOUN
  la **lluvia** fem
  **in the rain**
  bajo la lluvia
  **B** VERB
  **to rain**
  **llover**
  **It's going to rain.**
  Va a llover.
  **It rains a lot here.**
  Llueve mucho aquí.

> **It's raining.**
> Está lloviendo.

**rainbow** NOUN
  el **arco iris** masc

**raincoat** NOUN
el **impermeable** *masc*

**rainy** ADJECTIVE
**lluvioso** *masc*
**lluviosa** *fem*
**a rainy day**
un día lluvioso

to **raise** VERB
**levantar**
**Raise your left arm, everyone.**
Levantad todos el brazo izquierdo.
**to raise money**
recaudar fondos
**We're raising money for a new gym.**
Estamos recaudando fondos para un gimnasio nuevo.

**raisin** NOUN
la **pasa** *fem*

**Ramadan** NOUN
el **Ramadán** *masc*

**ramp** NOUN
la **rampa** *fem*

**ran** VERB ▷ *see* **run**

**random** ADJECTIVE
**at random**
al azar
**Pick a card at random.**
Escoge una carta al azar.

**rang** VERB ▷ *see* **ring**

**range** NOUN
la **gama** *fem*
**There's a wide range of colours.**
Hay una amplia gama de colores.

**rap** NOUN
el **rap** *masc (poetry)*

**rare** ADJECTIVE
1 **raro** *masc*
**rara** *fem (unusual)*
2 **poco hecho** *masc*
**poco hecha** *fem (steak)*

**rarely** ADVERB
**raras veces**

**raspberry** NOUN
la **frambuesa** *fem*
**raspberry jam**
mermelada de frambuesa

**rat** NOUN
la **rata** *fem*

**rather** ADVERB
1 **bastante** *(quite)*
**Twenty pounds! That's rather expensive!**
¡Veinte libras! ¡Eso es bastante caro!
2 **I'd rather ...**
Preferiría ...
**I'd rather stay in tonight.**
Preferiría no salir esta noche.
**Would you like a sweet? – I'd rather have an apple.**
¿Quieres un caramelo? – Preferiría una manzana.
**Which would you rather have?**
¿Cuál prefieres?
**Would you rather have water or orange juice?**
¿Prefieres agua o zumo de naranja?

**ravenous** ADJECTIVE
**I'm ravenous!**
¡Estoy muerto de hambre!

*Language tip*
Change **muerto** *to* **muerta** *if you're a girl.*

**raw** ADJECTIVE
**crudo** *masc*
**cruda** *fem*

**razor** NOUN
la **maquinilla de afeitar** *fem*

**RE** NOUN
la **religión** *fem*

**reach**

> **reach** *can be a noun or a verb.*

**A** NOUN
**Mum keeps the biscuits out of reach.**
Mi madre guarda las galletas fuera de nuestro alcance.
**The hotel is within easy reach of the town centre.**
El hotel está a poca distancia del centro de la ciudad.

**B** VERB
**to reach**
**llegar a**
**We hope to reach London by five o'clock.**
Esperamos llegar a Londres para las cinco.
**I can't reach the top shelf.**
No llego a la estantería de arriba.

to **read** VERB
**leer**
**I don't read much.**
No leo mucho.
**Have you read 'The Prisoner of Azkaban'?**
¿Has leído 'El prisionero de Azkaban'?

to **read out** VERB
**leer en voz alta**
**I'll read out the names.**
Leeré en voz alta los nombres.

**reading** NOUN
la **lectura** *fem*
**Reading is one of my hobbies.**
La lectura es una de mis aficiones.

**ready**

ADJECTIVE
**listo** *masc*
**lista** *fem*
**Breakfast is ready.**
El desayuno está listo.

**She's nearly ready.**
Ella está casi lista.
**Are you ready, children?**
¿Estáis listos, niños?

> **Ready, steady, go!**
> ¡Preparados, listos, ya!

**real** ADJECTIVE
1 **verdadero** *masc*
**verdadera** *fem (true)*
**Her real name is Cordelia.**
Su verdadero nombre es Cordelia.
2 **auténtico** *masc*
**auténtica** *fem (genuine)*
**It's real leather.**
Es piel auténtica.

to **realize** VERB
**darse cuenta de**
**Do you realize what time it is?**
¿Te das cuenta de la hora que es?

**really** ADVERB
1 **muy** *(very)*
**She's really nice.**
Es muy simpática.
**It's really hot today.**
Hoy hace mucho calor.
2 **de verdad** *(genuinely)*
**I'm learning German. – Really?**
Estoy aprendiendo alemán. – ¿De verdad?
**Do you want to go? – Not really.**
¿Qu eres ir? – La verdad es que no.

**reason** NOUN
la **razón** *fem* (PL las **razones**)

**reasonable** ADJECTIVE
**razonable** *masc & fem*
**Be reasonable, Joyce!**
¡Sé razonable, Joyce!

**receipt** NOUN
el **recibo** *masc*
**Keep your receipt.**
Guarda tu recibo.

**Language tip**

*Be careful! The translation of* **receipt** *is not* **receta**.

to **receive** VERB
**recibir**
**I received your letter yesterday.**
Recibí tu carta ayer.

**recent** ADJECTIVE
**reciente** *masc & fem*

**recently** ADVERB
**recientemente**
**He's been ill recently.**
Ha estado enfermo recientemente.

**reception** NOUN
1 la **recepción** *fem* (desk)
**Please leave your key at reception.**
Por favor, deje su llave en recepción.
2 la **celebración** *fem* (PL las **celebraciones**) (party)
**The reception will be at a big hotel.**
La celebración será en un gran hotel.

**receptionist** NOUN
el/la **recepcionista** *masc/fem*
**She's a receptionist.**
Es recepcionista.

**Language tip**

*In Spanish, you do not use an article with people's jobs.*

**recipe** NOUN
la **receta** *fem*
**a recipe book**
un libro de recetas

to **reckon** VERB
**creer**
**What do you reckon?**
¿Tú qué crees?

to **recognize** VERB
**reconocer**
**Do you recognize this boy?**
¿Reconoces a este chico?

**Language tip**

*Don't forget the personal* **a** *in examples like this one.*

to **recommend** VERB
**recomendar**
**What do you recommend?**
¿Qué me recomienda?
**I recommend the soup.**
Le recomiendo la sopa.

**Language tip**

*In Spanish you usually say who you're recommending something to. Can you find words for 'to me' and 'to you' above?*

**record**

*record can be a noun or a verb.*

**A** NOUN
el **récord** *masc* (in sport)
**the world record**
el récord mundial
**B** VERB
**to record**
**grabar**
**We're going to record the song.**
Vamos a grabar la canción.

**Language tip**

*Be careful! The translation of* **to record** *is not* **recordar**.

**recorder** NOUN
la **flauta dulce** *fem*
**I play the recorder.**
Toco la flauta dulce.

**rectangle** NOUN
el **rectángulo** *masc*

to **recycle** VERB
**reciclar**

**English Spanish**

## red

*red can be an adjective or a noun.*

**A** ADJECTIVE
**rojo** *masc*
**roja** *fem*
**a red rose**
una rosa roja

### Language tip
*Colour adjectives come after the noun in Spanish.*

**The traffic lights are red.**
El semáforo está en rojo.
**Gerald's got red hair.**
Gerald es pelirrojo.

**B** NOUN
el **rojo** *masc*
**Red is my favourite colour.**
El rojo es mi color favorito.

## to **redecorate** VERB
1 **empapelar de nuevo** *(with wallpaper)*
**I'd like to redecorate my room.**
Quiero empapelar de nuevo mi habitación.
2 **pintar de nuevo** *(with paint)*
**I'd like to redecorate my room.**
Quiero pintar de nuevo mi habitación.

### Language tip
*There's no single verb meaning both 'to paint' and 'to paper' in Spanish.*

## **red-haired** ADJECTIVE
**pelirrojo** *masc*
**pelirroja** *fem*

## **redhead** NOUN

el **pelirrojo** *masc*
la **pelirroja** *fem*

## to **redo** VERB
**rehacer**
**I need to redo my homework.**
Tengo que rehacer mis deberes.

## **reduced** ADJECTIVE
**at a reduced price**
a un precio rebajado

## **reduction** NOUN
la **rebaja** *fem*
**a five-percent reduction**
una rebaja del cinco por ciento

## **referee** NOUN
el **árbitro** *masc*
la **árbitra** *fem*

## **reflexive** ADJECTIVE
**a reflexive verb**
un verbo reflexivo

## **refrigerator** NOUN
el **frigorífico** *masc*

## **refugee** NOUN
el **refugiado** *masc*
la **refugiada** *fem*

## to **refuse** VERB
**negarse**
**She's refusing to say anything.**
Se niega a decir nada.

## **regards** PL NOUN
los **recuerdos** *masc pl*
**Give my regards to Lucy.**
Dale recuerdos a Lucy.
**Tim sends his regards.**
Tim manda recuerdos.

## **region** NOUN
la **región** *fem* (PL las **regiones**)
**in this region**
en esta región

## **register** NOUN
**I'm going to call the register.**
Voy a pasar lista.

## **registration** NOUN

after registration
después de pasar lista

**regular** ADJECTIVE
1 **regular** *masc & fem*
   **at regular intervals**
   a intervalos regulares
   **a regular verb**
   un verbo regular
   **You should take regular
   exercise.**
   Deberías hacer ejercicio con
   regularidad.
2 **normal** *masc & fem (medium)*
   **a regular portion of fries**
   una porción normal de patatas
   fritas

**rehearsal** NOUN
   el **ensayo** *masc*

**reindeer** NOUN
   el **reno** *masc*

**relation** NOUN
   el/la **pariente** *masc/fem*
   **my relations**
   mis parientes
   **I've got relations in London.**
   Tengo parientes en Londres.

**relative** NOUN
   el/la **pariente** *masc/fem*
   **all her relatives**
   todos sus parientes
   **I've got relatives in
   Manchester.**
   Tengo parientes en Manchester.

to **relax** VERB
   **relajarse**
   **Mum's relaxing in front of
   the TV.**
   Mi madre se está relajando
   delante de la tele.
   **Relax! Everything's fine.**
   ¡Tranquilo! No pasa nada.

> **Language tip**
>
> Change **tranquilo** to **tranquila** *if
> talking to a woman or girl.*

**relaxed** ADJECTIVE

**relajado** *masc*
**relajada** *fem*

**relaxing** ADJECTIVE
   **relajante** *masc & fem*
   **Cooking is very relaxing.**
   Cocinar es muy relajante.

**relay race** NOUN
   la **carrera de relevos** *fem*
   **We won the relay race.**
   Ganamos la carrera de relevos.

**reliable** ADJECTIVE
   **fiable** *masc & fem*
   **a reliable car**
   un coche fiable
   **He's not very reliable.**
   No es muy fiable.

**relief** NOUN
   el **alivio** *masc*
   **What a relief!**
   ¡Qué alivio!

**religion** NOUN
   la **religión** *fem* (FL las
   religiones)
   **What religion are you?**
   ¿De qué religión eres?

**religious** ADJECTIVE
   **religioso** *masc*
   **religiosa** *fem*

to **rely on** VERB
   **confiar en**
   **I'm relying on you.**
   Confío en ti.

**remark** NOUN
   el **comentario** *masc*

to **remember** VERB
   **acordarse de**
   **I can't remember his name.**
   No me acuerdo de su nombre.
   **Sorry, I can't remember.**
   Lo siento, no me acuerdo.
   **Did you remember to lock
   the door?**
   ¿Te acordaste de cerrar la puerta
   con llave?

a
b
c
d
e
f
g
h
i
j
k
l
m
n
o
p
q
**r**
s
t
u
v
w
x
y
z

### Language tip
In Spanish you often say **no te olvides** (don't forget) instead of **remember**.

**Remember to write your names on the form.**
No os olvidéis de escribir vuestro nombre en el impreso.

to **remind** VERB
**recordar**
**Remind me to speak to Daniel.**
Recuérdame que hable con Daniel.
**She reminds me of you.**
Me recuerda a ti.

**remote control** NOUN
el **mando a distancia** masc

to **remove** VERB
**quitar**
**Please remove your bag from my seat.**
Por favor, quita tu bolsa de mi asiento.

### rent

**rent** can be a noun or a verb.

**A** NOUN
el **alquiler** masc
**She has to pay the rent.**
Tiene que pagar el alquiler.
**B** VERB
**to rent**
**alquilar**
**We are going to rent a villa.**
Vamos a alquilar un chalet.

to **repair** VERB
**arreglar**
**Can you repair them?**
¿Puedes arreglarlos?

to **repeat** VERB
**repetir**
**Can you repeat that, please?**
¿Puedes repetir eso, por favor?

**Repeat after me, everyone.**
Repetid todos después de mí.

### reply

**reply** can be a noun or a verb.

**A** NOUN
la **respuesta** fem
**I got no reply to my letter.**
No recibí respuesta a mi carta.
**B** VERB
**to reply**
**contestar**
**I hope you will reply soon.**
Espero que contestes pronto.
**She always replies to my letters.**
Siempre contesta a mis cartas.

### report NOUN
1 el **boletín de evaluación** masc (PL los **boletines de evaluación**) (school report)

### Language tip
Although **el boletín de evaluación** is the Spanish for **school report**, Spanish children usually just talk about their **notas**, literally 'marks'.

**I usually get a good report.**
Normalmente saco buenas notas.
2 el **reportaje** masc (news report)

**request** NOUN
la **solicitud** fem

**reservation** NOUN
la **reserva** fem
**I've got a reservation.**
Tengo una reserva.
**I'd like to make a reservation.**
Quisiera hacer una reserva.

### reserve

**reserve** can be a noun or a verb.

**A** NOUN
el/la **suplente** masc/fem

**I was a reserve in the game last Saturday.**
Estaba de suplente en el partido del sábado.

**B** VERB

**to reserve**
reservar

**I'd like to reserve a table for tomorrow evening.**
Quisiera reservar una mesa para mañana por la noche.

## reserved ADJECTIVE
**reservado** *masc*
**reservada** *fem*

**This seat is reserved.**
Este asiento está reservado.

## resolution NOUN
**Have you made any New Year's resolutions?**
¿Tienes buenos propósitos para el Año Nuevo?

## resort NOUN
el **centro turístico** *masc*

**It's a resort on the Costa del Sol.**
Es un centro turístico de la Costa del Sol.

**a ski resort**
una estación de esquí

## responsibility NOUN
la **responsabilidad** *fem*

**It's your responsibility.**
Es tu responsabilidad.

> **Language tip**
> Have you noticed that **responsabilidad** has an 'a' in it in Spanish?

## responsible ADJECTIVE
**responsable** *masc & fem*

> **Language tip**
> Remember that the Spanish word ends in 'able' rather than 'ible'.

**He's responsible for booking the tickets.**
Es responsable de reservar las entradas.

**It's a responsible job.**
Es un puesto de responsabilidad.

## rest

> rest *can be a noun or a verb.*

**A** NOUN

**1** el **descanso** *masc (break)*

**five minutes' rest**
cinco minutos de descanso

**Can we have a rest?**
¿Podemos descansar?

**I need a rest.**
Necesito descansar.

**2** *(remainder)*

**the rest**
el resto

**I'll do the rest.**
Yo haré el resto.

**the rest of the money**
el resto del dinero

**B** VERB

**to rest**
descansar

## restaurant NOUN
el **restaurante** *masc*

**We don't often go to restaurants.**
No solemos ir a restaurantes.

## result NOUN
el **resultado** *masc*

**my exam results**
los resultados de los exámenes

> **Language tip**
> Change **los exámenes** to **el examen** if you're talking about only one exam.

**What was the result? – One-nil.**
¿Cuál fue el resultado? – Uno a cero.

to **retire** VERB
**jubilarse**
He's going to retire.
Va a jubilarse.

**retired** ADJECTIVE
**jubilado** *masc*
**jubilada** *fem*
She's retired.
Está jubilada.

**retirement** NOUN
la **jubilación** *fem*

## return

> **return** can be a noun or a verb.

**A** NOUN
1 la **vuelta** *fem*
after our return
después de nuestra vuelta
the return journey
el viaje de vuelta
2 la **ida y vuelta** *fem (ticket)*
A return to Glasgow, please.
Una ida y vuelta a Glasgow, por favor.

**Many happy returns!**
¡Que cumplas muchos más!

*Language tip*
*Have you noticed the upside-down exclamation mark at the start of Spanish exclamations?*

**B** VERB
**to return**
1 **volver** *(come back)*
I've returned from holiday.
Acabo de volver de vacaciones.
2 **devolver** *(give back)*
I've got to return this book to the library.
Tengo que devolver este libro a la biblioteca.

**reverse** ADJECTIVE
**inverso** *masc*
**inversa** *fem*

in reverse order
en orden inverso

to **revise** VERB
**estudiar para un examen**
I haven't started revising for my exams yet.
Todavía no he empezado a estudiar para los exámenes.

**revision** NOUN
Have you done a lot of maths revision?
¿Has estudiado mucho para el examen de matemáticas?

**reward** NOUN
la **recompensa** *fem*
There's a thousand-euro reward.
Hay una recompensa de mil euros.

**rhubarb** NOUN
el **ruibarbo** *masc*

**rhythm** NOUN
el **ritmo** *masc*

**rib** NCUN
la **costilla** *fem*

**ribbon** NOUN
la **cinta** *fem*

**rice** NOUN
el **arroz** *masc*
Would you like some rice?
¿Quieres arroz?

**rich** ADJECTIVE
**rico** *masc*
**rica** *fem*
He's very rich.
Es muy rico.

to **rid** VERB
**to get rid of**
**deshacerse de**

**I need to get rid of my chewing gum.**
Necesito deshacerme del chicle.

## ride

> ride *can be a noun or a verb.*

**A** NOUN *(on horse)*
**to go for a ride**
ir a montar a caballo
**Would you like to go for a ride?**
¿Te gustaría ir a montar a caballo?
**I'm going for a ride on my bike.**
Voy a ir a dar una vuelta en bici.
**B** VERB
**to ride**
**1** montar a caballo *(on horse)*
**I'm learning to ride.**
Estoy aprendiendo a montar a caballo.
**2** **to ride a bike**
montar en bici
**Can you ride a bike?**
¿Sabes montar en bici?

## rider NOUN

**1** el **jinete** *masc (man, boy)*
**He's a good rider.**
Es un buen jinete.
**2** la **amazona** *fem (woman, girl)*
**She's a good rider.**
Es una buena amazona.

## ridiculous ADJECTIVE
ridículo *masc*
ridícula *fem*
**Don't be ridiculous, Fiona!**
¡No seas ridícula, Fiona!

## riding NOUN
**I like riding.**
Me gusta montar a caballo.

## riding school NOUN
la **escuela de equitación** *fem*

## right

> right *can be an adjective, adverb or noun.*

**A** ADJECTIVE
**1** **correcto** *masc*
**correcta** *fem (correct)*
**That's the right answer!**
¡Ésa es la respuesta correcta!
**It isn't the right size.**
No es la talla correcta.
**We're on the right train.**
Estamos en el tren correcto.
**2** *(true)*
**That's right!**
¡Es verdad!
**You're right, Luke.**
Tienes razón, Luke.
**3** **derecho** *masc*
**derecha** *fem (not left)*
**Hold out your right hand.**
Extiende la mano derecha.
**B** ADVERB
**1** **correctamente** *(correctly)*
**Am I pronouncing it right?**
¿Lo pronuncio correctamente?
**2** **a la derecha** *(to the right)*
**Turn right at the traffic lights.**
Gira a la derecha en el semáforo.
**C** NOUN
**on the right**
a la derecha
**a step to the right**
un paso a la derecha

**You're right.**
Tienes razón.
**Right! Let's get started.**
¡Bueno! ¡Empecemos!
**Turn right.**
Gira a la derecha.

## right-hand ADJECTIVE
**the right-hand side**
la derecha
**It's on the right-hand side.**
Está a la derecha.

English Spanish

a
b
c
d
e
f
g
h
i
j
k
l
m
n
o
p
q
**r**
s
t
u
v
w
x
y
z

### right-handed ADJECTIVE
**diestro** *masc*
**diestra** *fem*
> **Tim is right-handed.**
> Tim es diestro.

### ring

> *ring can be a noun or a verb.*

**A** NOUN
1 el **anillo** *masc (for finger)*
> **a gold ring**
> un anillo de oro
> **a diamond ring**
> un anillo de diamantes
> **a wedding ring**
> una alianza de boda
2 el **círculo** *masc (circle)*
> **Stand in a ring.**
> Poneos formando un círculo.

**B** VERB
**to ring**
1 **llamar** *(phone)*
> **You can ring me at home.**
> Me puedes llamar a casa.
2 **sonar** *(make sound)*
> **The phone's ringing.**
> El teléfono está sonando.

### ringtone NOUN
el **tono de llamada** *masc*

### rink NOUN
1 la **pista de hielo** *fem (for ice-skating)*
2 la **pista de patinaje** *fem (for roller-skating)*

### ripe ADJECTIVE
**maduro** *masc*
**madura** *fem*
> **a ripe peach**
> un melocotón maduro

### to rise VERB
**subir**

### risk NOUN
el **riesgo** *masc*
> **It's a big risk.**
> Es un gran riesgo.

### rival

> *rival can be a noun or an adjective.*

**A** NOUN
el/la **rival** *masc/fem*
> **our rivals**
> nuestros rivales

**B** ADJECTIVE
**rival** *masc & fem*
> **a rival gang**
> una banda rival

### river NOUN
el **río** *masc*
> **across the river**
> al otro lado del río
> **the River Amazon**
> el río Amazonas

> **Language tip**
> In Spanish **río** is not spelled with a capital letter in names of rivers.

### road NOUN
1 la **carretera** *fem*
> **There's a lot of traffic on the roads.**
> Hay mucho tráfico en las carreteras.
2 la **calle** *fem (street)*
> **They live across the road.**
> Viven al otro lado de la calle.

### road sign NOUN
la **señal de tráfico** *fem*

### roadworks
PL NOUN
las **obras** *fem pl*

Ducks crossing

### roast ADJECTIVE
**asado** *masc*
**asada** *fem*
> **roast chicken**
> pollo asado
> **roast potatoes**
> patatas asadas

• • • • • • • • • • • • • • • • • • • • • • •

**Did you know...?**
*In Spanish you translate both* **roast potatoes** *and* **baked potatoes** *the same. If you want to specify, you can say* **patatas asadas con la piel** *for* **baked potatoes**.

**rob** VERB
**robar** *(person)*
**I've been robbed!**
¡Me han robado!
**to rob a bank**
asaltar un banco
**They're robbing the bank!**
¡Están asaltando el banco!

**robber** NOUN
el **ladrón** *masc* (PL los **ladrones**)
la **ladrona** *fem*
**a bank robber**
un ladrón de bancos

**robbery** NOUN
el **robo** *masc*
**There have been a lot of robberies in my neighbourhood.**
Ha habido muchos robos en mi barrio.
**a bank robbery**
un asalto a un banco

**rock** NOUN
1 la **roca** *fem (boulder)*
2 el **rock** *masc (music)*
**a rock concert**
un concierto de rock
**He's a rock star.**
Es una estrella del rock.
3 *(sweet)*
**a stick of rock**
un palo de caramelo

**rocket** NOUN
el **cohete** *masc*

**rod** NOUN
la **caña** *fem*

**rode** VERB ▷ *see* **ride**

**role play** NOUN
el **juego de rol** *masc*

**We're going to do a role play.**
Vamos a hacer un juego de rol.

**roll**

roll *can be a noun or a verb.*

**A** NOUN
el **bollito** *masc (of bread)*
**a ham roll**
un bollito con jamón
**B** VERB
**to roll**: Roll the dice.
Lanza los dados.

**Rollerblades**® P_ NOUN
los **patines en línea** *masc pl*
**a pair of Rollerblades**
unos patines en línea

**rollercoaster** NOUN
la **montaña rusa** *fem*

**roller skates** PL NOUN
los **patines de ruedas** *masc pl*

**roller-skating** NOUN
**to go roller-skating**
ir a patinar
**Do you want to go roller-skating?**
¿Quieres ir a patinar?

**Roman Catholic** NOUN
el **católico** *masc*
la **católica** *fem*
**He's a Roman Catholic.**
Es católico.

**Language tip**
**católico** *is not spelled with a capital letter. Remember that you do not use an article with people's religions in Spanish.*

**romantic** ADJECTIVE
**romántico** *masc*
**romántica** *fem*

**roof** NOUN
el **tejado** *masc*

**room** NOUN

1 la **habitación** *fem* (PL las habitaciones) *(in house)*
**My room is the smallest.**
Mi habitación es la más pequeña.
**a single room**
una habitación individual
**a double room**
una habitación doble
**the biggest room in the house**
la habitación más grande de la casa

> **Language tip**
> You can also use **el cuarto** to refer to a room.

**My room is the smallest.**
Mi cuarto es el más pequeño.
2 el **aula** *fem (in school)*

> **Language tip**
> Even though it's a feminine noun, remember that you use **el** and **un** with **aula**.

**the music room**
el aula de música
3 el **sitio** *masc (space)*
**Is there room for me?**
¿Hay sitio para mí?

**rope** NOUN
la **cuerda** *fem*

**rose** NOUN
la **rosa** *fem*
**a bouquet of roses**
un ramo de rosas

**rough** ADJECTIVE
**áspero** *masc*
**áspera** *fem*

**roughly** ADVERB
**aproximadamente**
**It weighs roughly twenty kilos.**
Pesa unos veinte kilos aproximadamente.

**round**

> **round** can be an adjective, preposition or noun.

A ADJECTIVE
**redondo** *masc*
**redonda** *fem*
**a round table**
una mesa redonda
B PREPOSITION
**alrededor de**
**Sit round the table.**
Sentaos alrededor de la mesa.
**It's just round the corner.**
Está aquí a la vuelta de la esquina.
**round here**
por aquí cerca
**Is there a chemist's round here?**
¿Hay una farmacia por aquí cerca?
C NOUN
la **vuelta** *fem (of tournament)*
**the next round**
la siguiente vuelta
**a round of golf**
un partido de golf

**roundabout** NOUN
1 el **tiovivo** *masc (merry-go-round)*

2 la **rotonda** *fem (at road junction)*

**rounders** NOUN

> **Did you know...?**
> **Rounders** isn't played in Spain. The nearest game for which there is a Spanish translation is **el béisbol** or **baseball**.

## row

*row can be a noun or a verb.*

**A** NOUN

1 la **hilera** *fem*
**a row of houses**
una hilera de casas
2 la **fila** *fem (of seats)*
**Our seats are in the front row.**
Nuestros asientos están en la primera fila.
3 el **jaleo** *masc (noise)*
**What a row!**
¡Menudo jaleo!

**B** VERB
**to row**
**remar**
**I can row.**
Sé remar.

## rowing boat NOUN
la **barca de remos** *fem*

## royal ADJECTIVE
**real** *masc & fem*

## rubber NOUN
la **goma de borrar** *fem*
**Can I borrow your rubber?**
¿Me dejas tu goma de borrar?

## rubber band NOUN
la **goma elástica** *fem*

## rubbish

*rubbish can be a noun or an adjective.*

**A** NOUN

1 la **basura** *fem (garbage)*
**Where shall I put the rubbish?**
¿Dónde pongo la basura?
2 las **estupideces** *fem pl (nonsense)*
**Don't talk rubbish!**
¡No digas estupideces!

**B** ADJECTIVE *(useless)*
**They're a rubbish team!**
¡Son un equipo que no vale nada!

**The film was rubbish.**
La película no valía nada.

## rubbish bin NOUN
el **cubo de la basura** *masc*

## rucksack NOUN
la **mochila** *fem*

## rude ADJECTIVE
**grosero** *masc*
**grosera** *fem*
**Don't be rude!**
¡No seas grosero!
**a rude word**
una palabrota

## rug NOUN
1 la **alfombra** *fem (carpet)*
2 la **manta de viaje** *fem (travelling rug)*

## rugby NOUN
el **rugby** *masc*
**I play rugby.**
Juego al rugby.

### Language tip
*In Spanish, you need to add* **al** *before the name of the sport.*

## ruin

*ruin can be a noun or a verb.*

**A** NOUN
la **ruina** *fem*
**the ruins of the castle**
las ruinas del castillo

**B** VERB
**to ruin**
**estropear**
**You'll ruin your shoes.**
Te vas a estropear los zapatos.

### Language tip
*In Spanish you usually use an article like* **el**, **la**, **los** *with clothes you are wearing.*

## rule NOUN
1 la **regla** *fem (of game)*
**the rules of the game**
las reglas del juego
2 *(regulations)*

**the rules**
las normas
**It's against the rules.**
Va contra las normas.

**ruler** NOUN
la **regla** *fem*
**Can I borrow your ruler?**
¿Me dejas tu regla?

**run**

> **run** *can be a noun or a verb.*

**A** NOUN
**to go for a run**
**ir a correr**
**Do you want to go for a run?**
¿Quieres ir a correr?
**I did a ten-kilometre run.**
Corrí diez kilómetros.
**B** VERB
**to run**
**1 correr** *(move fast)*
**Run!**
¡Corre!
**I ran two kilometres.**
Corrí dos kilómetros.
**She's running.**
Está corriendo.

**2 organizar** *(organize)*
**They run English courses.**
Organizan cursos de inglés.

**rung** VERB ▷ *see* **ring**

**runner** NOUN
el **corredor** *masc*
la **corredora** *fem*

**runner-up** NOUN
el **segundo** *masc*
la **segunda** *fem*

**running** NOUN
**Running is my favourite
sport.**
Correr es mi deporte favorito.

**rush**

> **rush** *can be a noun or a verb.*

**A** NOUN
la **prisa** *fem*
**I'm in a rush.**
Tengo prisa.
**B** VERB
**to rush**
**apurarse**
**There's no need to rush.**
No hay por qué apurarse.

**rush hour** NOUN
la **hora punta** *fem*
**in the rush hour**
en la hora punta

# S s

**Sabbath** NOUN
  el **sábado** *masc* (Jewish)

**sack** NOUN
  el **saco** *masc*

**sad** ADJECTIVE
  **triste** *masc & fem*
    **Don't be sad.**
    No estés triste.

**sadly** ADVERB
  **1 lamentablemente**
    (*unfortunately*)
    **Sadly, we haven't got time.**
    Lamentablemente, no tenemos
    tiempo.
  **2 con tristeza** (*sorrowfully*)
    **'She's gone,' he said sadly.**
    –Se ha ido, dijo con tristeza.

**safe** ADJECTIVE
  **seguro** *masc*
  **segura** *fem*
    **This car isn't safe.**
    Este coche no es seguro.
    **We're safe here.**
    Aquí estamos seguros.
    **Put it in a safe place.**
    Ponlo en un lugar seguro.
    **Don't worry, it's perfectly**
    **safe.**
    No te preocupes, no tiene el
    menor peligro.
    **You're safe now.**
    Ya estás a salvo.

**safety** NOUN
  la **seguridad** *fem*

**safety pin** NOUN
  el **imperdible** *masc*

**said** VERB ▷ *see* **say**

**sailing** NOUN
  la **vela** *fem*
    **His hobby is sailing.**

Es aficionado a la vela.
**to go sailing**
hacer vela
**I'd like to go sailing.**
Me gustaría hacer vela.

**sailing boat** NOUN
  el **barco de vela** *masc*

**sailor** NOUN
  el **marinero** *masc*

**saint** NOUN
  e **santo** *masc*
  la **santa** *fem*

> ### Language tip
> The masculine form **Santo** is
> shortened to **San** before names
> other than **Domingo** and **Tomás**.

    **Saint John**
    San Juan
    **Saint Thomas**
    Santo Tomás

**salad** NOUN
  la **ensalada** *fem*
    **Would you like some salad?**
    ¿Quieres ensalada?

**salad cream** NOUN
  la **mayonesa** *fem*

**salad dressing** NOUN
  la **vinagreta** *fem*

**salary** NOUN
  el **sueldo** *masc*

English Spanish

a
b
c
d
e
f
g
h
i
j
k
l
m
n
o
p
q
r
s
t
u
v
w
x
y
z

**sale** NOUN
1 la **venta** fem (transaction)
'for sale'
'a la venta'
2 las **rebajas** fem pl (with bargains)
There's a sale on this week.
Hay rebajas esta semana.

**salmon** NOUN
el **salmón** masc (PL los salmones)

**salt** NOUN
la **sal** fem

**same**

> same can be an adjective or pronoun.

A ADJECTIVE
**mismo** masc
**misma** fem
the same class
la misma clase
We've got the same colour T-shirts.
Tenemos las camisetas del mismo color.
B PRONOUN
They're exactly the same.
Son exactamente iguales.
Our trainers are the same.
Nuestras zapatillas son iguales.
It's not the same.
No es lo mismo.

**sand** NOUN
la **arena** fem

**sandal** NOUN
la **sandalia** fem
a pair of sandals
unas sandalias

**sand castle** NOUN
el **castillo de arena** masc

**sandwich** NOUN
el **sandwich** masc
a cheese sandwich
un sandwich de queso

**sang** VERB ▷ see **sing**

**Santa Claus** NOUN
**Papá Noel** masc

**satchel** NOUN
la **cartera** fem

**satisfied** ADJECTIVE
**satisfecho** masc
**satisfecha** fem

**Saturday** NOUN
el **sábado** masc
It's Saturday today.
Hoy es sábado.
I've got a Saturday job.
Tengo un trabajo los sábados.

**on Saturday**
el sábado
**on Saturdays**
los sábados
**every Saturday**
todos los sábados
**last Saturday**
el sábado pasado
**next Saturday**
el sábado que viene

*Language tip*
*Days are not spelled with a capital letter in Spanish.*

**sauce** NOUN
la **salsa** fem

**saucepan** NOUN
el **cazo** masc

**saucer** NOUN
el **platito** masc

English Spanish

a b c d e f g h i j k l m n o p q r s t u v w x y z

**sausage** NOUN
la **salchicha** *fem*
**sausages and chips**
salchichas con patatas fritas

to **save** VERB
1 **ahorrar** *(money, time)*
**I'm saving for a new bike.**
Estoy ahorrando para una bici nueva.
**It'll save time.**
Ahorrará tiempo.
2 **salvar** *(rescue)*
**He saved my life.**
Me salvó la vida.
3 **guardar** *(on computer)*
**Don't forget to save the file.**
No te olvides de guardar el archivo.

to **save up** VERB
**ahorrar**
**I'm saving up for a new bike.**
Estoy ahorrando para una bici nueva.

**savoury** ADJECTIVE
**salado** *masc*
**salada** *fem*
**Is it sweet or savoury?**
¿Es dulce o salado?

**saw** VERB ▷ *see* **see**

to **say** VERB
**decir**
**Say hello, Matthew.**
Di hola, Matthew.
**What did you say?**
¿Qué dijiste?
**I said no.**
Dije que no.
**Could you say that again, please?**
¿Puedes repetir eso, por favor?
**I don't know how to say it in Spanish.**
No sé cómo se dice en español.

> **How do you say 'hello' in Spanish?**
> ¿Cómo se dice 'hello' en español?

**scar** NOUN
la **cicatriz** *fem* (PL as **cicatrices**)
**He's got a scar on his face.**
Tiene una cicatriz en la cara.

> **Language tip**
> In Spanish you usually use an article like **el**, **la**, **los** with parts of the body

**scared** ADJECTIVE
**to be scared**
**tener miedo**
**Don't be scared.**
No tengas miedo.
**I'm scared of dogs.**
Me dan miedo los perros.

> **I'm scared!**
> ¡Tengo miedo!

**scarf** NOUN
la **bufanda** *fem*

**scary** ADJECTIVE
**It was really scary.**
Daba mucho miedo.
**a scary film**
una película de miedo

**scenery** NOUN
el **paisaje** *masc*

**school** NOUN
el **colegio** *masc*
**I love school.**
Me encanta el colegio.
**The children are at school.**
Los niños están en el colegio.
**I go to school by bike.**
Voy al colegio en bici.
**the school library**
la biblioteca del colegio
**There's no school next week.**

La semana que viene no hay clase.

**at school**
en el colegio

**schoolbag** NOUN
la **cartera** *fem*

**schoolboy** NOUN
el **colegial** *masc*

**schoolchildren** PL NOUN
los **colegiales** *masc pl*

**schoolgirl** NOUN
la **colegiala** *fem*

**school holidays** PL NOUN
las **vacaciones escolares** *fem pl*

**school uniform** NOUN
el **uniforme del colegio** *masc*

**science** NOUN
la **ciencia** *fem*

**scientist** NOUN
el **científico** *masc*
la **científica** *fem*

**scissors** PL NOUN
las **tijeras** *fem pl*
  **a pair of scissors**
  unas tijeras

**scooter** NOUN
  1 el **patinete** *masc (child's toy)*
  2 la **Vespa**® *fem (motorcycle)*

**score**

**score** *can be a noun or a verb.*

**A** NOUN
  **What's the score?**
  ¿Cómo va el partido?
  **The score was three nil.**
  El partido acabó tres a cero.
**B** VERB
  **to score**
1 **marcar** *(goal)*
  **I scored a goal.**
  Marqué un gol.
2 **obtener** *(point)*
  **City School scored fifty points.**
  El colegio City obtuvo cincuenta puntos.
3 **llevar el tanteo** *(keep score)*
  **Who's going to score?**
  ¿Quién va a llevar el tanteo?

**Scot** NOUN
  el **escocés** *masc* (PL los escoceses)
  la **escocesa** *fem*

**Scotland** NOUN
  **Escocia** *fem*
    **Glasgow is in Scotland.**
    Glasgow está en Escocia.
    **I'm from Scotland.**
    Soy de Escocia.

**Scotsman** NOUN
  el **escocés** *masc* (PL los escoceses)

*Language tip*

**escocés** *is not spelled with a capital letter in Spanish.*

**Scotswoman** NOUN
  la **escocesa** *fem*

**Scottish** ADJECTIVE
**escocés** *masc* (PL **escoceses**)
**escocesa** *fem*
   He's Scottish.
   Es escocés.

**Scout** NOUN
el **boy scout** *masc*
la **girl scout** *fem*
   I'm in the Scouts.
   Estoy en los scouts.

**scrambled eggs** PL NOUN
los **huevos revueltos** *masc pl*

**scrapbook** NOUN
el **álbum de recortes** *masc*

to **scream** VERB
**chillar**

**screen** NOUN
la **pantalla** *fem*

**screw** NOUN
el **tornillo** *masc*

**screwdriver** NOUN
el **destornillador** *masc*

**sea** NOUN
el **mar** *masc*
   I live by the sea.
   Vivo al lado del mar.

**seafood** NOUN
el **marisco** *masc*

**seagull** NOUN
la **gaviota** *fem*

**seashore** NOUN
la **orilla del mar** *fem*

   on the seashore
   a la orilla del mar

**seasick** ADJECTIVE
   to get seasick
   marearse en barco
   I get seasick.
   Me mareo en barco.

**seaside** NOUN
la **playa** *fem*
   at the seaside
   en la playa

**season** NOUN
la **estación del año** *fem* (PL las **estaciones del año**)
   What's your favourite season?
   ¿Cuál es tu estación del año preferida?

**season ticket** NOUN
el **abono de temporada** *masc*

**seat** NOUN
el **asiento** *masc*
   I'd like a seat by the window.
   Quiero un asiento al lado de la ventana.
   Go back to your seat, Mike!
   ¡Vuelve a tu sitio Mike!

**second**

**A** ADJECTIVE
**segundo** *masc*
**segunda** *fem*
   on the second page
   en la segunda página
   Tim came second.
   Tim llegó el segundo.
**B** NOUN
el **segundo** *masc*
   It'll only take a second.
   Solo tardará un segundo.
   My birthday's the second of July.
   Mi cumpleaños es el dos de julio.
   Today's the second of June.
   Hoy es dos de junio

English Spanish

a b c d e f g h i j k l m n o p q r s t u v w x y z

English Spanish

a b c d e f g h i j k l m n o p q r s t u v w x y z

**on the second of March**
el dos de marzo

*Language tip*
*Use the same set of numbers that you use for counting (**uno**, **dos**, **tres** and so on) when giving Spanish dates.*

**secondary school** NOUN
el **instituto** *masc*

**secret**

*secret can be a noun or an adjective.*

**A** NOUN
el **secreto** *masc*
**It's a secret.**
Es un secreto.
**Can you keep a secret?**
¿Me guardas un secreto?

**in secret**
en secreto

**B** ADJECTIVE
**secreto** *masc*
**secreta** *fem*
**a secret passage**
un pasadizo secreto

**secretary** NOUN
el **secretario** *masc*
la **secretaria** *fem*
**She's a secretary.**
Es secretaria.

*Language tip*
*In Spanish, you do not use an article with people's jobs.*

**secretly** ADVERB
en secreto

to **see** VERB
**ver**
**We're going to see Granny and Grandpa.**
Vamos a ir a ver a los abuelos.
**I can't see her car.**
No veo su coche.
**I can't see anything.**
No veo nada.
**Can you see the difference?**
¿Ves la diferencia?

*Language tip*
*Don't forget the personal **a** in examples like the following.*

**I saw Catriona yesterday.**
Vi a Catriona ayer.
**Have you seen Paul?**
¿Has visto a Paul?

**See you!**
¡Hasta luego!
**See you tomorrow!**
¡Hasta mañana!
**See you soon!**
¡Hasta pronto!

**seed** NOUN
la **semilla** *fem*
**poppy seeds**
semillas de amapola
**sunflower seeds**
pipas de girasol

*Did you know...?*
*Did you know that sunflower seeds, often referred to just as **pipas**, are a popular Spanish snack?*

to **seem** VERB
**parecer**
**She seems tired.**
Parece cansada.
**There seems to be a problem.**
Parece que hay un problema.

**seen** VERB ▷ *see* **see**

**seesaw** NOUN
el **balancín** *masc* (PL los **balancines**)

**selfish** ADJECTIVE

**egoísta** *masc & fem*
> **Don't be so selfish, Charles.**
> No seas tan egoísta, Charles.

*Language tip*
Even though **egoísta** ends in **-a**, you can use it to describe a man or boy.

**self-service** ADJECTIVE
**autoservicio**

*Language tip*
**autoservicio** never changes its ending no matter what it describes.

> **The café is self-service.**
> La cafetería es autoservicio.
> **a self-service restaurant**
> un autoservicio

to **sell** VERB
**vender**
> **He's selling his car.**
> Vende su coche.
> **The tickets are sold out.**
> Las entradas están agotadas.

**Sellotape**® NOUN
la **cinta adhesiva** *fem*

**semicircle** NOUN
el **semicírculo** *masc*
> **Get into a semicircle.**
> Formad un semicírculo.

**semicolon** NOUN
el **punto y coma** *masc* (PL los punto y coma)

**semi-final** NOUN
la **semifinal** *fem*

to **send** VERB
**enviar**
> **I'm going to send Sally a postcard.**

Voy a enviarle una postal a Sally.
> **Send me an email.**
> Envíame un e-mail.
> **My friend has sent me some photos.**
> Mi amigo me ha enviado algunas fotos.

**senior school** NOUN
el **instituto de enseñanza secundaria** *masc*

**sense of humour** NOUN
el **sentido del humor** *masc*
> **Our teacher has a sense of humour.**
> Nuestro profesor tiene sentido de humor.
> **He has no sense of humour.**
> No tiene sentido del humor.

**sensible** ADJECTIVE
**sensato** *masc*
**sensata** *fem*
> **Be sensible, Amy!**
> ¡Sé sensata, Amy!

*Language tip*
Be careful! The translation of **sensible** is not sensible.

**sent** VERB ▷ see **send**

**sentence** NOUN
la **oración** *fem* (PL las **oraciones**)
> **What does this sentence mean?**
> ¿Qué significa esta oración?

**separate** ADJECTIVE
**aparte** *masc & fem*
> **Put the green cards in a separate pile.**
> Pon las tarjetas verdes en una pila aparte.

**English Spanish**

a b c d e f g h i j k l m n o p q r s t u v w x y z

**September** NOUN
**septiembre** masc
**My birthday's in September.**
Mi cumpleaños es en septiembre.
**It's the twelfth of September today.**
Hoy es doce de septiembre.

**in September**
en septiembre
**on the fifth of September**
el cinco de septiembre

*Language tip*
*Months are not spelled with a capital letter in Spanish.*

**sequence** NOUN
el **orden** masc (PL los **órdenes**)
**Put the pictures in sequence, Peter.**
Pon las fotos en orden, Peter.

**series** NOUN
la **serie** fem
**a TV series**
una serie de TV

**serious** ADJECTIVE
**serio** masc
**seria** fem
**You look very serious.**
Estás muy serio.
**Are you serious?**
¿En serio?

to **serve** VERB
**servir**
**They're serving lunch now.**
Están sirviendo la comida ahora.
**It serves you right.**
Te está bien empleado.

**service** NOUN
1 el **servicio** masc (in restaurant)
**Service is included.**
El servicio está incluido.
2 el **oficio religioso** masc (in church)

**service charge** NOUN

el **servicio** masc
**There's no service charge.**
El servicio va incluido.

**service station** NOUN
la **estación de servicio** fem
(PL las **estaciones de servicio**)

**serviette** NOUN
la **servilleta** fem

to **set** VERB
1 **poner**
**I normally set the alarm for seven.**
Normalmente pongo el despertador para las siete.
**Could you set the table?**
¿Puedes poner la mesa?
2 **ponerse** (sun)
**The sun is setting.**
El sol se está poniendo.

to **set off** VERB
**salir**
**What time are you setting off?**
¿A qué hora sales?

**settee** NOUN
el **sofá** masc

to **settle down** VERB
**calmarse**
**Settle down, children!**
¡Calmaos, niños!

**seven** NUMBER
**siete**
**seven euros**
siete euros
**I get up at seven o'clock.**
Me levanto a las siete.

**She's seven.**
Tiene siete años.

*Language tip*
*In English you can say **she's seven** or **she's seven years old**. In Spanish you can only say **tiene siete años**. Have you noticed that in Spanish you need to use the verb **tener** to talk about somebody's age?*

## seventeen NUMBER
**diecisiete**
   **seventeen euros**
   diecisiete euros

**He's seventeen.**
Tiene diecisiete años.

### Language tip
*In English you can say **he's
seventeen** or **he's seventeen
years old**. In Spanish you can only
say **tiene diecisiete años**. Have
you noticed that in Spanish you need
to use the verb **tener** to talk about
somebody's age?*

## seventeenth NUMBER
**diecisiete**
   **on the seventeenth floor**
   en la planta diecisiete
   **We break up on the
   seventeenth of December.**
   Empezamos las vacaciones el
   diecisiete de diciembre.
   **Today's the seventeenth of
   March.**
   Hoy es diecisiete de marzo.

**on the seventeenth of January**
el diecisiete de enero

### Language tip
*Use the same set of numbers that
you use for counting (**uno**, **dos**,
**tres** and so on) when giving
Spanish dates.*

## seventh NUMBER
1 **séptimo** *masc*
   **séptima** *fem*
   **on the seventh floor**
   en la séptima planta
   **My birthday's the seventh of
   February.**
   Mi cumpleaños es el siete de
   febrero.
   **It's the seventh of April today.**
   Hoy es siete de abril.
   **on the seventh of August**
   el siete de agosto

### Language tip
*Use the same set of numbers that
you use for counting (**uno**, **dos**,
**tres** and so on) when giving
Spanish dates.*

## seventy NUMBER
**setenta**
   **My grandma is seventy.**
   Mi abuela tiene setenta años.

### Language tip
*In English you can say **she's
seventy** or **she's seventy years
old**. In Spanish you can only say
**tiene setenta años**. Have you
noticed that in Spanish you need to
use the verb **tener** to talk about
somebody's age?*

## several ADJECTIVE
**varios** *masc pl*
**varias** *fem pl*
   **Several children are
   absent.**
   Varios niños no han venido.

## sewing NOUN
la **costura** *fem*
   **I like sewing.**
   Me gusta
   la costura.

## shade NOUN
la **sombra** *fem*
   **It was thirty-five degrees in
   the shade.**
   Hacía treinta y cinco grados a la
   sombra.

## shadow NOUN
la **sombra** *fem*
   **my shadow**
   mi sombra

## to shake VERB
1 **temblar** *(tremble)*
   **My hands are shaking.**
   Me tiemblan las manos.

English Spanish

a
b
c
d
e
f
g
h
i
j
k
l
m
n
o
p
q
r
s
t
u
v
w
x
y
z

English Spanish

a b c d e f g h i j k l m n o p q r s t u v w x y z

### Language tip

*In Spanish you usually use an article like el, la, los with parts of the body.*

**2 sacudir** *(on purpose)*
**She shook the rug.**
Sacudió la alfombra.
**to shake hands with somebody**
darle la mano a alguien
**Shake hands with your best friend!**
¡Dale la mano a tu mejor amigo!
**Spanish people shake hands a lot.**
Los españoles se dan mucho la mano.

### shall VERB

### Language tip

*You can usually translate shall I...? using the present tense of the main verb.*

**Shall I shut the window?**
¿Cierro la ventana?
**Shall I go first?**
¿Empiezo yo?
**Shall I put the light on?**
¿Enciendo la luz?

### shame NOUN

**What a shame!**
¡Qué pena!

### shampoo NOUN

el **champú** *masc*
**a bottle of shampoo**
un bote de champú

### shape NOUN

la **forma** *fem*

---

to **share** VERB
**compartir**
**I share a room with my brother.**
Comparto la habitación con mi hermano.

### sharp ADJECTIVE

**afilado** *masc*
**afilada** *fem*
**Be careful, it's sharp.**
Ten cuidado que está afilado.

### she PRONOUN

**ella**
**She's got a radio but I haven't.**
Ella tiene una radio pero yo no.

### Language tip

*she isn't usually translated unless it's emphatic.*

**She's very nice.**
Es muy simpática.

### she'd

1 (= **she had**) ▷ see **have**
2 (= **she would**) ▷ see **would**

### sheep NOUN

la **oveja** *fem*

### Language tip

*When sheep refers to more than one animal, use ovejas in the plural.*

### sheet NOUN

la **sábana** *fem*
**clean sheets**
sábanas limpias
**a sheet of paper**
una hoja de papel

### shelf NOUN

el **estante** *masc*
**the top shelf**
el estante de arriba

**she'll** (= **she will**) ▷ see **will**

### shell NOUN

la **concha** *fem*

**shelves** PL NOUN
los **estantes** *masc pl*

**she's**
1 (= she is) ▷ *see* **be**
2 (= she has) ▷ *see* **have**

**Shetland Islands** PL NOUN
las **Islas Shetland** *fem pl*

to **shine** VERB
**brillar**
The sun is shining.
El sol brilla.

**ship** NOUN
el **barco** *masc*

**shirt** NOUN
la **camisa** *fem*
a white shirt
una camisa blanca

**shocking** ADJECTIVE
**escandaloso** *masc*
**escandalosa** *fem*
It's shocking!
¡Es escandaloso!

**shoe** NOUN
el **zapato** *masc*
I've got new shoes.
Tengo unos zapatos nuevos.
Put on your shoes.
Ponte los zapatos.

*Language tip*

*In Spanish you usually use an article like el, la, los with clothes you are wearing.*

**shoelace** NOUN
el **cordón** *masc* (PL los **cordones**)

**shoe shop** NOUN
la **zapatería** *fem*

**shop** NOUN
la **tienda** *fem*
The shop is shut.
La tienda está cerrada.
a sports shop
una tienda de deportes

**shop assistant** NOUN
el **dependiente** *masc*
la **dependienta** *fem*
She's a shop assistant.
Es dependienta.

*Language tip*

*In Spanish, you do not use an article with people's jobs.*

**shopkeeper** NOUN
el **tendero** *masc*
la **tendera** *fem*

**shopping** NOUN
la **compra** *fem*
I do the shopping for my
granny.
Le hago la compra a mi abuela.
I go shopping with my
friends.
Me voy de compras con mis
amigas.
Can you get the shopping
from the car?
¿Puedes traer las bolsas de la
compra del coche?

**shopping bag** NOUN
la **bolsa de la compra** *fem*

**shopping centre** NOUN
el **centro comercial** *masc*

**short** ADJECTIVE
1 **corto** *masc*
**corta** *fem* (not 'ong)
a short skirt
una falda corta
short hair
el pelo corto
a short walk
un paseo corto

**2 bajo** *masc*
**baja** *fem (not tall)*
**She's quite short.**
Es bastante baja.

## shorts PL NOUN
los **pantalones cortos** *masc pl*
**My shorts are green.**
Mis pantalones cortos son
verdes.
**a pair of shorts**
unos pantalones cortos

## short-sighted
ADJECTIVE
**miope** *masc & fem*

## shoulder NOUN
el **hombro** *masc*

## should VERB
**You should try it.**
Deberías intentarlo.
**You shouldn't do that.**
No deberías hacer eso.

## to shout VERB
**gritar**
**Don't shout, children!**
¡Niños, no gritéis!

## to show VERB
**enseñar**
**Show me!**
¡Enséñame!
**Shall I show you the photos?**
¿Te enseño las fotos?

## shower NOUN
**1** la **ducha** *fem (for washing)*
**She's in the shower.**
Está en la ducha.
**to have a shower**
ducharse
**I'm going to have a shower.**
Voy a ducharme.
**2** el **chaparrón** *masc* (PL los
**chaparrones**) *(rain)*
**It's just a shower.**
Es solo un chaparrón.

## Shrove Tuesday NOUN
el **Martes de Carnaval** *masc*

## to shrug VERB
**to shrug one's shoulders**
**encogerse de hombros**
**She shrugged her shoulders.**
Se encogió de hombros.

## to shuffle VERB
**You have to shuffle the
cards.**
Tienes que barajar las cartas.

## shut

*shut can be a verb or an adjective.*

**A** VERB
**to shut**
**cerrar**
**What time do the shops
shut?**
¿A qué hora cierran las tiendas?
**Open your mouth and shut
your eyes.**
Abre la boca y cierra los ojos.

**Language tip**
In Spanish you usually use an article
like **el**, **la**, **los** with parts of the body.

**B** ADJECTIVE
**cerrado** *masc*
**cerrada** *fem*
**The door is shut.**
La puerta está cerrada.

## shy ADJECTIVE
**tímido** *masc*
**tímida** *fem*
**He's very shy.**
Es muy tímido.

## sick ADJECTIVE
**enfermo** *masc*
**enferma** *fem (unwell)*
**He is sick.**
Está enfermo.

**I'm going to be sick.**
Voy a devolver.
**I feel sick.**
Tengo ganas de devolver.

**side** NOUN
1 el **lado** *masc (of object, building, street)*
**on this side**
en este lado
**It's on this side of the street.**
Está en este lado de la calle.
2 el **equipo** *masc (team)*
**He's on my side.**
Está en mi equipo.

**sightseeing** NOUN
**We're going to go sightseeing.**
Vamos a ir a visitar monumentos.

**sign**

*sign can be a noun or a verb.*

**A** NOUN
la **señal** *fem*
**a road sign**
una señal de tráfico
**B** VERB
**to sign**
firmar
**Sign here, please.**
Firma aquí, por favor.

Ducks crossing

**signal** NOUN
la **señal** *fem*

**signature** NOUN
la **firma** *fem*

**sign language** NOUN
el **lenguaje de signos** *masc*

**silence** NOUN
el **silencio** *masc*

**silk**

*silk can be a noun or an adjective.*

**A** NOUN
la **seda** *fem*

**B** ADJECTIVE
**de seda**
**a silk scarf**
un pañuelo de seda

**silly** ADJECTIVE
**tonto** *masc*
**tonta** *fem*
**Don't be silly, Ian!**
¡No seas tonto, Ian!

**silver**

*silver can be a noun or an adjective.*

**A** NOUN
la **plata** *fem*
**gold and silver**
oro y plata
**B** ADJECTIVE
**de plata**
**a silver chain**
una cadena de plata
**a silver medal**
una medalla de plata

**similar** ADJECTIVE
**parecido** *masc*
**parecida** *fem*
**His sweater's similar to mine.**
Su jersey es parecido al mío.

**simple** ADJECTIVE
**sencillo** *masc*
**sencilla** *fem*
**It's very simple.**
Es muy sencillo.

**since** PREPOSITION
**desde**
**since Christmas**
desde Navidad
**since then**
desde entonces

**sincerely** ADVERB
**Yours sincerely ...**
Le saluda atentamente ...

a b c d e f g h i j k l m n o p q r s t u v w x y z

**to sing** VERB
**cantar**
**I sing in the choir.**
Canto en el coro.

**singer** NOUN
el/la **cantante** *masc/fem*

**single**

**single** *can be an adjective or a noun.*

**A** ADJECTIVE
**1 individual** *masc & fem*
**a single room**
una habitación individual
**a single bed**
una cama individual
**B** NOUN
la **ida** *fem*
**A single to Barcelona, please.**
Una ida a Barcelona, por favor.

**singular** NOUN
**in the singular**
en singular

**sink** NOUN
el **fregadero** *masc (kitchen sink)*

**sir** NOUN
el **señor** *masc*
**Yes, sir.**
Sí, señor.

**sister** NOUN
la **hermana** *fem*
**my little sister**
mi hermana pequeña
**my big sister**
mi hermana mayor
**I've got one sister.**
Tengo una hermana.
**I haven't got any sisters.**
No tengo hermanas.

**Have you got any brothers or sisters?**
¿Tienes hermanos?

**to sit** VERB
**sentarse**
**I want to sit next to my friend.**
Quiero sentarme al lado de mi amigo.
**Can I sit here?**
¿Puedo sentarme aquí?
**Brian is sitting next to Megan.**
Brian está sentado al lado de Megan.

### Language tip
*Change* **está sentado** *to* **está sentada** *if it's a girl or woman who is sitting somewhere.*

**to sit down** VERB
**sentarse**
**Sit down, Anthony.**
Siéntate, Anthony.

**Sit down, children.**
Niños, sentaos.

**site** NOUN
**1** el **sitio web** *masc (website)*
**2** el **camping** *masc (campsite)*

**sitting room** NOUN
el **salón** *masc* (PL los **salones**)

**situation** NOUN
la **situación** *fem* (PL las **situaciones**)

**six** NUMBER
**seis**
**six euros**
seis euros

**She's six.**
Tiene seis años.

### Language tip
*In English you can say* **she's six** *or* **she's six years old**. *In Spanish you can only say* **tiene seis años**. *Have*

*you noticed that in Spanish you need to use the verb **tener** to talk about somebody's age?*

**sixteen** NUMBER
**dieciséis**
> **sixteen euros**
> dieciséis euros

**He's sixteen.**
Tiene dieciséis años.

**Language tip**
*In English you can say **he's sixteen** or **he's sixteen years old**. In Spanish you can only say **tiene dieciséis años**. Have you noticed that in Spanish you need to use the verb **tener** to talk about somebody's age?*

**sixteenth** NUMBER
**dieciséis**
> **on the sixteenth floor**
> en la planta dieciséis
> **We break up on the sixteenth of December.**
> Empezamos las vacaciones el dieciséis de diciembre.
> **Today's the sixteenth of January.**
> Hoy es dieciséis de enero.

**on the sixteenth of August**
el dieciséis de agosto

**Language tip**
*Use the same set of numbers that you use for counting (**uno**, **dos**, **tres** and so on) when giving Spanish dates.*

**sixth** NUMBER
**sexto** *masc*
**sexta** *fem*
> **on the sixth floor**
> en la sexta planta
> **My birthday's the sixth of October.**
> Mi cumpleaños es el seis de octubre.

**It's the sixth of November today.**
Hoy es seis de noviembre.

**on the sixth of August**
el seis de agosto

**Language tip**
*Use the same set of numbers that you use for counting (**uno**, **dos**, **tres** and so on) when giving Spanish dates.*

**sixty** NUMBER
**sesenta**

**My aunt is sixty.**
Mi tía tiene sesenta años.

**Language tip**
*In English you can say **she's sixty** or **she's sixty years old**. In Spanish you can only say **tiene sesenta años**. Have you noticed that in Spanish you need to use the verb **tener** to talk about somebody's age?*

**size** NOUN
la **talla** *fem*
> **It's the right size.**
> Es la talla correcta.

to **skate** VERB
1 **ir con patines** *(roller-skate)*
> **I can't skate.**
> No sé ir con patines.
2 **patinar sobre hielo** *(ice-skate)*
> **I like skating.**
> Me gusta patinar sobre hielo.

**skateboard** NOUN
el **monopatín** *masc* (PL los monopatines)

a b c d e f g h i j k l m n o p q r s t u v w x y z

**skateboarding** NOUN
el **skateboard** masc
**I like skateboarding.**
Me gusta el skateboard.
**I'm going skateboarding with Gavin.**
Voy a hacer skateboard con Gavin.

**skating** NOUN
**I go skating every Saturday.**
Voy a patinar todos los sábados.

**skeleton** NOUN
el **esqueleto** masc

**ski**

> **ski** can be a verb or a noun.

**A** VERB
**to ski**
esquiar
**Can you ski?**
¿Sabes esquiar?
**B** NOUN
el **esquí** masc (PL los **esquís**)

**ski boots** PL NOUN
las **botas de esquí** fem pl

**ski lift** NOUN
el **telesilla** masc

> **Language tip**
> Even though it ends in **-a**, el **telesilla** is a masculine noun.

**ski slope** NOUN
la **pista de esquí** fem

**skiing** NOUN
**Do you like skiing?**
¿Te gusta esquiar?
**I'm going on a skiing holiday.**
Voy a ir de vacaciones a esquiar.

**skin** NOUN
la **piel** fem

**skinny**
ADJECTIVE
**flaco** masc
**flaca** fem

**skipping rope** NOUN
la **comba** fem

**skirt** NOUN
la **falda** fem
**a black skirt**
una falda negra

**sky** NOUN
el **cielo** masc
**The sky is blue.**
El cielo es azul.

to **slam** VERB
**Don't slam the door.**
No des portazos.

**sledge** NOUN
el **trineo** masc

**sledging** NOUN
**Let's go sledging!**
¡Vamos a montarnos en trineo!

to **sleep** VERB
**dormir**
**My cat sleeps in a box.**
Mi gato duerme en una caja.
**Did you sleep well, Sonia?**
¿Dormiste bien, Sonia?

**sleeping bag** NOUN
el **saco de dormir** masc

**sleepover** NOUN
**My friend is coming for a sleepover tonight.**
Mi amigo viene a dormir a mi casa esta noche.
**We're going to Camilla's for a sleepover.**
Vamos a quedarnos a dormir en casa de Camilla.

**sleepy** ADJECTIVE
**I'm sleepy.**
Tengo sueño.

**sleeve** NOUN
la **manga** fem
**a shirt with long sleeves**
una camisa de manga larga
**a shirt with short sleeves**
una camisa de manga corta

**slept** VERB ▷ see **sleep**

**slice** NOUN
1 la **rebanada** *fem (of bread)*
2 el **trozo** *masc (of cake)*

**slide** NOUN
1 el **tobogán** *masc* (PL los **toboganes**) *(in playground)*
2 el **pasador del pelo** *masc (hair slide)*
3 la **diapositiva** *fem (photo)*

**slight** ADJECTIVE
**ligero** *masc*
**ligera** *fem*
  **a slight fever**
  una ligera fiebre
  **a slight problem**
  un pequeño problema

**slightly** ADVERB
**ligeramente**

**slim**

> **slim** *can be an adjective or a verb.*

**A** ADJECTIVE
  **delgado** *masc*
  **delgada** *fem*
  **She's slimmer now.**
  Ahora está más delgada.

**B** VERB
  **to slim**
  **adelgazar**
  **I'm trying to slim.**
  Estoy intentando adelgazar.

**slipper** NOUN
la **zapatilla** *fem*
  **a pair of slippers**
  unas zapatillas
  **Put on your slippers.**
  Ponte las zapatillas.

> **Language tip**
>
> *In Spanish you usually use an article like* **el**, **la**, **los** *with clothes you are wearing.*

**slow** ADJECTIVE

**lento** *masc*
**lenta** *fem*
  **The music is too slow.**
  La música es demasiado lenta.

**slowly** ADVERB
**despacio**
  **Could you speak more slowly?**
  ¿Puedes hablar más despacio?

**smack** NOUN

> **smack** *can be a noun or a verb.*

**A** NOUN
  el **cachete** *masc*
**B** VERB
  **to smack**
  **dar un cachete a**

**small** ADJECTIVE
**pequeño** *masc*
**pequeña** *fem*
  **This skirt is too small for me.**
  Esta falda me está demasiado pequeña.

**smart** ADJECTIVE
1 **elegante** *masc & fem (elegant)*
  **smart clothes**
  ropa elegante
2 **listo** *masc*
  **lista** *fem (clever)*
  **She's very smart.**
  Es muy lista.

**smell**

> **smell** *can be a noun or a verb.*

**A** NOUN
  el **olor** *masc*
  **a nice smell**
  un buen olor
**B** VERB
  **to smell**
  **oler**
  **Mmm, that smells nice!**
  ¡Uy, qué bien huele eso!

**smile**

> **smile** *can be a noun or a verb.*

**A** NOUN
la **sonrisa** *fem*
**a beautiful smile**
una bonita sonrisa

**B** VERB
**to smile**
sonreír
**Why are you smiling?**
¿Por qué sonríes?

to **smoke** VERB
fumar
**I don't smoke.**
Yo no fumo.
**He's smoking.**
Está fumando.

**smoking** NOUN
**Smoking is bad for you.**
Fumar es malo para la salud.
**'no smoking'**
'prohibido fumar'

**smoothie** NOUN
el **batido de frutas** *masc*

**snack** NOUN
**You can get a snack in the canteen.**
Puedes picar algo en la cafetería.

**snack bar** NOUN
la **cafetería** *fem*

**snail** NOUN
el **caracol** *masc*

**snake** NOUN
la **serpiente** *fem*

to **sneeze** VERB
estornudar

**snooker** NOUN
el **billar** *masc*
**I play snooker.**
Juego al billar.

*Language tip*

*In Spanish, you need to add **al** before the name of the sport.*

to **snore** VERB
roncar
**He's snoring.**
Está roncando.

## snow

*snow can be a noun or a verb.*

**A** NOUN
la **nieve** *fem*
**B** VERB
**to snow**
nevar
**It's going to snow.**
Va a nevar.
**It snows a lot in the mountains.**
Nieva mucho en las montañas.

**It's snowing.**
Está nevando.

**snowball** NOUN
la **bola de nieve** *fem*

**snowboarding** NOUN
el **snowboard** *masc*
**I like snowboarding.**
Me gusta hacer snowboard.

**snowflake** NOUN
el **copo de nieve** *masc*

**snowman** NOUN
el **muñeco de nieve** *masc*
**I'm going to make a snowman.**
Voy a hacer un muñeco de nieve.

## so

*so can be an adverb or a conjunction.*

**A** ADVERB
tan
**You talk so fast.**
Hablas tan rápido.
**It's so difficult.**
Es tan difícil.

**so much**
tanto
**I love you so much.**
Te quiero tanto.
**I've got so many things to do today.**
Tengo tantas cosas que hacer hoy.
**B** CONJUNCTION
**así que**
**It's Raymond's birthday, so I've got him a present.**
Es el cumpleaños de Raymond, así que tengo un regalo para él.
**I play football. – So do I.**
Yo juego al fútbol. – Yo también.
**Is Lisa winning? – I think so.**
¿Va ganando Lisa? – Creo que sí.

**so do I**
yo también
**so have I**
yo también
**so am I**
yo también
**I think so.**
Creo que sí.
**I don't think so.**
Creo que no.
**I hope so.**
Eso espero.

**soap** NOUN
el **jabón** masc
**a bar of soap**
una pastilla de jabón

**soccer** NOUN
el **fútbol** masc

**sock** NOUN
el **calcetín** masc (PL los calcetines)
**I'm wearing white socks.**
Llevo calcetines blancos.
**a pair of socks**
un par de calcetines

**sofa** NOUN
el **sofá** masc

**soft** ADJECTIVE
1 **suave** masc & fem (voice, texture)
2 **blando** masc
**blanda** fem (pillow, bed, ball)

**soft drink** NOUN
el **refresco** masc

**soil** NOUN
la **tierra** fem

**sold** VERB ▷ see **sell**

**soldier** NOUN
el **soldado** masc
**He's a soldier.**
Es soldado.

**Language tip**
In Spanish, you do not use an article with people's jobs.

**some**

some can be an adjective or a pronoun.

**A** ADJECTIVE
1 **algunos** masc pl
**algunas** fem pl (a few)

**Language tip**
When **some** refers to something plural and means the same as 'a few', you can use **algunos** or **algunas** depending on whether the word is masculine or feminine.

**Some children are absent.**
Algunos niños no están.
**I need some nails.**
Necesito algunos clavos.
**I've got some sweets.**
Tengo algunos caramelos.

**Language tip**
However, when **some** is followed by a plural word, it is often not translated.

**I need some nails.**
Necesito clavos.
**I've got some sweets.**
Tengo caramelos.

**2** *(a little)*

> **Language tip**
> When **some** *refers to something you can't count, it usually isn't translated.*

> **Would you like some bread?**
> ¿Quieres pan?
> **I need some sellotape.**
> Necesito celo.

**3 algún** *masc*
**alguna** *fem (one)*
> **some day**
> algún día

**B** PRONOUN

**1 algunos** *masc pl*
**algunas** *fem pl (a few)*
> **some of my friends**
> algunos de mis amigos
> **Have you got all her books? –**
> **I've got some of them.**
> ¿Tienes todos sus libros? –
> Tengo algunos.
> **I've got some, but not many.**
> Tengo algunos, pero no muchos.

> **Language tip**
> When the number of things referred to is unimportant, **some** *usually isn't translated.*

> **Chips? – No thanks, I've still got some.**
> ¿Patatas fritas? – No, gracias, todavía tengo.

**2** *(a little)*

> **Language tip**
> When **some** *refers to something you can't count, it usually isn't translated.*

> **Would you like some coffee?**
> **– No thanks, I've already got some.**
> ¿Quieres café? – No gracias, ya tengo.

> **Language tip**
> However, you can often use **un poco**, *which literally means 'a little'.*

> **I've got a bar of chocolate.**
> **Would you like some?**
> Tengo una tableta de chocolate.
> ¿Quieres un poco?

> **I've got some.**
> Tengo.
> **Would you like some?**
> ¿Quieres?

**somebody** PRONOUN
**alguien**
> **Somebody asked after you.**
> Alguien preguntó por ti.

**someone** PRONOUN
**alguien**
> **Someone asked after you.**
> Alguien preguntó por ti.

**something** PRONOUN
**algo**
> **Are you looking for something?**
> ¿Estás buscando algo?

> **I can see something green.**
> Veo algo verde.

**sometimes** ADVERB
**a veces**
> **sometimes, but not very often**
> a veces, pero no muy a menudo

**somewhere** ADVERB
**en alguna parte**
> **It's somewhere in the classroom.**
> Está en alguna parte de la clase.
> **I've got to go somewhere.**
> Tengo que ir a alguna parte.

**son** NOUN
el **hijo** masc
**her son**
su hijo

**song** NOUN
la **canción** fem (PL las canciones)
**We're going to sing a song.**
Vamos a cantar una canción.

**soon** ADVERB
**pronto**
**It'll soon be lunchtime.**
Pronto será la hora de comer.
**very soon**
muy pronto
**Please tell me as soon as possible.**
Por favor, dímelo lo antes posible.

**as soon as possible**
lo antes posible
**Write soon!**
¡Escribe pronto!

**sore** ADJECTIVE
**It's sore.**
Duele.
**My head is sore.**
Me duele la cabeza.

**Language tip**
In Spanish you usually use an article like **el**, **la**, **los** with parts of the body.

**sorry** EXCLAMATION
¡**Lo siento!**
**I'm really sorry.**
Lo siento mucho.
**I'm sorry, I can't.**
Lo siento, no puedo.
**I'm sorry I'm late.**
Siento llegar tarde.

**Sorry!**
¡Lo siento!

**sort** NOUN
el **tipo** masc

**What sort of bike have you got?**
¿Qué tipo de bici tienes?

**sound**

sound can be a noun or a verb.

**A** NOUN
**1** el **ruido** masc (noise)
**the sound of footsteps**
el ruido de pasos
**Don't make a sound!**
¡No hagas ruido!
**2** el **volumen** masc (volume)
**Can I turn the sound down?**
¿Puedo bajar el volumen?
**B** VERB
**to sound**
parecer
**That sounds interesting.**
Eso parece interesante.
**That sounds like a good idea.**
Eso parece una buena idea.

**soup** NOUN
la **sopa** fem
**vegetable soup**
sopa de verduras

**sour** ADJECTIVE
**agrio** masc
**agria** fem

**south**

south can be an adjective or a noun.

**A** ADJECTIVE
**sur**

**Language tip**
**sur** never changes its ending no matter what it describes. Did you know that adjectives that behave like this are called 'invariable adjectives'?

**the south coast**
la costa sur
**B** NOUN
el **sur** masc
**in the south**
en el sur

**the south of Spain**
el sur de España
**Málaga is in the south of Spain.**
Málaga está en el sur de España.

### southern ADJECTIVE
**southern England**
el sur de Inglaterra

### South Pole NOUN
**the South Pole**
el Polo Sur *masc*

### souvenir NOUN
el **recuerdo** *masc*
**a souvenir shop**
una tienda de recuerdos

### space NOUN
1 el **sitio** *masc (room)*
**There's a lot of space.**
Hay mucho sitio.
**Leave a space for a drawing.**
Deja un sitio para un dibujo.
2 el **espacio** *masc (outer space)*
3 la **casilla** *fem (in game)*
**Go back three spaces.**
Retrocede tres casillas.

### spaceship NOUN
la **nave espacial** *fem*

### spade NOUN
1 la **pala** *fem*
**a bucket and spade**
un cubo y una pala

> **Language tip**
> Be careful! The translation of **spade** is not **espada**.

2 *(in cards)*
**spades**
las picas *fem pl*
**the ace of spades**
el as de picas

### spaghetti NOUN
los **espaguetis** *masc pl*

### Spain NOUN
**España** *fem*
**Seville is in Spain.**
Sevilla está en España.
**He lives in Spain.**
Vive en España.
**We're going to Spain.**
Vamos a ir a España.
**They are from Spain.**
Son de España.

## Spanish

> **Spanish** *can be an adjective or a noun.*

**A** ADJECTIVE
**español** *masc*
**española** *fem*
**a Spanish girl**
una chica española
**our Spanish teacher**
nuestro profesor de español
**my Spanish book**
mi libro de español
**Spanish people**
los españoles

> **He's Spanish.**
> Es español.
> **She's Spanish.**
> Es española.

**B** NOUN
el **español** *masc*
**Do you speak Spanish?**
¿Hablas español?

> **Did you know...?**
> Did you know that Spanish is also called **el castellano** because it originated in **Castilla** in central Spain? Depending where you are in the country, you'll also hear other languages, such as **el catalán**, **el gallego** and **el vasco**, but **el castellano** is understood and used throughout the country too.

**the Spanish**
los españoles

**spare room** NOUN
la **habitación de invitados**
*fem* (PL las **habitaciones de invitados**)

**spare time** NOUN
el **tiempo libre** *masc*
**What do you do in your spare time?**
¿Qué haces en tu tiempo libre?

**sparkling** ADJECTIVE
**con gas**
**sparkling water**
agua con gas
**sparkling wine**
vino espumoso

to **speak** VERB
**hablar**
**Could you speak more slowly, please?**
¿Puedes hablar más despacio, por favor?

**I speak English.**
Hablo inglés.
**Do you speak English?**
¿Hablas inglés?

**special** ADJECTIVE
**especial** *masc & fem*

**speciality** NOUN
la **especialidad** *fem*

**specially** ADVERB
**sobre todo**
**It rains a lot, specially in winter.**

Llueve mucho, sobre todo en invierno.

**spectator** NOUN
el **espectador** *masc*
la **espectadora** *fem*

**speech** NOUN
el **discurso** *masc*
**The headmaster made a speech.**
El director dio un discurso.

**speed** NOUN
la **velocidad** *fem*
**a ten-speed bike**
una bici de diez velocidades

**speedboat** NOUN
la **lancha motora** *fem*

to **spell** VERB
1 **escribir** *(in writing)*
**How do you spell that?**
¿Cómo se escribe eso?
2 **deletrear** *(out loud)*
**Can you spell that please?**
¿Puedes deletrear eso, por favor?

**spelling** NOUN
la **ortografía** *fem*
**a spelling mistake**
una falta de ortografía

to **spend** VERB
1 **gastar** *(money)*
**I spent twenty pounds on presents.**
Gasté veinte libras en regalos.
2 **pasar** *(time)*
**We are going to spend two weeks in Scotland.**
Vamos a pasar dos semanas en Escocia.

**spicy** ADJECTIVE
**picante** *masc & fem*

English Spanish

a b c d e f g h i j k l m n o p q r s t u v w x y z

**spider** NOUN
la **araña** *fem*

**spinach** NOUN
las **espinacas** *fem pl*
**I don't like spinach.**
No me gustan las espinacas.

**spite** NOUN
**in spite of**
a pesar de
**in spite of the weather**
a pesar del tiempo

to **split** VERB
1 **dividirse** *(separate)*
**Split into two groups.**
Dividíos en dos grupos.
2 **compartir** *(share)*
**Let's split the money
between us.**
Vamos a compartir el dinero
entre nosotros.

**spoiled** ADJECTIVE
**mimado** *masc*
**mimada** *fem*
**a spoiled child**
un niño mimado

**spoilsport** NOUN
el/la **aguafiestas** *masc/fem* (PL
los/las **aguafiestas**)
**Don't be a spoilsport!**
¡No seas aguafiestas!

**spoilt** ADJECTIVE
**mimado** *masc*
**mimada** *fem*
**a spoilt child**
un niño mimado

**spoke** VERB ▷*see* **speak**

**spoken** VERB ▷*see* **speak**

**sponge** NOUN
la **esponja** *fem*

**sponge bag** NOUN
la **bolsa de aseo** *fem*

**sponge cake** NOUN
el **bizcocho** *masc*

to **sponsor** VERB
**I'm doing a sponsored ten-
mile walk in aid of the
homeless.**
Voy a caminar diez millas para
conseguir donativos en beneficio
de los sin techo.

> **Did you know...?**
> In Spain it isn't usual to sponsor
> people to go on walks, swims and so
> on for charity.

**spoon** NOUN
la **cuchara** *fem*
**I haven't got a spoon.**
No tengo cuchara.

**sport** NOUN
el **deporte** *masc*
**What's your favourite sport?**
¿Cuál es tu deporte favorito?
**Football is my favourite
sport.**
El fútbol es mi deporte favorito.
**What sports do you play?**
¿Qué deportes practicas?

**sports bag** NOUN
la **bolsa de deportes** *fem*

**sports car** NOUN
el **coche deportivo** *masc*

**spot**

> **spot** *can be a noun or a verb.*

A NOUN
1 el **lunar** *masc (dot)*
**a red dress with white spots**
un vestido rojo con lunares
blancos
2 el **grano** *masc (pimple)*
**He's covered in spots.**
Está lleno de granos.
B VERB
**to spot**
**encontrar** *(find)*
**Can you spot the odd one
out?**
¿Puedes encontrar el que no es
como los demás?

**spring** NOUN
la **primavera** *fem*
**It's the first day of spring.**
Es el primer día de la primavera.

**in spring**
en primavera

**springtime** NOUN
la **primavera** *fem*

**in springtime**
en primavera

**spy** NOUN
el/la **espía** *masc/fem*

**square** NOUN
1 el **cuadrado** *masc (shape)*
**a square and a triangle**
un cuadrado y un triángulo
2 la **plaza** *fem (in town)*
**There's a statue in the middle of the square.**
Hay una estatua en mitad de la plaza.

**squash** NOUN
1 *(drink)*
**orange squash**
la naranjada
2 el **squash** *masc (game)*
**I play squash.**
Juego al squash.

*Language tip*

*In Spanish, you need to add* **al** *before the name of the sport.*

**squirrel** NOUN
la **ardilla** *fem*

**stable** NOUN
la **cuadra** *fem*

**stack** NOUN
la **pila** *fem*
**a stack of books**
una pila de libros

**stadium** NOUN
el **estadio** *masc*

**staff** NOUN
1 el **personal** *masc (personnel)*

2 el **profesorado** *masc*
*(of school)*

**staffroom** NOUN
la **sala de profesores** *fem*

**staircase** NOUN
la **escalera** *fem*

**stairs** PL NOUN
la **escalera** *fem*
**Go down the stairs.**
Baja la escalera.
**Go up the stairs.**
Sube la escalera.

**stamp** NOUN
el **sello** *masc*
**a Spanish stamp**
un sello español
**My hobby is stamp collecting.**
Mi afición es coleccionar sellos.

**stamp album** NOUN
el **álbum de sellos** *masc*

**stamp collection** NOUN
la **colección de sellos** *fem* (PL
las **colecciones de sellos**)

to **stand** VERB
**Stand in a line.**
Poneos en fila.
**Stand over there, Andrew.**
Quédate ahí de pie, Andrew.
**I'm standing by the door.**
Estoy de pie junto a la puerta.

to **stand for** VERB
ser la **abreviatura de**
**'EU' stands for 'European Union'.**
'EU' es la abreviatura de 'European Union'.

to **stand up** VERB
ponerse de pie
**Stand up, Christine!**
¡Ponte de pie, Christine!

**stapler** NOUN
la **grapadora** *fem*

**star** NOUN
la **estrella** *fem*

**the moon and the stars**
la luna y las estrellas

**He's a TV star.**
Es una estrella de la TV.

*Language tip*

*Did you notice that you can use una estrella even when referring to a man?*

## start

*start can be a verb or a noun.*

**A** VERB
**to start**
**1 empezar** *(begin)*
**What time does it start?**
¿A qué hora empieza?
**It starts with a P.**
Empieza por P.

*Language tip*

*When start is followed by another verb it is translated by empezar a.*

**You can start writing now.**
Podéis empezar a escribir ahora.

**Let's start.**
Empecemos.
**Start now, children.**
¡Niños, empezad ahora!

**2 crear** *(set up)*
**We want to start a football team.**
Queremos crear un equipo de fútbol.
**B** NOUN
el **principio** *masc (beginning)*

**at the start of the film**
al principio de la película
**at the start of December**
a primeros de diciembre
**Shall we make a start?**
¿Empezamos ya?

**starter** NOUN
la **entrada** *fem (dish)*

**to starve** VERB
**I'm starving!**
¡Tengo mucha hambre!

**station** NOUN
la **estación** *fem* (PL las estaciones)
**Where's the station?**
¿Dónde está la estación?

**statue** NOUN
la **estatua** *fem*

## stay

*stay can be a verb or a noun.*

**A** VERB
**to stay**
**quedarse**
**Stay here, Daniel!**
¡Quédate aquí, Daniel!
**We stayed in London for three days.**
Nos quedamos tres días en Londres.
**We're going to stay with friends.**
Vamos a quedarnos a dormir con unos amigos.
**Why don't you stay the night?**
¿Por qué no os quedáis a dormir?
**B** NOUN
la **estancia** *fem*
**my stay in England**
mi estancia en Inglaterra

**to stay in** VERB
**quedarse en casa**
**I'm staying in tonight.**
Esta noche me quedo en casa.

**steak** NOUN
el **filete** *masc*
**I'd like steak and chips.**
Quiero un filete con patatas.

to **steal** VERB
**1 quitar** *(take)*
**Who's stolen my pencil case?**
¿Quién me ha quitado el
estuche?
**2 robar** *(thief)*
**Our car's been stolen.**
Nos han robado el coche.

**step** NOUN
**1** el **paso** *masc (movement)*
**a step backwards**
un paso atrás
**Take a step forward, boys.**
Dad un paso hacia
adelante, chicos.
**2** el **escalón** *masc* (PL los
**escalones**)
**Mind the step.**
Cuidado con el escalón.

**stepbrother** NOUN
el **hermanastro** *masc*
**his stepbrother**
su hermanastro

**stepfather** NOUN
el **padrastro** *masc*
**my stepfather**
mi padrastro

**stepmother** NOUN
la **madrastra** *fem*
**my stepmother**
mi madrastra

**stepsister** NOUN
la **hermanastra** *fem*
**my stepsister**
mi hermanastra

**stew** NOUN
el **estofado** *masc*

**stewardess** NOUN
**1** la **auxiliar de vuelo** *fem (on
plane)*
**2** la **camarera** *fem (on boat)*

to **stick** VERB
**pegar**
**Stick the stamps on the
envelope.**
Pega los sellos en el sobre.

to **stick out** VERB
**Don't stick out your tongue!**
¡No saques la lengua!

**sticker** NOUN
la **pegatina** *fem*

**still**

> **still** *can be an adverb or an
adjective.*

**A** ADVERB
**todavía**
**You've still got two cards.**
Todavía tienes dos cartas.
**I'm still hungry.**
Todavía tengo hambre
**B** ADJECTIVE
**Keep still, Ben!**
¡No te muevas, Ben!
**Sit still, David!**
¡Siéntate ahí quieto, David!

> **Language tip**
> *Change* **quieto** *to* **quieta** *if you're
talking to a girl.*

**stitch** NOUN
el **punto** *masc*
**I've got five stitches.**
Me han dado cinco puntos.

**stomach** NOUN
el **estómago** *masc*

**stomachache** NOUN
**I've got stomachache.**
Me duele el estómago.

**stone** NOUN
la **piedra** *fem*
**The boys are throwing stones.**
Los niños están tirando piedras.
**a stone wall**
un muro de piedra
**I weigh five stone.**
Peso unos treinta y dos kilos.

### Did you know...?

*In Spain, weight is given in kilos. A **stone** is about 6.3 kilos.*

**stool** NOUN
la **banqueta** *fem*

### stop

**stop** *can be a verb or a noun.*

**A** VERB
**to stop**
parar
**Stop, that's enough!**
¡Para, ya basta!
**Stop talking, children.**
Parad de hablar, niños.
**My dad wants to stop smoking.**
Mi padre quiere dejar de fumar.

### Stop it!
¡Ya basta!

**B** NOUN
la **parada** *fem*
**a bus stop**
una parada de autobús

**storey** NOUN
la **planta** *fem*
**a three-storey building**
un edificio de tres plantas

**storm** NOUN
la **tormenta** *fem*

**stormy** ADJECTIVE
**stormy weather**
tiempo tormentoso

**story** NOUN
1 la **historia** *fem (spoken)*
**I'm going to tell you a story.**
Os voy a contar una historia.
2 el **cuento**
*masc*
*(written)*

**stove** NOUN
la **cocina**
*fem*

## straight

**straight** *can be an adjective or an adverb.*

**A** ADJECTIVE
1 **recto** *masc*
**recta** *fem*
**a straight line**
una línea recta
2 **lacio** *masc*
**lacia** *fem (hair)*
**I've got straight hair.**
Tengo el pelo lacio.
**B** ADVERB
**straight away**
en seguida
**straight on**
todo recto

### Go straight on.
Sigue recto.

**strange** ADJECTIVE
**extraño** *masc*
**extraña** *fem*
**That's strange!**
¡Eso es extraño!
**a strange dream**
un sueño extraño

**stranger** NOUN
el **desconocido** *masc*
la **desconocida** *fem*
**Don't talk to strangers.**
No hables con desconocidos.
**I'm a stranger here.**
Soy de fuera.

### Language tip
*Be careful! The translation of **stranger** is not **extranjero**.*

**strap** NOUN
1 el **tirante** *masc (of bra, dress)*
2 la **correa** *fem (of watch, camera, suitcase)*
**I need a new strap for my watch.**
Necesito una correa nueva para mi reloj.

**straw** NOUN

**1** la **pajita** *fem (for drinking)*
**2** la **paja** *fem (material)*

**strawberry** NOUN
la **fresa** *fem*
**strawberry jam**
mermelada de fresa
**a strawberry ice cream**
un helado de fresa

**stream** NOUN
el **arroyo** *masc*

**street** NOUN
la **calle** *fem*
**in the street**
en la calle

to **stretch** VERB
**1** **estirarse**
**The dog woke up and stretched.**
El perro se despertó y se estiró.
**2** **estirar** *(arms, legs)*
**Stretch your arms!**
¡Estirad los brazos!
**Shall we go out and stretch our legs?**
¿Salimos a estirar las piernas?

> **Language tip**
> In Spanish you usually use an article like **el, la, los** with parts of the body.

**strict**
ADJECTIVE
**estricto** *masc*
**estricta** *fem*

**strike** NOUN
la **huelga** *fem*
**They are on strike.**
Están en huelga.

**string** NOUN
la **cuerda** *fem*
**a piece of string**
una cuerda

**stripe** NOUN
la **raya** *fem*

**stripy** ADJECTIVE
**de rayas**
**a stripy shirt**
una camisa de rayas

**strong** ADJECTIVE
**fuerte** *masc & fem*
**She's very strong.**
Es muy fuerte.

**student** NOUN
el/la **estudiante** *masc/fem*
**I'm a student.**
Soy estudiante.

> **Language tip**
> In Spanish, you do not use an article with people's jobs.

to **study** VERB
**estudiar**
**My sister's studying for her exams.**
Mi hermana está estudiando para sus exámenes.

**stuff** NOUN
las **cosas** *fem pl*
**Have you got all your stuff?**
¿Tienes todas tus cosas?

**stuffy** ADJECTIVE
**It's stuffy in here.**
Hay un ambiente muy cargado aquí.

**stupid** ADJECTIVE
**estúpido** *masc*
**estúpida** *fem*
**a stupid joke**
un chiste estúpido

**subject** NOUN
la **asignatura** *fem*
**What's your favourite subject?**
¿Cuál es tu asignatura favorita?

**subtitles** PL NOUN
los **subtítulos** *masc pl*
**a Spanish film with English subtitles**
una película española con subtítulos en inglés

a
b
c
d
e
f
g
h
i
j
k
l
m
n
o
p
q
r
s
t
u
v
w
x
y
z

to **subtract** VERB
**restar**
> **Subtract three
> from five.**
> Réstale tres
> a cinco.

**suburb** NOUN
el **barrio
de las
afueras** *masc*
> **a suburb of London**
> un barrio de las afueras de
> Londres
> **They live in the suburbs.**
> Viven en las afueras.

**success** NOUN
el **éxito** *masc*
> **The party was a great
> success.**
> La fiesta fue un gran éxito.

> *Language tip*
>
> Be careful! The translation of
> **success** is not **suceso**.

**such** ADVERB
**tan**
> **such nice people**
> gente tan simpática
> **such a long journey**
> un viaje tan largo
> **We've got such a lot of work.**
> Tenemos mucho trabajo.
> **such as**
> como
> **towns such as Alicante and
> Valencia**
> ciudades como Alicante y
> Valencia

**sudden** ADJECTIVE
**repentino** *masc*
**repentina** *fem*
> **a sudden change**
> un cambio repentino

**suddenly** ADVERB
**de repente**

**suede** NOUN
el **ante** *masc*

> **a suede jacket**
> una chaqueta de ante

**sugar** NOUN
el **azúcar** *masc*
> **Do you take sugar?**
> ¿Tomas azúcar?
> **More sugar?**
> ¿Más azúcar?

**suggestion** NOUN
la **sugerencia** *fem*
> **Have you got any
> suggestions?**
> ¿Tienes alguna sugerencia?

**suit**

> **suit** *can be a noun or a verb.*

**A** NOUN
**1** el **traje** *masc* (man's)
**2** el **traje de chaqueta** *masc*
(woman's)
**B** VERB
**to suit**
**sentar bien a**
> **Pink doesn't suit me.**
> El rosa no me sienta bien.

**suitcase** NOUN
la **maleta** *fem*

**sum** NOUN
la **suma** *fem*
> **I like doing sums.**
> Me gusta hacer sumas.
> **She's good at sums.**
> Se le da bien el cálculo.

**summer** NOUN
el **verano** *masc*
> **It's very hot in summer.**
> Hace mucho calor en verano.

We're going to Greece this summer.
Vamos a ir a Grecia este verano.

**in summer**
en verano
**this summer**
este verano
**last summer**
el verano pasado

**summer holidays** PL NOUN
las **vacaciones de verano** *fem pl*
   **in the summer holidays**
   en las vacaciones de verano

**summertime** NOUN
el **verano** *masc*

**in summertime**
en verano

**sun** NOUN
el **sol** *masc*
   **in the sun**
   al sol

to **sunbathe** VERB
**tomar el sol**
   **I like sunbathing.**
   Me gusta tomar el sol.

**sunburnt** ADJECTIVE
   **to get sunburnt**
   quemarse con el sol
   **I got sunburnt.**
   Me quemé con el sol.

**Sunday** NOUN
el **domingo** *masc*
   **It's Sunday today.**
   Hoy es domingo.

**on Sunday**
el domingo
**on Sundays**
los domingos
**every Sunday**
cada domingo
**last Sunday**
el domingo pasado
**next Sunday**
el domingo que viene

*Language tip*
*Days are not spelled with a capital letter in Spanish.*

**Sunday school** NOUN
la **catequesis** *fem*

**sunflower** NOUN
el **girasol** *masc*

**sung** VERB >see **sing**

**sunglasses** PL NOUN
las **gafas de sol** *fem pl*
   **a pair of sunglasses**
   unas gafas de sol

**sunny** ADJECTIVE
   **It's a sunny day.**
   Hace un día de sol.

**It's sunny.**
Hace sol.

**sunshine** NOUN
el **sol** *masc*
   **lots of sunshine**
   mucho sol

**super** ADJECTIVE
**estupendo** *masc*
**estupenda** *fem*

**supermarket** NOUN
el **supermercado** *masc*
   **We do our shopping at the supermarket.**
   Hacemos la compra en el supermercado.

**supper** NOUN
la **cena** *fem*

**supply teacher** NOUN
el **profesor sustituto** *masc*
la **profesora sustituta** *fem*
   **She's a supply teacher.**
   Es profesora sustituta.

*Language tip*
*In Spanish, you do not use an article with people's jobs.*

to **support** VERB
  **ser de**
    **I support Real Madrid.**
    Soy del Real Madrid.
    **What team do you support?**
    ¿De qué equipo eres?

**supporter** NOUN
  el **aficionado** *masc*
  la **aficionada** *fem*
    **a Liverpool supporter**
    un aficionado del Liverpool

to **suppose** VERB
  **suponer**
    **I suppose he's right.**
    Supongo que tiene razón.
    **You're not supposed to do that, Teresa.**
    No deberías hacer eso, Teresa.

**sure** ADJECTIVE
  **seguro** *masc*
  **segura** *fem*
    **Are you sure, Helen?**
    ¿Estás segura, Helen?

**I'm not sure.**
No estoy seguro.

**surf**

*surf can be a noun or a verb.*

  **A** NOUN
    las **olas** *fem pl (in sea)*
  **B** VERB
    **to surf**
  **1 hacer surf**
    **I like to go surfing at the weekends.**
    Los fines de semana me gusta hacer surf.
  **2 to surf the Net**
    **navegar por Internet**

**surface** NOUN
  la **superficie** *fem*

**surfboard** NOUN
  la **tabla de surf** *fem*

**surfing** NOUN
  el **surf** *masc*

**I go surfing.**
Hago surf.

**surname** NOUN
  el **apellido** *masc*
    **What's your surname?**
    ¿Cuál es tu apellido?

**surprise** NOUN
  la **sorpresa** *fem*
    **What a surprise!**
    ¡Vaya sorpresa!

**survey** NOUN
  la **encuesta** *fem*
    **We're doing a survey on pets.**
    Estamos haciendo una encuesta sobre las mascotas.

to **suspend** VERB
  **expulsar temporalmente**
    **He's been suspended.**
    Lo han expulsado temporalmente.

to **swallow** VERB
  **tragar**

**swam** VERB ▷ *see* **swim**

**swan** NOUN
  el **cisne** *masc*

to **swap** VERB
  **cambiar**
    **Do you want to swap?**
    ¿Quieres que cambiemos?
    **I'll swap you my stamps for your stickers.**
    Te cambiaré mis sellos por tus pegatinas.
    **Let's swap places.**
    Vamos a cambiarnos de sitio.

**sweat**

*sweat can be a verb or a noun.*

**A** VERB
**to sweat**
sudar
**B** NOUN
el **sudor** *masc*

**sweater** NOUN
el **jersey** *masc* (PL los **jerseys**)
**a white sweater**
un jersey blanco

**sweatshirt** NOUN
la **sudadera** *fem*
**a green sweatshirt**
una sudadera verde

**sweet**

*sweet can be a noun or an
adjective.*

**A** NOUN
**1** el **caramelo** *masc* (*toffee, mint
etc*)
**a bag of sweets**
una bolsa de caramelos
**2** el **postre** *masc* (*pudding*)
**Sweets: ice cream or
chocolate mousse**
Postres: helado o mousse de
chocolate
**B** ADJECTIVE
**1** **dulce** *masc & fem* (*sugary*)
**It's too sweet.**
Está demasiado dulce.
**2** **encantador** *masc*
**encantadora** *fem* (*delightful*)
**Isn't she sweet?**
¿Verdad que es encantadora?

**sweetcorn** NOUN
el **maíz dulce** *masc*

**swim**

*swim can be a verb or a noun.*

**A** VERB
**to swim**
nadar
**Can you swim?**
¿Sabes nadar?
**I can swim.**
Sé nadar.

**I can't swim.**
No sé nadar.
**B** NOUN
**I want to go for a swim.**
Quiero ir a nadar.

**swimmer** NOUN
el **nadador** *masc*
la **nadadora** *fem*
**She's a good
swimmer.**
Es una buena
nadadora.

**swimming** NOUN
la **natación** *fem*
**Do you like swimming?**
¿Te gusta la natación?
**I go swimming on
Wednesdays.**
Voy a nadar los miércoles.

**swimming costume**
NOUN
el **traje de baño** *masc*

**swimming pool** NOUN
la **piscina** *fem*

**swimming trunks** PL NOUN
el **bañador** *masc*
**I've got new swimming
trunks.**
Tengo un bañador nuevo.

**swimsuit** NOUN
el **traje de baño** *masc*

**swing** NOUN
el **columpio** *masc*

**switch**

*switch can be a noun or a verb.*

**A** NOUN
el **interruptor** *masc*
**Where's the switch?**
¿Dónde está el interruptor?
**B** VERB
**to switch**

● ● ● ● ● ● ● ● ● ● ● ● ● ● ● ● ● ● ● ● ● ● ●

cambiar de
**Switch partners!**
¡Cambiad de pareja!

to **switch off** VERB
apagar
**Switch off the computer, Jane.**
Apaga el ordenador, Jane.

to **switch on** VERB
encender
**Switch on the light, Neil.**
Enciende la luz, Neil.

to **swop** VERB
cambiar
**Do you want to swop?**
¿Quieres que cambiemos?
**Let's swop places.**
Vamos a cambiar de sitio.

**sword** NOUN
la **espada** fem

**swum** VERB ▷ see **swim**

**symbol** NOUN
el **símbolo** masc

**sympathetic** ADJECTIVE
**comprensivo** masc
**comprensiva** fem

**Language tip**

*Be careful! The translation of* **sympathetic** *is not* **simpático**.

**system** NOUN
el **sistema** masc

**Language tip**

*Even though it ends in* -**a**, **el sistema** *is a masculine noun.*

# T t

**table** NOUN
1 la **mesa** *fem (piece of furniture)*
**It's on the table.**
Está en la mesa.
2 la **tabla** *fem (chart)*
**the three times table**
la tabla del tres

**tablecloth** NOUN
el **mantel** *masc*

**tablespoon** NOUN
la **cuchara grande** *fem*

**table tennis** NOUN
el **tenis de mesa** *masc*
**I can play table tennis.**
Sé jugar al tenis de mesa.

> **Language tip**
>
> *In Spanish, you need to add **al**
> before the name of the sport or
> game.*

**tail** NOUN
1 el **rabo** *masc (of dog)*
**The dog wagged its tail.**
El perro movía el rabo.

> **Language tip**
>
> *In Spanish you usually use an article
> like **el**, **la**, **los** with parts of the
> body.*

2 la **cola** *fem (of horse, bird, fish)*

**Heads or tails?**
¿Cara o cruz?

to **take** VERB
1 **coger**
**Take a card, Susan.**
Coge una carta, Susan.
**Who has taken my ruler?**
¿Quién ha cogido mi regla?
**Take the first turning on the
right.**
Coge el primer desvío a la
derecha.

**Let's take the bus.**
Vamos a coger el autobús.

> **Language tip**
>
> *Don't use **coger** in Latin America as
> it's considered rude in some places.
> Use verbs like **tomar** and **agarrar**
> instead.*

2 **tomar** *(food, medicine)*
**I don't take sugar.**
No tomo azúcar.
3 **llevar** *(take along)*
**Mum's going to take me to
the fair.**
Mi madre me va a llevar a la
feria.
**Don't forget to take your
camera.**
No te olvides de llevarte la
cámara.
4 **durar** *(last)*
**How long does the journey
take?**
¿Cuánto dura el viaje?
**It takes about an hour.**
Se tarda más o menos una hora.

to **take away** VERB
**Thirty take away
nine is twenty-
one.**
Treinta menos
nueve son
veintiuno.

to **take back**
VERB
**devolver**
**I'm going to
take this book back to the
library.**
Voy a devolver este libro a la
biblioteca.

to **take down** VERB
**quitar**

**Take the posters down.**
Quita los pósters.

to **take off** VERB
**quitarse** (clothes)
**Take your coat off.**
Quítate el abrigo.

*Language tip*
In Spanish you usually use an article
like **el**, **la**, **los** with clothes you are
wearing.

to **take out** VERB
**sacar**
**Can you take the key out of
the lock?**
¿Puedes sacar la
llave de la
cerradura?
**I take the dog
out at about
six o'clock.**
Saco al perro a
pasear sobre
las seis.

**taken** ▷see **take**

**takeoff** NOUN
el **despegue** masc

**tale** NOUN
el **cuento** masc

**talk**

**talk** can be a verb or a noun.

**A** VERB
**to talk**
**hablar**
**You talk too much.**
Hablas demasiado.
**Today we're going to talk
about Spain.**
Hoy vamos a hablar de España.
**B** NOUN
**Let's have a talk about it.**
Vamos a hablar de eso.

**talkative** ADJECTIVE
**hablador** masc
**habladora** fem

**tall** ADJECTIVE
**alto** masc
**alta** fem
**Ian is tall.**
Ian es alto.
**My sister is taller than me.**
Mi hermana es más alta que yo.
**Mark is the tallest in the
class.**
Mark es el más alto de la clase.
**a very tall building**
un edificio muy alto

**How tall are you?**
¿Cuánto mides?
**I'm one metre thirty tall.**
Mido un metro treinta.

**tan** NOUN
el **bronceado** masc
**She's got an amazing tan.**
Tiene un bronceado increíble.

**tangerine** NOUN
la **mandarina** fem

**tap** NOUN
el **grifo** masc
**Turn on the tap.**
Abre el grifo.
**the hot tap**
el grifo del agua caliente

**tap-dancing** NOUN
el **claqué** masc

**target** NOUN
la **diana** fem

**tart** NOUN
la **tarta** fem
**a jam tart**
una tarta de mermelada

**tartan**
ADJECTIVE
**de cuadros
escoceses**
**a tartan
scarf**
una bufanda
de cuadros
escoceses

## taste

*taste can be a noun or a verb.*

**A** NOUN
el **sabor** *masc*
**It's got a strange taste.**
Tiene un sabor extraño.
**Would you like a taste?**
¿Quieres probarlo?
**B** VERB
**to taste**
1 **probar** *(try)*
**Would you like to taste it?**
¿Quieres probarlo?
2 **It tastes nice.**
Tiene buen sabor.
**It tastes of fish.**
Sabe a pescado.

**tasty** ADJECTIVE
**sabroso** *masc*
**sabrosa** *fem*

**tattoo** NOUN
el **tatuaje** *masc*

**taught** VERB ▷*see* **teach**

**taxi** NOUN
el **taxi** *masc*
**by taxi**
en taxi

**taxi driver** NOUN
el/la **taxista** *masc/fem*

*Language tip*
*In Spanish, you do not use an article with people's jobs.*

## tea

1 NOUN
el **té** *masc*
**a cup of tea**
una taza de té
**tea with milk**
té con leche
**Would you like some tea?**
¿Quieres un té?
2 la **cena** *fem (evening meal)*
**What's for tea?**
¿Qué hay de cena?
**to have tea**

cenar
**We're having tea.**
Estamos cenando.

**tea bag** NOUN
la **bolsita de té** *fem*

to **teach** VERB
**enseñar**
**Mrs Morrison teaches us English.**
Mrs Morrison nos enseña inglés.
**My cousin is teaching me to play the guitar.**
Mi primo me está enseñando a tocar la guitarra.

**teacher** NOUN
1 el **maestro** *masc*
la **maestra** *fem (in primary school)*
**Mr Price is our teacher.**
Mr Price es nuestro maestro.
2 el **profesor** *masc*
la **profesora** *fem (in secondary school)*
**a maths teacher**
un profesor de matemáticas
**She's a teacher.**
Es profesora.

*Language tip*
*In Spanish, you do not use an article with people's jobs*

**team** NOUN
el **equipo** *masc*
**a football team**
un equipo de fútbol
**She's in my team.**
Está en mi equipo.
**We're going to divide the class into two teams.**
Vamos a dividir la clase en dos equipos.

**teaspoon** NOUN
la **cucharilla** *fem*

## tear

*tear can be a noun or a verb.*

**A** NOUN
la **lágrima** *fem*

**B** VERB
**to tear**
**romper**
Be careful or you'll tear the page.
Ten cuidado que vas a romper la página.

**teatime** NOUN
la **hora de cenar** *fem* (supper time)
**at teatime**
a la hora de cenar

**tea towel** NOUN
el **paño de cocina** *masc*

**technology** NOUN
la **tecnología** *fem*

> *Language tip*
> *Have you noticed that there isn't an* **h** *in* **tecnología**?

**teddy bear** NOUN
el **osito de peluche** *masc*

**teenager** NOUN
el/la **adolescente** *masc/fem*

**teens** PL NOUN
**He's in his teens.**
Es un adolescente.
**She's in her teens.**
Es una adolescente.

**tee-shirt** NOUN
la **camiseta** *fem*

**teeth** PL NOUN
los **dientes** *masc pl*
**I clean my teeth three times a day.**
Me lavo los dientes tres veces al día.

> *Language tip*
> *In Spanish you usually use an article like* **el**, **la**, **los** *with parts of the body.*

**telephone** NOUN
el **teléfono** *masc*

**telephone call** NOUN
la **llamada telefónica** *fem*

**telephone number** NOUN
el **número de teléfono** *masc*
**What's your telephone number?**
¿Cuál es tu número de teléfono?

**television** NOUN
la **televisión** *fem*
**on television**
en la televisión
**What's on television?**
¿Qué hay en la televisión?
**I haven't got a television in my room.**
No tengo televisión en mi habitación.

**television programme**
NOUN
el **programa de televisión** *masc*

> *Language tip*
> *Even though it ends in* -a, **el programa** *is a masculine noun.*

to **tell** VERB
**1 decir** (say)
**Tell me why, Janice.**
Dime por qué, Janice.
**I'm going to tell my mum.**
Se lo voy a decir a mi madre.
**2 contar** (recount)
**I'm going to tell you a story.**
Te voy a contar una historia.
**I'll tell you about myself.**
Te contaré cosas sobre mí.

to **tell off** VERB
**regañar**
**She tells me off if I'm late.**
Me regaña si llego tarde.

**telly** NOUN
la **tele** fem
**I watch telly a lot.**
Veo mucho la tele.
**on telly**
en la tele

**temperature** NOUN
1 la **temperatura** fem (in centigrade etc)
2 la **fiebre** fem (fever)
**I've got a temperature.**
Tengo fiebre.

**ten** NUMBER
**diez**
**ten euros**
diez euros
**It's ten to three.**
Son las tres menos diez.
**It's ten past two.**
Son las dos y diez.

**I'm ten.**
Tengo diez años.

*Language tip*
*In English you can say **I'm ten** or **I'm ten years old**. In Spanish you can only say **tengo diez años**. Have you noticed that in Spanish you need to use the verb **tener** to talk about somebody's age?*

**tennis** NOUN
el **tenis** masc
**I play tennis.**
Juego al tenis.

*Language tip*
*In Spanish, you need to add **al** before the name of the sport.*

**tennis ball** NOUN
la **pelota de tenis** fem

**tennis court** NOUN
la **pista de tenis** fem

**tennis racket** NOUN
la **raqueta de tenis** fem

**tennis player** NOUN
el **jugador de tenis** masc

la **jugadora de tenis** fem

**tenpin bowling** NOUN
los **bolos** masc pl
**Do you want to go tenpin bowling?**
¿Quieres jugar a los bolos?

*Language tip*
*In Spanish, you need to add **a los** before **bolos**.*

**tent** NOUN
la **tienda de campaña** fem

**tenth** NUMBER
**décimo** masc
**décima** fem
**on the tenth floor**
en el décimo piso
**My birthday's the tenth of April.**
Mi cumpleaños es el diez de abril.
**It's the tenth of July today.**
Hoy es diez de julio.

**on the tenth of August**
el diez de agosto

*Language tip*
*Use the same set of numbers that you use for counting (**uno**, **dos**, **tres** and so on) when giving Spanish dates.*

**term** NOUN
el **trimestre** masc
**It will soon be the end of term.**
Pronto será el final del trimestre.

**terraced house** NOUN
la **casa adosada** fem

**terrible** ADJECTIVE
**terrible** masc & fem
**My English is terrible.**
Mi inglés es terrible.

**terrified** ADJECTIVE
**aterrorizado** masc
**aterrorizada** fem

**I was terrified!**
¡Estaba
aterrorizado!

**test** NOUN
la **prueba** *fem*
**I've got a test tomorrow.**
Tengo una prueba mañana.

**text**

> text *can be a noun or a verb.*

**A** NOUN
**1** el **texto** *masc (in book)*
**2** el **mensaje de texto** *masc*
*(from mobile)*
**B** VERB
**to text**
enviar un mensaje a
**I'll text you when I get there.**
Te envío un mensaje cuando
llegue.

**textbook** NOUN
el **libro de texto** *masc*
**an English textbook**
un libro de texto de inglés

**text message** NOUN
el **mensaje de texto** *masc*

**than** CONJUNCTION
que
**She's taller than me.**
Es más alta que yo.
**Are you older than him?**
¿Eres mayor que él?

**thanks** EXCLAMATION
gracias
**No thanks.**
No, gracias.
**Thanks for helping me.**
Gracias por ayudarme.

**thank you** EXCLAMATION
gracias

**Thank you very much.**
Muchas gracias.

**that**

> **that** *can be a pronoun, adjective or conjunction.*

**A** PRONOUN
**1** **ése** *masc*
**ésa** *fem*
**eso** *neuter*
**That's my brother.**
Ése es mi hermano.
**That's my friend Sonia.**
Ésa es mi amiga Sonia.

*Language tip*
Use the neuter form **eso** when that refers to something vague, something not very specific or to an object you don't recognize.

**That's right! Well done.**
¡Eso es! Bien hecho.

*Language tip*
Instead of **ése**, **ésa** and **eso**, use **aquél**, **aquélla** and **aquello** to talk about something or someone that's quite far away.

**That's my French teacher over there.**
Aquél es mi profesor de francés.

**What's that?**
¿Qué es eso?
**Who's that? – It's Stephen.**
¿Quién es ése? – Es Stephen.
**Who's that? – It's Sarah.**
¿Quién es ésa? – Es Sarah.
**I know that.**
Lo sé.

*Language tip*
Traditionally, the pronouns **ése**, **ésa**, **aquél** and **aquélla** were written with an accent to distinguish them from the unaccented adjective forms. Nowadays, you don't have to give the accents unless the sentence would be confusing otherwise.

**2 que** *(relative)*
**the man that lives here**
el hombre que vive aquí
**the girl that I saw**
la chica que vi

**B** ADJECTIVE
**ese** *masc*
**esa** *fem*
**that dog**
ese perro
**that woman**
esa mujer
**This man? – No, that one.**
¿Este hombre? – No, ése.
**This chair? – No, that one.**
¿Esta silla? – No, ésa.

**Look at that car over there!**
¡Mira aquel coche!
**C** CONJUNCTION
**que**
**I think that it's raining.**
Creo que está lloviendo.

**I think that Henry is ill.**
Creo que Henry está enfermo.

**the** ARTICLE
**el** *masc*
**la** *fem*
**los** *masc pl*
**las** *fem pl*

**the boy**
el chico
**the girl**
la chica
**the children**
los niños
**the oranges**
las naranjas

**We're going to the theatre.**
Vamos al teatro.
**a photo of the dog**
una foto del perro

**theatre** NOUN
el **teatro** *masc*

**their** ADJECTIVE
**su** *masc & fem* (PL **sus**)

**their house**
su casa
**their parents**
sus padres

**They took off their coats.**
Se quitaron los abrigos.

English Spanish

a b c d e f g h i j k l m n o p q r s t u v w x y z

# theirs → them

**They are washing their hands.**
Se están lavando las manos.

**theirs** PRONOUN
el **suyo** *masc*
la **suya** *fem*

### Language tip
*Remember that the choice of* **el suyo**, **la suya**, **los suyos** *or* **las suyas** *depends entirely on the thing or things referred to.*

**That isn't the Smiths' car. Theirs is red.**
Aquél no es el coche de los Smith. El suyo es rojo.
**Those aren't the twins' books. Theirs are here.**
Aquéllos no son los libros de los gemelos. Los suyos están aquí.

### Language tip
*After* **ser** *you can usually just use* **suyo**, **suya**, **suyos** *or* **suyas** *to agree with the noun referred to.*

**Is this theirs?**
¿Es suyo esto?
**This house is theirs.**
Esta casa es suya.
**These cases are theirs.**
Estas maletas son suyas.
**Whose is this? – It's theirs.**
¿De quién es esto? – Es suyo.

### Language tip
*Because* **suyo** *can also mean* **his**, **hers** *and* **yours**, *you can avoid confusion by using* **de ellos/de ellas** *instead.*

**Whose is this? – It's theirs.**
¿De quién es esto? – Es de ellos.

**a friend of theirs**
un amigo suyo

**them** PRONOUN
1 **los** *masc*
   **las** *fem pl (direct object)*
   **Where are the horses? I can't see them.**

¿Dónde están los caballos?
No los veo.
**There are some more biscuits in the cupboard. Do you want them?**
Hay más galletas en el armario. ¿Las quieres?
**I like these socks. I think I'll buy them.**
Me gustan estos calcetines. Creo que me voy a comprarlos.
2 **les** *(indirect object)*

### Language tip
*Use* **les** *when* **them** *means to them* or *for them.*

**Can you give them a message?**
¿Les puedes dar un mensaje?
**I'm going to buy them a present.**
Les voy a comprar un regalo.

### Language tip
*Change* **les** *to* **se** *when combining it with a direct object pronoun like* **lo**.

**I'll tell them.**
Se lo diré.

### Language tip
*Because* **se** *can mean to him, to her and to you as well as to them, you can add* **a ellos/a ellas** *(to them) after the verb for clarity.*

**I'm going to give it to them.**
Voy a dárselo a ellos.
3 **ellos** *masc pl*
   **ellas** *fem pl (after preposition)*
   **It's not for you, it's for them.**
   No es para ti, es para ellos.
   **Teresa and Victoria are here, and Graham's with them.**
   Teresa y Victoria están aquí, y Graham está con ellas.

**Language tip**
*Use **ellos** and **ellas** in comparisons.*

**I'm older than them.**
Soy mayor que ellos.

**Language tip**
*Use **ellos** and **ellas** after the verb* **ser**.

**It must be them.**
Deben de ser ellos.
**It's them.**
Son ellos.

## theme park NOUN
el **parque temático** *masc*

## themselves PRONOUN
1 **se** *(reflexive use)*
**They're enjoying themselves.**
Se están divirtiendo.
**They have hurt themselves.**
Se han hecho daño.
2 **sí mismos** *masc pl*
**sí mismas** *fem pl (after preposition)*
**They talked about themselves.**
Hablaron de sí mismos.
3 **ellos mismos** *masc pl*
**ellas mismas** *fem pl (for emphasis)*
**They did it themselves.**
Lo hicieron ellos mismos.
**The girls did it all by themselves.**
Las chicas lo hicieron todo ellas mismas.

## then CONJUNCTION
**luego**
**I get dressed. Then I have breakfast.**
Me visto. Luego desayuno.

## there ADVERB
1 **ahí** *(not far away)*
**Put it there, on the table.**
Ponlo ahí, en la mesa.
**up there**
ahí arriba
**down there**
ahí abajo

2 **allí** *(further away)*
**I'm going there on Friday.**
El viernes voy allí.
3 **there is ...**
hay ...
**There's a new boy in the class.**
Hay un chico nuevo en la clase.
**there are ...**
hay ...
**There are ten chairs in the room.**
Hay diez sillas en la habitación.
**How many biscuits are there?**
¿Cuántas galletas hay?
**There are lots.**
Hay muchas.
**There aren't many.**
No hay muchas.

**over there**
por ahí
**There he is!**
¡Ahí está!
**There they are!**
¡Ahí están!
**There is ...**
Hay ...
**There are ...**
Hay ...

## these
A ADJECTIVE
**estos** *masc pl*
**estas** *fem pl*
**these shoes**
estos zapatos
**these tables**
estas mesas
**Which books do you need? – These ones.**
¿Qué libros necesitas? – Éstos.
B PRONOUN
**éstos** *masc pl*
**éstas** *fem pl*
**If you need felt-tips, I've got these.**
Si necesitas rotuladores, tengo éstos.

**Of course we've got apples. Look at these!**
Claro que tenemos manzanas. ¡Mira éstas!

### Language tip
*Traditionally, the pronouns* **éstos** *and* **éstas** *were written with an accent to distinguish them from the unaccented adjective forms shown in the previous category. Nowadays, you don't have to give the accents unless the sentence would be confusing otherwise.*

**they** PRONOUN
**ellos** *masc pl*
**ellas** *fem pl*
   **We went to the cinema, but they didn't.**
   Nosotros fuimos al cine, pero ellos no.
   **I spoke to my sisters and they agree with me.**
   Hablé con mis hermanas y ellas están de acuerdo conmigo.

### Language tip
**they** *isn't usually translated unless it's emphatic.*

   **Where are your friends? – They're over there.**
   ¿Dónde están tus amigos? – Están allí.

**they'd**
   **1** (= they had) ▷ see **have**
   **2** (= they would) ▷ see **would**

**they'll** (= they will) ▷ see **will**

**they're** (= they are) ▷ see **be**

**they've** (= they have) ▷ see **have**

**thick** ADJECTIVE
**grueso** *masc*
**gruesa** *fem*
   **a thick slice**
   una rebanada gruesa

**thief** NOUN

el **ladrón** *masc* (PL los **ladrones**)
la **ladrona** *fem*

**thin** ADJECTIVE
   **1** **delgado** *masc*
   **delgada** *fem* (person)
   **I'm quite thin.**
   Soy bastante delgado.
   **2** **fino** *masc*
   **fina** *fem* (slice, book)
   **a thin slice**
   una rebanada fina

**thing** NOUN
   la **cosa** *fem*
   **I've got lots of things to do.**
   Tengo muchas cosas que hacer.
   **my things**
   mis cosas

to **think** VERB
   **1** **pensar**
   **What do you think?**
   ¿Qué piensas?
   **Think carefully, Harry.**
   Piénsalo bien, Harry.
   **I'll think about it.**
   Lo pensaré.
   **2** **creer** (believe)
   **I think he's here.**
   Creo que está aquí.

### Language tip
*Although you can say both 'I think he's here' and 'I think that he's here' in English, in Spanish you cannot leave out the* **que** *and have to say* **creo que está aquí**.

**I think so.**
Creo que sí.
**I don't think so.**
Creo que no.

**third** NUMBER
**tercero** *masc*
**tercera** *fem*
> **It's the third time.**
> Es la tercera vez.
> **I came third.**
> Llegué el tercero.

### Language tip
*Shorten* **tercero** *to* **tercer** *before a masculine singular noun.*

> **the third prize**
> el tercer premio
> **My birthday's the third of September.**
> Mi cumpleaños es el tres de septiembre.
> **It's the third of December today.**
> Hoy es tres de diciembre.

**on the third of March**
el tres de marzo

### Language tip
*Use the same set of numbers that you use for counting (*uno, dos, tres *and so on) when giving Spanish dates.*

**thirsty** ADJECTIVE
> **to be thirsty**
> tener sed
> **Are you thirsty?**
> ¿Tienes sed?
> **I'm not thirsty.**
> No tengo sed.

**I'm thirsty.**
Tengo sed.

**thirteen** NUMBER
**trece**
> **thirteen euros**
> trece euros

**I'm thirteen.**
Tengo trece años.

### Language tip
*In English you can say* **I'm thirteen** *or* **I'm thirteen years old**. *In*

Spanish you can only say **tengo trece años**. Have you noticed that in Spanish you need to use the verb **tener** to talk about somebody's age?

**thirteenth** NUMBER
**trece**
> **on the thirteenth floor**
> en la planta trece
> **We break up on the thirteenth of December.**
> Empezamos las vacaciones el trece de diciembre.
> **Today's the thirteenth of May.**
> Hoy es trece de mayo.

**on the thirteenth of August**
el trece de agosto

### Language tip
*Use the same set of numbers that you use for counting (*uno, dos, tres *and so on) when giving Spanish dates.*

**thirtieth** NUMBER
**treinta**
> **My birthday's the thirtieth of March.**
> Mi cumpleaños es el treinta de marzo.
> **Today's the thirtieth of July.**
> Hoy es treinta de julio.

**on the thirtieth of August**
el treinta de agosto

### Language tip
*Use the same set of numbers that you use for counting (*uno, dos, tres *and so on) when giving Spanish dates.*

**thirty** NUMBER
**treinta**
> **thirty euros**
> treinta euros
> **My aunt is thirty.**
> Mi tía tiene treinta años.

# this → those

## Language tip
*In English you can say **she's thirty** or **she's thirty years old**. In Spanish you can only say **tiene treinta años**. Have you noticed that in Spanish you need to use the verb **tener** to talk about somebody's age?*

## this

**this** can be an adjective or a pronoun.

**A** ADJECTIVE
**este** *masc*
**esta** *fem*
**this book**
este libro
**this man**
este hombre
**this time**
esta vez
**Which book do you want? – This one.**
¿Qué libro quieres? – Éste.
**That card? – No, this one.**
¿Esa tarjeta? – No, ésta.
**B** PRONOUN
**éste** *masc*
**ésta** *fem*
**esto** *neuter*
**This is my room.**
Éste es mi cuarto.
**This is my class.**
Ésta es mi clase.

## Language tip
*Use the neuter form **esto** when **this** refers to something vague, something not very specific or to an object you don't recognize.*

**Look at this.**
Mira esto.

**this morning**
esta mañana
**this year**
este año
**this afternoon**
esta tarde

**What's this?**
¿Qué es esto?

## Language tip
*Traditionally, the pronouns **éste** and **ésta** were written with an accent to distinguish them from the unaccented adjective forms shown in the previous category. Nowadays, you don't have to give the accents unless the sentence would be confusing otherwise.*

## those
**A** ADJECTIVE
**esos** *masc pl*
**esas** *fem pl*
**those shoes**
esos zapatos
**those chairs**
esas sillas

## Language tip
*Instead of **esos** and **esas**, use **aquellos** and **aquellas** if you're talking about people or things that are quite far away.*

**Look at those boys over there!**
¡Mira a aquellos chicos!
**Which books do you need? – Those ones.**
¿Qué libros necesitas? – Ésos.
**B** PRONOUN
**ésos** *masc pl*
**ésas** *fem pl*
**Those aren't my boots.**
Ésas no son mis botas.

## Language tip
*Instead of **ésos** and **ésas**, use **aquéllos** and **aquéllas** to talk about people or things that are quite far away.*

**Those are my classmates over there.**
Aquéllos son mis compañeros de clase.

**Language tip**

*Traditionally, the pronouns* **ésos**, **ésas**, **aquéllos** *and* **aquéllas** *were written with an accent to distinguish them from the unaccented adjective forms shown in the previous category. Nowadays, you don't have to give the accents unless the sentence would otherwise be confusing.*

**thought** VERB ▷ see **think**

**thousand** NOUN
   **a thousand**
   mil
   **a thousand euros**
   mil euros
   **two thousand pounds**
   dos mil libras
   **thousands of people**
   miles de personas

**three** NUMBER
tres
   **three euros**
   tres euros

   **She's three.**
   Tiene tres años.

**Language tip**

*In English you can say* **she's three** *or* **she's three years old**. *In Spanish you can only say* **tiene tres años**. *Have you noticed that in Spanish you need to use the verb* **tener** *to talk about somebody's age?*

**throat** NOUN
la **garganta** *fem*
   **I've got a sore throat.**
   Me duele la
   garganta.

**through** PREPOSITION
por

   **Our cat always comes in through the window.**
   Nuestro gato siempre entra por la ventana.
   **I know her through my sister.**
   La conozco por mi hermana.

to **throw** VERB
tirar
   **Throw me the ball.**
   Tírame la pelota.

to **throw away** VERB
tirar
   **Don't throw it away!**
   ¡No lo tires!

**thumb** NOUN
el **pulgar** *masc*
   **She sucks her thumb.**
   Se chupa el pulgar.

**Language tip**

*In Spanish you usually use an article like* **el**, **la**, **los** *with parts of the body.*

**thunder** NOUN
los **truenos** *masc pl*
   **There was thunder and lightning.**
   Hubo rayos y truenos.

**thunderstorm** NOUN
la **tormenta** *fem*

**Thursday** NOUN
el **jueves** *masc*
   **It's Thursday today.**
   Hoy es jueves.

English Spanish

a
b
c
d
e
f
g
h
i
j
k
l
m
n
o
p
q
r
s
t
u
v
w
x
y
z

**on Thursday**
el jueves
**on Thursdays**
los jueves
**every Thursday**
cada jueves
**last Thursday**
el jueves pasado
**next Thursday**
el jueves que viene

*Language tip*
*Days are not spelled with a capital letter in Spanish.*

## tick

**tick** *can be a noun or a verb.*

A NOUN
la **señal** *fem*
**Put a tick or a cross.**
Pon una señal o una cruz.

B VERB
**to tick**
señalar
**Tick the right box.**
Señala la casilla correcta.

## ticket NOUN
1 la **entrada** *fem (for concert, cinema, museum)*
**a cinema ticket**
una entrada para el cine
2 el **billete** *masc (for bus, train, plane)*
**a bus ticket**
un billete de autobús

## ticket office NOUN
la **taquilla** *fem*

## tidy

**tidy** *can be an adjective or a verb.*

A ADJECTIVE
**ordenado** *masc*
**ordenada** *fem*
**My room is tidy.**
Mi cuarto está ordenado.
**It's tidier now.**
Ahora está más ordenado.

B VERB
**to tidy**
ordenar
**You must tidy your room.**
Tienes que ordenar tu cuarto.

## to tidy up VERB
**Don't forget to tidy up afterwards, children.**
No os olvidéis de ordenarlo todo después, niños.

## tie

**tie** *can be a noun or a verb.*

A NOUN
1 la **corbata** *fem (for neck)*
2 el **empate** *masc (in match)*
**It's a tie.**
Es un empate.

B VERB
**to tie**
atar
**Let's tie the balloons to the door!**
¡Vamos a atar los globos a la puerta!
**Tie your laces.**
Átate los cordones.

## tiger NOUN
el **tigre** *masc*

## tight ADJECTIVE
1 **estrecho** *masc*
**estrecha** *fem (too small)*
**This dress is a bit tight.**
Este vestido es un poco estrecho.
2 **ceñido** *masc*
**ceñida** *fem (close-fitting)*
**a tight skirt**
una falda ceñida

## tights PL NOUN
las **medias** *fem pl*
**I'm wearing black tights.**
Llevo medias negras.
**a pair of tights**
unas medias

# till

*till can be a noun or a preposition.*

**A** NOUN
la **caja** *fem*
**at the till**
en la caja
**B** PREPOSITION
**hasta**
**He's staying till Monday.**
Se queda hasta el lunes.
**from nine till five**
de nueve a cinco

# time NOUN

1 la **hora** *fem (on clock)*
**What time is it?**
¿Qué hora es?
**It's time to go.**
Es hora de irse.
**What time...?**
¿A qué hora...?
**What time do you get up?**
¿A qué hora te levantas?
**What time does the train arrive?**
¿A qué hora llega el tren?
2 el **tiempo** *masc (amount of time)*
**I'm sorry, I haven't got time.**
Lo siento, no tengo tiempo.
3 la **vez** *fem* (FEM PL las **veces**) *(occasion)*
**three times**
tres veces
**this time**
esta vez
**next time**
la próxima vez
**the first time**
la primera vez
**two at a time**
dos a la vez
**Two times two is four.**
Dos por dos son cuatro.

**What time is it?**
¿Qué hora es?
**It's lunch time.**
Es la hora de comer.

**How many times?**
¿Cuántas veces?
**Have a good time, Amanda!**
¡Que lo pases bien, Amanda!

# timetable NOUN
el **horario** *masc*

# tin NOUN
la **lata** *fem*
**a tin of soup**
una lata de sopa

# tin opener NOUN
el **abrelatas** *masc* (MASC PL los **abrelatas**)

# tinsel NOUN
el **espumillón** *masc*

# tiny ADJECTIVE
**minúsculo** *masc*
**minúscula** *fem*

# tip NOUN
1 la **propina** *fem (for waiter, taxi driver)*
**It's a tip for the waiter.**
Es una propina para el camarero.
2 el **consejo** *masc (piece of advice)*

# tiptoe NOUN
**on tiptoe**
de puntillas
**He's standing on tiptoe.**
Está de puntillas.

# tired ADJECTIVE
**cansado** *masc*
**cansada** *fem*
**I'm tired.**
Estoy cansado.

# tiring ADJECTIVE
**cansado** *masc*
**cansada** *fem*
**Doing so much running is tiring.**
Es cansado correr tanto.

# tissue NOUN
el **Kleenex®** *masc*

English Spanish

a
b
c
d
e
f
g
h
i
j
k
l
m
n
o
p
q
r
s
t
u
v
w
x
y
z

**Have you got a tissue?**
¿Tienes un Kleenex?

**title** NOUN
el **título** masc

**to** PREPOSITION
**1 a**
**We're going to London.**
Vamos a Londres.

*Language tip*
**a** *combines with* **el** *to form* **al**.

**Can I go to the toilet?**
¿Puedo ir al servicio?
**I go to school with my friend.**
Voy al colegio con mi amigo.
**I'm going round to Mary's.**
Voy a casa de Mary.
**Give it to Jane!**
¡Dáselo a Jane!

**to my house**
a mi casa
**to the supermarket**
al supermercado

**2 de** *(for)*
**the train to London**
el tren de Londres
**the plane to Madrid**
el avión de Madrid
**3 hasta** *(up to)*
**Count to ten, everyone.**
Contad todos hasta diez.
**from nine o'clock to half past three**
desde las nueve hasta las tres y media
**4 para** *(in order to)*
**I'm doing it to help you.**
Lo hago para ayudarte.

*Language tip*
*Don't forget that* **to** *is often just part of the infinitive form of the verb.*

**to eat**
comer
**to work**
trabajar

**I want to buy a new camera.**
Quiero comprar una cámara nueva.

**toast** NOUN
las **tostadas** fem pl
**Would you like some toast?**
¿Quieres tostadas?
**a piece of toast**
una tostada

**toaster** NOUN
la **tostadora** fem

**toastie** NOUN
el **sandwich caliente** masc

**today** ADVERB
**hoy**
**What's the date today?**
¿Hoy qué día es?
**It's Monday today.**
Hoy es lunes.

**toe** NOUN
el **dedo del pie** masc

*Language tip*
*On its own* **dedo** *means 'finger'. So the Spanish* **dedo del pie** *literally means 'foot finger'!*

**toffee** NOUN
el **caramelo** masc

**together** ADVERB
**juntos** masc pl
**juntas** fem pl

*Language tip*
*The Spanish word* **juntos** *is an adjective so must agree with the noun.*

**Mary and Barbara are going to go there together.**
Mary y Barbara van a ir allí juntas.

**toilet** NOUN
**1** el **servicio** masc *(in school, café etc)*
**Can I go to the toilet?**
¿Puedo ir al servicio?
**2** el **baño** masc *(in private house)*

**toilet paper** NOUN
el **papel higiénico** *masc*

**told** VERB ▷*see* **tell**

**tomato** NOUN
el **tomate** *masc*
  **a kilo of tomatoes**
  un kilo de tomates
  **tomato soup**
  sopa de tomate

**tomorrow** ADVERB
**mañana**
  **Let's go swimming tomorrow.**
  Vamos a nadar mañana.

> **tomorrow morning**
> mañana por la mañana
> **tomorrow afternoon**
> mañana por la tarde
> **tomorrow night**
> mañana por la noche
> **the day after tomorrow**
> pasado mañana
> **See you tomorrow.**
> Hasta mañana.

**tongue** NOUN
la **lengua** *fem*

**tonight** ADVERB
**esta noche**
  **Are you going out tonight?**
  ¿Vas a salir esta noche?

**tonsillitis** NOUN
la **amigdalitis** *fem*

**too** ADVERB
  **1** **también** (*as well*)
  **My sister is coming too.**
  Mi hermana también viene.

> **Me too.**
> Yo también.

  **2** **demasiado** (*very*)
  **The water's too hot.**
  El agua está demasiado caliente.
  **You're too late.**
  Llegas demasiado tarde.

**Daniel, you talk too much.**
Daniel, hablas demasiado.
**It costs too much.**
Cuesta demasiado.

> *Language tip*
> When **too much** and **too many** are used to describe nouns, remember to make them agree.

  **too much noise**
  demasiado ruido
  **too much water**
  demasiada agua
  **too many mistakes**
  demasiadas faltas

**tooth** NOUN
el **diente** *masc*

**toothache** NOUN
  **I've got toothache.**
  Me duelen las muelas.

**toothbrush** NOUN
el **cepillo de dientes** *masc*

**toothpaste** NOUN
la **pasta de dientes** *fem*

**top**

> **top** *can be a noun or an adjective.*

**A** NOUN
  **1** el **top** *masc* (*T-shirt, sweater, etc*)
  **a black skirt and a white top**
  una falda negra y un top blanco
  **2** la **parte de arriba** *fem* (*highest part*)
  **at the top of the page**
  en la parte de arriba de la página
  **on top of**
  encima de
  **It's on top of the fridge.**
  Está encima de la nevera.
  **3** la **cima** *fem* (*of mountain*)
  **the top of Snowdon**
  la cima de Snowdon
  **4** el **tapón** *masc* (PL los **tapones**) (*of bottle*)
**B** ADJECTIVE
  **He always gets top marks in English.**

Siempre saca las mejores notas
en inglés.
**the top floor**
el piso de arriba

**torch** NOUN
la **linterna** *fem*

**tortoise** NOUN
la **tortuga** *fem*

**total** NOUN
el **total** *masc*

to **touch** VERB
**tocar**
**Don't touch that!**
¡No toques eso!

**tour** NOUN
la **visita** *fem*
**a tour of the museum**
una visita al museo

**tourism** NOUN
el **turismo** *masc*

**tourist** NOUN
el/la **turista** *masc/fem*
**There are lots of tourists.**
Hay muchos turistas.

> *Language tip*
> *Even though it ends in -a, you can*
> *use* **turista** *to refer to a man or boy.*

**tourist information
office** NOUN
la **oficina de turismo** *fem*

**towards** PREPOSITION
**hacia**
**Come towards me.**
Ven hacia mí.

**towel** NOUN
la **toalla** *fem*

**tower** NOUN
la **torre** *fem*
**a tower block**
una torre de pisos

**town** NOUN
la **ciudad** *fem*
**It's a beautiful town.**
Es una ciudad muy bonita.
**the town centre**
el centro de la ciudad
**I'm going into town.**
Voy al centro.

**toy** NOUN
el **juguete** *masc*

**toy shop** NOUN
la **juguetería** *fem*

**tracksuit** NOUN
el **chándal** *masc* (PL los
chándals)

**tractor** NOUN
el **tractor** *masc*

**tradition** NOUN
la **tradición** *fem* (PL las
tradiciones)

**traffic** NOUN
el **tráfico** *masc*
**There's a lot of traffic.**
Hay mucho tráfico.

**traffic lights** PL NOUN
el **semáforo** *masc*
**Turn right at the traffic
lights.**
Gira a la derecha en el semáforo.

**train** NOUN
el **tren** *masc*
**by train**
en tren
**We're going by train.**
Vamos en tren.

**trainers** PL NOUN
las **zapatillas de deporte** *fem*
*pl*
**a pair of trainers**
unas zapatillas de deporte

English Spanish
a b c d e f g h i j k l m n o p q r s **t** u v w x y z

**training** NOUN
el **entrenamiento** *masc*

**tram** NOUN
el **tranvía** *masc*

**trampoline** NOUN
la **cama elástica** *fem*

to **translate** VERB
**traducir**
> I can translate the menu into
> English.
> Puedo traducir la carta al inglés.

**translation** NOUN
la **traducción** *fem* (PL las
traducciones)

**trap** NOUN
la **trampa** *fem*

**travel agent's** NOUN
la **agencia de viajes** *fem*

**travelling** NOUN
> I love travelling.
> Me encanta viajar.

**tray** NOUN
la **bandeja** *fem*

**treasure** NOUN
el **tesoro** *masc*

**tree** NOUN
el **árbol** *masc*

**triangle** NOUN
el **triángulo** *masc*

**trick** NOUN
el **truco** *masc*
> I can do magic tricks.
> Sé hacer trucos de magia.

**trip** NOUN
el **viaje** *masc*
> We're going on a trip to
> London.
> Vamos a hacer un viaje a
> Londres.

Have a good trip!
¡Buen viaje!

**trolley** NOUN
el **carrito** *masc*

**trouble** NOUN
el **problema** *masc*
> The trouble is, it's too
> expensive.
> El problema es que es
> demasiado caro.
> Peter is always getting into
> trouble.
> Peter siempre se está metiendo
> en problemas.

**trousers** PL NOUN
los **pantalones** *masc pl*
> I'm wearing black trousers.
> Llevo unos pantalones negros.
> He's changing his trousers.
> Se está cambiando de
> pantalones.

**truck** NOUN
el **camión** *masc* (PL los
camiones)

**true** ADJECTIVE
> That's true.
> Eso es verdad.
> That's not true.
> Eso no es verdad.

True or false?
¿Verdadero o falso?

**trumpet** NOUN
la **trompeta** *fem*
> She plays the trumpet.
> Toca la trompeta.

English Spanish

a
b
c
d
e
f
g
h
i
j
k
l
m
n
o
p
q
r
s
**t**
u
v
w
x
y
z

**trunks** PL NOUN
el **bañador** *masc*
**I've got new trunks.**
Tengo un bañador nuevo.

**truth** NOUN
la **verdad** *fem*
**Tell me the truth.**
Dime la verdad.

**try**

> **try** *can be a verb or a noun.*

**A** VERB
**to try**
1 **intentar** *(attempt)*
**Try to remember.**
Intenta acordarte.
**I'm going to try.**
Voy a intentarlo.

**You're not trying, Richard.**
No estás haciendo el esfuerzo
suficiente, Richard.
2 **probar** *(taste)*
**Would you like to try some?**
¿Quieres probar un poco?
**B** NOUN
el **intento** *masc*
**his third try**
su tercer intento

> **Good try!**
> ¡No ha estado mal!
> **Can I have a try?**
> ¿Puedo intentarlo yo?

to **try on** VERB
**probarse**

**Can I try it on?**
¿Puedo probármelo?

**T-shirt** NOUN
la **camiseta** *fem*
**Put on your T-shirt.**
Ponte la camiseta.

> ***Language tip***
> *In Spanish you usually use an article*
> *like* **el**, **la**, **los** *with clothes you are*
> *wearing.*

**Tube** NOUN
**the Tube**
el metro

**Tuesday** NOUN
el **martes** *masc*
**It's Tuesday today.**
Hoy es martes.

> **on Tuesday**
> el martes
> **on Tuesdays**
> los martes
> **every Tuesday**
> cada martes
> **last Tuesday**
> el martes pasado
> **next Tuesday**
> el martes que viene

> ***Language tip***
> *Days are not spelled with a capital*
> *letter in Spanish.*

**tummy** NOUN
la **barriga** *fem*

**tummy ache** NOUN
**I've got tummy ache.**
Me duele la barriga.

**tuna** NOUN
el **atún** *masc*
**a tuna salad**
una ensalada con atún

**tune** NOUN
la **melodía** *fem*
**I know the tune.**
Conozco la melodía.

**tunnel** NOUN
el **túnel** *masc*

**turkey** NOUN
el **pavo** *masc*

**turn**

*turn can be a noun or a verb.*

**A** NOUN
el **turno** *masc*
**You miss a turn.**
Pierdes un turno.

**Whose turn is it?**
¿A quién le toca?
**It's my turn!**
¡Me toca!

**B** VERB
**to turn**
girar
**Turn right at the lights.**
Gira a la derecha en el
semáforo.

to **turn off** VERB
1 **apagar** *(switch off)*
**Could you turn off the light?**
¿Puedes apagar la luz?
2 **cerrar** *(tap)*
**Turn off the tap, please.**
Cierra el grifo, por favor.

to **turn on** VERB
1 **encender** *(switch on)*
**Could you turn on the light?**
¿Puedes encender la luz?
2 **abrir** *(tap)*
**Turn on the tap, please.**
Abre el grifo, por favor.

to **turn over** VERB
**dar la vuelta a**
**Turn over the cards,**
**everyone.**
Dadle todos la vuelta a las
cartas.

to **turn round** VERB
**darse la vuelta**
**Turn round, children!**
¡Daos la vuelta, niños!

**TV** NOUN
la **tele** *fem*
**on TV**
en la tele

**twelfth** NUMBER
doce
**on the twelfth floor**
en la planta doce
**We break up on the twelfth**
**of April.**
Empezamos las vacaciones el
doce de abril.
**Today's the twelfth of June.**
Hoy es doce de junio.

**on the twelfth of August**
el doce de agosto

*Language tip*
*Use the same set of numbers that*
*you use for counting (**uno**, **dos**,*
***tres** and so on) when giving*
*Spanish dates.*

**twelve** NUMBER
doce
**twelve euros**
doce euros
**I have lunch at twelve**
**o'clock.**
Como a las doce.
**It is twelve thirty.**
Son las doce y media.

**twelve o'clock**
las doce
**I'm twelve.**
Tengo doce años.

**Language tip**

*In English you can say* **I'm twelve** *or* **I'm twelve years old**. *In Spanish you can only say* **tengo doce años**. *Have you noticed that in Spanish you need to use the verb* **tener** *to talk about somebody's age?*

### twentieth NUMBER
**veinte**

**the twentieth floor**
el piso veinte
**My birthday's the twentieth of October.**
Mi cumpleaños es el veinte de octubre.
**Today's the twentieth of April.**
Hoy es veinte de abril.

**on the twentieth of May**
el veinte de mayo

**Language tip**

*Use the same set of numbers that you use for counting (***uno, dos, tres*** and so on) when giving Spanish dates.*

### twenty NUMBER
**veinte**

**twenty euros**
veinte euros
**It's twenty to three.**
Son las tres menos veinte.
**It's twenty past eleven.**
Son las once y veinte.

**He's twenty.**
Tiene veinte años.

**Language tip**

*In English you can say* **he's twenty** *or* **he's twenty years old**. *In Spanish you can only say* **tiene veinte años**. *Have you noticed that in Spanish you need to use the verb* **tener** *to talk about somebody's age?*

### twice ADVERB
**dos veces**

### twin NOUN

**Language tip**

*In Spanish you usually use different words for identical and non-identical twins*

**1** el **mellizo** *masc*
la **melliza** *fem (not identical)*
**They're twins.**
Son mellizos.
**her twin sister**
su hermana melliza

**2** el **gemelo** *masc*
la **gemela** *fem (identical twin)*
**They're identical twins.**
Son gemelos.

**my twin sister**
mi hermana gemela

### twin room NOUN
la **habitación con dos camas** *fem* (PL las **habitaciones con dos camas**)

### twinned ADJECTIVE
**hermanado** *masc*
**hermanada** *fem*

**Veracruz is twinned with Valencia.**
Veracruz está hermanada con Valencia.

### two NUMBER
**dos**

**two euros**
dos euros
**It's two o'clock.**
Son las dos.
**Get into twos.**
Poneos en grupos de dos.

**She's two.**
Tiene dos años.

**type** NOUN
  el **tipo** masc
    **What type of camera have you got?**
    ¿Qué tipo de cámara tienes?

**tyre** NOUN
  el **neumático** masc

English Spanish

a b c d e f g h i j k l m n o p q r s **t** u v w x y z

# U u

**UFO** NOUN
el **OVNI** masc

**ugly** ADJECTIVE
**feo** masc
**fea** fem

**UK** NOUN (= **United Kingdom**)
el **Reino Unido** masc
**in the UK**
en el Reino Unido
**to the UK**
al Reino Unido
**I live in the UK.**
Vivo en el Reino Unido.

**Ulster** NOUN
el **Ulster** masc

**umbrella** NOUN
1 el **paraguas** masc (PL los
paraguas) (for rain)
2 la **sombrilla** fem (sun
umbrella)

**umpire** NOUN
el **árbitro** masc
la **árbitra** fem

**unbelievable** ADJECTIVE
**increíble** masc & fem
**That's unbelievable!**
¡Eso es
increíble!]

**uncle** NOUN
el **tío** masc
**my uncle**
mi tío
**my uncles
and aunts**
mis tíos

**uncomfortable** ADJECTIVE
**incómodo** masc
**incómoda** fem
**The seats are very
uncomfortable.**

Los asientos son muy
incómodos.

**under** PREPOSITION
1 **debajo de**

> **Language tip**
> When something is positioned under
> something, use **debajo de**.

**The dog's under the table.**
El perro está debajo de la mesa.

**under there**
ahí debajo
2 **por debajo de**

> **Language tip**
> After verbs which express movement
> (like 'go' and 'run') use **por debajo
> de**.

**The tunnel goes under the
river.**
El túnel pasa por debajo del río.
3 **menos de** (less than)
**It costs under twenty
pounds.**
Cuesta menos de veinte libras.
**children under ten**
niños de menos de diez años

## underground

> **underground** can be a noun,
> adjective or adverb.

**A** NOUN
el **metro** masc
**by underground**
en metro

the London underground
el metro de Londres

**B** ADJECTIVE
**subterráneo** *masc*
**subterránea** *fem*
an underground car park
un parking subterráneo

**C** ADVERB
**bajo tierra**
Moles live underground.
Los topos viven bajo tierra.

## underneath

**underneath** *can be a preposition or an adverb.*

**A** PREPOSITION
1 **debajo de**

*Language tip*
*When something is positioned underneath something, use* **debajo de**.

The key's underneath the mat.
La llave está debajo del felpudo.
2 **por debajo de**

*Language tip*
*After verbs which express movement (like 'go' and 'run') use* **por debajo de**.

The footpath goes underneath the bridge.
El sendero pasa por debajo del puente.

**B** ADVERB
**debajo**
Look underneath, Rachel!
¡Mira debajo, Rachel!

to **understand** VERB
**entender**
I don't understand this word.
No entiendo esta palabra.
**Do you understand, Tim?**
¿Lo entiendes, Tim?

I don't understand.
No lo entiendo.
**Do you understand?**
¿Lo entiendes?

**understood** VERB ▷*see* **understand**

**underwear** NOUN
la **ropa interior** *fem*

**undone** ADJECTIVE
**desatado** *masc*
**desatada** *fem*
Your laces are undone.
Llevas los cordones desatados.

*Language tip*
*In Spanish you usually use an article like* **el**, **la**, **los** *with clothes you are wearing.*

**undressed** ADJECTIVE
to get undressed
desnudarse
I'm getting undressed.
Me estoy desnudando.

**unemployed** ADJECTIVE
**parado** *masc*
**parada** *fem*
He's unemployed.
Está parado.

**unfair** ADJECTIVE
**injusto** *masc*
**injusta** *fem*
That's unfair!
¡Eso es injusto!

**unfashionable** ADJECTIVE
**pasado de moda** *masc*
**pasada de moda** *fem*

to **unfold** VERB
**desplegar**
Unfold the map.
Despliega el mapa.

**unforgettable** ADJECTIVE
**inolvidable** *masc & fem*

**unfortunately** ADVERB
**lamentablemente**
Unfortunately it's too late.
Lamentablemente es demasiado tarde.
**Unfortunately not.**
Lamentablemente no.

English Spanish

a
b
c
d
e
f
g
h
i
j
k
l
m
n
o
p
q
r
s
t
**u**
v
w
x
y
z

**593**

**unhappy** ADJECTIVE
**to be unhappy**
**no estar contento**
**She's unhappy at school.**
No está contenta en
el colegio.
**You look unhappy.**
Pareces triste.

**uniform** NOUN
el **uniforme** masc
**We wear school uniform.**
Llevamos uniforme al colegio.

### Did you know...?
Uniforms aren't worn in most
Spanish state schools but they are
in most Spanish private schools.

**Union Jack** NOUN
la **bandera del Reino Unido**
fem

**United Kingdom** NOUN
el **Reino Unido** masc
**to the United Kingdom**
al Reino Unido
**in the United Kingdom**
en el Reino Unido

**United States** NOUN
los **Estados Unidos** masc pl
**in the United States**
en Estados Unidos
**to the United States**
a Estados Unidos

**universe** NOUN
el **universo** masc

**university** NOUN
la **universidad** fem
**She's at university.**
Está en la universidad.
**Do you want to go to
university?**
¿Quieres ir a la universidad?
**Lancaster University**
la universidad de Lancaster

**unless** CONJUNCTION
**a menos que**
**Don't do it unless your mum
tells you to.**

No lo hagas a menos que tu
madre te lo diga.

### Language tip
**a menos que** is followed by a form
of the verb called the subjunctive.
Alternatively, you can often use **si
no** (if not) and an ordinary form of
the verb instead.

**I'll have that biscuit, unless
you want it.**
Yo cogeré esa galleta, si no la
quieres tú.

**unlikely** ADJECTIVE
**poco probable** masc & fem
**It's possible, but unlikely.**
Es posible, pero poco probable.

**unlucky** ADJECTIVE
**to be unlucky**
tener mala suerte/traer mala
suerte

### Language tip
**to be unlucky** has two translations
depending on whether it means 'to
have bad luck' or 'to bring bad luck'.
Look at the examples.

**I'm always unlucky.**
Siempre tengo mala suerte.
**It's unlucky to walk under a
ladder.**
Trae mala suerte pasar por
debajo de una escalera.
**Thirteen is an unlucky number.**
El trece trae mala suerte.

to **unpack** VERB
**deshacer las maletas**
**Have you unpacked?**
¿Has deshecho las maletas?
**I'm going to unpack my
suitcase.**
Voy a deshacer la maleta.

**unpleasant** ADJECTIVE
**desagradable** masc & fem

**unpopular** ADJECTIVE
**poco popular** masc & fem

**unpredictable** ADJECTIVE
**impredecible** *masc & fem*
The weather is
unpredictable.
El tiempo es impredecible.

**unreliable** ADJECTIVE
**poco fiable** *masc & fem*
Our car is unreliable.
Nuestro coche es poco fiable.

**unsuitable** ADJECTIVE
**inadecuado** *masc*
**inadecuada** *fem*

**untidy** ADJECTIVE
**desordenado** *masc*
**desordenada** *fem*
My bedroom's always untidy.
Mi habitación siempre está
desordenada.
My writing is untidy.
Tengo mala letra.

**until** PREPOSITION
**hasta**
He's here until tomorrow.
Está aquí hasta mañana.
The supermarket is open
until ten.
El supermercado está abierto
hasta las diez.
not until tomorrow
hasta mañana no
When will it be ready? – Not
until next week.
¿Cuándo estará listo? – Hasta la
semana que viene no.
from ... until
de ... a
from nine until five
de nueve a cinco
from the tenth until the
fourteenth of May
del diez al catorce de mayo

**unusual** ADJECTIVE
**poco común** *masc & fem* (PL
**poco comunes**)
It's an unusual name.
Es un nombre poco común.

**up**

> **up** *can be an adverb, adjective or
> preposition.*

**A** ADVERB
1 **hacia arriba** *(upwards)*
She looked up.
Miró hacia arriba.
2 **arriba** *(at a higher level)*
He's up on the roof.
Está arriba en el techo.
It's up there.
Está allí arriba.
I'll come up later.
Subo más tarde.
**up to**
hasta
Let's count up to fifty.
Vamos a contar hasta cincuenta.
**up to now**
hasta ahora
It's up to you.
Lo que tú quieras.
What's up with her?
¿Qué le pasa?

> **up there**
> allí arriba
> **up here**
> aquí arriba

**B** ADJECTIVE
I'm always up before eight.
Siempre me levanto antes de las
ocho.
He's not up yet.
Todavía no se ha levantado.
**C** PREPOSITION *(along)*
We could walk up the road to
the bus stop.
Podríamos subir por la carretera
hasta la parada del autobús.
The post office is up
the road.
Correos está
más arriba.
The cat is
up the tree.
El gato está
subido al árbol.

**English Spanish**

a b c d e f g h i j k l m n o p q r s t u v w x y z

**upper** ADJECTIVE
**superior** *masc & fem*
  **on the upper floor**
  en el piso superior

**upset**

> **upset** *can be an adjective or a verb.*

**A** ADJECTIVE
**disgustado** *masc*
**disgustada** *fem*
  **She's still a bit upset.**
  Todavía está un poco disgustada.
  **I've got an upset stomach.**
  Tengo mal el estómago.

**B** VERB
**to upset**
**dar un mal rato a**
  **I don't want to upset my granny.**
  No quiero dar un mal rato a mi abuela.

**upside down** ADVERB
**al revés**
  **That painting is upside down.**
  Ese cuadro está al revés.

**upstairs** ADVERB
**arriba**
  **Where's your coat? – It's upstairs.**
  ¿Dónde está tu abrigo? – Está arriba.

**up-to-date** ADJECTIVE
**moderno** *masc*
**moderna** *fem*

**upwards** ADVERB
**hacia arriba**

**urgent** ADJECTIVE
**urgente** *masc & fem*
  **Is it urgent?**
  ¿Es urgente?

**US** NOUN (= United States)
los **EE.UU.** *masc pl*
  **in the US**
  en EE.UU.
  **to the US**
  a EE.UU.
  **from the US**
  desde EE.UU.

> ### *Language tip*
> As **EE.UU.** *stands for* **Estados Unidos**, *why are there two Es and two Us? It's to show that the abbreviation refers to something plural. Compare* **JJ.OO.** *for* **Juegos Olímpicos** (**Olympic Games**).

**us** PRONOUN
**1 nos** (direct and indirect object)
  **He hates us.**
  Nos odia.
  **Tell us the story.**
  Cuéntanos la historia.
  **to us**
  nos
  **She's going to write to us.**
  Va a escribirnos.
**2 nosotros** *masc pl*
  **nosotras** *fem pl*

> ### *Language tip*
> Use **nosotros** *and* **nosotras** *after prepositions.*

  **Come with us.**
  Ven con nosotros.

> ### *Language tip*
> Use **nosotros** *and* **nosotras** *in comparisons.*

  **He's older than us.**
  Es mayor que nosotros.

> ### *Language tip*
> Use **nosotros** *and* **nosotras** *after the verb* **ser**.

It's us.
Somos nosotros.

**USA** NOUN
(= **United States of America**)
los **EE.UU.** *masc pl*
**in the USA**
en EE.UU.
**to the USA**
a EE.UU.
**from the USA**
desde EE.UU.

> **Language tip**
>
> *As* **EE.UU.** *stands for* **Estados Unidos,** *why are there two Es and two Us? It's to show that the abbreviation refers to something plural. Compare* **JJ.OO.** *for* **Juegos Olímpicos** (**Olympic Games**).

**use**

> **use** *can be a verb or a noun.*

**A** VERB
**to use**
usar
**Can we use a dictionary in the exam?**
¿Podemos usar un diccionario en el examen?
**Somebody is using the computer.**
Alguien está usando el ordenador.
**Can I use your phone?**
¿Puedo llamar por teléfono?
**Can I use the toilet?**
¿Puedo ir al baño?

**B** NOUN
**It's no use.**
Es inútil.

to **use up** VERB
gastar
**We've used up all the paint.**
Hemos gastado toda la pintura.

**used** ADJECTIVE
**I'm used to getting up early.**
Estoy acostumbrado a levantarme temprano.

**I'm used to it.**
Estoy acostumbrado.
**I'm not used to it.**
No estoy acostumbrado.

**useful** ADJECTIVE
**útil** *masc & fem*

**useless** ADJECTIVE
**to be useless**
no servir para nada
**This map is useless.**
Este mapa no sirve para nada.

**usual** ADJECTIVE
**habitual** *masc & fem*
**my usual seat**
mi asiento habitual
**She's late, as usual.**
Llega tarde, como siempre.

**as usual**
como siempre

**usually** ADVERB
**normalmente**
**I usually wear trousers.**
Normalmente llevo pantalones.

**utility room** NOUN
el **lavadero** *masc*

English Spanish

a
b
c
d
e
f
g
h
i
j
k
l
m
n
o
p
q
r
s
t
**u**
v
w
x
y
z

# V v

**vacancy** NOUN *(in hotel)*
'Vacancies'
'Quedan plazas'
**'No vacancies'**
'Completo'

**vacuum cleaner** NOUN
la **aspiradora** *fem*

**Valentine card** NOUN
la **tarjeta del día de los enamorados** *fem*

**Valentine's Day** NOUN
el **día de los enamorados** *masc*

**valley** NOUN
el **valle** *masc*

**valuable** ADJECTIVE
de valor
    a valuable picture
    un cuadro de valor

**van** NOUN
la **camioneta** *fem*

**vandal** NOUN
el **vándalo** *masc*

**vandalism** NOUN
el **vandalismo** *masc*

**vanilla** NOUN
la **vainilla** *fem*
    a vanilla ice cream
    un helado de vainilla

**varied** ADJECTIVE
**variado** *masc*
**variada** *fem*

**variety** NOUN
la **variedad** *fem*

**various** ADJECTIVE
**varios** *masc pl*
**varias** *fem pl*
    There are various possibilities.
    Existen varias posibilidades.

**vase** NOUN
el **jarrón** *masc* (PL los **jarrones**)

**vegan** NOUN
el **vegetariano estricto** *masc*
la **vegetariana estricta** *fem*
    I'm a vegan.
    Soy vegetariano estricto.

**vegetable** NOUN
la **verdura** *fem*
    **vegetable soup**
    sopa de verduras
    **Would you like some vegetables?**
    ¿Queréis verduras?

**vegetarian**

vegetarian *can be an adjective or a noun.*

**A** ADJECTIVE
**vegetariano** *masc*
**vegetariana** *fem*
**vegetarian lasagne**
lasaña vegetariana

**B** NOUN
el **vegetariano** *masc*
la **vegetariana** *fem*
**I'm a vegetarian.**
Soy vegetariano.

**verb** NOUN
el **verbo** *masc*

**very** ADVERB
**muy**
**very tall**
muy alto
**not very interesting**
no muy interesante
**It's very hot.**
Hace mucho calor.
**I love you very much.**
Te quiero mucho.

> **very soon**
> muy pronto
> **very much**
> mucho
> **I'm very sorry.**
> Lo siento mucho.

**vest** NOUN
la **camiseta** *fem*

**vet** NOUN
el **veterinario** *masc*
la **veterinaria** *fem*
**She's a vet.**
Es veterinaria.

> *Language tip*
>
> *In Spanish, you do not use an article with people's jobs.*

**vicar** NOUN
el **pastor** *masc*
la **pastora** *fem*

**video**

> *video can be a noun or a verb.*

**A** NOUN
el **vídeo** *masc (film, cassette, machine)*
**We're going to watch a video.**
Vamos a ver un vídeo.

**B** VERB
**to video**
grabar en vídeo
**We're going to video the concert.**
Vamos a grabar el concierto en vídeo.

**video game** NOUN
el **videojuego** *masc*
**I like playing video games.**
Me gusta jugar con videojuegos.

**video recorder** NOUN
el **vídeo** *masc*

**video shop** NOUN
el **videoclub** *masc*

**view** NOUN
la **vista** *fem*
**There's an amazing view.**
Hay una vista increíble.

**village** NOUN
el **pueblo** *masc*
**in the village**
en el pueblo

**vinegar** NOUN
el **vinagre** *masc*

**vineyard** NOUN
el **viñedo** *masc*

**violent** ADJECTIVE
**violento** *masc*
**violenta** *fem*

**violin** NOUN
el **violín** *masc*
**I play the violin.**
Toco el violín.

**virus** NOUN
el **virus** *masc* (PL los **virus**)

**visit**

> **visit** *can be a noun or a verb.*

**A** NOUN
la **visita** *fem*
**a visit to Edinburgh castle**
una visita al castillo de Edimburgo
**B** VERB
**to visit**
visitar
**We're going to visit the castle.**
Vamos a visitar el castillo.
**I'm going to visit some friends.**
Voy a visitar a unos amigos.

> *Language tip*
> *Don't forget the personal **a** in examples like this one.*

**visitor** NOUN
el **invitado** *masc*

la **invitada** *fem*
**Today we've got a Spanish visitor.**
Hoy tenemos un invitado español.

**vocabulary** NOUN
el **vocabulario** *masc*

**voice** NOUN
la **voz** *fem* (PL las **voces**)

**volleyball** NOUN
el **voleibol** *masc*
**We play volleyball sometimes.**
A veces jugamos al voleibol.

> *Language tip*
> *In Spanish, you need to add **al** before the name of the sport.*

**volunteer** NOUN
el **voluntario** *masc*
la **voluntaria** *fem*

**vowel** NOUN
la **vocal** *fem*

# W w

**waist** NOUN
la **cintura** *fem*

**waistcoat** NOUN
el **chaleco** *masc*

to **wait** VERB
**esperar**
Wait Alison, it's not your turn.
Espera, Alison, que no es tu turno.

Wait for me!
¡Espérame!
Wait a minute!
¡Espera un momento!

**waiter** NOUN
el **camarero** *masc*

**waiting room** NOUN
la **sala de espera** *fem*

**waitress** NOUN
la **camarera** *fem*

to **wake up** VERB
**despertarse**
Wake up, Peter!
¡Despiértate, Peter!

**Wales** NOUN
**Gales** *masc*
Swansea is in Wales.
Swansea está en Gales.
Bronwen is from Wales.
Bronwen es de Gales.
the Prince of Wales
el Príncipe de Gales

**walk**

walk *can be a verb or a noun.*

**A** VERB
to walk
**caminar**
He walks fast.
Camina rápido.
I walked ten kilometres.
Caminé diez kilómetros.
Are you walking or going by bus?
¿Vas a ir a pie o en autobús?
**B** NOUN
el **paseo** *masc*
Would you like to go for a walk?
¿Quieres ir a dar un paseo?
It's a five-minute walk to the town centre.
Lleva cinco minutos andando hasta el centro.

**walking** NOUN
My parents like walking.
A mis padres les gusta caminar.

**wall** NOUN
1 la **pared** *fem (inside building)*
There are posters on the wall.
Hay pósters en la pared.
2 el **muro** *masc (outer wall, garden wall)*
Tony is sitting on the wall.
Tony está sentado en el muro.

**wallet** NOUN
la **cartera** *fem*

**walnut** NOUN
la **nuez** *fem* (FEM PL las **nueces**)

to **want** VERB
**querer**
Do you want a piece of cake?
¿Quieres un trozo de tarta?

**I don't want to play.**
No quiero jugar.
**What do you want to do tomorrow?**
¿Qué quieres hacer mañana?

**What do you want, Judith?**
¿Qué quieres, Judith?
**What do you want, boys?**
¿Que queréis, niños?

**war** NOUN
la **guerra** *fem*

**wardrobe** NOUN
el **armario** *masc*

**warm** ADJECTIVE
1 **cálido** *masc*
**cálida** *fem (weather)*
**warm weather**
tiempo cálido
**It's warm today.**
Hoy hace calor.
**warm clothes**
ropa de abrigo

2 **caliente**
*masc & fem (bath, water, hands)*

**It's warm.**
Hace calor.
**I'm warm.**
Tengo calor.

**was** VERB ▷ *see* **be**

to **wash** VERB
1 **lavar** *(thing)*
**He washes his car every Sunday.**
Lava el coche todos los domingos.
2 **lavarse** *(get washed)*
**At eight I get up, wash and get dressed.**
A las ocho me levanto, me lavo y me visto.
**I'm going to wash my hands.**
Me voy a lavar las manos.
**I want to wash my hair.**
Quiero lavarme la cabeza.

**Wash your hands!**
¡Lávate las manos!

*Language tip*
*In Spanish you usually use an article like* **el**, **la**, **los** *with parts of the body.*

**washbasin** NOUN
el **lavabo** *masc*

**washing machine** NOUN
la **lavadora** *fem*

**washing-up** NOUN
**to do the washing-up**
fregar los platos
**Who's going to do the washing-up?**
¿Quién va a fregar los platos?
**I often do the washing-up.**
Muchas veces friego yo los platos.

**wasn't** (= was not) ▷ *see* **be**

**wasp** NOUN
la **avispa** *fem*

**waste** NOUN
**It's a waste of time.**
Es una pérdida de tiempo.

**wastepaper basket** NOUN
la **papelera** *fem*
**Put your chewing gum in the wastepaper basket.**
Tira tu chicle a la papelera.

**watch**

*watch can be a noun or a verb.*

**A** NOUN
el **reloj** *masc*
**I haven't got a watch.**
No tengo reloj.

*Language tip*
*Did you know that* **un reloj** *is also* **a clock**?

**B** VERB
**to watch**
1 **mirar** *(look at)*

**Watch what I do.**
Mira lo que hago.

**Watch me, Mum!**
¡Mírame, mamá!

**2 ver** *(television, programme, match)*
**He watches television every day.**
Ve la televisión todos los días.

to **watch out** VERB
**tener cuidado**
**You need to watch out.**
Tienes que tener cuidado.

**Watch out!**
¡Cuidado!

**water** NOUN
el **agua** *fem*

**Language tip**
*Even though it's a feminine noun, remember that you use el and un with* **agua.**

**The water was very cold.**
El agua estaba muy fría.
**a glass of water**
un vaso de agua

**Language tip**
*Be careful! The translation of* **water** *is not* **wáter.**

**wave**

**wave** *can be a noun or a verb.*

**A** NOUN
la **ola** *fem*
**There are big waves sometimes.**
A veces hay olas grandes.
**B** VERB
**to wave**
**1 saludar con la mano** *(in greeting)*
**They're waving at us.**
Nos están saludando con la mano.
**2 to wave goodbye**
decir adiós con la mano

**Let's wave goodbye.**
Vamos a decir adiós con la mano.

**wavy** ADJECTIVE
**wavy hair**
pelo ondulado

**way** NOUN
**1** el **camino** *masc* *(to place)*
**I don't know the way.**
No sé el camino.
**Ask the way.**
Pregunta el camino.
**Can you tell me the way to the station?**
¿Me puedes decir cómo se llega a la estación?

**It's a long way.**
Está lejos.
**Which way is it?**
¿Por dónde está?
**It's this way.**
Es por aquí.

**2** la **forma** *fem (manner)*
**What's the best way to learn Spanish?**
¿Cuál es la mejor forma de aprender español?

**Language tip**
*As* **la manera** *and* **el modo** *mean the same as* **la forma,** *you could alternatively say* **la mejor manera** *or* **el mejor modo** *to mean* **the best way.**

**He looked at me in a strange way.**
Me miró de forma extraña.
**Do it this way, Katy.**
Hazlo así, Katy.
**by the way**
a propósito
**No way!**
¡Ni hablar!

**way in** NOUN
la **entrada** *fem*

**way out** NOUN
la **salida** *fem*
**Where's the way out?**
¿Dónde está la salida?

**we** PRONOUN
**nosotros** *masc pl*
**nosotras** *fem pl*
**Shall we do it?**
¿Lo hacemos nosotros?

> *Language tip*
> **we** *isn't usually translated unless it's emphatic.*

**We do sport in the afternoon.**
Hacemos deporte por la tarde.

to **wear** VERB
**llevar**
**He's wearing a hat.**
Lleva un sombrero.
**I wear glasses.**
Llevo gafas.
**What's she wearing?**
¿Qué lleva puesto?

**weather** NOUN
el **tiempo** *masc*
**What's the weather like today?**
¿Qué tiempo hace hoy?
**The weather isn't very nice.**
No hace muy buen tiempo.

> **What's the weather like?**
> ¿Qué tiempo hace?
> **The weather's nice.**
> Hace buen tiempo.

**weather forecast** NOUN
el **pronóstico del tiempo** *masc*

**Web** NOUN
**the Web**
Internet *masc/fem*
**Look on the Web.**
Mira en Internet.

la **webcam** NOUN
la **webcam**

**website** NOUN
el **sitio web** *masc*

**we'd**
**1** (= **we would**) ▷*see* **would**
**2** (= **we had**) ▷*see* **have**

**wedding** NOUN
la **boda** *fem*
**It's my cousin's wedding today.**
Hoy es la boda de mi prima.

**wedding anniversary**
NOUN
el **aniversario de boda** *masc*

**Wednesday** NOUN
el **miércoles** *masc*
**It's Wednesday today.**
Hoy es miércoles.

> **on Wednesday**
> el miércoles
> **on Wednesdays**
> los miércoles
> **every Wednesday**
> cada miércoles
> **last Wednesday**
> el miércoles pasado
> **next Wednesday**
> el miércoles que viene

> *Language tip*
> *Days are not spelled with a capital letter in Spanish.*

**week** NOUN
la **semana** *fem*
**two weeks**
dos semanas

> **this week**
> esta semana
> **last week**

la semana pasada
**every week**
cada semana
**next week**
la semana que viene
**in a week's time**
dentro de una semana

**weekday** NOUN
**on weekdays**
los días entre semana

**weekend** NOUN
el **fin de semana** *masc*
**What are you doing at the weekend?**
¿Qué vas a hacer el fin de semana?
**The shops are closed at weekends.**
Las tiendas cierran los fines de semana.

**at weekends**
los fines de semana
**last weekend**
el fin de semana pasado
**next weekend**
el fin de semana que viene

**welcome** ADJECTIVE
**Welcome!**
¡Bienvenido!

*Language tip*
*Remember to change* **¡bienvenido!** *to* **¡bienvenida!** *if you're welcoming a girl or woman. Similarly, change it to* **¡bienvenidos!** *if you're welcoming a mixed group or a group of men.*

**Welcome to Scotland!**
¡Bienvenido a Escocia!

**Thank you! – You're welcome!**
¡Gracias! – ¡De nada!

**we'll** (= we will) ▷ *see* will

**well**

*well can be an adverb or an adjective.*

**A** ADVERB
**bien**
**The team is playing well.**
El equipo está jugando bien.
**as well**
también
**We're going to London as well as Manchester.**
Vamos a Londres y también a Manchester.

**B** ADJECTIVE
**to be well**
estar bien

*Language tip*
**bien** *never changes its ending no matter who or what it describes.*

**He isn't well.**
No está bien.
**I'm not very well at the moment.**
No estoy muy bien en este momento.
**How are you? – I'm very well, thank you.**
¿Cómo estás? – Estoy muy bien, gracias.

**Well done!**
¡Bien hecho!
**Get well soon!**
¡Que te mejores pronto!

*Language tip*
*Have you noticed the upside-down exclamation mark at the start of Spanish exclamations?*

**well-behaved** ADJECTIVE
**well-behaved children**
niños que se portan bien
**He's very well-behaved.**
Se porta muy bien.

**wellies** PL NOUN
las **botas de agua** *fem pl*

**wellingtons**
PL NOUN
las **botas de agua** *fem pl*

**well-known** ADJECTIVE
**conocido** *masc*
**conocida** *fem*
**a well-known film star**
un conocido artista de cine

## Welsh

> **Welsh** *can be an adjective or a noun.*

**A** ADJECTIVE
**galés** *masc* (PL **galeses**)
**galesa** *fem*
**a Welsh town**
una ciudad galesa
**Welsh people**
los galeses

**He's Welsh.**
Es galés.
**She's Welsh.**
Es galesa.

**B** NOUN
el **galés** *masc* (language)
**the Welsh**
los galeses

> *Language tip*
> **galés** *is not spelled with a capital letter in Spanish.*

## Welshman NOUN
el **galés** *masc* (PL los **galeses**)

> *Language tip*
> **galés** *is not spelled with a capital letter in Spanish.*

## Welshwoman NOUN
la **galesa** *fem*

> *Language tip*
> **galesa** *is not spelled with a capital letter in Spanish.*

**went** VERB ▷ *see* **go**

**were** VERB ▷ *see* **be**

**we're** (= **we are**) ▷ *see* **be**

**weren't** (= **were not**) ▷ *see* **be**

**west**

> **west** *can be an adjective or a noun.*

**A** ADJECTIVE
**oeste**

> *Language tip*
> **oeste** *never changes its ending no matter what it describes. Did you know that adjectives that behave like this are called 'invariable adjectives'?*

**the west coast**
la costa oeste
**B** NOUN
el **oeste** *masc*
**in the west**
en el oeste

**western** NOUN
la **película del oeste** *fem*
**I like westerns.**
Me gustan las películas del oeste.

**wet** ADJECTIVE
**mojado** *masc*
**mojada** *fem*
**wet clothes**
ropa mojada
**I'm wet.**
Estoy mojado.

**It's wet today.**
Hoy está lloviendo.

## what

> **what** *can be a pronoun or an adjective.*

**A** PRONOUN
**1 qué**

**What are you doing, boys?**
¿Qué estáis haciendo, chicos?
**What's the matter?**
¿Qué pasa?
**What's this?**
¿Qué es esto?

*Language tip*

Use **¿qué es...?** in 'what is...?'
questions when asking for an
explanation or definition.

**Ask her what they are.**
Pregúntale qué son.
**2 cuál** (PL **cuáles**)
**What's the capital of Spain?**
¿Cuál es la capital de España?

*Language tip*

You usually use **¿cuál es...?** in
'what is...?' questions when asking
for specific information rather than
an explanation or definition.

**3 lo que**

*Language tip*

Use **lo que** when **what** is not a
question word. Because **que** is not a
question word here, it does not have
an accent.

**I saw what happened.**
Vi lo que pasó.

**What?**
¿Qué?
**What is it?**
¿Qué es?
**What do you want?**
¿Qué quieres?
**What's the weather like?**
¿Qué tiempo hace?
**What's your name?**
¿Cómo te llamas?
**What's your phone number?**
¿Cuál es tu número de teléfono?

**B** ADJECTIVE
**qué**

*Language tip*

**qué** never changes its ending.

**What letter does it start
with?**
¿Por qué letra empieza?
**What colour is it?**
¿De qué color es?
**What a pretty house!**
¡Qué casa más bonita!
**What delicious cherries!**
¡Qué cerezas tan ricas!
**What time is it?**
¿Qué hora es?
**What day is it today?**
¿Qué día es hoy?

*Language tip*

Don't forget the written accent on
question words like **qué** and **cuál**
nor the upside-down question mark
at the start of questions.

**wheel** NOUN
la **rueda** *fem*

**wheelchair** NOUN
la **silla de ruedas** *fem*

**when** ADVERB
**1 cuándo** (in questions)
**When's your birthday?**
¿Cuándo es tu cumpleaños?

*Language tip*

Don't forget the written accent on
question words like **¿cuándo...?**
nor the upside-down question mark
at the start of questions.

**2 cuando** (in other sentences)
**When it rains, we stay in the
classroom.**
Cuando llueve nos quedamos en
la clase.

**where** ADVERB, CONJUNCTION
**1 dónde** (in questions)
**Where's Emma today?**
¿Dónde está hoy Emma?
**Where are you going?**
¿A dónde vas?

**Where do you live?**
¿Dónde vives?

English Spanish

a
b
c
d
e
f
g
h
i
j
k
l
m
n
o
p
q
r
s
t
u
v
**w**
x
y
z

**2 donde** *(in other sentences)*
**the house where I live**
la casa donde vivo

## whether CONJUNCTION
si
**I don't know whether to go or not.**
No sé si ir o no.

## which

**which** *can be an adjective or a pronoun.*

**A** ADJECTIVE
**qué**

**Which flavour do you want?**
¿Qué sabor quieres?
**Which number is it?**
¿Qué número es?
**Which one would you like?**
¿Cuál quieres?
**Which ones would you like?**
¿Cuáles quieres?

**B** PRONOUN
**1 cuál** (PL **cuáles**) *(in questions)*
**Which would you like?**
¿Cuál quieres?
**Which is your car?**
¿Cuál es tu coche?
**Which are your suitcases?**
¿Cuáles son tus maletas?
**Which do you prefer, cricket or football?**

¿Qué te gusta más, el críquet o el fútbol?
**2 que** *(relative)*
**the car which we sold**
el coche que vendimos

**the film which I was telling you about**
la película de la que te hablaba

## while

**while** *can be a conjunction or a noun.*

**A** CONJUNCTION
**mientras**
**While you're here, we can do some sightseeing.**
Mientras estás aquí podemos hacer un poco de turismo.
**You hold the torch while I look inside.**
Aguanta la linterna mientras yo miro por dentro.
**B** NOUN
**a while**
un rato
**a while ago**
hace un rato
**after a while**
después de un rato

## whipped
**cream** NOUN
la **nata montada** *fem*

## whiskers
PL NOUN
los **bigotes**
*masc pl*

## white

**white** *can be an adjective or a noun.*

**A** ADJECTIVE
**blanco** *masc*
**blanca** *fem*
**He's wearing white trousers.**
Lleva pantalones blancos.
**My shirt is white.**
Mi camisa es blanca.
**He's got white hair.**
Tiene el pelo blanco.

> **Language tip**
> Colour adjectives come after the noun in Spanish.

**B** NOUN
el **blanco** *masc*
**The bride is wearing white.**
La novia va vestida de blanco.

**whiteboard** NOUN
la **pizarra blanca** *fem*
**an interactive whiteboard**
una pizarra interactiva

**white coffee** NOUN
el **café con leche** *masc*

> **Did you know...?**
> **el café con leche** *is made with hot milk. If you'd like a short, strong white coffee, ask for* **un cortado** *instead.*

**Whitsun** NOUN
**Pentecostés** *masc*

**who** PRONOUN
**1 quién** (PL **quiénes**) *(in questions)*
**Who wants to start?**
¿Quién quiere empezar?
**Who's that?**
¿Quién es ése?
**Who are they?**
¿Quiénes son?

> **Language tip**
> Don't forget the written accent on question words like **¿quién...?** nor the upside-down question mark at the start of questions.

**2 que** *(relative)*
**the girl who lives there**
la chica que vive allí

**whole** ADJECTIVE
**todo** *masc*
**toda** *fem*
**the whole class**
toda la clase
**the whole afternoon**
toda la tarde
**the whole world**
el mundo entero

**whose** PRONOUN, ADJECTIVE
**de quién** *(in questions)*
**Whose pencil case is this?**
¿De quién es este estuche?
**Whose turn is it?**
¿De quién es el turno?

> **Whose is this?**
> ¿De quién es esto?

**why** ADVERB
**por qué**
**Why are you crying?**
¿Por qué lloras?
**Why not?**
¿Por qué no?
**Why don't you eat meat? - Because I don't like it.**
¿Por qué no comes carne? - Porque no me gusta.

> **Language tip**
> The Spanish translations for **why** and **because** are very similar. When it is used to ask a question, **¿por qué?** is two separate words and has an accent on the **qué**.

**That's why I can't go.**
Por eso no puedo ir.

**wide** ADJECTIVE
**ancho** *masc*
**ancha** *fem*
**a wide road**
una calle ancha

**widow** NOUN
la **viuda** *fem*

**widower** NOUN
el **viudo** *masc*

**wife** NOUN

la **mujer** *fem*
  **She's his wife.**
  Es su mujer.

**wild** ADJECTIVE
**salvaje** *masc & fem*
  **a wild animal**
  un animal salvaje

**will** VERB
1 *(forming future)*
  **It will soon be my birthday.**
  Pronto será mi cumpleaños.
  **We'll get there quite late.**
  Llegaremos bastante tarde.
  **It won't rain.**
  No lloverá.
2 *(in requests and offers)*
  **Will you help me?**
  ¿Me ayudas?
  **I'll make the coffee.**
  Yo hago el café.

to **win** VERB
**ganar**
  **Who is winning?**
  ¿Quién va ganando?
  **I've won!**
  ¡He ganado!

**wind** NOUN
el **viento** *masc*
  **There is a lot of wind.**
  Hace mucho viento.

**window** NOUN
1 la **ventana** *fem*
  **Look out of the window, boys.**
  Mirad por la ventana, chicos.
  **a shop window**
  un escaparate
2 el **cristal** *masc (pane)*
  **He's broken the window.**
  Ha roto el cristal.

**windy** ADJECTIVE
  **a windy day**
  un día de viento

**It's windy.**
Hace viento.

**wine** NOUN
el **vino** *masc*
  **a bottle of wine**
  una botella de vino
  **a glass of wine**
  una copa de vino
  **white wine**
  vino blanco
  **red wine**
  vino tinto

**winner** NOUN
el **ganador** *masc*
la **ganadora** *fem*

**winning** ADJECTIVE
  **the winning team**
  el equipo ganador

**winter** NOUN
el **invierno** *masc*
  **last winter**
  el invierno pasado

**in winter**
en invierno

**winter sports** PL NOUN
los **deportes de invierno**
  *masc pl*

**wintertime** NOUN
el **invierno** *masc*

**in wintertime**
en el invierno

**wish**

*wish can be a noun or a verb.*

**A** NOUN
el **deseo** *masc*
  **Make a wish!**
  ¡Pide un deseo!
  **With best wishes, Lily**
  Un abrazo, Lily

**Best wishes**
Un abrazo

**B** VERB
**to wish**
desear
**He wished her a happy birthday.**
Le deseó feliz cumpleaños.
**I wish I could go with you!**
¡Ojalá pudiera ir contigo!

*Language tip*
**Ojalá** *is followed by a form of the verb called the subjunctive.*

**witch** NOUN
la **bruja** *fem*

**with** PREPOSITION
**1 con**
**Tea with milk?**
¿Té con leche?
**We're going to stay with friends.**
Nos vamos a quedar con unos amigos.
**I live with my dad.**
Vivo con mi padre.

*Language tip*
*Remember that* **with me** *translates as* **conmigo**.

**Come with me.**
Ven conmigo.
**It begins with 'b'.**
Empieza por 'b'.
**2 de** *(in descriptions)*
**a woman with blue eyes**
una mujer de ojos azules

**without** PREPOSITION
**sin**
**I drink coffee without sugar.**
Bebo el café sin azúcar.
**without speaking**
sin hablar

*Language tip*
*Just use* **sin** *on its own to translate* **without a**.

**without a coat**
sin abrigo

**witness** NOUN
el/la **testigo** *masc/fem*

*Language tip*
*Did you notice that the feminine form* **la testigo** *still ends in* **-o**?

**wives**
PL NOUN
las **mujeres**
*fem pl*

**wolf** NOUN
el **lobo** *masc*

**woman** NOUN
la **mujer** *fem*
**three women and two men**
tres mujeres y dos hombres

**won** VERB ▷*see* **win**

to **wonder** VERB
preguntarse
**I wonder where Caroline is.**
Me pregunto dónde está Caroline.

**wonderful** ADJECTIVE
**maravilloso** *masc*
**maravillosa** *fem*

**won't** (= will not) ▷*see* **will**

**wood** NOUN
**1** la **madera** *fem (substance)*
**It's made of wood.**
Es de madera.
**2** el **bosque** *masc (place)*
**We went for a walk in the wood.**
Fuimos a pasear por el bosque.

**wool** NOUN
la **lana** *fem*
**It's made of wool.**
Es de lana.

English Spanish

a b c d e f g h i j k l m n o p q r s t u v **w** x y z

a b c d e f g h i j k l m n o p q r s t u v **w** x y z

**word** NOUN
la **palabra** *fem*
**I've forgotten the word.**
Se me ha olvidado la palabra.
**What's the word for 'shop' in Spanish?**
¿Cómo se dice 'shop' en español?
**We're going to learn the words of a song.**
Vamos a aprendernos la letra de una canción.

## work

> **work** *can be a verb or a noun.*

**A** VERB
**to work**
1 **trabajar** *(person)*
**She works in a shop.**
Trabaja en una tienda.
2 **funcionar** *(machine, plan)*
**The heating isn't working.**
La calefacción no funciona.

**B** NOUN
el **trabajo** *masc*
**He's at work at the moment.**
Está en el trabajo en estos momentos.
**I've got a lot of work to do.**
Tengo mucho trabajo que hacer.
**to go to work**
ir a trabajar
**He goes to work at eight o'clock.**
Va a trabajar a las ocho.

**at work**
en el trabajo

**worker** NOUN
el **trabajador** *masc*

la **trabajadora** *fem*
**She's a good worker.**
Es una buena trabajadora.

**worksheet** NOUN
la **hoja de ejercicios** *fem*

**world** NOUN
el **mundo** *masc*
**the whole world**
el mundo entero
**He's the world champion.**
Es el campeón del mundo.

**worried** ADJECTIVE
**preocupado** *masc*
**preocupada** *fem*
**She's very worried.**
Está muy preocupada.

to **worry** VERB
**preocuparse**
**He worries too much.**
Se preocupa demasiado.

**worse** ADJECTIVE, ADVERB
**peor** *masc & fem*
**The weather is worse in Scotland.**
El tiempo está peor en Escocia.
**I'm feeling worse.**
Me siento peor.

**worst** ADJECTIVE, ADVERB, NOUN
**peor** *masc & fem*
**I always get the worst mark.**
Siempre saco la peor nota.
**Darren behaves worst.**
Darren es el que peor se porta.
**She's the worst in the class.**
Es la peor de la clase.
**Chemistry is my worst subject.**
La química es lo que peor se me da.

**worth** ADJECTIVE
**It's worth a lot of money.**
Vale mucho dinero.

> ### Language tip
> In Spanish, **valer mucho** *has two meanings. It can mean* **to be worth a lot** *or* **to cost a lot.**

**It's worth it.**
Vale la pena.

## would VERB
**1** *(in offers, requests)*

*Language tip*
Use the verb **querer** to ask what someone would like or to say what you would like.

**What would you like, dear?**
¿Qué quieres, cielo?
**My friend would like a sandwich.**
Mi amigo quiere un bocadillo.
**Would you like to play with me?**
¿Quieres jugar conmigo?
**I'd like a hot chocolate, please.**
Quiero una taza de chocolate, por favor.
**2** *(in polite orders)*

*Language tip*
Use the verb **poder** to ask someone to do something.

**Would you close the door, please?**
¿Puedes cerrar la puerta, por favor?

## wrapping paper NOUN
el **papel de envolver** *masc*

to **write** VERB
**escribir**
**She's writing a story.**
Está escribiendo un cuento.
**I'm going to write to my friend.**
Le voy a escribir a mi amigo.
**Write your names.**
Escribid vuestro nombre.
**Write to me soon, Sandra.**
Escríbeme pronto, Sandra.

**Write soon!**
¡Escribe pronto!

*Language tip*
Have you noticed the upside-down exclamation mark at the start of Spanish exclamations?

to **write down** VERB
**apuntar**
**I'll write down the address.**
Apuntaré la dirección.
**Can you write it down for me, please?**
¿Me lo puedes apuntar, por favor?

## writer NOUN
el **escritor** *masc*
la **escritora** *fem*
**He's a writer.**
Es escritor.

*Language tip*
In Spanish, you do not use an article with people's jobs.

## writing NOUN
la **letra** *fem*
**I can't read your writing.**
No entiendo tu letra.

**written** VERB ▷*see* **write**

## wrong

**wrong** *can be an adjective or an adverb.*

**A** ADJECTIVE
**1** **incorrecto** *masc*
**incorrecta** *fem (answer, information)*

**This answer is wrong.**
Esta respuesta es incorrecta.
**That's the wrong answer.**
Ésa no es la respuesta correcta.
**I got three questions wrong.**
Me equivoqué en tres preguntas.

2 **equivocado** *masc*
**equivocada** *fem (person)*
**You're wrong!**
¡Estás equivocado!
**You're looking at the wrong page.**
Estás mirando en la página equivocada.

**B** ADVERB
**mal**
**You're saying it wrong.**
Lo estás diciendo mal.
**Have I spelled it wrong?**
¿Lo he escrito mal?

**What's wrong?**
¿Qué pasa?
**What's wrong with you?**
¿Qué te pasa?

**wrote** VERB ▷ *see* **write**

# X x

## Xmas NOUN
la **Navidad** *fem*

## X-ray

> **X-ray** can be a verb or a noun.

**A** VERB
   **to X-ray**
   **hacer una radiografía de**
   **They're going to X-ray my leg.**
   Me van a hacer una radiografía de la pierna.

**They X-rayed my arm.**
Me hicieron una radiografía del brazo.

### Language tip
*In Spanish you usually use an article like **el**, **la**, **los** with parts of the body.*

**B** NOUN
   la **radiografía** *fem*
   **I'm going to have an X-ray.**
   Me voy a hacer una radiografía.

## xylophone NOUN
el **xilófono** *masc*

# Y y

## yacht NOUN
1 el **barco de vela**
   *masc (sailing boat)*
2 el **yate** *masc*
   *(luxury*
   *motorboat)*

## yard NOUN
el **patio** *masc*
**in the yard**
en el patio

## to **yawn** VERB
**bostezar**

## year NOUN
1 el **año** *masc*
   **a hundred years**
   cien años
   **an eight-year-old child**
   un niño de ocho años

**this year**
este año
**last year**
el año pasado
**next year**
el año que viene
**I'm ten years old.**
Tengo diez años.

2 el **curso** *masc (school year)*
   **What year are you in?**
   ¿En qué curso estás?
   **I'm in Year Six.**
   Estoy en sexto.
   **She's in Year Five.**
   Está en quinto.

### Did you know...?
*In Spain, children start primary*
*school at six and go on to secondary*
*school at twelve. Compulsory*
*education ends at sixteen but they*
*can stay on at school till they're*
*eighteen to do their* **Bachillerato**.

## yellow

**yellow** *can be an adjective or a noun.*

**A** ADJECTIVE
**amarillo** *masc*
**amarilla** *fem*
**I'm wearing yellow shorts.**
Llevo unos pantalones cortos
amarillos.

### Language tip
*Colour adjectives come after the*
*noun in Spanish.*

**B** NOUN
el **amarillo** *masc*
**Yellow is my favourite colour.**
El amarillo es mi color favorito.

## yes ADVERB
**sí**
**Do you like it? – Yes.**
¿Te gusta? – Sí.
**Orange juice? – Yes, please.**
¿Zumo de naranja? – Sí, por favor.
**Answer yes or no.**
Responde sí o no.

## yesterday ADVERB
**ayer**
**When? – Yesterday.**
¿Cuándo? – Ayer.
**I was absent yesterday.**
Ayer no vine.

**yesterday morning**
ayer por la mañana
**yesterday afternoon**
ayer por la tarde
**yesterday evening**
ayer por la noche

### Language tip
*Translate* **yesterday evening** *by*
**ayer por la tarde** *instead if you're*
*talking about a time when it was*
*still light.*

**yet** ADVERB
1 **todavía** (in negatives)
   **I haven't finished yet.**
   Todavía no he terminado.
2 **ya** (in questions)
   **Have you finished yet, children?**
   ¿Habéis terminado ya, niños?

**Not yet.**
Todavía no.

**yoga** NOUN
   el **yoga** masc

**yoghurt** NOUN
   el **yogur** masc

**you** PRONOUN

*Language tip*
*There are different Spanish words for* **you** *depending on whether it refers to one person or more than one person and how formal you are with them. The translation also depends on whether* **you** *is a subject (see senses 1-4) or an object (see mainly senses 5-8). The notes that follow each translation will help you find the word you need.*

1 **tú** masc & fem

*Language tip*
*Use* **tú** *to refer to just one friend, family member or person your own age when* **you** *is the subject of the verb.*

**You've got a cat but I haven't.**
Tú tienes un gato pero yo no.

*Language tip*
*But remember that* **you** *isn't usually translated unless it's emphatic.*

**You've got a new computer, haven't you?**
Tienes un ordenador nuevo, ¿verdad?

*Language tip*
*Also use* **tú** *in comparisons.*

**She's younger than you.**
Es más joven que tú.

*Language tip*
*Use* **ti** *instead after a preposition like* **para** *or* **de**.

**It's for you, James.**
Es para ti, James.
**I'll go with you.**
Iré contigo.

**for you**
para ti
**with you**
contigo

2 **vosotros** masc pl
   **vosotras** fem pl

*Language tip*
*Use* **vosotros** *and* **vosotras** *to refer to two or more friends, family members or people your own age when* **you** *is the subject of the verb.*

**You've got time but I haven't.**
Vosotros tenéis tiempo pero yo no.

*Language tip*
*But remember that* **you** *isn't usually translated unless it's emphatic.*

**You've got a new car, haven't you?**
Tenéis un coche nuevo, ¿verdad?

*Language tip*
*Use* **vosotros/vosotras** *in comparisons.*

**They are younger than you two.**
Son más jóvenes que vosotros dos.

*Language tip*
*Also use* **vosotros/vosotras** *after a preposition like* **para** *or* **de**.

**It's for you, girls.**
Es para vosotras, niñas.
3 **usted** masc & fem

English Spanish

a
b
c
d
e
f
g
h
i
j
k
l
m
n
o
p
q
r
s
t
u
v
w
x
y
z

### Language tip
*Use* **usted** *to refer to just one person that you treat with respect, for example your teacher or an older person, when* **you** *is the subject of the verb.*

**You have a lot of books but I haven't.**
Usted tiene muchos libros pero yo no.

### Language tip
*But remember that, like the other subject pronouns,* **usted** *is often omitted.*

**Have you got any more paints, Miss?**
¿Tiene más pinturas, señorita?

### Language tip
*Use* **usted** *in comparisons.*

**She isn't as nice as you.**
No es tan simpática como usted.

### Language tip
*Also use* **usted** *after a preposition like* **para** *or* **de**.

**It's for you, Mr Smith.**
Es para usted, señor Smith.
**4 ustedes** *masc & fem pl*

### Language tip
*Use* **ustedes** *to refer to two or more people that you treat with respect, for example your teachers or older people, when* **you** *is the subject of the verb.*

**You have a lot of books but we haven't.**
Ustedes tienen muchos libros pero nosotros no.

### Language tip
*But remember that, like the other subject pronouns,* **ustedes** *is often omitted.*

**You've got a huge garden, haven't you?**
Tienen un jardín enorme, ¿verdad?

### Language tip
*Use* **ustedes** *in comparisons.*

**They aren't as nice as you.**
No son tan simpáticos como ustedes.

### Language tip
*Use* **ustedes** *after a preposition like* **para** *or* **de**.

**They are for you, Mr and Mrs Smith.**
Son para ustedes, señor y señora Smith.
**5 te** *masc & fem*

### Language tip
*Use* **te** *instead of* **tú** *to refer to just one friend, family member or person your own age when* **you** *is the object of the verb.*

**I love you.**
Te quiero.
**I'll give it to you.**
Te lo daré.
**6 os** *masc & fem pl*

### Language tip
*Use* **os** *instead of* **vosotros/ vosotras** *to refer to two or more friends, family members or people your own age when* **you** *is the object of the verb.*

**I know you, Tracy and Sheila.**
Os conozco, Tracy y Sheila.
**I'll give it to you, boys.**
Os lo daré, chicos.
**7 lo** *masc*
**la** *fem*

### Language tip
*Use* **lo** *and* **la** *to refer to just one person that you treat with respect, for example your teacher or an older person, when* **you** *is the object of the verb.* **lo** *and* **la** *are the direct object pronouns that correspond to* **usted**.

**I can see you, sir.**
Lo veo, señor.

I can see you, Miss.
La veo, señorita.

**Language tip**
*Use **le** instead (for both masculine and feminine) when **you** means 'to you' or 'for you' and is the indirect object of the verb.*

**I'll give you my exercise book.**
Le daré mi cuaderno.
**I'll write to you.**
Le escribiré.

**Language tip**
*Change **le** to **se** when combining it with a direct object pronoun like **lo**, **la**, **los** or **las**.*

**I'll give it to you.**
Se lo daré.

**8 los** *masc pl*
**las** *fem pl*

**Language tip**
*Use **los** and **los** to refer to two or more people that you treat with respect, for example your teachers or older people, when **you** is the object of the verb. **los** and **las** are the direct object pronouns that correspond to **ustedes**.*

**May I help you?**
¿Los puedo ayudar?

**Language tip**
*Use **les** instead (for both masculine plural and feminine plural) when **you** means 'to you' or 'for you' and is the indirect object of the verb.*

**I'll give you the keys.**
Les daré las llaves.
**I'll write to you.**
Les escribiré.

**Language tip**
*Change **les** to **se** when combining it with a direct object pronoun like **lo**, **la**, **los** or **las**.*

**I'll give them to you.**
Se las daré.

**you'd**
**1** (= **you would**) ▷see **would**
**2** (= **you had**) ▷see **have**

**you'll** (= **you will**) ▷see **will**

**young** ADJECTIVE
**joven** *masc & fem* (PL **jóvenes**)
**You're too young.**
Eres demasiado joven.
**They're younger than me.**
Son más jóvenes que yo
**She's the youngest in the class.**
Es la más joven de la clase.
**my youngest brother**
mi hermano menor
**Stephen's the youngest.**
Stephen es el menor.

**your** ADJECTIVE
**1 tu** *masc & fem* (PL **tus**) (to someone you call 'tú')

**Language tip**
*Remember to use **tu** before a singular noun and **tus** before a plural one.*

**Is that your brother?**
¿Es ése tu hermano?
**your friend Helen**
tu amiga Helen
**your parents**
tus padres
**Wash your hands, Laura.**
Lávate las manos, Laura.

**Language tip**
*Remember that **tú** with an accent means 'you' while **tu** without an accent means 'your'.*

**2 vuestro** *masc*
**vuestra** *fem* (to people you call 'vosotros')

**Language tip**
*Remember to make **vuestro** agree with the noun that follows it.*

**Is that your car?**
¿Es ése vuestro coche?
**Is this your house?**
¿Es ésta vuestra casa?
**Write your names.**
Escribid vuestros nombres.
**Put on your coats, children.**
Poneos los abrigos, niños.
3 **su** *masc & fem* (PL **sus**) *(to people you call 'usted' and 'ustedes')*

**Language tip**
*Remember to use **su** before a singular noun and **sus** before a plural one.*

**your house**
su casa
**When's your birthday, Miss?**
¿Cuándo es su cumpleaños, señorita?
**Here are your books, Miss.**
Aquí tiene sus libros, señorita.

**you're** (= you are) ▷*see* be

**yours** PRONOUN
1 el **tuyo** *masc*
la **tuya** *fem (to someone you call 'tú')*

**Language tip**
*Remember that the choice of **el tuyo**, **la tuya**, **los tuyos** or **las tuyas** depends entirely on the thing or things referred to.*

**That isn't your coat. Yours is here.**
Aquél no es tu abrigo. El tuyo está aquí.
**Those aren't your boots. Yours are here.**
Aquéllas no son tus botas. Las tuyas están aquí.

**Language tip**
*After **ser** you can usually just use **tuyo**, **tuya**, **tuyos** or **tuyas** to agree with the noun referred to.*

**Is this yours, Frank?**
¿Esto es tuyo, Frank?
**Whose is this? – It's yours.**
¿De quién es esto? – Es tuyo.
**a friend of yours**
un amigo tuyo
2 el **vuestro** *masc*
la **vuestra** *fem (to people you call 'vosotros')*

**Language tip**
*Remember that the choice of **el vuestro**, **la vuestra**, **los vuestros** or **las vuestras** depends entirely on the thing or things referred to.*

**That isn't your car. Yours is here.**
Aquél no es vuestro coche. El vuestro está aquí.
**Those aren't your exercise books. Yours are here.**
Aquéllos no son vuestros cuadernos. Los vuestros están aquí.

**Language tip**
*After **ser** you can usually just use **vuestro**, **vuestra**, **vuestros** or **vuestras** to agree with the noun referred to.*

**These sweets are yours.**
Estos caramelos son vuestros.
**a friend of yours**
un amigo vuestro
3 el **suyo** *masc*
la **suya** *fem (to people you call 'usted' and 'ustedes')*

**Language tip**
*Remember that the choice of **el suyo**, **la suya**, **los suyos** or **las suyas** depends entirely on the thing or things referred to.*

**That isn't your coat. Yours is here.**
Aquél no es su abrigo. El suyo está aquí.
**Those aren't your boots. Yours are here.**
Aquéllas no son sus botas. Las suyas están aquí.

*Language tip*
*After* **ser** *you can usually just use* **suyo, suya, suyos** *or* **suyas** *to agree with the noun referred to.*

**Is this yours, sir?**
¿Esto es suyo, señor?
**These tickets are yours.**
Estas entradas son suyas.
**Whose is this? – It's yours.**
¿De quién es esto? – Es suyo.
**a friend of yours**
un amigo suyo
**Yours sincerely**
Le saluda atentamente

*Language tip*
*Use* **Le saluda atentamente** *when writing to one person. Use* **Les saluda atentamente** *when writing to more than one person.*

## yourself PRONOUN
**1 te** *(to someone you call 'tú')*
**You'll make yourself sick!**
¡Te vas a marear!
**Are you enjoying yourself?**
¿Te estás divirtiendo?

*Language tip*
*Use* **ti** *instead after a preposition.*

**Tell me about yourself!**
¡Háblame de ti!

*Language tip*
*Use* **tú mismo** *and* **tú misma** *in emphatic uses.*

**Do it yourself!**
¡Hazlo tú mismo!
**2 se** *(to someone you call 'usted')*
**Are you enjoying yourself?**
¿Se está divirtiendo?

*Language tip*
*Use* **usted** *instead after a preposition.*

**Tell me about yourself!**
¡Hábleme de usted!

*Language tip*
*Use* **usted mismo** *and* **usted misma** *in emphatic uses.*

**Help yourself, Mrs Day!**
¡Sírvase usted misma, señora Day!

## yourselves PRONOUN
**1 os** *(to people you call 'vosotros')*
**Did you enjoy yourselves?**
¿Os divertisteis?

*Language tip*
*Use* **vosotros/vosotras** *instead after a preposition.*

**Tell me about yourselves!**
¡Habladme de vosotros!

*Language tip*
*Use* **vosotros mismos** *and* **vosotras mismas** *in emphatic uses.*

**Do it yourselves!**
¡Hacedlo vosotros mismos!
**2 se** *(to people you call 'ustedes')*
**Are you enjoying yourselves?**
¿Se están divirtiendo?

*Language tip*
*Use* **ustedes** *instead after a preposition.*

**Tell me about yourselves!**
¡Háblenme de ustedes!

*Language tip*
*Use* **ustedes mismos** *and* **ustedes mismas** *in emphatic uses.*

**Help yourselves!**
¡Sírvanse ustedes mismos!

## youth club NOUN
el **club juvenil** *masc*

English Spanish

a
b
c
d
e
f
g
h
i
j
k
l
m
n
o
p
q
r
s
t
u
v
w
x
y
z

**youth hostel** NOUN
  el **albergue juvenil** *masc*
  **We're going to stay at a youth hostel.**
  Nos vamos a alojar en un albergue juvenil.

**you've** (= you have) ▷ *see* **have**

**yummy** ADJECTIVE
  **buenísimo** *masc*
  **buenísima** *fem*

# Z z

**zebra** NOUN
la **cebra** *fem*

**zebra crossing**
NOUN
el **paso de peatones** *masc*

**zero** NOUN
el **cero** *masc*

**zip** NOUN
la **cremallera** *fem*

**zoo** NOUN
el **zoo** *masc*
**We went to the zoo on Saturday.**
Fuimos al zoo el sábado.

a
b
c
d
e
f
g
h
i
j
k
l
m
n
o
p
q
r
s
t
u
v
w
x
y
z